Cover art: Skye Saunders - https://www.etsy.com/shop/NightSkyeDesigns

# Journal of a Deadman

## Omnibus, Books 4-6

## Alexander Collas

# Journal of a Deadman

## Volume 4 – Wrath

Quote: "When an inner situation is not made conscious, it appears outside of you as fate." - Carl Jung

# Entry 141

As I walked back to the inn, my mind kept returning to the beggar. Something was different about him. Though he'd been dressed in rags, his tattoos, the way he carried himself, the various instruments, all told me he wasn't as he wished to appear. Then it hit me -- it was those instruments. Where did he get those? Yeah, he was more than he appeared. With this being Hell, meeting someone who wasn't quite right shouldn't have surprised me, but for some reason it did. I continued to walk lost in thought. Finally, I realized the problem wasn't his appearance or what was off about him; it was almost like he didn't belong, he wasn't of this place. Hell, I mean.

I heard the crackling of flames and the smell of cooked meat, and was brought back to the present. Hell had no real time, no day or night, but this must have been the slow time of their 'day.' The merchants were opening the shops that had been closed for the evening. Creatures, strange ones of all sizes, were scurrying about. Some were cleaning the litter from the streets. Others were collecting and eating all the random bits of damned souls who hadn't made it through the previous evening's festivities. I came upon a square, and in the center was a bonfire. Well sort of, it was a pile of souls, horribly mutilated. I guess they were being burned to dispose of them. I paused and watched as the two large Demons took what remained of one soul and tossed it up onto the fire. It was missing its head, but then they all were. Those were lined up beside the cart watching their bodies be disposed of, each lost in its own phantom cries of pain, never heard since there were no vocal cords to produce the sounds. But then they didn't need a voice; their eyes told of how they could feel their bodies being consumed.

Back at the inn, it was, as always, full, crowded and loud. Sitting at the back of the room at what had become our normal booth was Usis. I had no more than closed the door behind me when his eyes found mine. It was like his mind was always searching, waiting for me to enter his field of vision. More and more I noticed there was very little he missed. Not just with me, but in his surroundings, everywhere. He was with Bell. I smiled and headed over with a mix of happiness at seeing them but also sadness. I had to deliver the news that it was time for us to leave the Plane.

"You're back. Did you enjoy your evening, by yourself?" asked Usis. I could hear just a hint of anger in his voice. The freshness of said bitterness told me that my night on the town, alone, must have been the topic of their conversation. It was confirmed when I saw Bell nudge him with her elbow.

"It was interesting..." I decided to throw in a lie. "It would've been better with you, our first night out on the town, but you were off doing whatever it is you wander off doing." I felt that not only covered my ass but turned some of the onus back on him. I'd hit the mark. I could tell by the expression on his face. A tinge of regret was birthed in my mind but I suffocated it quickly.

As I sat at the table, Bell instinctively poured me a drink and I drank it down. "We're leaving tomorrow for the Fifth Plane," I blurted out before even I knew I was going to say it. No warning, no build up, just there it was.

"We had already guessed that," said Bell with a nod.

"Yes, why else would you run off and leave us with no notice?"

"Usis, I told Kitar, he knew. Since you've not talked to him, I can only guess you've just gotten back as well, from whatever it is you keep vanishing to do." I was tired and this attitude was starting to rub me the wrong way.

As if he sensed he was going too far he scooched over beside me and put his arm around my shoulder. "It is as you wish, my Lord."

My eyes shot to him. Was he going to start pulling that slave bullshit with me again? I was relieved to find an ear-to-ear grin spread across his face. He just raised an eyebrow. Any response I had planned was silenced as we all turned to find Kitar enter the inn, his bark alerting us to his arrival. He clearly wasn't in a very good mood. When he made it to our booth he threw himself down beside Bell who handed him a drink. She truly was the consummate hostess.

Without any greetings to the others asked he asked me, "Are you ready to leave?"

I sat back, surprised. "Slow down there, hoss. We will rest tonight and head out tomorrow. I see no reason to traverse into a new territory until we are fresh." Pausing, I scrutinized him more carefully. "What are you not telling me? What should I know that I don't? Does it have to do with that beggar? There was something strange about him."

Any doubts I had about the beggar were quelled when Kitar changed the subject without as much as an acknowledgment of what I just said. "You are right; we are in no hurry. The next Plane is going to have its own challenges, what with the Overlord and all."

I cocked my head. "Oh gawd, what's this one's story?"

"You know I am not going to answer that. It is your responsibility to discover the Planes and learn them, not be briefed before you arrive. I am there to protect you from what comes, not prepare you for it."

"That might be the truest statement you've made so far. And if you're interested, it also makes you an asshole, just so you know."

"Ok, well drink up and then you two get packed so we can get out of here early tomorrow."

I had to laugh at how he just ignored certain things.

Usis jumped in. "I had backpacks made. I am tired of carrying things in bags like we are some kind of drifters. Though I guess in a way that is exactly what we are, but that does not mean we should accept it. Since we are slowly accumulating things, we need a way to carry them." He added, "Yours is on your bed and has your name on it and yes, before you ask, it is leather, which means souls. This is Hell, OK?"

We took the night and relaxed enjoying each other company. Even Kitar loosened up, and Bell spent a good portion of the evening with us. Kitar said there would be cities from this point on but there wouldn't be another place like "Another bad decision" or Bell. But no one could be like Bell, and boy she didn't hold anything back that night. She made sure we partied, drank, ate like we were celebrating a wedding. Before the evening was over the party had spilled out onto the streets, and most of the residents were involved as well. It was a glorious night for which I'll always be grateful. She had managed for a small while to help us forget where we were and the mission we were on.

I'd usually say around dawn we crawled up to bed. But there is no dawn in Hell, just that damned dull gray light, plus I think we partied through the day into another night. At some point, we did stumble up, for the last time on this Plane, and passed out.

# Entry 142

The following morning, I awoke before Kitar and Usis. How'd I know if I woke up before Kitar? Well, because he was passed out in the bed with us. I barely remember him helping me bring Usis upstairs. But it was now evident that he'd decided to pass out in bed with us instead of returning to his room. Usis was curled against his back, much like he slept with me. And no, I wasn't worried, jealous or anything else, so let's not go there.

I carefully got up and ran downstairs and brought up some breakfast, cheese, bread and wine. By the time I returned Kitar was in his regular spot smoking his pipe and Usis was running around like a crazy person checking corners ensuring we'd not forgotten anything.

Setting the food down, I asked, "So we are off to the Fifth Plane today?"

Shrugging, Kitar poured the three of us some wine. "Unless you have reasons for us to stay, I would say let us get this journey underway."

"Will you tell me anything?"

"It is the Plane of Wrath and Sullenness. As far as Planes go, it is pretty ordered. The Overlord runs a tight ship, as your culture used to say. Other than that, you know I am not going to tell you much. We probably will be staying in the Keep this time but can play that one by ear. I can see the benefits to staying in Dis if you want too."

"Dis?" I asked.

"That is the city on the Fifth Plane," answered Kitar.

"Whatever you think is best." I motioned Usis over to join us at the table. "Before we leave though I do want to bring something up. I have waited till we three were together alone. You both are becoming more intricate players in my story and the story of these travels. Therefore, from time to time, when something happens to one of you and I'm not there, but it's useful to include in my journals, I want you to let me know so I can interview you and make a record of it. I will write it, but it will be me telling your story, not me telling the parts of your story I've pieced together. I think this will add a level of depth that we have been missing with everything being only from my perspective. It will be important that I tell it as you see it, not as I think you see it. Does that make sense?" I explained.

"Completely, and I think that is a fine idea," commented Kitar.

"I understand and will keep that in mind. Any way I can help you, my love, you know I am eager to do so. Now with that being said, are we going to sit here and talk about the next Plane or are we going to go see it?" barked Usis, who stood up and crossed to the door, clearly impatient.

Both me and Kitar stared at my little companion. It was like time had stopped. Then Kitar shrugged. "I am ready, you?"

"I'm ready," I answered. Then smiling at Usis, I asked, "Are you?"

His answer came in the form of him throwing my new backpack at me. "What do I have that needs a backpack?"

"I got us some clothes, you know shirts, pants and tunics, so you do not have to keep running around asking the overlords for clothes. It's a little embarrassing, don't you think? As I understand it there are no more cold Planes so I did not get you anything thick," Usis explained.

We made it down to find Bell already wearing an expression like someone had run over her dog, or more to the point in this place, cooked it. "So youz guyz are leavin, are ya?" she asked, her Jersey accent in full display.

"Yes, it is best we get the introductions out of the way. I cannot help the feeling we are going to run into a few problems," answered Kitar.

Smiling a sad smile, she pulled Usis into her arms, giving him a long close hug. Right before she stepped back she kissed him on the cheek. "You're a good boy. Take care of this lug and keep him out of the pits."

Usis just stared at his feet. He didn't want to let her see how tears were filling his eyes.

She then turned to Kitar as she grabbed him by the balls. "I don't need to tell you to take care of them. They couldn't be in better hands. Come back soon, handsome, don't be a stranger. Eternity is not so bad when you're around." He too hugged her close.

Finally, she came to me. I shook my head as he pulled me into an embrace. "I can't tell you how much you've made my travels better. Seeing you and this place took me home for a little while, something I never thought possible. Thank you, Bell," I said.

She kissed me on the cheek then pulled her head back letting our eyes meet, still holding me tight. "You have become very dear to me. It is with that caring that I fear the path you will have to walk and what that path could do to you. Just remember, there is happiness here, there is light in this darkness. Sometimes all you have to do is move your hand a little to your left to find a bit of that light waiting to take it." Wrinkling my brow I reached out to find Usis' hand waiting. I nodded as she released me and we headed out the door. She stood in the entryway watching us as we worked our way down the street toward the Fifth Plane.

We took our time as we strolled through the city, out across the bridge, and through the mountain of heads. We paused briefly on the Fourth Plane to catch our breaths. The intense heat hit Usis harder than Kitar and myself since he hadn't been off the Third Plane for a while.

Kitar made sure we had both adjusted before we started on our way again. He said the heat would not be as humid but would continue to grow in intensity as we descended, getting closer to the furnaces themselves.

The path down to the Fifth Plane was like the others, just a tunnel entrance with a metal bound door. Kitar placed the key in the lock. I hadn't seen it since Calmet. Before the key had always changed shape to fit the Plane we were entering; now if it did, I didn't notice. Those little wonders had long ago stopped concerning me. Before, as we descended it often felt like we were moving to the next part of an incredible journey, now it was like we were slowly being led to the slaughter.

Trudging down the tunnel Usis and I stood several steps back. The last time we had descended into a new Plane of Hell we had been attacked and imprisoned by The Lovers, an issue that was, in my mind, still not yet resolved.

As we made it to the bottom of the tunnel I saw Kitar slow and then stop as a low growl slowly echoed up through the passage. It took me two more steps to see what he was looking at, two guards standing in the doorway, each with their pikes crossed. These were massive Demons, their faces like that of a black hairless dog, long teeth extending from their muzzle. They were nude with no genitalia, their skin the color of tar, having that black-green hue. Their arms were long ending in massive clawed hands, their feet elongated claws as well. I stood and watched as a drop fell from the cave ceiling striking my face. I saw a rush of faces, pain and lives lost in agony. I shook, wiping it away as if it had burned my skin. It wasn't my flesh it tormented but my soul.

Kitar in his most demanding voice barked, "Stand aside, we are here on The Dark Lord's business."

The Demons' only response was to stand taller as they replanted their pikes, crossing them. "You are not allowed to enter here. Our Lord has forbidden it." Kitar's eyes went wide as I heard a low guttural noise from behind me. I felt a hand start pulling me back up the stairs, it was Usis, leaning in he whispered, "Step back, my love."

I noticed the cave was low and narrow, a perfect place to try something like this. Kitar had no room to work, he couldn't assert his judge form. Again, we heard from our guide, "I order you to stand aside."

This time there was no response from the two guards. All three stood like statues. Usis hissed and pulled me back trying to place distance between us and their stillness, which creeped up the steps like a disease. Finally, just before we too were wrapped in this strange embrace Kitar ordered, "Back up the stairs."

We heard Kitar mumble a curse as he also turned and followed behind us. When we made the around the corner, blocking the guards' view, I stopped. "What's going on?"

"It appears the Overlord denies us access to her Plane," snarled Kitar.

"Can she do that?"

Shaking his head, he replied, "Clearly she can. I am all but powerless. Those sentries are created; they have no souls to speak of and therefore my powers as a Judge are all but useless. I could have an effect on her, the Overlord that is, but she is not here. We must return to Bell's until I can resolve this problem."

As we started up, I asked, "She…. the Overlord's a female? And…how exactly do you, as you said, resolve this problem?"

"For all practical purposes yes, the Overlord is female now." Shaking his head, Kitar continued, "But we will get to that after this issue has been resolved. It is far too complicated to explain now. As for the second part of your question, there is only one way I know to solve this problem. I am going to drop you two off then go pay a visit on our Lord and Master."

I stopped dead in my tracks. "You're going to go tell Lucifer? I can't imagine this is going to go over too well." I smiled though I think it was more to mask my fear.

Cocking his head to the side, Kitar answered, "You have no idea. Once you understand the relationship between Enepsigos and Lucifer, you will understand just how unpleasant this is going to be." Pausing, he added, "What is more concerning to me is you. Why are you smiling?"

"Are you kidding? I'm about to get to see Lucifer show up and kick some serious Overlord ass. I've seen what he does to souls. I can only imagine what a throw down between The Dark Lord and one of his Primary Servants must be like."

Shaking his head, he passed us and continued up the stairs. "You have no idea, my friend, you have no idea." Pausing, but not turning so we could see his face, he added, "Though it could be interesting to watch." I could tell he was smiling now as well.

# Entry 143

We walked into *Another Bad Decision* and there was Bell leaning against the bar. Upon seeing us, she stood straighter but seemed to relax once she realized all three of us were there. Walking over, the smile she first carried slowly morphed into worry. "Why are you back?" she asked me then pointing to Kitar, "And why is he so pissed off?"

"Is our room still available?" asked Kitar with no explanation.

"You haven't been gone long enough for me to get the cum stains out of the bed. You think I am that much in demand, sweetie?" When he didn't even crack a smile, she raised her eyebrows in question to me.

"You two stay here. I will be back," commented Kitar angrily as he left.

Like we were home again I walked over and slid into our booth as Usis grabbed both our bags and took them upstairs to the room. By the time he made it back Bell was on her way to the table with three goblets and a pitcher of wine. "What happened?" she asked.

"There were guards blocking our entrance. They wouldn't allow us to pass onto the Fifth Plane. The cave was too small for Kitar to do his thing. He also said something about them being constructs so he was powerless against them and brought us back," I explained.

She let out a low whistle. "Oh my poor poochie, he probably hasn't felt like that who knowz how long." She poured our drinks in silence. Eventually she added, "He will be one pissed judgie when he gets a chance to think about it. So where did he go?"

"To get Lucifer."

Her eyes went wide and I saw her mouth Lucifer's name and then turn and bark, "Stig, get the place in order. I have a feeling the boss is comin and he ain't goin to be in a good mood. Tie down what you can and kill the rest. This could get ugly quick." She waved and ran off. I could hear here yelling at the staff, "Be useful or be dinner tomorrow night, it's up to you. Clean this place up."

Just a few minutes later she came out of the kitchen carrying a large tray of food, several dishes, lots of meat, her version of vegetables and a stew. She moved in beside us and together we started to eat.

"I thought you were freaking out. You seem calm now," I observed.

She smiled as she took a bite of the stew. "I am the owner. I freak out only until I get the staff to freak out and then I have lunch."

As we ate I probed to see what she knew about the Fifth Plane but she knew only marginally more than me, which meant nothing. We ate and talked for a while but both Usis and myself were exhausted and it showed. Finally, Bell suggested we get some rest. "If Lucifer is going to get involved then when things get started they will start fast and go until they don't anymore. You will need to be fresh."

I nodded weakly as we headed up to our room.

I'd no sooner closed the door and turned around when I found Usis pulling his clothes off with an evil little smile. I shook my head trying to ignore the already growing problem in my tights. "Didn't you hear? They could show up at any time. We're talking about Kitar and possibly Lucifer, and you're wanting us to be doing what possibly?"

I had tried to sound like I thought it was a bad idea but probably failed since the whole time I was throwing off my clothing.

Pulling the last of his clothes off revealing his eagerness standing before him, he slid into the bed patting the mattress beside him. "Then the sooner we start, the sooner we finish."

Sex between Usis and I had become understandable, predictable; maybe the better word was comfortable. It's like that bathrobe you instinctually put on when the day became cold. That sweater when you had to run out. The taste of the first sip of coffee. A welcome, never tiring bit of comfort. Usis was a dish I never tired eating, pardon the pun.

I slid into bed and met Usis' body already under the covers, his warm nakedness sliding across the sheets spreading the scent of his flesh mixed with his horniness. Slipping in, he moved immediately on top of me, our bodies finding each curve. Each of us conforming to the other, out bodies becoming each other's second skin. His manhood slipped in close to my growing rigidness and we moved back and forth enjoying the feel of our flesh sliding across the other's.

He slipped down under the covers, all I could see was the bump of his head. I felt him though, first at my nipples, his tongue licking and circling, enticing the small buds to stand. Then the nip, a brief flash of pain that sent notice to the rest of my body, awakening its senses, causing me to shudder. My cock bobbed up, pressing against his chest in response. I was now fully erect.

I felt him continue working down my body, his kisses and licks on my stomach. The way he pulled at the little hairs between my bellybutton and my pubes. His soft breaths on the moisture left in his tongue's wake, all adding to my anticipation. Then a long pause where my breath caught waiting. Waiting...

I felt a brief touch to just the tip of my cock followed by the warm wet sensation as my companion sucked its length deep into his mouth, closing his soft flesh around my rigid shaft. My head relaxed back into the pillow as I felt him begin to move up and down. His breath rushing out at irregular intervals helped build my excitement. I let out a low moan as Usis began to move with a little more speed, his lips hugging my solid phallus. His hands ran up the lengths of each leg coming together at my balls as he began to massage the soft orbs.

I was lost in the wonderful feeling when I heard a commotion outside. My eyes shot open. *Oh gawd not now*, I thought but no sooner had the words escaped my lips in a gasp than the door flew open and Kitar was standing there.

"That is precious, but The Dark Lord is on his way. I suggest you get ready to leave," Kitar ordered.

Usis pulled back the covers, sticking his head out like some kind of plains creature. "Now, Really?"

"I can tell The Dark Lord you are busy giving his writer a blow job and maybe suggest he have a mug of wine or something," Kitar snarked then barked, "Yes NOW!"

I was already out of bed. My erection, and for that matter the urge to have sex, nothing but distant memories. I pulled on my clothes as did Usis. Grabbing our stuff, we headed downstairs. "Is he coming now?" I asked.

"All he told me was to get back here and make sure you two were ready. Clearly, he knew something I did not. What that seemed to be was that if you two were given one free second you would strip and start sticking things in each other," answered Kitar. "That order came after his anger had already caused most of the souls in the nearby vicinity pop out of existence, so I was wise enough just to bow and do as I was told."

"Really? I thought that could only happen..."

Kitar stopped on the stairs. "Really, you are going to ask questions about his powers right now?"

We'd just made it to the bottom of the stairs and over toward the bar when all Hell broke loose, pardon the pun.

The screams on the street told us something was happening. We all turned in time to see the inn door fly open as two winged Fallen marched in and snapped to attention. In the brief time I had to study them it was obvious that everything about these two Ex-Angels screamed fierceness. What made it disturbing was how that horrific countenance was embodied in such perfection and beauty. There's no written language to describe them properly so

I'll leave it to your imagination, which no doubt will be a pale comparison.

The crowd in the bar, which was large, let out a collective gasp as thundering footsteps preceded Lucifer as he entered in full battle armor. His face was set, and in his eyes, I could see the creature who had fought against The Father. This was not the person who visited me the couple of times I had been injured.

He marched in, found the three of us and barked, "Come," as lesser creatures by the droves stared to vanish from eternity. Both Usis and myself stood frozen in fear. I'd never seen Lucifer quite this angry.

"Go! Did you not hear him, you fools?" yelled Kitar almost in full panic as he pushed us forward.

Kitar's words broke through our paralysis and we raced to catch up. Once out on the streets the two generals fell in line behind us. We marched through town. The streets, normally crowded, cleared as Lucifer came storming up the avenue. I jumped when I felt two hands grip me under the armpits. It was the General. I looked back to see the other follow suit with Usis. All three in unison, the two Generals and Lucifer, expanded their mighty wings. Then with a single great flap we were airborne, rising smoothly up above the city. I struggled to see behind me and found Kitar powered by his own massive wings.

We rose up into the great dome until we were only feet from its rocky surface. It was easy to forget the Planes were nothing but massive caves. There for several seconds we hung, Lucifer shining like his namesake, The Morningstar, for all below to see. Then as suddenly as we ascended we plunged downward at a stomach-churning speed, headed for the great pit. Though the Fourth Plane did seem far below, the time it was taking to traverse the two Planes amazed me. That thought died a quick death when I realized we were headed directly for the boiling cauldron of gold directly under the opening we were currently dropping through.

My eyes followed Lucifer as he emerged from the opening. When his toe touched down onto the boiling surface, the molten liquid solidified. The thousands of souls suffering within became nothing more than guided effigies to pain and misery. Though their movement had stopped, their muffled cries remained, continuing to fill the cavern. As we came to rest in the forest of golden, drowning torsos, The Dark Lord, with a simple wave, sheared them off at the water line. Though the path was now cleared, instead of limbs there were pits where torsos lay open, their entrails and organs sliced clean so Lucifer could walk unobstructed. The heads still cried as they rolled off onto the cavern floor below.

Lucifer paused only long enough for the rest of us to catch up and then marched toward the ramp. As he passed, the crowds of souls vaporized, one after the other, his anger like waves flowing off of him. When we reached the opening, leading from the Fourth Plane, we didn't pause. The bound door Kitar had needed a key for was no longer there.

I struggled to quickly get my wits about me as I ran to catch up. I'd never seen The Dark Lord like this and I had no plans of missing any of it. I made it around the corner just in time to see Lucifer come face to face with the creatures blocking the way. I'm not sure what I expected but what happened was, in many ways, anticlimactic, but since this is Hell I guess I should have been surprised I was surprised. The Dark Lord simply waved his hand, just like he had at the cauldron, and the two giant guards crumbled into a pile of dust. Their pikes fell in a clatter as they marched down the wall onto the tunnel floor. The door which blocked us from the Fifth Plane blasted outwards, all of this happening without Lucifer as much as breaking his stride.

As we rushed down and out the opening I again found myself standing on a platform. I broke out in a cold sweat. There was that familiar sinking feeling in the pit of my stomach as I studied, spread out before me, the landscape of Wrath, the Fifth Plane of Hell.

# Entry 144

As I've come to learn, each Plane is different. Its terrain is affected by two specific forces. The first being the sins the Plane is designed to punish and the second is its Overlord. This was Wrath, and from what I could tell, the battles were part of the punishment and the order was probably due to its keeper. I was just starting to take in the regions, all aligned in meticulous rings, when again I felt a hand grip me under the arms. Yes, we were in the air and sailing toward the Keep in the center of the Plane like a series of fighter jets. Fast, in formation and following our clear leader, The Dark Lord.

I will save descriptions of the Plane for a later entry when I can do each of the regions justice. What I can tell you now is that it appeared to be laid out, as I indicated, in perfectly ordered circles, all moving toward the Keep at its center.

As we grew closer, the Keep came into focus. It rose above what appeared to be a city. The massive structure was made entirely from the stones of the surrounding mountains. In all ways, it was a proper keep. Long windowless walls rising some thirty or forty stories into sky hung over the city like a great vulture watching its prey. Placed in the center of the front was a drawbridge. At its end, between two great battlements, was a door set behind a retractable iron gate. The drawbridge was down as if expecting us.

We swooped in and landed in the center of the bridge. My eyes followed the smooth lines up the side of the structure, taking in its enormity. My examination was cut short as the cries and screams of agony found my ears. I turned to find lining both sides of the drawbridge a row of heads on pikes. Their bodiless heads mouthing soundless screams as their skin slowly rotted away, dripping into puddles at the base of the pike. That clearly wasn't the source of the cries. I walked to the edge of the drawbridge and glanced over the side toward the wails only find their source obscured by a thick murky fog. I listened closely eventually hearing gurgling, like something drowning. I knew already this was a concern for another day, so I simply turned away.

I was brought back to the problem by a slap to the back of my head. I turned to find Kitar urging me to keep up as The Dark Lord marched with no hesitation toward the entrance of the Keep. As he approached, the iron gates lifted as the two enormous doors slowly opened as if knowing their Master had returned.

I ran to catch up with The Dark Lord as he entered the main hall. Though it was the Overlord's domain, Lucifer entered with a sureness that left no doubt as to who its real Master was. The main chamber itself was a study in bleakness and size. Its enormity was almost overpowering. I had learned over time that a Plane's Keep in many ways would help define its Keeper, such as De Sade's ostentatiousness and Ramclick's littered chambers of pain and discarded souls. Here, as with the rest of this Plane, what little I had seen, was clean, stark and utilitarian. The walls were bare, the only ornamentation were souls suspended by their hands from long chains, swaying and twirling as they moaned in agony. Even they knew not to litter the room with unneeded sounds.

In perfect lines were intricately carved ornate columns. Some traveling up hundreds of feet until coming to their purpose, that of supporting the massive ceiling overhead. As my eyes traversed upward, I could see balusters where balconies for the upper levels must have been. From the center of the great ceiling hung two enormous candelabras, their light emanating from what I can only describe as bonfires. The chamber was busy as myriads of creatures both entered and left through the many doors that lined the walls.

At the end of this impressively barren chamber sat its focal point, an enormous throne. Bowing in front were thirteen rows of what I assumed were slaves. Each knelt, their head down and their hands placed gently in their laps facing the currently empty chair. Kitar explained, "They are here in case they are needed by the Overlord or one of the guests training here."

When I saw movement out of the corner of my eye I watched as a row of soldier Demons came marching into the hall, single file. Each took up position before one of the suspended souls. Then, what I could only assume was their commander, barked an order and they began using the poor creatures as target dummies. Like the entrails as they spilled out onto the floor, coating the damned's legs in blood and gore, so did the tortured silence as they began to cry and beg for mercy. With swords, pikes and all manner of weapons the soldiers inflicted nasty wounds upon their victims. It became clear the goal wasn't to dispatch them but instead to see how much damage they could do before the soul finally surrendered to its wounds.

We stood for several seconds watching as one of the soldiers made an impressive move severing the arms of the creature he had been torturing, causing it to tumble to the floor. The Demon yelled, "Another," and almost immediately two of the bowing slaves raced off only to return with another victim, chaining it in place and raising it up so its feet no longer touched the floor.

As much activity as there was before, now there was more. All the slaves rose, and in groups separated to attend the soldiers in training. When they weren't needed to secure the next victim, they were constantly cleaning and scrubbing, pushing the bits of bodies and puddles of suffering into long grates that lined the chambers walls. Even with all the carnage, the massive hall never became littered. It was clear cleanliness was demanded by whomever ruled over this domain.

I can tell you, dear reader, in all the ways I've seen for a soul to be abused, this by far seemed the most humane. You can only hope when you arrive that your suffering is, even for a brief time, interrupted by the simple serving as a target dummy for one of Lucifer's many soldiers.

Remembering I was with their master I glanced over to find The Dark Lord studying the soldiers as they trained. He stood quietly, almost hidden for several moments, then lifting his hands, he clapped once. Like thunder it rang through the room. Everyone stopped as Lucifer walked out into the center of the chamber. Immediately, both soldiers and slaves dropped down to one knee, bowing their head saying in unison, "My Lord."

In stark contrast, I heard from the back of the hall, "Why are you here?" All eyes followed The Dark Lord's as a creature stepped out from behind the large stone throne. As quickly as our eyes had shifted from Lucifer, they shifted back as he marched forward down the center of the room.

"Balic," barked Lucifer, "Where is your Master, and why is she not here kneeling before me?" Before the creature could answer he added, "Do not tell me she does not know I have entered the Plane. Surly she should be expecting me since she intentionally interfered with my servant's actions," he said, pointing to us. I could again see anger painting Lucifer's angelic face.

Kitar leaned in to me. "That is the Overlord's assistant."

"What is it? I've never seen anything like it before," I whispered.

In as quiet a voice Kitar answered, "Later."

Balic walked to within a few feet of Lucifer, then paused. I couldn't see The Dark Lord's face but knew he was daring the assistant to defy him further. Finally, as both generals let out warning growls, reaching for their swords, the overlord's assistant dropped to one knee and bowed his head. "My Lord, My Mistress does know you are here but is attending other duties. I have been instructed to show you to her private audience chambers." Any suspicion as to The Dark Lord's displeasure was put to rest when most of the damned, slaves and many of the Demons present cried out in shock. I saw a light form in each of their torsos glowing from under the skin, dimly lighting the room. Then much to my horror, like cinders from a disturbed fire, flames burst forth from their chests and slowly started traveling in all directions across their bodies, consuming them until nothing but piles of ashes were left.

Balic slowly rose. You could see he'd realized his insolence had pushed Lucifer too far. He kept his head bowed, not daring to meet the angry Dark Lord's eyes. He, like we, had noticed the creatures being destroyed all around us. The little piles of ashes where once souls had been. Lucifer didn't move for several seconds. Then he stepped closer, so close in fact their faces were mere inches apart, then backhanded the assistant sending him sailing across the room to slam into the wall. He didn't say a word as he walked off. When he again stopped, it was so sudden that we were all forced to backpedal so as not to run into him. Lucifer ordered Balic, "Go rattle the door and get her up here or I will summon her, and we both know how she loves it when I do that."

Something was strange about the way Lucifer was dealing with the assistant and the Overlord. True, several dozen creatures had just burst into flames but still it was like he was being patient. It was kind of weird and, dare I say, unnerving. Kitar glanced at me and when he saw I was thinking of asking a question he gently shook his head in warning.

I guess now is as good of a time as any to describe Balic. He stood about six feet tall, maybe a little taller. His entire body was covered in dark blue skin-tight armor, sorta like the batman armor, form fitting with nipples, you know the kind. The boots, gloves and cod piece were the same material but in lighter shades. A seriously long sword in a matching scabbard hung from his right hip. I don't know why but that made me wonder if he was left handed. Anyway, there was nothing of his body visible. I would say nothing but his head, but it's when I get to his head where things start to get strange. See his head, if that is what you want to call it, was, well, a donut stood on end. It connected to a neck like normal, but instead of having a nose, eyes, ears and mouth, which it did, they were not part of the head as such. I know this sounds confusing. So, let's try it this way, think of a donut with extra-large hole. The donut part about a hands width wide all the way around. The hole in the center just a little smaller than a normal head, but a hole, none the less, keep that in mind. At a dozen points around the inside of the hole were grommets where a flat piece of flesh with eyes, nose and a mouth was stretched with sinew running from the grommets in the skin to the ones in the donut. So, if that is still confusing you, imagine a donut with the flesh of a face stretched in the hole in the center and you have this thing.

Yes, the mouth moved, the eyes blinked and he showed expression. Now you might wonder what you saw from the other side. Well basically just a mirror version of what was on the front. I never got to ask him if he could see both ways at one time or if one, the front-facing or back-facing face was dominant. This fleshy sheet of face was only about an eighth of an inch thick. The eyes were flat as well, not orbs. So, overall if you have not figured it out, he was a very bizarre creature.

I guess I might as well jump in here and tell you what I learned later from Kitar since it seems like the right place to include it. This was my first time to meet a constructed creature. He was built in one of the labs in Hell. I am told I'll get to see one on the next Plane. Kitar said Balic was a very good example of what the labs can turn out. Now you probably have the same question I did, does he have a soul? Well yes and no. If you've been reading the other entries you know how much I hate that answer. The No is, he doesn't have a soul, the Yes is, many souls were used to animate and construct him. The next logical question, are those souls still conscious like seems to be the nature of souls in Hell. And to that question the answer was No. The souls were taken apart and their power used to build this dude. If that makes absolutely no sense to you, don't worry, you're not alone. I'm hoping we all understand it better when we get to one of the labs.

Ok, now back to the action.

We followed The Dark Lord to a door in the back of the massive chamber.

I'm going to cut the next part short. It was just a strange evening. The Overlord never showed up, let's start with that. Which only caused The Dark Lord to keep getting angrier. Finally, we were served dinner in the main dining room which put the one on the Second Plane to shame. Lucifer sat at the head of the table, all but ignoring us, talking to his generals. I did find out for sure that the two Generals were Fallen Angels, but little more than that. We were finally shown to our rooms, Lucifer and his Generals saying they were staying as well. This sent the whole Keep and the Assistant into an absolute turmoil. None of which we got to see because Kitar, at this point, having seen The Dark Lord's mood, decided it was best if we were just absent. So we went to our rooms. The rooms we would have, I assume, during this stay.

The rooms were nice, I mean very nice. They were huge like everything on this Plane seemed to be. But...and I mean this is a big but...it's was like we would be staying in a gothic orgy. All the walls were the dark stone and there was, surprisingly, molding which gave the impression of being wood. I asked Kitar about it and he reminded me we'd seen trees on the Judgement Plane. Well, they weren't exactly trees, they were Ents, Elves that had the appearance of trees. They, like everything else, were pealed, planked and used as building materials. So the walls were actually still living, well conscious is probably more accurate. It was a deep, dark wood if that helps. The ceiling was at least twenty feet high. Kitar's room was attached to ours through a door and the other door led to a balcony on which I could observe the Plane below. We had walked forever to get to the room, which had to be a hundred feet up, over the Plane. The furnishing were standard but very elegant and dark. Like I said, just think gothic.

# Entry 145

I was on the balcony when Kitar came out with two goblets, and together we stood watching the little creatures move below. I knew though they appeared to be tiny from this distance that they were actually huge Demons administering suffering to the masses. "As you can see the Plane is very orderly," Kitar explained. "It is broken into basically six regions. From the outside working in, you have the mountains which surround the Plane. The second is the river of suffering."

I broke in. "Another river? How much do you remember of Earth's literature?" I knew he was familiar with it. He had judged untold numbers of people from Earth. It was more about the range of that knowledge I wasn't sure of. He made a face indicating I should just ask my question. Everyone was still uptight from the day. "Ok, then, was the river when we first pass into Hell the river Styx or is this it?"

"I read your early entries and you assumed the first river was what your culture called the river Styx, that was, and is, incorrect. The one you encountered before is a river, with water, because it is technically not part of Hell. It is where souls go before they enter Lord Lucifer's domain. The river here is technically what you would call the River Styx. It is the one Dante called Styx. As you can now see, it is impossible for a newly minted soul to cross over the river Styx. That happens later and for some never at all. But it is a common mistake, one The Dark Lord never bothered to have any of his emissaries correct. As you can imagine, he saw no reason. By the time you understand the mistake, it is too late, you had already passed into Hell's jurisdiction. Some in Hell have placed significance upon this river, many believing it is a transition. Before Styx, the Planes are focused on the sins of the flesh and self. Afterwards, they are more cerebral, the sins of intent. That is mostly correct, though this Plane, the Plane of Wrath, in many ways still falls into the sin of self. But as you can imagine, and no doubt will learn, there are aspects of both, self and intent in the sins of wrath."

"OK, I guess that makes sense. So, another part of my original entries is wrong. Just what an author likes to hear, but fine. Keep going."

Laughing, Kitar said, "Oh don't worry about the accuracy of your entries. You are traveling into places you have never seen. As we move deeper, rules will change, that does not mean the old rules were not correct when you were wherever that rule applied in that form. Ok now back to the Plane. The third ring, for lack of a better way of explaining, it is the Fields of Battle, the fourth is The City of Dis, the fifth the Swamps of Sullenness, and finally we can call the Keep the sixth ring. The Overlord runs an extremely orderly Plane."

"I guess asking anything more about these 'rings' will get me the answer, *you'll see when you get there*."

"Pretty much."

"OK let's see if I can get an answer to this simple question. What is going on with The Dark Lord? Or more importantly between him and The Overlord? There seems to be something between them. Lord Lucifer just seems way more patient than he normally would be."

Smiling and raising a toast, Kitar said, "All in time. All in time."

We heard a cough behind us and turned, almost dropping our goblets. There in the doorway stood Lucifer. Kitar dropped to a knee as did I.

"Please stand. Neither of you are required to kneel when we are in private," said Lucifer. (Note: I do like the caveat in his comment, hope you caught it.) He walked over casually and poured himself a drink as two servants came in carrying food. "I know you have eaten but this discussion may require something to chew on, so to speak." Taking a seat then inviting us to join him he said entirely too casually considering what I was about to learn, "I am going to tell you who the Overlord is so you can focus on the rest of the Plane, which is your job after all. I am not going into the full story tonight. It is late and if the Queen Bitch is not in the Keep by morning I will summon her and then you will get to see what our relationship is really like."

"Thank you, My Lord, it just seems you are being extraordinarily patient with this Overlord. Forgive me if this sounds wrong, but I haven't, in my limited time writing about you and our domain, known you to suffer the folly of fools."

"I do like how you phrased that. Please make sure to repeat that to Sigos as often as you can," Lucifer said smiling broadly as I reached down picking up my and Kitar's goblets, refilling them in wine.

"Sigos?"

"That is the short version of her name. I call her Sigos because Enepsigos is just too long."

"I'm not even sure how to spell that. I'll go with your version for the entries. Now for the answer to my question?"

"I like your directness." He finished his wine and held it out to be refilled. For a second I thought he was going to ignore me. Finally, he said, "She, my dear boy, is my wife, the mother of my children and the Queen Bitch of Hell."

My eyes went wide as my jaw dropped, and then to my shock I began laughing. Worse still I couldn't seem to stop, even with The Dark Lord staring at me. I just kept going. I would almost get it under control and then seeing their faces would cause me to burst out again. When I could catch a breath and regain composure, Lucifer rose, set his goblet on the table and walked to the door.

Kitar was just shaking his head. "What, pray tell, is so funny?" he asked. "This is not the reaction I was expecting."

Slowly standing using the chair to support me. "I am so sorry, my Lord, it's an old habit. I tend to respond with laughter when something catches me completely off guard. It's proven to be very inconvenient many times in my life."

"I can see that. Laughing at me does not tend to go over well," commented Lucifer with a smirk. He was now leaning against the door frame just as he had only a few minutes before. "That did not answer my question though," he added.

I bowed my head, composed my thoughts. "So you are telling me right after I arrive on the plane that you have...had, a wife. She is now your ex-wife. And she runs the Plane of Wrath. Forgive me, Lord Lucifer, but would it be safe to assume that the marriage did not end well?" I started laughing again.

Kitar humphed, which I knew was him giving up all hope of me not sticking my foot in my mouth and instead decided just to bury his head in his hands. I managed to get control quickly this time, feeling I might be slipping into dangerous territory. Lucifer waited patiently, gave a small throaty chuckle and added, "Who said it has ended? So, to correct you, young one, it continues to not go well." Just before he left, he stopped and added, "Welcome to the Fifth Plane, my dear boy." With that he headed down the hall and I could hear him whistling to himself. Now in retrospect, I think he was most pleased with having gotten to break that news to me, as well as my reaction to it. Evil comes in so many forms.

"You are here to learn, not to be told. I would not have told you what The Dark Lord did. I would have let you discover it on your own," said our guide.

I was about to respond when I heard Usis snoring in the bed behind me. I knew he could sleep through anything but this was a bit much, even for him. No one, not even The Dark Lord, commented on his presence.

"I wouldn't be surprised if Our Lord did not have a hand in your companion's slumber. He wanted to talk to you, after all," Kitar commented as he noticed who I was studying.

I said my goodnights to Kitar and crawled in bed. I thought about how much harder each Plane was getting. As I drifted off to sleep, the last thing I remembered was what Kitar had said about the River Styx. Sins of intent...

# Entry 146

The next morning things seemed different. I was lying in bed trying to figure out how when my thoughts were interrupted by a knock on the door. Usis, who was awake and in his normal good mood, answered to find a small Demon standing there. He had dark red skin with swirling black patterns. In many ways, he reminded me of a one of the characters from a sci-fi movie in my youth. He wasn't very tall, maybe five feet with a small, compact body that was very well defined. He had clawed feet and normal fingers with long black nails. Down the center of his forehead and then across his brow were small sharp horns as well as a longer set which curled up and around the sides of his head starting at his hair line. His hair was black and long, braided down the center of his back, laying between two small greyish wings. Overall, as Demons went, he was cute. "The Master has summoned you down for a meal."

I pulled back the covers, still nude, but the Demon didn't flinch. "Is your Master back?" I asked.

"My Mistress has not yet returned, my Lord, but The Dark Lord, our Master, has instead summoned you."

"Tell him we will be right down after we dress," said Usis as I walked over and started to dig through my pack.

The small creature bowed as he stepped out and stood waiting just on the other side of the door. "The Master instructed me to bring you back down when I came, therefore I will wait if that pleases, my Lord."

"Fine, we won't be a moment," I said.

I found the clothes Usis had made in my bag. I was impressed with both the clothing and the backpack. They were well made and the clothes fit perfectly. He had gotten me a tunic made from what appeared to be a very elegant cloth. It was rugged but still very soft. I noticed while admiring the needle work that Usis had also left four flaps on the back, small ones, just big enough for that damn bug of mine to attach to my back. Out of what I think is preservation it did not spend as much time attached to my back anymore, choosing instead to stay in the room. But if I forgot to do my entries for longer than a few weeks it was always there to remind me.

Next I found tights, yes tights, and pulled them on. I have chicken legs so it's not the greatest thing but everyone around here seems to wear them so he felt we should go with the flow. To round out the outfit there was a belt, and knee-high boots, very much like hiking boots with a lace up front. Overall when Usis and I had finished dressing we were more suited for this place.

What I couldn't figure out was the clasp just above the center of my pecs on the outside of the garment. My curiosity was satiated when Usis reached under his collar, motioning for me to do the same, and pulled out the amulet. He then pressed it into the clasp where it was held in place, prominently displayed. We didn't need to take it off the chain, this just ensured that all who came upon us knew who we represented. It was a smart touch considering.

We followed the little servant down and into the dining room. I motioned to Usis silently as I noticed the scars across the slave's back only interrupted by where his wings probably would have been when retracted. He nodded and whispered to me, "I am sure it is not uncommon. Remember I had many when we met."

The dining room was the same one as the night before. Both Usis and myself could not believe our eyes. It was evident what having Lucifer in residence meant. Instead of it being the five of us, the room was full of servers, Generals, and other people and Demons I'd never seen before. The power emanating from this many Fallen in one room was almost visible. All these creatures had been myths and legends to me, and now I stood in awe, slack jawed, watching them scurry about. I guess it shouldn't have surprised me that my only thought was of all the stories they could tell.

Since I didn't describe the room last night I will, in short, this morning. Let's get the obvious out of the way, the walls are the dark stone, covered in tapestries, which I'll admit, after knowing the relationship between Lucifer and the Overlord make a lot more sense. There are tables around all the walls with statues, candelabras and now food, which was being scarfed up quickly by the crowd mulling about.

Usis rushed off to get us a plate. I stood at the door watching the Master of Hell at work. It was very interesting, it was like a real job. Demons and other strange creatures were, in an ordered fashion, coming up, kneeling to Lucifer and then presenting their case. If Lucifer was interested he would invite them to sit, if not he'd listen, make a decision and send them on their way. It was a flurry of activity.

While Lucifer was talking, he held out his cup and a well-dressed servant took his glass and went over to refill it. It would seem by now that it wouldn't affect me but it still does. I almost gagged when I saw the creature pull a small curved blade from his loincloth and open a wound along the leg of one of the dozen souls hanging around the room. The imprisoned soul let out a gurgled scream, his throat had been cut and then wrapped so he would not bleed on the polished stone floor. The servant held the goblet under the wound letting the blood (which is really suffering) drip into the glass as he poked at the poor damned soul with the end of his knife. Once he had filled the cup about a quarter full he reached over, taking a large pitcher, and topped it off with wine. The Dark Lord took the goblet without as much as a glance at the servant who then knelt awaiting his next instructions.

Kitar, who was sitting toward the other end of the table, saw me and motioned for me to sit beside him. I'd barely taken my seat when Lucifer rose from his chair. In an instant, everyone stopped talking and turned their attention to him. "I know many of you have heard the rumors," he said, extending his hand to me. Kitar whispered, "Rise." Lucifer continued as I stood up, "This is the writer that is gaining so much fame in my domain. His name is Keith, he is under my personal protection. I suggest you do whatever you can to help him and his marry band of tag-a-longs succeed in their duties."

All eyes moved from The Dark Lord to me as I swallowed hard. Then much to my surprise everyone in the room, except Lucifer, went to one knee and bowed to me. I paled and quickly sat back down, as did Lucifer. Everyone rose, and the commotion started again like it had never stopped.

# Entry 147

I watched and listened closely to The Dark Lord and his court go about their morning duties. I'd seen enough of Hell by now that several times the conversation turned to something or someone I knew. It was good to hear De Sade was still favored and firmly in control. Finally, as we finished our meal and things started to wrap up on the other end of the table I heard Lucifer announce in a normal voice, "OK, you can all leave now. I have other matters to attend to." Then with an almost imperceptible wave of his hand there were dozens of small flashes and the room was empty.

In surprise, I found Lucifer smiling as he rose from his chair. "Do not worry, little one, they are fine. I sent them back to the Keep. We have things to attend to which I know are not going to be pleasant." As he walked around the table he barked, "Balic," and just like his court the Overlord's assistant appeared standing beside him. "We will take wine in the sitting room, and I would suggest if you have any sway over that Master of yours you get her here. I have a few things to discuss with the writer. If Sigos is not here when I am done, I will be taking a more active role in arranging for her attendance. Are we clear?" Giving Balic a warning glare, his eyes glowing, Lucifer added, "And it will not fare well for you having let me down."

We three followed him as he left the room. We didn't need to be told. As we came around the corner both Usis and I jumped behind Kitar as a huge, lumbering beast came charging towards us. I would say it was a dog, but closer to the size of a SUV. Its eyes, ears and mouth blazed red with flames as his nose blew out long tendrils of smoke as it breathed. Its skin was covered in a thick black fur and its claws were easily the size of my head. In horror, we watched as it charged right for us. "Dozzer," barked Lucifer causing the creature to skid to a stop right beside him. "Do not eat my writer. He has been difficult to train and is just now beginning to grow a spine," explained The Dark Lord as he scratched the creature behind the ear, causing it to wag its barbed tail. We continued into the sitting room, the dog creature following beside his master, occasionally turning back to us and licking his lips. I was pretty sure it was intentionally taunting us.

As we sat down in what clearly was a library, I asked, "Forgive my bluntness, My Lord, but what the fuck is that?" I pointed to the large creature that was now lying on the floor at The Dark Lord's feet.

"That, young one, is a Hellhound. And he can understand you, so you might not want to keep referring to him as it," answered Lucifer who continued after seeing the look on my face. "They are created creatures used as pets, guards or as ways to keep the Planes cleaned up. We release thousands of them into the hills around most of the Planes to ensure any souls that wander off do not stay lost for long."

As Balic entered with a tray of wine, I asked, "Are they soulless as well?"

"Oh no, unlike Balic here who is soulless, hellhounds, though not as sophisticated, are but a single soul." A whine came from Dozzer as Lucifer said this. "But as demonstrated, like I said, he can understand."

"A single soul, and they can understand. So inside him is a person?"

"Basically, hellhounds are a single soul inside a constructed body. The soul used is often chosen based upon the temperament of the creature you wish to create. That in many ways is the same as Balic in the sense that Sigos clearly used sniveling cowards to create this thing..." waving at the assistant, "where Dozzer here is the soul of a very fierce warrior and still has the intelligence, cunning and courage of the original creature." Balic stood stone still. His head slightly bowed beside Lucifer as he listened to The Dark Lord talk about him. When Lucifer finally took his drink, the assistant muttered, "thank you, My Lord," and then offered us all a goblet.

"How can you know that a creature is going to be a hunter, a pet or something if it has the soul of a specific creature? I understand the choosing based upon their sins or character in life but is that enough?"

He continued, "No, there is preparation involved. See a soul will remain in the state it was in when it is pushed into the new construct. So, unlike Dozzer here, most candidate souls are starved for long periods before they are placed in their new host. It narrows the mind, making them vicious and aggressive, exactly what you want in a cleanup animal. The ones that hunt out in the mountains or on the Great Plane are wild and extremely dangerous, even to the public, so to speak. Wandering the Planes outside the area of the Overlord's control is always a risky proposition. Add to that the fact that the souls are often the lowest or most vicious souls while they were living. It makes them quite formidable and good at their job. When one is constructed to be a pet they are treated just the opposite. Normally, just before the soul goes in, they are pampered that way they spend eternity as docile, tamed beasts."

I heard a noise in the corner and glanced over to find a small collared humanoid restrained by a long chain attached to the floor. I studied him for several seconds. He was interesting. Pointed ears, small mouth, thin muscular frame with lots of body hair, but under fed. When he noticed me watching him he sprung to the end of his restraint snapping and clicking his teeth. I guess The Dark Lord noticed because I heard him say, "She might be saving him for a special occasion or as I said, the creation of a hellhound, though he seems pretty tame. Speaking of which..." Lucifer turned to Balic. "Time's up."

# Entry 148

There was a blinding flash followed by a roar that sounded like all Hell had broken loose, pardon the pun. When my eyes cleared, there in front of us stood a woman, a very attractive woman and very mad woman.

If she would've settled down for just a second I might've gotten a better look at her, but right now she was in the middle of blowing a gasket. I know I've said this a lot while traveling through Hell, but she wasn't what I'd expected. Though I did know a hissy fit when I saw one, and she was well on her way to building up to a good one. I could also tell Lucifer's reaction was not helping. He was sitting back in the chair, sipping his wine with that 'seen this before' expression on his face which always causes irate spouses to instantly calm down.

She was humanoid with black hair down to the middle of her back. She had braids hanging in front of her ears, which were delicate and pointed ending in bits of cartilage, causing them to swing when she moved. Her face was smooth, well-shaped with small almond eyes, nose and a mouth that probably on someone else would've been comfortable with a smile. Her horns emerged from the front of her head... Let's say it together, '...halfway out of her hairline'. I realize I'm saying that a lot, I think from now on I will just say horns and you can assume where they start. Hers curled up and back making a long, slow arch to behind her head where the sharp points were capped with silver cuffs.

She had that sultry well-toned body so many women envied. She wasn't very tall, maybe a little over five feet. Her breasts, which were covered by a leather vest, appeared to be round and well sized but not too large. Bits of the supple flesh peeked out between the top of the vest forming that elusive valley straight men loved so much. She wore tight brown leather pants that hugged her broad hips and muscular legs. Overall, she had the appearance of one of those women from NYC who cared about her appearance and went to Yoga, self-defense class and worked out three times a week. Emerging from the ends of her pants were hooves. I couldn't help smirking because, though they were Demon hooves, they were painted in dark red which offset perfectly against her pants. Oh, and she had wings, again not large, unlike most of the other wings I'd seen on Demons these reminded me in all ways like those on an eagle, long and graceful. They started in deep blueish browns and faded to lighter shades of cream along the ends and across the feathers. At the tip a long single feather plunged down to almost the ground like that of an ornamental bird. Not being as versed in describing females, I know I'm not doing her justice. I guess to give you a better overall impression it might help to say that I could see people thinking she was of a Native American decent. Whatever the case, I think if she weren't so angry she would be beautiful. If this was, in fact, Lucifer's wife I could understand the attraction.

In her screaming and rage I also noticed she had delicate fangs which hung down just slightly creasing her lower lop when her mouth was closed. Which I might add, at this moment was not often. "You God Damn abomination," she screamed, pulling my attention from her appearance.

Shaking his head not bothering to rise, Lucifer said, "Now, now dear, we have guests. You would not want them to think we are not the loving couple. You know better than to show your Lord and Master such venom. It is unbecoming of you."

"Well I can tell you now, you can take that Lord and Master shit and shove it up your ass. What gives you the nerve to summon me?"

"The simple fact that I can summon you should remind you who I am and who you are not, regardless of your own self-image. I requested your presence and you chose to ignore those requests. You should, by now, know I do not often ask twice and expect my commands to be promptly attended to. So, my dear, what choice did you leave me?"

"Commanded, commanded..." Her voice was getting higher and higher. I glanced over to see if Dozzer was cringing yet, actually his teeth were showing and there was a low growl coming from deep inside his chest. "You commanded *me*...How dare you!"

That is when Lucifer's patience reached its end. He snapped, simply snapped two fingers, and she was instantly bound in chains and her words cut off midsentence. He slowly stood, the smile now absent from his face. "I would strongly suggest you regain control over yourself. You know why I am here. This posturing is not going to change anything in my mind but it can, if it continues, cause you even more problems that it has numerous times in our history."

Her eyes narrowed as she shook slightly causing the chains to fall away. "Don't show off. As for 'doing something rash' Almighty Lord of Hell...bite me." Stepping casually out of the pile of chains she strolled over, clearly calmer, and poured herself a drink. Almost as an afterthought she pointed at me. "You brought that minion onto my Plane?" Walking over and throwing herself into the chair Lucifer had been sitting in, she continued as she propped a leg over the arm. "I assume I need to have the labs start on new guards?" With raised eyebrows, she added turning to me, "You know I am going to eat that soul of yours while your friends watch you scream."

Lucifer seemed to ignore the last comment as he walked over and refilled his goblet as well. I, on the other hand, sat on the couch squirming. Usis moved in closer beside me. Finally returning, he set the goblet down on the table beside her chair and leaned in placing a hand on each of the arms. When his face was only inches from hers he said in a deadly voice, "Now who is showing off? But I was hoping you would say something like that. I am leaving my guards here to help watch over my writer. Even as we speak they are arriving with a few hundred more of my troops. Your Plane is under my rule until Keith leaves. If I in anyway learn you have harmed, mistreated, hindered or even pissed off Kitar, Keith and his little friend, I will promise you, my dear, you will spend the next few millennia with no avatar through which to spit your vengeful venom. Do I make myself clear?" he stood slowly taking his wine and moving to a different chair.

"You would not dare!" she barked in more shock than anger.

Taking a long draw from his goblet, Lucifer closed his eyes and inhaled deeply. "This does not need to be a problem. You know why I am doing this. As I recall it was your idea some time ago. It has just taken this long to find the correct conduit." Lucifer undisturbed this whole time took another drink. "Sigos, you are just being obstinate out of habit."

The Overlord waved his comment off she was focused on someone else now, Usis. For several seconds, she studied him as if seeing someone she had not seen for years but recognized. Shaking her head, she asked, "Who is that?"

Lucifer followed her gaze. For just a second I saw The Dark Lord's left eye twitch, replaced by what appeared to be almost concern. "He is no one, the writer's traveling companion," he said dismissively.

"Greetings, Mistress, it is a great honor," announced Usis as he stood then deeply bowed to the Overlord.

Nodding her approval, she said, "See that is the way I should be greeted."

Rolling his eyes Lucifer continued, "And you probably would if you were not such a bitch. Am I going to have problems with you on this?"

"If I say I will comply, will you get your troops off my Plane?"

"No."

"And why not?"

"We are known for lying. I am called the Lord of Lies, not the Lord of Fools."

"That, my dear, is still very much up in the air," she replied as the room sank into silence. "I will allow them to stay but they had best watch themselves."

"You will give them protections."

As she shook her head, I could sense the fury starting to boil again. I could see why she was the Overlord of Wrath, her anger was always just below the surface. "Fine, but this is a dangerous place. I will not go out of my way to protect them. I will tell my people they cannot be harmed. I will do no more." In a quiet voice, the voice I would assume she used when not in a state of rage, she said, "Tell me, Lucifer, really what is it you want? What is it you expect him to accomplish?" It was disturbing the way she talked as if I wasn't there. Yes she was studying me, but not really acknowledging me as being in the room. I could see it in her eyes, she was already searching for our weaknesses.

I found myself leaning in. This was the first time I was going to get a description of my job directly from The Dark Lord.

"He has been touring the Planes and reporting on what is happening here. We are allowing these entries out among the living to try to shape their behavior."

"It sounds like it would work against us," the Overlord commented, seeming to be thinking about the ramifications. She never took her eyes off me.

"We can hope. We need more to go to The Host. They are starving and we are drowning. I am constantly enlarging the furnaces. We cannot expect The Father's return if we continue the wholesale destruction of his creations. We need less souls coming through the Judgement Plane."

She shook her head. "Are you still fighting that battle? Has not enough time passed? You always ignore the obvious problems. The Host does not want the souls. They, like we, think they are more trouble than they are worth. I think you should not only be expanding the furnaces, you should be expanding the Planes. We have the resources to make more Demons, so if we had more space we could easily introduce a thousand times as many souls into the production of suffering. You have always been so concerned about what that absent Father of yours wants. Forget him. He was incompetent then, do you really think he would be any different now? The best thing to ever happen was his leaving and him giving his authority over to you and Michael."

I watched Lucifer as the Overlord talked. For the first time, I saw pain in Lucifer's face, indecision. More importantly I saw the real devotion he still had to The Father.

"Sigos I am not having this discussion with you again. We have spent millennia fighting over this."

"No, Lucifer, you have spent millennia fighting over this. Those of us who followed you knew what we were doing. You always said we needed to let it go. It is past time for you to heed you own advice."

"The Father needs to be revered even if he is sometimes just a misguided old man. It also has nothing to do with the bigger issue here. I do agree we need to increase the size of the Planes, that is part of this process." He pointed to me. "I cannot tour the Planes. I cannot send my Generals to tour the Planes. Everyone is on their best behavior or hiding the real issues. No one would dare tell me what is going wrong. I need to get a grip on this, so far, this experiment has been working. My Overlords and Servants seem to ignore the writer since he is a living. By the very nature of the way they dismiss the damned, they pay him no attention, which is good. He has been doing an excellent job at capturing the flavor of the Planes and more over the quality of my Overlords." Leaning in Lucifer placed his elbows on his knees, holding his goblet in both hands. "Work with Kitar and get this done. Sigos, it's going to happen, you can either help or you will be made to help."

"Fine, just remember if he gets in the way I will destroy him."

"No, my dear, you will not. He will have safe passage on this Plane or you will not see the other side of your tomb until the last creation is but a distant memory. I need to go. I cannot sit here and babysit my emissaries. If you have issues, take them to Kitar and he will address them. Now I need you to kneel to my request."

She nodded and Lucifer shook his head. "I mean kneel." There was a warning in his voice that was so strong I felt the entire room go cold.

She rose from the couch and knelt before Lucifer bowing her head all the way down. "As you wish, My Lord and Husband."

"Good." Lucifer rose, letting the glass drop at the side of his chair. I can only guess he was confident someone would be there to catch it. There was. He added to Kitar, "I would still keep an eye on her." He nodded to both Usis and myself as he stood over the still bowed Overlord. He placed a gentle hand on her head, left it there for no more than a second before lifting it and walking from the room.

Sigos rose from the kneel and without a word left the room, followed by Balic and a gaggle of servants.

I sat drinking my wine still sorta stunned by what had just happened. Finally I asked Kitar, "This is going to be a challenge, right?"

"Oh yes, but probably not from her. She gave in too easily. I think Lord Lucifer was correct, this was just anger for anger's sake." Kitar was interrupted as three Demons in armor entered the room and stood at attention by the door, bowing briefly to Kitar.

"Who are they?" I said to Kitar, not taking my eyes off the Demons.

"Those are Lucifer's guards. You will have two and Usis one for the duration of your stay. There will also be many Hellspawn and Fallen here, so be very careful. They are not to be trifled with."

"More dangerous than everything else in Hell?"

"By far."

"Fallen? Will I get a chance to interview them?"

Pausing and thinking Kitar finally answered, "I will see what I can do. Why don't you two go back to your rooms and let me make sure everything is sorted out?"

As we left the room, no more confident than when we entered the three guards, in formation, followed us up the stairs.

# Entry 149

We had been up in the rooms for a while when Kitar came strolling in. Without even waiting he said, "I am sure by now you realize we are in a hostile environment. I am going to see what I can do to turn Balic to our side. He is his Master's servant but I know for a fact he is not blindly loyal."

"What makes you think he will help us?" Usis asked.

"Constructs have one fatal flaw. They fear destruction. Therefore, if they had choose between the lesser of two...evils...they most often choose the stronger one to align themselves with. Though not always openly. Would you choose Sigos or Lucifer if you were concerned about each's wrath?"

After he left we found ourselves again stuck in the room. We drank the limited supply of wine and talked about mostly nothing. Finally, Usis sat up and said, "Well since there is nothing else to do, want to fuck?"

That was about all it took. We'd, after all, been disturbed the day before and I was still hanging on to a big ol' set of screaming blue balls.

In case you're curious, since this entry was written the next day I originally included the wild and crazies of the sex we had. Usis was getting more aggressive with each passing day. Not in a bad way, but the submissive little slave was clearly a thing of the past. By the time, we were finished I had marks and was sore in several places I'd not expected. We feel asleep and I think got a couple of hour's rest before we were awoken with a single knock and Kitar walked in. We were, of course, both still naked and curled around each other.

"Do you two do anything else?"

"We were locked in a room with very little booze, no food or entertainment. Exactly what else were we supposed to do? Plus, I was horny," said Usis in an almost apologetic tone.

Kitar raised an eyebrow, hard for a dog to do. Yes, remember Kitar is a humanoid dog. Anyway, I just shrugged adding, "Yeah, what he said."

As we talked, there came another knock on the door. Usis jumped out of bed and answered the door nude, I think more to annoy our guide than anything else. To our surprise a procession of servants marched in, the first carrying a tray of food while the next three brought things we would need, including boxes, yes boxes, full of wine skins. They set them in the corner while the one arranged the food on the table. He was the same slave as the day before, the cute little red Demon. Today I had more time to study him, and how the loincloth he was wearing really showed of his almost perfect bubble ass. It was accented by the tips of his wings which covered just enough of his butt to make you study closer, especially the way the little claws on the tips kept running up and down the crack of his ass as he walked. I pulled the covers up, I was getting hard again.

"This is Cemal. Lord Lucifer sent him to attend to our needs while we are here at the Keep. He will be stationed at the slave's alcove two doors down," explained Kitar.

I walked over and extended my hand to shake. He flinched and stared at me confused. "Sorry it's a custom from my world. I am Keith, it's nice to meet you," I said.

He took my hand cautiously. "I am here to serve, Master," was all he said. When I released his hand he quickly headed for the door, bowing to Usis and Kitar then pulling the door closed behind him.

"This should take care of all our problems. The Dark Lord sent the Demon to serve you. Get to know him, we should be able to trust him," said Kitar.

"How did the meeting with the assistant go?" I asked.

"As expected. Balic being a construct is loyal to his maker, the Overlord, but he still understands how things work. Like any created creature, there is this independence and intelligence that the creator fails to recognize."

"Wait, what do you mean, 'fails to recognize'?"

"It is one of the failings of most advanced creatures, be them Divine or living. They see things that are not as advanced as them as lesser and tend to ignore them. Here it is constructs. On some of the more technological worlds in Creation it is Artificial Intelligence. They think they can control it, and through their arrogance give it more and more power until it no longer needs its creators to recreate itself. In many ways, you can say the same thing has happened with the living as a whole." He paused. "Well, until they die and then they again find themselves kneeling at our gates. Balic is loyal, but he also is smart enough to know who the real Master of Hell is, and it is not Sigos."

"That makes complete sense. It is the same way with slaves. We would bow and scape when the Master was around. When he was gone, though we might not do anything to actively damage his reputation, we did have our own agenda and ways to punish him for his treatment of us," explained Usis as he started to fix a plate. As if to punctuate his point he formally knelt before me offering the plate up in both hands, "Your food, My Lord."

I shook my head and smiled at Kitar. "Thank you, my boy. You seem to have left out the green porridge."

"This boy did not think Master would care for gelatinous brains. This one would be more than happy to bring Master some and even force feed it to him while this one sat on his chest." As I turned green he fell over laughing beside the bed.

"OK, OK, enough of the servant act. I get your point." I said as I tried to ignore Kitar who was feasting on the brain jello. "So we can trust him, Cemal I mean?"

"Yes, he will serve your needs and see that the table against the wall is stocked, and the foods rotated regularly. I am telling you this so you will not be surprised when he just shows up."

"With that ass, we might want to move him into the room," added Usis with a bit of a smile.

Kitar let out a low growl. "He is yours to do with as you please, I guess."

"Usis, if you don't mind, why don't you use some of that former slave logic and see if he can really be trusted?"

"I will do you one further," said Usis crawling up on the bed with his plate of food. "Kitar, don't you think if things are going to keep getting more difficult like you and just about everyone else has said that maybe we should get a servant of our own? One who travels with us. One we can trust. One Keith owns. One that does not possibly report to the Overlord or for that matter anyone else?"

I cast an eye to Kitar who nodded his approval. "Actually, that makes a lot of sense. Since Lord Lucifer assigned him to you, acquiring him as your own should not be a problem. The Dark Lord knows full well the importance of having trustworthy people surrounding him," he added.

"Fine, that can be one of your projects. See if this Cemal is trustworthy and if so we will see what needs to be done to… acquire… him." The last part of that sentence caught in my throat. It didn't go unnoticed by Usis.

"My dear, if we own him he will most certainly have a better life than with many others here in this damned place."

"Still… can't we just have him as a servant and not something we own?"

Shaking his head firmly, Usis said, "No…he is a slave. Roles must be established, and he needs to understand his position and expectations. Be it him or a different creature. It is important. I will find out if he enjoys being a slave. Many do, it gives them a sense of protection and being owned is part of that security."

I shrugged. "Whatever you say, you are used to this. We abolished slavery long before I was born and I've never dealt with it. Find out what you must, and I'll leave the final decision to you."

This was only the first of the business at hand, I could tell Kitar was ready to get to work. I raised both eyebrows which he took as his cue to do what he did best, make plans. "Have you formulated a plan?"

"Well since this Plane is so neatly laid out, let's just take it in rings. I'm still curious about the river. What's it made of?"

"Suffering, of course. The portal to the next Plane was reduced to form a river on this Plane. The main purpose was to redirect the suffering, the portal is no longer in the center of the Plane like it was before. The Dark Lord wanted it worked back to ensure it ended up behind Pandemonium when it reached the Great Plane."

"I don't remember seeing that much suffering. I remember being shown the flow from the Second to Third Plane and then what was condensing on the Fourth. Is there really that much already?"

"Yes, the Planes we just left produce more than you would think. It is also far purer due to the condensation process. Right now, you are still seeing rivers. Soon they will turn into falls and lakes that are quite impressive."

"I have to ask, is there a ferryman? In our mythos about the River Styx there's a ferryman you must pay to cross the river at death."

"I had heard that. It makes little sense. If you don't pay him do you not enter into the afterlife? That sounds like a convenient way to skirt your punishment. But yes, there is actually a ferryman. The river has two ways across, the ferryman or the bridge."

"There's a bridge? What do you need a ferryman for then?"

"It is called The Bridge of Souls. It is off to the side of the Plane and used by the souls that will be traveling through to the lower planes. That path leads to the torture pits, which are much like the ones on Lust but a little more well-kept and orderly. We can visit them if you wish."

"Yes, with De Sade having such a proclivity for torture, I'm curious to see how the other Planes compare. I'm guessing, unlike De Sade's, these other Planes are going to be more run of the mill and less art," I said.

"You would be correct. De Sade is particularly inventive. I will arrange for us to visit these, as well."

"Then let's start there. I prefer to take the rings in order. Let's go back to the river. I want to meet this ferryman, see the bridge and the torture pits."

As we finished our lunch Kitar pulled his pipes from their bag, packed his and then mine and handed one to me. Usis did what he always does, gathered and stacked the plates outside the door.

"You seem distracted, or should I say, unsure about your path moving forward," noticed Kitar as we sat blowing smoke up into the heavily beamed ceiling.

"I hate back tracking. If I go back, I must basically close my eyes to everything I pass so it doesn't leave an impression. If I see something important I feel I should write about it before I forget. Otherwise the Planes become convoluted and confusing."

"I can see that, but in this case that will not be a problem. With the amount of business and training done in the Keep, a set of elaborate tunnels were dug to ensure ease of transit. We will not need to travel the Plane unless we choose too."

"Perfect, so we can get started today?"

"If you wish," answered Kitar.

"Will you be coming with us?" I asked my companion.

Wrinkling his nose, Usis said, "If you do not mind, I want to stay here and talk to Cemal. It will help me gain his trust if you both are not around. No offense."

"None taken. Do what you must, we all have our jobs." Adding over my shoulder to Kitar, "I'm ready when you are."

# Entry 150

As we walked through the Keep I took advantage of my first real chance to check out our new, temporary home. I guess I realized I was becoming a bit jaded. I'd grown used to staying with the elite of Hell so I studied the furnishings and the tapestries less as a journalist and more like a spoiled guest. Just like the main hall, the entire place was clean and well ordered. Tables, occasional chairs, tapestries, from the dark stained beams overhead to the rugs on the floor, the Keep was immaculate. Clearly a home to royalty.

When we again made it to the main hall, I had to stop and take in the flurry of activity. It was very different from when we arrived. Now sitting on the throne at the end of the room was the Overlord and there were Demons of all sizes hurrying about, most with a small train of damned trailing behind them.

Kitar stopped and pointed to a creature that was mostly white and shades of grey. He stood a good fifteen feet tall, his wings pulled back tight against his back. He was dressed in a silver armor, chainmail loincloth, with a sword hanging on his hip. "That is a Hellspawn."

"What exactly is a Hellspawn? I've heard the word but I'm not sure I've ever really grasped how they are different."

"They are creatures born here in Hell. They have never, in anyway, interacted with Creation, but that is not what makes them Hellspawns. That distinction is only awarded to those creatures whose linage contains one of The Fallen in their family line. To many of them the whole concept of Creation is more of a myth than reality. It was believed there was no way for them to even enter Creation. That was a lie told by both The Fallen and The Host. But now that lie has been exposed and things have changed." Walking a bit closer I tried to get a better look. Kitar followed behind me, finally stopping me with a hand on the shoulder.

"He's like Xia Morningstar? But I thought Xia was in Creation? Can I meet this one?"

"He is, that is how the old lie died. As for meeting this one, I think I can arrange that. Elick would be a good Hellspawn to talk to. He is less aggressive, much more of an intellectual."

Leaning in, attracted by the mystery of such a creature as well as his beauty, I found I couldn't take my eyes off him. "So, he is like Xia Morningstar?" I asked.

"Oh no, no one is like Lord Morningstar. Also make sure to use formal names when this close to them. They are very picky about such things. Lord Morningstar is a unique creature, unlike any others. But then he is The Dark Lord's great-grandson. Where Lord Elick is calm and uses his intellect to find compromise, Xia is just vicious and uses his to dissect and overpower any obstacle in his way. I have always found it interesting that they are such close friends. Lord Elick is the great-grandson of Lord Leviathan, who is one of the most vicious and intense Fallen you will ever meet. The young Lord and his Great-Grandfather do not get along."

We continued to work our way through the Keep. It became clear that not only did training happen on the battlefields but in the castle as well. I guess doing training on Wrath makes a level of sense and continues the theme of the Planes having a specific larger purpose. What I found interesting was how they kept this place so clean. With some of the things they were teaching and the messes it was making, the cleanup staff (better known as slaves) clearly had to work overtime.

As we walked down through the halls, we passed chamber after chamber with Demons and torturers practicing their craft. One chamber which was nothing but a large room with rock walls, floor and ceiling, had several Demons setting souls on fire. They would materialize the fire, in several different ways; sometimes with a spell, while others with a torch, or fuel of some kind. It was the spell castings that caught my attention. Some of the poor creatures set ablaze died instantly in a great flash. Others would start screaming with no visible signs of damage until the fire ate its way out of them, often bursting through their chest then consuming what remained of their shell. As we watched I realized that it was not the fire the instructor was training but instead the ability to keep the soul conscious for as long as possible to ensure a higher yield of suffering. It was not about the device that caused the suffering specifically but how it was used to produce a desired result.

We past several more rooms. Bodies being tortured. I had seen some of these horrors in the torture fields but here with an instructor explaining how or what a young Demon was doing wrong made the crying and screams even worse. Finally, unable to deal with it any more I put my head down and stared at the marble floor. I was so concentrated on just walking I didn't notice Kitar had stopped. "Come, let me show you this," he said as he headed down a deserted hall.

We walked down the long corridor; it was crowded with cabinets, tables and paintings adorning the walls. The other parts of the castle had many of the same things but not like these. My guide stopped in front of a long series of paintings. He pointed. I followed his finger. There on the wall, was a magnificent painting of The Dark Lord. Beside it and of equal size, one of Sigos. But what drew my attention were the two Hellspawn (I think) beside them.

"Those are Lucifer's two sons. Neither still exists. Lucifer killed them both. What I wanted you to see is here." He led me to a smaller painting, when I say smaller it was still some six feet long and four feet wide. The person in it was the most magnificent creature I'd ever seen. I turned to Kitar, "Is that Lucifer when he was younger? Wait, do The Fallen age?"

Shaking his head, "No they don't and that is not Lucifer. It is The Dark Lord's heart and soul, that my dear boy is Xia Morningstar, the Dark Prince of Hell. Lucifer's most prized possession."

I was drawn to the painting. I just stood dumbfounded. He was the stuff of nightmares but with the same regal flare Lucifer had when he was manifested to his full glory. (Editor's note: the writer described Lord Xia at this point, but it has been removed.) At least now I had a face to put with the name. To Kitar I asked, "She has paintings of her full family?"

"Yes..." answered Kitar.

"I just find it strange, considering her hatred for Lucifer. So, she is fond of the rest of her family?"

"No not really. Xia is Lucifer's child. The two sons no longer exist and this..." he pointed to a picture of a truly horrific creature. I am not sure how the painter did it, but there was no sign of humanity in this creature, "...is probably Sigos most beloved spawn. This is Lamashtu, she is their grand-daughter."

"Xia's mother?"

"Yes...the greatest hatred ever spawned in all of Creation. Lamashtu and her son are bitter enemies. Their hate is the stuff of legend. Let's go," said Kitar. Before we left he added, "I showed you these as a favor to you, do not pursue this. The Dark Lord has set narrow parameters for you, his family is outside those and it would only endanger you to pursue them. So just use them as context, nothing more. Understand."

I could tell from the seriousness in his voice this was equally advice as much as a warning. I just nodded.

Kitar took my arm and led me away. We went back to the main hall and continued down the corridor passing a whole new series of disturbing sights. This was like the theater of De Sade's, only here they were being taught to administer the business of Hell not enjoy it for its beauty, if one found such, in these acts. Most who passed us in the halls stopped and bowed to Kitar. It was still hard for me to realize this was the Judge from when I'd first arrived. When Kitar joined us as our guide I was sure I'd never be able to see him as anything other than that massive Demon sitting upon the Throne of Judgement. Now he was just the handsome furry dog I knew he had been prior to being appointed. The terror of his old form now nothing more than a shield in our arsenal.

"This is the entrance to the tunnels," explained Kitar as we reached the door.

"These are commonly used?"

"Yes, with the Plane being as violent as it is, this is really the only way to travel without risking being attacked or pulled into a battle."

We descended the stairs and I found myself in a labyrinth of tunnels heading off in all directions. To call these things tunnels was probably a bit of an understatement. They were interstates carved through the very bedrock of the Plane itself. Long wide corridors of glistening black stone dripped the suffering that seeped through the rocks, pooling on the ground below. Kitar again cast the spell to protect me from the pain of the drops. In case you don't remember, for a drop to land on your skin is to suffer all the visions and pain of the creature who created that suffering. It is a constant reminder to the souls who travel these Planes that others are here sharing the pain they have grown to expect for the rest of eternity, or with luck, until their soul wore out, having nothing left to give.

We walked for what seemed an eternity, passing doors and stairs leading both up and down. Kitar stopped and read a sign written in a language I couldn't understand and we ascended the steps. At the top, we again found ourselves standing at the beginning of the Plane. The endless line of souls spanning down the public tunnel lead from the Fourth Plane. They parted as we emerged. Kitar didn't wait but led us through the crowd. Almost immediately upon stepping out of the tunnel the two guards assigned to me were standing just behind us. Their faces grim, hands resting on their sword.

# Entry 151

Unlike the other Planes that paraded the damned destined for the lower levels past the plethora of horrors designed for those who would stay, the Fifth Plane kept them separate, isolated from those who would become its residents. The Fifth Plane is about war and battles, those destined for lower levels would have never survived.

We first went back to where the souls entered the Plane. The bridge over the river leading into the mountain pass was spectacular. The river itself was probably not more than fifty feet wide with nasty greenish grey waters rushing through the pillars supporting the massive structure.

The description to follow is long, maybe too long, but it's one of the first sights I have seen in Hell deserving this much description. I find it interesting how I wrote that some see art in what is here, implying I do, or did, not. This was a work of art. A horrid, nightmarish monument to the level of craftmanship that suffering had been raised to here amongst the Damned.

The bridge itself was completely constructed from souls. Not the bones like the buildings back on Greed, but the full bodies. The pillars coming up from the water were great lizard creatures, each at least twenty feet tall. They were bound solidly with ropes in pairs, back to back. Their hands bound to the decking, their great muscles straining under the weight. Since the water was actually suffering, I could only imagine the torment they were going through as all the pain from all the souls who created that suffering crested around them as they cursed Creation.

The railings were made from small humanoids with long necks and snake-like heads (called Oolugie). The shorter males were lashed back to back serving as the posts while the females, the railings. Their heads moved in synch, back and forth. Kitar explained that this creature instinctually moved in unison, a secondary language of their species. These who were part of the bridge sang a silent song for the damned as they passed.

The supports holding the roof were the most impressive. It was an elven race, very rare. Every six feet the supports would alternate between male and female along both sides of the bridge. They stood on the creatures that formed the railing. To carry the weight, they were bound to solid posts, again back to back, but not by ropes, but instead with golden bands every two feet up their torso. Kitar explained this was done so not to hide their beauty. Their arms extended out and up, bound to angled supports, again by golden bands. They held the enormous roof which was constructed from the same lizard creatures, then shingled in alternating rows of male and females Oolugie, forming a covered bridge.

Finally, the deck of the bridge was human souls, all facing up. This was to insure they could suffer the pain of being walked across by the hundreds of millions of damned that endlessly trudging across the bridge. The male's genitals, the female's breast, their eyes and noses slowly being mutilated as the stream of souls tripped over them. Though damaged beyond recognition, these humans still tried to bite at the feet of those who walked over them. Their only power in a place where they were nothing more than planking.

I now understood why it was called "The Bridge of Souls" because it was truly a bridge made from souls. This structure was the work of a demented mind.

We had to cross the bridge to get to the opening leading down to the shore. That is how I know about the trouble the walking souls encountered as I unpleasantly tripped over this poor creature's genitals. My boot being the final thrust it needed to separate it, causing it to fall between the cracks (pardon the pun) and down into the river. The soul cried out as he felt his manhood ripped away.

I know this was a long description, but I felt it was important. The Bridge of Souls is, so far, one of the true landmarks in my travels of Hell.

When we reached the shore Kitar walked me to the dock where we stood until the fog started to roll in. It was preceded by the ferryman's barge. Here the souls who were destined for this plane, having been separated, were ferried across.

We walked up onto the dock and watched as a seer (remember them from the other Planes) asked each damned what their sin was, forcing them to tell, in detail, what brought them to Wrath. After each ragged soul, remember they have made it through four Planes so far, listed their transgressions they could board the barge. They didn't need payment; their suffering would be charged against their debt.

Where I'd always thought the ferryman stood upon the deck of the boat, guiding it, this wasn't the case. It was installed on the ships bow, much like a figurehead would be. It controlled the direction purely with its mind. The creature neither spoke nor acknowledge us as we stood watching the souls be loaded. Each ferryman served until they rotted away and could no longer perform their duties. They were just constructs much like Balic. They had no soul of their own, but instead were constructed from many souls, all still conscious and suffering as the form they occupied rotted away, slowly falling into the churning river below.

We made our way back across the bridge, the guards in front clearing our way through the endless masses. For just a second I felt important, the way I was being escorted through the line. That feeling didn't last long as a pitiful soul, a female, threw herself at my feet asking about her children, begging for me to save her so she could go to them. At first, I listened but as she begged, more and more people stopped and started to yell as well. The more they yelled the more other joined in. Before long, Kitar, the two guards and I were surrounded by angry souls screaming for us to save them from their fate.

I was, at first, impressed at how quickly the guards moved into action. As they pulled me back I saw Kitar go down as a horde of creatures jumped him. The guards moved in front of me. As the crowd rushed forward they began impaling the souls with their picks, lifting them and throwing them over the railing into the churning suffering below. A large barrel of a creature reached in from the side and grabbed me, pulling me down and into the crowd. The humans, part of the bridge, started to bite me as more creatures moved in and began wail blows down upon my head. I curled into a fetal position not knowing what else to do. Don't get me wrong, all of this happened in a matter of seconds. Thankfully it ended just as quickly.

I heard a thunderous cry as all the creatures attacking were blown back. Then in a scene from a horror movie I saw Kitar, in his full judge form, rise slowly until he was floating just inches above the bridge deck. His wings keeping him aloft, his anger judging all those captured within the field of his vision. He was the very personification of Wrath. His anger, a wave flowing from him. In another great roar he yelled, "I order you to be gone," causing the wave to travel across the bridge blowing apart every creature in its path. I let out a scream as the bridge crumbled beneath me and I started to fall. Just before I hit the river Kitar reached down and grabbed me by the shirt. He carried me over and set me down on the shore. I looked back toward the bridge, or more accurately what was left of it. He had destroyed all the souls, both those crossing and the bridge itself. What little was left were just bits of torso, arms and legs that were still attached to the supports that enforced the structure.

Below me was what remained of one of the elves. Nothing more than bits of raw meat and skin. Its head lay on the sand leaking brain matter at my feet, everything below the nose had been torn away. Then its eyes, which were still intact in its skull, shifted to me. In a hoarse voice, I said to Kitar, "Finish them, please." With a wave of his hand, the remains of that creature and the rest of those who were in pieces exploded in a spray of red mist. Everyone within the range of his voice was gone. Kitar put a hand on my shoulder and helped me up the path. My legs didn't last long and I dropped down onto a large rock.

"I am sorry, that got out of control quickly," said Kitar, shifting back to his original form.

"In all this time, I never imagined my fellow souls turning on me and attacking," I said to Kitar now standing beside where I was sitting. "How could this happen?"

"It should not. Both the guards and I failed you."

Movement caught my eye, it was the little rat creatures. I guess I should call them the cleanup crew, they had arrived and were already cleaning up what was left of the mess. I looked over to the bridge, well what was left of it. "As horrible as it was, it was magnificent, now it's gone."

"Not gone, just damaged. It will be rebuilt."

"With new souls," I said dropping my head into my hands.

"Of course. Stand, let's get you back to the Keep."

I did stand but shook my head. "No, I don't want to have to come back here. Show me the torture chambers then we can go back. Just give me a minute."

Both Kitar and I heard running. I tensed but there was nothing to worry about it was only our two guards coming up the hill. They had been trapped on the far side of the river. They swam back across. As they came up, they dropped to their knees, neither had their pikes anymore. "Please, My Lord, forgive us for this grave mistake," they said in unison.

I sat waiting for Kitar's response, but nothing. Finally, he said, "They are not talking to me. It is you who must decide their fate."

"Fate?"

"Yes, if you wish I will dispatch them to the Hatchery. Their punishment is in your hands."

I shook my head. "No, if I punish them I'd have to punish you. Wait... I don't punish, I'm a writer not a judge. They did what they could, we were all caught off guard. We learn from this and move on."

I promise you dear readers if I sound like I was taking what happened well the truth was I wasn't, as demonstrated by my shaky voice when I said, "You are forgiven, let's just try not to let it happen again."

They stood as quickly as they dropped, snapped to attention and brought their fist to their chest in one of those military salute things. I took a deep breath to calm my nerves. "One of you can run and get us some wine." Pausing I added, "...please."

He took off running and returned far faster than I expected, only a few minutes had passed. Come to find out the guard post at the entrance to the torture pits had wine. I drank most of a full skin then stood and motioned for Kitar to lead the way. They had said the Planes were going to get more dangerous, never had it occurred to me it could be from the rabble. (Note: "the rabble" I wonder if this is the beginning of my views about the damned changing. That seems like a harsh designation.)

We caught up with the line, remember a big chunk of it was on the rocks now. The mountain pass was only wide enough for the souls and us to pass through single file. The guards were taking no chances so Kitar and I were between them and both the crowd before and after were warned about getting too close. I watched as these bat-like creatures kept sweeping down picking at the soul, tearing bits of flesh away so quickly there was no way to react. Sorry I don't have more information about the bats. To be honest, with all that had just happened I barely gave them a second thought. It was only when I was writing this entry that I remembered them at all, and still not well enough to even describe.

As we walked the air grew hot almost stifling. Sweat rolled down the souls while millions, billions of little biting flies congregated at the open wounds, chewing, laying eggs that would breed the next generation of ravenous flying beasts. The only sounds were the wailing, the crying, the endless dragging of weary feet along the mountain trail, until they reached the Pits.

Kitar stopped. "What are you humming and more to the point why?"

To be honest I didn't realize I had been. I thought about it and discovered it was a song I had heard while alive. "I don't know what made me think of it. It's a song by a band on Earth called *Ghost*. The song was named "He is", strangely it's about Lucifer. I guess walking into the Pits reminded me of lyrics."

Kitar tilted his head in curiosity. "Do you remember them? What are they?"

I thought for a second, trying to remember. "We are hiding here inside a dream, and all our doubts are now destroyed, the guidance of the Morningstar, will lead the way to the void. He is…He's the shining in the light…without whom I cannot see and…He is…. Insurrection… He is spite…. He's the force that made me be… He is… Nastro Dispater… Nostr'Alma Mater…He is."

As I finished quoting the lyrics. Kitar and the guards bowed their heads for just a second. Then he motioned for us to continue but added, "Lucifer should read this. I wonder where they are now? Which Plane?"

Don't ask me why I thought of that song at that time, I was as confused then as I am now. This is the second or third visit by a ghost from my old life and world who had floated into my head to sing to me. I can only assume it had to do with Earth no longer existing. As we walked into the clearing I silently hoped Kitar found them, I would like to hear the lead singer's angelic voice again.

I, again, had to stop and rest against the rock face. All of the sudden, or more accurately, again, I could feel the weight of all of Hell descend on me. Kitar saw that I had stopped. "Are you sure we should not return to the Keep?"

"No, it's not that. It's the song again, quoting it. I remembered the video. I remembered the first time Lucifer walked toward me on the First Plane. I think I am guilty of being jaded. He is…" I paused,

"He is…He is The Dark Lord… that Dark Lord…Lucifer, the Morningstar…He has stood since before there was a firmament on which to stand…He really IS…"

Kitar smiled. "It is good you remembered that. You have been jaded. It would serve you well and more importantly your writing well if you remembered you walk in circles few have ever even dreamed of… You realize He IS… but you should never take for granted the honor you have in knowing…He Is. He is not just a myth, none of this is like many in Creation think. You have not only met him, walked with him, had wine one on one with him, but you have had something far more important, his attention, your reflection in his eyes, his council. You are now, in all of the Creations, Keith, a rare creature. Remember above all else. He chose you.

# Entry 152

There is so much more I could say about the last entry, but why? All the words in all the Creations could not convey what happened in that moment. What has been happening. I was beginning, again, to discover just how important what I'm doing is. Not only to me, but to the Creations and most surprising of all I think to The Dark Lord himself. Anyway, on with the show...here are the Pits, after all I have a job to do.

The clearing was as long as the Plane. (You know, at some point I should probably find out how big a Plane is.) I'd later learn the clearing curved around the side and traveled the full length of the back ending at the great pit. All of this area was carved from the mountains themselves with sheer walls flanking each side. Scattered throughout, like on the other Planes, were stations of torturers and implements. Behind the stations against the cliffs were cages carved into the rock face. Inside the souls were stored awaiting their appointment with pain. I didn't count during my journey through this area, but I feel it's safe to bet there were several thousand stations. So, you do the math.

*Note: The Pit is something I've not commented much about. It's just a big hole. I did learn more about it later and here seems like as good a place as any to correct something Calmet told me. He had said the Pit went all the way down. I assumed at the time in a straight shot. That was not the case, on each Plane it's located in a different spot. This was done for strategic reasons back during Hell's construction to make invasion more difficult.*

I could again see the Overlord's hands all over this area. It was so perfectly organized. Unlike on the Second Plane where most stations seemed very generic, here they had been designed for specific sizes, body shapes and even groups of damned. This allowed the torture to be as effective as possible.

Even here Wrath was in play. I'd not noticed at first that it wasn't the massive Demons that were doing the torturing, they were just lookers on, overseers as such.

Remember these tortures are not the punishment the damned have earned. (Again I catch myself, when did I start thinking of the tortures inflicted upon the damned as earned?) These souls were just passing through, they're just here to suffer one indignity, one reward for their life outside The Father's light, and then they'll be allowed to move on.

The Overlord of this plane is wise. How do you demonstrate wrath to a creature destined for something else, someplace where wrath isn't a part of their sins? You let those who know the sin demonstrate it for you.

I stood and watched one of the stations, always keeping my distance. I had learned long ago, a part of me, the human part, needed time to adjust. Always when I first saw things like this, my body's first reaction was to scream for me to do something. Then my new mind would remind me we were here to see, not save.

Tears were already forming. I'd been forced to learn that tears weren't just about sadness. Sometimes they were the body's way of saying that the journey, no matter how small, a person was required to take was unavoidable but still necessary. Like my eyes, my ears and my voice, my tears were part of my experience that allowed me to write what these sometimes-clueless souls were suffering.

Finally, I allowed myself to see the old woman. She wasn't human, sort of a cross between a human and a toad, long grey hair, warts, large mouth, massive eyes, there too were tears. In Hell, she'd not regained her youth, she was still wrinkled, stooped and frail. That was the fuel for her wrath. She hated who she had become. When I say hate I mean it in that gnawing, debilitating, single-minded hatred one suffers and endures sort of way. Wrath causes as much pain to its wearer as it does to those upon whom it is practiced upon.

In front of her was a handsome thing. I thought it was an elf, but no, just a very handsome young man. I was told he had taken his own life, and just passing through. The woman had won in the arena and this was her reward. Now she, wrapped in her wrath, the loss of her beauty, was delighting with blade and chisel at removing from this once divine creature his distinction, his handsomeness.

With each application of her wrath, the handsome figure would grow more wretched as her lines smoothed, her posture straightened, and the blemishes began to vanish. She wasn't only torturing this soul, causing his suffering to flow like water onto the muddy ground. She was stealing from it the very thing she coveted, its beauty. Like a drug addicts craving that first needle as they awoke from their last black out with the spittle still dried on their chin, she delighted at the pain, craved it. You could tell why they were chosen specifically for the victim clung greedily to their prize as badly as the old wretch yearned to steal it.

When her work was done and the male's head slumped down, dread washed across her now beautiful face. The Demon, her handler, grabbed her and carried her away kicking and screaming. He set her down in front of a mirror, nude, to admire her work. Then like a butter statue in the Tibetan sun, everything she had fought for started to melt away. Her body withered, and spots appeared. The upright stance of a proud woman fell away in a sweat of suffering, replaced by the stooped old hag she had tortured a soul in hopes to destroy. I saw a tooth drop from her once perfect lips. She was again the vehicle that fueled her wrath, greed and lust. (Please keep in mind I was seeing a young attractive frog woman. When I say she was beautiful that's actually a lot of supposition on my part since I can only guess it was her species idea of beauty.)

She shook off the hands of her handler and barked for a weapon. He handed her, first one sword, then another as she raced off crying and laughing both.

To Kitar I asked, "Where is she going?"

"Back to the arena to win another match in hopes they will allow her to return so she can hold in her hands that which she covets most, her beauty. At least for the short time they will allow it. As long as she wins, she can extract her pound of flesh. If she loses, she will be exiled to the fields of battle to start again working her way up through the masses to possibly earn another place in the arena."

"How many times has she won?" I asked.

Kitar paused and walked over to the Demon. When he returned, he answered, "According to him over three hundred and forty times."

I whistled. "And every time she chooses to come back here and disfigure and abuse another just to see her old form for a fleeting second? Is that not vanity more than wrath?"

"For her, yes it could be, but sometimes when more than one sin finds its home in a soul we must look for the one which has be tended with more care, and in that one we find their suffering. Yes, she is vain, but her vanity, or the loss of it, is the banquet she sets for her wrath. Her life was good until she lost her beauty. Then in life, her anger and wrath was used to force model after model in her world to struggle to achieve impossible perfection. Her anger caused others to suffer. It was not the need for her own beauty anymore, but with the loss of it, her wrath ensured others would destroy themselves trying to live up to a standard outside their grasp. Wrath was her sin, vanity was the tool she used to empower it."

I shook my head surprised and impressed, yes sorry, impressed. I'd have never thought of that as wrath. It amazes me how we, the living, can so cleverly disguise our flaws behind other flaws then wrap skin and consciousness around them to construct the creatures we become.

# Entry 153

We moved through the tables. Some were like the old woman, souls lamenting the loss of something. Others were just the simple anger you would expect on wrath. One of the worst and hardest punishments was a guy who had a shape shifter strapped to the table, beating it. The Demon keeper was in control of the skill, shifting the creature through the members of his torturer's family. The wrathful soul endlessly saw the wife, child, family members who allegedly robbed him of what he thought his life could've been.

On other tables, a wife betrayed by the husband and her best friend. An overzealous business partner that was passed over one too many times. Table after table of souls screaming at other souls as they brought into reality the very embodiment of what introduced them to wrath.

Each soul sadly, in the end, was given the moment of satisfaction they thought they needed. That apology, that heart felt compliment, the thanks from a spouse or child. Whatever action they had let tarnish their soul until it became a wrath they shared with everyone around them. The supplies needed to build wrath I discovered were varied but it always led to the same closed, isolated soul. And then once obtained they discovered it wasn't the salve they had hoped it would be. Then as Hell did, they stripped the victory away leaving the soul crushed. The agony of their heartbreak fresh as they picked up arms and raced toward the arena to again engage in a fight that would never end.

"I thought these were the souls passing through. How are they going back to the arena?" I asked.

"The ones on the tables are those passing through. They are chosen based upon the needs of those souls waiting their time at one of the tables. The ones dispensing justice are here until we use them up."

I nodded. "Why do it this way, show them over and over?"

Kitar smiled, he knew I knew the answer already. I just wanted to hear him say it. "They fight in the fields and are chosen for the arenas because just throwing souls who have found themselves here into a battle they have no stake in produces nothing but a field full of defensive souls, all feeling like they are being punished. But, instead give them just a bit of what they crave while letting them torture others for us, then strip it away, over and over, ripping open the wounds of their pain and hate. Then when they are sent back to the arena each knows their opponent wants their moment again as much as they do. It feeds not only their original wrath but builds the fires of new ones for them to nurture and add to their suffering. So they fight to deny the other what they themselves crave. Now instead of victims fighting an endless battle they become renewed warriors of wrath eager to ensure in their suffering, others suffer more. It is an elegant design."

We were near the rock ledge and I leaned against it as my lips curved up a bit. "That's not the whole story and you know it. All this was designed by a woman scorned by a lover she must for eternity serve. Forced to live in a place she hates, to do a thing she doesn't want to do, as the very things she loved, her children were destroyed, controlled and turned against her by the man she has been scorned by."

Kitar had a sparkle of pride in his eyes for me. "Yes, Keith, Hell has no fury, or wrath, like a woman scorned. The Dark Lord, in his urges to fulfill his own needs, made the Overlord of this realm by offering her all of eternity. Then when he had what he wanted he abandoned her. After all, he had other things to attend to."

"That's a harsh explanation of The Dark Lord's intentions. I find it odd that you would draw such an assessment of him."

"Why? I am and always will be a judge. He did what he did. Like all of us here, the decisions that brought us to this place are in our past, they are what they are. Hell is nothing more than a series of understandings one makes with one's self about our motivations. So many sins are piled up on our back, collected like those things we hold precious. The skill of Hell is finding the one that ties them all together. The one that can cause the most pain. Anger is often the fuel, not the fire. You will see, as we travel downward, that the living do not stumble into their sins, they take them, at first, like clay and shape them. The very things that will damn them becoming their most prized possession which they hold to tightly, guarding and nurturing it like one does, say a fine wine."

"Still, wouldn't The Dark Lord be angry with you?"

"No, his greatest strength has always been seeing all things for what they are, that includes himself. He is called the Lord of Lies in many cultures. What they do not understand, until they stand here in his realm, is that the lies they condemn him of are not his, but only his nurturing of those we tell ourselves."

# Entry 154

As I wrote the two previous entries I realized I wasn't giving a blow by blow of the horrors being visited upon the victims. I've told you about the types of brutality done to a soul and I'm sure I will again. I think the two previous entries needed to be about the definition of wrath. So often we forget in the telling of all this violence and suffering that under it lies honest pain. The kind of pain that the person inflicting it doesn't even know they are administering. Which type of sin justifies more the punishment of Hell? The sin that is intended, acted upon eagerly, planned and executed? Or the ones that happen by accident, over and over, because of the self-perceived short comings and insecurities we amass over the course of our lives? So, in these entries I left out the visuals of the abuse in hopes that in their words you will see the intent and underlying foundations of their constructs.

We worked our way back toward the tunnel. "Do you have some superpower that will let you contact Usis from here?"

"Superpower, well I would not call it a super power, but yes, why?"

"I want him to meet us in town. Let's not go back to the Keep right away. This didn't take as long as I thought, and I'm not tired. It might not be the formal introduction to the new city, but can't we find a place to eat, get a drink and maybe see a little of the sights?"

"You want drinks, dinner and a little random violence?" asked Kitar.

"Well I wouldn't necessarily phrase it like that." I motioned around me. "I've had the random violence but otherwise, yeah."

"Well, Usis is already in town, and he is already seeing to one of your wishes."

I smirked. "I'd assume it isn't dinner or drinks."

"You would assume correctly. I just let him know we were coming to him. He seems to have paled."

"Tell him to relax, if he knows a place to go, tell him we will meet him there. Since we have UPS...haha, ups..."

"What is UPS?" asked Kitar.

"Usis Positioning System," I stated laughing. (Note: I know, it's a bad joke, but torture comes in many forms, doesn't it?)

"Right....to get to town we should take this tunnel," added Kitar as we back tracked a bit and headed down a different path.

The city of Dis was as different from Xictic as you could get. When we stepped out, instead of getting a rustic medieval village, I basically got what I imagined Pompeii would be like, you know before the volcano. The buildings were arranged in neat rows along cobblestone streets. Not like the cobblestone from before, these were clean, well ordered, and cared for. I could see the Overlord's hand and meticulousness at play here.

As we walked along the streets I marveled at how Kitar could stroll casually but still have the crowd part for him as he passed. I'd known several people in life who always seemed to be nothing but business even when they didn't plan to. Kitar was like that. I, on the other hand, was rubbernecking as we liked to call it.

I grabbed Kitar's arm as I stopped outside a shop. They had clothes, not loincloths and stuff but real clothing, pants, tops and armor. "That is a shop for the residents of Hell," explained Kitar.

"I've a feeling when you say resident it has a different meaning, explain," I asked.

"Resident means anyone who is Fallen, born or created here. It also covers those like myself, you and Usis, those who have been raised up. That is unless you screw up and get thrown back to your Plane of punishment after you have completed your assignment." Kitar smiled a devilish little grin.

"Thanks for the words of support. Have you tried motivational speaking? While we're stopped, I've another question. The first city, the one Usis was from was very medieval as was the one on the Third Plane, this one's more Roman by my world's standards. Why the great differences in architecture?"

"Good question, it is based upon who founded the city. This is one of the oldest cities in Hell. Pandemonium is the oldest, of course. The founder of Dis must have been from or knew of the Roman style, as you call it. And before you ask, no, I have no idea who that was."

"Wait, there's something you don't know? Does Lord Lucifer know this? He'll be shocked. We should contact The Host, the newspapers and see if there's been a mistake," I barked.

"Have you started to finally lose your mind?" he asked, shaking his head.

Oh, one thing I left out, all through the otherwise clean town were bodies hanging from chains every twenty feet or so, like back in the keep, except these were in little nooks set into the walls. Each one a different race. It seems to be a thing on this plain, hanging people from chains. I was about to ask when I noticed two grubby little Demons, like imps, approach the soul. They ran up and began gnawing on its leg, tearing large chunks of meat off and eating it. The creature screamed in pain as blood fountained from the open wound flowing down a grate just below him. I turned to Kitar; he had been watching as well. "Like everywhere else in Creation there are also vagrants even here in Hell. The Overlord takes pity on them by hanging out food for them to eat."

"Food? That is a soul," I insisted. "And why are none from the same Creation?"

"Yes, and you are about to sit down in a nice, clean establishment and eat the exact same thing, so is there a point to your indignation or is it just you being naive? As for them all being different, well you know that variety is the spice of life, right?" He walked off smiling as I followed shaking my head trying to ignore the sound of two little imps feasting on the soul while it screamed.

The Tavern spanned almost the entire block. Its sweeping columns culminated at a high tiled roof made from the stones quarried from the mountain. In front, there were clay pots with a server selling street food and drinks to the passersby. The other half was an outdoor dining area with low tables and chairs behind a large wall. The other side of the courtyard was the Tavern proper which was open to the outside with only curtain to separate the areas.

A waving hand caught my eye. It was Usis sitting at one of the tables. I was glad to see it was outside. As we walked up I noticed he had already ordered. There were three clay mugs, a pitcher and some steaming food on a large metal plate. There was also bread. "How'd they get grain?" I asked. I've traveled Hell long enough to know certain things just weren't available.

Usis shrugged but Kitar was quick with an answer. "It's one of the reasons I started to get us a room in town. Here due to the influence of Sigos, things are brought in from all the Planes as she sees fit. So, the variety of ingredients, both for consumption and creation, are far more varied."

As I sat down Usis asked, "I am surprised you wanted to meet me in town. Is something wrong?" I could sense the stress in his voice.

"Actually no. The Torture pits went as well as could be expected. We had some problems just before them, but our guide here managed to do his job and save my ass, so over all I can't complain." I decided Usis didn't need to know about the bridge incident. He'd just freak and I wanted to relax tonight. Seeing his eyes shift between me and Kitar I added to throw him off topic. "I needed to see the town and figured you would be here. Plus...." I let my voice trail off.

"Plus, what, Keith? Please do not do that, you know it makes me nervous," insisted Usis as Kitar poured us both a drink and pulled out his pipe pounding it louder than I thought necessary on the side of the table.

"Would you stop panicking? I just wanted to see the seedier side of one of these towns. You two shield me from too much…" Seeing them waiting to see what else I was going to say I added, "probably for good reason, but not tonight. So I thought maybe a club or tavern where they do the more exotic things."

I could tell by the way both Kitar and Usis narrowed their eyes at me they weren't buying it. "That is very un-you," said Kitar getting a, "Yeah" from Usis.

"To be honest I found the club in Xictic to be very informative. I saw and got to interact with more creatures than I have the whole trip. I mean ones that were not being actively tortured at the time. The only place to come close was Bell's, but that only bolsters my argument that there are things to be learned, people to see. The way the Damned and Residents interact so casually with not only torture but in their daily lives intrigues me."

Kitar nodded but Usis clearly still wasn't buying it regardless if it was true or not. Which for the record, it was. I did have a slight ulterior motive, I planned on getting Usis drunk and seeing if I could coax that darker side out while we were in town. Hey, It's not what you're thinking, dear reader. I know something's up with my boyfriend and I plan on figuring out what.

# Entry 155

As we had dinner out under the great dome it was one of the few times I've ever gotten to study where I am from a calm objective perspective. Just its enormity is normally enough to cause me to move on to something a little more within my understanding. The cave ceiling arched up hundreds of feet above us. I watched as winged creatures sailed around its expanse, swooping and playing. Some, just like us, enjoying the night. While others, clearly out hunting for those strays that had wandered away hoping to hide in the hills around the Plane. Occasionally, closer to the ground, I'd see a winged Demon shoot across the sky. Never lingering, they always seemed to be in a hurry. I'd grown used to seeing humanoid creatures sail by, it was a common occurrence in Hell.

As we ate I watched the traffic outside the wall through the gate and the different creatures stopping to pick up dinner from the street vendor before heading home. This is what I loved about being in the cities. "They seem so normal, I mean other than their appearances," I commented to Kitar between mouthfuls of bread.

"That is why I thought the cities were an important part of your journey. In many ways, the denizens of Hell are living lives like those in Creation."

"I know, it's what we have in common and that's what you want them to understand. Even here, where your eternity will be punctuated by pain there is still normality to be found and strived for."

"Well, that is a bit hopeful but yes," quipped Kitar.

"The question is, how do you move from being out there having your intestines pulled out, to here living a life or serving a less tragic existence?"

"You have heard of Xia's minion, Sam. He was Earth born and now he serves one of the most powerful creatures in Hell. Even here, you can choose to accept your fate or fight it. If you fight it, really fight it, there is a chance you will be noticed. True, it helps to have a skill or craft that Hell is in short supply of. When I say fight it I do not mean rebel, its more about accepting what you did and showing you can contribute to the overall running of Hell, no matter how small that contribution might be. Of course, with the number of souls that come through the gates it is extremely rare for a single soul to stand out, but it happens."

"What was Sam's gift, do you know?"

"Oh yes. First was his ability to study something Xia created and then make it more efficient. Forget what it is, a torture device, it's still just a device to him. But his most valuable skill, is his ability to handle a creature no one else in Hell is able to. It has been said he is working on a book called, "How to train your Hellspawn". I don't know if that is true, but he is qualified."

I laughed. "From what I've learned about Xia, he'd hate that."

"Completely," answered Kitar.

I was about to ask something else when I heard a huff of impatience from beside me. All during dinner Usis had been peppering me with an endless barrage of questions, trying to see if I had some underlying ulterior motive. I ignored his attempts. I would answer his question with a vague answer, then turn back to my conversation with Kitar. It was driving him crazy, and I was loving it.

After dinner Usis all but rushed us into the city. As we walked I tried to pay attention but mainly it was a chore just to keep up. I was however able to take in some of my surroundings, catalog the new creatures, not so much for your reading pleasure but more just to know which were dangerous and should be watched out for. It becomes a habit after this many years in Hell. I also spent a good portion of the night listening in on others conversations. It's amazing how many times I was mentioned, not directly but something about my travels as well as the given creature's speculation about what it really meant. Most times they were wrong. It felt like a night out on the town with friends, if you overlook the oddity of the environment and those moving through it.

I still could not get over how different this city was. Like I said earlier it was very Romanesque in the sense that it had columns and lots of drapes instead of solid walls. Every few feet there were iron sconces lighting the streets, fueled by bits of bone and flesh. Unlike Rome with its white marble, here everything was a mat black since the stone had been mined from the mountains. The columns in many places were carved with intricate details. The Demons and weird creatures were holding up the balconies and roofs. Most of the public buildings were open on the first floor. Those that weren't had high walls and gates hiding their interiors from the passersby. Just when you thought you could forget where you were, a soul hanging in a shop window, a strange creature, a twenty-foot-tall hooved Demon would remind you, this was Hell.

When Usis and Kitar stopped, we were standing in front of one of those gated buildings. I could hear the muffled cries and moans coming from within. I know I only occasionally point out the sounds, but don't let that lead you to believe that it is something that just drifts in on the nonexistent wind. Agony is our constant companion here, as on all Planes. It doesn't matter if we're alone in the tunnels, in our rooms, or on the streets, the cries are an ever-present part of our daily lives. But to those here, it becomes like the traffic outside the window in a busy city like New York, just background noise. Something you don't hear until you listen for it. If all the cries stop, as it has a couple of times, you tend to dunk under a table and hope not to find out what new danger has drawn everyone's attention away from their pain. Normally, it's Lucifer. Today, he wasn't here, and so the Plane was alive with its symphony of suffering.

Usis and Kitar walked casually through the arched gate as a smile crossed Usis' face. I could see he was excited. As is always the case when I experience new sights, I stopped in the doorway just to let my eyes take in what they were seeing and my mind try to interpret, analyze, and then come up with a story I could live with that didn't include curling up in a ball crying. Most of the time it worked, as it did tonight. "What the Hell am I seeing?" I asked.

"This is *The Overlord's Playhouse*, that is its name. The Overlord does not actually own or operate it," explained Kitar.

Usis with a guilty look added, "I asked around about the best place to come and experience…well…"

"Just spit it out," I said in a bit of a stronger voice than I'd intended. I smiled a cheesy smile to make up for it.

"I was told it is the best place in the city for food and drink. They are also known for their "extreme" entertainment, as you put it. In the back are elegant rooms to entertain or be entertained in, if you know what I mean."

"Sadly, I think I do," I said causing a ripple of fear to visibly race through Usis's face. Holding up a hand, I said, "That's fine, it's what I said I wanted. What's going to happen? Surprise is the last thing I want in situations like this."

"I would think first we get a table," answered Kitar as he pointed to the one he wanted when the host walked up. His voice made it clear it was not a request. I personally didn't think the gruffness was necessary since the host was staring at my necklace. "This way, My Lords," he said, leading us to low table at the edge of what appeared to be a pit, or performance area, set a good eight feet below the dining area.

A slave brought plates of food, many I'd never seen before, two large gold pitchers of wine and goblets for everyone. "What is supposed to happen?" I asked. I watched the slave as he placed the dishes. His nude blue body glistened with sweat. I couldn't take my eyes off one of the beads of moisture as it rolled down his back, around his short tail, finally dropping into the crack of his ass to continue its journey. I saw something out of the corner of my eye; Usis was watching me. Actually, he was glaring. I smirked, I could tell he was faking his indignation. As the boy began to leave Usis whispered something in his ear. He nodded and headed off.

Kitar started to eat some disgusting blue thing. I had never noticed how he attacked his food. Whatever it was, he was firmly holding it in both hands, well paws and I could swear it was moving. Between bites he said, "Well, you had best prepare yourself, first there will be a show and then if you are still up for it we can go back into the private bars where there are dancers and less elaborate tortures to keep the visitors entertained. If you wish you can get a room, torture your own slave. Or hire as many as you want and do pretty much anything you can imagine to them. Every slave here is expendable."

I narrowed my eyes. "Expendable..."

"Yes expendable," he said as the show began. I watched as a handler led a vicious looking creature out into the performance space. He then clipped the chain around its neck to a hook in the floor. This thing appeared to be part jackal, with patchy hair covering his grey/white body. Of course, he had a large erect cock shooting up from the sheath that normally protected it. His hands and feet were claws and his snout extended out with long grey colored teeth leaking a putrid blue saliva. Kitar pointed to where the spittle was landing, as it hit, small wisps of smoke rose up from the rough stone floor.

"I guess this is a sex show? I'm surprised at how sex is so prevalent in Hell and almost always used to degrade," I commented.

"It is a universal taboo across all Creations. The Father found violating someone abhorrent therefore he installed a disgust of such acts in all his creations. Unfortunately, it backfired, and the denigrating aspects were quickly embraced as a form of both attraction and belittlement. It has been a constant study, more on the Plane of Lust, for how it titillates as it upsets." Pointing, he added, "I am a little worried about you seeing this show. This will not be the light stuff you consider extreme. I am not sure what will happen but I am familiar with this race and it will not end well.

If it gets too much just let me know and we can go back to one of the inside bars," cautioned Kitar.

The second combatant was brought out. Where the first creature had come willingly this one was fighting every inch of the way. She had to be dragged out. The chain leading from the thick collar around her neck was also clipped onto the floor. I shook my head; I knew how this was going to go. It was going to be some form of rape. I was already ready to leave but forced myself to at least see what was going to happen. I had after all said I wanted to see this.

# Entry 156

(I'm doing the show and afterwards in a different entry for reasons which will become obvious. For the record, I think this is about the most horrific thing I've reported on to date. Normally I'd leave something like this out for so many reasons. One being I don't want to relive it as I write it. But since I keep getting warned it's only going to get worse, I guess it's time to start easing you in as well.)

The female scooted as far back from the jackal as she could, but it did no good. Licking his lips, he lunged across grabbing her by the arm, dragging her into the center of the pit. The crowd cheered as he forced her down onto her back and unceremoniously shoved his cock into her. I've never been one for straight sex, and to be honest I'm not even sure how to describe what I'm seeing. I can tell you due to the already pooling blood on the floor and the size of his manhood, he was ripping her open inside. His thrusts grew faster and harder as he let out an ear-piercing howl drowning out her screams. This caused the audience to go wild. I started to notice red splotches appear on her body. I focused on them in hopes it would help me ignore the brutality of the rape being played out before me. Kitar leaned in. "His saliva has a mild acid." My eyes went wide as they went back to his mouth where long thick lines of spittle were trailing down and dropping onto her white flesh as she writhed and struggled. Each time his saliva hit, a new wound would open, little bits of smoke rising, exciting the jackal even more. It didn't stop there, the spittle continued to bore its way down through the female's body. Glancing around the table I found Kitar's cold calculating eyes apprising the battle while it was clear Usis was riveted to the scene going on below us.

The jackal extended his tongue, licking the female across her right breast leaving a long raw trail where the skin had been dissolved away. Instinctually her hands came up and she tried to push his head back. That is when the scene truly turned horrific. As she pushed on the end of his muzzle he moved quickly, catching her fingers in his mouth and biting them all off.

The crowd roared their approval as coins started to rain down upon the two in the center of the pit. The audience was actually tipping. I could tell the male was starting to become lost in the intensity of the moment. Pushing hard into the female as he continued to howl louder and louder. When I didn't think things could get worse I watched in shock as he plunged down with his mouth digging deep into her torso pulling out several of her internal organs. He flipped his head upward as the long bits of intestine flung shit and viscera into the audience causing them to go insane with blood lust. She now lay wide eyed in horror as the creature continue to thrust in and out as he feasted upon her body. She couldn't die, she was conscious and a spectator at her own disembowelment and rape.

I felt the bile rise in my throat as I threw my hand over my mouth almost in unison with the creature lifting its head and shaking to tear away a large chunk of meat from the female's stomach. Through my fingers, I said quickly as I stumbled to stand, "Ok...I've seen enough." I felt arms around me. Still fighting the urge to vomit, both Kitar and Usis moved to support me as they led me into the building proper and away from the growing frenzy happening in the courtyard. I could tell, even though my haze, the crowd too was becoming violent. The heat of the air, the smell of shit, sex and sweat of all the creatures around me only made matters worse. We bumped into something and I lifted my head long enough to realize our way was blocked by a massive four-armed Demon. He was so tall I was starting at his cock and the smell of his musty genitals almost sent me over the edge. Thankfully Kitar, sensing the issue, caught the creatures' eye, pulling his attention away from me. I have no idea what they exchanged but the vision our guide projected into his mind must had been bad, he gripped his eyes, ripping them out as he took off into the crowd screaming in agony and mental pain.

I stopped in the doorway, putting my hands on my knees, and took several deep breaths through my nose. After a few minutes, I had my stomach under control and was starting to block out the frenzy of sounds behind me. I stood and together the three of us walked into a large Peristylium. Around the edges were couches with a bar at the back. The center, where the yard should have been was a shallow pool with dancing slaves, both male and female. "Nothing is going to happen to them, is it?" I asked Kitar.

"Not here, they are simply for entertainment."

As we found a group of chaises and I collapsed, Usis ran off to get wine. "I was thinking, should I be calling them slaves. I mean like the two in the pit…" I asked Kitar as my head dropped back and a flush raced across my face. I closed my eyes and took a deep breath trying to calm my stomach, the images of the rape were still too fresh in my mind. I added, "These dancers here. Are they slaves?"

"I don't know if I will ever stop being amazed at how your mind works. You get upset and sick over what you saw and to distract yourself by asking the most benign of questions. But to answer, technically yes, they are slaves, we all are. The definition of a slave is one who is owned and forced to work against their will. These souls were purchased by the club owner and as you have already seen they can be used for anything the owner wishes, from sex to torture."

I leaned back and stared up at the painted roof above me. "That was intense. We've seen things like that before but it's always been out on the Planes in the torture pits. There's something about it happening for sport that made it exponentially worse."

"I know. To my surprise, it was not as brutal as I had feared. That species is a very nasty creature. Your reaction is common. The mind has a way of putting things into context. That is why saying a violent game causes violent actions is normally a sign that the person making the assertion is not themselves capable of making that distinction. What you saw was exponentially worse because it is not 'acceptable' in an entertainment situation where it is more or less expected in a torture scenario."

"Was that creature actually created or was it a damned like me and everyone else?"

"It is a damned. In their creation, they were dumb animals until the ruling race, which was technologically advanced, started to genetically alter them for a war with a rival species. What they had not banked on was the creatures becoming sentient, and thus acquiring a soul. They did end up putting an end to the war as hoped but not exactly in the way intended. The two warring sides ultimately had to start working together to hunt down and kill all of the creatures you saw out there. There are no more of those living inside of Creation. They are coveted now for their aggressiveness and are often used either as guards or in situations like this. Their lusts, both blood and sexual, basically override their mental capabilities. That is why when I saw it being brought out I knew this was not going to end well."

While Usis was away Kitar leaned in. "I am not sure if you have noticed and if not I am hoping for your discretion until I can research it more. But have you seen the strange bumps Usis has begun to develop just below his hair line." Before I could say anything, he added, "Where horns normally grow." As you know I had noticed but hearing it out loud was like a slap in the face. I just groaned. Great, something else I needed to worry about.

"Of course, I've noticed and no I'm not going to keep it under wraps. He and I talk about such things. I'll see if he brings it up. If he does I'm not going to play dumb."

"Fair enough," said Kitar as I collapsed back onto the chaise. The enormity of the show coupled with this new problem sent my mind into overload.

When Usis arrived, he was trailed by three servants, two males and a female, carrying trays. Each tray had a pitcher, mug and some cubed meat. Usis pointed the one to me, he was the one from earlier that I'd liked. The female he directed to Kitar. "I assume you are not of our proclivity," said Usis as Kitar nodded and began to appraise the girl. "Very nicely chosen." The final male followed Usis to his seat. Usis then said to all three, "It has been a rough evening, you are now in front of your charges. Do what you do best." He pulled the little male he had chosen up into his lap as mine fed me a drink of wine. I moaned and closed my eyes. I did love my companion. He knew just what to give a man after a long night of watching psychotic dogs sexually abuse and then eat their partner.

I can't tell you for sure what was happening around me. My ears were ringing and my eyes saw nothing but the big white disk of my mind in overload. I lay there taking sips as the goblet was pressed to my lips. Eventually the wine started to take effect as did the little kisses on my face and chest. The blue slave was clearly trying to distract me. I could feel his hard-on against my stomach as his cute little ass was causing much the same reaction as it ground against my cock. I watched as Kitar headed off with his girl and heard Usis moan from his own attentions. Not sure where he was it took a sec for me to find him on the ground behind the chase. He was getting his manhood serviced by his own little slave boy.

Smiling at the blue boy, I asked, "What is your name?"

He cocked a crooked grin. "Does it matter?"

I nodded. "If for no other reason that I know what to moan later. I am Keith. You can scream that name at will."

"My name is Alegrate, Master Keith."

The rest of the night I've got to say went as good as the start had gone badly. Kitar and his little girl got along well from what I learned later. Usis and myself also found a room and, separately at first and then together, spent an enjoyable evening with our two little slaves. I say enjoyable. I was like a shell-shocked soldier going through the motions. Don't get me wrong I enjoyed it, a lot, but my mind stayed fuzzy. Alegrate kept feeding me wine which helped overall. Oh, and speak of Alegrate, what that boy can do with that tail. If you ever get a chance to have sex with someone with a tail, I highly recommend it.

We spent the night there and I was awoken to the smells of breakfast the next morning. Kitar was in our room sitting on the balcony smoking as the three slaves brought in the morning meal, again going to their charges and brought us into the day in a most pleasurable way. By the time we started our way back to the Keep I was fed, bathed and well rested. Dis had shown me both its brutal and gentle sides all in one evening.

# Entry 157

When we made it back we found Cemal kneeling in the corner of the room awaiting our return. Having learned that I was assigned to write about my journeys, he had arranged to have a larger table and three chairs moved in. I nodded approvingly to Usis as he went over to talk to the boy. The new furnishings were quickly forgotten when we were told Balic wanted to see us. Kitar ran down only to be told Sigos wanted to meet with me. It didn't improve my comfort level when both of our guards shifted on their hooves and stood straighter. This would be our first meeting since The Dark Lord left. It appeared it wasn't just me who didn't know what to expect.

We found Balic standing just outside the main hall. He ushered us quickly along. As always the main floor was bustling with activity. As we entered the main chamber I expected to see the Overlord on her throne, but it was empty. Bowing deeply, he informed us, "My Lord wishes a private conversation with you and your companions in her quarters."

Kitar shrugged. "The guards will be coming with us, you understand."

"That is fine. They can wait outside in the hall. Please, this way." He motioned for us to follow.

When we made it back to the hall with the Morningstar family pictures, I realized where we were. This was her private area of the Keep. At the end of the Hall stood a set of double doors. Balic knocked once and entered, not waiting for a summons.

Inside was a comfortable living room. Most of the walls had tables against them with pictures above. All the surfaces were covered, to say it was cluttered would be an understatement. It wasn't messy but still stood in stark contrast to the organized image I'd grown to envision of the Overlord. The only light came from candles scattered around the room and a small fire burning in a large ornately carved fireplace.

She was sitting in a large chair to the left of a set of massive couches, the largest of the two facing the fireplace. Motioning for us to enter, she invited us to sit; she didn't stand. Her voice immediately caught me off guard. She had spoken when we'd first arrived with Lucifer but then it had been a heated conversation with a lot of yelling. Today she was calm and her voice sultry, like a song you were familiar with that played in the back your mind and made you smile. I guess I should've found her tone calming but instead I sensed magic at work. I thought to myself, "She's trying to manipulate us." To which my mind answered, "Of course she is."

"Welcome, please have a seat. Balic, fetch us something to drink, please," she said in that calm voice. Two pleases already, yeah I needed to watch myself. As Balic did her bidding, she turned her attention to us. "I'd like to apologize for our initial meeting. You know how it is when old flames show up. It is quite easy for the old angers to resurface, especially if your old flame is the Lord of Flames." She smiled. Yeah, I was growing very nervous.

The gentle tap from Kitar on the side of my leg brought my attention back. He wanted me to speak instead of him. It was time for my first move in this new chess game. I took a deep breath letting the silence stretch on for several seconds before bowing my head slightly in respect. "I can only imagine, Mistress. We've been greeted with a variety of reactions and I understand how having us here could present challenges. I've seen how our presence can cause disruptions on other Planes. Though in our defense, none that I know were earth-shattering, pardon my pun. Now that I've had the opportunity to speak to you personally I would like to ask, not have you ordered, if I might spend time here, with your blessing to write about how you manage those in your charge and produce the precious suffering needed to keep all of Creation running."

As I finished speaking she tapped a finger on the arm of her chair. As a small smile curved the corners of her lips she said, "I can see why Our Dear Lord chose you for this task. You are quiet a well-spoken soul." With a flip of her eyes her attention again shifted, this time to Kitar. "It is wise you sit silently, servant of Lucifer. I prefer your silence to your opinions."

Again, her eyes moved, this time to the door just seconds before Balic entered carrying a tray with four goblets. He presented one to the Overlord first, then myself, Kitar and Usis finally. I knew the order had not been a choice but an indication of importance as the Overlord saw it.

"I will not mince words with you, writer. I do not want you here. With that being said, we are all but subjects to Lucifer and therefore I must bow to his wishes, however much it displeases me. Since your arrival, I have reflected on your presence and have also come to the conclusion that you are not worth the fight it would require to expel you from my realm. Therefore, you are hence allowed to travel freely as long as you do not get in the way."

As she talked she kept glancing over at Usis. Over and over I saw her eyes shift to my companion. I was beginning to worry we were about to have a problem but nothing came of it. I took a sip of my wine and set the goblet on the table in front of me. "Might I ask, Mistress, would you allow me at some point to interview you?"

I knew it was a long shot so I wasn't surprised when she said with a smile, "Most certainly not. Now if there is nothing else, I will leave you to your duties as I resume mine. This bit of folly Lucifer has gone on has already taken up far too much of my time."

We rose, bowed and were quickly shown from the room. As we reached the end of the hall Kitar thanked Balic who added, "You are now allowed to travel freely within and without the Keep and my Master's realm." Not waiting for us to say anything or to ask questions, he bowed deeply then left. With that our first meeting with the Overlord ended as quickly as it started.

# Entry 158

"Well that went better than I had feared," commented Kitar as we headed back to our room. "You're asking to interview her shows you are still stupid enough to have balls, I might add. I was surprised she did not overreact, as is her nature, and instead just told you no. Otherwise, you did very well, you have quite a gift when it comes to sucking up."

Rolling my eyes, I snarked, "Gee thanks, that's both a glowing endorsement and a slap down. If I might say, you have an ability to be a real smart ass. In case you hadn't been told before."

"Well when in the presence of a master, one is remiss if they do not observe and learn," he commented as he headed up the stairs, chuckling to himself.

I spent most of the rest of the day in our room getting my entries in order since my little bug had again decided to attach itself and start digging into my back. The little fucker. It, and I say it because I still have no idea what it is. I'm pretty sure it has a personality. Knowing what I know now it's probably a construct of some kind. I wouldn't be surprised to find out it has the soul of a fucking editor trapped in there, always bitching about commas and that kind of shit. Now in Hell it was attached to a writer and could exact its own kind of wrath. I say that but overall, we've come to a tacit agreement as to when it starts becoming a bitch. It originally had been made aggressive so the "editors" or whoever could ensure they got their entries. Now after all these years, I and to a lesser extent we, meaning Usis, myself and Kitar had settled into a routine where I was left alone once I started writing.

I worked most of the afternoon until Kitar and Usis came in suggesting I take a break and we go down and get food instead of staying in the room. When we found the dining hall, there was a buffet unlike anything I had seen spread out on the tables along the walls. "This is quite a setup. Is it like this every day?" I asked one of the Demons sitting beside me. I thought I was being nice but from the way he was staring at me I think he was trying to decide if he should pinch my head off and have me as part of his lunch. It was then that Kitar stepped in and in an overly polite tone said, "I do not think you have met Keith, have you Olic? This is the writer you have heard so much about. You know the one under The Dark Lord's protection." He smiled a disturbingly innocent smile with that last part.

I could see the change in demeanor almost instantly. "Oh no, this is not normal. There are several Hellspawn on the Plane right now training so with so many royalty and…" he paused then added, "…and special guests it seems her Mistress has decided to increase the level of grandeur." He rose slowly then bowed to us. "It was a pleasure to meet you finally…what was it, Keith, but if you will excuse me…" And he rushed off like his ass was on fire.

"That was mean," I said to Kitar.

"This is Hell, mean is what we do," he replied.

Once we were back in the room Kitar excused himself saying he needed to meet with The Dark Lord, something he did now on a regular basis. I was hoping one of their agenda items was going to be the developing issues with Usis. As he pulled the door closed Usis strolled over, completely nude, of course, and straddled me, "Do you have plans now that we are alone, My Lord?"

I raised my eyebrows. "Actually I do and I'd like you to be involved." I led him along just to amuse myself. It was fun but to be honest I was ignoring the bumps on his forehead. Even close up they were not that obvious but there was no mistaking they were there. I sent a silent prayer, I know funny, to Kitar in hopes that he could find an acceptable explanation that didn't include my boyfriend becoming a Demon.

Reaching up he began to unbutton his top. "Oh thank you, My Lord, that is very kind of you to include me in your plans."

"Well, then you'll need to get dressed."

He made a confused face. "What? But I thought? Wait, what is it you want?"

I let my eyes drift over to the door. "They say we can go anywhere on the Plane. After seeing those pictures the other day, I'd like to know what else is going on in this castle."

Usis couldn't hide the surprise on his face. "You want to go sneak around? What has gotten into you? First you say you want to see the more extreme side of Hell and now this?" With both hands he gripped the sides of my head so he could look me in the eyes. "What have you done with my boyfriend? Who are you, oh mischievous spirit?"

I burst out laughing but played dumb. "What? You don't like the idea?"

"Oh no, I love it. It's just not you. I do it all the time."

"See, that's why I asked for your help. When in need, find an expert. Lead the way, master spy. We've been told we have full access. I want to test that."

I'd never seen Usis forget about sex so quickly. He was up, dressed and ushering me out the door before I could rethink the wisdom of this decision.

We both realized pretty quickly that neither of us could remember the way to the tunnels. We stumbled into the main hall and hid behind one of the massive columns. As had become my habit, I wanted to see what was happening today. This place was always busy, even when the Overlord wasn't here. Tonight, for example, there were rows and rows of what appeared to be damned, all stripped naked, in neat lines, kneeling to a winged Demon sitting on the throne at the far end of the room. Throughout the room several other Demons were walking about swinging incense burners, the smoke curling up like confused caterpillars until it became lost in the haze that hung just above the damned's heads. The Demon on the throne was chanting loudly, and both Usis and I stood in awe as the damned started to glow, from the inside out.

They were silent at first but as they grew brighter their wails began to fill the room. Soon they were so bright they were almost blinding and their cries so loud as to be almost deafening. It was then in a great flash they blew apart. Their bodies vaporized leaving behind only small balls of light maybe two inches in diameter. The winged Demon intoned what sounded like a chant while holding up a small ornate gold cylinder. As he finished all the Demons in the room stopped and together said "*Dominus dominus noster*, Lucifer," causing the balls of light to race into the small tube. Just as the last one zipped in the Demon placed a cap over the opening. Extending his arms out another Demon came up and bowed, raising a long black candle before him. He then knelt, went down flat on the floor, all the time the Demons chanting, "*Dominus dominus noster*, Lucifer," the candle never moving from vertical. After several prostrations, the one holding the candle rose and walked up the steps to the throne. He then poured some of the black wax over the end of the tube, sealing it.

Usis shrugged. Neither of us understood what had just happened. I motioned for us to move away, as we watched Balic head off down the hall. Keeping our distance and hiding behind columns, we followed him and sure enough he led us right to the entrance to the tunnel just like we were hoping.

# Entry 159

As Balic disappeared we waited huddled together behind one of the pillars. Me in front, Usis behind, his hands playing over my chest as he hugged me close and giggled in the midst of our covert operation.

When we were sure the assistant was gone, we darted across the hall and ran into two large souls coming up from the tunnel. The leading one was female and I ran smack into her large tits and bounced off. They both burst out laughing as did Usis. When the laughter reached the floor, I too joined in.

"Watch yourself. Had they been smaller you might have been injured." She again laughed as they hurried down the hall. Usis reached down and helped me up. "Guess it's been a while since you have pounded your face against a female's breasts?"

"I don't think I have since my mother."

He laughed as I walked past him and down into the tunnels, closing the doors behind us. Now that we were here we had no idea where we were going. We stumbled and skirted along picking halls at random, mostly worried that we would get lost. We came upon a room, there was silence in it, which was uncommon for the rooms in this hall. The door was ajar, so we assumed it was empty, both of us had been curious about what was stored in them, so we peaked.

There in the room sat a man in a chair in front of a canvas. Spread out around him were paints, no more like pigments. We quietly walked behind him. He was painting at a furious speed. Usis walked slowly around him and then stopped motioning for me to come. I did, he pointed, the man had no eyes, they had been violently ripped out. Again, my companion pointed and there on the table sat the bloody orbs.

I couldn't stand it anymore. "Why are you here? Who are you?"

The painter paused as if roused from a dream, "Oh, sorry I did not hear you come in. Are you someone I should bow too?"

"No, I am just a soul passing through. What are you painting?"

"My home."

"Forgive me but it doesn't appear to be anything but a bunch of blotches. I don't see a home."

I stood watching, the way he put large patches of blacks, reds and blues on the canvas at random. Just the application of color with no rhyme or reason. At first I didn't see anything but eventually images began to appear as if stepping out from the canvas. I was amazed at how the picture started to emerge from the chaos, "You are good. If that is your home, was it destroyed?" I asked.

He shrugged, "Yes. At my hands."

"Why?"

"I was angry. I was their king and they had betrayed my orders. The citizens that is, they had not followed my commands. So, I had them killed and the city of my birth destroyed."

I realized this was one of those random moments I kept saying I wanted. "Was it so bad as to merit their deaths?"

"Of course not..." he paused, "well I say that now. At the time it seemed like the most important thing in the world. They had joined with the ones we were at war with."

"Why were you at war?" I asked.

"The raiders, they were nasty desert nomads, had stolen and freed our slaves. It was our kingdom's lifeblood." As I listened to him I felt Usis stiffen. "The city was at the edge of the kingdom. The raiders took it and the citizens joined willingly. I was so angry, so betrayed. I sent everyone, all my troops. I led the army and we surrounded them. The nomads feeling secure had left, the slaves freed. The citizens, seeing our force, surrendered. I did not want their surrender. I did not want them to kneel before me. I wanted only one thing, their deaths. They had embarrassed me, my birth city, they had risen against their king. We took it, we captured all the adults and in mass made them watch as we slaughtered their children. In horrible brutal ways, we made the children scream. Some so young to not yet know words but they knew agony. Then with their young laying in piles before them we left them chained to the walls and razzed the city. Burnt it to the ground. I sat in a tent just outside drinking wine and toasting their screams."

We were speechless. He continued, though he had no eyes I could tell he was reliving it in his mind. "My child, my beloved son, he walked up to me. I could see the anger in his eyes. I was not the man I had become. We fought. I had him taken away in irons. That night it seems he talked to his guards and while I slept they rallied the troops. The last image the desert ever saw was me hanging crucified upon the burned-out walls of a city I was born and ultimately died in. My last act was to spit out the name of my only child as my blood flowed onto the sands and I watched them place my crown upon his head. When I awoke next, I was here, in Hell and began my journey to this room."

I was amazed, horrified and feeling justified by his story. It was Usis who recovered first, his nails digging into my hand. His anger causing his next question to impact me more. I didn't understand. "You were a painter in life as well? Where do you start? I have never understood how one painted."

He stopped and set down his brush. His wounded face just staring at the canvas. Eventually he answered, "I never painted. I have never seen what I paint now. I am not allowed, she will not let me. It is my rage I paint...." He paused for a long time. "Painting, in many ways, is like rage. You must get past the big blotches, find the colors then, what shapes it, and only then, can you start to put the details to it.  We deconstruct our world to paint it, and we deconstruct our minds to find the primary colors of our wraths and disillusionments. They are much the same, if you think about it," he said as he resumed his work.

We stood and watched as he painted himself into the conflagration. As his figure took shape I could see him hanging there in the center of the canvas spread eagle on a cross. His chest open, his internal organs splayed out before the masses. Usis let out a gasp as the same horror were visited upon the old painter. My hand went to my mouth as we watched as his chest split open and his entrails cascade down the front of his body and onto the floor.

Usis grabbed my arm and started to pull me back toward the door. We both smelled smoke and were then frozen in shock as the canvas and then its painter burst into flames. The cries filled the room. We backed into the tunnel and closed the door. I thought of what had just happened. We had thought it was an empty room. I remembered what David Hockney once said as I stood staring at the door as smoke rose from the thin gap at the bottom. "Do we know what an empty room looks like?" I felt a hand take mine as I followed Usis down the hall and the wails of suffering had returned.

We wandered for a long while, passing souls, Demons, abominations, with each corridor there was something new to discover. It was like the tunnels were a separate part of this Plane. Then we came around a corner and there before us was a dark hall. Two guards, blue Demons with small wings, large hooves, stood blocking the path. Usis and I stopped, if this was guarded what was it guarding?

Shrugging remembering what the Overlord had said I walked up. I was free to explore anywhere. They stopped me, I lifted my amulet, don't ask me why. They stepped aside, not a word was said. Both Usis and I stepped past the two protectors and continued down the ever-darkening hall. The walls wept moisture, like a fool I touched it, I felt the surge of anguish, it was suffering, I should have known.

We reached the end of the hall, it was a long one. It was almost pitch black. There were torches but they seemed to be losing the battle. Before us stood a door, ornate with large rings. I slowly pushed, it slowly opened, making not a sound.

I carefully peaked around the door using it to protect my body. Before me was a stark concrete room. I'm sure it wasn't actually concrete, but it had that color and texture. On both sides of a wide path were square pools of suffering that took up the entirety of the room. The path itself led down the center and stopped at an ancient Egyptian tomb. Just a stone box about ten feet on all sides. In center front were a set of carved doors being guarded by two sphinxes, one on each side.

We stepped in, and it was then we noticed, not all the room was the pool. Against the side walls, both left and right were ledges, raised slightly above the water and some thirty feet away. On each ledge sat six hellhounds. Their bodies black as pitch, as big as lions, their eyes dancing with the fires of Hell. They lay like simple statues, matching the two sphinxes who lay sleeping with their heads on their paws.

As I took in the still elegance of the room until I heard a noise behind me. In the doorway stood Dozzer, Lucifer's Hellhound. He growled and walked closer. Tilting his head, he studied us and then moved past and walked into the room. We followed. Now all the Hellhounds were watching, as Dozzer led us down the stone path, just an inch, no more, above the pools of suffering. As we approached he let out a small roar, waking the two sphinxes.

In unison they lifted their heads. They were the same color as the stone with eyes that glowed a dark green. As if orienting themselves their eyes first found me, then Usis, and finally Dozzer. For what seemed a long time nothing happened. Then the two sphinxes bowed their head just slightly, and Dozzer took a couple of more steps forward. We stayed where we were.

The doors to the crypt opened slowly, no one initiated it. There was something inside. Like a magnet, I was pulled closer. Dozzer had laid down across our path blocking me from getting too close. Inside I could now see a figure, male, no wait, female with wings. They were white. This creature was wrapped, neck to toe, in bandages, like a mummy. Only its head wasn't covered, even it had been shaved. I leaned in getting a small growl of warning, as horrific as this creature was its appearance was still angelic. From its body and wings, span thousands of wires, taut from the weight. Each starting at some point on the figure then traveling to the chamber, anchored in the walls, floors and ceiling. Suspending the creature angled from front to back in its tomb. Its feet a mere inch from the floor. The wires on the wings pulled them out, taut. I stood in wonder at the beauty of the installation. Was this another piece of art? Like the painter in the room?

Its eyes moved and focused on me. I took a step back in surprise. It then spoke, in a sultry voice I recognized, "I guess it is time for that interview you wanted." And the doors framing her closed.

Dozzer rose and started to walk from the room. Stopping halfway he waited for us. It was clear we were to follow, and we did. As we left the room the large doors closed behind us. We continued up the hallway and through the tunnels a ways until eventually seeing the dim light of Hell's dusk just ahead of us we emerged just outside the Keep walls. There in the thick fog stood Kitar and our two guards. The hellhound nodded then walked back into the blackness of the tunnel. Kitar said, "You remember I can track you, right?"

# Entry 160

I was both shocked and angered at having been led right back to Kitar. From behind, Usis put his arms around me. "It seems we are not as sneaky as we had hoped."

I smiled. "How did you know we were here? Who was that in the tomb?" I started to ask another question, one I could no longer remember, when my attention was drawn to what was below me. I could barely see through the haze. We were standing by the moat.

"I told you, I can track you. Do you really believe after all the trouble Our Lord has gone through he would allow you to just wander off? One would have thought even you would have learned that lesson by now. As for who is in the room you just violated, that is not my tale to tell." As I walked to the edge, he added, "since we are here and clearly you are not near as tired or behind as you seem to have thought you were, maybe it is time for you to see one of the punishments that awaits those who hide and guard their wrath. This is the Stygian Marsh, where the sullen are exiled beneath the water for their unexpressed rage. For eternity, they are secluded from all that is, nothing interrupting their pain, never again given the opportunity to see The Father, The Dark Lord, or his Creations. They wander lost here in the moats surrounding the Queen of Hell's Keep.

"Wait, what?"

"The sullen," answered Kitar.

"You are going to need to explain more than that. I thought sullen was just pouting."

"These are those who while living develop and nurture a great rage or wrath against another, be it a single person or a group. In forever hiding their wrath, most see themselves as virtuous due to the misguided belief that by doing nothing they have spared those they despise. They never realize that it is the carrying of wrath that is the sin. It does not matter whether it is seen or unseen. Also, sullenness often manifests itself in a grumpy, or evil-tempered attitude toward life. Sullenness causes the soul to begin seeing themselves as the victim and often they cut themselves off from the world around them. The Father hates this most of all and sees it as the creature removing themselves from his Creation. Therefore, once here, we sentence them to an eternity cut off from everything, drowning in their own pain and loathing, in other words, their suffering, thus they fill the moat."

"All of this is their suffering and from simply being submerged like the souls back on the Gluttony Plane? Why is there so much?"

"Because, as you know, interacting with someone else's suffering causes one to experience their pain as well. As has been demonstrated several times in your travels."

"I very well remember, it still causes me to shutter. The question is, are we bringing one of them up? Otherwise how will I see what they are going through and possibly interview them?"

Kitar turned his gaze downward at that point and I knew this wasn't going to be the answer I wanted to hear. "As I have said on several occasions, Keith..." again with someone using my name. "...as you travel down the Planes it is going to grow harder on you to complete your duties. Sadly, you will need to enter the waters so you can walk amongst the damned."

"NO! I will not allow it," screamed Usis as we both turned in surprise. "No! Do you hear me? NO!"

Shaking his head, Kitar said in a soft, but firm tone, "This, little one, is something you need to stay out of. You are suggesting you are going to 'not allow' The Dark Lord's writer to do his job?"

"Yes..."

"No," answered Kitar in a flat dangerous tone.

"The Dark Lord does not understand what is required here," barked Usis grasping at straws. I reached over and put a hand on his arm trying to calm him.

As I did, I noticed Kitar stand up straighter. "Are you suggesting that Lord Lucifer be informed as to a possible unpleasantness his charge might be required to endure? That said Lord would not have considered all the implications of having a soul tour and document his PLANES?" The last word Kitar barked out with such force as to cause Usis to take a step back. I, on the other hand, stepped forward and in front of my companion, my natural instincts to protect him overriding any anger or fear.

"No what I am saying is that your callous uncaring heart would force Keith to do something regardless of the ramifications to promote your own selfish agenda no matter how it impacted him. Your goal, I believe, is completely self-serving. Keith freed you from being a judge and the way you repay him is by ignoring the pain he will have to suffer to fulfil his charge and all because you want to prove your worth to that Lord and Master you so worship. Maybe if you do not already have the worth you seek you will never have it. Did you ever think of that?"

As Usis finished speaking I realized I agreed with him. That coupled with the way Kitar addressed my companion sent me into a rage. "Now listen here, when you speak to Usis, you speak to me. You will never again raise your voice or use that tone with him or me. He, my dear guide, was with me before you came along and will be here long after I decide to replace you. So, you should remember your place. Do I make myself CLEAR?" I yelled the last word as well...

Kitar paused for a moment and then leaned forward so our faces were just barely touching. "If you for one second think that creature in anyway figures into your duties, you, my dear servant, are sadly mistaken. If he interferes with or becomes a detriment to your appointed, not voluntary, duties then I will remove him from the equation. I personally think he is good for you. I personally think he is a stabilizing force in your travels. I personally feel he should stay with you for as long as possible. I do not, however, have any delusions as to whom my loyalties are to. I will tell you now, little one, it is NOT to you and less to him if he interferes in my obligations, which are to see you finish this assignment. And I will do just that even if I am required to strap what is left of you to a Demon and extract the words from your writhing soul as you are tortured on one of our many forms of amusements. Now do I make myself clear?"

Kitar snapped his fingers and walked into the tunnel followed by the two guards. Surprisingly, now thinking back, it wasn't his words as much as that fucking snap that sent me completely over the edge. Just before he was outside earshot he added, "Now you take some time and get your head where it belongs. When I return, you are either going into that suffering voluntarily with the spell I can give you for protection or I can throw you in without it."

I screamed, "You dare remove my guards. They're assigned to me, you mutt. As you yourself have pointed out, this is MY assigned task. You'll stop right there and return to my side where you've been instructed to serve. NOW. That is a command, boy."

They didn't immediately respond but my small victory was I also no longer heard footsteps walking away. I turned to Usis instead, he was who I was worried about. Walking over, I wrapped him in my arms. "Don't let him upset you. You know Kitar, he will say whatever he feels is necessary to ensure I do what I've been tasked with." Pulling him back a bit, I continued, "You never doubt that if they do anything to harm you, or try to remove you from me, nothing in Hell or that The Dark Lord could ever do would convince me to continue in his service. We are in this together, and I know Kitar holds you dear as well. So, don't let his little bit of puffery scare you. I'm under The Dark Lord's protection not his. And you, my love, are under mine. And nothing in The Host or Hell is strong enough to change that."

Together we sat on the edge of the moat, his head resting on my shoulder while I wrapped him in my arms. Finally, I snapped a command and from out of the tunnel walked Kitar and the two guards. Leaning in I whispered into Usis' ear, though I knew our guide could hear, "See, he talks a good game but it's clear who he serves."

We both heard a low growl. Since only Usis could see my face, I smiled at him letting him know we were still in this together. He nodded almost imperceptibly.

# Entry 161

To recap since so much other shit has been happening... Remember we are on Wrath and there are two main parts of Wrath. The first is the battlefields which I have not yet visited and the second is sullenness.

After the exchange Usis and I continued to sit quietly staring into the fog. I wanted to make Kitar wait. I wanted him to stand there and know, I knew, he was being forced to wait. Eventually I asked Usis, "Are you alright?" He nodded. "Good, then let's get this show on the road." (Note: Don't get me wrong, I was still seething, but I knew nothing could be resolved right then, right there, so I decided to drop it until next I saw The Dark Lord. Then some things were going to be cleared up, for everyone. Regardless of the outcome.)

"Are you going in?" Usis asked.

This time I nodded before saying, "You know I have to. The argument wasn't about what I needed to do but about how he treated you. I knew I was going in, there wasn't a question about that. I just was not having your concerns dismissed by him because he thought his were more important. They're not."

"So, I just step off into the moat?" I asked in my most cheery voice.

"Well yes and no," answered Kitar with a smile as I shook my head. He reached out and placed a hand on my shoulder. I thought he was about to give me a good shove but instead I felt lightning shoot through my body. "Now you can, you're protected to a limited degree."

I heard Usis growl.

"First, what do you mean by 'a limited degree'? Second, why don't you tell me what to expect. That always seems to go better." I was using a very condescending tone. I couldn't help it.

"There is nothing I can do to stop you from feeling the pain of the souls within. What I did was help keep your conscious mind from getting absorbed into the suffering. You will feel what they feel but it will be like you are watching yourself experience the feelings, if that makes sense."

I nodded. "It makes complete sense. I'm not sure how helpful it will be, but I guess we'll see. You're telling me I go in alone? Just to check, you know this sucks, right?"

"Yes, on both counts. Rest assured I can bring you out if you get stranded, or absorbed too deeply into the images and appear to no longer be able to function. But know that I will only pull you out if I am absolutely sure you have become lost."

"I understand." I kissed Usis whose worry was painted on his face. "I'll be fine, see you in a few." I walked over and stepped off into the moat.

Instantly I choked, not only from drowning, something Kitar had not prepared me for, but also from the sheer intensity of the wave of emotions that besieged my mind. Though I could feel myself being pulled down I tried to swim back up as fast as I could. I think a hand broke the surface because the next thing I knew, on the verge of passing out, was me being lifted out of the water and laid on the shore. I've no idea how long I lay with my eyes closed, weeping from the overwhelming pain and hatred I felt from the suffering still wetting my clothes and clinging to my body. When I opened my eyes, there standing over me was Kitar and my head was cradled in Usis' lap.

"Well that did not work as I had hoped," was all our guide said.

Hearing him, my head hit the ground followed an instant later by Kitar. In shock, I reached over and took Usis' foot trying to stop him from advancing. He'd punched Kitar. Our guide rose and I could see him starting to shift but Usis didn't budge. "Go ahead and change you son of a bitch. I can wear a fur coat or Demon scales, I really don't give a shit. You said your spell would protect him," he barked.

In a frail but apparently adequate voice I snapped, "Stop it, both of you, *now*." Hoping it would break the tension, I said, "Well, you're correct, that didn't work. Do you have a plan B?"

"No, your insignificant pathetic judge does not, but I do," said the Overlord as she hung above us. Her colorful eagle wings kept her lazily afloat. I watched as she centered herself and then relaxed, allowing body to gently touch down, first a toe, then foot, then both. Everyone bowed, I didn't I was still flat on my back, after all. Nudging me with her boot, "I had a feeling our beloved Lord, if that's what you want to call him, would not provide as he should. It is a trend with him..." Kitar started to say something again the Overlord's eyes warned him against interrupting. "You will keep quiet, little judge. You might think yourself important or special, but to me you are just another damned in need of punishment and a reminder of your place. Make one sound and I will personally consume your soul and send the leftovers to our master." Touching my forehead with a finger she added, "I can help you with your problem, though." I felt a sharp pain that vanished as quickly as it started. "There you will be protected when you enter the water. Remember it is I who provided for you, not Lord Lucifer."

Usis asked, "No discomfort?" He was still being very protective.

She stopped, clearly was fighting a smile as she noticed Kitar who was still rubbing his jaw. "None, but more importantly did you just punch your guide? Did you, to use his (pointing to me) crude vernacular, hall off and punch a judge of The Dark Lord's?" She was smiling widely and Kitar was growling.

"He sent Keith into that shit with basically no protection and then told us we just had to live with it. I am not sitting by and watching my love suffer needlessly." Usis was so adorable when he was indignant.

Sigos smirked as she said to Kitar, "You know I am starting to like this one." The comment clearly hit the mark as Kitar's growl grew louder. She walked over and punched him on the arm. "Do not tell me you are upset. I know you, of all people, respect strength.

Admit you are impressed or you can go sit in the mouth of the tunnel and turn that judge eye on yourself, a little self-reflection might do you some good."

Kitar stood for several second seething until eventually huffing twice and walking back into the tunnel, where he sat down against the wall. I couldn't help but start laughing. Kitar's eyes shot up to the guards when he heard a snicker from them as well.

I sat up. Any emotions I felt from the suffering that dampened my body had vanished. I stood and shook a bit. I don't know why I felt like a dog after a bath. Walking to the edge, I paused beside the Overlord. "Is there a time limit to this spell?"

"No, you have all the time you need. It will dissipate when you have not been emerged in suffering for a length of time. You can even come back if you need a break. And before you enter the moat, keep in mind they cannot talk or see. You will not be able to communicate with them in any way, but you will be able to see their visions. This will provide you the information you seek."

I wasn't sure what she was talking about but realized there was only one way to find out. I stepped into the water again. I hadn't warned anyone, and just before my head entered the suffering I heard Usis cry out. I raised my hand above the surface and signaled that I was fine.

I sank, this time allowing the downward pull to have its way with me. I floated as if in slow motion. I kept dropping further and further. I began to worry that maybe there was no end. Panic set in. I struggled to see through the murky water. At first there was nothing then…. Darker shapes started to appear in the water below me. (Please remember when I say 'water' it's not water, it's just easier to write this way.) I continued down like a sunken ship racing to the bottom of the ocean. As I watched, the shapes began to grow firmer, more substantial, but I still didn't see the bottom until I hit it. Hard.

I stumbled and caught myself on the body of a nearby soul. I didn't have a chance to see why he was standing in that spot or what he was doing before I was plunged into his experience.

He had lived on a strange world. What I saw through his eyes made very little sense to me. It appeared to be a cave, but I knew from the information the vision was feeding me that this was his home. He stood and walked to the other room, there was screaming. As we walked by a reflective surface for the first time I saw myself, well him actually.

The upper half of his body was that of a mantis and the lower appeared to be more human, all of it was brown and scaly. From his face extended two short mandibles. They didn't come together so they must have been purely decorative. His long arms ended in sharp point, also much like a praying mantis. But today they hung to his side, dejected and angry. Much like his emotions.

As we walked I realized I couldn't control what I was seeing or doing. I was just a rider. I could however search his memories, his thoughts. But it wasn't just the thoughts. I could feel his anxiety, the way his heartbeat sped up as he relived the hatred and pain of his life. All his emotions. When he sat alone and cried, my eyes filled. All that he had been, I temporarily became. I don't want to go into the full story of his life. My mind was flooded with everything. I was him. I knew him. I had his memories, and still do even now as I write this. I'm torn, do I do him justice or do I stick to what is applicable for this Plane?

It sucks not having Goodreads where I could get feedback from my readers. I'm pretty sure most would hate the journals anyway. After all, they are living and believe they have a firm grip on everything. It's amazing when I think back and realize just how foolish we were. I guess the only consolation is there are ten creations, or maybe nine now, I don't know. Anyway, however many there are, everyone in all of them think the same thing. It goes back to the old question, slightly changed, of course. If all of Creation is foolish who is really the fool, the Creator or those who follow him? Ok, that had nothing to do with the story I have just had a couple of glasses of wine and thought of that. Sorry.

Here is what's applicable. His society in many ways was like a mantis. The males of the society were bred, weaker, and disposable. So much so they were often consumed by the wife and her family when the offspring was born. It was a tradition, part of what made a man a man. His wife though was one of those equal rights for the sexes type mantises. She thought it was bad what happened to men. She loved her husband. He hated her and their three children. Yes, they had three not just the one. He should be dead, consumed in a brutal fashion by his wife's family but no she wouldn't allow it. She didn't think it was right. She loved him, she said. How could she love him and disgrace him like she had? Did she not see the looks they got when walking in town with their children, him at her side, people knew, people could see? He carried that rage with him like a poison. It destroyed their marriage, his relationship with his children, one he shouldn't have. The kids hated him, they were picked on in school, he should've been feasted upon. He lived his entire life, a long life by their standards, and then one day as an old man, he died. He died having never been given the rights other men had been given. He took that hidden hatred, that wrath with him to his grave and into the afterlife.

I pulled my hand away. I sat down on the rocky bottom of the moat and cried. My feeling mixed, he was angry because his wife loved him above all others, he was angry because he hadn't been consumed as was their custom. He hated his children like they hated him. He hated his wife. All his life he suffered quietly, keeping that wrath hidden inside, that unexpressed rage. I didn't understand, I felt he should've been thankful. Did all of us have self-destructive actions that we insisted upon though would lead ultimately to our own destruction, I wondered.

I crab crawled back against the side of the moat, away from all the bodies. Now I could see a bit more clearly but still not far in front of me. Hundreds of creatures filed by, wailing and crying while many more just curled up on the ground ignoring those who stumbled over them. All suffering. Many had horrific wounds on their bodies. At first I thought they might had been attacked, which could also be the case, but others were mutilating themselves as they lived out their own private recollections of Hell. To isolate them even further their eyes, mouths and ears had been removed, now nothing but wrinkled scars. These souls had been separated from everything in Creation. I studied them. Watching as their bodies ripple in the murky depths. I realized what I was seeing was suffering. It's physical manifestation wafting off them like heat from a pavement on a hot summer's day. They were making real their pain, filling the moat with gallons of wrath. I stood and started to step forward when a female bumped into me. Again, I was sucked in; this time just flashes of her past. Nothing much, a woman who gave up everything for her husband and spent her life passively aggressively hiding her wrath. She died, she's here, like her life, nothing then, nothing now.

I immediately pushed myself back up against the wall. I became scared to move, not knowing whose life I would be thrust into next. Each time it happened I felt like I was going to be physically sick. I began to forget I was on the floor of a moat with millions of gallons of suffering surrounding me. Thanks to my protection, it just felt like water, nothing more. The Overlord had said to reach out and touch the soul if I wanted to know their story. I did not have to, they would bump into me, sucking me in, then throwing me out as they walked out of my reach. I had to hold on if I wanted to stay and see their stories.

# Entry 162

I couldn't just sit here and worry about who bumped into me next. I pulled myself up, sucked in my nerves and stepped away from the wall. As I worked through the crowd, weaving and dodging, I stopped when I saw a soul curled up on the ground. He appeared to be choking. I touched him, he was a fresh soul, newly introduced to the moat. I saw them seal his eyes, ears and mouth, then the terror of not knowing what would happen next. His body convulsed when he was thrown into the suffering. At first his mind responded believing he was drowning but that was quickly elapsed by the images from all the others pain taking hold of his mind. While he drifted like a pebble in the waves he curled up into a ball until finally coming to rest on the sandy bottom where he lay awaiting his own nightmares to begin. I could only guess, after time untold, his mind would adjust and just leave him lost in an eternity of his own wraths.

Through the cloudy water, I saw a creature sitting quietly in a little nook. The wandering souls seemed to change their path to avoid him. I worked my way over, experiencing souls along the way. Nothing of note. As I approached I saw him motion for me to join him. That was strange. There was just enough room in his little nook for another person. I sat cross legged with my hands resting on my knees. He lifted his hand and placed it over mine. I was no longer there in the moat on the Fifth Plane, now I was in a starship.

The creature sat in what appeared to be the captain's seat staring out at a planet, well to say it was still a planet would be a mistake. It was what appeared to be parts of one. There were two large pieces and hundreds of smaller ones. Steams of what must have been water floated in space, undulating bubbles of freezing liquid. The creature whose vision I was seeing, magnified the view on one of the large globules. I could see the razors of crystal arching through the quickly chilling sphere. It was clear, whatever had happed, had just. Inside were masses of plants, sea life, creatures, some looked sentient, all struggling to figure out what to do, of course they were powerless to change their fate.

The image on the screen was focused on one of the creatures, his arms swimming wildly as he tried to escape the frigid tendrils rushing to cradle him in its icy arms. When they finally caught up, all movement stopped as his form was embraced by the solidness of its new tomb. As the image pulled back, where there had been an undulating ball of water there was now a solid irregular sphere of ice with little impurities trapped inside. The chair turned suddenly as the creature rotated around to see his crew all standing watching the deaths below. He stood and walked away, saying nothing, he didn't need too. Years of hatred and war had just ended. The remnants floating outside the ship were not only the planet. Some were parts of a small moon the enemy, like the mind I was in, had dragged into orbit, the gravity taking hold causing it to crash into the planet. They had hoped to just destroy the surface of the world not wanting its complete destruction. He was now angry at the scientists who had miscalculated. As he entered his quarters and threw himself into his bunk I realized inside this creature was wrath, hatred, of so many other things. His bitterness was his life support, it was what put him to bed at night and what awoke him each morning.

My first thought was, this is not sullenness. It had been acted out. Having been in several heads now I was beginning to understand how to dig around to find what I wanted and I did. I raced back through his past and then forward until the time of his death. The race he hated had many worlds and over the course of his life he had watched most of them destroyed. It was when the damned soul removed his hand that I realized, sitting there, he had never shared this hatred. He was not the leader ordering these acts. He was just a soldier doing what he was told, it was, after all, just a war. I read how through his entire life he had been trained, brain-washed, to see 'them' as the enemies. He carried a wrath for a species he had never met. He killed billions but never stood before one.

I sat their thinking about how this was so much like people back when I was living. Though not destroying entire planets so many populations carried the shortsighted ignorant views that their race was the best and others were less than them. It amazed me how they spent all their time indoctrinating their children from birth to hate people who didn't fall into their limited scope of what a person should be. These same people claimed they loved The Father, all they were really doing was teaching their children to hate. Justify it anyway you want, you are sending your children to Hell when you teach them to see people for their differences. Not one of you have ever made it to The Host, I can assure you of that, right now. Now more than ever it makes me wonder how The Father had created such stupidity and it appeared never bothered to correct it. How flawed was *he*? But then maybe he didn't create the differences. Maybe that was done after he was gone by The Host. They didn't want us deplorable creations in their The Eternal City. So, I guess carried hate, even taught from childhood, is sullenness. Again, I find myself not pitying those who are here, they fostered their sin and deserved their punishment. I know this paragraph is a bit preachy, live with it or die ignoring it. I will see you when you get here.

I stood and started kicking my feet, it was hard but slowly I began to ascend to the surface. For some reason, I'd started to feel the suffering of the souls around me again. Was the spell wearing off? By the time I breached the surface my mind was screaming. It wasn't as bad, but as I was pulled ashore I still passed out.

# Entry 163

When I again clawed my way back to consciousness I found myself in our bed back at the Keep. I rolled over to find Kitar sitting with his feet on the table, his chair tilted back, smoking his pipe, as had become the custom.

"Welcome back," he said.

His words were like fingers being pulled from the dam. The torrent of memories rushed down upon me as the experiences in the moat hit me full force. My hand went to my head as I tried to rein in the flood of thoughts. "What if it was religious?" I blurted out. I don't know why I asked that, so many other questions were fighting for their place.

"What?"

It took me a moment to realize myself what I was asking. It was the question on my lips, well in my head as consciousness had been ripped from me. "The soul, the last one I saw, he'd been trained his whole life to hate another species he'd never met. He carried that hatred, that wrath, if you will, helping kill billions. It wasn't a religious wrath, this time, but so many are. What then?"

From behind me I heard a voice, it was the Overlord's. She was standing in the doorway. "Wrath and hatred can be many things. Like most, few sins are singularly based."

I wrinkled my brow, rubbing my head. "I'm not sure I understand."

*(NOTE: the next bit is a very complicated explanation of the nature of Wrath and the sins associated with it. I've already started to notice a trend and expect it to continue. That is that sins are becoming more complicated to understand and explain as we move down the Planes. I tell you this now, to prepare you. This gets tricky.)*

"Let's use Wrath, since you are here, as an example. First let me explain Hate and Anger. Anger is to negatively feel emotions toward another due to something you feel they did to either you or someone else. It does not become a sin until it is allowed to make a home in your soul, it then becomes Hate. The execution of the Hate becomes Wrath. Now I say that, but not always does Hate have its seeds in Anger, as you saw with prejudice, which is instilled, like in the soldier. That is Ignorance, the belief that someone should be hated for no reason other than you have been taught they should. So now Ignorance, not Anger, is the conduit for the sin of Hate. If that Hate is acted upon it becomes Wrath; if it is not, it is then Sullenness. Sadly, the sin of Prejudice is often practiced by those who follow The Father. Just because The Father is displeased with a soul's actions does not give license to his followers to be Angry or Hate that sinner. That is Judgement, and only The Father can judge a soul. Anger, Hate or Wrath for religious reasons falls into a different primary sin. Which is the sin of Judgement. Which means the soul sees themselves equal to The Father, and then the soul's damnation is no longer based in Wrath. But I will come to that."

"And Sullenness?" I asked shifting in the bed. This was way more than my mind could absorb having just regained consciousness. But since we were already this far, we might as well finish it.

"Sullenness, is much the same, but the focus of that Hatred will never be openly expressed. Though it is not openly acted upon, it will still affect all of that soul's future relationships and behaviors in negative ways. The worst is, as you saw, with the soldier, is when a society, or to a far greater degree, when a parent transfers their perceived Hatred to a child, be it theirs or others. To make it even more complicated, if the child when reaching the age of accountability chooses to nurture that taught Hatred, they can possibly become condemned due to the sin of Ignorance. The only way out is if they practice forgiveness and it does not turn into Hatred. So sadly, a child can, for all practical purposes, condemn their souls to our charge here in Hell before they have even really begun life. As Kitar will attest, many say they carried that Hatred because it was taught to them. That does not hold merit after the age of accountability. No one, ever, makes a soul act a certain way. They can influence it, but the adoption of a belief rest squarely on the shoulders of that soul. Each creature is responsible for their own soul. The teacher, be it parent or otherwise, does however also become guilty of Treachery due to the inherent trust the child had in them. You will learn about that on the next Plane. See it is a cascading link, one sin leads to another, the only way to stop the process is to cut out the original tumor and in most cases that is nothing more than forgiveness or acceptance."

"So, religious sins are the same?"

"No, when a soul performs any sin in the name of The Father, meaning it is their justification for their sin, then the container, to use our old example, would not be Wrath but Heresy or Blasphemy."

"Why those two?" (Hang in there, we're almost done.)

"It's based upon the soul. If the soul does not know they are sinning against The Father, they tend to end up on Heresy. If they know their actions are against The Father's wishes and ignores that knowledge, not changing their beliefs or behaviors, then they are guilty of Blasphemy. Those responsible of betrayal of The Father are cast down to the bottom Plane, the Great Plane as we tend to call it for there is no greater sin than knowing The Father's will and choosing to ignore it."

Something about what she said struck me, but I couldn't put my finger on it. She waited, like she knew. Finally, it hit me. "The Great Plane, where The Dark Lord and the Fallen live?"

She didn't answer but just nodded.

"So, they are on the Plane where the damned go when they ignore The Father's wishes. A Plane, I might add, which was created for the Master of ignoring The Father's wishes, Lord Lucifer himself?"

"Yes, little one, if you have not learned by now then let me be the one to instruct you. Lucifer might have created Hell and assigned each Plane its purpose, but he committed Blasphemy and like a magnet he has drawn those like him down to him."

"Thus the soul doesn't have a weight that causes it to sink through the Planes of Hell like I had originally thought, but more accurately a soul is drawn closer, as they descend, to the greatest of all sins..." I paused.

"Yes, you are correct, little one. He is drawing them closer to his bosom based upon how like him they are." Smiling, she turned to leave. "You rest now...I think you have just discovered there is still much for you to learn."

# Entry 164

*(Note: I hope I didn't lose you with that last entry, and that you understand the importance of it. I think it marks an important moment in my travels. Again the responsibility of where I am and what I'm writing is beginning to be driven home.)*

I woke from the nap and Kitar, like a rock, was still exactly where he had been earlier. "Where is Usis, have you seen him?" I asked.

"He has not been back to the room. If you are ready to stop lazing around, I can take you to him."

I gave our guide a sideways glance. Why couldn't he just tell me where Usis was? I shrugged. "We will talk about what happened in the moat later or you can just read about it." As I pulled back the covers I realized something for the first time. "I never thought of this before? Do you get to read the entries before they go out?"

"Of course, it is great insight into your mind. I find it interesting how over time your approach to them keeps changing."

"How so?" I asked as I pulled on my clothes.

"You used to write them like a journal, as was originally intended. Not written to anyone in particular. Your more recent entries are more like you are talking directly to the reader. Are you interested in knowing my thoughts about that?"

I shrugged. "I hadn't noticed but sure, tell me, oh wise one, why has my writing style changed?"

"I think it has to do with you missing your life as a living creature and this allows you to feel closer to the living again."

"I can't say I miss living but maybe you're right. I feel like I'm talking to my readers now, even though I don't know anything about them. They're not even from my world anymore since it's gone." I frowned, that was still a bitter pill to swallow.

I followed Kitar out of the room and down into the tunnels again. I started to quiz him about my conversation with the Overlord but decided to leave it for now. I was curious where he was leading me. The last time he decided to show me what Usis was up to, I found two imprisoned angels being tortured in the most brutal of ways, so needless to say my apprehension was growing. We traveled a different set of tunnels this time. Finally, we came to a locked door and ascended a set of steps up. When windows appeared, I could see the city below us. "We're in the city?"

"Just the other side, this is the wall surrounding Dis."

He opened another door at the top of the stairs and we stepped out onto the battlements surrounding the city. They were wide and sturdy. "What's with the battlements, for that matter the wall? Why is it so serious?"

Kitar smiled. "Sigos rebuilt this town almost from scratch after she took over. Once you get to know more about her you will understand, but suffice it to say she was a general during The Great War. When she came here she built this city like she thought it should be built. That includes walls. They are often used in the war games."

He pointed out into the distance. Then for the first time I could see the true purpose of Wrath. I had seen bits of the war games, as Kitar called them, but now they were spread out before me.

Off to the sides were tents and camps, everything I remember seeing back when I watched period movies of the middle and roman ages. That made me think. "Kitar, if there are so many species from so many technologically advanced planets, why does it all look like the middle ages on Earth, and why do the weapons seem so primitive?"

"Well, first the buildings only look like the middle ages, as you call it, from Earth because that is your only reference. There are vastly different buildings, but your mind probably chooses to overlook them since you could not, with the flow of information, process them. As for the weapons, swords and the like were a creation of

The Host. You surely have noticed Lord Lucifer and the others all wear swords of office. They have just filtered into Creation over time as many things do. As to why the weapons and, for that matter buildings, are not more advanced, it is because this is Hell and they use what they are given. We would not give laser rifles to the damned, not only because some never saw them, but also because someone here in Hell would have to manufacture them."

As fast as he started, he stopped, but then it made sense. I turned my attention back to the Plane, where the bulk of the expanse was nothing but an ongoing battle, isolated skirmishes with overseers watching from tall platforms. Then off to the right was a free for all, total war, no organization, no structure, just hand to hand combat. Kitar pointed as I surveyed the scene. Then, with a cough, I saw what it was he was waiting for me to see. In a small training area was my companion, Usis, and he was sparing with that handsome Hellspawn I'd seen back in the Keep.

Their movements were like a dance. Usis would lunge and the Hellspawn would parry. The Hellspawn, oh what's his name...wait...Elick...I had to check. Elick would spin bringing his sword around only to be met with a high upward swing deflecting it off to the left. "He's good."

With a wrinkled brow Kitar answered, "Yes, he is, he is very good."

I watched a while longer then my attention was drawn to our guide. He was rubbing his chin and watching very closely. Every once in a while, he would react with surprise and then shake his head making this clicking sound with his tongue. "What is it? You keep making that noise. Tell me what you are thinking." I asked.

"He is very good, almost too good...Against...Hoooo..." barked Kitar as I turned to find Usis with his sword at Elick's throat, the Hellspawn flat on his back. Now everyone in the area was watching.

"Ok, what is wrong with my Usis kicking someone's ass?"

"Well nothing exactly..."

"Well then broadly..."

"You see, first is should be extremely difficult to best a Hellspawn, especially not one as trained as Elick. Secondly, Usis was a slave, he did not have fighting abilities as I recall."

A little defensive at him picking apart my companion I added, "Well clearly he does, since he just kicked that winged bastard's ass."

Kitar shot me a disapproving look. "Don't be crude. It would be wise to make friends with that 'winged bastard'. He is experienced, receptive and one of Hell's royalty. He is an interview gold mine, that is if he or The Dark Lord will allow you to talk to him. Come," ordered Kitar as we walked across the wall into a tower and down onto the fields themselves.

Stopping just before we reached the area where Usis was fighting, Kitar said, "Might I make a suggestion? Do not let them know the extent of your knowledge about Hellspawns, or your surprise at Usis' skill. There is something happening with him. Let us see what they say. If they are sparing they had to have worked out some acceptable understanding. Just run with that for now."

"Boy, you sure can make playing dumb sound complicated."

"I was trying not to use the word dumb, since I am not always sure you are playing." He smiled broadly.

"Asshole."

"See that is more succinct. Work with that." I walked past him and headed toward Usis who had seen us approaching, so had Elick.

Usis came up smiling and hugged me. He was bare from the chest up and wearing only a thin leather loincloth and boots. The Hellspawn, though dressed similarly, was in chainmail and leather. His body was the definition of manhood. The muscles across his pale chest, down his stomach and on his arms rippled with moisture from the workout. His hair was stark white with streaks of grey giving it an almost monochromatic appearance. His wings, of the same color, were pulled in tight against his back. His boots, the only other clothing he wore, stopped just below his knee, hugging his muscular calves. The way he walked, with the loincloth swaying back and forth just covering his manhood had my eyes focused on his thighs which were exquisite. I heard a cough and smiled when I found Usis scowling at me with a disapproving smirk.

Kitar broke the silence. "Lord Elick, I would like the honor of introducing Keith, The Dark Lord's writer."

He smiled, my knees almost gave out. "So you are this writer everyone is talking about, especially your companion here. It is a pleasure to finally see you in the flesh." His voice was like a gentle breeze on a spring day as it brushed across my ears. He inspected me up and down as I felt those said ears go red.

"Yes, this is *my* companion. Normally his ears are not so colorful. And don't you mean while I was kicking your ass," corrected Usis in an acerbic tone, causing both me and Kitar to shot him disapproving glances. He simple smiled, having gotten the reaction he had hoped for.

"Yes indeed, you are far stronger than any soul I have encountered before. I am not sure what His Lordship did to increase your strength but it is quite sufficient. It was a pleasing workout I hope we can repeat."

Smiling, I watched Usis almost melt now as well. It was clear Elick knew the fine art of diplomacy. "Yes, that would be nice. I truly did not know I had any skills. I have never spared before."

That remark got him a long stare from both the Hellspawn and our guide. I jumped in wanting to change the subject. "My Lord..."

"Don't stand on such formalities with me. Elick will be fine."

I bowed my head slightly. "Elick, then. Would you do me the honor of an interview one evening, maybe over dinner?"

Thinking as a smile played across his perfect lips, he replied, "I am not sure my Great Grandfather would be very receptive to that idea." Then he paused and his smile widened. "Yes, I think I can do that, yes that would be fun. Just have your guide here..." I heard a growl, "contact me with the time and I will ensure I am there. Now if you will forgive me, I must return to training."

Without another word he headed off toward the side of the camp where a large tent was erected. I watched his perfect ass as he walked away. "Well he is absolutely charming," I said.

"He is absolutely charming," I heard in a mocking tone from beside me. I had to smile as I watched Usis just glower at the Hellspawn as he vanished beside the tent.

"Yes charming. Is there a problem?"

"You seem very taken by him."

"You're not? You were the one out bumping chests with him just a few minutes ago. Hell, you already had him out of most of his clothes. You're good. Oh by-the-way where did you learn to fight like that?"

"Yes, I would be curious to know that as well," added Kitar.

Shaking his head, his mood softening a bit, Usis replied, "I have no idea, really. The General said he has seen the damned, as he called me, learn new skills the longer they spend on the Planes. He thinks with all we have been through I might just be adapting." Kitar and my eyes followed his hand as it went to one of the bumps on his forehead. "I was just sparing with one of the souls when I accidently cut its head off." He shrugged. "When I turned around the General in charge was standing in the distance watching me. He said I had good form and next thing I know I am paired with Elick." In a lame attempt to change the subject he added, "Did you watch? I did not see you, when did you arrive?"

"Just as the fight was ending," I said, "Who is this general you are talking about? Is this who I need to see about getting a tour of this area?"

"Yes, probably," answered Kitar as he headed across the field to the larger tents set further back than the one the Hellspawn entered. "Let's get the introductions out of the way."

As we arrived at the tent, I stopped. "What do I need to know?"

"I am not sure which general is in charge right now. Elick did not mention a name. Different Fallen are on duty based upon when their legions need to be tested or trained. We will just have to play this by ear."

# Entry 165

Kitar walked up to the tent, pausing at the door. I couldn't see past him. I don't know what he saw but as quickly as he looked in he let the flap drop and stepped back taking us with him. We stepped a short distance away as he started to explain, "The Fallen in charge is Kimaris." He bowed his head and thought for a moment then his shape started changing slightly. We watched as he shifted, but not fully, into his judge form. He was taller now but not by much, his great horns and hooves appeared and his body took on its original countenance. He might not have been all he was but that was only in appearance, his mannerisms, presence and authority were all business now. "Follow my lead," he ordered in a whispered tone.

Kitar walked in first trying to exude an air of authority. It failed when he stopped short and became a comedy as I ran into him and Usis into me. I felt the growl through Kitar's tunic. "Greetings, Lord Kimaris," exclaimed Kitar in a commanding voice.

Excluding the screams behind us, common for Hell, I heard nothing at first. Then a smooth enticing baritone voice boomed from the tent, so alluring it caused my cock to harden as shivers traveled down my spine in fear. "Greetings to you as well, Lord Judge. I hear you are traveling with our Lord's latest whim." He paused as I peeked around. "Is that, by chance the writer hiding behind you like a scared mouse? Get out here, boy, show yourself." That last part so booming, I swear I whimpered.

Sucking in a breath and straightening my shoulders I stepped around our guide. "Yes I'm The Dark Lord's latest whim, though most call me Keith." I swear I sounded like a child trying to appear important when finally getting asked something by an adult.

With a hearty laugh, Kimaris said, "Well now that you are not hiding behind your guide, let us see what all the fuss is about." I walked about two steps and stopped. "You are from the first creation are you not, I recognize your flaws."

*My flaws, really?* I thought. "Yes, I'm from a planet called Earth."

Laughing loudly, he said, "No, little one, you *were* from a planet called Earth, our Dark Lord's Great Grandson has seen to that." My heart sank anew at hearing again what Xia had done to my home.

"Yes, I just learned about that recently, but thanks for bringing it up. Nothing like pulling the scab off a fresh wound. Want us to relive my first puppy dying as well?" I snapped.

Kimaris with surprise turned to Kitar and raised an eyebrow as he burst out laughing. "Well said, you do have a spine. I was about to send your friend here…" pointing to Usis, "…out to see if he could dig you one up, there should be an abundance of them lying about."

*(Note: Something I keep forgetting to tell you, and before I describe Kimaris, let's get it out of the way. The Powers can be hundreds of feet tall, even taller. It has been said Lord Lucifer if fully manifested can fill a creation, then why are they always so short when I describe them or meet them, even The Dark Lord himself? I finally remembered to ask Kitar, and the answer is painfully simple. They must deal with the living, well the damned to be more accurate, and most of the damned are somewhere between five and ten feet tall. That is the average size of a humanoid in the ten creations. Therefore, if the Demons and Powers were huge, they couldn't easily interact with those they torture. It's just a matter of logistics. See, simple.)*

Kimaris stood about ten feet tall with horns that are almost as big as he was. The first set come out about a foot from the sides of his head and curve down and back forming a half moon, ending in sharp points. What was most interesting and unlike the others I've seen, these horns didn't just emerge from his skull but seemed to be part of it. Where they met his head, the hard bone spread wide covering the entire sides and front of his forehead and top half of his skull like a helmet. Higher on his head just behind a bone shield was another set which curled back and looped twice before ending in sharp points, as well. Behind this massive shield of bone was hair hanging to his shoulders. It was probably the most impressive set of horns yet. Sorry, Lord Lucifer, but this guy has you beat.

Not to sound corny but that was just the beginning. As impressive as the horns were there were also three glowing orbs of purple fire about the size of tennis balls weaving and dancing through them. His face as a whole had the look of a person with a long mustache and beard. But it wasn't hair but bone. His eyes glowed red and danced with a mesmerizing fire. His body was strong and stout, but I could tell you nothing of its detail since he was covered from head to toe in armor. It formed large shoulders, not quite as big as WOW shoulders, that tapered down till blending with the waist. Think of a Viking, big burly man. His arms from the elbow down were visible and dark red with veins running all through them, ending in long, clawed fingers.

The interesting thing about his armor was that all through it were faces, just the front, you know like the face had been peeled off. They were clearly made from the same metal as the rest of the armor but all the faces, from the large ones covering his chest to the smaller ones on his shoulders, were alive and moving. When he addressed me all their eyes turned to face me. Finally, his legs ended in massive red hooves and he had wings which were like those of bats but the membrane was weathered, not torn but clearly had seen better days. He was through and through a warrior.

He walked around the table and with a finger reached under my chin lifting me from my kneeling position. I'd not even realized I'd dropped down. This was one of The Fallen, as horrific and terrorizing as he was, there was still that beauty of The Host peeking out wherever it could. Short of Lucifer himself, this was by far the most intimidating creature I'd yet encountered.

"Welcome to Wrath, little monkey. I think you will find what our Queen Bitch does here worth your pen. I can only assume you have met Sigos? If you have then it speaks well of you, since you are neither clawing your hair out or on a plate with something stuck between your teeth." Walking to the door, he motioned for us to follow. I hung back, letting Kitar go first. As he passed he stopped and whispered in my ear, "So far so good, you have survived the introductions."

We both heard Kimaris chuckle as we hurried to catch up.

We walked a short distance to the side of the tent where there was a raised viewing stand. "Your young... friend here..." Kimaris motioned in Usis' direction, "already knows what I am about to tell you since he has been here for most of the last two days sending creatures to regenerate or causing them to simply flee in terror. Spread out before you are the Mistress' fields of battle. Here is where those damned, due to their blatant wrath and anger, will spend eternity fighting their fellow damned. They fight for a reward most will never see. That is because there is no real reward in holding on to wrath. It is a fruitless endeavor pursued by wasted souls."

"But some get to go to the arena, correct?" I asked.

"Yes, those are the final winners. That will become clear as you tour the area. There are three simultaneous events going on here. The punishment and extraction of suffering of those who in life let their wrath make them victims. The punishment, extraction and futility of those who clung to their wrath while living, only to learn it earned them nothing. And finally, most importantly as far as I and many of my brethren are concerned, the training of our legions in the wargames."

"I've a question about that, and I know it will be answered in time but I'm curious now. Why here? Why train your soldiers here?"

"Is it not obvious? With the help of a lie, those who lived by wrath now get to battle with the futility of their struggles. They are led to believe there is a chance, and I guess in some ways there is, as in all battles, they can defeat the source of their rage and move on to The Eternal City. In truth, it is not their wrath but instead one of our soldiers whose guise shifts and changes based upon who they are facing. The damned rush in eagerly and fight furiously against an often-self-created adversary. What most never seem to understand is there is no defeating wrath or rage, it is an endless struggle against an invisible foe."

"I'm not sure I understand but let's get on with it," I said as we stood watching the carnage. Creatures of all sizes and shapes were fighting with bladed and blunt weapons inflicting mind numbing damages upon each other. Those who had no weapon, their wrath their only armor, fought with hands, teeth and other creatures' body parts, anything they could find to manifest their anger upon their foe. In every eye, you could see the shear hatred the soul carried as they were lost in the visions I thought only they could see. In that I was wrong.

Kimaris nodded curtly and headed down off the viewing stand. "Let us start with a small group so you can get used to the ability I am about to give you."

Kitar stepped forward quickly. "Those are the kind of decisions I make as I recall. What are you wanting to give him?"

Kimaris shot our guide a warning look and stepped closer to Kitar. "It will do you well to remember, Lord Judge, while you are in my presence who I am and more importantly who you are, which is simply a soul, nothing more. What I do needs no permission especially from someone as low as yourself. I have no interest in your directives whatever they may be." He added over his shoulder, "and do you presume I am here by accident?"

I had two different feelings about the exchange. First, I was glad to see Kitar getting slapped down after all the shit we had been putting up with from him lately. On the other hand, I was also getting tired of all these, so called, divine creatures deciding what I was going to experience or, more accurately, suffer through without ever consulting me. "How about asking me what I think, both of you? I'm not going into anymore heads if I can help it. I'm not a Judge, I'm not a Fallen or whatever you call yourselves. I'm a writer and I'd prefer to only have to suffer through the punishment of my own sins not those of countless others," I growled through my teeth.

Kimaris nodded with a smile. "I can understand that. If you find an interesting soul, I can allow you to see their past but for now we will limit your visions to only seeing a soul's manifestations." He touched me before I could respond, and the entire Plane shifted. I reached over, putting my hand on Usis's shoulder as he held me up while my legs tried to remember their purpose. Seeing an opening I added, "Oh and you have to agree to an interview."

Shaking his head, he replied, "No, I do not. I will however let you ask questions, and we will see if I will choose to answer them. As I recall you have already arranged to have dinner with one of Leviathan's grandchildren. He will be a good source for the information you seek as well as a gentle reminder to your companion that he does not control you." He smiled. "Yes, I can see all your intentions, little writer.

I heard the now familiar sound of Usis' displeasure. Really, I tried not to smile but how could I not? It was becoming almost like a button I could push to get a reaction. As he grew louder I noticed Usis had not limited his displeasure to just me, but Kimaris as well was also enjoying my companion's irritation. I kissed Usis on the cheek. "It's my job after all."

In a mocking tone, he snarled, "It's my job after all... Bite me."

"What exactly did you do to me?" I asked the general.

Patting my shoulder with his long taloned hand, he answered in an almost soothing tone, "I am not one of those who just inflict things upon my charges. I train soldiers to fight and to do that they need confidence. One does not gain confidence by jumping at shadows. Fear comes from not being ready. All you need to do is find a soul and say to yourself *Let me see their wrath*."

This was one of the great things about Hell. Since I had not being born in a magical world, it always amazes me when things like this happened. Everything shifted in front of me. Now not only could I see the souls but over their real opponents I could see the blue ghost they were projecting from their rage-filled minds. "So, the ghosts are the source of their wrath?"

"Yes, that is the phantom that houses the wrath these souls will spend eternity fighting. Once they vanquish it, another, if there are more, will appear. Sometimes if the soul feels even the slightest hint of remorse the phantom will fall wounded and beg for forgiveness or mercy, it almost never comes."

"What if it does?"

"We get the added suffering of the soul's remorse when the phantom inevitably appears to die. Eventually the phantom, as well as memory of this specific fight will fade, and the soul will be embittered anew. Watch..." He pointed to a soul who was fighting a Demon. "See how the Demon is overlaid with an image of a different creature, but the soul attacking the Demon is not? It's because the soul is seeing the person they housed their anger in, but the Demon is not being punished but just training so they have no phantom to fight. Now there..." He pointed again. This time it was two damned fighting each other and over each was the transparent projection of a different creature. "They are each fighting someone from their past, not seeing the soul they are actually combating."

"So until one of them falls, they'll continue beating the shit out of each other?"

"A colorful way of putting it, but yes."

# Entry 166 (continued from before)

"Can I walk down?" I asked.

We heard a cough from behind us. Kimaris snapped at Kitar in a dangerous tone, "Do judges catch colds? Hush."

I added because I could, "Yes, hush." He growled, giving me what I was hoping for. I wanted to make a point, not to him but to you, my readers. Take for instance the growling. I keep pointing it out because I want you to see how we are starting to take on each other mannerisms.

Kimaris started down. "You will be safe. They are trapped in their illusions, none will harm you." He pointed where I saw one particularly vicious attacker turn from one person to the next as the old opponent fell. The image before him, the subject of his wrath moved instantly to the other.

"So, if the other person falls, or they simply look a different direction, the subject of their hate will shift as well?"

"Not if they are only distracted, then it would be an unorganized frenzy. Once an image is placed upon another soul it will stay there until that creature is defeated. Then it will shift to another. This allows a continued pursuit if one of the two decides to retreat. It makes the battle more interesting that way. Consider if one's opponent falls as they fight beside two others who are engaged. When the victor of the one battle searches for his next opponent there is a chance he will then project his wrath on one of the two who are already fighting, thus the one will now end up with two attackers."

"Wait, I'm confused. If the image doesn't shift until the person falls, then the victor turns and attacks someone who is already enthralled with another, what does the newly attacked person's first opponent see? Does that make sense. Does the person attacked who is already in battle see a subject not of their wrath attacking?"

"Yes, the attacker will manifest their wrath upon the new person. When that attacked soul responds to the second attacker they will not manifest a second projection but instead will see the new attacker for who they are. What makes this so wonderful is the creature attacked will now see the new attacker as aiding the subject of their wrath and thus begin seeing them as an enemy as well. Sometimes this can have a cascade effect where different soul attack each other in just the right combination ending in a full battle between dozens if not hundreds of souls. It is quiet exhilarating to watch when it happens. You can see the cascade occur as moves through the field."

We stepped out onto the field. Directly in front us two short multi-armed creatures were in a fierce battle. Neither was armed except for their limbs of which each had four. When one was pushed away landing at our feet I could also see the wide mouth full of razor sharp teeth. I'm not going to describe each creature we encountered because I saw a lot of new varieties but this one was like a kobold, if you know what that is. If you don't, think of a thirteen-year-old with scales. The fight was vicious, they were both ripping each other apart. "Is there a way I can know their motivation without necessarily suffering the feelings themselves?" I asked.

"Of course, there is nothing we cannot allow you to see," answered Kitar this time. With a nod of his head he added, "Now just focus on the one you wish to learn more about and ask, *what is your sin*, and you will see their motivation, and history."

As one was thrown at my feet I again asked, "What is your sin?" I felt a breeze brush across my face and arms causing goosebumps to rise. The creature froze as our eyes locked. At first nothing changed, at least with the surroundings. I turned my gaze to the other one, he too was frozen and now I could see their intentions, their past. It was like seeing a person I had known for a while and remembering their history. I said to Kitar, "I'm keeping this skill, its useful." He nodded his approval.

The two fighting before me were from a lesser world that revolved much closer to their sun than Earth had ours. To my surprise they were brothers, which explained a lot, they looked so much alike. They had found each other here in Hell. Their hate for each other was so strong that each had promised they would track the other down so they could continue their blood feud. Now they fought for eternity, an endless battle over possessions and status of a life they no longer possessed. It was then that I realized why I'd noticed them first. They didn't have the blue ghosts over the other, that was because they had gotten their wish, they were fighting the source of their wrath. "How do they keep finding each other? From their memory, this battle has to have been going on for some time here in Hell," I asked Kimaris.

"It is very rare for two siblings to end up on the same Plane with the same sins and able to find each other. Keep in mind, due to the sheer number of souls that come through Hell, when I say rare, it still happens. These two have been battling for a long time and they have developed a way to tell if it is actually their brother or not. I'm unsure how, maybe instincts. One of the reasons is that neither will take the final blow that would vanquish the other. They will stop, wait while the other heals, and then start again. It is a wonderful thing, so we have allowed it. The amount of raw suffering that flows off these two could power a small planet," said Kimaris.

"We are in the section where its one-on-one?"

"Yes, we are near where the souls arrive on the Plane." Pointing, Kimaris showed me where the Seer was. "They enter there, then must fight their way across the Plane. It is individual combat here, then groups, then full battles. Creatures even start pairing up so they can together grow stronger."

We started to move deeper into the crowd so I could get more samples. It didn't take long. We came across three creatures fighting and their overlays, for lack of a better word, were blurry. Kimaris pointed. "See, more than one projection on the same creature. See how they blend together, thus no single one is clear to us? The combatants do not have this problem since they do not see the others projection."

I stopped when I heard crying behind us. On the edges of the fighting were thousands of souls knelt down, weeping. I learned it was the confusion of entering the Plane and seeing their wrath manifested before them. Most had hoped that upon their death they would be free of the endless hatreds and torments of their life. Of course, that wasn't the case. The pain and suffering, the hope that their sins would vanish was as much an illusion as the soul that stood before them attacking or waiting to be attacked. Also, there around the edges, were whole groups of souls whose wrath wasn't of a violent nature. Most lay in fetal positions, trying to hide, while others stood with their arms out simply accepting the assault of those who saw them as their adversary. Kimaris said these would be dispatched soonest to be regrown and thrown back into the fray. They would be allowed to remember the earlier attacks and over time many would learn the only way to delay the pain of regeneration would be to fight back. Therefore, they would slowly go on the offensive instead of just being punching bags. The ground was thick with suffering; it was like walking through a muddy area just after a heavy rain. Our feet were sinking up to the ankles in the muck. Kitar again shielded us from the effects of the suffering as it soaked into our boots.

I watched as one of the attackers defeated his enemy. The defeated fell to the ground, his arm missing, his chest an open wound. The attacked, instead of dispatching the creature, started kicking, spitting and yelling at him, its wrath not as physical but as violent. I was told this happened a lot, the focus of that soul's hatred not being allowed to die, they wanted to drag it out, their vitriol never satisfied. No amount of suffering they inflicted would ever be able quell the fire of hatred in their souls.

For clarity, I'm going to break this area into several posts. This will make the editors less grumpy and I'll be able to focus on the specific areas. This was the individual area, about a quarter of the total battlegrounds. The next area, group battles, was about the same size with the final area being a full half.

# Entry 167 (Group battles)

To our left through the crowds of fighting souls I noticed a large work area. "What is that?"

"That is where the weapons are manufactured. The souls consigned to that area are the creatures who dealt in war but never saw the pain they facilitated." We walked over and I was amazed at how many there were working and more importantly how ragged and damaged they were. Their bodies had been brutally abused. Fingers, missing part, things like their noses or ears cut off.

I turned to the General, but he anticipated my question. "Do you think we let them get off that easily? They spent their lives making or selling the weapons of war but refusing to see the fruits of their labors. Now here, they are not only forced to watch, but like when living, they continue to make the instruments needed to mutilate those around them, though no longer unseen. Now they get to experience the pain their weapons cause. Every strike to a foe out on the fields is also felt here by its weapons creator. That is why they are so damaged. No blow can be fatal, so they are forced to endure until their bodies are too injured to continue plying their craft, then they are dispatched to respawn."

Shaking my head, I asked, "Why don't they just stop? Stop making the weapons. I mean I'm sure you could force them but for some reason it seems that isn't Hell's style."

"You are correct, on both accounts. It is not our style to just let them stop, though strangely they could but they don't. It is in their nature. That is the interesting thing about the living. No matter how easy it would be to just stop hating each other, more often than not the living still chose to walk that path. As for making the weapons, we also instilled an incentive. The faster they work and the better they make their weapons the less they suffer. If one of these souls just stopped, they would feel the full force of the pain their weapons cause brought down upon their bodies. But as long as they work they reduce their own suffering by a small amount." He smiled as the deviousness of the plan sank in.

"They make weapons to do damage they never wanted to witness. They can but don't stop because if they stopped they would suffer the full pain of those weapons. So, by making more weapons they reduce their pain, thus increasing others, which by its very nature increases theirs. This Plane, so far, is laced with subtlety."

"Yes, very much so."

"Wait, where does the metal come from?"

"It is what I think your species called steel and iron."

"But I thought there weren't any metals other than gold?"

"No, gold, like many of the complicated compounds, are created on Avarice but the lesser ones are manufactured in the furnaces below The Great Plane, less care is needed in their production. That is also where the forges used to smelt steel are, which is what most of these weapons are made from."

I commented to Kitar, "See I'm getting confused. It's like I'm not being told the whole story."

"In some ways, you are not. Simply because if we tried to explain every insignificant thing, like how weapons are made, you would get bogged down with details. We are not wanting you to explain how The Dark Lord's domain makes weapons but more about the suffering of the souls. You are told what you need to know as we descend the Planes. This is a good example. The iron and steel are not as abundant on the Planes above. I mean they have it, for example the knives used in the kitchen are made here. The tools the torturers use are manufactured in the many areas like this that are scattered around Hell. Not here since this Plane's demand for weapons is so high. But if we explained everything at your first interaction with something you would never get to the real point. You will be introduced to new things as we grow closer to the Great Plane."

"I really don't like that answer. It makes my previous entries wrong."

"Not really, but by the very nature of your Journal, everything you are saying is from your point of view. There is, of course, much you don't understand and probably never will. We are not going to run around correcting you. It would take too much time. We will let you correct yourself as you learn more about the workings of Hell. (As you can imagine this really pisses me off, but he was right.) Pausing, he added, "You know for yourself you have learned many things which have contradicted something you thought earlier on but, like us, you have chosen to leave it out of your journals because it is not relevant. Correct?"

"I know, still I don't like it. Let's deal with this one so I can get the metal issues out of my mind. Hell has all the metals, it's just not always shared or they use what is mostly abundant. Like most of the stuff on the Third Plane at Bell's was gold because gold was so abundant on that Plane?"

At this point Kimaris stepped in. "Also do not forget who you are dealing with. We are the creators of all that is. If we run short, for whatever reason, one of The Fallen, as you like to call us, can just produce more." He walked over to a large boulder which had fallen from the mountains behind the blacksmith area and touched it causing it to begin to gleam. "This was just rock, now it is the purest steel that can be created. No creature in all of Creation could manufacture something as perfect as this. There is now enough steel in that one bolder to make many very strong, sharp blades. We just don't do it because, well to be honest, it is below us. Why spend our time doing labor when we can get everything Creation needs in one way or another by processing souls? You are, after all, made from most of the elements of Creation. Couple that to the fact you produce a natural by product, suffering, which is your only real purpose, or so many of us believe regardless of The Father's original intentions."

Deciding to ignore the whole discussion about what I should or should not know, I instead returned my attention to the battles.

"So what am I seeing?" I asked as we walked out of the blacksmith area, past the tables of weapons. "Can anyone just grab any weapon?"

"Yes, the more skilled choose carefully where the less experienced just grab a weapon with no forethought, normally something they cannot wield, and charge into the fray." I didn't need to watch long to see an example of both. A humanoid female took a sword from the table then turned and attacked the male beside her who was still choosing a weapon. He was much taller and the only way I can describe him is to say, think of a troll. He was also, clearly, more skilled. Without as much as a second glance he dodged then made three precise blows, two talking off the female's arms and the final one, her left leg. As she toppled over onto the ground screaming he laughed and walked casually into the battles.

I looked out across the dusky light of the Plane as untold numbers of creatures engaged in the carnage of war. Some huge, bigger than three men with the ability to take out entire groups with a single massive swing. Others, smaller than the average height humanoid darting in and out with small weapons stabbing, poking, clobbering anything they could reach.

I watched as a whole group of little possum creatures with blades no longer than a few inches ran under several beasts clearly from Lovecraft's Chuthulu novels, and in perfect unison lopped off their low hanging testacies while laughing loudly. The larger ones, let out a startled scream as their tentacled hands swooped down, with incredible speed, grabbing the little creatures and tossing them into their sharp tooth-filled mouths, swallowing them whole. I thought that was the end of it but no. To my amazement a few seconds later the beasts let out another cry as the possum things emerged from weeping wounds they had cut in the large creature's abdomen.

"It is common for races to find each other and group up. I have always assumed it gave them a renewed sense of their home while alive," commented the General as I watched impressed. As the large creatures fell with a thunderous glup into the muddy suffering pooled ground, the small ones let out a cheer running off to find their next victims.

"Why are they cheering? They seem almost like they are enjoying themselves."

"These creatures do not see projections of their wrath. They are often from the same worlds and still carry a specific hate toward races or creatures who were responsible for their persecution while living. Here the tables often turn and those of like races band together to exercise their wrath upon any and all of their tormentors they can find. Or it could just be an unspecific wrath and they are just having fun while hunting for their true hatred." Again anticipating my question, he added, "Unspecific Wrath is the hatred of a species or group of people with no defined parameters other than them being a member of the said group. Sometimes that "said group" can be anyone within the range of your weapon. These souls hate for hate's sake, little else. As for the cheering, Wrath does not always need to be a somber affair even if it ultimately leads to pain and suffering. It is not uncommon for groups, like you just saw, to come together to wreak random havoc. Most of the time when you see a race working as a unit it is to wage full out war against another group for which they carried Wrath while living. This type of behavior is more prevalent in the planet bound races. Their anger toward each other stems from their differing interpretations of basically the same beliefs. Once they begin traveling space they tend to evolve past these primitive behaviors and become more tolerant," explained the general.

"Are you referring to religion? It seems to be the main source of hatred and conflict, at least on my world," I added.

"Yes the belief or lack thereof when it comes to The Father and his teachings has always been a great source of conflict in all of the Creations. It is commonly believed that The Father might have intentionally made it this way to weed out those worlds that did not stand any chance of entering The Eternal City. If it was not

The Father, then it was most certainly installed shortly thereafter by a member of The Host to ensure the Holy City remained uncluttered by those from Creation."

I watched in morbid fascination as most of the surrounding battles stopped as their combatant's attention was redirected to tearing apart the massive creatures and consuming them. When the crowds had cleared, going back to their own private wars, I saw the rat things, which have been present on all the Planes, swarm in to clean up the remains. I nodded, "As gruesome as it is, I must say these battles are a very well-oiled self-maintaining machine."

"You can thank the Overlord for that. If Sigos is anything, it is efficient."

# Entry 168 (War Zone)

As we passed into the biggest zone I realized how each area had increased not only in violence but also in the intensity and skill of the fighters involved. Here, to put it simply, was the art of war. I could see many creatures that weren't damned engaged in the wargames as well.

I was never good at war reporting. When I worked for a paper just out of school I tried to cover one of the riots that started because of the aforementioned President from my old world, the dipshit. But I couldn't explain chaos. Here was no different, there was nothing to focus the eye or mind on. Everywhere around me there were creatures hacking and slashing at each other. Some with weapons they were randomly handing out, yes there were weapons carts that wove through the crowds offering souls a new or better weapon. They were like hawkers. "Oh that one won't do against a wontalic, you need something with more of an edge. Here try this one." And the Demon handed the creature this huge long blade on a pole. With glee the soul snatched the weapon, swung it a couple of times to get the feel and then hurried back into battle.

I watched as one vendor distracted a creature by suggesting a longer weapon against his current opponent. As the would-be attacker reached for the suggested sword his opponent took that opportunity to separated him from his head. It flew up into the air, circled twice and landed neatly on a spike sticking up from the side of the cart. The Demon threw the weapon back on the stack as he exclaimed, "And we have a winner" as he headed off into the crowd. I find it interesting the little bits of humor scattered about. It's almost like souls, both the damned and those who live here, search for places they can insert happiness, no matter how dark, just to add that second of joy to their existences.

We worked our way into the crowds, don't ask me why. All around us souls were chopping and hacking each other to bits. I felt like a president, no not that one, I mean a real president. My guards stood on each side, in front of me was Kitar and Kimaris with Usis walking beside me. We were working our way toward the center. There in the middle of the fighting was the Hellspawn and several larger Demons. "That is one of my brigades. The Hellspawn is Leviathan's great-grandson who I know you have met."

"Again, with the great-grandsons, like Xia. Where are the sons or the grandsons, or daughters for that matter?" I asked.

"They have all reached maturity and are working on the Great Plane. You probably will not see many of them," answered the Fallen.

We walked into the clearing. It was only a clearing because no matter how wrapped up these souls were in their own rage and hate, they were still smart enough to not come too close to the big scaly Demons or the guys with the wings.

I made a small circle now that I stood in the center of all these millions of souls fighting, hurting each other, and screaming. Some of the words filtered through to my ears, much of it I didn't understand, some I did. They were yelling about The Father's love, how they hated this person or that group. I turned as Kimaris started to say something and I held up a finger. "Why is this area so big?"

Kitar answered, "Because these are those who pretended to carry Wrath and Rage in The Father's name. They pretended to believe but in truth only used bits and pieces of what The Father taught to fuel their own agendas. These are the righteous whose hatred produced nothing but suffering around them. These are the truly damned. That is why they..." he motioned at the Hellspawn, Kimaris, and the Demons, "...train here. There are few creatures on this Plane as worthy of personally being punished by those who rule Creation, be it a lowly Demon or someone as exalted as Kimaris, as these."

"In that case I want to see some of these creatures and know their stories. I've been thinking about what I would like to do when I finally meet those fuckers who pretended to do The

Father's work but in actuality were nothing but shitheads. The ones whose own sadistic streak caused them to encourage others to torture and ostracize those who were different from them." As I finished my tirade I saw both Kitar and Kimaris staring at me in surprise. "What?" I said innocently.

Kimaris nodded as if in approval. "You will do fine on the upcoming Planes. Hang on to that wrath. It will soon serve you well. I see Rage and Hatred inside you, little one. If not here then on one of the Planes to come, take the opportunity to exercise some that that anger on a few deserving souls? We love it when the damned decide to become the executioners, as you have most certainly already noticed."

"We will see. I try to stay detached if I can," I said as my mind raced back to the comment Kitar had made when he judged me, *you can lose yourself and become a monster or you can hang onto who you were.* I didn't care, I suffered for years listening to these pieces of shit stoning trans children, booing kids because they were different. These fuckers deserved what they had coming and if I could bring them just a little bit more pain it was worth a little monster in my soul. "Let's continue the tour and I will revisit the places if I need to fill in some blanks later."

"All that is left is the Main Arena. Would you like to see it next?" asked Kimaris.

"The Arena?"

"Yes, think of it like the coliseums in your world's Roman times. We stage hand-to-hand battles and exhibitions there," explained the General.

"I noticed you didn't say mock battles," I said raising an eyebrow.

"There is no such thing as 'mock' in Hell, do or do not as I recall."

I smirked at the *Star Wars* reference. Smiling Kimaris just said, "I am omnipotent remember, well to an extent, anyway." He saw me pause then finally he added, "We will have the private box which is saved for visits from Hell's royals. We can talk there."

"Hell's Royals? You mean The Dark Lord?" I asked.

I watched as his smile faded. I'd already realized my mistake. "We all stood shoulder to shoulder against The Father's disappointment, little one. I, no we, are all as royal as our dear Lord Morningstar."

I bowed my head in a sign of respect. "Please forgive me, My Lord. I didn't mean any disrespect."

He started laughing. "No disrespect taken, my sin is not Pride."

We followed him across the field. As we walked the combatants either moved or vaporized into a cloud of dust clearing our way. He never as much as slowed or showed a reaction. I felt a hand move down my arm and then fingers curl between mine. Usis did as he always did, supported me. With my companion, I smiled as we turned and walked together through fields of Wrath.

# Entry 169 (The Arena)

When our escorts, both guides and guards, weren't protecting me from those trying to attack us, Kimaris was making comments to his soldiers about how to improve their fighting technique. I saw a lot of creatures dispatched just during that walk. Some from the battles but more because they didn't move fast enough. This was my first time to walk a Plane with one of The Fallen and I was starting to see just how, well, holier than thou they felt they were. I'd think, and I'm being conservative, that probably several hundred thousand souls were dispatched in the time it took us to walk from the fields to the Arena.

They kept talking about the Arena but the problem was I didn't remember seeing one even when I flew over. I mean I saw the small one on the fields but that wasn't the one they were talking about. Come to find out there was a reason. It was in the mountain itself and it was a sight to behold.

(This was the second landmark on this plane. The first was The Bridge of Souls. Now the Arena. I point this out simply because we are starting to see, as we move to the lower Planes, that not only the brutality is increasing but also the spectacle. As much as I fear the Planes to follow I am beginning to eagerly anticipate the architecture.)

Walking down the path into what appeared to be nothing more than a cave, I didn't expect much. What I saw once inside again showed me the grandeur of Hell. Not the pain and suffering, oh there was that, but here on display was its majesty. This Arena was clearly manifested through eyes which had beheld the divine. The cavern itself had to be some three hundred feet high and two to three times as long, how far back I've no idea.

As is always the case with sights like this I wonder how to explain it. The roadway was a dark brown worn cobble stone. Off to my right were several sets of doors leading into what I was told are the private quarters used by visiting soldiers of Hell's Legions. The VIPs, if you want to call them that, could choose to stay in the

Keep. I wasn't surprised to learn that Kimaris stayed here with his troops. He was the consummate warrior. I honestly would have expected nothing less from him. The barracks were made from the same stone as the street with great banners hanging along the front representing each of the major legions currently in residence. In total, I was told, there were several thousand troops currently housed here, most were Kimaris' since he oversaw the battles right now.

Across the street to the left and past the Arena was another large building. It boarded the slaves and gladiators. At first, I thought he was talking about the ones brought from other Planes but learned they also housed and trained slaves here, as well. These trained slaves could become gladiators, warriors, and of course, entertainment. It was becoming clear that the slave trade was a serious industry on all the Planes. I guess I was noticing it more now since we were talking about acquiring one ourselves. I'm still not sure how I feel about that.

As for the Arena, picture the Coliseum in Rome but constructed from the same brown stone as the other structures in the underground complex. The outside, was four circular stacked rows of columns and arches, each at least forty feet high. Before us, and directly across from the entrance to the complex was the steps leading up to the Arena. On each side of the steps towered two large Demon statues. From their raised hands hung great smoking braziers suspended from chains. Their flames lit the entire entrance and roadway.

The first floor was awash with creatures, both important and not, rushing about. Kimaris led us down the inside path to the left and up a flight of stone steps. We switched back twice until we came to another opening. When I stepped through I broke out in a big grin. It was really like being in Roman times. Circling the battle area were several rows of seating rising halfway up the Arena, just simple stone benches. The combat area in the center was about half the size of an American football field.

We stood in a box, surrounded on three sides by railing about twenty feet above the arena floor. Instead of stone benches there were half a dozen large ornate thrones. The biggest being in the center with the others to each side. Kitar nudged me. "The large one is for the highest-ranking Hellion in attendance. Today that would be Kimaris. You will sit to his right and I to his left."

"And Usis?" I asked.

"He sits beside you."

As we moved around and took our seats, Kimaris clapped twice and two servants scurried up bringing wine and foods which they set on the small tables beside each chair.

Without waiting Kimaris launched into an explanation. "Dis is the second, well third if you count the First Plane, city you will have encountered. This is the first with an arena. You will see them on most of the planes hereafter. The largest and most grand, of course, being on the Great Plane."

I laughed. "This isn't grand?"

"It is nice but nothing compared to Pandemonium's."

I quickly became engrossed when the first two competitors entered the arena. Two damned. One was large with six arms standing and about seven feet tall where the other was a short green creature with long K9's. The smaller one reminded me of a troll from old science fiction. You could tell the large one was confident in his ability to win but quickly realized he wasn't near as fast or flexible as the little guy who kept running between his legs. They fought for a while, just typical gladiator stuff but then with no warning a bell rang. "They can now use any racial or learned skills," said Kimaris, leaning over to me.

Before I could ask what he meant the little one shot across the ring, did a double front flip in the air catching the big guy off guard and buried his sword in the creature's skull. I actually found myself standing and cheering as the little guy wrapped his legs around his opponent's torso and started pushing the weapon down, slowly cutting the creature in half. It was horrific but equally awesome. When the little guy reached the neck the two halves of the big guy's brains fell out onto the sand. As he started to fall forward the little guy rode him down continuing to slice his opponent in two.

Finally, the battle was over and the little guy was declared the winner. "Do they get some kind of award? I don't know a day off from being tortured?" I asked trying to sound funny. Well clearly, I wasn't.

"No," answered Kimaris with no humor. Then added with a half grin, "It is better. Remember the torture of the souls headed for the lower Planes? Well this is how they get the honor of going over there and living out their fantasies."

"Oh, that's right," I nodded. We were still deep in conversation when I heard Kitar choke on his drink. The next thing I knew he shot past me and was staring wide-eyed into the arena. I followed his gaze and almost fainted. There in a loincloth was Usis. It was then I noticed his chair empty. "When did he slip off? And why is he in the arena?" I bellowed.

I almost jumped over the railing until I felt a hand on my shoulder, it was Kimaris. "He signed up therefore you will not interfere," he said as my blood turned cold.

"But..." I choked out.

In a low tone, he said as his eyes blazed up. "It is forbidden. I would suggest you sit down and enjoy the battle. Give the writer more wine."

I lowered myself slowly into my seat.

Kitar started to say something as the General added, "This is only an exhibition. Neither will be dispatched. Chopped up, limbs severed, disemboweled, sure, but both will remain on the Plane." With each adjective, my eyes grew wider. What kept ringing in my ears was that he'd signed up for this, it wasn't against his will. I was seriously thinking about putting a collar back on that boy. As my eyes refocused I could see both Kitar and Kimaris enjoying the hell out of my reaction. With anger in my eyes I said to no one in particular, "Can I get a collar and leash at the training facility?"

They both broke out laughing. I'm going to skip how disturbing the image of Kimaris laughing is, but it appeared he felt sorry for me. He added, still chuckling, "Do not worry, I will put your little friend back together when Elick finishes with him."

Again, I choked. "He's fighting a Hellspawn!"

"Did I leave that part out? Apparently, he is feeling a bit jealous about how you reacted when you and Elick met. I suggested they should settle it in the ring," commented Kimaris.

"WHAT...they're fighting over me?"

"It is so sweet," mocked Kitar with his tongue hanging out. I shot the finger at him.

"Well not over you, as such. Neither is seriously upset or anything. Well Usis might be a little. Since they were sparing earlier it was suggested they do an exhibition."

"Suggested, what fucking idiot would suggest that kind of bullshit?" I barked.

"That would be me," answered Kimaris in a tone I was starting to recognize. I was pushing my luck.

"Oh, I didn't know." I tried to smile and look contrite. I really wanted to strangle the motherfucker. Clearly, he could tell.

"Are you telling me you would not have thought this was suggested by a...how did you say...fucking idiot if you had known it was I who recommended it?" asked Kimaris now clearly prodding me.

"No, I just wouldn't have said it that way. I would have still thought it." I winked and did a fake mock bow. He raised a glass.

Snapping for the boy to pour more wine, he added, "So just sit there and watch the battle as your little boyfriend shows you how much he loves you by getting his ass kicked by a Hellion."

I decided this conversation was over. I settled back in the chair, downed the glass of wine and held it out for another, it was refilled and this one lasted longer.

Elick walked into the arena. He too was in nothing but a loincloth and like Usis carried only a sword. Had this been any other opponent I probably would've missed the fight completely, too busy staring at the Hellspawn's body. It was a thing of beauty. He was pale, I mean really pale with muscles everywhere they needed to be. His shoulders were broad, cascading down in the front to perfect pecs that dropped like a cliff onto his muscled abdomen. His back was broad and both faded down to a thin waist. Though the loincloth hid the front, his ass was there for all to see. Had I been a religious man I very well might have dropped to my knees and thanked The Father for creating such a work of art. I heard off to my side, "Close your mouth. It is good to see you are correct. There is clearly nothing for your companion to be worried about. You are the model of reserve." I ignored the comment but accidentally growled.

I heard a cough from Kitar who motioned towards Usis. Oh shit…. He had been watching me assess the Hellspawn. As anger flashed across his face, he didn't wait for the match to start but lunged, bringing his sword down in a long unexpected arc.

Elick let out a loud 'umph' as he quickly moved to block. Knocking Usis away, he parried and brought the weapon around as Usis jumped back, but not quick enough as a thin line of blood formed across his chest. I let out a yell. Turning to Kimaris I squeaked, "What are the rules?"

"There are no rules, this is Hell," He said in a way that made it sound like I had lost my mind. I was starting to notice he had a sarcastic streak. Not having one myself it was amazing I would notice…Hush readers.

I jumped up and ran to the edge of the box closest the arena. "NO RULES!" I yelled to Usis as my fury was unleashed. I spun on them both in a blind rage. "He's protected as I am. He's wearing the amulet which makes him an extension of me. Do something! *Stop this, Kitar!*"

"Do you see the amulet on him?" asked Kimaris.

"What...WHAT...he took it off?"

"It would not have mattered. I overruled it so he could spar," commented Kimaris casually.

A grunt brought my attention back to the action in the arena. I'm not sure what happened but there was something... "Is that blood..." across the Hellspawn's back and a notch taken out of his wing. "GO, USIS!" I yelled.

Even though I no longer needed to breathe I still found myself holding my breath. I was told early on it was only a muscle memory. I sat riveted watching Usis and the Hellspawn jabbing and stabbing back and forth. Neither had been seriously wounded but both carried injuries. In addition to the cut on his back, Elick had gotten a slice across the face, both legs and sadly across that spectacular ass (hey sue me, cute is cute). Usis was equally as injured, having taken several hits to the chest, one pretty bad. His arm was bleeding and he was now limping, but still not badly.

It was Kitar who finally broke the silence in the box. "He is doing far better than I would imagine a soul could do against a Hellspawn," he said to Kimaris.

"Yes, he is indeed," replied Kimaris. I watched as he studied Usis' fighting style more closely. "I noticed the spots on his forehead. He seems to be changing in some way but still I did not think for a moment he would hold his own. There is no way this should be happening." I watched as he closed his eyes, not for more than a second. As they popped open in shock, he exclaimed, "Damn," as he stood. With a clap of his hand everything froze. I mean time literally stopped, the crowd, the slave in mid pour, the combatants, me and Kitar as well. I can only assume the reason I saw what happened next was due to the protections of my necklace. I couldn't move but I was still able to watch.

Kimaris extended his great wings flew out over the arena. Dropping down between the two combatants he wrapped an arm around Usis' waist and flew him back to the box where we were sitting. He removed Usis' sword and set him down toward the back. With another clap, time resumed. Usis finished his swing, with no sword, and fell forward to slam his face into the chair and then collapsed to the floor. Elick swing came around and he spun in circles and then fell flat on his ass with a confused expression.

"What the fuck," I barked.

Kimaris turned towards Usis, then back to me, then back to Usis, then again to me. He started to say something but stopped himself, again he started, again he stopped. Finally, I yelled, "WHAT?" In any other situation, I would've been amused to see a Fallen so dumbfounded.

Nodding to himself, he said, "I reached out to The Dark Lord and he instructed me to stop that battle now. You and your little companion seem to be under more protection than I thought."

I spun on Kitar and screamed so hard spit flew from my mouth hitting him in the face. "Like I said..."

If Kimaris thought he was having trouble with me he clearly had not planned for what happened when Usis woke up. At first, he sat calmly with no reaction as I explained why the General had stopped the battle. As I walked back to the chair, Usis sprung to his feet and jumped on The Fallen's back pounding on his head, cursing. I have to give Kimaris credit because other than some really creative curses involving The Father, Gabriel and Michael, he handled it pretty well. Pulling my companion off again frozen mid-swing he sat him down. "Now you will calm down or I will fly up and place you in one of those empty arches outside the Arena where you will stay for the rest of eternity. You can speak..."

Usis grumbled a few undistinguishable curses. Turning I added, "Tell him you will behave. He just saved your life."

"He did not save my life. I was winning and I am dead already," Usis growled. I raised an eyebrow as Kimaris stood with his arms crossed. Finally, Usis added, "Fine…"

Kimaris smirked and Usis fell forward but didn't attack again. He did grab the pitcher from a still very stunned slave boy and drank it completely down.

# Entry 170

Everyone looked at me. My mind was racing. This whole dog and pony show felt like it was quickly barreling down a hill, and I didn't know what the fuck was going on. I took a deep breath, had my wine refilled and announced that I was going to watch a few more matches, which is exactly what we did. Usis finally plopped down in the chair beside me, pulling one of the slave boys up into his lap. I started to say something when he said in his defense, "He is treating my wounds."

Laughing I glanced at his raised loincloth. "I don't remember that being wounded?"

"That is why he is sitting on it, to protect it," Usis replied. I just shook my head but I heard Kimaris chuckle.

What I did find interesting was how Elick took the match ending. He didn't say anything. He just bowed to Kimaris who shook his head, letting the Hellspawn know it was over. He shrugged and walked from the Arena. Everyone else went on like normal. On our way out I detoured over to the barracks and found Elick. I invited him to dinner at the Keep the next day. He asked, of course, if my *companion* was going to lose his mind. I told him not to worry about it.

Thankfully nothing happened as we worked our way back, after all we took the tunnels. I think all Planes should have tunnels. It really cuts down on problems, horrid sights and, well, the overall pressure on my nerves. What did change as we walked back was my mood, it kept getting worse.

We made it in, said our farewells and headed up to our room. Usis walked through the door first, still grumbling, and I followed behind him. As Usis prepared to start in on me with his own anger, the slam of the door brought him up short. I spun around and screamed, "What the fuck are you doing going into an arena without your amulet against a Hellspawn, you stupid mother fucker?" I immediately regretted the last part. I was angry, scared and well worried.

Usis blinked a couple of times before he realized I was actually expecting an answer. "Well, you just seem so interested in him, I was jealous. I do not want to lose you and he is just so much more than me." He dropped to his knees and buried his face in his hands. "I was nothing but a slave and...and...well what hope do I have against something as amazing as him."

I rolled my eyes. "You've got to be fucking kidding me. Haven't we been through this like a hundred times by now? Yes, he is hot, I mean fucking hot, I'm still not sure I don't want to spend a night with him..." Usis' tear-stained face popped up out of his hands and I heard a shocked growl. "Oh sorry, I got distracted from my point."

"Which is..." Usis wasn't crying anymore and his anger was exacerbated by the fact I started laughing at the look on his face. Hey, I've had a rough afternoon.

I sat down beside him pulling him in close. "You are part of me. I couldn't replace you if I wanted to. Just as I hope you couldn't replace me. We're in this together. How many times have I told you that? Why would anything change?"

Usis was now wearing his damned pitiful face, the one he employed when he was trying to apologize without actually having to say the words. Reaching up and touching the bumps on his forehead, "Well...it is just...I mean...he just so...and something is happening to me. I was not sure you would still want me."

"Finally, I was wondering if you were ever going to bring that up. Both Kitar and I were questioning if you were even aware of it or just not talking about it." Kissing him on the top of the head, I added, "But first let me finish your partial sentences. ... It's just...I am so insecure, I mean...I am silly to ever question you, he is just so.... hot, sexy and smoldering in manliness..." I smiled.

"I am sure none of those are correct," he answered defiantly. Wiping his face as he stood and walked over and getting us both a glass of wine. "I am just a little scared...I mean what does this mean and are you going to be mad at me?"

"I can understand why you're scared, I am too. Did you do anything to cause your body to change?" My mind went back to The Lovers. "Kitar and Kimaris seem to think you are becoming a Demon." As the words left my mouth I knew they were a mistake. His eyes went wide and began to fill. "No, don't freak out. This is Hell, Usis, we have no idea if this is normal or not. Think about everything we've gone through. The Lovers, De Sade's Theater, all the other traumas and horrors, this could be natural. We'll just need to find out more. Whatever it is, we're a couple, that I can't see changing. I'm on the payroll, after all, of the entity that helped create Creation, I'm pretty sure I have some pull."

Biting his inside lip, he said, "No! I did not do anything to cause this to happen..." Again his hand found his forehead. "These are not all. My legs are getting hairier and my toenails look like they are turning black." He was trying to put on a strong face, but failing, I could tell how miserable he felt.

"We will figure it out, Usis, I promise."

Lowering his head and kicked his foot in a staggeringly cute, shy way. "Are you going to bed him?"

"Who?"

"The cute Hellspawn."

"Oh...I doubt it. But I'm going to dinner with him tomorrow. As I recall you have bedded how many other than me? We have an agreement and I haven't really exercised it. Either way, it in no way changes my feelings for you."

"Well, yeah, but I am not as civilized as you," he said as we both rolled our eyes as he crawled into bed.

I followed, adding, "Don't worry. He will be a wealth of information and if sleeping with him is the currency needed to access that library then it's what I'll do."

"Oh now you are full of shit. The currency...really...you slut... I know you want the information. Do not try to feed me the line that you are making a sacrifice to get the interview by forcing yourself to have hot steaming sex with that gorgeous specimen of a man. I know you, Keith. You want to get into that kilt because he is sex on hooves."

"Well, yeah, there is that." We both laughed. I decided to change the subject. He had given in, so now was time to let it go. I stared up at the ceiling for a long time. Something was changing about him, and I knew The Lovers was where it started, but I just had to wait and see how this played out. He'd been awake more than me. Who knows what he saw, what was done to him. Sadly, I found myself closing part of my heart. I'd suffered too much. I had to protect myself. That's not saying that my love for him diminished in any way, it didn't.

He wrapped himself around me as we lay cuddled close together both lost in thought. That was until they were disturbed by a knock on the door followed shortly by Kitar walking into the room.

He stood in the door and rolled his eyes at the two of us. "Can you two do anything else?" he asked. We held up the wine goblets. "Yes, we can fuck and drink. Right now, we are drinking and talking but soon it will be drinking and fucking. Is there any part of that you'd like to join us in. I hear you like it doggy style." Kitar let out a growl as I smiled and added, "Fine, since I'll probably never get to fuck you, I'll settle for fucking with you."

"And exactly how do you plan to do that, little one?" said Kitar with a smirk. (You know how hard it is for a muzzle to smirk, but he was good at it.)

"Funny you should ask," I said. "Usis, could you run down and see if you can procure us dinner?"

He hopped up and pulled on his clothing again. Oh, I did point out we stripped, right? I only tell you in case you're keeping count. He nodded and headed out the door, stopping only long enough to give Kitar a pity pat on the back.

"So what is this you are up too?" asked our guide as he walked over and sat down.

"It's your turn," I said.

"My turn to what?" He stopped as he saw my bug crawl up onto the table. "Oh no, I am your guide, not one of your subjects."

I got up as well and went over to the table, sitting down across from him. "I've interviewed Usis and you have been with us long enough now that we need some context. I know what you told me back on the Judgement Plane, but it's time you suffered the slings and arrows of outrageous fortune as a famous author on my world once said." (Shakespeare, in case you don't know.)

"No. Plain and simple, no. I will give you my story but not now," answered Kitar as he rose from the table and walked from the room.

I sat dumbfounded. This was the first time he had refused to help me. I'd originally only wanted his story for the context I mentioned, now I wanted it because he was being a dick about giving it to me.

# Entry 171

I ran across the room and threw open the door, planning to chase Kitar down. I was stopped when I ran face first into Cemal, the boy we had been assigned. Rubbing his forehead where we had bumped and said, "You have been summoned." He then bowed and headed back down the hall only stopping to motion for me to come with him. I ran back into the room and got dressed. As I hurried to catch up Usis came around the corner. "Where are...." he asked.

I shook my head. "I've been summoned. I'm assuming by the Overlord. I will be back. Stay here in case something goes wrong." As his eyes went wide I ran to catch up with Cemal.

As we made our way through the Keep and down the Overlord's private hall the butterflies in my stomach became *Cirque De Solei*, the little fuckers. When we reached the door and Cemal knocked, I thought I might pass out. I closed my eyes, took a deep breath as we heard, "Enter" and in we went.

This time the room felt more comfortable, more inviting. There were still books and stuff scattered about. I again found that interesting. She was again sitting in the same chair to the left of the fireplace. I noticed this time how throne like it was, last time it didn't seem so regal. She was still that handsome youthful nymph I'd seen back with Lucifer. Her wings were absent this time as well. She was wearing leather pants, laced up the side and a leather shirt that tied at the shoulders, very Joplin-esk. She motioned for me to come in and I took a seat on the couch. Cemal poured us both a glass of wine, left the pitcher and then vanished from the room.

"As I said before, I think it is time for our talk," she said.

"So that was you?"

"Yes, that is me. What you see here is a manifestation."

"I don't understand. This is not the real you?"

Shaking her head, she answered, "No...the real me, as you call it, is suspended in that reliquary."

"Why?"

For several seconds she stared at the wine goblet she held with both hands in her lap. I couldn't tell if her expression was sad or dejected, maybe a little of both. When she finally took a sip she continued, "Making a pact with any entity has both positives and negatives but when that entity is Lucifer, one outweighs the other. He tends to be very passionate..." She paused and I sat quietly. I wasn't going to interrupt my chance to get this story. "Maybe passionate is not the word. Single mindedly focused would be a good way to see it. Do not get me wrong, he is also a self-centered, egotistical, fucking shithead who deserves to burn in the furnaces he now rules over until the last creation burns out and The Father dies on the toilet from an excessively strong fart." I went wide eyed and then burst out laughing.

She sat quietly, her face no longer showing any hint of emotion, even when she had been railing against The Dark Lord. Finally, as my laughing stopped, helped by wine, I asked in a quiet voice, "Who are you?"

That made her smile, the first real one if think. She understood the importance of what I was asking. "I am Enepsigos, one of The Fallen. I served with Lucifer when we tried to bring change to The Host."

When she finished I took a second to construct my next question carefully. "You chose to be female? To have children?"

I could tell this was a serious conversation. Any humor from her earlier comments gone. This was not the time to be flippant. It was slowly sinking in, I wasn't only talking to the 'wife' of Lucifer, like that wasn't enough. But this was one of the original Fallen. It took all the strength I had not to start blurting out questions at the speed of light.

Inclining her head, she thought as well. "I agreed to it. When we fell, I hate that word, and Lucifer used his powers to give us genders and reproductive abilities, we were not forced to choose, male or female. Lucifer, like The Father I think, saw strict genders roles as a simplification for the livings mind when dealing with such issues. A dumbing down for those who were too closed minded or ignorant to contemplate or experiment with the full spectrum of who they were created to be. Yes, he made male and female, but that was purely for the reproductive process. There were all variations of gender other than that, all branching off those two but still a wide variety of choices. Sometimes nature made the choice or made the wrong choice, he allowed that as well. Since we are not temporal beings to start with, there is no need for us to be one or the other, male or female. We should be able and are able now to be either, well most of us. Lucifer came to me, told me what he wanted and I agreed. But for me to be able to do what needed to be done, I, sadly, had to lock myself into one gender." She stood so I could get another look at her. If you recall I said she was sort of tom-boyish before and she is. "As you can see I am still relatively...what is your world's word...androgynous. Gender unspecific...in my appearance but internally I had to be fully...I will not say female...that is just a word...capable of housing a reproductive system. Otherwise, there would be no way for me to produce children from a creature as powerful as Lucifer."

"So, The Father didn't specifically plan on just male and female?"

"Yes, he did, but he knew by allowing nature to do the development, what do you call it, evolution, that variations would arise. That was fine as long as a certain population remained viable to produce more of that civilization. It was almost required in many ways to have other, non-producing genders since eventually a population, like that of Earth, would overpopulate. Genders choices like non-gender, male/male, female/female, and the many transient genders would become the caretakers of the children. Something your planet did not do so well. Those of your world, for example, choose to follow the more extreme views of the living creature Paul or worse still The Power known as Gabriel, both who were extremists. Paul moved away from The Father for a while where Gabriel was never a fan of the living and worked to ensure they would do everything they could to wipe themselves out."

I thought about what she said. "Gabriel? It sounds like you don't hold him in very high esteem. He is credited with being the inspiration or helping inspire the founder of one of Earth's major religions."

"Yes, I know and, yes, I and most of The Fallen do not hold Gabriel in very high esteem, to use your words. As for inspiring one of your belief systems, he was responsible for doing that on many worlds. All with one common thread, they tended to be extreme. Not so much the teachings but the belief's ability to attract those who wished to interpret and worship it in extreme and perverted ways. Which, regardless what you are told otherwise, is precisely what Gabriel hoped for. He is blindly loyal to The Father but also hated, I choose that word carefully, you little monkeys. He found a way to not take a hand in destroying you directly since that would have disappointed The Father, but used a weakness The Father left in you so that you could destroy yourselves. But we are getting off topic. I do not think you came here for a history lesson."

I laughed, I couldn't help myself. "I'm walking through Hell, interviewing Angels, The Powers and The Fallen. To say I'm not here for a history lesson is sort of like saying I'm not here for art as I walk through an art museum."

She nodded her approval. "I really can see why he chose you. So, little one, what exactly do you wish to know?"

"Ok, let me back up. You were convinced to become a child bearer so you could host Lucifer's children? Is that correct?"

"Yes, and very carefully and accurately worded. I did agree and things went well. The first child was born as I ran the building of Pandemonium. The other Fallen worked on stabilizing Hell as Lucifer worked to stop the war and bring, if not peace, at least an accord between The Fallen and The Host." She paused, there was that sadness again. "I do not really wish to talk about our children."

"I understand but will you at least tell me how many and how they serve now?"

As quickly as the sadness appeared it vanished, replaced with such anger I recoiled out of reflex. But I could also see that she knew, as I, the question needed to be answered. "There were three and now there are none. Lucifer, their father, destroyed them. All that remains of the family I gave up all eternity for is my granddaughter and her son." When she said the last part she all but growled.

"That would be Xia?"

"Yes, but I prefer you not speak that name in this house."

"As you wish," I answered even though I was jumping up and down in my head having a hissy fit. I really wanted to coax information out of her. "Forgive me, I only ask because he comes up so often in my travels."

"Yes, of course he does. He is Lucifer's shining star."

Without thinking I said to myself, "Lucifer's morning star."

Approvingly she nodded, "Indeed."

"Can I ask one question, just a yes or no, to clarify something I've heard?"

"Fine, what is it?"

"Is he a twin? Is there a sister?"

"Yes," she answered but said nothing more. True to my word I didn't pursue it.

I sat there for several minutes respecting her silence. Finally, I asked, "So what happened?"

"We fell for a very long time, having wings only prolonged the process. Lucifer was trying to pull together the power needed to produce someplace we could land. He waited for as long as he thought reasonable as we passed all the existing creations and were free falling through the openness of the void. Finally when Lucifer had a plan, he worked in reverse order, clearly he had more than one plan. First, he talked to me and convinced me to choose to be a female so we could produce children, he and I. You have to understand, I was a member of The Host but not a well-known one, nothing like Lucifer, being the first created and all. I saw his offer as a chance to carry a bit more prominence in wherever Lucifer planned for our new home. He then created Hell, well the Great Plane, the others came later. With the last of his great reserves, before we all touched down, he gave us all the ability to reproduce. It was the last great slap in the face of those who had fought against us and stayed with The Father. Since the ability for the living to reproduce was what had started the war in the first place. Well, one of the things. Since he had already secured my oath, he installed in me the strength and ability to produce children from his seed, and made the alteration permanent.

"When we eventually set down, the next few millennia were occupied with the construction of Hell proper. Lucifer promoted many of The Fallen and made them his generals while others were assigned various duties, mine being the organization and creation of our capital city. He wanted it to rival The Eternal city, which it did for a very long time. That was when the souls started showing up. At first, they just piled up outside the gates. The Father had vanished by this point and Michael was now in charge of The Host. Lucifer was pulling Hell together. He finally, in an accord with Michael, agreed to take the souls of the damned. He was the first to discover their potential. The completion of Pandemonium and building of The Great Keep were the first punishments assigned to the souls. Now I had an ever growing contingent of souls to work with. Lucifer, on the other hand, spent most of his time studying the arriving souls himself, documenting and learning the scope of their capabilities. That is when the Planes were created. A series of specialized regions dedicated to the extraction of suffering from souls in specific ways based upon their sins, weaknesses and individual needs. The labs were also opened at this time and the creation of the Demon class began. Lucifer, after all, needed creatures who could execute the tortures with no consideration of the rocks from which they were mining this new-found source of power, the souls of the living.

"I will not go into the rest of the building and organization process. Finally with Hell and The Host at a fragile truce Lucifer focused again on his other plans, mainly the production of a family."

I broke in not thinking. "Production? That sounds very clinical."

"It was. He had a plan. No one was, or for that matter is, really sure why or what this plan consists of. Whatever his reasons for wanting a family did not seem to be coming to fruition since in time he would execute all three of his sons for one reason or another. Two of our sons never had children. One because he did not survive long enough and the other because he chose to rise up against his father. I assume you can guess how that went. Our final son did. He had a girl. I will not go into those details either, but suffice it to say she produced his Xia."

I started to ask about that but she held up her hand and wiggled a finger. "No information or discussion about that spoiled brat, remember."

She continued, "At this point, Hell and The Host were fully at peace. As much as they could ever be. Lucifer and Michael had things pretty much running smoothly. Both the Keep and Pandemonium were complete, and I was itching for something else to do. Lucifer kept putting me off until finally when one of the skirmishes broke out, I think you met a couple from that, The Lovers, I joined them. We lost and Lucifer punished all the rest. But what to do with me, since we had been much closer, sex does that you know, Lucifer could not decide how to properly punish me. So, he did what he does best, made an example of me by allowing his Generals to spend years torturing and humiliating me, three times they went too far, destroying me, and sending me to the Hatchery.

"Over the years, Lucifer and I grew apart. I say that but to 'grow apart' would mean we would have to had been attached somewhere and we were no longer. As the years passed and my anger grew, I was finally able to break free and lead what almost was a successful rebellion against him. That was the final straw. He had recently disposed of the Overlord of Wrath. I now hated him above all other creatures in Hell or The Host. While he still had me bound, I was moved down into the tunnels, encased in this tomb and hung from the ceiling. He knew if I could ever touch the ground again I could possibly work free. He put the guards in place, those fucking hellhounds and his final bit of punishment was to allow me to create this guise which enables me to move freely on this Plane but no others. Never can I truly walk Creation again. So, my dear boy, as your saying goes, 'There is no wrath like a woman scorned'. I have thus been trapped on this Plane ever since. Just like Rumiclick on Gluttony, I am free to serve but not free to roam."

We sat silently for quite a while. I could see the anger, pain and frustration laced through her body and face. Finally, all I could muster to say was, "He's not really the forgive and forget type, is he?"

This caused her to laugh. "My boy, you have no idea." Shaking her head, she finished her wine. "Anything else?"

"Do you taste that wine?"

"What an interesting question," she observed as she again turned that steel gaze upon me. This time I couldn't help it, I shifted uncomfortably in my seat. I saw the hint of satisfaction, but she played it off by answering, "Yes, this body is fully functional, it just cannot leave this Plane."

"Does the rest of The Fallen know you are trapped like this?"

"Of course, why do you think Lucifer put the training grounds on this Plane? He wanted as many of The Fallen, their children, the damned, Demons and abominations as he could parade past me to be forced to come here so it would constantly be rubbed in my face how truly trapped I am. But do not mistake it for just revenge; it also serves as a warning to those who might wish to rise against him. I hear about what is happening out there, but I can never leave or visit it. I was taken away from The Father by joining Lucifer in the war. Then Lucifer took Creation away from me, forever cutting me off from the few remaining wonders of The Father I could still enjoy. It is a punishment above all others." Then leaning in with a cold anger I have no words to describe she added, "and I hate him for it."

I bowed to her, more to her anger than to her actually. Silence filled the room until finally a knock came at the door and Cemal walked in. He motioned for me to follow him out. I rose and again bowed to the Overlord. She gave a curt nod with her head. As I turned to leave, just before I stepped out she added, "There are many things going on that you are not aware of, be aware of the little details." Then with a wave she dismissed me.

# Entry 172

When we made it back to the main chamber I found Kitar. "Come, I want to show you something. We must hurry."

"This can't wait? I just had a taxing interview with the Overlord."

"No," was the only answer I received other than a measured gaze. I could tell, for some reason, he didn't know.

We rushed through the keep to a section I'd never explored before. The area was dark and had a musty smell. As we hurried along I noticed crowded on the walls dozens of unfinished tapestries, some little more than loose hanging threads of various lengths, sizes and colors.

We reached a door and Kitar ushered me in motioning for me to keep quiet. The room was dark, lit only by braziers with bright orange flames dancing in them. In the chamber were twelve large blue creatures at least fifteen feet tall, each with long tentacles hanging like hair down their back. They had six arms, all evenly spaced along the sides of their torso. Even as alien as they looked they still carried a very regal aura. They were moving in unison, swinging incense as a thirteenth creature genuflected before three females sitting on ornate thrones at the end of the room. Around and behind them were more of the unfinished tapestries. The three were focused on the threads of one. Studying a single delicate fiber, they all held as it draped lazily from chair to chair.

I whispered to Kitar, "Who are they?"

"I wanted you to meet them but I urge you to be careful when you do. They, my dear Keith, are the Fates," he answered.

"As in *the Fates*? Clotho, Lachesis and Atropos?"

"That was Earth's name for them, yes."

"But how do they fit into the working of Creation? As I recall they were responsible for weaving, manipulating and then cutting the threads of the living. That makes it sound as if all things were predestined?"

"Not all things, but somethings have to be predetermined. When a Creation needs to be adjusted in ways that are not befitting its longevity, one of The Powers intervenes. If it is minor then the sisters are not needed, representatives in Creation can normally arrange whatever small adjustment might be needed. But if something larger or specific to one individual is needed that should affect the entire fabric of a people, world or Creation, then the sisters would need to arrange the necessary threads for that event to take place."

"Is there a tapestry for every Creation?" I asked.

"Sometimes as few as one, sometimes many. The tapestry of fate is sometime specific to something or as broad as a full Creation, but more often it can be a single planet, time, culture or even an individual based upon what intended outcome is desired. If, for example, it was based on an individual, it would start with their birth and end when the final thread is cut. In some cases where a soul is destined or predetermined for a specific goal, even the creature's birth may not be a random act. It will have been decided that someone needs to be introduced to effect a desired outcome."

"In that case, the creature is little more than a puppet?" I wasn't liking where this was going.

"Basically, yes, though they will live a life that appears to be of their own free will. Events, teachings, whatever is needed will be sent their way nudging them along the path they are expected to walk. As time goes on, since free will is a bitch, adjustments might need to be made which is what we are watching happen here today."

"Can I get closer?"

"Yes, but remain quiet and out of the way."

As I walked along the side of the chamber followed by Kitar I watched the blue creatures move about their ritual. Leaning in close, I asked, "Who are they?"

"Those are Manifestations. They are responsible for projecting the actions of the Fates down into Creation, setting the events in motion. They are a failsafe. It takes both The Fates and the thirteen Manifestations together to alter Creation. If any one of the sixteen deems the action as frivolous or unnecessary, they can refuse to allow the change to be revealed."

"Even if it is insisted upon? I can't see Lucifer accepting his orders being rejected," I questioned.

"You are correct. Some events are forced but rarely since The Fates do see The Powers as the final arbitrators of what should occur within Creation."

Now that I was closer I could see the three females more clearly. Though these were Fates they were very different than I expected. In Greek lore one was a maiden, one a matron and the final, a crone. In other words, the birth, life and death of a single thread. What they were here was the three primary colors, blue, red and yellow. The first, which I guess was the maiden was blue from head to toe. She was nude, as were they all, with long bat wings and hair slicked back as it flowed down her torso. Above her was a circular halo of what appeared to be intestines or umbilical cord that curved around her head. From even points around its circumference were long, thin pins puncturing the halo and running down into her scalp. Her face was serene. She was kneeling with her legs spread apart and from her vagina she was pulling a long, thin strand of thread. I glanced over to Kitar and was relieved to find him disturbed by this scene as well. He whispered, "She is producing a new event that will be added to the greater tapestry they are currently working on. All interactions with Creation in this manner must have a specific starting and ending point. As she produces this thread she is laying out its intent. As you can see, it is then being inspected and then woven into the final work itself."

The Second, I guess the Matron was red, again nude but instead of wings she had long thick tentacles like the Manifestations extending from her back. Her face showed no emotion and her hair was made of thick strands, each about as thick as a pencil and three feet long. They writhed and wiggled across her shoulders like they had a mind of their own. The thread being pulled by the first one was draped across this one's hand. She had her head down and was closely examining the sinew, as Kitar explained I assumed she was checking it for flaws.

The last Fate, the Crone character was much the same but yellow. She had no wings or tentacles and her ashy cracked skin was hairless from head to toe. My eyes followed the folds of skin down until finally they came to rest on her vagina which was saggy and worn. Nothing more than a relic of a younger woman who had now gone to seed. My eyes moved back up to her withered face. Where the first Fate had showed promise and the second intense scrutiny, this final withered shell reflected nothing but resignation. Like that of a parent who knows she is powerless as she watches her young child grow sickly as they prepare to die. As she was feeding the thread, her many hands worked to weave it into the tapestry beside the dais.

"They weave the destiny, for lack of a better word, and then the big guys here pass it down into Creation?"

"Correct."

Pausing I thought. "So who decides what needs to be done?"

"The Dark Council and/or The Holy Council."

"Wait Dark Council? This is the first I'm hearing about a Dark Council."

Shaking his head like explaining to a child, Kitar said, "Keith, it is all of the Generals with Our Lord Lucifer at their head. Together if either side decides that a creation needs to be adjusted, or pushed in a specific direction they approach the other and come to an agreement as to the outcome. Then they present the problem to the Fates who will work out the pattern and then weave it in. Once it is complete, it will be set into motion."

"Two things, so you're telling me that Lucifer or someone in The Host doesn't have the power to change the fate of creations? How did Xia destroy Earth?

"Of course, they can. Any of The Powers have the ability to alter a creation or anything in it. This was a compromise, an attempt to instill some order after The Father left."

I nodded, that made sense. Watching the crone weave, I asked, "So a tapestry like that one can last for years?"

"Sometime the entire life of a Creation."

"Is there one for Earth?"

"Of course, that is one of the most intricate because they were the first."

"I want to see it."

"After this, now watch." As the Crone finished weaving she sat back, her twelves arms coming to rest on her lap. The other two came over and reviewed the work. Nodding but never speaking then bowed their heads deeply to the Manifestations. The thirteen Manifestations came together into a ring around a painted pentagram on the floor and started to chant, each now carrying a staff. At first it was hard to hear but over time the sound continued to grow louder until finally out of the floor rose what looked like a ghost of a creature. "That creature is the center of their focus. Its destiny is being altered," explained Kitar.

The thirteen started to sway, and I noticed the tapestry had begun to glow as well. As they moved faster and faster an image, smaller but much the same as the figure in the center of the pentagram, floated out from the weave and across the room toward the chanting.

When the figure was floating just above the ghost of the creature all chanting stopped. With one swift movement, the Manifestations dropped the ends of their staffs to the floor. It was done with such perfect timing that they made but a single sound. As it echoed through the room the small figure descended into the larger ghost and then vanished again into the floor, leaving the circle empty. The Manifestations turned to the platform inclining their heads to the Fates who nodded back, rose and left the room through a back door.

I asked Kitar, "That's it?"

Shrugging, he answered, "Yes, this clearly was the manipulation of an individual and it went successfully. Had it failed, the weave would not have entered the figure but instead fallen through and landed on the floor as a jumble of thread. The Fates would then need to figure out what they had done wrong, remove the previous weave from the tapestry and repeat the process with the correct pattern."

I watched as the Manifestations walked towards us. They bowed to Kitar who returned the acknowledgement out of respect. "Greetings, Lord," they said in unison.

"Greetings to you as well. I'm here under the orders and protections of The Dark Lord. This here is Keith, a traveler in these realms writing the story of Our Lord's domain."

When they heard who I was they leaned into each other, almost touching heads and talked. When they finished as one they stepped closer clearly studying me, "Yes, we remember working his weave. We are pleased to see it was successful."

My knees almost gave out as I reached over to steady myself on a pillar. "What, what do you mean you enjoyed working my weave? You manipulated my life?" I was surprised to hear I was screaming.

With complete calm they answered, "Of course, small creature, it was determined that you would write Hell's story from before you were born. It fell upon us to prepare you."

My mouth fell open as the color drained from my face. "Did you know this? *Did you*?" I growled at Kitar not bothering to face him.

Without hesitation he answered, "No, but I suspected. The Dark Lord leaves little to chance."

This time my knees did give out. I dropped flat on my ass where I had been standing. For the longest time I just stared at them. "Did you arrange my death?"

"Of course, it was the final weave in your tapestry."

Together they turned, not waiting for any more questions, and left the room. I sat stunned until I was able to gain control of my mind again. Boy was I angry. When I stood I just stared at Kitar with my arms crossed. Finally, I asked, "Why did you feel the need to rush me here to see this?"

"I rushed you here because this does not happen often. I thought this was an important ceremony for you to witness. Your life having been manipulated is as much news to me as it was to you. I can assure you, had I known, I would not have brought you here."

My eyes grew even wider and my anger flared. I knew it, he wasn't on my side, he was just here to make sure I did my part. Then like a cold slap across my face I realized that wasn't a secret. He had told me time and time again what his duty was. Why was I mad? It didn't matter the reason, he was here to keep me...yes, me...safe. All these thoughts flashed through my mind in a split-second but it in no way quelled my anger.

"Show me Earth's tapestry," I whispered. Kitar studied me for a second and then headed toward the door the Fates had gone through. He paused just before entering and I think he was going to say something. I stopped him by motioning for him to continue with my hand. I didn't trust me speaking, I wasn't yet in control of what I might say.

We walked into an enormous candle lit room filled from floor to ceiling (hundreds of feet up) with balcony after balcony of tapestries. Picture one of those old Libraries where there were several stories of bookshelves, one above the other, with spiral staircases leading up to each level. That is what this was like only the balconies were deep and filled to bursting with textiles.

Kitar walked up to the Fates who sat in a pit in the center of the room. "Ladies, my friend here, the writer for The Dark Lord, wishes to see the tapestry from his world. Would you be so kind as to retrieve it?"

I noticed he didn't say which world was mine but then it was clear he didn't need to. The blue fate turned and hurried across the room. When she returned beside her floated a massive tapestry. It moved over and stopped in front of me. There on this glorified rug was the history of the world laid out in thread. Now don't get me wrong, it was not simple blocky depictions but almost photo realistic weaves. It was truly a work of art. I studied it but stopped when I reached the bottom. The end of the fine cloth was ragged, with hundreds, maybe thousands of tiny tails of threads hanging tattered like they had been cut off. "What happened, why is the end so ragged?" I asked.

This time it was the Red Fate, The Matron, who answered me. "That is because your world's weave was cut short when Xia Morningstar altered its fate. At that point all threads were severed and fell away unexpressed."

I said under my breath again, "Xia Morningstar, Xia Morningstar. Is there no where I can go that I don't hear that name?" I hadn't realized I was yelling until I saw the Fates recoil. I cannot say if it was surprise or just fear of my anger. I felt Kitar take me by the shoulders as he said in a reverent tone, "Thank you for your time, we will leave you to your work now."

I tried to protest but he would hear none of it as he all but drug me from the room. When we were back in the corridor he said, "Do not hold them responsible. They only enact what others wish set into motion. We can talk more about this once you have calmed down."

# Entry 173

When we arrived at our rooms, I found additional guards at our door with Balic pacing back and forth. I threw my hands in the air and marched past Kitar who obviously wanted to take control of the situation before I chimed in. "There seems to be no end to the problems we are having. What is this?" When he saw us come around the corner he exclaimed, "Where have you been?"

Kitar immediately went to high alert as did I. "What happened?" he barked.

"The writer's companion dispatched one of The Fallen's sons," explained Balic.

"How? That should be impossible," gasped Kitar.

"I know but it has happened. Lord Leviathan has arrived, and his Lordship is not at all pleased. My Mistress has ordered the writer's companion…"

I corrected in a louder than necessary voice, "His name is Usis."

Without missing a beat Balic corrected, "More like was. You do not know Lord Leviathan. He will not allow this to go unpunished."

"Over my dead body," I barked as I pushed my way passed the guards. I know I make it sound impressive but to be honest they just stepped aside. After all, two of them were mine and responsible for my safety.

Entering the room, I found Usis sitting on the bed with his head in his hands. I could tell he'd been crying. As he saw me he threw himself at my feet pleading, "Please do not let them take me from you. I am sorry. I do not know what happened. I just got lucky."

I spun around to find Kitar, the guards and Balic standing at the door. "There, you heard him, he got a lucky shot. What else is there to say?" I met Kitar's eyes and knew he realized that I was a ticking bomb on the verge of exploding. I might not be a Fallen but I was protected, and the shit I could stir up would force

Lucifer himself to come up here and deal with me. Kitar, the Overlord, Balic and, really for that matter, me did not want that to happen. I knew who to push and The Dark Lord wasn't one of them.

Kitar walked into the room. "A lot, Lord Leviathan is not one to be trifled with. Whatever he decides will stand until I can get to The Dark Lord and beg him to intervene."

I heard a stomp on the floor as the guards, all of them, drop to one knee, followed by Kitar visibly paling. Which is hard for a creature covered in fur. I knew someone had shown up and moved to stand in front of Usis as both Kitar and Balic dropped to a single knee as well. What came around the corner into view was by far one of the most ungodly, pardon the pun, creature I've ever seen. Then to make matters worse, the Overlord was with him and she was slightly paler than normal as well. Sweet fuck.

The creature that entered the rooms stunned me into silence. His authority radiated from him like flares from the sun though his appearance was the coldness of space. He stood at least ten feet tall, standard Fallen height, with a skin of dark blue almost black. But it was not the color of his skin as much as its appearance, it was like looking into deep space. He was covered in thousands of tiny glowing stars, I don't know how else to describe it. If you've ever seen pictures from the distance reaches of space, where the starts are scattered everywhere then you can begin to understand what he looked like. His entire body was like looking into a star field. His legs were thick canon bones with black hair running down stopping at the hooves. His fingers were long with shiny black nails that ended in points some two inches past the last digit. He had no hair and his face was beautiful, which told me he was one of The Fallen. His massive horns rose up two feet above his head, from just above and to the side of his eyebrows then split. The upper section rose another foot or so before branching again into three sets of smaller sub-horns that curled all the way down to his shoulders. His eyes were pitch black, as were his lips, almost lost in the darkness of his skin.

His ears were like that of an elf and over both and his face were an assortment of piercings. From each side of his chin, just below and beside his mouth, were a series of short horns curving up and stopping just to the side of each eye. The backs of his arms had long arching spiked horns, as well. His wings were pulled in close but again resembled that of a bat. They curved up over his head and down his back causing the horn at the bottom to just scrape the floor. Later as he was leaving I saw he also had several long spikes curling up from his spinal cord, extending about a foot behind him. Like this was not horrific enough between all the horns, all over his body, danced arches of electricity. He wore black pants embroidered in gold dragons that stopped where his hooves began just below his knees. His chest was bare but on each shoulder were deep golden dragons skulls. Though they were clearly dead the small two-foot-long one perched on the left was very much alive. He was like a void standing in the doorway sucking up and destroying the light and life of all that had the misfortune of encountering him. I didn't need to be told, this was Leviathan. I dropped to my knees, not to kneel but to protect Usis in my arms.

He stepped into the room, his hooves striking the floor causing the Keep to shudder. As we walked further in he ignored me, his eyes focused on my companion. "You are the one who dispatched Yaclom?" he boomed in a deep voice sounding like death.

My eyes shifted to Usis who just nodded.

The creature stepped closer to my companion causing me to rise between the two. With no more than a movement of two fingers I was thrown across the room to slam into the wall. I crumpled to the floor dazed as the monster studied Usis closer. He bent down and their eyes met. I heard a muffled cry of terror come from deep inside my companion as the Fallen stood and considered him. He then closed his eyes and for what seemed like an eternity just stood there.

When he opened his eyes again, his frightening gaze found first Usis and then me. "You are responsible for this one I am told."

Pulling myself up the wall, trying not to show the fear that was painted on my face, I stepped closer, squared my shoulders and said, "Yes I am, and though I do not know who you are nor for that matter do I really care, I will tell you now you will not harm my companion." I was surprised at the defiance in my voice.

I saw a smile interrupt his countenance for just a second before again being subjugated. "So you are the writer. What is your name?"

"Keith," I said then like a fool added, "...and yours?"

Now the smile was visible showing me his pointed yellow teeth. "I am Leviathan."

"Oh, that was your man," I said.

"No, that was my son. My second-in-command, or well now my former second-in-command. He has been defeated by that." He dismissively waved in Usis' direction, causing my companion to suck in a breath of anger. I reached back putting my hand on his shoulder.

"I will make a note of that in my Journal, not all The Fallen have children equaling them in stature," I said as Kitar, the Overlord and Balic sucked in a breath. I fully understood their surprise. What the fuck was I doing? I guess I was playing this one by ear.

But, it got me a laugh this time. "Oh I can see why he chose you, yes indeed."

"I've been hearing that a lot," I said before thinking again. Seems to be a trend right now.

"Well, your little companion is in no danger. I just came to see who or more to the point what could have defeated Yaclom. Now I know and he will come with me."

"Like hell." There I went again.

Leaning down he reached forward with one of his clawed finger and lifted the amulet up off my chest. "Do not overestimate the protection of your little trinket. As for your friend coming with me, I do not remember requesting anything. I am telling you and the rest of the rabble what is happening and what is happening is he *is* coming with me." Dropping the amulet back and turned for the door. "Come, little one. I will not ask twice."

This time Kitar took a step forward and blocked The Fallen's way. "Do I have your assurances he will not be harmed?"

With another brush of his hands, everyone in front of him, including Kitar, was flung aside. The only person standing was the Overlord. "I give you assurances of nothing." He paused, I swear for effect, then added, "You talking monkeys seem to have forgotten yourselves. The next word from any of your mouths will result in you becoming food for my son when he awakens in the Hatchery." Turning again to Usis he barked in a chilling tone, "Come."

Kitar quickly motioned for me to keep quiet since we were most certainly outside our depth, but if you've read much of my travels in Hell then you know that didn't stop me. Usis stood and, with his head bowed, walked over to Leviathan. "Kitar will be going to see The Dark Lord immediately," I said hoping to ensure him I wasn't giving up. That is where I probably should've stopped talking, but...nope...no way. We were being separated again, and again I didn't know what was going to happen, to him, to me, or to us. What the hell did it mean to be under the protection of that fucking Dark Lord? No wonder he lost his god damned war.

As they walked out of the room my anger exploded out of me as I burst out running toward the door only to have Balic and Kitar grabbed me by the arms and pull me back. "You worthless piece of shit. I see why they threw your deer headed ass out of The Host, you horny son of a bitch. You must have made your parents proud. Oh, wait you don't have a mother, and your father ran out on your ugly ass after you disappointed him." Kitar slapped a hand over my mouth as Usis and Leviathan vanished around the corner. I looked up to find the Overlord standing in the doorway shaking her head. Kitar added, "I will attempt to keep this burgeoning

Demon under control if you can see what you can do about getting Usis back." The Overlord headed down the hall but I heard her add, "I think I might have the easier task."

Once the Overlord was gone, Cemal reemerged from wherever he hid during the encounter and closed the door. Kitar released me as he barked, "Have you lost your mind!"

By now reason had set back in and wide eyed all I could think of to answer him was, "Clearly. Now what do we do?" I threw myself on the bed, pulling a pillow over my head.

He shrugged. "Are you listening? I personally think removing your tongue would be the wisest place to start. That is one of the most vicious of The Fallen, and you just went off on him like he was some store clerk. As much as you may not like it, this is one of those situations where we must just wait. Starting to yell and curse will end up only making things worse. He said Usis would not be harmed..." He started to say something else but paused, instead adding, "If I might make a suggestion. Why don't we go into Dis and get drunk and get this out of your system? It appears a good torture pit might help, beat the shit out of something."

Lifting the pillow and raising an eyebrow at him, I asked, "What did you leave out? You were about to say something."

He shrugged. "My only concern is the differences in your and Leviathan's definitions of harmed. For some reason I don't think they are the same."

"Oh great, that helped."

"And now you understand why I reconsidered saying it. Maybe don't ask questions you don't want answers to."

I threw the pillow across the room. "Great, so I just deal," I shouted to Kitar. We just stood there staring at each other. I thought he would say something and I was out of words. I felt numb. Finally, I just threw my hands in the air. "Fine, as you said there is nothing I can do and if I sit here I'm just going to get angrier. You know if Usis *is* harmed, we will be going wherever we need to go to save him. I hope that is clear. I suggest in addition to seeing The Dark Lord you start working on a plan to get us in and out of that Hatchery I keep hearing so much about. Let me finish dressing then I, not you, only I will go into town while you get my companion back."

"By yourself? I am not sure I can allow that," said Kitar.

My head snapped around as I corrected our guide, "At this point I don't give a shit what you can 'allow' so YES I am going by myself. If you can't understand one of those words please tell me so I can break it down for you. And for the record, since it seems to be the statement of the day, I don't remember asking. You have things you need to do, like start hunting down Lord Lucifer." Pointing to the two guards, I continued, "If I must have an escort, those two can come… but at a distance." Walking by I tapped one of them on the chest as I said over my shoulder to Kitar, "Do they even talk?" The guard never moved and when it appeared he wasn't going to answer I looked up at the brute. "Do you talk?" I barked louder than I had intended.

"Yes, My Lord," was the extent of the guard's answer.

"See, that is what I should be hearing from your sorry ass, Yes My Lord," I said with a smirk to Kitar.

He raised his eyebrows. "I agree, but you calling me My Lord every time will get cumbersome."

"Funny." I sneered and said to one of the guards, "If I ordered you to stab him with that big pointy stick of yours, would you?" Both guards mouths dropped open as they turned first to Kitar and then back to me. "Well, My Lord, I guess if I was ordered." I smiled, crossing my arms over my chest and with a smug expression turned back to Kitar. "This is where you run off and start trying to save my companion. If you think I'm a handful now, you just try to guess what kind of world class bitch I'll become if he is injured. I'll make both The Host and Hell wish they had never come across me."

"I am starting to think you might have already accomplished half of that goal. And watch what you say, we never know who is listening."

"Well if anyone is listening then they better know what they need to do and get it done," I said as if talking to an invisible microphone. "Do I make myself clear?"

I ignored Kitar's protests as I walked past him and headed down the hall followed by my two guards. Once we were around the corner I stopped, "Is there any way you two can appear less...I don't know...guardy?"

I was surprised when they just shrugged and started to change before my eyes. Their bodies became malleable and the next thing I knew they were just two run of the mill Demons, just like the ones you would run into on the streets of the city. "Why didn't you do that sooner? It's far less intimidating."

"My Lord, we are your guards. It is our job to be intimidating. That ensures creatures do not start troubling you. But for tonight we can do our job and appear less imposing."

"Cool... can you also keep a bit of distance, so I don't give the impression to be... well again... guarded?"

"Yes, My Lord."

# Entry 174

Again we made our way through the tunnels and, with the help of the guards, to the city itself. This time we stepped out into one of the back allies, clearly not a commonly used exit. "Have you two been to Dis before?"

"Yes, My Lord, we are both stationed here."

"In that case, where would you suggest I go? This is only my second time in the city. As you no doubt noticed back at the Keep, shit is starting to piss me off and I want some place that keeper of mine, meaning our over protective judge, would not pick. I want to see where the average working Demon (I chuckled) goes."

"We are not sure that is safe, My Lord."

"Isn't that why you're here, to protect me? I should be fine, I trust both of you with my life... Well, if I had a life, I'd trust you with it. Take me someplace that will make me sick enough that I'll forget how much I want to strangle most of The Fallen in this fucking place."

Looking around like they were about to be struck by lightning they bowed and led the way. We stepped out from the deserted alley onto a really busy street. I mean *busy*. We were almost run over by the wash of creatures moving like waves down the street. As I removed my face from a Demon's chest, I observed to no one in particular, "This place is far busier than I remember."

As the massive creature stared down at me like he was about to rip my legs off I just smiled and pointed to the two guards behind me. They smiled, which was disturbing on its own level, which caused the Demon to remember he was late for something else. He stepped around me and was taken away into the tide of creatures before I realized what had happened. Not even missing a beat, one of my guards said, "It is shift change so there are more people on the streets. It is the perfect time for you to see the real Dis."

We stood in the entrance to the alley just watching, getting our bearings. The roman architecture still floored me, it really gave the place a civilized feel if you could ignore the creatures that populated it.

I'll skip the travel brochure since I've no idea where we went. We took so many twists and turns I was completely lost before I knew what was happening. If the guards had wanted to kidnap me they had the opportunity but they didn't. What they did do was lead me to a less maintained part of the city. I was going to say run down but that is the wrong idea to give you. All of the city was amazing, this area unlike the cleaner areas had trash in the streets, bodies passed out, the columns, roadways and buildings were on a whole more utilitarian. This part of the city showed all the signs of a working-class area.

The establishment we ended up at was loud and crowded. The first guard, I asked their names twice but never got an answer, said, "We could get in real trouble bringing you here. Is this what you want? There is a fighting pit, good drinks, and as you can see it is loud. The boys, which I know you like, are very affectionate and attentive." Just the way he said it made me think about Usis and it must've shown on my face, "Oh, I am sorry, My Lord, I did not mean to displease you."

I shook my head. "You didn't. I'm worried about my companion...but yeah this sounds like what I want. In my mood, I could use some gratuitous violence and strong booze."

"Then this is your place. Unfortunately, we will need to stick close to you otherwise you will get tussled about, but many of the more important creatures, even merchants, have guards. In this form, we will not be as noticeable as legion soldiers."

"That's fine. If something happens to me, we all three will get our asses handed to us."

"You would only get your ass handed to you, My Lord, it would be more severe for us. Shall we go?"

I motioned for them to lead and we pushed our way into the bar. To give you the short on the bar, it was the same open design as the other one with sloped roofs on four sides with open courtyards in the middle. Unlike the first place where we passed into a closed bar there were no closed rooms here. It was a combination of about six of these open pavilions, four of them had gardens in the center where the final two had fighting pits surrounded by cushions and low tables.

"Where would you like to sit, or would you prefer to wander?" asked one of the guards.

"I think finding a place to perch would be best. It'll make it easier to guard and I'm not in the mood to just keep pushing through crowds."

They led me to the back rooms, one with a fighting pit. It was, for the moment, mostly empty, down in the arena were four little goblin creatures cleaning up what must have been the remains of the last fight. Through some not so subtle persuasion the guards got us a table by the edge. The pit was deep enough that I had to lean forward to look down into the arena, thus allowing me to avoid the carnage if I chose, which I liked. As we had walked in I'd commented on one of the serving boys who was running around. He was humanoid and sexy (don't judge) so one of the guards ran off to arrange from him to serve us.

Within minutes I was situated, had a cute nude, dangerously affectionate creature feeding me steaming chucks of meat and sips of wine. The guards did everything they could think of. They sat with me talking about the different species that walked by and just about anything else they thought I might be interested in. Overall, they were really trying and I know I should've been appreciative but my mind was still with Usis. Was he out there someplace suffering?

To my surprise, they knew what drinking games were and together we started doing what I can only describe as shots. I think they were cheating, it seemed like I was doing two for every one they were drinking. Then the night took another slight twist, not a bad one, just an unexpected one. In all the kerfuffle, I'd forgotten about the dinner with Elick. It's not that I suddenly remembered. I was reminded when a handsome pale Demon walked up to the table, who at first I didn't recognize. He was dressed in tights and a very nice tunic, with his snow-white hair pulled back in a ponytail. Seeing him the two guards moved to the table beside us and sat down. Stopping at my table he announced, "There you are. Did you forget something? As I recall you wanted to have dinner." That is when my embarrassed face told him the memory of our appointment had again come flooding back.

"Oh fuck, I completely forgot. Sorry… Something happened at the Keep and our date just slipped my mind." Looking around I said, "Is this place too beneath your status? We can go somewhere else."

"Our Date?" he said with a smile then continued before I could answer, "No this is fine. I prefer the more real places myself. May I join you?"

"Oh yes, please…" I motioned for him to sit. As he took the pillow beside me, remember these are low tables with only pillows to sit on, he snapped motioning for the boy to bring him a drink.

That was the night I got to know what it's like to be born and live in Hell. I think I also made an ally, well more than that actually but we will get there. The ally part was something that it was becoming very clear I needed if I expected to survive this fucked up assignment and not end up on one of the torture racks I so often don't want to talk about.

# Entry 175

"This is a different look than the one I saw before. I'm not sure how to say it but you appear very...normal," I commented to Elick. It was like my writer senses had awakened fully, or it could just be the booze.

"I heard something happened at the Keep and that you came into the city. I toned down my appearance so not to attract unwanted attention and headed off to find you. From what I managed to glean from that uptight guide of yours, it seems like you could use some company that is not as involved in The Dark Lord's grand schemes." He smiled as he said it. I almost melted, not from the smile as much as someone just understanding what it was like to be wrapped up in all of this.

"You can't come into town in your true form?" I asked.

"I can, it is just if a descendent of The Most High walked into a place like this would ensure it would not continue as normal so to speak. It would clear out before I could have found you. I do not think that is what either of us wants tonight."

"Do you disguise yourself often?"

"Yes, we travel the Planes of Hell often in disguise. Even The Dark Lord often goes out in a guise. The residents of Hell would find it very disturbing if they knew how often he walked among them."

"I can imagine. He makes me nervous just knowing Kitar is reporting to him." I watched him take the glass from the serving boy. I smiled when he ran a hand down the little boy's back and along his bare ass. He might hide his appearance but his movements and general demeanor, if studied, gave away his identity. His movements were like silk, judged and deliberate. "How often does a person like you get to actually interact with Lord Lucifer?"

"It's based upon where we are assigned. Since I am friends with Xia, I get to more often than most I would think. Though most of

The Fallen and their families are familiar with His Lordship." I wanted to ask about Xia but felt this was too early and for some reason it just didn't seem like the right question at the time. He must've sensed something since he changed the topic. Not to one I was particularly happy to talk about. "I understand my Great-Grandfather is on the Plane today, or more accurately was on the Plane, he is gone now."

I sat dumbfounded. Not only had I forgotten the dinner date, I'd also forgotten who his family was. This was Leviathan's great-grandson. "He has left?" I asked as fear and terror washed across my face.

Taking a sip of his wine then making a face he handed it back to the serving boy. "This is horrible, bring something better. If this place has nothing send someone to the Keep to fetch some real wine." I could tell as the boy started to shiver that he was now aware of who he was really serving. With his disarming smile I heard Elrik whisper to the boy, "Our little secret, young one, understand?" The boy nodded and hurried off.

"Is it not counterproductive to hide who you are and then show it to the slave?" I asked.

"He will not talk, I made sure of that as well. He will be able to pass my request along at the Keep but if he tries to reveal his discovery he will expire," Elrik said as he pushed away the old glass ignoring my indignation. "As for my Great-Grandfather, it is rare for someone to be so displeased when they learn he is no longer on the same Plane as them. What do I not know?"

I took a long drink. Actually I drank all of my wine. "It appears my companion has come into the orbit of your Great-Grandfather's domain. Meaning, well...he kinda killed his second-in-command."

Elick burst out laughing. "What...your little companion bested Yaclom. Oh, that is great, that pompous ass deserves to be taken down a few notches." Then raising and eyebrow and smiling, there was that damned smile again. "Wait, what happened when Great-Grandfather found out a soul dispatched his son?"

"He came to our room..." I said but was interrupted.

"At the Keep?"

"Yes, and took Usis with him."

Rubbing his chin with his hand. "That is probably not good, you realize that, right?"

"Oh yes, but he assured me Usis would not be harmed."

"Harmed at all or harmed but repairable? You need to learn to get specifics."

Shaking my head, I sat silently. "I don't know."

Snapping his fingers, he summoned a Demon, again dressed way down but clearly was not trying to hide his fierceness. "Go find what has become of the writer's companion. Last time he was seen my Great-Grandfather was leaving with him. See if you can locate him. Oh and find out what shape he is in." It told me a lot about the fear Leviathan garnered because when this massive Demon heard the order he visibly paled.

"Yes, My Lord," he answered then walked to the empty pit jumped up into the air extended his wings and vanished from view.

"You guys aren't really good at the whole subtle thing, are you?" I asked since the Demon leaving had not only called attention to him but to us as well.

"Do not worry. This is Hell. Demons are everywhere, and trust me they may not know who I am but everyone is acutely aware of who you are. Not only does your reputation precede you. Not only have you been the talk of all the planes for some time now, but that amulet screams Lord Lucifer's power and protection. I am surprised everyone is staying as calm as they appear to be. It might be time for you to realize, Keith, that you are a 'power' (I used a little 'p' because it sounded like he did when he said it, I got the gist) whether you like it or not. I am willing to help you with that if you so wish."

"What do you mean? You will help me?"

"In a place where power and strength is everything, it is good to have allies. That judge of yours is useful but I warn you about where his loyalties lie and it is not completely with you."

"I've become disturbingly aware of that, trust me," I said then added, "I'll take any help you're willing to give. I need friends at this point especially considering..." My voice trailed off. I bit the inside of my lip as my mind wandered off to Usis. I might not have known where he was but my heart and mind was with him. I still didn't feel comfortable being out on the town but...I didn't know what else to do at this point.

"Well I would be glad to do what I can, which is considerable. You do realize the position you are in, or more accurately, currently ascending to?"

"I'm starting to, yes. I've had several people now tell me that news of our arrival precedes us. What is being said? I mean if you don't mind telling me."

"I don't mind, and it is pretty simple. Any time someone who has direct interaction with The Dark Lord, The Host or any of their generals comes onto a Plane everyone gets a little careful. After all, here in Hell, patience and forgiveness is often said to be the tenant of the other guys. To the average resident your visits are not that important but to the ruling class it could carry more impact. You seem to have a skill at attracting the Powers like The Dark Lord and my Great-Grandfather, so creatures such as The Overlords justifiably get a bit...."

"Twitchy?"

"That is a very good word for it. On a different but related topic, why were you interested in talking to me? I ask both for that aforementioned twitchy reason but more out of curiosity. I am not, like most of the young Hellspawn of my generation, as interested in the Power struggle. We have never seen or been involved with anything outside of Hell itself, so we care little about the old ways."

I was given some time to think about my answer as the boy came back carrying a very dusty bottle. He pulled the cap and poured a test for Elick. The Hellspawn tasted it and nodded his approval. As the boy poured us both a glass I decided on my question. I tasted the new wine and it was way better. "Ok, I have a question. I'm going to just ask with no pretext to see what you say."

Elick nodded but I could see the hint of a smile.

"Tell me about Xia," I said.

"You wanted to talk to me about the brat prince?" I saw a hint of a frown. It might be arrogance but he seemed disappointed.

"No, that isn't the only reason. I'm actually asking about him to gauge your level of forthrightness." I smirked. "In you I find several topics I'd be interested in exploring." I couldn't help it, I broke out in a grin and think I even blushed.

"I can understand that and I will tell you honestly that we, his close friends, have been instructed quite strongly to not help you with that particular interest. With that being said, what do you want to know? After all, not following the rules set by authority is sort of a bench mark for a Hellion. As for your other interests in me, I am intrigued what those might be as well." He laughed.

"He destroyed my home?"

"I heard. You would not believe the mess that caused. But then, that is Xia, if he is not stirring up a mess The Powers start getting worried about what he is up to. The Host pretty much lost their mind from what I saw. I happened to be at Lord Lucifer's keep the day that bit of news filtered down, and trust me there was a lot of yelling ringing through the halls of the Great Keep."

"Really, it was passed off to me like it was no big deal."

"Of course they passed it off as 'no big deal' to anyone outside the inner circles. That is the way both sides work. They explode in private and then walk out and act like nothing is wrong and all the chaos is just part of the 'big plan'. Trust me, they are barely keeping Creation held together."

"Really? What can you tell me about Xia? Also, this will be my only question about him. I want to interview you about what it's like to be you and what it's like being a member of the Royal houses. Your perception of Creation, The Host, Hell and things in general."

He thought for a while, then moved around beside me as one of the matches started in the pit below. I'm not going into the details since this interview is what matters. Just suffice it to say, two creatures tore each other limb from limb and the winner ate the other.

# Entry 176

"I'm not sure what to ask you first. I feel that any question I ask will be based upon my understanding of things. There is no way you and I can have the same starting place. I guess, tell me what it's like to be a grandchild of The Fallen."

Elick laughed, louder and harder than I thought the question deserved. "You have seen many things since entering Hell and yet you have really seen nothing. The true Planes of despair are still before you. But to give you a starting point, to be born of the linage of one of The Fallen is to instantly have the weight of all of Creation on you. We are instantly targets. We are instantly envied. We are instantly expected to live up to a standard I dare say even The Fallen themselves could not achieve. My Great-Grandfather is one of the most feared Generals Lord Lucifer has. He is walking condemnation. You have seen him, he is pitch black. What could be worse? Even in my disguised form I am as I have always been told 'a pale comparison' and yet I am one of the most competent fighters Hell has."

He paused and though I didn't direct it as a question to him he heard me say under my breath, "What must be being a Morningstar be like?"

Again, he laughed. "You have no idea. This I will tell you about Xia, he is my dearest friend. But...he is the brat prince. He is the most hated...well maybe feared...of all our generation. His gift is pain. He can create devices of suffering that put all others to shame. Then you add in that little minion of his, that human, and there is no stopping him. Xia has just outside The Dark Lord's Keep a set of swamps where he hangs members of The Host who displease him. If an Angel or one of their messengers comes to Hell and even slightly upsets him, he has hung them up. That is not the impressive part. What is, is that no one will go against him to take them down."

"Even Lord Lucifer?"

"Lord Lucifer would not think of it, not because he cannot or because he fears his Great-grandson. Lord Lucifer does not because he, for lack of a better word, worships his Great-Grandson. Xia is the light in his eyes."

"That's what The Overlord told me. Xia is Lord Lucifer's morning star. And yet with all your harsh descriptions still Xia has friends? You are his friend?"

"I am and that is a very good way to put it. It is surprising no one has made that connection before. As to why Xia has friends. Xia is loyal. Xia is honest. Xia has no fear and will do anything for those he cares about. In the same breath I will add, he will destroy without second thought anyone who displeases him. I value Xia because he is what we all wish we could be, ruthless and unassailable. As you can imagine from what I have told you about my Great-Grandfather and what I am called, we do not always see eye-to-eye. But I grew up with him, I know to fear him. There are few who do not, Xia is one of those few. He has intervened several times on my behalf.

"To be a Hellspawn is to hear your entire existence about this 'creation' we must protect and nurture. We must witness these pathetic creatures this all-powerful father was supposed to have created. You living, forgive me, are sickening. This supreme being who is supposed to be so amazing created nothing but a flawed repository for the only thing they are good for, suffering. Then when it became too much and he was told what needed to be done to repair his faulty creation by his first born, what did he do? He ran away like the coward he is. If it were not for Lord Lucifer and the third of The Holy Host who followed him, Creation, you pathetic creatures as well as the divine Fallen and the weak Powers of The Host would all be gone. All of Creation should be kneeling down before The Dark Lord, not cursing him."

He paused and smiled then finally added, "But it is with much joy, that we finally see The Dark Lord fighting back by choosing to dispel the myths and lies of The Host. He has finally decided to speak the truth to the weak and foolish who choose to follow that incompetent father."

I was completely taken back. "How...what has he done? This is the first I'm hearing about this. How is The Dark Lord spreading his side of the story?" It was then I went pale.

With a mock toast, he said, "Yes, there it is. It is you, little one. You are showing the living just how weak, flawed and cowardly their beloved father really is. You are Lord Lucifer's messenger. And if you will take a bit of unsolicited advice... I have read your journals. I know of your journeys up till now. You have reported well and accurately but with an almost disrespectful disregard of the awesome opportunity you have been given. I know this has not gone unnoticed. To those in Hell, as I said, you are considered in many ways an ill omen. To The Fallen you are a foolish disrespectful bit of folly. Luckily for you The Dark Lord clearly does not see it this way. But based upon what you have produced so far, many are starting to think this might have been an ill-considered mistake by our Lord and Master." Leaning in and looking me in the eye, he continued, "I on the other hand do not. You, I think, can do this. And you, I think, have potential The Dark Lord sees, which would not be the first time. My suggestion to you is the same as what your guide told you. Maybe you will listen to me. I recommend you remember who you are and that of all the creatures, in all of time, and in all of the Creations, Lord Lucifer choose you to tell his story."

At this point the interview all but ended...I was too stunned and...well shocked by hearing again about the incredible weight that had been placed on my shoulders. It really drove home the realization I'd been trying to ignore, I was a child playing at a god's game. He was right. I needed to see, understand, and use the power I'd been given to tell the best story I could.

He did that smile thing again, I mean a big smile, I really wish he would stop doing that. "What is so funny about placing the weight of all of Hell on my shoulders?"

"Oh, did you not see. I answered your original question. You know where you asked what was it like to be a Hellspawn. A child of one of The Fallen. I just pointed out to you the unbelievable responsibility on your shoulders and the staggering weight that comes with it. Now, young one, you know what it's like to be the great-grandchild of one of The Fallen. Was that not your question?"

I closed my eyes, downed my drink and then asked the final question weighing on my mind. "Can I ask you something and get a blunt answer?"

"Of course, what is it you would like to know? If I can answer it, I will."

I simply asked, "Should Usis have been able to dispatch your grandfather?"

"No... I have fought against your companion. I have never in all my years of battle and training seen a damned who could fight like him. He is the sweetest creature I have met in a long time but when he steps upon the battlefield or for that matters watches a battle, something about him changes. His focus is absolute."

"Did you know The Lovers?"

"Yes, they were imprisoned by Lord Lucifer for instigating a war."

"If you read the journals then you know what they did to us."

"No, I mustn't have gotten that far. Only a limited number were available at the time. Why, what happened? I did hear rumors they had captured you at one point. I just assumed that necklace of yours kept you from harm."

"Yes, they did capture us and no the necklace didn't work for some reason. Lucifer showed up and freed us. I was badly injured and taken to the Keep. He left their punishment to Usis. I only went back to their cave once, with Kitar. They had both been brutalized."

His eyes went wide. "Why would Lucifer allow a soul to punish two of The Fallen, and what do you mean by brutalized?"

"The male's chest was cut open, a fire had been lit in its cavity. His genitals had been cut off and stuffed in the female's vagina. And there was more." I couldn't go on.

"And your companion did this?"

I simply nodded.

As if he'd been summoned, the Demon Elick had sent dropped from the sky, landing beside his master. He leaned down and whispered in the Hellspawn's ear. Cocking his head to the side I saw him steal a glace over to me, finally saying, "We should return to the Keep. It appears there are some complications with your companion's release."

# Entry 177

As Elick was about to say something else someone walked up behind him and quickly grabbed him around the neck placing a dagger at his throat. My eyes went wide but he winked letting me know not to worry. "Excuse me, but you seem to have slipped and placed a knife at my throat, did you by chance notice? Might I suggest you remove it before you make a mistake we both will regret," said Elick in a calm, smooth tone. I could listen to his voice all day and the hint of danger only made him more alluring.

"I need whatever you have in that little bag, if you don't mind," said the bandit. As he finished I realized the room was silent, the only noise was the exchange of money as all around watched and betted on who would win. Clearly, they didn't hold out much hope for Elick. I smiled, this was probably going to be a mess.

And it was, I know you probably want a long battle scene or something but if that's the case this wasn't the battle for you. Elick rose, dropped his guise, causing the entire room to break out in pandemonium. Gawd he is stunning. But that's not what ended the battle. There was a collective "oh shit" as his hoof hit the ground. He placed a hand on my shoulder, probably for the better, so I wasn't injured. As a shock wave traveled out, rippling the air like heat on a hot summer's day, it hit creature after creature causing them to explode. Within seconds, the entire building was painted in the many colors of the various creatures' blood, the only sounds were those of my breathing, which was abnormally loud in my ears. Once it was over, again only a couple of seconds, we two were alone, not even my guards remained.

"Are my guards destroyed?" I asked.

"Not destroyed but they will be waking up in the hatchery. Sorry about that, we will get you more." As I stood horrified at the devastation Elick added in a very casual tone, "Just so you know, that was a tiny version of what Xia did to your world. Imagine that shock wave as it traveled around a planet, so powerful even the atmosphere could not withstand it."

"Oh thanks, that's just the image I needed in my head." I said as the Demon who served Elick walked up behind him and stood at attention. Both Elick and the Demon extended their wings as the Hellspawn put a hand around my waist, pulled me close and gave me the most electrifying kiss I'd ever had. "I was hoping tonight would end in a little sex, but that seems less and less likely considering..." he commented as we rose into the air.

I was just barely able to get my next words out. "You have no idea how much I would enjoy that but with all that is going on coupled with my concern for Usis I am not sure I could...rise...to the occasion. But for the record, hang on to that thought." I can't believe I was making jokes and setting up sex dates with the mess my companion was in. What the hell was I becoming.?

"I fully understand, but at least you have given me an incentive to help you resolve the problem." He smiled evilly as we rose over the city and headed back toward the Keep.

Now I don't know if you managed to catch everything that happened at that little dinner. What I wanted was to relax and try to get my mind off the fact Usis had been hauled off. What ended up happening was me getting schooled by a Hellspawn about the responsibility of my task. By the time, we made it back to the Keep and up to my room, I was fit to be tied.

# Entry 178

As we walked into the room I saw Kitar sitting in his normal spot smoking like nothing was wrong, and my anger flared immediately. Shaking my head, I roared, "What the fuck is your purpose? Tell me, right now, why the fuck are you here, my so called protector? Where's my companion? Where's The Dark Lord? Where's any of the things I ordered you to do? Where...Tell me...Tell me." I marched across the room and slapped his feet off the table. "If you think this vacation you're on is going to continue, you have another thing coming."

Kitar was so stunned, the first few attempts to respond ending up being little more than a series of stammers. I waited until he finally seemed to have regained himself and then just as he started to say something I held up a finger to shut him up. I heard Elick walk in, leaving the door open. I looked over and smiled. "I had a wonderful night, thank you. If you need to go I understand but you're more than welcome to stay while I rip my guide a new asshole."

With that engrossing smile, he said, "Oh I think I have some time," making a motion toward Kitar, "please don't let me stop you. Enjoy yourself. I will just be over here. When you are finished, if you do not mind, I have some thoughts as well."

Now I was curious. Putting on my most innocent look I returned my attention to Kitar. He was still prepared to start arguing but when he saw the smile he came up short. "So what exactly is your issue?" he asked.

"Let's start with the basics. What is my job in Hell?"

"You know your job," he said.

"I most certainly do, what I'm questioning is whether you do. So, for shits and giggles, why don't you tell me what you think my job is, so we can see if we're on the same page."

Shaking his head, he replied, "You are to tour Hell and write about it."

I raised an eyebrow, "Is there anything else you want to add?" Thinking, he shook his head, not sure where I was going. I added, "Maybe you wanted to include that I didn't fall into this role. Maybe you want to include that my life was manipulated by The Fates to ensure I'd end up in Hell. Maybe you want to include that I wasn't recruited by The Dark Lord, that is Lord Fucking Lucifer to you, but forced into writing his side of the story. Me...a simple guy, who's only claim to fame is an unpublished book about two modern guys being transported to another world. You know the book I was delivering to my publisher when I was run over by a FUCKING cab. And you telling me all this, *'Above all the other creatures in all the other times in all of the Creations he picked me.'* ME...I think those were your words which for some reason were repeated to me again tonight by this handsome Hellspawn standing behind me. How does he know your words? Do you motherfuckers get a newsletter or a talking points memo?"

Elrik coughed behind me. "I might be able to help with that. See I have been watching you since you arrived on this Plane. Like the rest of Hell, I was curious. So tonight, when the opportunity came up, and seeing as how I had just been given the responsibility of your oversight, I decided to see if I could make my job a little easier by helping you along a path you were already headed down." He smiled at me and blinked his eyes twice. Damn... (I missed the 'given my oversight' part at first, we'll circle back around to that in a moment.)

Shaking my head, I asked, "Is Usis the only one not manipulating me?"

Kitar tipped back in his chair, placing his feet up on the table and took a long drag from his pipe. "First, it is not manipulating you, it is preparing you. Something you keep saying you want to happen. Now I ask you, do you remember what my job in Hell was, before I was saddled with you?"

"You were a judge, yeah, what does that have to do with anything?"

"My job was to render a verdict on how creatures conducted their lives. Not to tell them how they should conduct them, where they went wrong, how they could have made it simpler. No, those are all things they need to figure out for themselves. You would have never taken this job seriously if I had tried to get through that stubborn head of yours how important what you are doing is. You would have crumbled under the weight of the knowledge. Instead, I waited till you got the hots for this Hellspawn and decided to go out for drinks while your true companion was who knows where, having who know what done to him by one of the most fearsome of The Fallen to walk Creation. So you ask what my job is? Well my job is to help you realized for yourself how important what you have been told to do is before we get to the Planes where that lack of information very well might get your scrawny little ass destroyed." Taking another long puff, he added, "And if you ever raise your voice to me again --"

That is when Elick decided to step in again cutting Kitar off. "See there is where the problem lies..." I tried to say something, I know I did, but nothing seem to be coming out. Finally, Elick spoke up. "First, it is sweet everyone is in agreement as to how handsome I am, but Keith here does have a point. You are doing a woefully pitiful..." Kitar started to say something then decided better of it when Elick glared at him, "keep quiet, soul. That is one of your major issues. You try to speak when you mouth should be closed. I am *your* overseer now, you *will* sit there and listen. You might have served the Dark Lord well for many years as a Judge but you clearly have forgotten yourself. I am still one of the Royals of this domain and you are still just a scrawny little soul. Your job as guide has been woefully inadequate and it is time you stop lecturing The Dark Lord's chosen about his responsibilities and start performing your own. From this moment forward, I will be checking in on his progress personally. Lord Lucifer asked me if I would be interested and at first it did not sound like something that would spark my curiosity, well now it has. As you like to point out, little judge, you are his guide. Well now I am your Master, so you will put away your arrogance and start doing what you were ordered to do." Walking closer he reached down and picked Kitar up by his neck. "Is there any part of what you were just told you need me to clarify?" Kitar could barely move his head but I saw the small shake. As he was lowered back down onto the ground, Elick said, "Good" as he slapped me on the ass. I swear... and headed to the door. "I will see what I can find out about Usis. Finish up here, I think you are ready to move on."

Still angry with Kitar, I walked over and poured myself a glass of wine, grabbed the pitcher and threw myself in the chair across from him. Neither of us spoke. Eventually Kitar pulled what had become my pipe from his pouch, filled it and offered it to me.

As I took it I commented, "We have clearly gone off the rails here. Let's figure out what needs to be done so we can get on the same page and then go and get my *fucking* companion back."

Again, there was silence. A really long silence, so long it almost became impossible for either of us to break it. Thank gawd someone showed up and knocked on the door. I was about to get up when Sigos came walking in, behind her Cemal was carrying two bottles of wine. "Get me a cup and open the other two bottles," she ordered as she walked over to the table, taking a seat. She sat back in the chair, stretching her legs out before her and crossed her hooves at the ankles. "Since your house is in disarray and you seem to have an endless procession of Powers bringing you advice I don't want to feel left out, since this is, after all, my Plane, so here is mine." She turned quickly to Kitar and added, "I know you are not again about to make the mistake of interrupting me."

Seeing that Kitar wasn't going to say anything she said, "First let me get the insignificant business out of the way. After talking to your now absent companion I have arranged with Lucifer for you to take this one with you," she said pointing to Cemal, who almost dropped the bottle of wine. "He is yours. Consider him a gift. He is not on loan. You own him. He is beholden to you, body and soul.

Do with him as you will." I watched as Cemal with both hands set down the bottle and steadied himself on the side of the bed.

"Me, My Lord?" Cemal finally got out.

Not even turning, she replied, "Yes, you are now owned by Keith here. Any authority his companion or guide has will be given by him. Do you understand?"

"Yes, My lord," answered Cemal, his lip quivering.

I watched the scared boy, when he turned I caught his eye and mouthed, "Don't worry." I made a mental note to chat with him once the Overlord was gone.

"Now to the part you are not going to like. Please do not mistake this as me caring. But since you both were here in my house under my protection I feel it is my duty to inform you that your companion was taken by Leviathan to his Keep on the Seventh Plane." When she stopped talking she held up a hand. "Please do not upset me by interrupting."

"But…"

I took a deep breath and tried to not explode as the Overlord continued, "If you want my suggestion, there is nothing you can do for him right now. Something is happening with your young companion and though you may not like it, he might be in better hands for now. Don't bother asking me what that might be, only Lucifer knows and he is, as is his way, playing his cards close to his chest. Welcome to Hell. I can offer you a small consolation, mainly just to piss off our Lord and Master and get revenge against Leviathan for betraying your group's safety, which I had promised." She paused closing her eyes for a second then opened them again. "We can now not be over heard. I have a slave there, he is of a Demon class. I will give you the ability to see through his eyes. He has been told to find your companion and keep tabs on him. He will do nothing to aid Usis and has been forbidden from offering assistance in any way."

"Why, if you have someone there, can't we just rescue him?" I insisted not really caring what her excuse was. All I could here was the ringing in my ears and the urge to run to wherever Usis was and save him.

"And go against The Dark Lord and Lord Leviathans wishes? I might be strong, little one, but I am already at a marked disadvantage and my power is limited to this Plane. I will not risk for you or anyone having what few liberties my dear husband has left me stripped away. I am already taking a great risk by allowing you access to my spy...slave. Use it and don't over tax my patience. You know where he is. Do you job and you will get to him." She released the spell as she said, "The Dark Lord has entered my Plane."

Kitar and I finished our wine at the same time and held out our glasses. Cemal was there to refill them without missing a beat. The Overlord stood. "If there is nothing more you need, I would make the same suggestion as Elick. It's time for you to move to the next Plane. My last bit of warning for you, Keith..." She used my name. I didn't like that. "Is you prepare yourself for what is to come. The Planes change dramatically after this one."

"Why do people keep saying that?" I asked. "Maybe it is time for you to fill me in on what I have to look forward to." I was about to start up again when I heard a noise behind me. I knew by how Cemal's face had just turned white and then seeing Kitar bow as the Overlord's growled that Lucifer was standing there. Without moving to face him I said, "Greetings, My Lord." My voice didn't fully disguise my anger.

"And to you as well. If all the yelling, advice giving and other merriment is any indication, it is clear you have grasped and decided to practice the underlying tenants of this Plane. The air is thick with Wrath. Not being one to enjoy being left out, to quote my beloved Sigos here, I decided to come to see what aid I might be able to render. With that being said, I understand you have some questions about my instructions to your guide?" The Dark Lord said in a calm smooth tone.

I turned now and bowed to The Dark Lord. He was dressed all in black this time, about seven feet and still had his horns, tail and hooves. "It's just things have been happening more and more that have caught me off guard. Everyone keeps telling me how dangerous the upcoming Planes are but won't tell me why. Usis has been abducted and both of us..." I rose slowly deciding to no longer hide my anger, "were led to believe you had given us a level of protection."

With a *tsk tsk* sound Lord Lucifer walked into the room. "I have and he has not been dispatched, so there is that. As for your concerns about what you should or should not be warned about, I guess I have not made myself clear." Walking over to Kitar he lifted him up so he could look him in the eyes. "When I say do not tell him anything, I mean anything. Which includes warning him that a Plane is going to be more challenging. Does everyone understand now?"

Trying not to smile, Kitar's eyes shifted from Lucifer's to mine. Yes my mouth was hanging open, big surprise there, and said, "Yes, My Lord."

"But..." was all I could get out.

Before letting Kitar go he leaned in. "Here is the advice I mentioned and it is for you Lord Judge. I will not lecture you since your new overseer already has. But know I have noticed your perceived self-importance beginning to interfere with your duties. One of your original sins which seems to have only grown more pronounced since you joined us here in Hell. You are now a guide. You might still have many of your powers but that is only because I have allowed it. It is time you begin understanding you are in service just like this slave. I can assure you, judge, your powers, your continued standing within Hell, and for that matter your existence in eternity, are in your hands and how well you execute your duties. Serve this soul well or you very well might find yourself patrolling the mountains around a Plane in a hellhound's body."

Lucifer added as he walked by, "As to the subject of your companion. He is going through some challenges of his own. What those are and how they will ultimately affect him or you is at this time of no importance to your little writing assignment. What I suggest is, if you wish to be reunited with him, you do your job, write your entries and the sooner you get to Usis the sooner he will be at your side again. But do not for a moment think you can rush through or force an outcome. I will tell you what I told your guide. Your assumption of your importance is quickly becoming inflated past where it might be healthy for you. I would suggest you remember whom you serve as well as understanding that the rumors of my patience have been greatly exaggerated. Lastly, but I know you have already been told, Elick will be keeping an eye on you. There are several events happening in Creation that will require my full attention therefore I will not be able to check in on you as often. I trust Elick to keep you safe and out of unneeded trouble." Adding to Sigos he said, "See, problem solved. You have done well while the writer has been visiting your Plane. I will ensure you are rewarded the next time I visit."

As he walked out the door we all heard the Overlord say, "Oh joy, I so enjoy our moments together, my beloved husband." Lucifer did not respond as he pulled the door closed behind him.

# Entry 179

The silence drug on for several seconds after Lucifer had left until finally the Overlord burst out laughing. "Damn he can be a pain in the ass when he wants to." As I stood and glanced over at her she added, still smiling, "I guess that will teach you to complain, now wont it."

"But..."

"It seems all you have been saying for the last several minutes is 'but...'. Should I arrange for you a thesaurus?" Stopping at the door, she turned and gave me one of those rare friendly smiles. "Much to my surprise it has actually been a pleasure to have you visit. You were not near the trouble I had been told you were. I cannot say the same for that little companion of yours but then he has his own issues to deal with. Since our business is concluded, I will bid you well now. Feel free to leave when you are ready. My protection will stay with you until you step off this Plane." Walking out the door we heard as she pulled it closed behind her, "Happy Hunting."

I leaned against the door, a little out of fear that someone else would show up to throw yet another wrench into this mess. I walked back into the room and gave Cemal a nod then to Kitar I said, "We seem to be at an impasse." I handed the boy my empty glass as I ran my fingers through my hair, "I think it has just been made clear to both of us that we are in this together. Kitar, I trust you. We might have our differences but that's not uncommon when two people are placed in difficult situations. I want to know you have my back and I want you to know I have yours. I want to be able to trust you and know you don't have a hidden agenda. We've enough of those it seems. As for this not telling me about the future Planes. Now, and I hope The Dark Lord is listening, if you two want these journals, then your jobs, both of you, is to prepare me in any way needed to ensure I'm clear minded when I reach the next torments. You want an objective telling of my journey, and that, my dear guide, can't be done if I can't ensure my wellbeing. So, you need to decide what it is you're planning, and then do what you need to do to make that clear to the powers that be. On top of all of these other problems now Usis is missing and clearly there is something The Dark Lord isn't telling us. Even I'm smart enough to know pressuring him won't do any good, so all we can do is get to the Seventh Plane and rescue the man I love. Can I count on you to help me with that?"

"Keith, it has never been my intention to do anything other than help you. I see now that we have both been caught up in events swirling around us and it was my job to buffer you from that. I will do better in the future, you have my oath. The Dark Lord was correct. I have allowed my former station to cloud my actions. I am also wise enough to see what he just told me for what it is, a warning. We have both made mistakes. I hope you can accept my apology and we can start anew?"

"Of course," I sat down on the grown in front of Cemal who had been kneeling beside me, "Now I must ask you. Who do you work for?"

Bowing his head, he said in a worried voice, "Master, what The Lord told me means I am yours now, My Master. Master, I listen and have heard what you have said to Lord Judge and what has been discussed here today." He paused for several seconds and I could see he was choosing his words carefully. "I am yours, Master, that has been made clear to me." He lifted his head. "My only loyalty is now to you, no one else, ever. I will give my life, my soul, my heart and my body to your service for as long as you will allow me to do so. This, Master, is an absolute. There are no shades of grey or hidden agendas. The Dark Lord himself could give me an order at this point and I would await your approval before carrying it out. He carries more sway than the average damned here on the Planes of Hell." I nodded then a slight frown formed along the edges of his mouth. "What is my purpose, and if it is not being presumptuous, what is Master's feelings about owning this one? I have heard you mention reservations."

I shook my head. "I have no idea. This was my companion's idea. I understand and agree it was a good one, but I've no clue what your duties should be or how you should be instructed. I'm trusting since it appears you have served for some time that you know what you are doing. Do that. What I can tell you, what I'm absolutely sure about, is that you're part of this group now and as long as I can trust you fully, without question, you will be treated as a member of our team. You will be expected to do your duties. Your job is to ensure, we and our lodgings, wherever they may be, are cared for and kept optimal.

"In touring these Planes and writing my journals I'm often exposed to sights and experiences that are emotionally hard. Your job will be to do whatever you can to aid in making our lives easier. When I'm writing, it will be helpful to have you here to serve, allowing me to concentrate. I may at times ask your opinion or bounce something off you. Know that you won't be punished for whatever your answer is as long as I can trust that it is truthful. When we step into our quarters I want to know we are safe, things are handled, and we can count on you to be here, ready and willing to serve us. If you have questions or concerns, come to me. You don't let them fester or waste time worrying about them. You will be given coin to purchase whatever supplies you need. Don't waste or spend that money frivolously. You will be treated with respect as long as you behave in a way that is conducive to that. Does that make sense?"

Smiling broadly Cemal moved to a kneeling position and bowed all the way down until his forehead touched my legs. Then sitting up and placing his hands perfectly on his thighs, palms up, he said, "Yes, My Master. I am yours, and of that you will never need to question."

I leaned in and hugged him. I could feel him tense but then he carefully put his arms around me and hugged me back. When I released my hands, he did his as well. I got up. "OK, well, that is taken care of and I'm pleased with the outcome." Kitar nodded.

"Now that we are all on the same page again. I'm going to take one last look around the Keep while you two get our shit together. Kitar started to say something but I cut him off. "I'm safe inside the Keep and if I'm not that door isn't going to protect me." I left.

When I reached the end of the hall I found both Lucifer and Sigos leaning against the wall talking. Hearing me come around the corner, The Dark Lord started lazily clapping, "That was a very nice series of speeches, and yes I was listening. The only mistake you made is in challenging me. Never do that, little one. You are but a bug in the cracks of Creation and I have fought wars that have brought The Host to its knees. As for your other comments, you are correct. This is Wrath and I needed to see if you had any. You have been a blithering idiot since you arrived in Hell but I have had faith in you. Now you are about to enter the Hell you have always heard about. If you cannot control your guide, you would never survive what is to come. You did well, that being said do not get a head about you. You are the master of your little group and your guide knows that. Many of his actions were acting as I ordered, some not, we needed to test you. You have passed." He walked up to me and as he did he shifted into his full angelic form. "So you may continue as my writer and I still have confidence I have chosen well. Just remember your place."

He walked to the door in the wall beside us and stepped out onto the balcony as I watched his wings form and extend out behind him. He lifted into the air as a flash and a shockwave traveled through the door knocking me back against the wall. I guess having heard the noise, both Kitar and Cemal came running around the corner. "Great, he probably just wiped out most of the souls on my Plane." She commented as she reached out a hand to help me up. "You did well and do not worry he is not angry. It showed balls lecturing him as you did." The last thing The Overlord of Wrath would say to me as she walked away was, "Remember Lucifer respects strength, you just showed him you have some." She waved and disappeared down the steps.

Raising an eyebrow to Kitar who said, "I have to follow his orders as well. I am sorry if it caused a rift between us. That is something I truly hope will heal."

I smiled, "No problem, we are all at his mercy and as The Overlord once said, he can be a real ass."

"I heard that," rang through the Plane of Wrath, loud enough for everyone to hear.

# Journal of a Deadman

## Volume 5 – Blasphemy

## Alexander Collas

# Entry 180

It's been a few days since my last entry. I'd waited in anticipation of my mood improving. Well that didn't happen, it only got worse. Nevertheless, a lot *has* happened and as I said almost all of it had pissed me off. I usually try to give you an update as we begin our trek to the next Plane. I don't know why. I guess it's because I've no idea how much time passes between entries for you. I'm told my writing is distributed to independent servants in the different creations for dispersal. Who knows how long that takes? Down here -- that's Hell if you're new -- time moves differently than for the living. If I remember correctly, there's no set time for you since it's based on the movement of your planets around your stars. As for The Host and Hell, they follow a long-standing agreed upon measurement of time. With all that being said, the time it takes for the words I have written to reach you could be anywhere from days, months, to even years.

Anyway, I'm not really in the mood to do too much catch up. Since I see this is entry 180. If you're lost I'd suggest you go back and read the earlier 179 entries to get caught up. For those of you who might be curious, I don't number the entries; when I start one, it's done automatically. I've noticed from time to time how the numbers have skipped. I am sure you know better why than I do. This is just another thing that has been annoying me of late.

To bring you up-to-date, we've just completed our tour of the Fifth Plane and should be on our way to the Sixth, but no! I, or should I say we are on our fucking way back to the Second Plane because it seems I need to get my god damn head together. (Listen, editors, you can bite me if saying God Damn pisses anyone off. They can tell me themselves. Don't you dare change it.) The only upside to this little vacation to Lust is De Sade; he's about the only person in this whole damn place I'm really in the mood to see. Just in case you don't know, the "damn place" I'm referring to is Hell. Yes, that Hell. I've already told you to go back and read the earlier entries. You're going to get a headache, and I don't want to hear about it when you get here.

As for what is happening right now. Well, Kitar and Elick are getting the last of the plans made to leave, and currently, Cemal is running around like a beat dog, no I haven't beat him, no one has. He's just nervous. With a new owner, master, boss...whatever...me... stomping around screaming, I can understand why he is running around like a cat with its ass on fire. So, there you have it, that's all you get, so on with the show.

# Entry 181

It wasn't until we were packed and ready to leave that I noticed I'd slipped into a better mood. It was probably because I didn't have the bug thing on my back, literally, reminding me I needed to get an entry written. It was only my second time to travel between the Planes through the air. Elick carried me in his arms, mine wrapped around his neck, while Kitar and Cemal used their own wings. I won't lie, I enjoyed the feeling of being clutched to Elick's pale, muscular chest, but at the same time, it made me miss Usis. We sailed up into the massive cavern which was the Fifth Plane, the landscape of suffering spread out below us. Then at an incredible speed, we continued up until the blackness of the great void which separated the Planes engulfed us. For several seconds there was nothing, then we emerged in the inky greyness of the Fourth Plane, me disoriented. Elick's wings never seemed to strain against the extra weight as we rocketed across the Plane and up again into nothingness and onto the Third and finally the Second where we slowed and for several seconds hovered motionless in mid-air. Elick explained this was to let the Overlord, De Sade, know we had arrived. In case you haven't done your homework as instructed, The Second Plane is Lust.

Fearfully I watched as we soared from the heights of the cavern toward the black Keep, growing ever closer. Then with a disturbing suddenness, we stopped, just feet from the front façade of the upper floors. We hung suspended mid-air before dropping vertically straight down until Elick's foot gently touched the flagstones. With care, he held me out and placed me on my feet, my legs a bit wobbly, at the base of the black marble steps leading up to the large ornate entrance. I hadn't as much as gotten my bearings when the doors swung open to reveal Lust's Overlord, the Marquis De Sade, standing there with a broad smile, in all his glory.

I won't lie, it was like coming home. He was the first person since arriving in Hell that I'd known from my world, even if only by reputation. He'd welcomed me in and for the first time made me feel like this could be my place too. Don't get me wrong, he's one warped mother fucker, but in all the ways I've learned to like. Except maybe for his proclivity for torturing souls horribly in cruel and entertaining ways. Though I can't hold that against him, it's his job after all.

As I walked up with a smile, he took me in his arms and gave me a big hug. It was nice. Then holding me back at arm's length while looking me over he added in his ever so comforting style, "Boy you've really stuck your dick in it this time. I have read your entries, thanks to Elick. Got that cute Usis hauled off, and half of hell wants to destroy you." With a loud laugh added, "so, I guess this calls for booze and food to celebrate. You are finally making yourself at home."

"That's why I was happy when they told me they were bringing me back here. If anyone can lift my spirits and help find a silver lining it's you," I said sarcastically as the others walked into the Keep. I, on the other hand, pointed to a figure sitting just to our left. "What's that?" On one of the landings beside marble steps was a lady sitting on what appeared to be a park bench. She was dressed nicely except her chest was open from just below the neck to her waist with all her internal organs spilled out onto her lap and overflowing onto the bench beside her. Small bugs were buzzing around the intestines, zipping in and out of her open chest cavity. She was awake, conscious and in a lot of pain. On the ground at her feet were hundreds of those little rat creatures that had been so prevalent on all the Planes. Each was fighting to grab the bits of meat the weeping lady was tossing onto the ground from a bowl she was holding. Overall it was a truly gruesome sight and had all the earmarks of a De Sade created torture.

"Oh, after you left I felt the place needed some a little more culture, I had this installed," he said like it was no big deal. "As long as she keeps the little fellows fed they won't start eating her. Cleaver, don't you think? I call it 'Ne pas sass le suzerain.'"

("At the time I had no idea what the 'title' of the performance art meant. It wasn't until later that I discovered the translation from French was 'Don't Sass the Overlord.' From that I gathered the lady must have had a bit of an attitude when she arrived. As gruesome as this sense of humor is, it' a perfect example of the reason I love the Marquis so much. I've seen almost all the Planes now, and no one goes out of their way to give their atrocities a sense of style. De Sade finds art in his creations. They challenge and delight the eye while terrifying the mind. You can feel however you want about his odd sense of humor but let me assure you, after days, months, years of seeing the same ol' mutilations of millions of souls it's refreshing to see someone doing it more eloquently. I think it in some ways shows a bit of respect for the creature who is suffering. They aren't just another nameless, lost face amongst the crowd being herded along like cattle into the suffering production of Hell. It, in many ways, shows an Overlord taking pride in their work, regardless of how horrific that work might be.)

He could see the repulsed admiration on my face as he threw his arm around my shoulder and walked into his Keep.

"You know, in all my travels I've never met anyone who can turn pain into an art form like you can."

As expected De Sade laughed. "I know, it's a gift, and thank you for noticing."

I hadn't taken two steps into the entrance hall before I stopped in surprise. Sitting on one of the ornate chairs was the beggar from the Third Plane. When he noticed me, his expression changed from a smirk to a grin. "Well, greetings once again, young one," he said. I barely heard him; my attention was on his clothing. No longer was he in ragged tunic and tights but instead in a delicate outfit of golds with startling white tights clinging to his muscular legs. He wore knee-high boots of white with silver buckles and from a great belt hung a finely detailed trumpet. As he stood to greet us, I heard the Marquis say in a derisive tone, "I beg you all not to judge me by the unwelcomed company I keep..." Seeing my eyes widen, he continued, "Do you two know each other? Gabriel ungraciously invited himself to dinner. But then, when The Host shows up, you have to let them in, or there's Hell to pay." He laughed. No one else did. "Get it, hell to pay if you don't let in The Host?" Still nothing. De Sade shook head. "Ok clearly we will be serving a sense of humor with dinner followed by a stick up your ass removal ceremony." Turning to the Archangel, he added, "If you want to invite a few of your friends to that last part, feel free."

When Cemal snorted in laughter it was De Sade's turn to stop mid-sentence. He seemingly hadn't noticed the young demon boy until now. "Well, well, who do we have here?" Walking over he lifted

Cemal's face with a finger and looked deep into his eyes. I could see shudder travel down my young slave's spine. As the Overlord released the boy's chin, he started a slow trip around the now frightened youth. I was fascinated watching how De Sade took in all aspects of our new travel companion, lifting his tail, patting each ass cheek, running a hand across his broad shoulders, around and down his firm abs past his pubs and along his cock. It was like watching a tailor inspect a new suit. When he again stood beside me, he nodded his approval. "Very nice. I guess my admonishment earlier was uncalled for; it seems you have already replaced the old one. This way everyone."

Defensive I stuttered to explain, "No...he's a slave... I mean he was given to me... I mean he's joined us... Oh hell..."

With that, I heard Elick leaned in close to Kitar and say, "And he is our writer."

I didn't seem to care about Cemal's uncomfortableness; I was still focused on Gabriel. I don't know why it had shocked me so much. I had dined with Lucifer. We had drunk wine together as he gave me counsel in the privacy of my room. Gabriel was different; he's an Archangel. An actual member of The Host. Still, I don't think that was what was causing my sensory overload. It would have been one thing if it'd been our first meeting, then it would probably have been more detached. But I'd spent an evening sharing booze from an old bottle while sitting under a makeshift lean-to, all the time thinking he was just another pathetic soul here to suffer for eternity. Can't anyone be trusted in this place?

The Overlord clapped twice summoning two slaves. As they came running the first thing I noticed was how healthy they appeared. It was clear these were not rabble brought in from the planes; these were De Sade's permanent slaves. "Take our guests to their rooms," he ordered. The two young servants led us up the grand stairs to the third floor. (De Sade never picked slaves older than their early twenties and usually always male. Strangely one of these was female.)

When I entered my room, immediately I noticed it was the same one we'd used during our first visit. Again it felt like home, though an empty one. My mind's eye could see Usis sleeping in the bed, sitting at the table, leaning nude on the railing outside the back door, his little tail swishing as his ass cheeks flexed with his thoughts. I miss him, but I guess that's clear. Still, it was nice to be someplace I was accustomed to, less chance of some horrific surprises being just around the corner. This was all part of *their* plan, hoping the familiarity would help me get back on my feet.

As I sat down the packs I looked for wine and found none; I already knew I was going to need something. I sent Cemal with the two servants to find us something to drink and snack on. Mainly I just wanted to be alone for a few minutes. I knew things would quickly get their own inertia. I turned to find my pack still on the bed. Usis' had rolled off spilling its contents on the floor.

I knelt down to collect them when I noticed a small box still lodged in the bottom of the pack. It was about seven inches high and wide and about a foot long. At first, I didn't pay it any attention. That was until I noticed it was wood (which is strange considering how rare lumber was in hell) and had a golden latch. Curiosity got the better of me, and I opened it.

Looking back as I write this I don't know what I expected to find. I can't even remember. Any assumption was quickly eclipsed and then eradicated by the box's reality. What I'm sure I'd not expected to find were two hearts surrounded by straw, both still beating slowly. Which was sad, because that is precisely what the box contained. I dropped it and just sat frozen staring at it. As one of the hearts beat a small amount of black liquid leaked from the bottom of the organ where a bite had been taken. I covered my mouth as my eyes went wide. So much for no horrific surprise around the corner. I heard a noise behind me. It was Cemal returning. I slammed the box lid shut and quickly shoved it back into the pack.

"Master De Sade said not to eat much, he has dinner planned," said Cemal as he walked in setting a crate of wine down on the floor. I jumped up and rushed across the room, pulling the top off one of the bottles and drank it down as Cemal stood wide eyed still holding out a glass which I'd ignored. I sank into the chair beside the table and just stared ahead. It was only after several tries that I heard him ask "Is everything alright, sir?"

I shook my head a couple of times to clear it. "Yes, Yes...everything's fine. I accidentally knocked Usis' backpack off the bed, and it made me think of him," I lied.

In case you're wondering, as of the time I wrote this I hadn't yet told anyone what I'd found. I needed to process this new wrinkle in the fabric of my life. I knew what they were, or at least thought I did, and you'd think that would help, but no, it didn't. And the bite...

# Entry 182

I all but jumped out of my skin when a loud knock came at the door. Standing I saw Cemal was already across the room seeing who was there. He found a cute nude slave with a bit more arrogance than I would have thought safe in De Sade's house stood holding a stack of clothes. He handed them to Cemal, all but ignoring him, and announced in a clear voice, "Dinner will be ready soon."

"What's with the clothes?" I asked.

"My Master thought you might wish to dress…" He gave me a look up and down as if not approving of my current attire. "…for dinner."

I was about to say something when the boy screamed. Cemal had stomped his foot. "He might not be your master, but he is mine, and you will respect him as is your place or I might serve you for dinner," growled Cemal, giving him a smile befitting his demon nature. Like the boy, I shivered at the look and show of teeth. It was the first time I'd glimpsed the demon resting inside this little one. It'd probably behoove me to learn a bit more about that side as well as his history, of which I knew little.

Both the boy and Cemal, whose face was red with anger, turned to see how I'd react. I just shrugged. "Yeah…what he said. I'll be down soon. You may go."

With a much less cocky attitude, the boy added with head bowed, "Master is also expecting your servant to assist with dinner."

"What do you think, Cemal?" I asked with a shrug.

"It's customary, Master," he said.

"Then fine, you're free to go with this one." Feeling I needed to add something I threw in, "I expect you to treat Cemal as if he were me and if I get no reports back after dinner, we will let this matter of your insolence slide." I felt like a complete dork saying such bullshit, but I could tell from Cemal's half smile I'd done well. Usis handled this part of our relationship. Boy I missed him.

The boy bowed deeply. "Yes, My Lord."

I got dressed and went downstairs. There was plenty to tell about the dinner, but I'm not going to do it. My Host and our surprise guest spent a lot of time filling me in on the Planes to come. All of that I'm leaving out. Sorry, I feel it would be better if we got there at the same time, it'll give us context. What I can tell you is that Lucifer would be pissed. He didn't want me warned about what I've not yet seen. Oh well, that's what happens when an Angel comes to dinner.

Here's what I can tell you about dinner. When I arrived, I noticed Cemal. First, he was dressed in a very formal coat with an open front and no back. He was dressed formally but still mostly nude. He stood with about six other slaves, one of which was the smart ass one from earlier. I noticed he looked a bit more disheveled than the rest. I didn't need to ask because Marquis answered the question without prompting. "This one's..." he pointed, "rudeness has been corrected." I let it go. The eighth slave, and he stood out, firstly because he was fully dressed in white silks. Secondly, unlike the others, he was mostly dressed and amazingly stunning. I would say handsome but handsome is a masculine trait, I think, and he was not so much masculine. His skin was the color of porcelain, so unless you looked carefully, at times, it was hard to tell where his skin stopped, and his robes began. His face was angelic, his ears slightly pointed, I just stood and stared for a second, he was intriguing. What I found out during the meal, and I will recount part of it momentarily, is that he was Gabriel's slave. Yes, let that sink in, he was an Angel's slave. His name is Zacul.

"Please join us," said De Sade rousing me from my staring. I don't think it was his voice but the tone that got my attention. There was anger, annoyance, in it. I looked where he was pointing. The first seat on the left side of the table. He was across from me with Elick seated beside him. Beside me was Kitar. As I walked over I realized what it was; The Overlord was not at the head of his own table, Gabriel was. Now it made sense, the anger. He saw this as a slight; I tend to agree.

As my eyes looked between them, it was Gabriel who explained. "The Overlord is showing respect, that is all."

My gaze shifted back as De Sade growled, "Respect is given. Disrespect is taken. I gave nothing."

The Angel just inclined his head and dismissed the comment. "Please, join us."

Already not in the mood I took my seat. "I'm sure I wasn't brought back here and forced to delay getting to Usis to listen to an age-old struggle between competing sides. Can everyone stick to the point, say what they have to say so I can tell you how much better I feel and get on to the Seventh plane and my companion?"

"You will learn, young one; patience is divine, all in time. But for the record there are no competing sides, The Host won the war, it is that simple."

"Yet here we are a hundred million years later, and no one seems to be sure of that. It seems the only people who agree with you are those who have always agreed with you. We used to call that spin back on my planet. Keep saying it long enough, and someone will eventually believe you. Now can we get on with it?" Slamming my seat in I held out my cup which Cemal moved around and filled.

Elick decided to step in. "Look around you. This is not The Host, and you are the only thing divine in the room. A room I might add owned by the Divine creature you claim to have defeated. Then why, dear Gabriel, are you here and he not there? Who comes, crown in hand, to whom? Regardless, Keith is right, and we are not here to settle that old thorn today. So maybe we should just eat before our food gets cold."

I was sure when Kitar jumped in he was going to try to play peacemaker, the asshole. He might have been a Judge in Hell, but he still had his nose firmly up The Host's ass as far as I was concerned. "I think we could all use wine," he added.

I was glad to see I was wrong. "That I will agree with," I agreed.

De Sade made a subtle wave of his hand causing the slaves to scurry away only to reappear a few seconds later with plates. Of course, the Angel's meal was different from ours, and no I didn't ask. I can only say for sure that the wine was his. It was better than most I've had in Hell excluding when Lucifer brought his own.

"So why is an Angel in Hell?" I finally asked, bored with the banality of the conversation.

"The Host and Hell have business together. More so now than before. So it is not uncommon for us to visit The Dark Lord. After all, we must come to him since he cannot come to us," answered Gabriel, shooting a look at Elick.

At first, I didn't catch on, then, "Oh that's right, the whole thrown out of The Host thing. That's still in effect?"

It amazed me how quickly Gabriel's countenance changed. "Yes, it is most certainly still in effect. The abomination will never again see The Father's realm."

"Wow, how long has it been?" I asked. "Seems a long time to hold a grudge. I thought forgiveness was divine as well?" I couldn't help noticing both Elick and De Sade cracking a grin. The latter lifting an eyebrow. "Yes, explain to us about forgiveness?"

Sitting back in his chair and taking a long drink of his wine, Gabriel said, "Look around, you little one. Forgiveness has its limits. That is why you, them..." he tilted his cup toward the others at the table, "...are all here. The Father forgives, but only to a point."

"Yes, up to the point where he has to admit he was wrong," growled Elick as he quickly regained his smile and nodded to the Archangel.

"I've met several souls in my travels that don't belong here. They made mistakes, and yet they are sentenced to eternal punishment."

"The Father has rules. The Host was not created for those who are almost perfect; it is there to reward those who are truly The Father's love personified."

Elick again couldn't hold his tongue. "So The Host welcomes the living who meet their requirements with open arms."

Focusing his gaze upon the Hellspawn, he answered, "With open arms."

"Lie!" snapped Kitar. My eyes went wide as Gabriel's gaze shot toward our Guide.

"I would watch yourself, ex-judge. Would you like to relive your sins? I can list them if you wish. Don't presume to challenge a member of The Host."

"Then I will say it...that's a lie," I said softly. "I know my sins, I've been judged. I know why I'm here. I know what I've been tasked to do. And what I've been tasked to do is explore, analyze and then write about my travels through this place. Now you, My Dear Most High, are part of those travels. Therefore, you are now within my purview, so I'll ask you any fucking question I want. If you choose not to answer, then I'll move your refusal up the line, and you can then explain your reticence to my boss. As I understand it, you two know each other." Sorry I've already had enough of this little side trip. Though seeing De Sade is nice, I don't want to be here, and I most certainly don't have the patience for this arrogant fuck. Finally taking a deep breath and a deep drink I looked around the table. It was silent, everyone including Gabriel sat almost wide-eyed at my outburst. But I also know that if I want answers, this isn't the way to start. Setting my glass down I added to Gabriel, "Forgive me. As you know this trip has been grueling and due to recent events, my nerves are a bit frayed. We have all been bickering since we sat down. Let's all take a step back and start again." With that, I bowed my head to the Archangel who returned it with a forced smile.

Looking over at Kitar, I asked in a casual tone, "So, what questions have you always wanted to ask?"

"Just one, I have always wondered, even while I lived, but never received a direct answer. I have heard rumors but did not want to believe them."

"And what might that be?" I asked.

He smiled a sad smile. "Are the living welcome even in The Eternal City? Even if they are perfect?"

That was such a loaded question. I could see in my guide's eyes the answer he expected and the pain it brought him. This wasn't the question of a judge, but one asked by a believer, and it didn't matter if that person was living or dead.

All eyes turned to the Angel sitting at the head of the table. He sat quietly for several minutes, occasionally sipping from his golden chalice. "No...we do not want you talking monkeys littering our streets..."

Kitar let his head drop, almost on the verge of tears. You could see the pain written all over his body. Quietly he said, "So it is true?"

"...but Father wished them there, and we do not question our Father. Therefore, we welcome those who are worthy."

That's when I remembered several comments from past conversations. "So as long as they follow the correct path they are welcome. And who paves this path?"

"We do since Father is away."

"Have those rules changed much since his departure?" I asked, taking a sip.

"Some..."

I nodded. "I have my answer. So, let me get this right since I *will* be writing about it. And correct me if I'm wrong. But do you see each new soul entering The Eternal City as a triumph or as a bug in the fabric of time that still needs to be fixed? Is it a joy to see a new member of The Host or something to correct in hopes that it will not happen again?"

Gabriel gave the question some thought. I had to respect that. As he held out his goblet for the boy to fill, he answered, "Probably a little of both. We look at each soul that enters to see if there is some flaw, something unworthy inside them, which does need to be corrected in the future to ensure others like them do not enter accidentally. With that being said, we also rejoice because each new soul that arrives is proof of Father's work. Though it is tainted by the fact we were never happy with his decision to create another sentient class of souls."

"Interesting. In your eyes is there a point at which The Host will know you have accounted for all the flaws and are confident that only the truly worthy can enter?"

The angel smiled. "We already have that answer. All those who should ever be there, in the presence of Father, were already there before he started this endeavor. It is only us, his first children who truly deserve an eternity in his home."

It was my turn to take a second. All eyes were now on me, including Gabriel who had leaned forward, resting his elbows on the table. Copying his move, I leaned in. "It sounds to me like that didn't go so well, since a third of 'those perfect beings' choose to follow The First, The Most Loved by The Father, against you." Turning and looking at the boy, Gabriel's slave, I asked, "You have a slave? I find that interesting. A slave. But then it was promised we would be allowed to serve The Father and The Host for all time. I wonder if the faithful ever realize they should take that passage so literally. By serving their entire life faithfully they will be rewarded with an eternity in servitude. I guess my question now is, Lord Gabriel, did Lord Lucifer, get thrown out, or did he break his chains and leave? Did he choose to give up servitude, picking freedom instead?"

We, Gabriel and myself, were now staring into each other eyes. That was until another hand slammed down on the table. This time it was De Sade. "Now that is the writer that needs to finish this trip. It is good to see your balls have finally dropped since you were last here. Good for you."

I smiled a half smile as De Sade finished then turned back to see what Gabriel would say. His chair was empty. "He left? Did I upset him?"

"They are easily upset," answered De Sade. Looking at the other two. "It seems your concerns are unfounded. Our boy here seems quite prepared for what is to come."

"We are as surprised as you are," answered Kitar.

I sat eating while listening to my three dinner companions talk about me like I wasn't there. Trust me I've grown used to it. Most of those in power, both above and below, seem to see the souls of the living as nothing more than inanimate objects. After we had finished dinner, I decided it was time to address the elephant in the room. "I know there have been concerns. I think, and Kitar will back me up, I've been undergoing this change you've all been hoping to see for some time now." Pausing and taking a long swallow, I continued, "So I want to get moving. Let tonight's little display demonstrate that I have every intention of taking this job more seriously. No one is getting off, regardless of how powerful they are. That all being said, as far as I'm concerned, I have a single goal and that is to save my companion. Now if you think these two goals are contradictory, let me assure you they aren't. Usis is my strength, and with him by my side, I can do anything. While he is not, my determination to return him to me will drive me forwards. Therefore, I can promise you I'll give you no further reasons to delay our drive forward and ultimately enact his rescue. If there are any other issues I want them brought up and discussed so this can be the last I have to hear of this topic."

That is about all of this dinner party I am going to share. The rest I will bring up as we move through the next plane.

# Entry 183

Back in my room that night I couldn't shake a feeling of restlessness. So many bits from dinner's conversations were still stuck in my teeth. I drank a glass of wine, then a bottle, then a second. It was good stuff. I was drunk by the end of the third bottle, something which was getting harder to do since wine was my only available drink. Cemal came in halfway through my first and asked if he could hang out with a few of the other slaves, which I thought was a great idea. I did suggest he keep an ear open to see what he could overhear and off he went.

I stood on the balcony looking out across the dusty grey Plane of Lust. My eyes moved casually over the torture pits below as I listened and inhaled its cries and smells of suffering. From time to time I'd focus on a single area and for a few moments watch the souls being moved into place and then tortured. Their cries were punctuated by bits of flesh and drops of raw suffering as it rained down upon the hard-grey ground. I watched a session end, the defeated, often dissected soul pulled down still screaming; its body parts quickly gathered up, all in the span of time it took to bring the next one in from the overflowing holding cages. Over and over, these hundreds, maybe thousands of stations systematically moving through soul after soul. I watched as the Demon in the section closest to me took a break and sat down to rest, the soul he was torturing still strapped to the device. He paused, looked over, and then unclasped the creature's leg, lifting it and took a large bite from the four-toed foot. The unfortunate creature screamed but was quickly silenced by the shock of seeing his own foot devoured. Both the damned and I watched the torturer as he snacked on the creature's body indifferent to the fact he was being observed.

To me, all of this, after all these years, their cries, their pain, their oneness had been lost. They were nothing more than a symphony, the background noise of this horrible place where I stood in a suite having just dined with an Angel. My traveling companion, a Judge who had sentenced untold millions of souls to this pain. Who was I, this little man from New York City? That is wrong, this little man from Earth, cities don't matter. A world that no longer existed. Every single soul who had ever walked that great blue globe was now here, except for a handful that were told they would be tolerated as slaves to spend eternity amongst the elite. I saw Gabriel's arrogance tonight at dinner. Did walking through those gates blind those who were there to such disdain, I had to believe, not. As an atheist, I think I finally discovered there was an afterlife but had now also learned there was no justice. Kitar had told me when I'd first arrived at some point I'd be required to make a decision; would I remain myself or become one of the monsters. I think I was beginning to realize that all I could keep of myself was what was inside of me, my experiences, my history. The rest sadly had no choice but to become the monster. I knew at that moment, that if me becoming a monster would save Usis, then that's what I'd become.

When I finished the second bottle, I thought of the disco. That's right, one of De Sade's chambers of pain. Where souls who had spent their lives feasting at the banquet tables of debauchery, drugs, and excess were sent to continue their party in euphoric suffering. On my planet they were called Raves for a while, in truth there was a version of it on most worlds. From the dark dances of tribesman hoping to find enlightenment to the meticulously structured movements and sounds of the cybernetically advanced planets where computational order was what passed for perfection.

I changed clothes, something less dressy and more suited for what I knew was coming. As I headed down the hall with my third bottle in hand, I started to hear the music. I had to smile. This was where I needed to be tonight, and obviously De Sade agreed. An American (a place on my world for those not from Earth) singer was blaring down the hall as the light undulated from under the crack in the door. It was Rob Zombie.

Here is part of the lyrics that welcomed me to De Sade's house of sin:

This is the house
Come on in
This is the house
Built on sin
This is the house

Nobody lives
This is the house
You get what you give

I cut the flesh
And make it bleed
Fresh skin
Is what I need
I let it dry
Out in the wood
All your crying
Did no good, yeah

As the white ornately carved doors swung open, they were immediately stopped by the bodies dancing just inside. Right away I was pushed back by the overpowering mass of stimuli rushing to escape. The smells of rot, shit, and decay. The blare of the music, the crash of the light all combined to cause my body to recoil as if being plunged into boiling water, but I trudged ahead.

Tonight, in the beginning, my vision was not filtered the way it had been the first time. The Marquis wanted me to see the real rave. For now, I saw the room as it was. Thousands, maybe tens of thousands, of figures locked in their own private ecstasy. It would be easy to mistake this as a reward more than a punishment, but you would be wrong, terribly wrong. This was a frenzied stupor of deep chaotic hunger ever yearning for a fulfillment that was always just out of reach. An incessant desire to be addicted. Here in the Marquis' domain, the damned spent the only currency they had left, their souls. Here their bodies writhed and slammed against each other, ripping new wounds, smearing blood and viscera onto their partners trapped in a dance that would never stop. Chipped fingernails tearing at bits of exposed flesh, sweating rotten skin rubbing against bleeding open wounds until finally, unable to take any more, the skin fell away only to be stomped to a pulp and pushed through the grates in the floor. There it would be collected and either sent on to the great rivers of suffering or recycled, putrefied and redistributed to the dancing masses to be consumed in the guise of their favorite drinks. In truth, the refreshments they consumed only served to make their insides churn, causing them to vomit and retch all over each other as they reached for yet another disguised glass of pain hoping this one would wash away the sick. This was but one of De Sade's masterwork.

As I stood on the shores of bedlam, letting my body, mind, and senses adjust, I wasn't surprised to see a drink appear in front of me. It wasn't one of the illusional beverages for the decadent masses; this was a real drink, held out by our host. I took it and smiled. De Sade, like before, had shed his formal clothes and was now a t-shirt and jeans which hugged his thin, almost emaciated form. I looked down to read the writing on the shirt. The last time I was here it had read "Hell's not for pussies," and this time, with no disappointment it said, "Fuck an Angel, it's divine." I had to laugh.

As I sipped the drink, it was cold and delicious; we headed into the center of the dance floor flanked by two colossal golem-like creatures whose only purpose was to keep the rabble at bay.

Leaning in, "Can I have the guise," I asked. De Sade waved his hand dismissively causing the disfigured souls to morph into sweaty healthy revealers. We danced together as songs blasted away. As much as the illusion of the souls helped there were still times when the guise would falter. Not the look so much as what it could not mask, a leg finally rotting off and dropping away causing the seemingly healthy person to topple over, only to be trampled under the other dancers. I drank, the Overlord drank. Finally, sometime later he motioned for me to follow as we made our way to the back of the room where a red velvet rope and two of the giant guards protected a lavishly curved booth and table. The Marquis ushered me in and together we sat as the noise of the room faded into the background, no longer overpowering.

"I was hoping you would turn up. I feel you could do with some counsel," started De Sade.

Laughing and downing my drink, I replied, "I'm pretty sure that's why they brought me back. You've heard what happened to Usis?"

"Of course. I also know that Sigos gave you a link to a boy in Leviathan's keep. Have you seen your little boyfriend since they took him?"

Shaking my head, I looked down. "No. I've tried several times but the boy is never where he should be. I'm starting to think she was trying to add to my pain instead of helping relieve it."

"It is what we do after all. I could see her doing something like that if for no other reason than to passively strike out at Lord Lucifer," commented De Sade as he had two more drinks brought over. I hadn't realized I was staring into space until I felt the cold drink against my hand. "Listen, little writer, you can either start talking, or I will chain you to something and administer my special charms until you decide to spill your guts, pardon the pun. Which will it be?"

I shrugged. "What's there to say?" I Motioned out into the crowd. "We don't get do-overs, and I think it's finally started sinking in what I've been tasked to do. Lucifer, even after meeting him, well more the concept of Lucifer, was such an esoteric thing. I spent all this time with him, and I knew 'who' he was but never really put it together, I think. Until the last Plane, and then it hit me like a brick. It was learning about his past and all that happened in the lead up to Hell's creation which opened my eyes to the enormity of who I was serving and where I was. In all of history, he has never spoken. Never defended himself from the propaganda of hate produced against him. He let all of Creation think whatever they wanted. And now...." My voice trailed off.

"...And now he has chosen you to write part of that story. It is an awesome weight," said De Sade finishing what I left unsaid. "And, at least I hope, you are starting to realize you have neglected those duties. I mean your entries are good, often very good but there is still something disrespectful about them. It is like you feel you have been thrust into this situation and everyone should be thankful you are playing along. That is preposterous. Let me tell you, my naive friend, you have been spared a much worse fate. You could be out there..." he waved his hands toward where I assumed the fields of torture were, "suffering for all eternity or until we used up your soul. Instead, you are running around acting all high and mighty, living with the royalty of Hell, having creatures big and small cringe upon your arrival and you sluff it off like yesterday's dandruff. In case this is news to you, it is probably about time for you to realize you have all of creation in your hands, there in your pen or whatever it is you write with these days."

"It's not only that, its Kitar, Lucifer, all of them; they treat me like I'm nobody."

"So we have finally arrived at the whining part of the evening?"

"See, 'young one.' Isn't that a dig right there?"

Shaking his head, De Sade corrected, "Not in my case. I like you, Keith. As far as the rest of them are concerned, I have already told you the problem. You have not been taking your important job seriously so how do you expect them to take you seriously? You treat all of this like either a joke or a favor. You are dealing with creatures who have walked Creation since before there was a Creation, and yet you act like a petulant child. What do you expect? Respect is earned. I have welcomed many to my Plane who lived during the time you walked the Earth. I have seen how they expect respect. We often use that self-absorption as a component in their suffering. They are fools, as are you. Earn the respect you think you deserve. For that matter stop thinking you deserve respect. If you should have learned anything by now, it is you do not 'deserve' anything. You are not given anything. You earn or take it, and respect cannot be taken."

We sat quietly watching the throngs dance. The song changed again, this time it was some grinding thereminey sounding music from another creation. To me, it just sounded like two cats having an ogry with a blender while listening to an AM radio off station. De Sade noticed when I cringed and changed the music to "I Feel Pretty" from *The Sound of Music*, the bitch.

"Seriously?" I barked as it changed again, this time Metallica, "Seriously, now this feels more like Hell."

"See prissy, self-important," snarked De Sade.

"Then what am I to do? Isn't that why I'm here, to bask in your wisdom?"

"Yes, and it is probably the first wise thing you have done. My wisdom is what you need, old boy, writer to writer. You're dead, you have a divine assignment, and four Planes to go. You are barely halfway through Hell." He paused and shook his head.

"What?"

"Oh, nothing. It's just...and I say this with all deference to myself. You are no longer at the kiddies table. You need to grow up because soon you will be dealing with grown-up sins. Blasphemy, Violence, Treachery, you know the big boys."

I downed my drink and ordered another. When I say I ordered 'a drink,' it was one of De Sade's boys, who were ever-present bowing at his feet, they ran and got them. "See and then there is that. Everyone is saying it's only going to get worse and look how fucked up it's already been. How am I..."

I cringed as De Sade hit me on the arm, hard. "Please, stop whining, if I wanted to hear this, I could go outside. The Dark Lord chose you, so clearly you have what it takes. Allow me to give you a little more free advice. After all, that is what I am supposed to be doing."

"Imagine, you, working for the man."

"Oh hush," scolded De Sade.

"But seriously you kicked ass when you were alive. You were imprisoned, institutionalized, hated, despised by the rulers and church. Where did you find that strength?"

"See Keith.. (he never called me Keith) ...it was not strength, it was conviction, it was need. Writing was an addition. Those stories were not just stories; they were cancers, demons I had to exercise from my soul otherwise deal with their growing tumors and discomfort. You write because you feel you have been told to write. There are times, a few, in your entries where you forget your writing as an assignment and start writing because you need to vomit forth some horror you have seen. You don't write about Usis; you recount how your love affair has grown. Often your best work is when you first step onto the Plane, when it is all new and not just the grunge of reporting on the same old punishments. But always there is this fear in the back of your head, and it is obvious in your writing, that you don't want to say the wrong thing. I have always assumed it was because you're scared you might end up there with those you are writing about. Fuck that; you have to say, "Fuck you" and write what you want. Not what you think they want. Fuck Lucifer..." he cringed, we waited, nothing happened, ... "fuck them all. Shake things up. They have taken your devoted loved one. They have saddled you with that insufferable judge. And what have you done, just take it. They torture you when you don't turn out enough work. Fuck them, kill that god damned bug or better yet, turn the little bastard over, pull out your cock and give it an input it won't soon forget, then have it fried and served with onions. You are in Hell. You are damned. Unless you really fuck up, which you are well on your way to doing, you will spend the rest of eternity in Pandemonium. There are worse fates. You can go as "The Dark Lord's writer" with undertones of 'that pathetic suck-up who was too afraid to tell everyone just how screwed the whole place is. Or you can be 'The Dark Lord's Writer" capital "W" the one creature every one in Hell, and The Host says had the balls to write it like it is and The Powers be damned."

(Note: I'm writing exactly what De Sade's last bit of advice to me was. It was the strongest most intense bit of advice I have ever received, and I want it to read exactly as he said it. It should, I hope, also act as a warning to you, my dear readers, because this is advice I plan on taking to heart.)

"Yeah but I could end up in those torture areas," I said.

"You already are, in your mind. What is our most powerful weapon against the Damned? Their memories, their fears, their minds. You are already chained to one of the torture tables; your mind is the Demon administering your punishments. The Dark Lord respects strength buck up and write like it doesn't matter. Scare the shit out of those little ass kissers back there reading these entries thinking, 'Isn't that cute. It's just fiction. Hell ain't real.' Make it real, scare them, make turning the page an exercise in fear. When they see there is a new entry want them to say, "Oh shit... I don't want to know." Give them a fucking train wreck. Better yet, not just a train wreck, make it the ogre of train wrecks. All the eviscerated bitches found scattered across the pristine county side, like spring flowers, with their lover's cock still in their mouths, cunts, and asses. Make your readers hear the dogs and wolves mingled with the cries of little Billy as they nibble at his face and he cries for mommy. Don't tell them about the blood, pain, and shit, feed it to them. After they read your entries they should not roll over and go to sleep; they should want to take a bath and scrub it off, knowing all the time, they will never be clean again."

And just like that the lecture ended, as quickly as it had started. De Sade stood, smiled at me, waved and disappeared onto the dance floor with one of his little slaves. I sat there for a long time watching the damned dance.

# Entry 184

When I reached my room, I found Cemal curled up in the bed. Hearing me come in he scrambled off and went to his pallet in the corner of the room. "No, you can sleep on the bed. I don't want you sleeping on the floor. We will get you a room when...." I paused, "...if Usis gets back."

In a sleepy voice, "He will Master, he will.." I walked over and poured myself a glass of wine. Yes I know I'm drinking a lot. I'm mid-crisis, give me a break. I need some air.

As I walked out onto the balcony, I found a high wing back chair and a small table sitting in the perfect spot. I looked back into the room to find Cemal smiling his sleepy smile. "I put them out; Master seems to enjoy sitting outside and thinking."

"Thank you, now go back to bed."

He bowed and crawled back into the bed. Almost instantly I could hear his light snoring. I had to smile at how he had pushed himself as close to the edge as he could get. Gawd forbid he touched me while we were sleeping. He was cute, and already I saw him more like a little brother than a servant. I'd never get used to the slave thing. He handled all our lives while I wrote about others' death.

As I settled back into the comfortable chair, I was quickly lost in thought. I had to figure out not only how to get Usis back but also how to get my head back in the game. I sat there for who knows how long and eventually decided nothing. There is no way to plan; I'd just have to wait and see what happens. I know I needed to be more conscious of what I'm afraid to say and then say it anyway. It'll probably help me figure out what my trigger points are. Great now I'm playing psychoanalyst to myself, that always works out well. I guess we'll both see how my decision to make no decision works out. So good luck to you as well.

* * *

The next morning I awoke still in the chair. I guessed it was morning since I heard people moving and it wasn't as dark, but only by a few degrees. Cemal stuck his head out, and I sent him down to get food. Just as my mind started to drift back to those places I didn't want it to go I saw a hand reach around me and set a plate down on the little table. It wasn't the boy's, following it up I found Kitar instead.

"Your slave says you have been here all night," he said as he pulled another chair out onto the balcony and joined me.

"Are you expecting an answer? I didn't hear a question."

"That is clear; the question, if there were one, would be, what are you doing?"

I shrugged. "Thinking..." I shifted so I could look at him directly. "As you guys keep telling me, things are about to get intense. I had a long talk with De Sade, and I think I finally see the point all of you've been trying to make."

"Would you care to tell me what you have interpreted that point as being?"

"I am here, very little is going to change my status and the only things that probably will is what I am already in the midst of doing. Therefore, it is time for me to shake things up, both in my writing and my travels through the remainder of the Planes."

"I cannot say I disagree. We have both been walking on pins and needles, is that not your world's expression? I think I have been helping hold you back for fear of what might happen to me as well. It was made very clear my current course of action is not meeting with the desired outcome."

We sat in silence as I picked at my food. Eventually, I asked, "So what's our plan? It appears, though I'm supposed to be in charge of this little adventure that you guys have taken over, so tell me what you have in mind."

We both turned in surprise when we Elick answered from behind us. "I wanted to bring you back here to give you a new starting place for the rest of your journey. Plus, and it sounds like I was correct. I thought it would help for you to have some time with another writer and the one creature in Hell you have always written fondly of."

Today the handsome Hellspawn was dressed in simple white tights and tunic held by a thick black belt from which hung his sword. The tunic stopped at that magical point where it just covered about half of his generous bulge. His hair was pulled back in a ponytail secured by a gold and what looked like a ruby cuff, which matched the ones he wore around each wrist. His wings were pulled in tight, the tips no more than an inch off the floor. Damn, he knew how to dress. If you don't recall, he is often called a "pale comparison" of his Great Grandfather. This is two-fold. First, he isn't as brutal and secondly where Leviathan is like the depths of space, he's so dark, Elick has both pale white skin and hair. "So how long do you plan on us staying? I think last night helped. I understand what I need to do and more importantly what I've been doing wrong. But none of that changes the fact I want to get to Usis."

"We can leave whenever you are ready. I am turning this expedition back over to you."

"Good, let's spend the rest of the day here and get a fresh start tomorrow. Am I correct in assuming we will go directly to the Sixth Plane?"

"Yes, if you have no longer had business on the Fifth."

"I don't. I want to get to this next Plane, after our dinner with Gabriel the other night I look forward to seeing what Blasphemy looks like."

I could tell I hit a cord when both Kitar and Elick looked at each other and frowned. I let it go. "As you wish, I will inform the Marquis of our plans. We all know he will want to have a farewell dinner; it seems a thing with him."

"It's the French way. During the time he lived people traveled for weeks to visit someone and stayed for a while. So arrival and departure was a big deal. It was never a true visit until there was enough food and wine to float a barge," I added.

I turned to Cemal. "Let the Marquis know what we have decided and ask him not to plan anything extravagant this evening, I want to rest. As for you, Elick, do you need to run ahead? I don't particularly want rouge Fallen Angels blasting Kitar to bits if I can help it." I then gave my attention to Kitar. "And you do whatever it is you do." As they all stood there looking at me with a bit of surprise I couldn't help adding, "that is all."

As everyone shuffled out of the room, I got up, stretched my legs, got dressed and headed downstairs. I found the Marquis in his office on the first floor. After knocking, he looked up and smiled. "Good day Keith, and how might you be feeling after your night of dancing?"

I was about to ask for wine when one of the slaves knelt and offered up a goblet. As I took the glass, De Sade dismissed the boy, ordering him to close the door behind him. After he was gone, I decided it was the perfect opportunity to find out something I'd been curious about since our arrival. "The other day when we arrived the boy you sent up had a bit of an attitude. Not bad or anything, just more confident than, forgive me for saying, I'd grown accustomed to your slaves being."

The Marquis laughed loudly, "That, dear boy, is a remnant of your last visit. I saw how you dealt with my slaves and how they seemed to go that extra mile for you. I decided to try it myself and was somewhat surprised by the outcome. My permanent slaves, after being given more latitude, became more helpful, attentive and productive." He leaned forward and crossed his arms on his desk. "This is a perfect example of the impact you are making on Hell. I know of several other instances where your visit has altered one of the Overlords or their assistant's actions in a positive way. As I have told you, you need to trust your instincts more. You are leaving a far greater mark upon this place than you give yourself credit for. And now is most certainly the time to embrace change."

I couldn't hide the smile. That was probably one of the best bits of news I'd heard in a while. "Did Cemal find you?"

"Yes, and we will keep it simple tonight. Everything will be ready for your departure in the morning."

"Thank you. I wanted before things get out of hand, as they have a tendency of doing, that coming back here was as needed and helpful as they had hoped it would be. I thank you for all your counsel and support. I hope, here in this place, I can count you among those I can trust and call a friend."

De Sade gave a small bow of his head, and said, "You may, and I hope you will find your way back here in the future. If you ever need a place to lay your head, my Keep is always here for you." He rose, extending his hand and we shook.

Stopping just before I left, I turned back, "One last thing. Do you know if Usis is still alive, well alive as such?"

"I was curious if you would ask. Of course, he is alive. Lucifer has a hand in all of this. Don't ask me how or what it is, but nothing is going to happen to that boy. All you can do is play along. As to why he might do this, it is also important to remember Lucifer is not above doing all of this just as a reminder that you have not been performing at the level he expects. Buck up and start playing the game. I have tried to give you the best advice I can, but it is still important to remember, it is now time for you to either play the game or lose it."

# Entry 185

The night was, in fact, uneventful. Kitar sat smoking his pipe. He and I were still trying to smooth over our differences, and I'd say by the end of the evening we were getting back to normal. Cemal sat kneeling by the bed -- I really hate that -- and contributed where he thought he could help. De Sade came in for a while, but he too only stayed a brief time. I wanted to sleep, so I slept.

We left with no ceremony or fanfare. De Sade was dressed casually, something I've never seen outside the disco. Today his shirt was clearly meant to poke at our Archangel visitor. It simply read, "Gabriel come blow my horn." The only odd thing I noticed was how he kept looking up, like he was expecting someone. I assumed it was Lucifer, but he never showed. No one did. The last thing the Marquis said as we left was, "Remember my boy, in Hell there are monsters. To no longer fear them you must become one; then they carry no sway over you."

We made our way through the Plane of Lust, to that now familiar path down. As we approached the corner where Calmet was destroyed, I started to feel a tension in my stomach. Then I saw the opening in the stone wall, the Lover's Cave, and I froze. Not only from the shock of the moment and location but from the fear that I could hear the hearts in Uris's bag starting to beat louder. I looked around; everyone was looking at me. Did they know? Could they hear them? The question was answered by Kitar.

"Come, you do not need to relive this," and in unison, they turned, and I followed. When we reached the locked door to the 3rd Plane we walked on by, then the Fourth, Fifth, and finally we stood at the entrance to the Sixth Plane.

"Why didn't we fly?" I asked.

"I wanted you to take a walk. I thought it was an important reminder of where you have been. Much time has passed since you wrote about some of the aspects of these Planes. I felt you needed the time to remember and reflect on the past, so you could move forward with a new beginning as I said before," answered Elick as he unlocked the door. I noticed he had a shifting key. This time it looked like a cross.

As he swung the door open, I instantly knew all the rumors about things changing were true. I was knocked back by the wave of heat as it hit me. With a flourished bow Elick motioned for me to lead the way. As expected, we stood upon a rock precipice looking out over the Plane with a path leading down from the left. I know I've said this before but again I must, I stood with my mouth agape.

This was the Hell I'd been warned about in my youth. This Hell was the Hell I'd begun to believe only existed in the minds of those who wished to enslave and control the masses. I'd been wrong in that burgeoning belief, the Hell of my world lived here on Blasphemy. This is the Hell of fire and brimstone.

As I stood and stared out over the expanse all I could find to say was, "It's huge. It seems bigger than the other planes."

"It is about three times the size. From here on out, all the Planes will grow as we move downward." Answered Kitar.

Here's a rough rundown of my first impression of the visible sections of the Plane. I'm sure there will be more. First and foremost, the entire place is ablaze. As far as I could see around the edges of the vast expanse were two rows of mountains. The inside row, jagged and short, maybe no more than a hundred feet high. Behind them set back against the very edge of the plane were volcanos spewing forth rocks, ash and long winding trails of lava which vanished between the two rocky expanses.

Below us and taking up at least a third of the visible plane was a forest of what appeared to be trees. Not happy little trees like that guy on PBS used to paint but odd looking trees in an ocean of thorny bushes with yellow-orange boulders scattered amongst the madness. These rocks, some small, others as large as cars were often ablaze with dancing blue flames. It was not until later when I asked Elick about them that I discovered they were pure sulfur. So already we had fire, thorns, and Sulphur, which as I recall was the trifecta of suffering.

Oh, but wait it gets better. Where the forest stopped, roughly a third of the way across the plane was the Overlord's Keep. Unlike the earlier Keeps which had mostly been built from rocks quarried from the mountains surrounding the Plane, this one was constructed of white marble with black and gold veins. In many ways, it reminded me of the seat of Earth's Catholic faith, St Peter's Basilica in Rome. I could tell from its shape it wasn't a cross. I can only assume crosses were specific to my planet since it's how we hung their representative when he last visited. The center and main part of the building was rectangular fronted with massive black columns. To each side were wings of the same marble with rows and rows of arches, some with windows, while others had doors. It was tough to see much more detail from this distance. On top of the center structure was, of course, an enormous golden dome which rose high above the Plane's landscape.

As I studied the Keep, I was startled by a massive explosion from the volcanos. All at once the hundreds of mountains around the plane belched forth great pillars of lava so high it cascaded against the curved roof high above. The shock and heat from the blasts was so intense it blew back against Elick's chest. Almost immediately I felt his arms wrap around me as he caught me and kept me from falling. (No, I swear I didn't slide down along is firm abs to feel his cock rub against my lower back. That would be opportunistic and wrong. I know what you're saying, 'Remember your boyfriend, Usis?' As a matter of fact, I do, and he would have been disappointed in me had I not taken this opportunity to cop a feel. I did it thinking of him. Yea...let's go with that. Smiles.).

As Elick helped me stand he explained that what we were seeing was the exhausts from the great furnaces on the lowest plane of Hell. The volcanos were vents. They were belching forth flames as the Keepers tossed in another large group of discarded souls. If you remember from earlier entries, Hell is overcrowded. Therefore, most souls never see the tortures administered by each plane but instead are sent directly to the furnaces to be incinerated. Now if you think this sounds like a pretty good option after reading what is in store for those who are sent to the Planes, think again. Once a soul is introduced as fuel into the furnaces, which I'm told eventually all souls become, they aren't instantly destroyed. If I recall it can take as little as a few hundred to millions of years. I am hoping we find out more about that as we move down. It appears to be based upon the amount of The Father's energy still contained within that soul. Those who suffer on the planes are often empty vessels by the time they reach the furnaces and thus consumed quickly. Those who are sent directly there immediately after judgment should expect hundreds of thousands of years of endless suffering in the fires that power eternity. Also, keep in mind that the raw suffering, which has been collected since the second plane, and now flows through the Planes in raging rivers also is used in the furnaces. But not so much as fuel, as I initially believed, but more as an accelerant to increase the intensity of the flames within. The energy created by these furnaces are what fuels not only the many creations but The Host and Hell as well. Without these fires, all of Creation would have already died away.

I know this Planes explanation is short, and I'm keeping it that way. Since I'll be visiting each region during my stay, I'll leave the detailed description till then. But lastly and probably most important, other than the Keep, was the creature which hung from the top of the rocky dome high above the Plane itself. It was very Chuthulu-esque. The large bulbous body, which had to be a hundred feet across, clung to the roof while hundreds of tentacles moved down and over the plane.

"What is that?" I asked in disbelief.

"That is Detaltuchiaca; he is the Overseer of the Plane. He is the one responsible for assigning new souls destined to spend eternity on this plane to their physical location."

Well, I'm not sure about you, but though that technically counted as an explanation, it wasn't a very clear one. So I did the only thing I could think to do, I stared at Kitar like he'd just spoken Latin to me. He pointed, and I watched as a single tentacle moved to the crowded clearing of Demons and souls and plucked one from the masses. As the arm and the screaming creature -- I assume he was screaming. With all the noise of the Plane I couldn't hear that soul specifically -- traveled across the plane, it eventually stopped and with a fast-downward movement deposited the soul into the trees. From this distance I couldn't make out what was happening, so I left it for later as well.

"I don't know what I just saw," I explained.

"The arm of Detaltuchiaca moved over and picked up a soul ready to be moved out into the Forest of Pain," explained Kitar.

"He just dumps them into the forest with the thorns?" I asked.

"Not exactly. You will understand better once your tour the forest. Suffice it to say for now it is not 'just a forest with thorns.' It is the forest of blasphemers and heretics."

If that didn't help you, believe me, it didn't help me either. I guess we'll understand in time.

"Let's get you to the Keep and in your rooms. Then we can sit down with The Overlord and talk about the parts of the Plane, so you can get a layout and start putting together a plan," suggested Elick.

"Perfect," I said.

# Entry 186 – The Walk to the Keep

You ask, and I deliver. What did they mean by a forest of Heretics and Blasphemers? Well, I learned soon enough. As we walked down the trail leading to the Keep, past its switchbacks and guards standing at every turn, I began to see what the forest was made of.

This wasn't a forest, it was millions, tens of millions of spiked posts. Each with a single body impaled upon it. The post was no bigger around than a chain link fence post, maybe 3 inches in diameter but this varied according to the size of the creature it ran through. See, it entered between the legs and exited out just behind the head to the right of the spinal cord.

We stood on a raised path some six inches above the rest of the fields. There was no fire, thorns or spikes here. It was a clear, "safe" path for those having business with the Keep but needing to walk to enter the Plane. To each side was the forest of spikes.

"Why do some have more thorns than others?" I asked.

"The ones with thorn encompassing them are the ones who led followers astray. This is where your guide would be if he had not been recruited as a judge," answered Elick as my eyes widened and I turned to find Kitar standing, mouth agape, walking in a slow circle.

"There are so many," was all I could find to say.

"Since this is a major part of the Plane it might be best to wait until you have someone who can better explain the why's and how's of the punishment. Let's get to the Keep and get that over with."

We started down the path, but even though I said I didn't want to explore this area yet, that didn't stop me from being amazed, curious and horrified at what at the scene that surrounded us. There was row after row of impaled bodies. Around some the area was clear, just the soul on a stick, writhing, screaming and roasting. Remember, the ground was littered with patches of flames. Others souls were surrounded, sometimes encased in thorny vines. The barbs were a variety of lengths. The short ones just pricking the body, the wind from the dancing flames causing the thorns to rip gashes into the soul's flesh. Other times the spines were long and impaled the creature. Those same winds causing the thick barbs to move in and out, back and forth. Now don't get me wrong, they weren't one or the other, long or short. Like any briar bush, there were a variety of sizes and lengths. The only thing they all had in common was that every one of them was in some way causing pain upon its victim. I couldn't wait to find out how this applied to sin.

When we finally reached the Keep, we paused at the bottom of the steps leading up to the intricately carved golden doors. On each Plane there had been a Keep but nothing like this one. The others were bleak and stark where this one had been designed to carry the assumed majesty of The Host's Eternal City. To be honest, the difference from the other Keeps almost caused me a sense of vertigo when looking at this one; I had grown used to the other Planes' starkness.

OK I guess now is a good a time as any. Here's one of those tidbits of information I withheld from the dinner the other night. If you didn't catch it, I just alluded to one in the last paragraph. I told you I'd say when it was time. Well, it's time. This plane of Hell isn't overseen by a Demon, Ex-living or any member of Hell's army. The Host rules it. For future reference, I'll be using the word 'Angel' from time to time to denote a member of The Host; it's just faster. From what I understand they take turns on this Plane as The Overlord. Here is what I know at this point. Gabriel told me that the sins of this Plane are directly against The Father and his teachings. Therefore, The Host wants to administer their appreciation for, as they see it, attacking The Father directly. It was agreed early on that the Master of Heresy, Lucifer, or any of his people shouldn't run this place. This Plane is The Father's wrath personified against those who bastardized his teachings for their own benefits. Oh, one last thing, Gabriel is the Angel currently in residence. That's why he was in Hell in the first place. Happy, Happy, Joy, Joy.

# Entry 187

Let me start by saying as I sit and write this entry I find myself not liking this Plane's Keep. It's too...I don't know... light, welcoming, something. It's just wrong for where we are. Anyway.

The front like I said earlier is black granite columns against a façade of white streaked marble. The entrance was two golden doors with scenes of The Great War, each about forty feet tall, showing an engraving of Lucifer and his followers being cast from the City of Light. That is the first correction I noticed about the telling of Lucifer's expulsion. Instead of being kicked out, Lucifer and his followers are being shown out. The representation didn't even really look violent, almost like an ill-behaved patron being asked to leave a restaurant. Still, even here, in the Host's depiction of the event, As always, Lucifer carried all his confidence. He was leaving, but it appeared to be on his terms not those of The Father. Now did the door show The Father you would ask, no not exactly. He is or was I'm assuming the bright sun-like figure hovering over the city. The other thing I found interesting was the Angel on the wall blowing the trumpet; I wasn't sure if he was sounding the end of the conflict or letting everyone know they had expelled the usurper. Either way, that Angel was Gabriel.

At the top of the stairs in a classic military pose were two soldiers, I have no idea if I should call them Angels or servants or what. They were dressed in gleaming armor with long spears. As we climbed the seven steps, they moved and together swung the great doors open. Standing in the center of the veranda was Gabriel in his full glory. I'm sure he wasn't his full height, but his body was clad in long flowing white robes. His hair, now loose, cascaded down his back.

As we entered he smiled. "Welcome." I followed Elick's lead when he bowed deeply and did the same. I had no idea how to great an Angel.

"Thank you for welcoming us..." Kitar said.

"Why would I not? In this young one's travels it is only here he will hear the truth."

I smiled as Elick in a sarcastic tone said, "Now that is more befitting the greeting I expected."

I was trying to listen, but honestly, I was a bit gobsmacked at the surroundings. All of Hell is dark; the sky is always dusk, the rooms are lit by low candles or fires. The Keeps are black stone. Everything about Hell was like waking from an intense dream only to look out the window to find a gloomy winters morning shrouded in a dense fog. Here though, it was light. The ornately carved white walls of cherubs, angels, and heavenly hosts all shone brightly in the optimistic light of a warm summers day. I have no idea how long I've been in Hell, but standing there in the entrance to the Keep I knew I was now a resident of this damned place. I had the urge to slink back outside and hide my eyes from the harsh glare of Light's appraisal.

I know I keep harkening back to the analogy of how this place reminds me of the Vatican but then it was the seat of The Father's power in my world. This central chamber consisted of almost the entire center section of the massive keep. There were several doors on both sides leading to, I would assume, other rooms. In the center of the floor in the long hall was a circular crest inlaid into the stone highlighted by what looked to be rays of sunlight. When I followed them up I could see the light pouring into the keep through small windows around the bottom of the massive dome. Yes, you heard me right, sunlight. The ceiling around the dome was painted with frescos while the walls were littered with paintings of all sizes. Scattered along the great chamber were groups of couches, tables, chairs, and sculptures, all positioned on beautiful rugs which reminded me of the tapestries from The Fate's rooms. What caught my attention more than the opulence of the room was the subject matter of both the paintings and the Sculptures. They were scenes and carvings of figures from The Host and almost always they were subjugating or stepping over fallen Demons and what appeared to be the living. I made a mental note to ask about that later.

The whole place looked a lot like the great cathedrals from the Renaissance. Not the darkening times of the Gothic period when even the houses of worship became shadowed with the misguided interpretations of The Father's words. Just standing here in the entry I could almost see when the fall for my world began. It started when even The Father's light was extinguished from his most holy of places.

I came back to myself to find everyone staring at me. "What? I'm trying to remember my impressions of this room; I have to write about it later. Who did all the art? I mean the artists?"

With his usual smugness, Gabriel said, "That is fine, I am sure after so much time in the darkness it is hard to stand in The Father's Light. As for the artists, sadly that is one of the advantages of Hell. We have access to some of the best artisans in Creation. They rarely make it into The Eternal City. There is something about being creative that tends to taint a soul." He paused and with a devious smile added, "Writers usually are the most afflicted. We would have to relax a myriad of rules to see a writer walk through our gates. What is it about you writers that cause you to be such rebels?"

"I'm not sure, probably because we create worlds. Therefore, those attempted by others don't impress us. After you've created a universe as well as its worlds, residents, and rules it seems easy for us to find the flaws in others' creations. How does the old line go? 'In The Father's house there are many rooms'? Well in The Father's creations there are many flaws." If you can't tell, I was a bit annoyed. His little crack about The Father's Light sort of pissed me off, maybe because it hit a little too close to home.

"Well, when you get to Pandemonium you will be in good company. Possibly one of the most famous writers in all of Creation by then. That is if you survive, which has yet to be seen." That sneer of his was starting to get on my nerves.

"Can I be shown my rooms now? I'd like to settle in. Please tell me this whole place isn't this bright. Does The Father's Light come on a dimmer?"

Elick burst out laughing, not only from my comment but the expression on the Angel's face which was quickly followed by a growl from Kitar. Gabriel took it in stride saying, "He did pick well. I'll have the servants show you to your rooms."

# Entry 188

As I expected the guest rooms were all on one side of the Keep, the right wing one to be exact. Each wing consisted of eight floors each being about thirty feet tall with open galleries on the second through eighth looking down onto the first. Two slaves lead Cemal and me to our room. I still need to check into this slave thing. It was on the eighth floor. The fucker, no elevator and I didn't have wings.

The room was huge and took up the entire end of the top floor. If that had not been enough to catch me off guard, it's elegance was. I mean De Sade's Keep was over the top but that was to be expected, he was French. As we walked through the suite taking in the furnishings and art, my first question was how they had gotten all this stuff into Hell in the first place. But then I guess being deities they can 'create' anything if they want. Cemal even suggested that since Hell tends to rely on its own resources, The Host probably brought the stuff in from the Creations just to prove they could. We found a door against the side wall and walked out to discover, that since we were on the end of the building, we had a balcony which wrapped all the way around the three outside walls. I liked that a lot.

Back inside we discovered two more doors, one on each side of the suite's main entrance. The one on the right turned out to lead to Kitar's room while the left one led into a less ornate slave quarters. Though Cemal seemed to be impressed, I didn't like the idea of him having to sleep on the small pallet stuck in one of the corners. Again, the boy surprised me when he was honest enough to admit that some time alone would be nice when he was released at night. I could fully understand that. As we stepped back into the main room, I realized the two female slaves, who had shown us up, were still standing by the door. Come to find out they had been assigned to me as well. I gave them to Cemal and told him to manage them. Which he did right away, sending them to get wine and some snacks. That's my boy.

Now for the main suite, which I'm guessing doubles as my room, or vice-versa since it's a single chamber. I mentioned this to Cemal as we walked through. "Why do you think they would give a guest just a single room: Livingroom, dining room and bedroom all together?"

"If this one was to guess Master, the bedroom furnishings have probably been added. The only guests The Host would normally expect would be either from The Host or Hell and with this room being designed for an important guest, they probably would not sleep."

I nodded my approval at Cemal. "Excellent point. Thank you." I could see his pride at having answered my question so well.

Anyway, the layout of the room. To one side, against the wall, was the canopied bed with a small chaise at the end. On each side were nightstands upon which set small suffering fueled lamps. In the center, in front of the fireplace and across from the entrance were two sofas and chairs with tables beside each. There was a low coffee table in the center. Behind the couch sat a sofa table with another two lamps and two statues of stunning detail. On the far side of the room, the side with the slave's quarters sat a long six-person dining table in front of the door leading out onto the balcony. There were two very gaudy chandeliers hanging from the high ceiling which fortunately could be extinguished allowing us to use the assorted smaller lamps scattered around the room. Thus, giving me the type of lighting I'd grown accustomed to. As Cemal and I finished walking the suite, I stumbled over a small cushion on the floor. "What is this?" I asked.

Cemal waked over and knelt down on the cushions. Looking up at me he straightened his back, placed his hand's mid thighs, palms up and then bowed a very low exaggerated bow, "It's for me, Master." I just shook my head not only at the boy's comment but how much what he'd just done reminded me of Usis when he'd explained similar things like this in the past. I tried to mask my sadness but could tell I failed. The boy's lip quivered as I reached down and raised him up. "Don't look like that. You just reminded me of Usis, and I couldn't be more grateful."

Any further discussion was interrupted by a knock at the door which Cemal ran to get. It was Elick. Walking in he looked around impressed. "This bodes well. It seems our Overlord is not too angry about the other night if he gave you one of the nicest rooms. Since it appears you are in good hands, I will leave you for a while to attend to some personal matters. If you need me, do not worry I will have an eye on you."

"You have personal matters? I didn't think your type had..."

"See and you would be wrong. Xia and I own several businesses in Pandemonium, and as you know, he is no longer in Hell to attend and intimidate. Therefore I must do it." He winked.

I raised an eyebrow. "But you are such a pussycat." I smiled.

"Keep thinking that. If you must know my intent, I am going to visit my dear Great-Grandfather. It has been a long time since I have seen him and as a dutiful grandson I really should show my respects," he answered. "Plus I am curious if Yaclom had gotten back from his little vacation in the Hatchery."

I smiled as he laughed and started to leave. "You'll find out how Usis is, right?"

"That is why I am going, Keith. Do you think I would subject myself to my Great-Grandfather if I did not have to?"

"Thank you, Elick; I owe you."

"Yes, you do, and I plan to collect."

As the door closed behind Elick, I heard Cemal announce, "You should eat before all Hell breaks loose."

"Is that a phrase from your world as well?" I asked.

"No, Master, I learned it from you."

On the table, dinner was already prepared. The boy had been very through; there was a plate, cutlery, a napkin and a glass of wine in a lovely crystal goblet. I held the glass up. "Crystal?"

"I do not know, Master. It was in the cupboard in the slave quarters along with the rest of the dishes."

As I began to eat Kitar marched into the room without as much as a knock. I gave him a hard look which he didn't see. These were the kinds of things I needed to fix while I had the chance.

As Cemal rushed off to fix him a plate he asked as he sat down, "Are you settling in?"

"I'd think the first question should be, 'May I join you?'"

"May I?" he said with a disapproving tone.

"Of course you may join me. That doesn't change the fact we've become lax, and it's started to cause too many problems. You've said so yourself. Well, it's time we start pulling ourselves back together and get some organization in this...this...whatever you want to call it. I have a feeling whether you like it or not that we are about to go to war with an Archangel. We can't...I can't be second-guessing myself or you guys. So, I start where I can, and that means you respecting my rank in this group and me respecting the job you have been given as my guide."

As Cemal set down the plate and started to walk away, I gave him a look to stay. Kitar picked up his fork and began to eat as I just stared at him. Cemal stared, not sure what I was doing but still, he mimicked me. He was absolutely adorable, the way his tail swished like a cat reminded me of Usis. I stifled a frown.

As Kitar stuck the first bite in his mouth, he realized both of us were watching. He paused, "what?"

I looked at his plate and then at Cemal and then him.

"Seriously?" Seeing I was dead serious he turned to Cemal and said, "Thank you."

"It was and is always a pleasure, Lord Judge," answered the slave in a syrupy sweet tone as he bowed and turned to leave.

I threw in as the boy walked away, "Now fix yourself something. You can eat on the couch."

"Thank you, Master," he said as he flashed a look at Kitar.

Turning back to the guide, I asked, "So what can you tell me about Gabriel and this Plane? What do I have to look forward to?"

He finished chewing, took a sip of wine. "I am not even sure where to start. Gabriel is old school. Michael and Raphael are progressive, as I understand it, and see the necessity for The Host and Hell to stay peaceful and work together. Gabriel and his group of Angels still hold grudges from the war. There is probably no single entity in all of Creation that hates Lord Lucifer as much as our current host. Though at this point his feelings for Xia might outstrip any hatred he has for The Dark Lord, if so, only by barely."

"That I'm sorry to tell you isn't a secret. I could see his feeling toward Lucifer every time the Dark Lord's name was mentioned. But it's good to have my suspicions verified. Now the Plane?"

"You are relentless. To be honest, I am a bit worried about this Plane and you. More than once you have had some very negative things to say about religious clergy and now you are on a Plane full of them."

I smiled an evil smile. "Yes I know, and I have a list of names I want you to look up while I'm here. You two took me back to De Sade for advice, and now I plan on exercising some of it. He said to enjoy my anger and hatred and when given the opportunity to use it. I plan to reward some of the pieces of shit who used their influence to suck the elderly dry of their life's savings, so the fucking preacher could buy a jet or five."

"I am not sure that is a wise idea. Keith, they were clergy. The mouthpieces of The Father."

"You hit the nail on the head Kitar, right there. WERE...they started out that way. They chose to become abominations who used The Father and his words as a weapon instead of a tool to help those in their charge to change their lives for the better. Now they're in Hell where they belong. You said yourself, this is the Plane of Blasphemy, and The Host rules it because THEY...not The Dark Lord, not you, not me, The Host sees it as a direct attack against them. Well, I have lived through those fuckers' existences and seen what they have done to the gay communities, the poor, the weak. The way they condemned rape victims and made them feel bad for getting rid of a fetus before it became a child they would never love because of the pain associated with its conception. I saw it all, the planes, the million-dollar houses, the refusing to let their church members find refuge in their sanctuaries during major disasters. I SAW IT ALL. DO NOT TALK ABOUT FORGIVENESS TO ME. ANYWHERE ELSE...BUT NOT HERE, JUDGE...THIS IS HELL; THIS IS NOT THE HOME OF REDEMPTION." I slammed my fist down on the table causing the plates and silver wear to jump and the goblets to topple spilling wine on the floor. Taking a deep breath, I sat back as Cemal rushed to start cleaning up the mess.

Kitar was silent for a long time, eventually nodding, "There is a good chance you and Gabriel will get along just fine."

"We'll see. Now the Plane please."

Shaking his head, he picked up his fork and started picking at the scattered remains of his plate. "There are four areas you will probably want to tour. The first is the fields of blasphemers. Second is The Repentant shrine. Thirdly is Buddha, and finally the catacombs. I also assume you want to see the torture pits and the pass-through for this Plane as well?"

I nodded as I pushed mine away. "Buddha?"

"Yes, he is here. You have always been interested in the Angels who did not choose a side. On your world Raguel was known as The Buddha," answered Kitar.

"Oh, that's right. Yes, I'd like to meet him. I followed Buddhism for a while," I added as Cemal took both plates away.

"Would Masters like to have wine in the living room?" he asked.

"That would be nice," said Kitar in a friendly tone. I smiled, Cemal didn't know my plan but none the less he was walking Kitar right into my trap. As we sat and drank, we talked. When I thought he was about where I wanted him, and we in full reconcile mode, I pounced.

"Keith, We have had many disagreements. We will always see thing from different perspectives, but that does not change the fact I will do whatever necessary to help you bring this tour of our Lord's domain to a successful conclusion."

"Anything?" I asked looking over my glass. I saw a twitch at the corner of his mouth; he knew he was in trouble.

We stared at each other for several seconds until finally, he said, "Yes, anything."

"Then tell me your story…"

# Entry 189

Kitar started to object but then just shook his head. "I knew the time would come. Here on this Plane, I guess it is now time. You have heard a lot of it."

"I know you were a member of the clergy and used your power over your flock to manipulate them. What I don't understand, especially after seeing the rest of Hell, is what you did to move yourself up to the ranks of Judge instead of getting yourself deposited on a post out in the fields there." I motioned to the window.

Kitar let out a long sigh. "I know that is what I told you, and in a greatly simplistic way, it is true."

"But..."

"I guess I should start with a brief explanation of my Creation. The world I was born on created my species. Not exactly created, our ancestors always existed, it's just over time my race, the Clivoc were genetically altered. My ancestors, as your world would call them were wolve., Isn't that your world's word?" I nodded as he continued, "I was born about fifty generations after my species, through the experiments, was brought into consciousness..." Seeing I had questions he paused saying, "Ask your questions as we go. I will not revisit this."

"Brought into consciousness? The Father didn't create you to have souls?"

Shaking his head, "No, we acquired them eventually. This is an aspect of Creation you have not delved into yet; you will on the Eighth Plane."

"We *will* come back to that, but for now, go on, please."

"I suggest you let the soul acquisition topic rest until we get to Fraud, there it is a significant aspect of the Plane's purpose. As for me, I was born conscious, as were most of my species after the third generation. The problem was the ruling species, the Latroves. They had grown to hate us."

"Why?" I asked.

"There were aspects they never could or choose not to breed out of us, our aggression being one. That coupled with our growing intellect caused the rulers to segregate us away from their population centers. I was told that the first camps were nice, not as good or technically advanced as the Latroves had, but still adequate. As time went on, more and more of our enclaves began to descend into squalor, until finally, when I was born, we were living in nothing short of filth.

"My family was poor but very close and loving. My parents tried to give us everything they could to ensure we had opportunities. They also taught compliance, not to rock the boat or bring attention to ourselves. It was not safe. My people at this point had very little hope for their future, and from a young age, I wanted to give that back to them. This desire, of course, flew in the face of not drawing attention to myself as I had been taught. I wanted, no insisted, we have better. It was a dream from as early as I can remember and the cornerstone of my downfall."

"Before you tell me what, 'it' was that let to your 'downfall' as you call it, let me ask, would you do it the same all over again?" I wanted his answer to help taint my hearing of his story.

"Yes, without a doubt."

"Ok, sorry, continue..."

"I came to The Father in my early adulthood. It was not our belief. Historically we did not, as a species, have a religion. Still, I saw value in The Father's teachings. I was not alone; do not think I was an innovator. In the naivety of youth, I formed a church. Over time it grew, my voice grew, the power of my opinion in our community and the other Clivoc communities increased. The Latroves continued to become more hostile. We had started to develop our own technologies, no longer relying only on what they created. We used them, for sure, but now more as the springboard for our own developments which over time began to surpass what they had. The Latrove leaders did not take this well, especially when we refused to share.

"In my congregation as well as other Clivoc churches we preached self-dependence. Our knowledge, since we had been forced to fight for it and then hated for it, was ours not theirs. That is when the battles began. Many in our community taught compliance. Even though they did not want to give our technologies away or share them necessarily, they did want to provide the Latroves with at least access to them. I did not agree. By this time I ran the largest congregation, and as is often the case, one of my flock was killed, actually three, two young girls and a boy. I was outraged, as was our community but still the other churches taught peace. I did not want peace. It was becoming more and more evident that the situation was spiraling downward and the planet could not house both the Latroves and the Clitovs. "Then there was another attack. That was the final step for me. Many in my congregation were screaming for blood. The whole eye for an eye thing, your culture has it as well.

"So slowly, in small ways, I started to suggest to eager ears in our church that maybe retribution should be visited on this specific influential person, or that one. Little things started happening. A member of the ruling Latroves would be discovered dead. Their media would condemn it. I, in my church, would preach its justice. This only encouraged more violence, which I did nothing to discourage. Being the largest church now, we had almost unlimited resources, and we used them.

"I do not think I need to go into all the details. You, yourself being from one of the most violent races in all of Creation, know where we were headed. It continued to worsen, and more people died. Casualties started to mount on both sides. That, believe it or not, was not the turning point. It was when the ruling government finally asserted that since they brought the Clitovs into consciousness, and the ungrateful mutts had not shown the proper gratitude, it was time to reduce us back down to what we had once been, mindless animals.

"Eventually, members of my congregation were abducted, and experiments done to them. I do not think we were singled out. They just happened to be part of my flock. What the Latroves scientists discovered was by using this new drug they could lobotomize those injected. Reduce them back down to unintelligent creatures. By now, I was preaching the divinity of fighting for our rights, our autonomy, I had become a rallying point. You have to understand the drug was slow and painful as it caused the subject to cease to be conscious.

"When they abducted my wife, this became the catalyst for my hatred and wrath. I would learn while judging that this was a typical manifestation when something like this happens."

"With that being said, don't you feel it is justified? Should The Father condemn you to Hell for what seems to be a perfectly normal reaction to such an assault?"

"I cannot answer that, Keith. They, The Host, would say we are to turn the other cheek, but since I did not do that and still to this day carry that hatred in my heart, I am unfit to argue for forgiveness, as you will see."

"Go on…," I said. I did not want to interrupt.

"Over the next few years I arranged for two of our brightest scientists, who were not members of my congregation, but part of the resistance, to apply and find jobs working as traders with the other side. They were like you, both unbelievers. It was not unheard of; many had turned on their people in exchange for their families safety. So these two defected. At first, they were put on low-level projects, but over the course of months and their talents became obvious they rose through the ranks. They took a lot of persecution from other Clitovs as more and more of our peoples suffered the cruel experiments.

"Finally, they came to me one night and told me the government was now satisfied with the vaccine, as they called it, and wanted to start the forced vaccination of the entire Clitovic race. The first step was to produce enough of the drug to ensure no interruption once the next phase began. I told them to continue doing their jobs, mainly to ensure we knew how the production was going. They were instructed to report back before the next phase, the injections, started.

"I knew we could not fight a war; all such actions would do is subject my people to years of struggle, senseless deaths and untold amounts of pain. The problem was the Latroves as a population. I knew we needed to do something, what that something was I was not sure. Still, I started preaching a message to change the mindset of my people. I recruited other ministers and leaders to promote the same message. They thought it was to prepare for war, which I guess it was to an extent, but mainly it was me stalling while we tied to find a solution. My fall happened quietly one night as I sat in silence reading a report which had been smuggled to me. It was an internal memo about two of the Latrove scientists who were accidentally infected, as I called it, with the drug. The same effects happened to them. They became fools, mindless idiots. This, of course, horrified the leaders of the Latrove government, and the scientists were ordered to develop a vaccine. No matter how they tried, they could not create anything to reverse the effects once the mind wipe drug had run its course. At that point, the person was beyond a cure. The vaccine did work if it was administered beforehand thus rendering the effects of the other drug mute.

"My power with my flock and my population continued to grow. I was now openly leading the rebellion against our ruling class. At this point, those of us who were sacrificed were considered martyrs. It was the greater good that mattered. As far as I was concerned all the Latroves needed to be wiped out, I was ruled entirely by my hatred of their race at this point. So I convinced several groups to break in and steal quantities of the wipe drug and then place it in water supplies and to release it into their public spaces. Hit and run attacks. More and more Latroves were wiped. I was satisfied with this, until the night when I received a message that the Government had decided that the only way to stop the problem was to round us all up and administer the drug in mass. At the same time, they would start vaccinating their own population against any future attacks. That night the war to begin. Since they had us ten to one, we were driven back. More and more government services were cut off forcing us to replace essential services like water, trash and such with our own. This proved to be the pivotal event.

"The government decided since our population was about a tenth of theirs and we were already gathered into small communities, all the Latroves had to do was introduce the drug into about two dozen water supplies. Which due to the war were now sperate from theirs. Now keep in mind, the only way we knew this was going to happen was because of our inside sources. What we also learned was that the government did not want it known by their population for fear it would change public sentiment. See they had been lying to their population telling them it was just evolution correcting itself. We were reverting to our earlier dumber selves. Our war against them was purely out of anger at realizing we were a doomed species and our bitterness moved us to try to take them down as well.

"To make a long story shorter, we managed to switch the antidote and the drug in eight of ten of our enclaves. You see there was only one molecule difference between the two; they were virtually identical. So what was introduced into our water supply was the cure. No one ever found out, and there the story should have ended. It would have just become two races on the same planet fighting it out until one won. But no, by now, with my wife having been mindwiped, I was a creature filled with hate. I started to push my flock harder and harder until finally, I whipped them into enough of a frenzy that groups of civilians agreed to break in and steal large quantities of the mind wipe drug."

Kitar buried his head in his hands. This was the first sign of emotion he had shown. Finally, he lifted his head, downed his wine, looked me in the eyes and finished, "We filled massive bombs with the drug and dropped it on the Latrov cities. The ones who did not breath it in eventually ingested it in their food and water, just as they had planned to do to us. In a matter of less than one of our years, we mindwiped over 85% of their population. We, of course, were safe, we had been vaccinated. After it was over, I declared publically our success as the remaining 15% of their population was hunted down, killed or enslaved. I lived out the rest of my life in luxury and was revered as a hero of my people. As far as I know, I still am."

We sat quietly for a while lost in our thoughts. I found it interesting how at times Kitar's face showed extreme sadness while at others nothing but pride. I had to ask, "Do you now regret your actions?"

"No, if I have to spend eternity in Hell to ensure the survival of my race then that is a price I am and was willing to pay."

"Can't any extremist use the same excuse? They believe, or at least want to believe, they are doing what is best for their people, race, religion or god. Does that absolve them of their atrocities?"

"No, as was the case with me, and ultimately why I was placed in the position I was. Once you pass from the living, each person will be judged, and then only the laws of The Father hold sway."

"I'd like to say I'm not sure how I feel about what you've told me. My logical mind says I should say that genocide is wrong, but you were just stopping what they were going to do to you. So was using their sin against them making it your sin?" I asked.

"As the Overlord of Wrath pointed out, Hell finds the seed or in my case the fertilizer that causes all your sins to grow. Had I stopped, I would be in violence, hate or wrath. It was using my power as The Father's representative to urge people to believe that what they were doing was the Father's will. That was my greatest sin. It was labeling my hate as his."

"Jihad. It's what one of our religious cults believed as well. I want to say this because I know someone or several people are probably listening. Though I understand, kinda, what you're saying. If I've started to learn anything during my travels through Hell, it's that the ultimate sinner isn't the one being punished. You led your flock to commit sins in The Father's name and you are judged for having led them astray. Those in your flock who carried out those sins are probably somewhere here in Hell for having committed such sins against the living. Those who the sin were committed against, the Latrovs, are probably here in Hell because they treated your race horrible, they created the drug, they planned on lobotomizing your race, so many things. But has no one..." I paused and smiled, "realized the problem goes deeper. You're punished for what you led your followers to do; they're punished for what they did. All of this could have been stopped if your creator, The Father, had the...courage or strength... to admit his creation was flawed and in doing so worked to correct it. But instead, he vanished when the only creature in all of Creation, his first son, stood up to him and told him he was wrong. So I guess that answers my question, 'did no one realize' because yes they did. It was Lucifer and one-third of The Host all those many years ago."

Kitar was staring at me wide-eyed as I concluded, "You're not the sinner, you're the victim of a much greater sin, arrogance."

We both turned as we heard a fist slam against the wall outside our door and footsteps angrily walk away. "I guess someone was listening."

"Keith, that is a very dangerous opinion to speak aloud, on this Plane in particular."

I shook my head. "Sorry, no, De Sade said tell it like it is, that is how it is, like it or not. Kitar, I've learned many things during this little jaunt, and I'm sure I'll learn more. And one of the things I've learned is The Father isn't what we were led to believe. That is proven in the collection of the Overlord on Greed. In that Keep is a chronicle of all the attempts The Father made to make a dream only he could see or understand. He failed an untold number of times and stopped with this.." I motioned around my head, "Are you sure this isn't just another flawed creation from a flawed being with an untold amount of power?"

Kitar studied me for longer than I was comfortable. Sitting back and pulling his and my pipe out, he started to load them. "I never thought I would say this because I have always suspected you were more than you let on. But your insights, whether I agree with them or not, are much deeper than even I gave you credit for."

"Maybe that's the reason Lucifer came up with this little exercise and picked an 'outside' source to do it. To get a fresh perspective," I replied.

He again paused as he handed me my pipe and we lite them. As he blew out the first smoke ring, he added, "I hope your time here with Gabriel will help soften your opinion of The Father. We cannot know..."

I cut him off, "Yes I know, it seems all of Creation agrees with at least one things, right or wrong. The Father moves in mysterious ways. What I'm starting to wonder about more, is how does that compare to how The Dark Lord moves. Did the Father leave the game while it was still being played or is it already over and no one else has been told....but there is also the chance it is he who thinks it's over when it's not? Now I will share with you one of my world's quotes - To win you must first show up."

# Entry 190

The rest of the night was quiet. Kitar and I talked and drank continuing to mend our formerly fractured relationship. I won't lie, it felt good to have someone I thought I could trust to talk to again. I'd missed the Kitar I'd met back at the beginning. The one with my best interest at heart. I can't hold anything against him. I, of all people, know how fast things have gotten out of hand. I'm also pleased to report that after awhile I even managed to break through Cemal's hard servant shell and he relaxed into a sitting position on the floor. That kneeling thing was making me nuts. We also learned two things, one that night and one the next morning. That night we discovered Cemal couldn't hold his liquor and the following day we found out our little slave was an incredible bitch and really uncoordinated when he had a hangover. His cute quotient didn't change though. He could string together a creative set of curse words when he slammed into a wall by accident or tripped over his tail. My constant snickering didn't improve his mood though.

As he prepared the morning meal, I strolled around the room. What I was interested in was the view outside. I'd grown used to using the balconies as a way to help me organize my plan of attack. As I walked out toward the front of the Keep, I could see the Forest of spikes and thorns down below and noted bodies moving between the posts. As I turned to go back in, I noticed something else out of the corner of my eye. I looked up to find the creature dutifully going about its duties. What I hadn't seen before were the millions of what looked like caskets hanging from chains to one side of the massive cavern ceiling. It gave that entire side of the Plane's roof a look of honeycombs after the cells had been filled. I'd have to check that out as well later.

To the side of the building were mountains, a cave entrance and what appeared to be another large building. Ok, that could wait as well. Finally, as I made my way around back inside, I knew my first visit. As if he could read my mind, Kitar walked up beside me. He looked me up and down before saying in a sarcastic tone, "So it was not Usis who kept you naked."

To be honest, I'd forgotten I was nude. This plane was hot. "Actually, I forgot, but even had I thought about it, I still probably wouldn't have dressed. Clothes are itchy, and it's hot." I then looked at him and did the same as he'd done to me. "You're not going to start shedding on the furniture, are you?" He let out a growl which also sounded slightly mixed with a chuckle as I pointed asking, "What's that?"

"That is the processing area for the souls passing through to the Lower Planes. The same as all the other levels."

I looked closer. "There doesn't seem to be as many as before."

"There is not. Remember you are now half-way into Hell's Planes, and a substantial portion of the souls stop on this plane. The ones that proceed are, as you have been told, the serious ones."

"Is it going to break some divine edict if I ask you to remind me what the remaining Planes are?"

Shaking his head, "No it will not. The seventh is Violence as you know, ruled over by your buddy Leviathan. The eighth is categorized as Fraud, but as you will learn...IF YOU GET THERE...that is not a very comprehensive designation. I will tell you this; it is also the technological Plane. Then lastly is the ninth Plane, which is the Great Plane. For all intents and purposes that is the end of the punishment planes, but as you already know the Furnaces are at the very bottom. They don't count since they are just waste removal, more or less."

"Waste removal, where what 70% of all souls go right off the bat?"

"Somewhere in that range, yes."

Looking back, I said, "I can't help noticing, at least from this distance, there aren't the normal torture stations."

"There are no stations, as you call them, on this Plane. Remember this Plane is run by The Host, they have a different outlook on punishment."

Slapping him on the back as Cemal appeared behind us announcing breakfast, I said, "Good, that's our first stop." I was about to invite him to breakfast when he pushed passed me and sat down to fill his plate.

Leaning in close Cemal whispered, "There are ways to drug him if Master wishes."

My eyes went wide. "Are you suggesting we sedate our guide?"

His brows wrinkled, "Oh, yeah, sedate, yes, yes, that's what this one meant Master. Your boy would never suggest poisoning him, that would be wrong..." pausing, "right? That would be wrong, right?"

I couldn't keep from laughing at the look on his face. "You have an evil streak, my boy."

He slapped me on the butt with his tail, "Your humble servant is a Demon, after all, if Master will recall."

It was my turn to lean in and whisper, "You know he can read your thoughts, right?"

"Yes, Master, this one knows," he answered with a smirk as he turned and went back inside.

I stood in stunned surprise. Strangely the whole exchange made me miss Usis. He'd personally picked Cemal. I'd initially assumed it was just because I thought the boy was cute and he thought we needed a personal servant we could trust. Now I saw that he'd taken into consideration what could best serve our journey, which it seemed turned out to be all of the above with a hint of an evil streak and the capability to cause absolute chaos.

As I walked in, I watched Kitar watch Cemal as he headed toward his room. Loading my plate with food I sat down as the young slave poured me a steaming cup of wine. "This will be new to you Master; it is wine with a few additional ingredients which adds to the flavor and acts as a bit of a stimulant."

"Like coffee?"

"This one is not sure what that is Master, but this is popular on the Lower Planes."

"What is the secret ingredient?" I asked.

"It is probably best you not ask," added Kitar.

I raised my hands in surrender. I knew when not to peruse some things. The drink tasted good and as far as I was concerned that was all that mattered. Once breakfast was completed Kitar headed downstairs as I got dressed. When I finally made it down as well, I found Kitar in the middle of a conversation with Gabriel. "Greetings, young writer," said the angel in a far better mood than I'd expected.

"Greetings to you Lord...Um...how should I address you?"

"Normally it would be My Lord, but for your stay, since you are technically not a soul in residence, you may call me by my name."

I don't know why but I didn't like that idea at all, so I answered, "Yes, My Lord."

With a nod, Gabriel added, "So do you have plans today?"

"Yes, unless you can offer suggestions I was considering the pass-through for the lower Planes."

Inclining his head, Gabriel replied, "Seems a reasonable starting place. I will leave you to it, oh but first." Walking over he placed a finger upon my forehead causing a great flash to blind me and almost knock me on my ass.

"What the Hell was that?" I barked.

"Watch your language. It was my mark. It will ensure your safe travel on this Plane."

I reached down and pulled out the amulet Lucifer had given me. "This isn't good enough?"

"It is, but since many here are not under The Dark Lord's rule, it is best if you carry mine as well. Don't worry, you will not be keeping it," answered the Angel in a matter of fact tone.

"Understood, and thank you, My Lord." Turning to Kitar, I said, "lead the way."

As Gabriel turned to leave, he looked back. "If you are feeling up to it this evening, you are invited to dinner. I am sure you will have many questions. I have set aside time to assist you where I can."

I bowed my head. When we were outside I stopped Kitar, "Is it just me, or does he seem to be taking this all very well? I mean almost too well?"

Nodding, "Yes. I suggest you stay on your guard. You have been a pawn in The Dark Lord's game since you started. Now you have simultaneously been recruited into The Host's...well, at the very least you are part of Gabriel's game now as well."

"Great."

# Entry 191

As we walked toward the back of the main hall, I continued to study the paintings and sculptures. I was not only amazed by their ornate beauty but I wanted to see if the trend I'd noticed earlier continued, and it did. Most of the works were of higher beings, like The Host, trampling souls underfoot. As we walked by one of the sitting areas I looked down to admire the detail in the rug and was shocked to see the woven figures shifting and moving. Looking up at Kitar I raised an eyebrow. "They are souls who have been woven into the strands used to make both the rugs and tapestries. Many of the higher power's both here, and I assumed in The Host, have them in their homes and offices. The souls are conscious, and they feel themselves being tread upon. It's just another way Hell has found to utilize its overabundance of resources. Great now I have to tiptoe through this place. As we reached the back of the long hall, we came to another set of doors, just as intricate and as the ones at the front of the Keep.

As the doors opened the heat and sulfur of the plane slapped me upside the face knocking me back. So overwhelming was the effect that all I could do was bend over and put my hands on my knees while I tried to catch the breath I didn't even need. As I inhaled slowly, I started to cough just from the density of the air outside.

"Why is it so bad now, so hard to breathe. It wasn't like this when we arrived or even this morning?" I asked.

"Our arrival was during a lull in the furnaces firings; now it seems they are back to a more regular schedule. Not only was the air clearer but as you noticed the Plane had cooled quite a bit as well. Did you not hear the loud booms earlier in the morning? That was the furnaces belching heat, lava, and sulfur onto the Plane. It is always worse right after a venting." Thinking back, I did remember some loud sounds this morning while I was dressing. I'd ignored it at the time, having grown used to Hell's soundtrack.

As my body adjusted, now coated in sweat, I looked around to find us standing at the top of a set of marble steps. At the bottom was a bridge spanning a wide chasm. Looking at Kitar, he explained, "This is one of the vents like the volcanos. The eruptions and excess heat from the furnaces travel up and are vented here and through the volcanos. There are several of these openings scattered across the Plane which are essentially large stone tubes. Needless to say, they also manage to keep the entire Plane at this insufferable temperature and maintain the fires you will see burning randomly across the landscape." Pointing to the other side, he added, "Across the bridge is where those passing through receive their punishment. Three bridges lead into the central plaza. This one from the Keep. The left one is the intake where souls enter from the above Plane and finally the right one leading from the plaza and down to the Planes below.

"Wait, so the vents travel under the rock," I asked leaning over the railing looking down into the black void.

"Yes, the furnaces vent on both this and the Seventh Plane."

"So not the Eighth or Ninth?"

"No, as I said, the Eighth plane is more technological, so heat is not conducive to that Plane and with all the Royalty of Hell and our capital city being on the Ninth it was decided early not to vent onto that Plane either. The Great Plane is still somewhat warm since it rests directly over the furnaces themselves. I think its Lucifer's way of reminding everyone they are just one step away from their ultimate demise."

The Plaza, again very Vatican, these guys can't seem to stray far from a theme. I wonder if other planets in the Creations have the same over the top gaudy feel? Anyway, it was a colossal plaza ringed by columns. Between each column were golden panels of scrolled latticework which enclosed the entire area. I was about to take a step down when Kitar grabbed me and pulled me back just as a massive wall of flames shot up from the pit and crashed into the ceiling some three hundred feet above. This conflagration lasted a good minute before dying down and again vanishing into the depths of Hell. As the flames died, I realized I was screaming. Though my skin only looked red, it felt like the entire front of my body had been burned off. This had to be one of the most intense pains I'd ever experienced. My knees gave out, and I dropped to the marble step gasping for breath as my body screamed in agony.

"WTF?" I screamed.

"What does that mean?" asked Kitar.

I took several seconds to calm my nerves, and the pain began to subside thanks to my amulet, I think. It had started to glow almost instantly. When I was able to form rational thoughts again, I said, "What, Oh…it means 'What The Fuck.' It was an Earth expression of shock."

"That was the fires of Hell. Oh, that's right, it's the first time you have ever felt them. Not nice, are they?" explained Kitar.

"That was fucking horrible. I've never experienced anything that painful in my life, or well afterwards and remember I had my head squashed by a taxi cab; I was imprisoned and tortured by two ex-Angels and so on." All the sudden a thought hit me. I turned to face Kitar. "Is that what the souls in the furnaces are feeling?"

He shook his head. "No, Keith, this was just a residual venting from the gasses created when new souls are introduced in mass. The pain the souls inside the furnaces are suffering are thousands of times worse than what you just experienced."

"Thousands of times worse?" I can't begin to tell you the level of pain I'd just experienced. As close as I can get would be getting a terrible direct fire burn while you were living. Now multiply that all over the front of your body. Then multiply that again by say, oh I don't know, five hundred. Now if that isn't bad enough, slice that burned area up with hundreds of razor cuts and douse the whole thing in alcohol while listening to a Justin Beaber album. Then you might get close. Now if Kitar is to be believed, the souls in the furnaces are suffering that pain over their entire body, a thousand times worse for sometimes hundreds of thousands of years. My mind couldn't even comprehend such pain.

I sat there recovering for quite a while. Kitar ran back inside and brought me a goblet of wine which I drank slowly. Remember, not only did I just get toasted, but the Planes temperature rose again due to the outgassing, it must have risen another hundred degrees. The air was so think you could've cut it with a knife.

"Do you wish to continue?" asked Kitar.

I just nodded. As I again approached the bridge, I paused and gingerly looked over the edge and then darted across at a dead run. I turned to find Kitar casually strolling. When he reached me, he commented casually, "They have, it appears, introduced two large groups of souls into the furnaces this morning. There should not be any more added for a while."

I breathed a sigh of relief at hearing that. "So, the temperature will drop?"

"Yes, it should. By morning it should be back to where it was before this last venting."

"So still horrible, just not this bad?"

"Correct."

"Wait, one more question. You've said that this happens when they introduce new souls in mass. Define 'in mass'?"

After thinking a second, he said, "Probably about a hundred million or so. This last one was relatively small."

"A hundred million souls have just been thrown into the fiery furnaces just this second."

"To be accurate, a few seconds ago but yes, you could say that."

I closed my eyes and took a long breath. This morning was becoming one Hell, pardon the pun, of a learning experience. Hell had become real to me a long time ago, but I guess no mind can ever grasp the enormity of what was happening in The Dark Lord's domain. Finally trying to shake it off, I said, "OK, wow...fine...let's see what we have to see. I have a feeling I'm going to need a drink or twenty." Just as we turned our attention back to the plaza, I added, "You guys said the Hell we were entering as of the Sixth Plane was worse than anything

I'd seen or written about thus far. I've only been on this Plane for a day, and already I want to crawl up in a ball under the covers and never come out."

Kitar in his most comforting tone said, "you were warned."

"Even against Lucifer's wishes. I'll be talking with our little Dark Lord once he decides to show back up."

"Careful who you challenge Keith, it is not too late for you to end up in those furnaces," replied Kitar. Before I could say anything, he led me into the plaza. In the center of the great courtyard stood a tall statue of an angel with his foot on the neck of a man. "It seems to be a trend?" I commented.

"Yes, it does. This Plane has many depictions of The Host treading on the throats of the living."

"Why?"

"That question might best be directed to Lord Gabriel."

"Makes sense," I said liking Kitar's new honesty.

As you can imagine the plaza wasn't empty, not by a long shot. Being a pass-through, souls destined for other areas, entered here, were punished and then left to move on to the next plane. As I said before, there were not as many, but there was still a lot. What was missing were torture stations, no great Demons with implements of pain. Here instead were hundreds of thousands of souls in neat, orderly rows. As they entered, they were sorted at a table by a Seer, who would announce their sin. A Cherubim would then take them by the arm and lead them to a table where they would choose the implement of their punishment. After which they would be directed to an empty spot in the central plaza, forced to kneel and then start flogging themselves. Yes, no one imposed their punishment upon them, they were made to do it to themselves.

At this point, one of the Cherubim ascended the steps stopping before us. "Greetings, I am Nakeb. I have been tasked with attending to your needs while you are in the plaza. Please, this way."

As we walked down and into the walkways between the rows of souls, I could hear each one announcing a number, asking The Father for forgiveness and then flogging themselves. "How many lashes are they forced to endure?" I asked.

"That is up to them and how gravely their sins have displeased The Father."

I started to say something when Kitar put a hand on my shoulder, "It can be as low as ten thousand or upwards into the millions."

"And they must count each one off?"

Again, Nakeb answered, "Yes, and if for any reason they lose count their body will be healed to as it was when they arrived, and they must begin again."

"That seems time-consuming considering the number of souls waiting to pass through," I pointed out.

"The damned took the time to commit the sins against The Father; it is only fair we should allow them an equal amount to atone."

As we reached the center of the circle, I stopped and slowly took in the low chatter of counting, the muffled cries of agony and the swoosh of the lash followed by that disturbing thwack as it struck the creatures' backs. And the smell, oh the smell: shit, urine, rotting flesh, all swirled together in the breeze created from the millions of moving cords as they swung forward and then back striking the penitents raw weeping flesh.

"Please this way," said Nakeb as he led us around the plaza toward the gate where souls exited.

"Is it correct to assume that I can't talk to one of the souls?"

"I don't see why you cannot."

"Will it not mess up their count? I wouldn't want to subject them to additional suffering on my account."

Smiling he reminded me, "I would personally not worry about such things. You were not responsible for bringing them to their suffering so why concern yourself with its duration. This was brought upon them themselves, and it is without a doubt far better than what is in store for them in the Lower Planes. Here at least they are being allowed to show The Host their remorse at having sinned against the Most High."

Turning to Kitar, I said, "I find it interesting how people like Nakeb see this as a reward."

Kitar started to answer but didn't get the chance. The Cherubim said, "A reward is a recognition given for service or effort. In the case of these damned souls, whether they intended or not, their service was clearly in that of The Dark Lord, and their effort was in bringing themselves here."

"Isn't that punishment?" I asked.

"Punishment or reward. Are not both nothing more than a matter of perspective, as your friend, De Sade would point out. To a child being spanked is punishment, to a masochist its considered reward. Or more to the point, to most waking up in Hell is a punishment, but for you, it proved to be more of a reward, would you not think? If you considered the alternative?"

"I'll agree it's perspective. But, if we are to follow your train of logic, isn't it possible that too much reward can eventually turn into punishment?"

Looking around as we walked I noticed other Cherubim walking between the kneeling souls. "Why are so many of your type here. You must find this place abhorrent. Is working here a punishment or a reward?"

Making a clicking noise with his tongue, Nakeb replied, "It is safe to say being assigned here is both a reward and a punishment for us, according to whom you ask."

"I'm asking you."

"A punishment, clearly A PUNISHMENT," his tone grew angry for a split second, but he caught himself as he continued, "As for why so many of my kind. As you can see with the soul there, he is only pretending to reward himself for his behavior; there is no conviction behind it. It falls upon us, to remind them of how important repenting is and therefore encourage them to renew with vigor their actions."

"Ahh, but are they not past repenting? They are now confined here for eternity; there is no repenting."

"There can be as you will see when you inevitably meet The Buddha."

"Right, one of the Angels who didn't choose a side," I said.

"You mean the Fallen," corrected Nakeb.

"Again a matter of perspective," I added. "Also, I notice a lot of what appears to be humanoids like me, almost disproportionately."

"That is because they have started to arrive after the incident with The Dark Lord's Great Grandson."

"Oh yes, Xia…" pausing I realized I'd had been given a gift, "So tell me Nakeb -- may I call you by your name -- how do you feel about what Lord Morningstar did? Is that punishment or reward, and how does The Host see it?" He started to speak but I cut him off. "After all, as I understand it, when he arrived on Earth and saw what they'd become, something I wouldn't disagree with, he destroyed every living thing on the planet. Clearly he was punishing them for their sins. But…." I motioned to those bowing around us, "according to your definition of atoning, was not his actions, that of The Dark Lord's Great Grandson, actually nothing more than rewarding them for those very same sins. That must put you guys, The Host that is, in a precarious situation. You, by nature and deed, hate Xia for everything he is, but this one time do you not agree with his actions? So should he be punished or rewarded?"

Shaking his head, Nakeb said, "That is not for someone in my station to decide."

"I'm not asking you to exact the punishment, only what your opinion is about what The Dark Prince did."

"I would agree that your world deserved what they had coming. But as undoubtedly you have been told during your journeys, no one but The Father should judge the living for their actions, so therefore it was not that abomination's place to make that decision for himself."

"Do you still think The Father moves within Creation?" I asked.

"Of course, just because we do not, or have not seen him in some time does not change the fact all things act according to his will."

"Then with that being said, is it possible that Xia Morningstar was, in fact, an instrument of The Father's will?"

Again, I saw a flash of anger dance across the Cherubim's face. "It could indeed, The Father does not always reveal his plans to us." I was about to twist the knife just a bit deeper when we arrived at the gate, and he changed the subject. "To answer an earlier question. How might you interview a soul? I have brought you here, so you might find an applicable candidate from those who are about to leave. Therefore, sparing a soul the suffering, or reward, of starting their count over while gifting them a few additional moments before they will be required to travel further into this accursed land. I will leave it to your decision if putting off their eventual fate, even temporarily, is a punishment or a gift."

I liked how this guy's mind worked even if I was still a bit annoyed that I hadn't gotten to finish my line of questioning. "That sounds good. Is there a place around here where I can take them so we are not disturbed?"

The Cherubim motioned for us to follow and walked through the gate and turned right into a small cave which was surprisingly nice for Hell. "This is our refuge away from this cursed place. Its where the servants of The Father go to revive themselves and shake off the filth of the Plane. If you find this acceptable, you may use it."

"Can you get some food and wine brought down? I want the soul to feel at ease. I've found that helps lubricate their sense of cooperation and encouraged them to talk. After all, as I'm sure you already know, a little kindness goes a long way."

Nodding his approval, Nakeb said, "Yes, Yes indeed it does. I can arrange to have some refreshments provided."

"Perfect, I will start looking for a soul while you stock the grotto."

"And how might you do that?" Nekeb asked.

"I've given him the ability to see a soul's sins," answered Kitar.

"And why would you do that?"

"Is that not obvious, so he can better perform his duties," again answered Kitar.

"How very odd. None the less, I will arrange for your food and drink," Nekeb said as he walked off.

I almost skipped into the cavern and threw myself down on the grass. Yes Grass, can you believe it? It looked like a forest grove complete with trees, flowers, chirping birds, butterflies and did I mention the grass. I found myself squinting at the intense light, but then that seemed to be a thing wherever The Host hung out. "This is nice."

Kitar sat down and joined me. "I agree, we might want to set up a camp and stay here."

"Don't tempt me."

As much as we didn't want to leave we had to if I was going to find a subject for the interview. With great pain, we made our way back through the gate and stood for a while watching souls filter by, and there were a lot. Hundreds of creatures of all shapes and sizes limping by covered in shit, all with the shredded backs. I shuddered, it was surprising at how just seeing grass and sun again, even for a few minutes and then returning to the pain of the Plane caused my stomach to clench up and my head to start aching. Of course, part of that might have been the fucking smell of sulfur and the heat. It did cause me to consider what it must be like for The Host, to come from

The Eternal City to here. I could see how Nekeb would see this as punishment. It was.

# Entry 192

Kitar and I stood off to the side of the steps as the crowd of damages souls walked by, most with a resigned look on their face. That made a degree of sense due to the untold number of years they'd already been in Hell, the tortures they'd experienced and the Planes they'd traveled. By now, the old saying was probably accurate, "Abandon all hope ye who enters here." All hope was gone. I was curious if this was part of what they talked about when they said the 'real Hell' started on this Plane. Before this, those condemned to this eternity might have thought there was maybe an end. As they traveled down from Plane to Plane, I could only imagine how increasingly the damned finally realized there was no hope left. They had in actuality abandoned all hope back on the shores of the river on the Judgement Plane.

As we watched, I finally saw an unusual looking creature in the center of the crowd and pointed it out to Kitar.

"That would be a perfect choice. It's a Paiston," he said as if that should mean something to me. The creature looked like a lama with two heads, each on a long serpentine neck. Its body, and extremely long tail appeared to have, at one time, been covered in a course, thick tan hair, as was its Mohawk. His neck and legs were bare. When I say 'at one time' I'm only guessing because now his back and sides were ripped open weeping blood and behind him trailed several long strands of internal organs. What caught my eye was not so much his appearance, I'd seen many strange creatures while in Hell. It's just this creature seemed so much more injured. Its body was so damaged and abused. Something about it made me wonder. All the beings passing through this Plane were responsible for their own punishment. Why were his wounds so much worse?

The crowd parted as Kitar walked over to the creature. I watched as my guide leaned down and gently picked up the organs and not so gently stuffed them back into the creature's body. With a single hand, he closed the wound, not healing it, just closed it. The gash still wept. "The Dark Lord's emissary wishes to have a word with you. This way."

I nodded to the creature as he approached and together we turned and followed Kitar into the grove. I heard two gasps as we entered the lush surrounds. "Have we been forgiven?" he asked.

Shaking his head, Kitar said, "No, you have been given a reprieve. As I said, Keith, The Dark Lord's writer wishes to hear your story."

Bowing both heads, "It is not a pleasing tale, but if his Lordship's emissary wishes to hear what we have to tell, then we will consider it part of our deserved punishment to recount our sins."

I walked over and placed a hand on his back just below where one of the necks met his torso. "While you are with me you have nothing to fear. I've asked one of the Cherubim to bring food and drink. Please join me." I started to turn and walk away then stopped, "Forgive my rudeness, I'm Keith. I've been tasked with touring and writing about Lord Lucifer's realm. Like you, I'm just a soul, nothing more."

As we reached the center of the clearing Kitar and I sat and watched as the beleaguered creature, with a hidden grace from a life he no longer lived, knell down like one of those trained Arabian horses. Just as I was about to start Nekeb showed up with two slaves. They rushed in, set down several platters of food between us, along with two goblets, a strange looking bucket with what appeared to be a straw and several bottles of wine. Nakeb stepped back and crossed his arms and looked at me expectantly. Raising an eyebrow, "Is there something you need? You can go but leave the two slaves. If I need you, I'll have them summon you," I ordered in a tone leaving no room for debate.

In shock, the Cherubim turned and marched out making a 'stay' motion with his fingers to the two slaves. I watched in amusement as the Piaston's head kept switching between the Cherubim and me with a surprised look.

Finally stopping on me I commented, "He is just a servant of sorts and considering where we are, for the wrong team at that. Do you have a name?"

The left head looked at me, "We are called Tinolic."

"Let me start there, we?"

The two heads looked at each other saying nothing. Then the left addressed me, "Yes, we are one, but each is also separate. We are both independent and combined. We have our own emotions and opinions but are also aware of the others as well. We are two, but also we are one."

"How do you not talk over yourselves?" I asked.

"It is part of our upbringing. We learn, over time, which one of us is better at addressing the world while the other is often better at observing it. It takes time to come to this agreement, and even then if the other wishes to speak, they will and can." Turning to the other head, "Would you say that is correct?"

"Yes, indeed," answered the right head.

"Interesting. Before I begin would you like something to eat or drink?" I motioned to the food which had been placed between us. It was then I discovered how this creature functioned with no hands. His, its, theirs, whatever, tail whipped around as one side picked up the bucket with a straw and the other a bottle. I hadn't noticed the two sides of the tail. Tinolic poured an entire bottle into the bucket and sat it down in front of him. Looking over at the food both heads snatched a couple of bites; then the left one turned to me as the right one took a long drink from the straw. "Thank you; we are ready to assist you in any way we can."

# Entry 193

Here is my interview with Tinolic. It gets interesting.

"Let's start with a broad overview. If you had to sum up your primary sin, we are in Hell after all, as explained to you by the Judges on the first plane, what would it be?" I asked, thinking it was broad but would give us a starting point."

Thinking for a second, he answered matter-of-factly, "We were the destroyer of worlds." The right head lifted and looked at the left who said, "Would you not say that is accurate?"

"Yes, we think that is precisely what we are."

I sat just stared at the creature a bit surprised. It wasn't so much the comment as the nonchalance of their assessment. Thankfully I didn't have to look like a stunned idiot for long. I felt a tap on my arm and looked to see Kitar offering me a full mug of wine. "You might need this."

"Yes, I think I will." Returning my attention to the Piaston, I said in a calm tone after a long drink, "Would you care to explain?"

"Where to start, how to start?" We waited. Bowing its head it started, "We think first you need context, about our species. We are advanced compared to many others, including yourself. You are from a small blue planet orbiting a yellow sun if memory serves, are you not? I think it is called Earth?"

"I was, Earth is no more. Well, the planet still exists but not the life it housed."

At that, both heads turned to look at me. "We are not surprised, but could you explain how that occurred?" I could not see caring but detached, almost clinical, interest.

"I'd prefer not to talk about it, to be honest," I answered.

"Understood, but, in fact, it might have a bearing on our story."

"How?"

"We do not know until we first know the cause of your species extinction."

Taking a deep breath, I answered, "Xia Morningstar destroyed my planet."

"In that case, your former planet does not hold any bearing to our story."

"Fine, can we get on with it then?" I barked, having momentarily lost my patience.

"Yes, we can. As I said, we are an advanced species. Far more advanced than about 56% of the sentient species in the known universe. That number was, of course, accurate as of the time of our death. We cannot as of this time give you an accurate number," he commented as I growled. I took a deep breath to get control of my anger. No, I have no idea why either, I guess having Earth thrust back upon me hit a nerve.

(Here is where they finally start telling me their story. I'm summarizing since the conversation took several hours and went down many different roads, as you will see they tend to enjoy hearing themselves talk. What I'm including is what I think is important in both their story and personality.)

"For many eons, the Piaston have led a broad consortium of species scattered across the universe. Our mission was to find young, potentially sentient planets and ascertain from their early behaviors, as well as testing if they would or could be guided to develop into a peaceful member of the universal community. We had not as of yet decided on your planet, by the way; we had visited several times. Our estimations were correct if a Hellspawn decided you were unworthy to continue." The left head paused and looked at the right, them both turned to face me. I could tell they were studying me.

"What happens if you decide a species is unworthy?"

"That is determined by the governing body. In most cases, they are, as you would expect, eliminated. Thus ensuring they do not develop into the analyzed threat."

"Eliminate? How?"

"If we feel they could eventually leave their planet or more importantly their system then their planet is sterilized."

"That's what you mean by the destroyer of worlds?"

"Yes, it is, in our lifetime we were responsible for several dozen worlds being neutralized." He could tell from my face I was appalled. "If it helps you, Lord Keith..."

"Just Keith"

"If it helps, we also admitted or saved three times as many from the same fate."

Sitting back and taking a few bites of food and a drink, "I guess what I don't understand is who or what gave you the authority to make such decisions?"

Following suit and taking a drink themselves, left answered, "Our species, the Piaston, are one of the oldest members of the federation and the most technologically advanced. We were given additional deference since, having destroyed our own world in our younger years, then surviving and thriving we felt we knew what was required of a young civilization to succeed and not become a threat once they joined the universal family."

This is where Kitar stepped in. "I would like to add that their species was also responsible for many of the technologies needed for deep space travel, and correct me if I am wrong, jealously guarded that technology thus ensuring their sway with member systems."

I looked back and raised an eyebrow, to which left answered, "Absolutely, at no time have I asserted that our members, or for that matter ourselves, are enlightened. Success amongst other advanced societies is often dependent upon power, money, and strength. We did what was necessary to ensure our species continued longevity. So yes, there was more than good feeling involved in ensuring we continued to carry sway in the high council."

I interrupted. "What I find interesting and so very different from all the other interviews I've done in my travels. You haven't yet spoken of your personal life. Normally those are the sins that have brought souls to Hell."

"Not in our case. The Piaston tend to bond only out of necessity, not out of emotional or physical attachment. There are times when two do find themselves considering their personal desires over those of the universal good and our species continued domination..."

I interrupted again. "Now we seem to be hitting upon the heart of the matter... domination?"

The right head looked at the left when I said domination and the tone I used, and I swear they smiled at each other like a couple of parents thinking something a three-year-old said was cute. "As cultures continue to age, if they survive, they tend to grow not only technologically, ideologically but also in arrogance and ego. The Piaston being no exception if I dare say the only difference is we deserved our arrogance."

"As most believe they do..." added Kitar under his breath.

"You are most certainly correct Lord Judge. Arrogance is after all, as we have learned, a sin." Turning back to me, "As you will no doubt discover if you explore a soul's society as much as you do their lives, as a civilization grows older sins are something they tend to collect like power, at least if they wish for longevity."

My mind drifted off for a bit while the Piaston and Kitar debated the more delicate points of societal rights and wrongs. Finally, when I'd had enough, I asked, cutting them both off, "Then you died, ended up here and since you are passing through you must be headed for one of the three remaining lower planes. May I ask which one?"

"This might surprise you but Treachery, the final Plane if we are not mistaken," said the right head speaking to me directly for the first time.

"Really, how does treachery come in based upon what you told me. Is it the betrayal of all the worlds you had murdered?"

"That did not play into our ultimate punishment..." The left head paused and looked to Kitar who nodded his agreement. "It was based upon our turning on our own culture and using the trust they had given us against them." I decided to stay silent. Telling your life story after arriving in Hell is hard enough without having someone interrupt you with constant questions. I should know, I'm constantly interrupted.

They waited to see if I had a question. When I didn't the left one continued, "Our downfall started when we were assigned to evaluate a planet in a relatively distant part of space which had been overlooked. Now the species on the fourth planet was not only sentient, advanced but had developed FTL technology."

I had to stop them. "FTL?"

"Faster than light."

"Oh, OK, continue."

"We traveled there and were met with a restrained hostility, which is not uncommon. We started negotiations, explaining who we were and why we were there."

"Not including the part where you would exterminate them all if they didn't meet your approval, I assume?" OK, fine, I said I wouldn't ask questions, but the ability to refrain from snarky comments is beyond my control.

"That goes without saying; we don't normally ever tell them that part of the procedures manual until we are obliged to terminate their world. It keeps things simpler."

Looking over to Kitar, I said, "These guys are charming…" Then I paused, "Are you guys?"

The shoulders of the beast shrugged. "We do not have genders either, not assigned one at least. We choose them based on the role we wish to assume during the coupling process."

"Assume, how do you decide who is what?" I had to ask.

"Normally it's contractual," answered the right one.

Again looking at Kitar, I commented, "Romantics as well." He couldn't hide his laugh. "Go on, so you arrive in this system?"

"Yes, and, as we said, were met with guarded hostility. Just the normal reaction when a species is visited by another species for, what we assumed, was the first time. We negotiated landing rights with a marginally high degree of certainty against counterproductive actions."

"Counterproductive actions?"

"It's a Piaston way of saying, being attacked," explained Kitar.

"Oh, I see, go on."

"Once we landed and after some tense negotiations and interrogation we were actually shown to quarters and treated reasonably well. After a week, yes, we weren't allowed to leave, they even granted us access to their planet."

"Did you explain your mission?" I asked.

"Oh Yes, we saw no reason to hide any information from them and to be honest, we could not. They were able to read thoughts. It was that ability coupled with our openness about our mission that facilitated their rudimentary trust in us."

"I guess that makes sense, anyway continue."

"Over the next few weeks, we integrated into the community. As we said, we were treated well and in time began to understand and respect these peace loving people. We learned that over the years the reason they had not been identified was that they had chosen to hide from the rest of the universe. They knew of the Alliance, and they had heard of the Piaston, though most of their information was dated or simply wrong. What we did learn while there was that in the realm of technology they exceeded anything the Alliance had, even our species. We strove to learn all we could while keeping an air of detached interest. We did not want them to know we were now spying as much as we were gathering information. This is where we developed the problem that would eventually lead us to our great betrayal. We grew to enjoy our life on Santerian 5, the people were friendly, and their social structure was far more lax than that of the Piaston. Going back to your original comment about motivation, you could say in the end; personal feelings did play into our decisions. We were welcomed, embraced for our differences and treated with respect simply because we were us, not because of what we could contribute."

Here Tinolic paused and took a long drink from his bucket. Looking back, the left continued, "Eventually we convinced our hosts of our need to return to our people. We had assured them that not only would they be left in peace, but that if we could, we would someday return."

Again there was a long pause. I felt like the two were talking to each other mentally, don't ask me why. The right, this time, continued, "I do not have the story telling abilities of my other, so I will be blunt. When we returned to our world and made our report, what we knew would probably happen, did. Our ruling body decided to raid the world, terminate the population and absorb the technology. We knew we could not allow that to happen. We tried, in vain, to convince our leaders, just this once, to ignore this world, but they refused. There was too much strategic and financial gain to be made from the advancements their technologies offered. We watched helplessly as the Piaston fleet moved into Santerian 5 space." The right one stopped.

The left one continued, "We were guilt-ridden. You must understand for us this was a new experience and one we were not equipped to deal with. We acted rashly. We convinced our leaders to allow us to lead the attack. They believed it was to prove our loyalty. While the planning was underway, we were also permitted to return to the surface. We were sent to deliver an ultimatum that the species would be spared if they only turned over their technologies and wiped all information of it from their systems. Well, that was the message we were instructed to give, not the one we in fact delivered. We warned the Santerian's about the impending attack and proposed a solution. One I might add their peaceful nature would not allow them to support. We had already decided it was not up to them. We told them purely to inform not to recruit."

Left paused, turned to look at the right. When they turned back, together they finished their story, "We returned to our base ship which housed roughly 75% of the Piaston population. We planted explosives and destroyed the ship. Due to the size of the initial blast, it set off a chain reaction extinguishing the rest of the fleet. We did not learn of the extent of the damage until we reached Hell and a Judge told us." They together bowed to Kitar. "There was but a minimal number of the Piaston population left to carry on our race."

Lifting his head the right one added in a very decisive tone, "We, who had been trained to assess and pass judgment upon species, found our own wanting and in so finding passed sentence and sterilized the universe of the inferior race, the Piaston."

Each of us sat quietly sipping our wine while we digested our feelings about Tinolic's story. When I realized they were all looking at me, I asked a question that even I, at the time, did not understand. "Why are you so much more injured than the others leaving this Plane?"

Shrugging their llama-like shoulders, the left one said, "Did you not understand what we said? We destroyed our entire species. We awoke in Hell, were judged and finally understood the true nature of life, death, and creation. We then, as we had always done, passed judgment upon ourselves. We found ourselves wanting. We had personally presided over hundreds of worlds sterilization, even more societies were greatly diminished due to our strategic removal of their thinkers, slowing or stopping their advance. Then finally, we destroyed those who had put faith in us always to have their best interest at heart, our species. Therefore, having decided our sins were worthy of the punishment we were given, an eternity in Hell, we did what any good Piaston would do in such a situation, we embraced it. We have thrown ourselves eagerly into each of the Planes punishments, knowing none of them are in fact sufficient for our sins. Here on this Plane, we were tasked with administering punishment upon ourselves, so we did, with eagerness and to the fullest of our ability. We will not lie to you, just like every time before, we were disappointed when we were told it was time to move to the next Plane. But we console ourselves with the knowledge that with each subsequent Plane the punishment grows more fitting of the sins we have committed. Therefore, we welcome our eternity of pain, though, in all honesty, it is but a pale reward for the atrocities we have carried out."

Now I was really in shock. Turning to Kitar, "They are repentant. Does that carry no sway in Hell?"

Shaking his head, Kitar replied, "Keith, you already know the answer to that question. Their judgment has been passed, their punishment assigned. No one revisits past decisions, it is just carried out." He stopped and took a bite of the food before adding, "I do feel you should know that if Tinolic had not repented, as you call it, their crimes would have been sufficient enough to ensure them a place of distinction on the Great Plane. They probably would have lived out eternity as a torturer, or possibly given a life inside the capital city. But due to them having rejected their sins and in fact regretting them, they have ensured that they will eventually pass from eternity in the fires of the furnace."

Before I could voice an objection, the left one added, "As it should be." With that, the Piaston stood, bowed and added, "If you do not mind, telling our story has renewed our desire to continue our punishment. If you will excuse us." Then just like that, with their heads held high, they walked from the meadow.

# Entry 194

After watching the Piaston leave, I started to ask Kitar a question but was cut off, "No there is nothing you can do. Keith, consider what they did, and how they are embracing their punishment. Show them the respect they deserve for understanding the consequences of their actions and working to atone by accepting their punishment with a resigned understanding."

"I guess…" I was searching for more to say but nothing came. I still felt I should've been fighting to spare them some of what was in their future if you can call it that. Sadly, I had nothing, eventually giving up, I said, "If we're done I want to get back and get this written down." Kitar motioned for me to lead, we exited the grove and was again slapped by the stench and heat. Just as we reached the bridge leading back to the plaza Kitar once again stopped me as another blast, though smaller this time, shot up incinerating all the souls on the steps. As we recovered and I tried to catch my breath, I asked, "Were those souls destroyed?"

"No, they will awaken eventually in the hatchery."

"Oh, that's right," was all I could muster.

We walked along the path between a row of souls all beating the shit out of themselves. Having heard Tinolic's story, I looked to see if I could identify those who were taking their punishment seriously. It was surprisingly easy. Just up from us was a Ukillesg, a tentacled blue octopus looking, creature, I'd seen before, using four of his twelve arms, all with whips. He was administering a proper beating upon himself.

A little further down was a human female, probably from Earth. If you cleaned her up, she'd look like one of those well-treated sacks of shit they raised in California. Not saying everyone from there was like this girl, but they did seem to produce more than their fair share of blond, mindless whorish females, and males for that matter. She was one of those Nakeb had mentioned who didn't 'embrace their punishment.' She'd whack herself and then break out in tears and start whining about how much it hurt. Several times as I watched I saw one of the overseers come up, take the whip, give her a good pop to demonstrate how it was to be done, only to cause her to start crying harder. I asked Kitar, "Are you telling me that people, like that girl, even after this much time in Hell and all the punishments they've had to endure still whine like little self-absorbed millennials?"

"Do I need to answer, when the answer kneels right in front of you? Some creatures, no matter how long they are in Hell, will never embrace the reality that they are here due to their actions. Many until the very end believe they were wrongly judged and the universe is out to get them."

I just shook my head. "See those are the ones even I want to tie to a table and beat the Hell out of. I hated people like that when I was alive but here, after all of this..." I just stood watching the little crying cunt. "They're one of the reasons humans don't exist anymore." Not being able to restrain myself any longer, and to the Kitar's surprise, I marched over, grabbed the whip and beat the ever-loving shit out of the girl. Screaming the entire time how their family was gone, their friends were gone, and the human race is gone. By the time I'd finished I was completely drenched in sweat and panting. When I made it back to my guide, I turned to see the girl splayed out on the ground in shock, her back completely torn open. Walking off, I said, "Let's get Tinolic's story taken down before I forget it."

Before we could make it back, I saw a brute of a creature arguing with one of the Cherubims as he urged the soul to "properly" administer its reward. Springing forward, the damned pushed the Overseer backward, lunging at him before he could right himself. As the Overseer's wings took over and set him firmly down on his feet, it quickly became apparent the level of the mistake the soul had just made. The Cherubim picked the creature up by its neck, casually walked over and dropped him over the edge of the platform. It was amazing how long we could hear the beast screaming as it plummeted down the exhaust tube. Oh and in case you're interested, the creature was a Eulicos, they're a huge brutish species. Some nine feet tall, just as wide, dark-skinned and covered in hair. Now if you think I'm describing the males, you'd be wrong, the females looked much the same. The only visible difference was the males two-foot-long cock or the females massive underinflated breasts. I'd interviewed one once but didn't include it since their world was just too brutal. It almost made Hell's tortures at the time seem tame.

I guess here is a good place as any to do a little housekeeping. In case you're wondering, I don't just stumble upon the right soul to interview. I talk to lots of different races. Most of my days, even when I don't report my activities to the journal, are full of studying, learning and talking to those who serve in Hell, as well as those being punished. The reason I don't report every interview I have is twofold. First, there would be hundreds of pages of soul interviews. Secondly, and probably more importantly, most of the stories are boring. Just the run of the mill soul having done the run of the mill stuff that would sentence them to one of the Planes. As sad as it sounds, and I've said this before, the vast majority of souls here in The Dark Lord's realm have lived lives of quiet desperation, as a writer once said. Their actions, while they were living, had little to no impact on their world. Now to be clear, they must have had more than those who end up going directly to the furnaces, but not by much. Now that they are here, their suffering carries the same weight as their lives and are not worth recording or passing down to future generations. Let this be a lesson, one I wish I would've learned myself: if you're alive, live fully, even if you fuck up and make a complete mess of your time, at least you made an impact. Your life doesn't ensure your memory, and your death doesn't guarantee your eternity. You're only what you leave behind. No one in this place, and I fear The Host as well, really cares about who you are or what you did. It is only the impact you make while breathing and the memory carried down by your people which will ensure you are more than fertilizer for worms after your soul has finally arrived at its enteral destination.

With that being said, let's get back to Blasphemy.

# Entry 195 – Elick's entry

It has been suggested by those overseeing the distribution of The Dark Lord's writers work that it might serve the narrative if I were to contribute at times. Keith's tale has begun to branch into areas where events he is not present for will directly impact the story he is telling. I questioned the logic of infecting the writer's works with other opinions and insights only to be reminded this was not setting a new precedence; there have been augmentations before, as needed.

Having served at the whim of The Dark Lord for as long as I have, I knew their instructions to contribute were not a request but an order. I have therefore capitulated.

To start, let me tell you who "I" am. I am the great-grandson of Leviathan, keeper of The Dark order and Overseer of Lord Lucifer's latest whim. When I say whim, I am talking about his new found need to have his domain documented by a somewhat feisty creature from Earth. I am Elick Lancestrider.

If you have been keeping up with the entries of our dear writer then you know I am on my way to visit my great-grandfather to learn about the fate of Keith's companion, Usis. As you might have gathered by now, this is not a visit I relish. My Great-Grandfather and I do not see eye-to-eye.

So here I was dropping down through the pit onto the Seventh Plane. Now since Keith has not been on this Plane and I am not a writer, nor in the mood to do descriptions for you pathetic talking monkeys, you get none. As I emerged, a chorus of suffering greeted me from below. I had grown up to these sounds. Our Plane, the Seventh, like all the others, had a specific pitch, a sound unique to that Plane. To me, it was the sound of home. The next thing to greet my return were two of Great-Grandfather's winged guards. This was not a sign of his displeasure; it was just the Seventh Plane. This Plane is always on alert. This Plane is always ready for war, holding its breath until that day when The Dark Lord unleashes it upon the pitiful minions of a tired old Father. With precision, they flew up, flanked me on both sides as we continued down to the Keep itself. As we landed, one of the two guards said in a friendly tone, "He is not in a good mood since the incident on Wrath. Did you see it?"

I just shook my head as the doors to the Keep swung open. The guards slapped me on the back as I walked in and said, "Good Luck. We always have respected your bravery." I had to laugh.

When I had decided to come home, I planned to get in, discover where Usis was being held, assess his condition, hunt down this slave Keith could see through and clarify his instructions to check on the writer's companion regularly, and then get the Hell, pardon the pun, out of there.

As I entered the great hall, I knew my plans were mute. Standing at the bottom of the grand staircase was the Archangel himself, my great-grandfather, Leviathan.

"So you return. Are you here for a loving embrace or to spy for that pathetic creature Our Lord has tasked with spying on his Planes," remarked Leviathan as he walked up with an inspecting eye. "Have you been working out? Practicing with your sword?"

"It is wonderful to see you too Great-Grandfather," I said as I bowed deeply. He might be a pretentious viscous prick, but he is still Hell's royalty, and I know what boundaries not to cross. "I have been practicing, but it seems that question would be more suited for my Uncle Yoclom, do you not think?"

I kept my head bowed waiting for him to release me to rise but could feel his disapproval of my comment. I counted his hoof steps as he came closer. Finally feeling his finger under my chin, I rose and looked up into his pitch black face. We turned and walked toward the sitting area. "In all actuality, it is probably best you have come. The creature is not well, and none of my staff can figure out why. I wanted to question the soul, not destroy him. With all that is happening in Hell and Creation right now, this is not the time to turn The Dark Lord's already angry eyes toward this house."

"So you had planned on allowing the creature to live?" I said somewhat surprised.

My Great-grandfather was all but showing weakness and concern, but any spark of compassion was quickly extinguished with his next words. "I had planned on seeing if he would prove useful until the writer left this plane. Then I would probably have had him dissected to see why he was so strong. Having bested my son, there are certainly aspects of this creature that do not add up. We can all see something is different about his energy. But what, no one is sure. I sense a Morningstar family hand in this, and that in itself is grounds for concern."

His choice of words got my attention. He would not have said Morningstar family if he had meant Lord Lucifer, one does not generalize when referring to Hell Lord and Master. "I heard he was changing?" I asked as I followed. Grandfather (yes, Great-Grandfather but that is too much to keep writing, so figure it out) was in a talkative mood; I planned on milking it for all I could.

As we walked into the family room, I watched the spirits of souls dance in the flames of the fireplace. These were pixies from some obscure creation. Many of the Most High had them installed due to their dances of pain and cries of agony as the flames licked their delicate bodies. Grandfather took his customary seat; it was amazing how almost all of the Fallen arranged their public living areas as The Dark Lord did. A single big throne against the wall and then couches and several chairs on each side around a massive low table. I took one of the chairs as a handsome, though battered slave immediately knelt beside me offering me a goblet of wine. Grandfather noticed the smirk on my face but ignored it. He was not fond of boys liking boys, but this was Hell after all. A female slave in much better condition served him.

"Yes, he is changing. That in itself is not uncommon. It happens often, but this soul does not have the proper temperament for such a manifestation."

Typically it was only the most depraved who changed over time. Demon hybrids were often used in the torture pits or to run the day to day activities of some of the more necessary shops in Hell's many cities. Grandfather was right about Usis. I had spent many days sparing with the soul, and though he was ruthless and very good with a weapon, deep down he was not the kind of creature to spontaneously mutate into one of Hell's more vicious creations.

"You said he was in pain?" I asked.

"Yes, it is suffering greatly. There are times when it is lucid, but most of the time it is writhing and screaming in agony." Pausing and taking a drink, he said, "You have spent time with them both. Is there anything you can contribute to the limited knowledge we have on its history?"

"Honestly I wish I could. I have no idea. Usis, that's his name, by the way, showed no signs of pain or discomfort while I have been traveling with them. As you pointed out, he had to be at the top of his game, even beyond it to have defeated one of Hell's best warriors."

I was surprised when Grandfather dismissed my compliment. "Yoclom is a lot of things, but Hell's best warrior is not a title I would not honor my son with. He did, after all, get sent to the Hatchery by a soul. His next trip will probably be shortly after he returns home at my own hands. The fool."

As he talked, and I drank, I could not shake the feeling that I was being played. I mean, obviously I was. Grandfather was never this pleasant or talkative, well at least not to me. Our conversations usually consisted of him giving an order and me shooting back with why I did not want to do whatever it was he was demanding. Then he would inevitably threaten me, and then I would bow to his authority. Don't think I am weak. Other than the back talk he gets from me, it was the same for everyone who interacts with one of the Fallen. My status as part of his family extends to me the luxury of at least firing off a complaint or counter argument from time to time. It was his concession to our strained relationship.

Standing and handing the cup to the slave, he asked, "Are you staying? I thought you were Lord Lucifer's little toy's keeper now. Or have you failed in that as well?"

Closing my eyes I took a deep breath, then through clenched teeth, answered, "As I said, I came to check on Usis' status. Keith, you know

Lord Lucifer's little toy, will not be able to concentrate until he gets word on the status of his companion. So to ensure both your house's reputation and my continued ability not to visit the Hatchery, I have to figure out a way to calm the writer's mind and get him back to work. May I see Usis?"

Waving dismissively as he walked away, he said, "If you wish. He is in the guest room on the third floor." And with that, my audience with the Great Lord Leviathan was over. Thank The Father. (Yes, we say that here as well, though it means something quite different when used by someone with my lineage.)

# Entry 196

Just before we stepped back into the controlled splendor of the Keep, I saw a soul I recognized. He was the son of a political figure on Earth during my time. Like all the others he was kneeling, and with languid insignificant slaps, he would lazily loop the cat of nine tails up into the air and then let it fall onto his back. I didn't like this person. I didn't like his family. I didn't like his father. This was good; my adrenaline level was still up from the little valley girl. I held up a finger to Kitar and walked over just as the attendant was about to scold the human for his laziness in administering his most just reward. I asked with a smile, "May I demonstrate how it should be done?"

The Cherubim shrugged as I snatched the whip from the creature's hand and with ten very measured blasts of my rage tore open his back. The first two I did in rapid succession only stopping to lean in and whisper, "I was alive when your father pretended to be president. I've seen him; he's an overlord's toy on another plane. I'll find your brother and sister, especially your sister and I'll make sure a whole platoon of Demons takes her until they punch straight through and out her ass. As for now, it is your turn to atone. Scream for me, let's make Hell great again." Again, two hits. Again, leaning in, I said, "I remember your insensitive remarks, you're holier than thou attitude. Here let me remind you where you are." With that, I finished my part in his suffering with six more amazingly succinct whacks to his back. I'd have to remember to thank De Sade for teaching me how to use one of these things. When I finished, having handed the whip to the Overseer I leaned in for the final time, "You are traveling down I see. So to make you feel less alone here in this place know I *will* look for you again and maybe once more we can visit and discuss the past." As I said the last word, I dug my finger into one of the deep lacerations. I let my nail find a sensitive nerve causing the damned soul to let out such a cry that for several seconds all those around us went silent. I stood, wiped my bloody finger on his greasy blond hair and walked back to Kitar. "Shall we?"

Just as I passed I realized Kitar was not following; I looked over my shoulder to find him standing with an incredible look of shock on his face. "May I ask what that was about?"

"Just someone from home who went too far and harmed too many for no reason other than to make himself feel important. Rarely do we get a chance to show them just how much they meant to us."

Kitar gave me a hard look. "There is that monster."

"Yes, you should grow used to him. I'll be seeking his counsel more often, I think."

Any satisfaction I might have felt quickly vanished when we were met just inside the door by Cemal. "Master, did you forget about the dinner with the Angel? To say he is upset might be considered an understatement."

"Oh shit, how long has he been waiting."

"That is the thing Master, he has only waited a little bit, but that does not seem to matter. This one would guess for an eternal being, time flows differently but..." added Cemal.

"It is not the time; it is the slight of being made to wait. They snap, and worlds end, and you have him cooling his heels in his own Keep," explained Kitar.

"Cooling his heel? Have you been studying Earth sayings?" I asked.

Like Gabriel being led to feel that we were making him wait was not enough to stress my already overloaded mind, what Cemal said next from behind me almost caused me to collapse under the pressure. "Master Elick is back. He will be at dinner as well."

It was like he'd hit me in the back of the head with a brick. I stopped dead in my tracks as I visibly saw time slow down before me. Now all I wanted was to get back to my room to hear what the Hellspawn had to say but I also knew there was no way to get out of this dinner. Gabriel was already angry and knowing Elick had news about Usis I suddenly felt like the Archangel was standing before me like a linebacker unwilling to let me pass.

"Thank you," is all I said though I could feel both sets of eyes, Cemal's and Kitar's, on me. As the two servants opened the eighteen foot tall door leading into the dining room, I took a breath and walked in. There sitting at the end of a long table was Gabriel, he was dressed immaculately. I, on the other hand, had an asshole's blood all over the front of my tunic and bits of who knows what on my shoes. "Sorry, we're late. I didn't expect the interviews in the pass-through area to take so long." Brushing off the mood of the Overlord or the cautiousness aura Kitar was actively trying to exude, I took a seat to the right of the angel and said, "Is there wine?"

# Entry 197

"I was told you were interviewing one of the damned," said Gabriel as he motioned for the servants to start serving and for Kitar to join us. I didn't hear him. I wasn't listening. Where is Elick, was all I could think? Then, as if I'd summoned him, in he walked and my mouth dropped. He was stunning. Pale white skin, chalk-white hair with streaks of black scattered, just enough to break up the starkness. Tonight, he wasn't wearing a tunic, but instead a white leather vest. You'd think it would be hard to tell where the vest stopped and the skin began, but it wasn't. His skin was as smooth as porcelain where the leather had the grooves of the creature who had contributed the hide. Around his neck hung a long chain with a glowing red crystal which matched the ones in his wrist cuffs. Finally, and I saved the best part for last, he was in black tights which appeared to have been painted on. Every curve, sinew, and bulge hugged tightly like a child wrapped in his mother's arms. To finish all this off was a series of black and gold belts, maybe four, with a sword in a pale blue scabbard hanging from them.

"It appears I am not as late as I had feared," he said in that husky tone of his.

Yes, if you haven't noticed, I'm in deep lust for this Hellspawn. Something I might add I feel like shit about due to Usis' situation. That is why I plan on waiting till my companion gets back so we can jump Elick's bones together. Don't worry I intend on it being a welcome home present for Usis.

"It appears no one chose to be on time for a dinner with me tonight," commented Gabriel in an almost comical growl.

Needless to say, the meal was a bit awkward and uncomfortable. You know, imagine Thanksgiving when your sister shows up pregnant from a person your extremely Christian parents hate. Also, you've decided today is a good day to tell them you're coming out and have accepted an offer to move in with a guy you met at a bar a week ago. Upon arriving at your parents' house, you and your sister's new baby daddy discovers he is also your new boyfriend, and he hasn't gotten around to telling your sister he is leaving her for another person, a man, who just also happens to be you. Now everyone is sitting around, poking at their turkey, waiting to see who cracks first. Tense... yes, in a word, tense.

Surprisingly it was Gabriel who broke first. "So here I am, I have heard about these grueling interviews you have given the other Overlords. What do you wish to know?"

"You're giving me carte blanch to ask a member of The Host anything?"

"You can ask, I will answer what I choose too."

"Ok, that sounds more like what I expected."

"Before you start I do have a question of my own. I observed what happened out in the plaza. Would you care to explain?" Seeing that my expression was like a kid being called into the principal's office, he added, "Do not misunderstand me, young writer. You could have dissected the entire lot, and it would not have mattered to me. To be honest, it might be a relief as we are so far behind. I was just curious, in my understanding you have always been restrained and...oh what is the word..."

I interpreted, "weak?"

"I might not have chosen that word but, yes, it will do."

"The girl I didn't know, she just represented one of the things I thought was wrong with my world at the time. The embracing of materialism, the rushing toward ignorance, the mindless parasitic obsessions with others to make yourself feel you had worth. As for the guy, well his father is on display in Rumclique's gallery on Gluttony as Earth's perfect example of excess. The soul out in the plaza was a carbon copy of everything that was wrong with his father, his family and most of those who were in a political party at the time called Republicans. Having been told by De Sade that I needed to start embracing my inner monster, I decided to practice on that one. I would not object to having an entire Plane just for me filled with Republicans. I could find few things more enjoyable than spending the rest of eternity torturing the whole racist, misogynistic, holier than thou, bible hugging bunch." I paused, looked up and smiled, seeing everyone's eyes on me. "Oh sorry about that last part."

"For some reason, I feel you are not, sorry that is, but I understand your point. They were after all followers of, as you said, your world's bible. Which in its final presentation had little if anything to do with The Father and his teachings."

"Yes…" I barked, "Thank you…"

"You can do to these souls whatever strikes your fancy." I watched as Gabriel paused, closed his eyes and sat quietly for a moment. Not sure what was happening I looked to Kitar to find him wide-eyed. When he saw me looking, he motioned for me to return my attention back to the Angel.

When Gabriel opened his eyes again, he said, "Forgive the pause, I was looking at the history of your world during your life and death. I can see, and now more fully support, your anger out on the plaza. Many of these Republicans, you mention, had already offered their souls into The Dark Lord's service and had become his representatives."

"You mean like Demon possession?" I asked

"Not exactly. As much as I would like to feed into your teachings about how Lucifer works, I cannot. Not saying I approve of his tactics but he, like The Host, does have representatives on all the evolved worlds in Creation. I did not look into the motivation behind these souls agreeing to be possessed, but there appears to have been many in that party's leadership, possessed at the time. I am not sure what the opposing political faction was, but many of them were also Lucifer's minions. I can only imagine he did this to provide different types of stimuli to ensure your population chose one path over another."

"So most of the Republican Party and many in the Democratic party, as well, were possessed by representatives of Hell? And what is this path he was leading us down?"

"It was not just your politics being shaped; it seems battles were being waged on many fronts all over your world. Both The Host and Hell seems to have been actively manipulating activities there. I find this interesting since we had all but given up on your species some time back. As for why and what outcome Lucifer might have been wanting, I cannot say. But…" he paused and studied me, "it is possible, and this is only speculation, that the outcome he might have been working toward was a well-prepared vessel to tell his story. You have after all discovered he had a tapestry on you and was directing your experiences." Gabriel could see the anger surfacing in my eyes and smiled. "Calm down, little one. It is standard practice for both Hell and The Host to step in when we see potential in a soul or need to produce a specific type of person to help guide events of the time. Lucifer manipulated your life to prepare you for your potential arrival in Hell, just like we have manipulated others' to move a specific situation or society in a given direction. Like it or not, little one, the living are nothing more than the fuel which runs all of Creation in our eyes. The powers of The Host, like myself, would most certainly prefer not to have you talking monkeys stinking up The Eternal City but that does not change the fact we also do not wish Lucifer to get the upper hand. As much as you might not like to see the game which is being played, you have to keep in mind that to us, The Most High, it is little more than just that, a game. As for these politicians' motivation, you can ask them yourself when you reach Treachery. Most of them have ended up there. It also appears that two, one called Pence and another called Cruz where full fledge Demons. Those you can no doubt find in Pandemonium when you arrive there."

"So Pence was a Demon?"

"Is that not obvious to you by now? He believed and promoted the belief that the way The Father created a soul could be changed through torture, or as he called it conversion therapy. Have you not paid attention during your travels? Which side, The Host or Hell, chooses torture as the means to an end?"

I thought for a second. "So this all goes back to when Lucifer taught us the difference between good and evil? This manipulation thing?"

Now Elick jumped in. "It was not good and evil. That is an example of The Host interfering to change the story. Lord Lucifer taught the living how to think for themselves. How to objectively view both sides of a situation and draw their own conclusions. He taught them not to follow The Host blindly."

"I am not sure I would phrase it like that but to answer your original question, yes, he opened the door for interference, and we walked through as well."

"As was always the case, Lord Lucifer was leading the way," added Elick causing Gabriel to shake his head.

"I will not be getting dragged into that old argument tonight," snarked the Angel.

We sat for a while sipping our wine after that. I had mentally summoned the bug down from our room. Since I still hadn't gotten the Piaston story recorded I knew I was going to need assistance remembering all these conversations. After all, this was a very rare opportunity. To have an Angel, actually an Archangel, one of The Host ruling council willing to sit and let me ask questions, I wasn't passing up this opportunity.

To you, my dear readers, if you don't like the religious, blasphemous or intense parts of my journal you might as well skip the next few entries, in many places they tear down the very foundations of organized religion. I'll say before we start, if Creation followed this version, I guess what you'd call The Father's correct version then they would probably have more followers, souls in The Host and less hatred in all the Creations. To quote *All About Eve*, "Hang on, its going to be a bumpy night."

# Entry 198 – Religion

Leaning in and putting my elbows on the table, I asked, "Let's get the basics out of the way first. Remember I'm using my world's belief systems since that's all I know. If you want to expand your explanation to other cultures, please do. On Earth, there were many religions, but let's limit it to the main ones, Wicca, Christianity, Buddhism, Hindi, Judaism, Muslim, and Satanism. (I won't lie I threw that last one to see Gabriel's reaction.) Is any specific one the "right" one and if so how were we to know? And what happens to the other ones, in the end?"

Gabriel sat back and rested his left arm on the side of the chair, "First, Satanism is not one of The Father's religions, it's an atheistic religion, named as it was, to elicit a reaction, as you tried with me. As for the other ones and most societies are pretty much the same, at the basest level. In the beginning..." he smiled, "...pardon the pun, as civilization begins to build itself, it does so in little pockets. In your list Wicca, Buddhism, Hindi, Judaism, Christianity and a version of Muslim were all aspects of the true religion."

I started to say something, but he held up a finger. "Do not interrupt, it is rude. To begin with, there were many more aspects of The Father's teachings than the few you listed above. For our purposes and simplicity, we will limit the scope to these six, and you can extrapolate from there. The mistake most of your religions made, was to believe theirs was the only one. The Father did not plan it this way. Since the burgeoning civilizations had little to no contact or communications, representatives from The Host were sent to test each of the cultures. Those who showed promise were nurtured, those who did not, we helped to fail. This is another example of our earlier topic about The Powers stepping in to manipulate societies as we saw necessary. So each culture was given specific parts of The Father's teachings, no single one the complete story."

Seeing my look he went on to explain, "you must understand, with the limited intelligence of most of the living. There was no way a single culture could fully understand The Father's will. Therefore, he decided it best to give specific parts to each culture and let them grow into a full understanding of that aspect. Then in time they would travel to other cultures and share their part of the teachings allowing the two cultures to piece together an even greater understanding. The Father hoped this would help unite them with a common bond. Even if only a few of the cultures worked together, we expected some attrition over time as cultures died or were weeded out, then the remaining cultures would be able to fill in the missing parts since the concept was not that difficult. Also, and this is important, this was the 'proof' you living kept insisting upon. It would have proven, through many different sources, The Father's existence. We hear all the time how if we would have just confirmed our presence then you would have believed. Then you would have accepted not believed. If you had not closed your eyes to other cultures and just cross-referenced all these teachings, focusing on the similarities instead of the differences, most of which were added by the living, you would have seen the grand design and thus had the proof you so begged us for."

"Clearly that idea did not work," added Elick under his breath. He was speaking what I was thinking.

"Clearly. The Father had far more faith in his creations than most of us did. Therefore over time, instead of learning from each other, you did what many expected. You allowed your insecurities to close your minds and refused to believe anyone else could hold a part of the total truth."

I could not help myself. "You understand why, right?"

Giving me a look like I was an idiot, Gabriel said, "Because the living are justly insecure in their place in Creation and wanted to elevate themselves to the stature of those of us in The Host."

Leaning in, I replied, "You sound a lot like you believe what Lucifer believed. As I understand it, he didn't support The Father in his misguided belief that the living should be gifted with a soul. And correct me if I'm wrong, but more importantly, the ability to recreate."

For the first time I saw anger in the Archangel's eyes. "The living should have never...NEVER...been given the gift to procreate."

Tilting my head and locking eyes with Gabriel. "Why? Because it was making them too much like The Father or because it was elevating them above you, his firstborn?"

I swear the temperature in the room rose several degrees when our host replied, "Let me be clear. The living should never have been given the ability to recreate."

"I heard you the first time. What I'm trying to figure out is if you, one of The Father's still loyal followers, is saying he made a mistake. From all I've learned in my travels, is not what you just said exactly what Lucifer tried to tell The Father, who refused to listen. Is that not the entire reason for the Great War?"

"If you can understand, Lucifer led a self-indulgent war against Father. There were other options..." He slammed his hand on the table causing us all to rush to keep our goblets from falling over. "His actions cost many good Host their existence, not to mention he was attacking Father at his weakest."

I'd noticed Gabriel had now removed the 'the' from The Father's title and was simply calling him 'father.' "His weakest?" I asked.

"Yes, Father put a lot of love and care into Creation, sadly most times it did not work out as he had hoped."

"Oh, yes, I saw the collection Rumclique had on Lust."

"I have never been sure if that is a dedication to Fathers power's or a gallery of failure designed to remind him of the pain of his early work."

"The word is failure, not work. His early failures," corrected Elick.

The two exchanged very hard stares. "Based upon your earlier comments you as well didn't approve of the living having the ability to procreate. The same as Lucifer and the third of The Host. I don't understand why there was animosity."

Gabriel rose from his chair. He was almost screaming now. It might have been a scream of anger, but I don't think so. It seemed deeper, more pained. It was almost a cry of agony I believe. "They rose up against Father. Tried to overturn The Host and rebuild it in their image, ultimately causing him so much disappointment that he left..." Gabriel's voice dropped to almost a whisper as he collapsed back in his chair, "... and he has not returned." Silence overtook the room, when Gabriel finally looked up he met my eyes and added, "We miss him so..." He let his head drop till his chin rested on his chest.

I looked at Kitar; his eyes were trying to tell me to shut up, where Elick's were almost eager to see me continue to press my point. "Forgive me for asking, but I've heard that you above all others in The Host hate Lucifer the most. Is this true?"

In a defeated voice, he said, "He caused Father to leave. My Father, I will never...NEVER...forgive him for that."

There was silence for several minutes. I had many more questions, but at this point, I wasn't sure I should ask them. "What would have happened if the Great War had not happened?"

Looking up and wrinkling his brow, Gabriel asked, "What do you mean?" His voice still carried that tiredness.

"If Lucifer hadn't led the armies against The Father, Hell wouldn't have been created. If Hell wasn't created, where would the souls of the living have gone? From everything I understand they're not welcome in The Eternal City." At this point Elick leaned in, smiling.

"Father is all knowing and all seeing. He wanted to create the living to populate Creation and to worship him. Those of us who supported him...WITHOUT QUESTION... believed he would eventually tire of this little experiment. Then we, his true family, could eliminate the smell of you talking monkeys from Creation as a whole and return it to the way it was."

"All knowing and all seeing, but yet, if I understand you correctly, you're saying he would've eventually realized his MISTAKE and ceased his folly to create a new creature. Putting that aside, why did he feel he needed to create something new if he had The Host? No disrespect intended, but were you not what he wanted? Another failed experiment? And if the living were failed experiments as you say, why did he give them souls and the ability to recreate, something he hadn't given you?" I spoke softly; I was no longer on the attack. I felt like this was kicking a person when they were down. But I had to keep going; I had to know.

Shaking his head, I realized I'd been right; it wasn't anger I saw on the Angel's face. There was anger, but only around the edges, it was hidden behind the sadness. It was then I realized he didn't know the answer to these questions. And that for a being who can see and understand all must have been a private Hell in and unto itself. As much as Gabriel was a creature, which he was in the sense that The Father created him, he, like the rest of us did not understand why The Father did what he did. Why he left. Why he chose to let Lucifer live. Why he had not returned or for that matter made any contact. I was beginning to wonder, maybe The Father had decided this whole experiment was a failure, from Lucifer down to Creation. The entire show. Was there someplace else for him to go and start again, differently?

We'd gone as far as I felt comfortable going, so I picked up my goblet, finished the wine and carefully placed the cup on the table. Bowing to Gabriel to show respect, I said, "If you'll forgive me, this has been a long, taxing day. I'd like to retire for the evening. And if you're so inclined, might I have the honor of another interview? I would appreciate it."

Gabriel was now looking tired himself. "You should rest. There is still much for you to see. As for another interview, I will see what I can do."

Together, Kitar, Elick and I rose, bowed and started for the door. Stopping I turned back. "Lord Gabriel, I hope you understand I'm just a soul, of a once living creature, forced into an almost impossible position. I've been told to write about something, that until I awoke on the shores of the Judgement Plane, I didn't believe existed. I follow where my questions lead me. I in no way wish to disrespect you or The Host. To me, it sounds like we, the living, were given another unintended gift, that is death, where the questions for us are finally answered. You were left without warning and explanation. In life we lose people too; I'm not saying it is in any way equal to The Father leaving. As much pain as we might feel from that loss, and no matter how long that pain continues, sometimes for the rest of our lives, we know it will eventually end when we take our last breath. I cannot imagine what it must be like to be as powerful as you and have such painful lingering questions. I again thank you for your time and understanding." With that, I bowed, and we walked from the room.

# Entry 199

As Cemal pulled the door closed behind us, I looked over to find both Kitar and Elick staring at me shaking their heads.

"You never cease to amaze me," commented Kitar.

"The Dark Lord most certainly knew what he was doing. For a while there I saw no way for you to pull that conversation out of the fire, and then you turn completely around and do what the living do so well. Admit you do not know. That is the single thing, both Hell and The Host could learn from your kind. Admitting you do not know is not admitting defeat."

I nodded. They were giving the conversation way more thought than I had. Looking over at Elick and motioning, I said, "Let's go...now...to the room. I want news about Usis." I watched his response and knew instantly from the look he tried not to have, his news wasn't going to be something I wanted to hear.

When we got to the room, I went over and dropped down onto the sofa. I was exhausted and impatient, but I tried to stay calm and give them a chance to get situated. I was glad to see Cemal got it. He rushed in, filled a goblet and was at my side before I had a chance to realize wine was what I wanted. Elick grabbed two more bottles and joined us in the sitting area taking the chair across from me and started to pour the wine fastidiously. I think he was intentionally trying to drive me mad. Finally, after taking a sip, he said, "You are not going to like this."

In a sarcastic tone, I replied, "I've already figured that much out. But get on with it and don't leave anything out."

"After talking with my Great Grandfather, a meeting, I might add that went better than I had expected, I went up to see your companion. Well, and to be honest, I heard him before I saw him. He was screaming in agony. My first thought was that Grandfather (he explained he would be saying, grandfather because Great grandfather was just too much) was having him tortured. I raced to his room, drew my sword and threw open the door. What I saw next caught me off guard.

"His room stank and was humid and musty. They had the doors to the balcony open, but since Grandfather's Plane is as hot as this one, it did little for the room's climate. Standing inside the room on each side of the door were two guards with long pikes. Big burly fellows with massive, fleshy wings and misformed hooves. The pikes, each ten feet long, were standard issue.

"On the bed was Usis in a lot of pain. Due to the hide they had covering him I could not see his body. Turning to one of the guards, I asked, 'How long has he been like this?'

"Knowing who I was, the guard bowed. 'My Lord the soul became ill on its second day and has been growing steadily worse.'

'Did Great Grandfather have him tortured?'

'No, My Lord. The creature was showing discomfort, then on the second day collapsed and his body began to mutate.'

"I found it odd the guard used the word mutate. Walking over, trying not to show my concern I pulled the covers back. I think at this point it is important to remind you Usis was never conscious of my presence. I am not sure he was aware of anything."

I screamed, "Get on with it. Tell me about USIS, goddamnit."

Everyone froze for a second, surprised.

"I was wondering how long it would take you to snap." He leaned forward resting his elbows on his knees and set his goblet on the floor between his hooves. "He looked bad, Keith, I will not lie to you. I could tell it was him; he still looked familiar. Sweat and blood were rolling down the sides of his face, disappearing into his hair. The blood was from the open wounds on his forehead where those two knots had been, just below the hairline. Now there were two black horns which curved up, each about six inches long, coming to a sharp point. His ears, which I could barely see through the matted hair were now pointed. His entire body was scabbed over, from his hairline to his knees. When I pulled down the fur to expose his lower body I saw he now has the rough, I mean rough, emergence of clawed feet. It will probably be more like a dog's than our typical hoof. I could not yet tell if it was going to have fur since it too was scabbed over. The other was still roughly humanoid but the toes had dropped off. I have seen this before."

I was almost in tears hearing Usis' condition; one hand clutched the goblet, the other the side of the chair in a death grip. In a cracked voice, I asked, "You said the toes were gone on one foot but not the other?"

"Yes, but do not worry about that. If one leg changes the other will follow, of that, I am sure. The only other thing I noticed and cannot tell you what is going to happen, is his tail. It, like the rest of his body, was scabbed over. I know he had a tail to start, but now it is just a bloody raw string of muscles and cartilages. I could not tell what was happening there, he might keep it, or it might fall off." Stopping and looking over at me, he picked up the goblet. "As I said, he looked bad, very bad. I have heard of souls transforming; it is not uncommon. What we could not figure out and what Grandfather did not understand is Usis had none of the signs of a creature that would normally change. And the pain he was in, that is also uncommon, some other stimuli is causing this. If The Dark Lord was around, he might be able to help, but he is not in his Domain right now."

As worried and horrified as I was, I already knew what was happening and why. I hoped I was wrong and but I am pretty sure now. But I had to get rid of Kitar; I didn't have the strength right now to deal with his hysterics. I needed to send him away for a little while. Realizing what to do, I said almost too aggressively, "He has to be somewhere..." Shifting my eyes to Kitar I added, "You are technically my go between..." Looking at Elick, "...no disrespect..." back to Kitar, "So you go find Lucifer or someone and see if something can't be done...NOW." Kitar started to offer an objection, but I cut him off with, "NOW...OUT."

In a huff, Kitar bowed and left. "I will see what I can do. I should be back by morning," he said sadly as he walked out pulling the door closed behind him. I felt like shit for having been so short with him.

I turned to Elick. "Good, now that he's gone, I have a question and a possible revelation."

Raising an eyebrow, Elick replied, "Fine, what is the question? I will open another bottle of wine for the revelation."

"What could cause Usis to start changing?"

"Like I said, I don't know. It is not uncommon for severely evil souls to mutate into Demons but Usis does not fall into that category. Plus, this manifestation is more severe than anything I have ever seen or heard of. Even Great Grandfather did not know what could cause this."

Shaking my head, I said, "What if Usis ingested say a piece of a higher being?"

Eyes going wide, Elick murmured, "Maybe two bottles..." He stood and used magic to remove the corks then he returned to pour us drinks. While he filled our goblets, I found Usis's backpack and pulled out the box with the hearts in it. As he finished, I sat the box on the table and opened the lid, saying nothing.

Elick, for a long time, just stared at the two hearts, still slightly beating. "Are those what I think they are?"

I nodded then picked one up. "And this one has a bite out of it."

"Let me make sure I understand. Those are The Lover's hearts which your companion, I am guessing, removed while torturing them and am I correct in assuming he is the one who has been nibbling on them?"

"As far as I know," I answered as I finished my full goblet in one drink. For the record, so did Elick. He refilled both.

We sat in silence for a long while. Then he sat up and said, "Wow..." After finishing his next glass of wine he added, "You know that would also explain the suffering."

"How so? Please don't tell me he's dying. Well, Hell's form of dying."

"Of that, I am not sure. He very well could be."

"Shit. Is there anything we can do? Kitar has to find Lucifer now."

"I can tell you for sure Lucifer is not in Hell." As Elick chewed the inside of his lip, he reached down and picked up the heart with the bite out of it and closed his eyes. I saw a glow appear around his hand and the heart. "Interesting, it seems most of the energy of the Lover this heart belonged too is still contained within the organ." Raising a hand, he said, "Do not ask me why, I have no idea. How The Most High are made is beyond my pay grade, to use one of your world's sayings."

"But..." I prompted.

"But...there is a good chance what Usis is suffering from is energy depletion."

"I don't understand."

"Simply put, the energy from The Lover's heart jumpstarted the transformation. That energy has now been absorbed and his body is starving for more."

Quicker than Elick could respond, I grabbed a knife from an old plate sitting on the table and sliced off the tip end of the heart. A piece about two inches in diameter and about a quarter of an inch thick. "Take this to him then."

Elick sat back and just stared at me. "You are something else. That was a quick and decisive decision. I am impressed."

"Be impressed while you head back to the Seventh Plane. As an added incentive when we get Usis back we might reward you with a night you won't soon forget. But for now, will you please go feed this piece of an Angel's heart to my companion?" Pausing and rubbing my hand over my eyes, I said, "I can't believe some of the things that come out of my mouth anymore."

"Wait, so you are saying I am not going to be able to bed you until we get Usis back?" he asked.

"That is all you took from this? Seriously?"

He just shrugged. "With such incentives, of course, I will feed a piece of one of The Most High's heart to your companion. And for the record, that is even a strange statement in my book." I was still holding my hand out with the piece. "You mean now?"

I nodded.

# Entry 200

After everyone left, I sat alone for a long time just sipping wine, lost in thought. At some point much later, a knock came on the door scaring the shit out of me. As I got up to answer Cemal came racing from his room. "Sorry, Master, I will get it," he exclaimed as he opened the door, squeaked and dropped to his knees.

Gabriel was standing there. "May I come in?" he asked very nicely as he looked down at the boy. "You may stand."

I stood as well and bowed my head. "Of course, it's an honor to have you visit. I wasn't sure we were still on speaking terms after dinner."

He waved that away. "Please, I have spent an eternity dealing with Lucifer. Do you think a bit of cross-examination from a soul is going to spoil my day?"

Without looking, he extended his hand to the side and was correct to assume Cemal would already have a goblet poured and ready. He took it and smiled at the boy, who almost fainted. "He's never almost fainted from my nods," I observed.

"Give it time..." Gabriel motioned to the couch. "May I?"

"Yes, of course." I sat down after he did and smiled to myself as Cemal assumed a kneeling position to the left of my chair. "Forgive my bluntness. The day has been very taxing, and I'm a little tired and frazzled. What do I owe the honor of your visit?"

"A couple of things. First, I wanted to let you know, as I said before, I can see why Lucifer chose you. You seem to be walking a fine line between reporting what he wants while not choosing sides."

"I'm not sure that is true. I've found myself, more and more, questioning the overall competence of The Father and his ability to make decisions. If you'll forgive my honesty."

"Honesty is never a bad thing regardless of how wrong or, in this case, speculative the opinion might be. But if you must know, many have wondered the same thing, on both sides."

"That forces the question. Then what makes either side different?"

"Simple, we choose to stay loyal. He is our creator, and just as he demands loyalty from the living, he requires the same from us."

"I can understand that... but again I feel I must point out, if he demands loyalty then you're not staying loyal by choice...and the second."

He smiled as what appeared to be a guilty look crossed his face. "I could not help overhearing your discussion earlier." His eyes shifted to the now-closed box still sitting on the table."

"You were ease dropping. Has anyone ever told you that is rude?"

"Dear boy, it is part of the job assignment. We listen to what old ladies do in the privacy of their one-room shacks on dark nights when their husbands are away playing cards. Do you doubt we do not keep an eye on what is going on under our own roofs?"

"Tosha." I paused and took another drink. And yes, for the record, I was starting to feel all the wine. "So are you here to extract some kind of holy retribution on me?" Before he could speak, I went on. "Regardless of what you're here to do, don't even for a second think about harming my companion. He is under my charge and therefore I'll take any negative ramifications from his or our actions."

Shaking his head, Gabriel replied, "That is very loyal of you but do not worry. I am not here to bring divine wrath down upon you or him, for that matter."

"Then why exactly are you here?"

"Again, right to the point. To answer your question about those..." He pointed to the box, "Yes, if your companion ate a piece of the heart it would explain his condition."

"But it sounds like he is changing into a Demon. Why? It was an Angel's heart."

Gabriel hissed like a cat. "It was a Fallen's heart and the energy contained therein is nonspecific. It pulls from its environment..." He paused, then added, "and the proclivity of the creature who consumed it."

"Are you saying Usis wanted to be a Demon?"

"Not necessarily. Having viewed his past with you..." He paused and raised a hand. "Do not ask, trying to explain how we see time would take eons. Nonetheless, he probably did it wanting to protect the two of you, and here in Hell he probably thought it would just make him stronger."

"If you saw his past, then you saw what happened on the Second Plane. How much stronger does he need to be?"

"Yes, I saw that, and much more you do not know about..."

"All of which I'm guessing you won't reveal to me?"

"See you are getting smarter. That is his responsibility, not mine."

"Anyway."

"He probably did not realize how drastic consuming such a strong power source laced with an incredible amount of Father's creative spark was and what it would do to him. You did the right thing by sending the Hellspawn to give him more. It will be interesting to see what happens next."

"I thought you could see through time. You don't know?"

"No, it does not work that way. If he were still living I could, if I was that interested, but now that he is in the abomination's domain, he is outside our jurisdiction."

"But you saw his past."

"That is now written into the fabric of Creation, plus I have been in Hell for a while. Had I not already been here it would not have been as easy to eavesdrop, as you call it."

"So, you can see the past and future of living. The past and future of those in The Host and the past of those in Hell if you happen to be around?"

"That is a simplified version but yes."

"That leads me to my next question," I added.

"Which is?"

"Why are you telling me all of this?"

"That should be obvious. I am both curious and concerned about what might happen if your companion continues to consume the heart."

"It has nothing to do with this possibly causing The Dark Lord a massive headache, does it?" I said with a half-smile over the top of my goblet.

"That, young one, is simply a bonus," Gabriel answered, returning my devious smile.

I eyed him carefully. "I thought you were the wholesome ones? That seems devious."

Smiling and taking another sip, he replied, "We all have our reasons, but if you must know I like you. What you did back in the dining room shows style. You knew when to push and when to back off. More importantly, you showed respect. I like that."

"Still, possibly pissing Lucifer off is also a big part of it."

He clanked my glass, adding, "And you are observant, as well." Finishing his goblet and then handing it to Cemal who was now standing, Gabriel rose. "Now, if you will excuse me. I have some matters that need attending."

I also rose and then bowed. "It was a pleasure to have you visit. Please feel free to drop by anytime. I'm sure I can think of more questions."

As he walked out, I heard him say, "Of that, I have no doubt."

# Entry 201

Like my mind hadn't been preoccupied enough already after Gabriel left I couldn't seem to settle it down enough to sleep or even rest. It wasn't until I heard a loud bang that I was brought back to the moment. Instantly on alert, I looked up only to find Cemal straightening up. The noise was apparently an attempt to get my attention.

I watched as he removed the empty bottles, cleaned the goblets and tidied up the table. As I studied his little body, which I still thought was wonderfully Demonish and sexy, an idea hit me. "Cemal could come here for a second?"

Setting down the rag, he came over and knelt beside the chair. Shaking my head, I motioned to the couch. "I want your advice, and when I ask such favors, you are not my servant but a friend and therefore will be treated as such."

With a little smile he tried to hide, he rose and took a tentative seat on the couch. "How may I help you, sir?"

"I was thinking about something Usis once told me when we first met. That one of the servant's job was to be invisible in plain sight. I never really understood what he meant until I realized you'd been here for almost all of the conversations that have occurred since you joined our little group. That led me to two thoughts. First, and I know I don't need to remind you this, but you swore allegiance to me above all others. Now don't think you've done anything wrong, you haven't, quite the opposite, you've been amazing. The reason I'm asking is I need to know if there is anything that has occurred when I wasn't here that I should know about?"

Cemal mouth made several strange movements, and then he said, "Sir, and this one does not feel he is betraying any trusts. Everyone in your 'little group' as you call it is very loyal to you. Master Kitar barks a lot…" he giggled, "…but has said several times that though he might not always agree with your decisions, they seem to be serving you the best considering the situations in which you have found yourself. As for Master Usis, this one has not been with him or the two of you other than the brief time during my interview. That being said, it was obvious during our talks just how much he loved and cared for you, Master. His eyes, concerns, and soul are only for you. When it comes to Lord Elick, he wants to bed you so badly his sizable Hellspawn balls are about to explode." He smiled as I turned a couple of shades redder. "Does that answer Master's questions?"

"Yes."

"And the second question, sir?"

"This heart thing, I'm sure you heard the conversation with Elick and Lord Gabriel. What are your thoughts?"

"Thoughts about what?"

"Usis, and what he probably did with these hearts. I know we haven't had a chance to sit down and talk. At some point, since you are part of our team, I'll need to interview you and get your story, but right now I need to focus on this Plane and getting my companion back. That is why if anyone knows anything that can help I need to be told. I can't have secrets when it comes to what Usis might be going through."

Nodding his understanding, Cemal said, "Master, as far as my backstory there isn't one. This one was created here in Hell and have served ever since." I started to say something, but he held up a finger to stop me, causing me to raise an eyebrow. "Oh sorry, sir..."

"No go ahead, my reaction was more to the fact you felt comfortable enough to do that. Which is good."

"Oh, thank you, sir, but this one will not overreach. Having served under several lords of Hell, and having seen numerous transformations, this one can say with some certainty that your companion will no longer be who he was. Do not get me wrong, sir, he will most probably still be who he was inside, though that will change over time due to his new senses and understandings. That is just a guess, Master. His body will change, as clearly it has already started to do."

"How can you be so sure?"

"Master, using bits of higher beings is how creatures like myself are created. Now normally in cases where they create a servant class, such as myself, the higher being might only be the souls of the living, never someone as exalted as that of an Angel or Fallen. If Master Usis consumed the heart of a Fallen, as you think, his transformation should be more extreme."

"In what ways?"

Shaking his head, "Master, sadly there is no way to know. As Master Elick said, Lord Leviathan was even at a loss as to what was happening. This one is basing his guesses purely on having seen creatures like myself and those of slightly higher stations created while working in my creator's lab. This one is not an expert, Master."

I smiled what I hoped was a gentle smile. "I wanted your opinion, and that is what you gave, and for that I'm thankful. If you don't mind, I need to get some writing done. Could you get me another bottle and bring it to my desk?"

Standing, smiling and then bowing he said, "Right away, Master."

"One second, I have one more question."

"Yes, Master?"

"Do you enjoy what you do? I mean being a servant. Are you happy?"

Making one slow nod ending in a bow he answered, "In you, Master, there is little more a servant could hope for. This boy has had vicious and cruel Masters in the past; you are neither. Just to ask this one if he is happy is more than one could have ever imagined. It is a great honor to serve you, and yes indeed, this one is happy." I nodded as he turned and went to get my wine.

# Entry 202

When I awoke the next morning, I found Kitar sitting in the living room. I could tell from his demeanor that his mission, if you wanted to call it that, was a failure.

"I take it you didn't find our Boss?" I asked sitting down taking a glass of warmed wine from Cemal.

"No, and I did not expect to, you do not seem to understand. Lord Lucifer is NOT in Hell."

Deciding this line of conversation wasn't going to go anywhere, I settled for honesty, "I know, I only sent you away because I was tired and needed to talk to Elick about a suspicion I had and did not have the energy for your hysterics. If I'm right, Usis should be feeling better soon, well at least temporarily."

Looking over his glass, Kitar asked, "Is this the kind of information you should share with your guide?"

"If my guide is not acting like a complete dick and promises he won't blow it all out of proportion like he tends to do."

"I most certainly do not."

I was about to respond when we heard Cemal snort from behind us. Looking at Kitar, I smirked, "I rest my case."

Kitar was about to start again when I reached over and flipped open the lid to the box which clearly, he had not bothered to look in. His mouth moved up and down several times as his eyes went wide. "Please tell me those are not what I think they are."

"Well unless you think they are something other than The Lovers hearts then I'll be able to do that."

"Why are they here?" He started moving down the couch like he didn't even want to be near them.

"It appears Usis ripped them out while he was seeking retribution for the tortures they heaped upon us."

Never taking his eyes off the hearts, which were very slowly beating. Beating is probably the wrong word. Just every so often they would do a single pulse and then stop. "Explain to me how these have anything to do with Usis' condition."

"You don't know? I thought you knew everything."

Looking me in the eye, he said, "Do you want me to do that to you?"

I quickly looked down, "No and you better never do it." Since this conversation was moving into the uncomfortable territory, I decided to get it back on point, so I reached down, picked up the left heart and showed Kitar where it was missing a bit.

His eyes went wider. "What happened to that heart?"

"Well, actually two things. The first, it appears, Usis ate a bit of it." He started to scream something, but I interrupted, "Before you go off the deep end, something you promised not to do. The second event to happen to this heart is I cut a piece off, which Elick is taking to the Seventh Plane to feed my companion in hopes it will ease his suffering. Since we are pretty sure…" I didn't get to finish; he did that for me and at the top of his lungs."

"His feeding on the heart is what started his transformation. Oh, my fucking god of…." He continued to curse, throw his arms in the air and stomp around the room. I don't know what he said after 'fucking god of' because he changed into a language I didn't understand, and it seemed Hell wasn't willing to translate. I sat back while he raged. I know I should've been worried or upset, but I was just amused. Not at what Kitar was doing but instead at watching Cemal race in front of the pissed off Judge grabbing things off the tables and running away with them so Kitar didn't have anything to start throwing.

Finally, he made it back around to the couch and sat down. The hurricane, or at least this part of it, had blown itself out. "Are you better?" I asked. Which for the record was the wrong question, it got him started again.

I watched Cemal watch Kitar carry on for another several minutes. If you're wondering what he was saying or the point he was making; you're asking the wrong person, I wasn't listening. I was too busy with important things, which was watching our servant shake his head and throw out a single word or a question which acted as fuel to keep Kitar at full burn. When the storm had run its course the second time, I merely asked, "You're familiar with the word Queen right? You're such a drama queen when you get like this."

I guess that was just what was needed, he huffed, threw himself on the couch like a duchess just being told she wasn't getting this season's shoes and turned to me. "This is tragic."

"Why?" before he got started again I added, "explain, exactly, calmly and succinctly."

"Your companion is now going to be a Demon. You understand that, correct?"

"Yes, but as it was explained to me, his personality probably will not change very much."

"Who told you that? He is going to be feared. He is going to have powers, who knows how much power. He has eaten the heart of one of The Host...Oh My Lord...."

Calmly I said, "Kitar, your starting again." He huffed once more.

Taking the offered goblet from Cemal, he finally turned to me. "So what are we going to do?"

"I need to go see the Forest out front. Let's do that; it will take your mind off all the other things."

"Other things..." he growled as he walked off toward his room. Just before he vanished, I heard him say, "What did I do? I was made a Judge and suffered years of other's horrors because of my sins while living. What, dear sweet Dark Lord did I do to be assigned to him? How..."

As the door shut behind him cutting off the rest of the sentence. "Well that went well, Master," I heard Cemal say as he collapsed on the floor, holding his stomach, laughing causing me to start as well.

# Entry 203

After getting dressed I walked out on the balcony and let the heat and the sulfur smell wash over me. I stood there looking out at the forest of souls I was about to visit. I reminded myself not to miss the small things. It was becoming easier the longer I was in Hell. It's so easy to become engrossed in this place, its sheer size, the enormity of the Keep, the ruling bodies on both sides, the weight of the sins encapsulated in the masses of souls. I need to continually remind myself you aren't here, as De Sade told me, it's my writing's job to drag you down here with me.

As we walked down the steps of the Keep Kitar was quiet. As we reached the bottom, we ran into one of Cherubim I'd not yet met. We greeted each other and just as I was about to walk off I asked, "I'm about to visit the Forest of Pain for the first time. It will be my introduction to Blasphemy and what it means. If you could give me one thought to carry with me, what would it be?"

He thought for a second, then answered, "I can see you are from Earth. To quote the book used on your world, "Allow me, then, this day, to show you, first, the great enormity of the sin of blasphemy; and secondly, the great rigor with which The Father punishes it." He smiled, bowed and walked off.

This was a quiet day. I'm not sure if we were caught up in the troubles and dramas of our travels or if it was this place. The juxtaposition of walking from The Host's realm, contained inside the Keep, out into Hell's horrors, which surrounded it like a ring of bullies, seems to have left me both disoriented and a bit uneasy.

I stood at the top of the steps and cringed as the massive Keep doors slammed shut behind me. I closed my eyes to block out the visual allowing me to adjust myself to the now familiar sounds and feelings from the cries and pain.

When I took the first step down I heard from over my shoulder, "Here are those who sinned against The Father. Sins against the living hold no sway here." It was Kitar.

We walked down the steps and along the path we'd taken as we arrived on this Plane. Halfway through I stopped, "Should we just turn in? How does this work?"

Again from behind me, I need to start paying more attention, I heard the same voice I'd just met, the Cherubim. I raised an eyebrow. "I hadn't intended for you to accompany us."

"Lord Gabriel suggested you might need a guide who understood this Plane and its intricacies."

"Agreed. So now I'll direct to you the question I just asked Kitar. Do we just turn in?"

Taking the lead, he said, "There is a path right here allowing us to enter the souls' domain."

As we turned off onto the path and stepped into the pillars of suffering, the posts that impaled the souls, the light faded. The already normal gloom was made darker, and it became a challenge to see. There were fires, the blue dancing flames of the sulfurous stones scattered about the landscape as well as small fissures where flames would occasionally flare up. But still it wasn't enough to light our way; it was like they didn't want to shine too brightly for fear they would also be subjected to the suffering that surrounded them. Then with a simple snap of his fingers, the cherubim caused fire pots to burst to light. I know I shouldn't have smiled, but I found it interesting how they wasted no opportunity to torture. Though the braziers ran along the sides of the path, each was still positioned at the base of one of the impaled souls, thus burning its feet. As we stepped into the Forest of Pain, I also noticed how the sound shifted to something like a chorus of tiny flies on a warm day in the southern swamps, just a low hum of moans. I would grow louder the further in we went.

"What is your name? I assume you have one," I asked.

"Yes, it is Cleosdege."

"Fine, I'll call you Cleo. Both of you give me a second I want to take in what is happening around me before you both start talking to excess."

I noticed them look at each other as Kitar just shrugged. Why I wanted to watch is because you'd expect a bunch of souls impaled on spikes to be a very still event, but you'd be wrong. First, let me give you a rundown of what was happening to the specific soul I was watching. The creature was humanoid, about my height, from what I could tell, after all, she was bayonetted on a spike. As I just said, it was a female and appeared to be a humanoid version of a frog with four long saggy breasts. She was impaled upon a roughly ten-foot-tall pole that was about the same diameter as a rounded 4x4 fence post. The post itself entered through the anus, traveled up the back and out just to the side of the head near the collarbone. This allowed the head, arms, and legs to move freely, which they did, as her cries of pain added to the din of the forest around us. Lastly, the creature was almost entirely encased in an undulating bush of thorns. Sometimes the bush would merely be wrapped around the creature's legs and then like a flame catching on a scarecrow it would explode upwards, encasing the creature, wrapping it tightly as the many thorns pushed their way into the soul's greenish mottled skin. The barbs themselves ranged from an inch to a foot or longer and were as varied in thickness as they were in length. Though there was no wind, the entire bush moved and shifted continually causing the thorns to slide in and out, back and forth, tearing at the soul's skin, undulating and jabbing like a horny teenager having their first intercourse. With each puncture, the clear pinkish nectar of suffering would ooze out and drip down onto the hard rocky ground. Now multiply that by millions, and you get the idea of why I called this area The Forest of Pain.

Looking down the path as I took in the size of this area, I asked, "All these souls are people who led their congregations astray?"

"No, those are reserved for greater suffering. These are the souls who in the course of their lives misrepresented The Father's words thus bringing sadness, pain and often self-hate upon those they wished to diminish."

I tilted my head slightly. "So these are the cult people like David Koresh?"

With a look of disgust, he paused as he closed his eyes. When he opened them, he said, "I needed to see to whom you were referring. And yes, that is an excellent example. The leader led his flock down a path by praying upon their hatreds and insecurities. Had he achieved more notoriety, he would be suffering the same fate as those who commit the Great Blasphemies. But overall his effect were minor but still worthy of note. From your world, we got (I noticed the past tense) a lot of cult leaders. They had a great impact on the lives they touched but did not cause a larger ripple in the greater scheme of things. This area is reserved for them, those who chose to misinterpret The Father's words repeatedly in an attempt to make themselves feel important or to harm. These are the believers who wielded The Father's teachings as a weapon instead of a tool of enlightenment."

I nodded as we started down the path, "What are the thorns? They seem to have a mind of their own."

"An astute observation. They, in fact, have several minds of their own. They are the souls the crucified sinner led to hell through their words. They are the souls who fell because they chose to believe another's interpretation over their own ability to read, meditate and understand The Fathers word's for themselves."

"First, why are they thorns? And secondly, why tie them for eternity to the soul who led them astray?"

"It is quite simple. They are now thorns, so they can help us punish the one they put before their Father's words. As you see, at times the thorns are small, then grows to its full size. This is also a representation of their choices in life. They started out as babes in The Father's words but often grew to become false prophets, spreading the false teachings. Thus, these sheep have lain eternally at the feet of the shepherd they chose instead to follow."

"I don't understand. Don't most souls who were led astray, lead others astray themselves?

"In most cases you are correct, that is why there are far more thorns than crucified souls. These souls did not take the time to read and learn for themselves, thus trusting, incorrectly, the words of the creature that damned them. Where the ones on the post knew they were misrepresenting The Father's words, and still for their own personal reason chose to wield those teachings as a weapon to lead others down a misguided path."

"Are you telling me that if a parent misleads a child about The Father's teachings, the child will end up here?"

"Not necessarily. Age must be taken into consideration. If the child is under the age of accountability, then whatever they were taught or chose to believe is irrelevant. If they die before becoming aware or accountable, it will not matter since they would not have a soul yet and therefore would not join us in eternity. After such time as they do become responsible if they then continue to live by their earlier teachings, knowing full well The Father's correct beliefs are available to them, then yes, they would arrive here."

We continued to walk down the path. I passed a bizarre looking creature, look up a monkfish then give it a brawny torso, four arms, four legs and ears like a cocker spaniel. This one's mouth was open in a constant silent cry. Why silent I wondered. Looking closer, I realized I could see the stake, which impaled it, visible in the back of its throat; someone had aimed wrong when placing it. It's many arms and legs spasmed while hundreds of little thorns jabbed and poked its flesh as suffering dripped from its toes. Only then in the shadow of this creature's silence did all the others cries come again into focus. For a while, they'd faded into the background. Not because the conversation was stellar, or they'd stopped, it was merely because after so many years in this place the sounds of suffering had become like that old fan, nothing more than white noise. The sound still there but unnoticed.

At one point I stopped, the posts from here to the cliff face off in the distance were many different sizes. The ones closest to us were tiny. The creatures, what looked like fairies were no more than a foot tall. The post may be a quarter of an inch in diameter. As the creatures got bigger so did the columns from which they hung. Near the back where the souls were easily as big as a Demon, a dozen feet tall or larger some of the posts were as big around as my waist. It was like walking through an old growth forest.

# Entry 204

The Cherubim stopped me and pointed down a small path leading deeper into the forest. It looked spooky. "If we go up this path we will start encountering souls with more serious sins. The path we are currently on ends, as you can see, at the mountains and all the sins are of the same severity."

Kitar reached out to grab me but was too late. The next thing I knew my eyes were briefly filled with a black fog, and I was submerged into a landscape I didn't recognize. This wasn't where I'd just been; this wasn't Hell.

I now stood in a meadow. It was night; there were crickets chirping as fireflies languidly bounced around in the blue and green expanse. I thought I felt a breeze brush my face and that was confirmed when I heard the leaves in the trees nearby rustle. I looked around, the landscape was a swamp like back home but in many ways very different. The undersides of large mushrooms as tall as buildings hung over the blue trunks of the moss-laden trees. The bases around the mushrooms were aglow with a soft light. All around, the trees tingled with fluorescence that reflected off the water. An odd shaped bird swooped down pulling a growling fish from the water then flew back up into the canopy.

Where was I? I saw different trees off in the distance, more like willows. This place reminded me of World of Warcraft. Great now I was in a game. Hell, with as many people who played it, at this point, I wouldn't have had a problem believing Blizzard (registered trademark) was an extension of The Dark Lord's domain. For some reason that caused me to think about how much I wanted to be a blood elf. Oh, that means Illidan Stormrage would be around, boy I'd like to get a piece of that. Ok wait, I digress.

As quickly as I popped into the vision, I popped out. If you caught that last sentence, then I told you what happened. It was a vision. The reason Kitar grabbed me was an attempt to pull me out of the path of a Wraith, yes clearly, they do exist. It was an evil looking creature made of smoke with deep red glowing eyes. As it moved through the forest, it passed through me, or maybe more accurately I through it. When this happens, I learned I get to see their world briefly. All I can tell you is I plan to find another and try it again. It wasn't that horrible. Actually, if you knew it was going to happen, it was pretty cool.

"Are you alright?" Kitar asked. I nodded, and he proceeded to explain what I just told you. Sadly, I learned that not all visions are the same, some can be quite bad. It's dependent upon the soul used to create the Wraith's programming. It seems the creators get to pick the type of experience the victim will experience from the specter.

It appears that some Wraiths spread happiness, while others pain, anxiety, and suffering. This is done so the souls the creature encounters sometimes suffer worse fates than their own while other times they are given a relaxing vision like the one I had. When they burst back into their reality, impaled on a post or part of a giant briar bush the pain they feel is reset anew and thus the suffering is even more palatable. Kitar told me creatures like the Wraith are created on both the Seventh and Eighth Planes in the labs of Hell's alchemists. We will be sure to visit that place, well if I survive to get there.

It was again a very creative way to remind the souls of what they'd given up or could've had if they'd lived a different life. Signaling I was ready, we continued down the path when again I stopped. (I know I keep getting distracted, but lots of things are going on) I had to strain to see what was moving deep back in the sea of blasphemers on a stick. I wasn't sure if I was seeing anything or just imagining it. What I thought I was seeing was a plant. I heard the Cherubim start to say something but again motioned for him to be quiet. The creature...plant...was tall, maybe seven feet and thin. Its arms were just vines, and instead of legs, it moved along on roots. I swear I'd seen a creature like this in the Rumclique collection. In the center of its shoulders, where a head should be, was just a curved neck ending in a giant jagged-toothed mouth.

I watched as the plant creature wiggled and weaved its way through the posts, ripping parts of thorn bushes out of its way, eating them, as it drew closer. Lifting my eyes, I realized there were more than one. Actually looking around, now that I knew what to look for I could see dozens moving through the forest. At times one would stop and run its tentacles along the impaled creature, then move on. To make matters worse, I noticed a herd of those little rat creatures that have been present on every Plane clustered behind, following along.

Looking to my guides, the Cherubim pointed for me to watch. I turned back to see one of the plant beasts run its tentacles up a creature's side. This time it didn't move on. It paused, then ran its arms further up. Stopping it shuddered in what appeared to be delight. Its neck mouth shot forward and tore a chunk out of the creature's side. The neck continued to expand longer than it had looked initially as it tunneled deeper into the impaled soul's torso. I could tell it was eating the creature from the inside; chunks were traveling down the plant's neck as it swallowed. As you would imagine the impaled soul was screaming bloody murder. I could only imagine the pain.

Slowly the plant devoured the main body of the creature, at first one leg, then the other, then an arm, and the other falling away to be pounced on by the little rat creatures. As the neck again emerged covered in the viscera of the now destroyed soul, it moved up to the head and in one bite ripped it off the post, chewed and swallowed it.

I turned pale and bent over putting my hands on my knees trying not to throw up. When I could talk again, I asked, "You cannot tell me that soul is still in existence. Oh wait, did it go to that damn Hatchery I keep hearing about?"

Cleo answered, "No, it resides in the Xitra (the plant creature) until it can hold no more and then it goes down to be disposed of in the furnaces."

"Does it just randomly pick its victims?" I asked as I saw off in the distance another creature start to be devoured.

"No, it only chooses souls that are almost used up. It makes room for new souls," he said as he pointed toward where the one had been devoured. Now the post stood empty; already I could see the thorns begin to wither and decompose.

Kitar pointed up. I looked up just in time to see the roof creature capture another soul in one of its tentacles. I watched as the entrapped creature moved closer, all the time gaining speed. The massive beast on the ceiling constantly making minor adjustments as they grew closer to the post. Then, as I cringed, the soul was slammed down onto the spike, with such a disturbing sound that we all three winced from the impact. The cry from the now impaled soul as the post entered its anus and traveled through its body and out, just beside its head, temporarily muted all the other noises around me. I watched in sick fascination as the tentacle released its victim and with a quick motion opened a gash along the soul's back. Blood started to flow, well actually suffering, and spilled out onto the ground. As it was absorbed into the stone new brown buds began to spring up. They quickly began to grow into the bush that would eventually house the thorns of the misguided followers who would torment the damned shepherd until it too was used up and consumed.

"Wait I don't understand. I thought you said the thorns are the many souls influenced by the soul on the stake. Why is the bush springing from its suffering?" I asked.

"Simple, as you will see..." Cleo explained. I'm waiting to tell you about this until we get to that part of the Plane. I've not seen what happens, though I've been told. Kitar recommended I wait to document it. I tend to agree.

I watched as another soul was eaten. It truly was intense. The Xitra that was nearest worked its way toward us. "Are we safe?" I asked.

"Yes, you are of no interest to it," answered Cleo.

Sure enough, when it got within touching range, it stuck out its toothy neck, which I might add stunk horribly, sniffed all three of us and moved on. Its body, which initially looked like multi-colored leaves were, in fact, millions of tiny thorns and the faces of the souls it had devoured.

"Let me guess, those souls continue to suffer while entrapped inside the Xitra," I asked.

Smiling Cleo said, "Not only do they continue to be digested, which I would imagine is painful. They suffer not only their pain but the pain of all the other souls imprisoned within the Xitra." Seeing my face, he added, "Think of it as a cancer which slowly consumes the Xitra, once it is full and can no longer perform its duty it is disposed of."

"Is the Xitra a damned?"

Shrugging, "Souls are used when creating the Xitra so in some respects it could be considered conscious and possibly damned since it suffers an unending hunger which ensures it keeps searching for expended souls to devour. They are created on in the labs on the Seventh and Eighth Planes. Creatures like the Xitra and your familiar are both produced in those facilities."

"Damn, you guys are serious about their suffering," I said shaking my head. Then that last part of what he said struck me, "My familiar?"

Cleo looked first at Kitar and then back at me. "Yes, the familiar that serves you currently."

To Kitar, I asked, "What's he talking about; I have a familiar?"

"Cemal. Cemal is a familiar class Demon."

"There's a classification for him?"

"Of course, all the lower types of created Demons fall into classifications. Cemal is a servant class and general assistant. They are known as familiars. If it helps, Cemal is a higher level familiar. The lower level ones are the ones sent into Creation to serve high ranking living souls," answered Kitar as I just stood there with a dumb look on my face.

I started to say something to Kitar as Cleo began to walk toward the next area he wanted to show us. For some reason, I noticed movement above me. That's not really uncommon, creatures, both Demon and otherwise are always flying around. But for some reason, I knew who this was. It was Elick, and he was back. "This tour will have to continue at another time. I'm needed at the Keep," I said as I ran off, not giving them a chance to stop me.

# Entry 205

I was back in our room by the time Elick landed. I swung the doors to the balcony open as his foot touched down. Our eyes met. He smiled. I knew it had worked, which meant our suspicions had also been confirmed. Then my knees gave out. Usis, my love, my companion, my partner, had been consuming an Angel's heart. He lied to me, back in the bed that day when he said he didn't know why he was changing. He knew what he was doing and what it was doing to him. To us.

Elick reached down and picked me up, effortlessly taking me to the couch. After he set me down, he went and poured us both a drink. When he returned, handing me my goblet, he merely said, "He did it to protect you."

I looked up in tears. Those simple six words were like a gut punch. He was in eternity. There was no going back from this. His entire existence hung in the balance and he did it to protect me. I cried. I cried hard. I hadn't cried like this since I left the Second plane. All I've seen, the horrors, none of that mattered if Usis wasn't beside me.

"He should not be in this place," I said, motioning around me with my hand.

Inclining his head, Elick replied, "On this occasion, I cannot say I disagree."

Lifting my eyes from the glass, I went on. "Do you think Lucifer is responsible for him being here? Him meeting me. Him being who he is, was, what he's becoming?"

Taking a drink, Elick answered, "I would say he did not arrange for Usis to come to Hell. He would not have arranged for you to come to Hell either."

"I saw the Fates, the tapestry."

"Keith, that was him shaping you, that is all. We do not know how many others might have been traveling down that same path but at some point either took a different road or you beat them here."

"But why me, how would he pick me?"

"His relationship with time, like all The Powers, is complicated and I do not doubt that he set a series of parameters and your name came up. Just like what you would do with a computer. He probably went forward to look at possible outcomes and decided you carried the highest probability. Therefore, he set in motion the engines needed to shape you. That does not mean he decided your fate; they don't work that way. Yes, he might have prodded you along. Offered you options that were attractive to help you choose the path he wanted you to follow but then all of The Powers do that. The living are the playthings of those like us. You do not have to like that, but there is also nothing you can do about it."

"So you don't think he damned Usis to come to Hell to manipulate me?"

"Do you hear yourself? How big is your ego? Usis was here, by his own accord. With that being said, I would almost guarantee Lucifer saw the potential of what Usis could become to you and in that arranged for you two to meet. You can see that as manipulation, or you can see that as him giving you a wonderful gift. Usis for eternity. So did he arrange it, in some ways? Probably yes."

I looked around several times trying to find my words. Finally, I asked, "Do you think it's wrong of me to say I am glad about that?"

"No...I know this place. I have no delusions about what it is. You needed, we all need, someone we can count on here. For you that is Usis." I met his eyes. "Yes, for me it was, or is Xia and the other Hellspawns in our group."

We sat in total silence until the door burst open and Kitar came marching in already yelling. Elick's head popped around, and for the first time I saw Hellspawn anger in his face, he snapped, just snapped, yes with his fingers, and Kitar could no longer speak. Sort of anti-climatic, but it worked. The gravity instantly sank in, and our former judge came around and took a seat. I swear he looked like a puppy you'd just scolded.

"Give him back his voice; he'll behave," I said then looking at Kitar added, "Won't you?"

Elick didn't do anything this time. The snap had been for our benefit.

In a quiet voice, Kitar asked, "What has happened?"

"As you know I took a slice of one of The Lover's heart down to Usis. He was suffering badly, and we thought it might help. Plus, we needed to confirm that it had been him who had taken the bite. So I temporarily calmed his pain, just enough to get one answer from him," explained Elick. Then turning to me he said, "he said he did consume the heart. So I pulled the piece and gave it to him. He ate it hungrily. The change was instantaneous. His body relaxed, his pain subsided, and he became fully lucid."

I fell back on the couch, relaxing. "This is a temporary fix. I guess my next question is, is there a way to reverse it?"

"Probably not," answered Elick.

"Lord Lucifer could step in. I am sure he could reverse the effect, but I am not sure we should ask him," added Kitar.

"To be honest, I'm not sure I want to. Did Usis give you any indication why he did this?"

"Once he started to feel better I asked that very question. You should not be surprised as to why he did what he did. As I said earlier, it was to protect you. After the attack by the Lovers and the growing intensity of the Planes, he felt you guys needed a little more protection."

"They have both you and myself," snarked Kitar.

"True, but Usis feels that Keith and himself will not always have high powered retainers around them and need to start thinking about how to protect themselves. To be honest, he has a point. I am not sure I would have suggested the path he has chosen, but then, as we all know, here in Hell you have to take what you are given and learn to use it or be destroyed," explained Elick.

Kitar and Elick continued to discuss the subtler points of Usis' decision. I sat quietly; I didn't care what he did, it was why. I understood what he was thinking and sadly he's right. We were now in eternity, and thanks to my writing our choices had expanded from two to three. We could end in the furnaces, return to our original suffering or find a way to survive in this new landscape in which we've found ourselves.

Cemal walked over and filled my glass; I was holding it on the arm of the chair beside me. I looked up when he finished finding them all staring at me. "You know what I'm going to say. We need to get there. We need to find out what your fucking Great-Grandfather intends to do and we need to rescue my lover. If him eating that heart and growing into something that can bust its way out of that place and return him to me is the only way then all I can say is more power to him."

Kitar started to say something, but I stopped him, "I know, we can remain who we are, or we can become a monster. That's easy for someone to say who's already had the decision made for them. You're one of those monsters. You walk around here proud, confident in the power having become that monster has made you. So don't lecture me about keeping my soul. I know the status of my soul. It's here in Hell and its either time to adapt and learn to survive or become yet another suffering soul in the hands of those who rule this place."

I saw Elick nod his approval. It was Kitar again who broke the silence. "You are right. As Elick said, I am not sure your companion's course of action was the best, but it was all he had. He did what he needed to do. Since there is no turning back, we move on. He is part of our family and therefore, no one shall stand between us and getting him back."

It was my turn to nod approval. "Thank you. Even if you don't fully believe what you've just said you're at least starting to realize what I've tried to build from the start. We're a group; we stick together, it's not my fight to survive, it's not yours, it's ours. Let's call it a night, I need to make notes about what I saw today and tomorrow I want to get to the next part of this Plane. The only thing keeping me sane right now is my writing." Holding up a finger, I said, "But do not worry, I'm not rushing or skipping anything but I'm also not going to sit around and waste time. At this point I don't give a shit how I feel about what I see, it's not going to change the outcome or my reporting of it, but it will keep me from my companion."

We all stood and just before Elick left I asked, "How much resistance are we going to get when I finally do get to your Great-Grandfathers Plane?"

Without flinching, he said, "Probably a lot."

"See what you can find out. See what you can do to lubricate that process, if anything." Pausing and getting very serious, I said, "If we have to find some way to send the leadership of that whole damn Plane to the Hatchery so I can get Usis out, then that's what I'll do. I'm not leaving without him."

# Entry 206

After Elick left I went and knocked on Kitar's door. "Can we talk for a moment?" I asked.

When he came back in, I handed him a goblet and invited Cemal over as well. Since Kitar was here he insisted on staying kneeling on the floor. I wasn't in the mood to fight that battle with what I was about to do.

"Kitar, I need to know if you have my back."

Nodding, Kitar said, "Yes, Keith, regardless what you do I'll be here for you."

"Because you've been ordered to or because you want to?"

"Does it matter?"

"Yes, it does," I answered.

"In that case, I guess my answer is, I was ordered to make sure you could perform your duties. Since joining you and doing some soul searching, I want to. Keith, though I may not always agree with you, you are loyal and have become a light in this dark place. After our problems on the last Plane, I thought about how I felt traveling with you and if I was looking forward to this assignment's end. What surprised me was the pain I felt at thinking about it being over. Being a Judge, I turned my eye on myself, as had been suggested, and realized you were more to me than an assignment. You had proven you are a friend, and I have not reciprocated. I am working to do that now."

"I think we all are. It's going to get hard soon I fear, really hard."

"I am sure of that," agreed Kitar.

"I think I'm going down to see if I can find someone to finish the tour of the forest," I added as a voice from the doorway to our suite said, "I will take you for this part of your tour."

I was shocked to see Gabriel. Actually, seeing the Archangel in his own Keep wasn't surprising, but seeing him dressed again in simple clothes was. It reminded me of Gluttony when he had pretended to be a beggar. "Might I ask why you're dressed the way you are?"

"Those condemned to this place have not earned the right to look upon a member of The Most High as we normally appear."

"I guess I can understand that." Turning back to Kitar, I said, "If you'd like to get some rest I should be safe with Gabriel... I think." I smirked, causing both my guide and the Angel to raise eyebrows.

"Yes, we should fare well enough, just the two of us," Gabriel agreed. I won't lie, I like this guy.

We walked down the steps, me following Gabriel into the main hall of the Keep. As we made our way past the statues, and paintings across the polished floors, I asked, "Why are there no living in these pieces?"

He turned to see which painting I was asking about. "There are damned in the paintings and most of the statues. See here..." He pointed to a pile of souls one of The Most High was standing on. Another, a painting, the souls were all dead and disfigured, scattered along the sides of a golden pathway leading up to a set of bright pearly gates.

"They are all dead or trodden upon," I observed.

"Yes, as they should be. The living are unworthy of being represented in depictions of The Most High."

"With this being Lord Lucifer's domain, I would have at least expected some representation of him."

Though he didn't say anything directly, again I could see the open hatred he had for The Dark Lord in his eyes. "The Abomination should not have only been thrown from the walls of The Eternal City but blotted from Creation completely." As quickly as his anger flared it vanished as he shook his head. "You do enjoy looking for a person's weaknesses, do you not? We have already discussed the intricacies of what might or might not have occurred had we been so lucky as to have rid ourselves of our Father's first creation."

I let it go. It didn't make much sense pissing off your guide and guard as you were about to walk out onto the Planes of suffering. As the massive golden door swung open, we were bucketed by the heat and smells of pain and sulfur. Even Gabriel staggered a bit. "It is a smell, you must give it that," I said.

"That it is little one, that it is."

As we reached the bottom of the steps, Gabriel said, "First I will take you to where the souls out in the 'Forest of Pain' as you call it are introduced to those they lead astray. Then we will visit those who have, as far as The Host is concerned, led an active war against The Father and his Teachings."

Gabriel turned and headed down a path leading off to the right of the Keep. I hadn't seen this area when we arrived; we'd come in from the other direction. From my balcony I'd seen the ceiling creature pulls souls from this area, I hadn't explored past that.

As if reading my thoughts, he said, "We will visit first the staging area where the shepherds are reunited with their flock."

"I was thinking about the Forest of Pain while I was typing my entry yesterday. When do the flock, as we have resorted to calling them, discover they've been misled by their spiritual leader? Is that at judgment?"

"Yes, but here is the first time they will be reunited and prepared to assist in justly rewarding the enemy of The Father."

Briefly, we entered the forest, me walking beside the Angel. He ignored the souls and their cries. The only light again from the small patches of flames which spontaneously sprang up and equally as quickly died. "Why are there flames? Is this entire area over the vents?"

In the distance, I started to notice the forest beginning to clear. I didn't ask any questions; it didn't seem my guide was yet in the mood to talk. When we stepped off the path, Gabriel stopped, me beside him. I looked out at the scene before us as my hand came up over my mouth.

I found us standing in the mouth of a large clearing, to the right was a cave entrance through which souls entered and were classified, either sheep or shepherd. The largest of the two pens were for the sheep, and the much smaller holding cell, for the shepherds. Now to give you scale, the sheep's pen was probably about the ten times that of a football field. It went all the way back to the cliff face and was some hundred and fifty yards wide, remember I'm eyeing this. Yes, it was massive. The shepherds, on the other hand, was a tenth the size. Souls were judged and added from the near end, closest to where we were standing, eventually being pulled from the far end to begin their torture. What I found strange were the furnaces lined up along the back of the smaller, shepherds, pen.

We walked into the clearing and almost immediately were flanked by two Cherubim. I looked back at Gabriel and motioned to one of them. "They are just doing their duty, pay no mind to them."

The souls, upon seeing someone of import arriving, began begging for mercy as we walked toward the area in the back, where the furnaces were. Each large furnace was made of metal and about the size of a small walk-in closet. The front had a door and the top an exhaust. You could tell which were in use and which sat silent by the plumes of smoke rising from the smokestacks. Leading to each furnace was a fenced in queue, think of cattle pens. If I recall they're called lanes, but I can't remember. There were in total probably a thousand furnaces stretching back as far as the eye could see. It was all very organized and, in many ways, gave the feel of a processing plant, which I guess, in fact, it was.

Gabriel lead us to a furnace that was currently not in use. "I have arranged for a soul to be prepared for the spikes they will later suffer once they are placed in the Forest of Pain," he explained as he looked at me, adding, "I do like that name, we will probably keep it."

I nodded as he motioned for them to bring the soul out. I could see Gabriel's attention to detail; this soul was from my world. He was ragged, but then most souls were by now, having suffered all these Planes and their assorted tortures. He was old, balding, nude, a dried-up husk of whatever he'd once been. He was weeping and begging, again common and somewhat annoying at this point.

"Should I know him?" I asked.

Gabriel answered without looking at me. "His name was Phelps. Do you know it?"

As had been done to me so many times, I walked up and lifted this poor creature's chin to look into his eyes. He attempted to spit in my face, but his mouth was so dry it was nothing but a sound. It was then I froze, just for a second, as I recognized him. I said in a growl, "God hates fags." He smirked and nodded. Looking back over my shoulder, "He'll not be released from this body, right?"

"Correct, why do you ask?"

"No reason." I reached down taking both his hands in mine and smiled. "We're from the same world. I'm one of those fags." As I spoke each word, I bent a finger back, listening to it snap as the nail touched the top side of his hand. He screamed. When I was done I walked back to Gabriel. "Let's get this show on the road."

Just before Gabriel gestured to start, I said, "Wait, I do have one question."

The Archangel motioned for me to ask. Looking back over to the preacher, I said, "Did you love your flock?"

In a weak, sad voice Phelps said, ignoring me as his eyes stayed on Gabriel, "More than words can explain."

Gabriel shifted his eyes to me as he lifted an eyebrow. I said, "Good that will make this easier. Carry on." I watched the Archangel close his eyes and stand motionless for a second. I knew what that meant. He was delving into the database of Creation to find something.

When he opened his eyes, a series of emotions flashed across his face in quick succession, surprise, shock, sadness, hurt (I think) and finally anger. Walking over to the soul, he bent down -- remember he is tall -- "Did you think we would not ask about this?"

Weeping as he realized who the Power in the plain clothes was, Phelps said, "I thought it was The Father's will."

"It is past the time for lying. I know and you know The Father never told you to hate," commented Gabriel as his angry face looked to the Cherubim who would be administering the punishment. "As the writer said, carry on."

# Entry 207 – Minor Blasphemy Punishment

The Cherubim motioned to someone back at the sheep's pen. Seconds later a steady stream of souls started to lumber down the path, single file. As they grew closer, one of the first Demons I'd seen on this Plane gripped the preacher by the shoulders forcing him to watch their approach. The Cherubim then asked Phelps, "Do you know this person? Were they a member of your congregation?"

I could tell from his eyes what the answer was. He confirmed my suspicions with a simple, "Yes."

The entire mood changed, not that it was ever pleasant. The Cherubim, "Open the door to the furnace in front of you," he instructed Phelps. I noticed the authority in his voice.

Gabriel leaned into me. "The Cherubim has used the Voice of The Father. It is a command no soul can refuse. He will comply. That does not, however, mean he does not understand what he is doing."

I didn't need to be told he was being forced to obey. He looked like a person trying to walk against hurricane force winds. He opened the furnace, then stood there.

We all watched as flames exploded to life inside the metal enclosure. As I realized what was about to happen my knees went weak and without thinking I reached over to steady myself by placing a hand on Gabriel. As I regained my balance, I looked up to see him staring at my hand, touching him. I quickly removed it, but he continued to stare.

I felt I shouldn't ask which, of course, means I did. "Was that wrong? Me touching you."

His look as he shifted his eyes to me was more of curiosity. "I am not sure when a soul last touched me." Pausing he added, "No, it is not an issue, just surprising."

I looked back when the preacher was instructed to return and stand beside the soul at the front of the line. Again, the Cherubim commanded, "Speak their name."

I looked up the line, there were only a couple of hundred souls. Turning back to Gabriel, "He didn't have many followers, did he?"

"I instructed the Cherubim to find an eligible soul from your world with only a few followers. These creatures do not deserve the honor of my presence, nor do I have the patience to stand and listen to an endless list of the livings sins against The Father."

"He is a minor blasphemer? I would have thought he would be in with the big boys."

"No, it appears for some reason that many blasphemers are, as you would call them, local clergy with little to no understanding of The Father. They often, as with this one, lead their flock based upon their own prejudices. Still, it does not matter, they have betrayed The Father and condemned the souls of their flock to this infernal place. You should note that this is one of the distinguishing characteristics which separate the lesser blasphemers from, the greater. The concern they carry for those they have brought with them. It is unfortunately common that the greater and more successful the shepherd becomes, the less they seem to care for their flock. They are the true enemies of The Father, as you will see when we reach those who committed the greater blasphemies. We were fortunate, if you can call it that, that there were many from your world just arriving. We saved the assignment of their rewards for you to see." Gabriel smiled. This was the first time I'd heard Gabriel use the word 'reward' for the punishments they administered. It had been common with the Cherubim.

So enough talk, here's what happened. At this point, it was like watching a person in those old movies about demon possession. He was fighting the commands but failing. He cried out the name of the first person. Then he was ordered to take them by the arm and lead them to the furnace and throw them in. Gaining just a bit of control over his body he turned back to us and screamed, "Please, please don't make me do this."

I looked up to Gabriel to see if he would address the sick fuck. Surprisingly he held up a finger and walked over to the preacher and asked, as he motioned to the row of people waiting their turn with their pastor. "You sent us this trash. Who did you think we would use to clean it up? Now do your duty."

Again, the will of the Cherubim took over, and the preacher lost control of his body. He gripped the first person, a lady, and dragged her, as she screamed, toward the open-door belching fire so hot that both souls began to smoke as their skins began to blacken. The smell drifted over causing me to pull a part of my tunic up to breathe through. In an agonizing scream, he then pushed the woman into the flames.

As he walked back, I couldn't take my eyes off the entrance. The glare from the fire was almost blinding, but still I could see the woman dancing a dance of agony as her body was consumed. I turned back when I heard Phelps announce the next name. Again, he pulled the person -- this time a male -- forward and again shoved him in. All the while begging to be forgiven, imploring, to all that was holy, to understand he hadn't known. His lies continued, he thought he was doing The Father's will. But you could see in his eyes that the truth was finally starting to show its face to him.

Gabriel said in a quiet voice, but I could tell it was the same command as the Cherubim. "Tell them the real reason."

Though I didn't think Phelp's face could become more distorted with rage and agony, he screamed, "I hated myself for who I was and wanted to be, but I couldn't. I wanted to make others suffer as bad as I did. I wanted everyone to hate anyone as much as I hated me." Again, he announced a name. Again the soul was thrown screaming into the flames.

I turned, I hated this guy, but I couldn't watch. Unfortunately, there was no relief. Gabriel had brought us to the center of the clearing. Everywhere I looked was a soul, of all different races and languages, announcing names as they drug their followers into the fires of The Host's fiery wrath.

I closed my eyes, but only for a second. I knew I needed to watch this. I'd spent hours back home listening to this man and his followers as they disrupted the funerals of veterans, gays, and anyone else this distorted fuck could brainwash his little flock into hating. I thought about the Cherubim back in the Pass-through Plaza and remembered what he said. I straightened my shoulders and turned to face this demented soul. 'He was being rewarded,' that is what they considered it. This was his reward. Name after name, soul after soul, into the flames. Now I could see them all packed together, their eyes having exploded from the heat. Their noses burned off. Their limbs ablaze as they were being consumed. Finally, the cries stopped when there were only around 14 people left in the line. I looked back at the preacher to find that he wasn't seeing any of the remaining souls except the last one, a female.

You have heard me mention many times the sounds of the cries and pain which is the background noise for Hell. Still, I don't think I've ever heard anything like what left Phelps mouth next. The amount of absolute despair was so massive I couldn't see how one human could produce this level of anguish. He screamed...."NO.............." as the Cherubim barked, "Announce the name."

Again, he said the name as he begged the soul he'd just condemned to the fires to forgive him. "Son, I didn't know," he wailed as he took the pathetic soul, who was kicking and screaming, toward the furnace. My mouth dropped, it was his son.

Any pain the evil pastor had felt only grew worse as he, one after the other, announced and then tossed his other twelve children into the fire.

Now only one person remained. Phelps took small steps, cried, begged, stepped, pleaded, bargained, stepped until his short journey of a lifetime ended standing before the last person in the line.

In an almost undecipherable chocked voice he announced the last soul's name, his wife's name.

She, unlike him or the other followers, was silent. He took her arm, no longer begging Gabriel or the Cherubim not to force him to do this, he was instead talking to his wife as he led her to the furnaces. I could hear him asking her for forgiveness, crying how he had been wrong.

He said, "I never doubted our mission. I thought The Father hated them as much as I did. I thought The Father called me."

The two stopped just before the furnace. Her skin was already beginning to blister and burn, dropping off great greasy slabs. She reached up and placed a hand on her husband's cheek, and said, "I knew The Father, and you did too. You knew it wasn't his will. My dear, you were called, but it wasn't by The Father. We deserve to be where we are. You for your sins and me for supporting you while you committed them." And then she stepped into the furnace of her own free will as Phelps collapsed onto the ground, a smoking mass of crying pain.

The Cherubim didn't care about the drama unfolding before him. He announced, "Close the door," and like a tragic puppet on a string the preacher stood, reached over and gripped the handle, pushing it shut. When it was closed, and the cries of those inside were muffled, I watched him pull back his hand only to see all the charred skin come off leaving nothing but the skeletal remains.

For a long time, he just stared at his hand. Then he turned to the Cherubim and asked, "May I please leave now?"

The two Demons again stepped forward and picked the preacher up by his armpits. They carried him to a small table and sat him in a chair. I looked up at Gabriel with tears in my eyes only to find him watching me. "You feel for this soul?"

"Not specifically, it is the pain of a soul, not particularly this soul. It transcends my hatred of what he did. In the end, he is just a sad man who through his hatred led dozens into the fiery pits of Hell."

The corners of the Archangel's lips curled upwards. "That is The Father's compassion, even now still evident in you. But you are here to see how they are bound so he may be placed on a post in the Forest of Pain."

In shock, I said, "That's not it?"

"No," he answered as he, and I following his lead, turned back toward the furnace. Now the smoke was no longer coughing forth from the chimney. The metal still glowed red but was cooling quickly. We watched as one of the Demons opened a small door at the bottom and began scooping out a black-grey dust, the ashes of the incinerated souls.

"That is all that's left? I don't understand, I thought it took thousands of years to destroy the souls," I asked.

"Who said we were disposing of their souls? Only their bodies," explained Gabriel as we watched the Demon get every bit of dust. "The souls of the damned are still contained in those ashes. As they together made others suffer in life, they now as a group suffer together."

The Demon stood and handed the pail of dust to the Cherubim, almost reverently. Taking the container, he turned and walked over to the defeated soul of the preacher and set it on the table. "Now eat."

At almost the same instance as the preacher looked up to the Cherubim in shock, so did I to Gabriel who explained. "He will now consume their souls, ingest them, make they're suffering his."

As I watched the preacher scoop up a hand full of ashes and start forcing it into his mouth, I said to Gabriel, "I cannot take any more of this. Tell me how it ends so we can leave."

Nodding his understanding, the Archangel said, "Watching this creature disgusts me as well. We can leave, the ritual is all but completed. He will be forced to devour all the remains of his followers, licking the bucket clean. Once that is complete, he will be led to a holding area to await space for him in the forest. From there you have seen what will happen.

I merely said, "Yes..." then turned and started back up the path.

# Entry 208

Gabriel caught up to me, it wasn't hard, and led me down a different path. Again, along the forest and off to the right of the Keep. He stopped briefly asking, "Would you like to rest?" I shook my head, so we continued along the path. As we crossed a bridge, I looked down and saw the churning river of suffering some fifty feet below as it worked its way across the landscape and down to the Lower Planes. I stood there for a second thinking about when it had started, oh so long ago on the Second Plane, nothing more than a trickle. Now it crashed and crested in massive waves against the canyon walls.

"As we walk, can you give me your definition of the more serious forms of Blasphemy?" I asked.

"This sin is probably the simplest in its definition. It is a sin against The Father himself. Be that in denunciation, which is a lesser form. In ignoring or denying him completely, again a lesser sin. Or through your actions misrepresenting him or his teachings thus leading others down the path of Blasphemy on a large scale. These are the most grievous."

"Wow, I have lots of questions about that statement. First, so being an Atheist is blasphemy?"

"Technically yes, but as you surely understand there are often two types of Atheists. Those who choose not to acknowledge the existence of The Father, neither supporting or undermining him to others. This type of soul is not necessarily condemned to this Plane since The Father teaches us to judge a soul based upon its actions. I have encountered several Atheists who, though they did not enter The Eternal City, their primary sin was not their lack of belief. A soul does not have to acknowledge The Father to live as he has instructed. But a soul cannot live as he instructed and openly wage war against the belief in him. Does that make sense?"

"Yes, so I would probably have committed the sin of Blasphemy while living?"

"Oh yes, that taint is upon your soul. But it was not what brought you to this place as you were told during your judgment."

"You mentioned those who misrepresent The Father's teachings. I assume you're talking about the Clergy?"

"Not specifically. It is completely possible for a soul to help lead others down the path to blasphemy without having dedicated themselves to the teachings of The Father. Though, if a soul has in fact offered themselves up as a leader in their religious teachings and claims to represent The Father, and then they teach contradictory beliefs, they then become damned and most hated by us in The Host. We see them as little more than warriors against The Most High. Even those we loved and called brothers that led a war against The Father were eventually defeated and expelled from The Eternal City. Imagine what we would do to an abomination like you talking monkeys who would choose to wage war against our Father openly. There are few greater sins in all of Creation and therefore, few greater punishments. As you will soon see."

"I don't understand. How is my indifference worse than say a priest leading his flock astray?"

"You were a writer; therefore, you spoke to the masses. Your contempt was not only directed toward The Father but often toward your own kind. Your indifference was a blasphemy against The Father and all he created."

"So which Plane would that have destined me for, in your eyes."

"Oh, most certainly Treachery, the final Plane."

"Really? That sounds horrible. Isn't that like for the worst of the worst. I mean in your eyes." I was so surprised I tripped over one of the paving stones.

"What is the definition of Treachery?" he asked.

"I know what I think it is, but if I've learned anything, it's not always what you guys think it means."

He paused for a moment. "I think we can use one of your world's definitions which is: an act of deceit, faithlessness, or treason. All three are a betrayal of all that The Father wished."

"Strangely, my dislike of my species, in many ways mirrors that which you in The Host hold as well. So how can it be blasphemy to agree with The Host about a creation I feel is flawed and holds no merit. Of course, I cannot speak about other cultures since I didn't know there were any until after I was dead."

"That very fact is one of the reasons I feel Lucifer chose you for this assignment. You carry many of the same beliefs as we in The Host do. In our defense, not that we need defending, where the sin comes in, is we believed The Father was not wise to create the living, but we accepted and followed him regardless of our doubts. We believed he had a long-term plan which we were not privileged to know. Therefore, we could not and would not say he was wrong. Lucifer, on the other hand, felt he knew what was best for Creation and The Host and then attempted to overrule The Father's wishes and seize control. That is where betrayal comes in."

"You would agree, I'm guessing here, that since Lucifer was with The Father from the start, maybe had a better idea of where Creation was headed. Where it had originally been intended to go and whether or not The Father was still adhering to that plan. The Father made The Host promises when he started, as I recall. Was his plans still staying true to those original assurances? Maybe Lucifer knew something you didn't. And before you say it, don't tell me that doesn't count, since you extend to The Father that same grain of Faith. I'm not saying Lucifer had any additional knowledge but is Hell really a result of The Great War, as you all call it, or because The Host wanted to find a place to dump The Father's great flawed experiment?"

All I got in response from Gabriel was an inclined head. I took that to mean he was neither agreeing nor disagreeing with my remark. Since I could go on forever about this topic, having the key players to give me input, I decided to stop. I'm here to write about Hell not who was or was not mistaken in what appears to be little more than assumptions. The only one who can answer any of the crucial questions is MIA. But don't worry, if I can hunt him down, I don't plan on going as easy on him as I have his representatives.

I'm sure you've already noticed. This Plane's entries have much more to do with religion. What can I say, It's not very often you get access to such an exalted group of players from both sides of the issue. I'd be remiss to not seize upon it.

"We just saw the mild blasphemers, though I have a hard time considering our last example, mild. And there are the extreme blasphemers. Are there any in between?" I asked.

He pointed down, and it was then I realized it wasn't just a path we were walking on but the soot-covered faces of thousands of souls. They were grouted in, unable to move. Their eyes staring up and their mouths sealed shut. Forever silent. A metaphor for the blasphemy they spewed while living. I'd tripped several times, I thought the stones were just uneven, but that wasn't the case. It was a nose or eye I was tripping over. I'd been so absorbed in the conversation I'd forgotten to do my job, observe. "Oh Gawd..."

"Thank you; we thought it was a nice touch as well. They will for eternity, or until they are replaced, be nothing but the stones upon which, we The Host and our servants, walk upon."

We walked on, I tried not to appear like I was walking differently, but I was. Almost tip toeing. We eventually made it around the corner, and I found myself standing at the entrance to the massive chamber I had seen when we arrived. I'm not going to describe the outside, think of an auxiliary of the Vatican, yeah that covers it. When we walked inside I froze... (yes, I know I say that a lot...bite me.)

# Entry 209

This time my freezing was not out of shock but amazement. We were standing in the doorway to a massive gothic auditorium. I'm not sure gothic is the right term, that might lead you to believe it was dark. It wasn't. On the contrary, it was constructed of light grey marble with gold and black veins wandering through the stone like a drunken sailor. To save us both time, I learned it was The Host's version of a mega church. You know one of those massive stadiums looking altars to greed and gluttony where the hopeless and gullible go to hand over their money to self-interested charlatans. My first reaction was to look at Gabriel. "Isn't this very earth specific? Surely Creation isn't full of foolish god-fearing people willing to believe that if you gave enough money to a mindless puppet master The Father will love you more."

"You would be surprised. Many, too many, worlds have charlatans...."

I finished the sentence for him, "...that suck the pus off the wounds of the weak and foolish?"

"The imagery is close, but I am not sure I would have phrased it like that," observed the Archangel.

"That's because I'm the writer and you're not. That's because I have lived with these talking monkeys as you call them. Trust me; I fully understand how much of a fuck up The Father made when he stopped creating and declared us his greatest creation. In the little time I have spent with The Powers, both above and below, you all seem far more evolved than anything that came along later. How old was The Father when he did all of this? Could he have been losing his faculties? "

I got no response from Gabriel, but for the record, his face went through several phases during my rant. Sometimes he showed approval but toward the end, not so much.

We were standing to the right on a large stage. Splayed out before us was a room filled with seats as far back as I could see. Each row slightly higher than the one before it until they became lost in the back of the massive building. As expected they formed a semi-circle around the stage. The front row probably held about eight hundred seats, and I have no idea how many the back rows contained. It was standing room only. A captive audience consisting of the sinful clergy from every world in Creation. It appeared all species were represented, some I'd never seen before. The collector on Greed had nothing on this place. Gabriel took my arm and started to lead me down off the stage, but I stopped him. I wanted to take in the scene. The stage, which was probably a hundred feet across and twenty deep, complete with rows and rows of hot lights shining down upon it, was covered in grizzled bits of flesh, shit and who know what else. The only clean spot, a single circle, in the center of the stage directly under a bright white spotlight, how dramatic. The stage was bare. "The light on center stage is a nice touch. So bright and blinding, sorta like The Father's light," I commented.

Gabriel smiled. "I was curious if you would recognize the symbolism. Well done."

I turned and followed the Angel down off the stage. I again paused at the bottom of the little steps and looked at the first creature seated in the first chair on the first row. It was then I noticed the seats were made from bones, all lashed together. I never found out where the bones had come from, but later I was shown how each new clergy member was required to make their own bindings. They would shear the sinew, muscles, and hair from a few of their most loyal followers, then weave the strands into a cord which was then used to lash them in place until their time on stage.

I was shown the process but have decided to not go into detail, only offering you the short explanation. I will add this to conclude the description. When the clergy member was taken to their seat carrying their cord it would be set on the floor before them and then snake up, by its own power, to secure their arms, legs, and head in place, ensuring they could not move or look away. To further guarantee they couldn't escape the spectacle upon the stage a small Demon would walk along the rows slicing off the damn's eyelids. I was reminded that this needed to be done regularly since the soul would regrow their damaged body parts.

"What am I looking at?" I asked.

"Here is where those who pledged to The Father, to spread his word, to help lead his flock to The Eternal city, are allowed to relive their blasphemy. Not only theirs but their peers. Collectively they share the pain and damnation they rained down upon each of the innocent souls who came to them hoping for little more than a place of solace."

"Unlike the punishments of the lesser blasphemers and the others I've seen in Hell, here a single individual's reacquaintance with their sins can take a long time," I noted.

"Yes, based upon the size of their flock, it can last months, years or even millennia."

He directed my attention back toward the stage. In an inset against the back wall upon an ornately carved pulpit sat a multi-faced Demon. This wasn't one of those tall menacing Demons. He was about my height and was seated on a gilded gem-encrusted throne. His head was like a cylinder with several faces, one looking forward, one left and one right. On top of his head where hair and horns would have been instead burned a green flame about a foot tall. His body was nude, scaly and dark grey. His hands and feet both ended in four clawed talons. "This is the Tacarta; he ensures all the residents enshrined here are given the opportunity to review their treachery against The Father.

"Three faces?" I remarked.

"One sees the past, the sins of the damned as well as the lives of disappointment and pain of those they led astray. One sees the now, the pain and suffering administered while they stand in his domain. Lastly, one sees the future and the pains the lost souls will suffer due to the blasphemer's actions. This ensures each warrior against The Father full understanding of the damage they caused with their greed and absorption of self."

I think this was the first creature in Hell, this Tacarta, that I'd met who could see the future.

I raised an eyebrow and did what I usually do. I looked for my world's representatives. Don't ask me why. I can only imagine it's because they are familiar and more accessible. Seeing what I was doing, Gabriel pointed off, and there were many of the famous liars from my world, all together, lashed to their seats awaiting their turn in the light. It indeed was a friar's roast of all the greatest pond scum from my childhood, youth and adult years. My eyes immediately fell upon Robertson, Crouch, Bakker, and Falwell, both one and two. Robertson was the first I noticed; I guess because he was the most pathetic in his later years. His only good trait was he became so insane, in the end, he was little more than a joke to his followers and detractors. Seeing Bakker, a smile crossed my lips. Never, and I mean never, in all my time in Hell had I ever seen a soul I was so happy to run into here in the land of the Damned. Bakker, James Orsen Bakker. I pointed, "Him, I want him." Turning to Gabriel, I asked, "Would you mind demonstrating on him? He was a particularly reprehensible creature from my time. Several times his blasphemy included him telling his followers that he had stood before The Father and personally received instructions. Something even The Host hasn't been honored with, of late." Yes, I threw that last part in as a jab. I could tell immediately that it had worked, Gabriel's eyes narrowed, and I heard him growl.

The Archangel looked me in the eyes; I mean hard. I don't know if I'll ever grow used to staring into the face of eternity, the eyes of an Angel. Don't think it's honor wasted on me. I know the gift I've been given. He then turned to Bakker and just stared for a moment. I knew he was reviewing the televangelist's soul. After returning his attention to me, he said, "Though you are correct about the blackness of this one's soul I do not think he is the greatest abomination currently present from your world." I was honestly surprised. "I will have him brought up, so you can see as well, just how many of those seated around him served in the training which led to his damnation. As you should have discovered by now, this is the main part of the sin of Blasphemy, the passing on to others the improper teachings of The Father and then sending them out to sin more. So this one..." pointing to Bakker, "is a good example of both the sin and the sinner."

Now as you know, I'm writing this after the fact. This isn't a narrative where I'm parroting to you what is currently happening. So I'll say this up front. Some of the things I learned this day changed my opinion of the man to whom I hastened his sentence. I'm not writing a biography. Therefore I'll only dance across the strings of his life instead of examining them. I want you to see how he was shaped, but more importantly, and more to the task at hand, how he was to be punished for the paths he was both led down by others or chose to take for himself.

To the Overseer on the throne, Gabriel inclined his head toward my choice. Then in a thunderous voice, as he exclaimed, "Bring our next penitent."

Two Demons I hadn't noticed before walked down from the back of the arena with one of the seers. The seer stopped, checked its book and pointed to my choice. The Demons, one in front and one behind, moved up the aisle toward the damned. Now standing before him, the one in the front with a curved blade sliced the sinew holding Bakker in place. As the one behind, gripped him under each armpit and lifted him up out of his seat. Already I could hear that same pitiful cry for mercy I'd seen so many times on the news when Bakker had been arrested and hauled out in disgrace in handcuffs. Carrying him up, followed by the seer, they placed him in the bright circle on the stage. He tried to run but couldn't.

They stepped away leaving him just standing there, nude, crying, the bright light ringing his body, casting his shadow back along the stage, stopping just short of the throne.

I watched as the seer walked up the side of the stage and like at the Oscars, handed the Overseer a sheet of parchment. He read through it and then announced in a loud voice, "You were born, and much of your young life is without consequence. You were raised religious and attended a religious school, I see. In the beginning, it appears you were determined to dedicate your life to the teachings of The Father, but that changed. You met and married, started your ministries and things seemed looked promising for you. But as is often the case, wealth, fame and lust soon became your gods. I can see in your eyes the justifications. The lies you told yourself. You cheated." With a movement of his finger, he spun Bakker around. "Did she know? Your wife." Before the preacher could answer, the overseer answered for him, "No...well not at first. She trusted you. She believed in you. As so many others did."

As time went on, he continued to deteriorate. Was jailed for fraud, for duping money from the poor hopeless people who turned to him for guidance. As I listened, I continued to grow madder. Finally, unable to stand it anymore I turned to Gabriel. "May I question him?"

"Yes," he said without pause. He walked up onto the stage and, as expected, the Overseer stopped recounting his account of Bakker's life. "Our young writer here is from this damned soul's world and has a few questions." Bakker's body slowly rotated toward me as the Overseer bowed his head in acquiescence.

"He is all yours," commented Gabriel as he walked back to the side of the stage. From behind one of the columns, Gabriel's slave appeared with a tray on which sat two goblets and a bottle of wine. He set the tray on the edge of the stage then filled both cups. Lifting one, he first presented it to the Archangel. Then the second to me. I took it. I'd probably need this before I was done.

Turning back to Bakker as I approached him, I asked, "Do you know what's in this goblet?" I lifted it and poured a small amount into his mouth. He took it hungrily. "That is Hell's wine; it's purified, I'm told, from the suffering of a special flock of souls." Shaking my head, I added, "you're not one of them." I asked, as I cleaned the edge of the goblet and took a sip, "You know where you are, correct?"

In a broken voice, he answered, "Hell..."

"You can do better than that. Which Plane?"

"Blasphemy," answered Bakker.

"And why would that be, do you think?" I asked.

He stood up straight, stopped crying, wiped his nose on his arm. "Because I knew this was my fate. Do you think I was blind? It took a while, but I realized what I'd done. The sins I had committed. The person I'd become." Turning and pointing at the others from my world, all clumped together unable to move. "But they...they led me down this road." Pausing knowing I was about to say something, "Don't get me wrong. I committed the affair. I got the ministry in too deep. I knew about the payoff. I knew we were not using the money for the things I was telling my flock it was for. Before all of that, I wanted to do The Father's work. Things just got out of control." Looking past me at Gabriel, "I know that isn't an excuse, and I know that it's not why I'm here, on this Plane. That's of my own doing. I mean all of it is, but this, right here, Blasphemy, that was an intentional choice."

Turning his head to me again, "Do you know what they put me through?" He yelled, "DO YOU…"

I was curious. "Continue…"

"I started the Trinity ministries, and that one stole it…" He pointed to Crouch. "Then negotiated to get Tammy on his program…" He pointed to Robertson. "…all I wanted was a talk show at night, The 700 Club. I made it work then he took it from me. We left and started PTL, that is where I started to fall, things were working, money was coming in, we became celebrities, we lived a life I was sure, just years before, would never be ours. Then I fell again; I cheated on Tammie Faye, I tried to cover it up, money was going out so quickly. You must remember I was a preacher, not an accountant. I didn't know. I trusted those around me." Again, turning to Gabriel, "…as the bible said, I trusted. Then he showed up, a wolf in sheep clothing and stole again from me what I'd worked so hard to created…" he pointed at Falwell senior. "He made promises and lied, he wept with us and schemed, he smiled to the cameras while his demon's tail swished wildly behind him. I went to jail. I served my time. I emerged a laughing stock, hated by the flock I'd hoped to lead. But during my time in jail, I reviewed my life, my works, those I'd followed, and those who'd followed me. I found them all wanting. It was then I made my decision; I'd come back. I'd start a new ministry. But…but…this time I'd do what I knew The Father wanted. I'd lead these sick unworthy lemmings, not to his gates but instead to the one who deserved them. I would lead them here…to Hell…and that is exactly what I did."

Picking up the story, the Overseer added, "You did not seem to understand. It was your duty to be ridiculed, held to account, and even maligned by those who pretended to believe. It was your duty to stand up and shine as the light of The Father to your flock and all those who looked upon you. But no. According to the numbers our seer has given me, in your time you led 128,750,421 souls to their damnation here in Hell. Not all those souls made it to this Plane or any of the other Planes of Hell. Instead, because you convinced them to fund your sin at the cost of their hopes and dreams, their lives, in the end, amounted to nothing of consequence. Due to their choice and your actions, their souls now burn in the fires of the furnace until the last spark of their pitiful existence blinks from Creation, sparing The Father the pain of looking down upon them. For these actions, you find yourself here, as a warrior against The Father and for that, I raise the same number of flies as those souls you led astray. For the remainder of eternity, their hunger shall never be sated as they feed upon your flesh. Because like your actions and your life, in you no creature found sustenance. Do not assume the pitiful biting of these insignificant creatures is the totality of your reward as an enemy of The Father. With each bite you shall see, feel, hear and relive the lives you so led astray. Their despair, dread, self-loathing and sadness shall become your constant companion until the fires of Hell cool and all of Creation is no more."

I watched as a horde of pea-sized flies rose up from the floor, and started to circle the damned soul. For several seconds nothing else happened. Then came the first scream as one by one the small creatures began to dive in, ripping tiny bits of flesh from the tormented soul. I watched in silence as more and more wounds opened up and began to weep tiny rivulets of suffering down onto the floor.

I turned when I heard the thousands of souls in the audience all start to cry and beg for mercy. Knowing they too would soon suffer the same fate.

It was then the Overseer announced, "Secure the Damned," as the two Demons walked up onto the stage carrying what appeared to be a coffin filled with two-inch-wide holes. They sat it down on the floor then turned to the Bakker. Lifting him, as he fought, they lowered him into the box. His new flock, the flies, buzzed around hungrily waiting for their next chance to feast upon their shepherd. The Demons lowered the lid, sealing the coffin as its new resident begged for forgiveness. Throwing out bible verses as if they would sway those who had just passed judgment upon him. As they lifted the box to their shoulders, the two Demons turned and walked off the stage, past both Gabriel and me. They exited the building with the swarm of flies following close behind, Gabriel took my arm, and we followed them out. We walked for several minutes toward the side of the Plane, near the mountains of lava. I turned to find Gabriel pointing up. As I followed his finger, I discovered the honeycomb patterns on the cavern ceiling again, only now did I realize that the entire roof of this plane was filled with billions of coffins just like this one, each suspended by chains and obscured by the swarming clouds of tiny flies.

The procession stopped as a length of chain was lowered toward the ground. When it was within reach, the Demons took the end and attached it to a ring on the top of the small metal prison. With slow steady movements, it was then raised up to join the masses of other souls, all crying in pain. I started to step forward when Gabriel stopped me. "You should not get within range of the suffering." It was then I realized that below the cloud of flies was a steady rain falling like a spring shower down upon the barren ground. I would learn later that it would rain down across the landscape letting all the souls in residence suffer the feelings of those who knew true Blasphemy. I had not felt it due to the heat; it was evaporating. He pointed to the rocks where it eventually condenses, during cooler times, to flow down into the river of suffering. Again, I was amazed at the elegance of Hell's systems. The way nothing was wasted, and every opportunity was taken to augment the pain of those in its charge.

As the coffin reached its eternal resting place, a massive flame shot up, engulfing all the coffins and killing all the flies. I turned and raised an eyebrow, "You killed the bugs?"

"Oh no, it is but a short respite to allow all the damned to heal while the flies are reborn to start again." I looked up as a new round of cries rang out across the Plane, louder than before, the coffins, all of them, were now glowing bright red cooking their inhabitants anew. "Heal? How with the coffins burning their skins?" I asked.

"Yes, it seems we overlooked that. As you like to say, Oh well...," I couldn't help smiling when he tried to look innocent and then grinned. "The heat will take weeks to dissipate."

"So they will suffer the eternal biting of the souls they have doomed as well as the agony of the scalding metal?"

"Yes, considering their infractions against The Father, it seems the least we can do."

I took a single step forward and looked up, in many ways it looked like an art installation. The way the metal, across all the many coffins, rippled and changed through the colors of red as the heat danced across their smooth surfaces. I tried to envision what it would look like when the flies were active, and the boxes were still slightly heated. I imagined it looking like an aerial view, looking down, of a city clouded in fog.

Together Gabriel and I turned and walked back to the Keep.

# Entry 210

As we walked back my mind again returned to Usis and what Elick would say this time. I know I don't seem like I've been worried but trust me it's just a ruse. I've been worried sick. I wish this Plane were more like Lust; I could use the distraction. There is only so much you can do with a bunch of unrepentant assholes whose entire life was about pretending they were holy. Seriously, boring Plane. It didn't help that the overlord was a fucking Angel...am I allowed to use those two words, one after another... fucking angel...well no lightning, I must be good.

Back in the room, I found Elick had already returned. He was embroiled in a conversation with Kitar. I shut the door a bit harder than I needed to get their attention. Cemal came up, handing me a goblet. I could tell from the look on his face our news was not going to be good.

"SO...?" I asked in a loud voice. "What do you have to tell me. Remember I've been out reviewing how The Host punishes those who disappoint him. You might say taking lessons."

They waited until I joined them in the sitting area. "I wish I had better news, but I do not. First, Usis is fine. He is doing well. I took several portions of the heart to hold him over."

"That sounds like good news. Is he functional now?"

"Mostly, he still sleeps a lot, and he has severe mood swings. He cannot move a lot since the scabs are now starting to harden and they tend to crack."

I wrinkled my nose at the thought of the scabs, it sounded painful and itchy. "Then what's the bad part?"

"It is my great-grandfather. When I confronted him about letting Usis go when you arrived, he said that was not going to happen. He plans to force the boy into service to him, as one of his troops."

"Can he do that? How can he force someone to serve?"

"He is a Fallen. Usis is a damned. Have you forgotten that? If he issues his will upon a soul that soul has no choice as to their actions."

I could tell from his mood he thought that was the end of the discussion. As you can imagine it wasn't. "So what are we going to have to do to get Usis back?" I asked.

Shaking his head, Elick said what I feared he was going to say, "I do not know if there is anything we can do. About all you can do is change Grandfather's mind, once you get there."

"No, I don't accept that." Turning to Kitar, I asked, "Can we get Lucifer to intervene? Or more to the point, you are one of Xia Morningstar's friends. I know he would not allow anything to go against his wishes. Are you not of the same rank and stature? He, as I recalled, has fought the Lord of Hell, we only have to fight one of his little henchmen."

Elick's eyes went wide. "Are you challenging me...ME and calling me a coward?"

As he walked up and got in my face, I said in a firm tone, "Not yet, I'm hoping I don't have to." Pausing I asked again in a calmer tone, "Will Lucifer intervene?"

"I would not count on it," answered Kitar adding, "also, Keith it is dangerous to disparage one of the Fallen."

"Fuck that. I have the Dark Lord's protection, as you said, challenging me is offhandedly challenging Lord Lucifer. I have studied Lucifer; he will not allow that to happen. So..." and I marched to the balcony doors, threw them open and yelled, "FUCK YOU, Leviathan."

Neither said anything for several seconds as I walked back over and refilled my glass. Before I could say anything Elick added, trying to remain calm, "There are several reasons why Lucifer will not get involved. First, Lucifer has his hands full with Xia in Creation right now. Plus, I doubt he would step in and start a war with one of his Generals over a soul. There is just no upside to him intervening."

"I could stop writing, then what would he do?"

"He would compel you. Like I said with Grandfather forcing Usis to serve. Can you imagine what power Lucifer has over a soul?"

"Wait what you said goes both ways. Is your Not So Great-Grandfather willing to start a war with Lucifer over a soul?" When they didn't say anything I added, "Are you telling me you two have already given up?" I asked as an idea started to form. "Wait. You both have said Lucifer respects strength. What we need is someone to champion us, so to speak."

"Against my Great-Grandfather. I seriously doubt that."

"Just bear with me. What would we need?"

"We would have to find someone who could challenge Great-Grandfather and be able to win in a fight. Lucifer would, most certainly, side with the winner. The Dark Lord would probably even approve such a challenge; he likes testing his Generals. If, and it is a big if, the agreement was to release Usis and your champion won, Lucifer would most certainly force the terms of the agreement to be respected. The problem is, Grandfather is one of the best, if not the best, fighter The Dark Lord has. No one would go against him."

Again, silence descended like a veil over the room. I looked up. "What if we got someone who already had Lucifer's protection?"

Kitar's eyes went wide. "No."

Elick looked between us. "What are you thinking?"

"Me. Lucifer protects me by decree."

Elick thought, "First, let's skip the obvious, which is he would rip your soul apart. Also, forget you are no fighter. I worry when you try to put on your shoes that you might fall over and send yourself to the Hatchery. The merits by themselves are sound, and you do have a point. With you having The Dark Lord's protection, if you challenged Great-Grandfather, it would probably cause him to think twice whether to even accept the challenge. If you were lucky and he refused the challenge, you would then have a case for your companion's release. The problem is if Great-Grandfather refused, it would be a mighty blow to his reputation. Therefore, he would never refuse. Thus, you would be forced to fight him, and there is no chance a soul could defeat such a mighty Fallen."

I smiled slightly. "What if I found a way to even the playing field?"

"And how, pray tell, could you do that?" growled Kitar.

I leaned forward and flipped back the lid of the box on the table. Inside was what remained of the one heart that Usis has been eating and beside it lay the whole heart of the other Lover. Kitar jumped up and started screaming about how insane I was. I ignored him; I was watching Elick, who sat back stroking his chin.

While Kitar raged and Cemal ran around cursing, collecting the breakables, Elick sat in silence. Finally, reaching up and placing an arm on Kitar's to calm him, he motioned for our guide to take his seat. Cemal was there to fill his goblet, which he downed and took another refill.

"The problem I see is clearly the heart Usis is eating is Enepsigos', that means the other is Zepar."

"I don't know why that matters," I said.

"Enepsigo was the fighter. After you told me Usis was consuming a heart, I did some research and am pretty sure that is the one he is consuming. Her heart would bestow on him some of her traits, usually the stronger ones. Since he was able to kick my ass as well as several others it only makes sense that he is consuming her heart."

"So, I'll eat the other one."

"NO," barked Kitar. "We are not even talking about this."

Elick looked up at him raising an eyebrow. "That sounded a lot like an order. I know you are not issuing orders to me are you, Lord Judge?" The look of danger in the Hellspawn's eyes caused Kitar to set back down slowly.

"As I was saying, Zepar's gift was magical not combat. Therefore, if you consume his heart, it will not help you in a physical battle against

Grandfather as much as the other heart would. Thus probably not giving you a real chance of defeating him."

"Can they be mixed?" I asked.

"I do not know, but I cannot imagine why not. There is no precedent for consuming a member, present or past, of The Host's hearts. I am not sure anyone knew what would happen before Usis did. He might be the first."

"Have either of you thought about what Usis has gone through," injected Kitar.

"It doesn't matter. If there is a chance to save him, I must try." Pausing I added, "Does Leviathan know about the hearts and what Usis has done?"

"I doubt it," answered Elick.

"We should probably keep it that way," I said.

There was a long pause, then Elick turned to Kitar, "Also, and correct me if I am wrong Lord Judge. I might point out the long-term ramifications. The Dark Lord will probably allow them to live out eternity in Pandemonium after they complete this task." He paused and looked at me, "That is of course if you do not screw up before then."

"Like consuming a Fallen's heart," snarked Kitar.

"I don't think The Dark Lord will have issues with that. He destroyed them already, so that is done. The point I am trying to make is the potential complications of being a somewhat exalted soul living at the epicenter of Hell's power structures. You both would stand a better chance of not becoming eternal pawns on the chess board of Hell's politics if you had some powers to protect you," commented Elick.

For the first time I saw a break in Kitar's anger. "He does have a point. Once this assignment is over, regardless of how much Lord Lucifer gives you, it will only be temporary. He will not come running every time you get into trouble. You saw how he discarded his wife, and she was one of his followers during the Great War."

"Exactly, but that would not matter. Many powers in Hell would still see you as a way to strike at The Dark Lord, either to show their defiance or in hopes of drawing him out."

We sat quietly until Cemal came and refilled our goblets. In surprise, we all shot forward when he reached down and picked up the partially consumed heart. "Calm down my Lords; I just wanted to see how much was remaining."

"And..." asked Elick eyeing the boy.

"The parts you have removed are from the small end, so there is more than half left," answered my boy as he sat the heart back down carefully. As he knelt beside me, he added, "I can feel the power in it. There is a great amount."

"By just picking it up?" asked Elick who then did the same. "Yes, yes indeed. These hearts contain a massive amount of creation energy."

Looking up into at the ceiling like I was talking to a hidden microphone, I said, "What do you think Lord Gabriel?"

# Entry 211 (cont)

The door opened as the Archangel stepped in. "You know that is rude."

"The listening at the door or the calling you out while you do it?" I asked as Cemal snorted.

Shaking his head, he ignored my comment. "The only two things I would interject here is it might work. And you are correct; this has never been tried. But based upon what your companion has already gone through and the new talents he has exhibited it is clear the hearts are bestowing on him some of Enepsigos' powers."

"And secondly," prompted Elick with a slight smile.

"You already know what I am going to say. If you are going to do this, I would suggest you get on with it since The Fallen Abomination is not in his domain right now to interfere. And while you are here you are under my protection, there are few better conditions for you to attempt such a fool hearty exercise," added the Archangel.

"I am not sure. Are you supporting this insane idea or not?" asked Kitar.

"I am doing neither. I am confirming your suspicions and suggesting that if you wish to travel down this path, now is the best window of opportunity. As to my personal views of its outcome, I do not have or, for that matter, want enough information to speculate."

"Can't you look into the future and see?" I asked.

"As I have told you before, this is Hell; it is outside our jurisdiction. Therefore, I have no power to foresee the future of its inhabitants. As I also said, I do not want to know because of all the possible ramifications of me having that knowledge."

"Ramifications?" I asked.

Elick answered, "If he knew, for a fact, it would work then since he hates Lord Lucifer as much as he does, he would feel the need to step in and offer any sway he might be able to contribute just to watch the mess it would cause here in Hell." Smiling Elick asked, "Am I close?"

With a deadpan expression Gabriel just said, "As I said, I do not want to know."

"Whatever, but you wouldn't object to hosting me while I went through the rough parts at the start?"

"No."

"Again, because you know this is going to drive Lord Lucifer up a wall, so to speak."

"There is that perk, yes. But then I can always say it was probably something you ate," smirked Gabriel.

"Which would not be a lie, as such," added Kitar shaking his head.

Nodding, Gabriel said, "as such."

"Since we are getting official reaction to this foolish idea, I want it on the record that I am dead set against it," barked Kitar.

"You have made that abundantly clear, Judge," growled Elick.

I just let them bicker as I stared at the hearts. When I cut them off, I asked Elick, "Will you train me?"

Kitar raised an eyebrow at Elick. "You want me to train you to raise a weapon against my Great-Grandfather? One of the most powerful creatures in all of Creation. Is that what you are asking?" I started to respond when he added, "Against the creature who has made my life a living hell. A Fallen who has said on many occasions that I was a sad representation of our family's lineage. A person who has often mused on how much honor I could bring to the family if I would just sacrifice myself to eternity. It would be an honor. If there is even a chance I could see that bastard on his knees, I would train an army. Sadly, or strangely, regardless how this turns out, it will probably raise me in his eyes. Well after the anger passed, of course."

Turning to Gabriel, I asked, "And you will ensure my safety while I am getting my feet back under me?"

"I can assure you no one will enter this keep while you are recovering," answered the Angel.

"Anyone?" commented Kitar.

"Even he would not dare besiege this Keep over such a small affair. The rift it would cause between his Domain and the Host would set relations back for centuries."

Looking at me, Elick added, "Plus, regardless how this turns out, it will resolve itself. I could see The Dark Lord thinking this could bear interesting fruit regardless of what happens. It is more his style to let anything that does not directly challenge him play out. If for no other reason than a lesson to everyone else."

Kitar held up a hand. "Are we actually entertaining this idea?"

Turning to each person and finally to Kitar, I said, "I'm past entertaining. As far as I'm concerned the decision is made." I paused, turning back to Elick. "There's no way Leviathan can find out about this and prepare is there?"

"He would have to be told since he cannot see your actions in advance of them happening. Regardless of that, he has not given you a second thought, I can assure you. After all, you are still, in his eyes, as with most of Hell, just a pathetic soul. The thought you would challenge him would never enter his mind; it is just too ridiculous."

"Yes, there it is, ridiculous," exclaimed Kitar.

I nodded my approval, "Oh hush," I said to Kitar. Then turning my attention back to the Hellspawn and the Archangel, (there is a line you don't get to use often), I said, "Fine. Gabriel what else on this Plane should I see before we start this little experiment? I have a feeling I'll need to complete my tour first."

"I agree and will come to you after you have rested. We will see what outstanding business you have left on this Plane. I am also going to post guards outside all entrances to your apartments. Do not be alarmed; this is only to ensure no one has access to these chambers without us, or mainly me, knowing."

"Thank you, Lord Gabriel. Both in this and in your support."

"Dear boy, my support will neither help nor hinder your effort. What you are suggesting is almost certainly doomed for failure. My involvement is simply to sow discord amongst Lucifer and his accursed Fallen. If there is anything I can do to facilitate that after all the problems he, those who followed him and now his cursed great-grandson, has done, it is my pleasure." And with that, the Archangel smiled, finished his wine and left the room.

From behind me, I heard, "You hated being a pawn in Lord Lucifer's games. Now you have just become a pawn in the ongoing struggles between The Host and Hell. Congratulations, you are moving up in the world," commented Kitar.

"As you said I've always been," I remarked.

"Well yes, but before it was a passive role, it is no longer. You have become an active player if you choose this course of action."

"So be it, if it gives me even the slightest chance of getting Usis back."

"Ahhh, such is love," added Elick.

# Entry 212

Shortly after Gabriel's departure, Elick left as well. He took parts of both hearts with him. This would be Usis' first part of the second heart. Sadly, whether I liked it or not, Usis was already under the effects of The Lover's heart, so we decided to give him the first piece of the other heart and monitor the results. I mean it's not like it mattered, I was moving forward. I'd already decided we were either going to succeed together or fail together.

I sat for a while lost in thought until I heard a small cough from behind me. When I looked back, Cemal was there with his customary smile, his little-pointed teeth in a neat row pressed against his lower lip. He motioned to the table; there were two places set for dinner.

"Is Kitar joining me?"

"If you do not mind," came the answer from the door between our rooms.

"Of course not. Please," I said as I walked over and sat down.

Though he was willing, maybe even wanting to have dinner together, it was still a very quiet affair, little was said.

After dinner, I walked out onto the balcony and just stared across the Plane. I watched as Detaltuchiaca's tentacles moved methodically across the forest. Picking up and placing new souls upon their spits. You would see the flailing damned, so small in the great beast's grasp, move across the sea of spikes and then the sharp movement downwards punctuated by the scream of unimaginable pain.

Hearing movement behind me, "Is Detaltuchiaca a Demon, soul or was it created? Do you know?"

"It is a created Demon," answered Kitar from behind me, I looked back with a questioning look, "Most creations use souls, some get the energy that drives them from Demons instead. It is one of them, as is Cemal," Kitar explained.

"Does it talk? Can it talk? If so can I talk to it? I guess thats what I'm asking."

"I will see what I can arrange. It has a smaller more humanoid shape."

"Good to know," I said taking the offered drink from our guide as he joined me on the balcony. "So you are dead set against this?"

Shaking his head, he replied, "No, it is a tremendous risk. But maybe the only option we have. Based upon what Elick said, you are not getting Usis back any other way, and I know how much he means to you. Therefore, if you do not try, or try and fail, the result is the same, you eternal suffering and second-guessing yourself. This is probably the only way you will ever have a chance, though small. As much as I hate to say it, I also agree that if you do not transform into something else you will always be a target. If you want a life after this assignment, you will need to do something; Pandemonium is a dangerous place."

"It's a great relief to hear you say that, thank you," was all I could say.

"You know you will need to become a gifted fighter quickly. Thankfully you have Elick who is probably one of the best." Inclining his head and smiling, Kitar said, "I mean if you ignore the fact your boyfriend kicked his ass several times. If you truly inherit some of the ability of the heart's previous owners, that will most certainly help. I will see what I can do to get Lucifer or someone in the upper power structure to intervene."

"Upper power structure, who would that be?"

"You have a point there, whether you know it or not, other than Lucifer, there is no one else. All his generals hold the same sway."

"That's what I thought. Is there a town on this Plane?"

"No...The Host would not allow it. They bring their servants in from The Eternal City."

"Like the Cherubim?

"Yes, and some souls."

"What did they do wrong to get stationed here?" I laughed at my joke, Kitar did not.

"That is closer to the truth than you know. They bring the souls down here if they are having trouble with them to remind them what their alternative is."

"Scared straight, so to speak. Can a soul get kicked out of The Eternal City?"

"Yes, it is rare, but it has happened."

"Find me one; I want to talk to them. It would make a great addition to the journal. Compare and contrast."

Shaking his head, Kitar replied, "I am certain Lord Gabriel will not allow you access to any they have brought with them, but I will see what I can do. Based upon what I have learned since coming to Hell, The Host is not all that people believe it is. I will see if any of the fallen souls are on the upcoming Planes."

"Good, as for The Host not being all they advertise, I've already figured that one out."

"I will see if I can arrange for you to talk to Gabriel's slave. He could probably tell you about both the lower and upper levels of the hierarchy. Since he started as a soul in the street of The Eternal City and worked his way up to serving one of The Most High."

"That's a great idea. I'd forgotten about him," I commented. That got a cough from behind me. Turning and finding Cemal kneeling, I said, "Do you have something to add?"

In almost a shy tone my little slave reminded me of something Usis often said, "Remember, Master, invisible in plain sight."

Kitar nodded his approval. "Yes, we should be cautious of who is around both obviously and not from this point on." Turning back to the boy, Kitar said, "Good catch young one." Cemal just bowed his head to the Judge.

I changed the subject, not liking this line of conversation. It was making me uncomfortable. "I'll see if I can corner the slave. It might not be until after I start the…. I wonder what I should call it… change? Transformation? Evolution?"

"I would probably say transformation, it seems more accurate. More to the point, I would not call it anything if you can help it. Again, you do not wish to be overheard."

# Entry 213

That night I tried to rest, but my mind was racing a thousand miles an hour. I worked on entries, sent them to the editors. In case you're wondering how they get them and prepare them to be sent into Creation and you, I've no idea. My typewriter bug handles that, and yes, I've never asked. I treat the entries like I'd treat a book after giving to the publisher. They can do with it as they see fit.

A few hours into typing I ran out of wine, I know I drink a lot, sue me, and went to find more. When I opened the door, I found Cemal curled up on a mat on the floor. Don't think that, it looks comfortable and I have already said I don't approve. I watched him for a bit. I remembered when I thought he was sexually attractive. Now he was like a brother or a son; I couldn't imagine having feelings like that for him now. They'd changed into something new and good. I snuck in to get a bottle off the shelf as he rolled over, his snoring temporarily stopping. It was the first time I'd really gotten to look at his wings and how he pulled them so tightly against his back. From the front, they were barely visible if he didn't have them extended. As I pulled the door shut and started back to my desk, I let out a small cry, startled by Gabriel standing in the sitting area.

"You know you should give a person more warning. You almost gave me a heart attack," I gasped.

"Technically not possible but my apologies."

"No problem. Is there something you need?"

"Yes, I think there is someone you should talk to before you set your plans into action."

"If it's to convince me not to do it, that won't happen unless you can come up with another way to get Usis back."

Shaking his head, Gabriel replied, "I have no interest in changing your plans. Please follow me."

Not saying another word, he turned and left. I rushed to follow behind him as we made our way through the Keep and out the front. He turned to the left, together we walked in silence through the Forest of Pain until we reached the mountains, in the cliff face, was an opening.

I looked at the Archangel. "You are safe, you have my word. This is the home of Raguel. He is one of the Fallen."

"And you are bringing me to him? I thought you hated these guys."

"Hate is strong. Raguel is one of The Host who chose not to choose. As you already know, they were cast out as well. This particular time my feelings about him are inconsequential, I think he can help you along the path you are about to walk. He is also part of this Plane and someone you would have needed to visit anyway."

Shaking my head, "I can't figure you guys out. I was given the indication we would receive no help from you or any of The Host while we were here. You have proven to be a valuable friend."

He smiled. "Keith, I have set my feelings about Lucifer and his Domain aside. Even had I not, I would have probably still ended up helping you. But it is not at the wishes of that accursed beast that I have chosen to give my aid. We are trained to judge people based upon their actions. Even though I originally wanted to dislike you but found your merit outweighed any prejudices I wished to impose upon you. If Lucifer insists on this folly I cannot think of a more impartial soul he could have chosen to write it. Now go, Raguel is awaiting you."

In stunned silence, I stood and watched the Archangel walk back up the path and vanish into the forest.

# Entry 214

Entering the cave, however reluctantly, I walked down a long tunnel. The narrow path twisted and turned until eventually, I could see a wall of light which sparked a distant memory of a sunny day. This was the second place on this Plane which betrayed the dark gloom of Lucifer's domain.

Standing at the entrance, blinded by the light... (sorry just had to say that) I heard from inside, "Please come in, you are safe here and most welcome." The voice was smooth, calm and a lot like Gabriel's. Have I pointed out, every time Gabriel speaks it's like getting a warm bath after a long day? And boy have I had a long few days.

As I stepped through the curtain of light, I found myself standing on the grassy shore by a small pond about a hundred yards back and wide. Across the water, a short distance was a tiny island upon which sat a single room Asian building. On the porch at the front of the shack stood an average size man dressed in long flowing robes, a lot like a Tibetan monk. His head was bald and his face young, carrying the glow I'd seen in both Gabriel and the Cherubim, it was positively radiant. He bowed to me as I stood there taking his measure and then, I swear, he started to walk across the water. When he reached the shore, he again inclined his head. "Welcome, I am Raguel."

Bowing myself, I replied, "It is a pleasure to meet you. I'm Keith, Lord Lucifer's writer, as I'm often called."

"It does not matter what you are called; it is what you call yourself. But yes, I know who you are. I have been expecting you. Please take my hand; I have tea prepared." I did as he asked as we walked out across the water, sorta cool. I could see the fish and waving plants under us as we passed over them.

I would describe the Angel's house as austere but ornate and not very large. Just paper screen walls cornered by columns leading up to a terracotta tile roof capped with golden dragons decorating each corner. On the porch were two cushions and a low table upon which sat two cups and a pot of tea.

He extended a hand inviting me to sit as he moved across and took the seat opposite. With long thin, pale fingers, he reached out and poured us both tea. "It is jasmine, if that meets with your approval."

"That would be nice. I haven't had tea in a very long while, well since I died."

"I can imagine, the drinks in this place are, how would you say, less than wholesome." He smiled.

He was welcoming and sweet, but boy was he making me nervous, "Do you know why Gabriel wanted me to meet you? I mean other than as part about the journal. Do you know what I'm thinking about doing?"

"Why Gabriel wants anything is normally very easy to understand, he is not that deep. As to why he wanted you to meet me, I would imagine it is for me to tell you how to succeed against The Leviathan. As to your last question, yes."

"If you don't mind, can we address the issue with my companion first? I'm having trouble focusing on anything else. I guess it's the idea of having to outsmart a Fallen that has me a bit worried. Then if you would allow, I would like to chat about your past more casually, your relationship to The Host and, of course, Hell itself."

"That is understandable. I can see your mind is troubled."

"Thank you," I said as I took a sip of the tea. Setting it down I blurted, "Not to put too fine a point on it, what can you tell me?"

"First let me correct a misstatement you made. You will not 'outsmart' Leviathan. All you can hope to do is outplay him. As you have been told on many occasions, you are now part of an intricate game. Up to this point, you have been a reluctant player. That will have to change. You now need to embrace the game and play it well if you wish to be successful. As for your adversary, Leviathan, what I can tell you is that you cannot hesitate. Any show of reluctance or doubt he will seize upon and use against you. You must be ready to lose everything and to make him believe he stands to risk the same. If you do not think he will use you and your traveling companion's weaknesses against you, you have already failed."

"What about the hearts? Do you have any idea what consuming both of them will do to us?"

He shook his head. "You are moving in uncharted waters there, dear boy. Which is quite something considering the company you now keep. No one can tell you what the ramifications will be. Seeing how you have already started down that path, you have no choice but to continue and see where it leads."

"When he took Usis the choice was taken from me," I said sadly.

"You speak like that is a bad thing. You sit here and tell me that once your love was taken, saving him was the only action left to you. What greater statement can there be said by anyone for another. Even The Father would approve." Inclining his head, he said, "Your methods, maybe not so much, but then, considering again the company you keep, it could be considered restrained."

I smiled and sipped my tea. "Speaking of The Father..."

"I will not discuss with you the details of the Great War; you have already recorded that story."

"Will you tell me your thoughts about the events leading up to and thereafter?"

"I will not presume to speak for others. As far as I am concerned the war against The Father was in the best case, handled wrong, and in the worst, a mistake. The reason I say this is because after all this time and much reflection I am not sure how else the Morningstar could have made his point.

"The fact that Lucifer and an army of one-third of The Host's population felt they needed to rise against The Father, sacrificing all they had, is in itself an indication of just how far afield the situation had gone. The Father was no longer listening to his advisors, his firstborn. He was acting out of selfishness and dare I say, in many ways, in the same destructive manner as has since been manifested in most of his living creations. As I recall it was your world's book which said, 'Man was made in The Father's image.' Sadly that was both in appearance and temperament.

"As unpopular as my opinion is, neither side was entirely in the right, or for that matter, the wrong. Both The Father and Lucifer made mistakes and/or intentionally did things which would leave no outcome but a full uprising. I have often asked Lucifer, when he visits, why, but he will never give me an answer. His opinion, like so many others, is 'It is done, and it is time to move on.' But I know my older brother, and he does not 'move on'. He is planning something, and no one in Creation knows what that is."

"You explained how Lucifer failed, how about The Father? What did he do wrong?"

"I have already explained part of it. The final straw, so to speak, the act which led ultimately to the war was simply that The Father betrayed those who served him. His greed and obsession to be worshipped without question led those who rose against him down a path with few other options."

"You didn't walk that path, as you call it, you didn't choose a side. Why?"

"Because mine is the path of the middle ground. I have, in my manifestations to many worlds, yours included, tried to teach the destructive nature of possessions, self-love, and extremes on either side of any given belief system. It is a wise man's job to find the extremes and help disillusion those who carry them by pointing out the middle way. Only then can a solution hope to be found, with neither side being truly happy. I tried before The Great War, but no one would listen. In fact, it led to me being one of the first cast out." He paused as if weighing his next words. "One of the loudest voices for my removal was the current Overlord of this Plane as well as your host. Gabriel is a blind follower. I can see in your mind that he has been generous and helpful. Going back to our original discussion about the decision you are facing, it would do you well to keep in mind that Gabriel would do anything to disrupt, cause turmoil and even destroy the Master of this Domain. Where Lucifer is my oldest brother, Gabriel is among the youngest and in so being the most wounded by Father's disappearance. He will never forgive the Morningstar for the pain he brought Father."

"Do you think he or anyone can destroy Lucifer?"

"No, Lucifer is older than us all. We all carry large amounts of The Father's creation energy. Lucifer, on the other hand, is completely creation energy. With The Father gone, no one, even Gabriel, would deny that the Morningstar is the most powerful entity walking Creation. Michael would be a close second, maybe almost an equal, but still not fully. And when you are talking about the amounts of power a creature like Lucifer holds in comparison to say, Michael, even a small difference is a vast amount." Again, he paused. "Which leads me to you."

"Me? How so."

"Why do you think your presence and more importantly your assigned activities have caused such a stir?"

"I've always assumed it was because Lucifer has decided to report the true intentions of Hell."

"Surprisingly, you are mostly correct but have you not carried it thru to its logical conclusion. Why now? Why with Xia, his favorite grandson, wandering throughout Creation? Why, when he and Michael seem to be working so well together?" He smiled. "I know you are going to ask if I have answers to these questions, and no I do not. But it is a fact, these questions and others are causing many to wonder if a larger game is afoot. And if that is indeed the case, and Lucifer is playing it, what might our oldest brother be planning."

"You keep referring to Lucifer as your brother. No one else has done that. Why do you and why don't they?"

"Because those who serve Lucifer see him as their Lord, and even a prince bows to his King. As for everyone else, many, like your host, do not call Lucifer as who he is, hoping that in its silence the truth will no longer be true."

I sat lost in thought for several minutes. It was not until Raguel refilled my tea that we resumed our conversation. "Do you think, since Lucifer arranged for me to eventually become his writer, that its possible he arranged for Usis to become my companion?"

"Yes, The Fates. I can assure you Lucifer will see Kitar taking you to visit them as a mistake. I would venture a guess; he did not want you to know he had a hand in preparing you. But now that you do, does that not also answer your question about your companion?"

I frowned. "Sadly, I think it does."

He nodded, "But do not let that change your opinion of Usis, or for that matter Kitar. You would go crazy if you try to run the circles to find Lucifer's, or any Most High's long-term intentions. There is no way for your mind to fathom such complex equations. I will say if it helps to ease said mind just a little, Lucifer is also a big believer in rewards for services rendered. He could have given you Usis as nothing more than payment for what you are doing for him. But as is our way, he gave him to you early enough to let your relationship cure in the heats of Hell before it turns into the intended payment for said services."

I looked at him sideways. "Do you believe that?"

"No, but I did not say I believed it, I said, if it would help ease your mind. Look around you, though Lucifer might be a 'big believer' of rewards, it is also clear that he tends more toward punishments for failures than compensations for success. That one observation should be considered when weighing the possible future conflict with Leviathan."

I smiled, and though he tried to control it, he smiled as well. "I know you guys don't tend to answer directly, but I feel I must ask you bluntly. Do you think I should eat the hearts as well?"

"Honestly, dear boy, I do not think you have any other choice. For the obvious reasons, it will possibly help Usis return to you. One of the less obvious reasons is simple; there is a good chance Lucifer did not see this one coming. I have known Lucifer for many millennia and knowing him as well as I do I can see no way where this would have been in his plans. Therefore, at the very least it will serve as an object lesson for our older brother. Where the living is concerned, you cannot completely predict their actions. If I might also point out, Gabriel and Elick are correct when they say it is probably the only way to transform you from a victim in Hell to a resident of Hell. And that single factor will have eternal ramifications upon your future existence."

He stood and quietly walked into his little house. After a few moments, he returned holding a small bag. "Here is some of my tea. Take it with you and enjoy it. Drink it when your mind needs to relax, and you seek clarity. Meditate."

I stood and took the bag, "May I visit again sometime?"

"It is why I am here, dear boy. Before you leave, I think there is one more topic you wish to discuss."

I thought, and like a light going on, I told him the story of Piaston. "I don't know why I felt you needed to hear that story."

"It may have something to do with the place I have found for myself here in Hell. Many who were cast out remained angry, as you know, you are consuming their hearts. I choose to see if I could find a way to help those few who do repent and realize the error of their lives. I will look into this one you have mentioned. If he is truly repentant, then I can arrange for his soul to be sent back to his world to be reborn. This will give him an opportunity to choose a different path. It is probable he will not, but one can never tell."

"Reincarnation? You mean it's real?"

"It was not originally planned. It took millennia for me to convince Lucifer, who eventually allowed me to petition Michael and The Eternal Council. Luckily, I was permitted to use my unique talents as long as I did not abuse them. Therefore, the number I can return is small. I must choose well. As I said, I will look into this case for you."

I smiled. "Thank you, Lord Raguel." He nodded as he took my elbow and began to lead me back across the waters.

"I wish you well on your travels. If you find yourself in need of a place to rest your mind or my modest advice, you are always welcome to visit again."

I don't know why, I guess because he was an Asian figure in my old world, but I bowed deeply to him. A gesture he returned. I realized when I was writing this that some might see that as "racist." I don't. If any other worlds are as hypersensitive as the world I left then I'd point out that the reason for a bow, and also my reason for bowing, was to show respect. I've had very few opportunities to genuinely show respect since I died and found myself here in Hell.

As he stood at the doorway to his cave, I asked, "Does meditation work?"

"Of course, most see it as talking to a higher power. And I guess in some ways you are, yourself. In my experience, the one voice the living least like to listen to is the one given to them by The Father in the form of their eternal spark. The one inside them which suggests the right path regardless if it is the one they wish to follow."

# Entry 215

As I walked into the Keep, I smelled food and heard conversation coming from the dining room. When I walked in, I found the whole group, Kitar, Elick, Gabriel and a couple of other people I didn't recognize sitting at the table eating. Cemal was there as well. When he saw me, he rushed up and threw his arms around me and then quickly vanished into the other room, returning with a place setting and some food.

Everyone had stopped their conversation. "Well it's about time you return," said Elick breaking the silence that had descended upon the chamber.

"What? I just went to talk to Raguel. It was not even a particularly long conversation," I responded.

It was Gabriel who cleared up the confusion. "Time conforms to the desires of the powers which inhabit it. Raguel's cave moves at a much slower pace than most of the rest of Creation, he sees it as mindfulness. He says it allows for more consideration in a shorter time."

"How long was I gone?"

Kitar answered, "About two weeks."

"WHAT," I barked.

"Please calm yourself. You have returned, and all is in order. Please join us," said the Archangel calmly as he resumed eating his dinner.

My eyes flashed immediately to Elick who just nodded and subtly, with his hand, suggested patience. As I took a seat it was then that I noticed the other guests at the table. Two took my breath away, where the third stole my appetite.

Gabriel seeing me studying them turned to the two who were clearly Angels, "Allow me to introduce The Dark Lord's much talked about writer. This is Keith." Turning to me, "Keith you have the honor of dinner this evening with Raphael and Cerveil. Our third guest is by your request, but most welcome. This is Detaltuchiaca, the Overseer of this Plane's punishments."

I forced my eyes back to the creature I'd just learned was Detaltuchiaca. I don't know what I was expecting, having seen the massive beast hanging from the cavern like a gelatinous stalagmite, but I'm sure a semi-human form wasn't it. I swallowed hard, took a drink of wine returning my gaze to the two Angels. "It's a pleasure to be in your company, My Lords." Then to the overseer I simply said, while trying not to sound shocked, "And you Lord Detaltuchiaca, It's a pleasure. I hope we can have a few moments to chat."

Looking back to Gabriel, Detaltuchiaca quietly said, "Chat?"

Smiling, the Archangel explained, "It is a term from his world meaning, to talk. Yes, you are the next victim in the Dark Lord's writer's wheel of inquiry."

"Oh yes, it would be a pleasure," answered the Overseer as his eyes returned to me. "It is after all, why I have been summoned." He had a deep rumbling voice, almost Slavic in some ways but the way he rolled certain letters gave it a French flow if that makes sense.

I nodded my agreement and tried to not look too surprised. I can tell by the looks on my friend's faces that I was failing miserably.

Dinner went well, and I'm not going to bother to describe the two Angels. Suffice it to say they were handsome, youthful with just a hint of stern unyieldingness behind their eyes. I'll, however, describe the Overseer Detaltuchiaca. His body was about seven feet tall and somewhat bulky. It was proportional. I guess slightly bloated would be a good way to describe it. He had the standard humanoid frame, two arms, legs and was dressed in a pair of tights, a vest covering his upper torso, boots and, strangely, gloves. Now that is a fundamental description so let's break it down.

First his face. I cannot say what his actual face might look like; I think there mightn't have been one. The structure of the front of the face: eyes, nose, mouth, forehead, and chin were all on a stretched piece of skin. It was like a flexible mask, somewhat like Balic from an earlier plane. Where they differed was Balic's face was stretched in the center of a donut of a head. Here the skin of Detaltuchiaca's face was pulled tight over the standard humanoid shaped structure. At several spots, there were holes, just above and to the side of each eye, on each side of the mouth along the edge, a couple along the chin and several along the top of the forehead. Each of these spots had a cord laced through them that traveled to the back of the head to secure the face to the front. What I found most interesting was how tightly they were pulled, it seemed almost to the point of tearing out the holes. The part of his head, excluding his face, the top, sides with ears and back in many ways looked like one of the knit stockings one would use on a cold day or to rob a bank.

What I would learn later while we were talking, which I will get to, was why he appeared to be bloated. See he is strange. You'd think he would be a monster, based upon the service he provides in Hell but that would be wrong. He's a quiet and insecure creature. When hearing he would be meeting with me, The Dark Lord's writer, he forced his actual form into the skin of a humanoid. Yes, you read that right, he pushed his malleable body into another form, hoping it would make me feel less uncomfortable. Close up I noticed it when I saw the stitching down the back of the arms, vanishing into the vest he was wearing. It seems he pulled the skin from someone, stuffed himself into it and then laced it up to hold him and it in place.

After dinner, we went and found a spot away from the group and chatted for several hours. He was a frightfully gentle soul, almost disarmingly so. As you will see, it was the conversation, not his look which gave him his fierceness.

"I'm not sure where to start. I hope this isn't a rude question; I was told you were created?"

He nodded. "Yes, I'm a construct, my Lord. The souls of the living and the essences of Demons which reside inside this shell have been moved several times from one body to another based upon the Overlord's wishes for how I am to perform my duties."

"You carry on from body to body?"

"Yes, one of my greatest struggles is changing forms. When the residing Overlord chooses to relocate me, for one reason or another, or if the current shell is damaged then I must be pulled out and placed into a new body. It is most inconvenient since they tend never to make me the same twice. I must relearn how to perform my duties within the limitations of the newest construct."

"Based upon what I saw the other day while watching you work, your current form seems very suited for your responsibilities."

"Yes, this is one of the better shells I have inhabited. And thank you for noticing, My Lord."

"I am just Keith. Just a soul, doing a job, just like you," I corrected with a smile.

"Yes, My...Keith," he replied almost demurely.

"I must say I find your personality surprising; you seem very shy."

"My...Keith, you must remember I spend all day rewarding souls with their eternity. Rarely am I allowed to come down, and in all the millions of years since my creation I have only been invited into the formal parts of the Keep twice. So today, having entered the Overlord's residence. Having consumed food with you and the three Most High. Now I am being allowed to sit in this beautiful room and talk like a normal creature is, if you will forgive me for saying, a real honor and treat which I will look back upon and savor for millennia to come."

I noticed the pride that glistened in the eyes behind the stretched fleshy mask. "You enjoy what you do?" I asked.

"Oh yes, Lord...Forgive I mean Keith...I am serving to ensure those who have offended The Father receive the payment for those sins. Their screams to me are a testament to the quality of my work. The suffering that drips from their bodies as they struggle in agony upon the spit I see as a direct indicator of how well I have applied my craft."

I just sat watching him talk, his taut face, the way the strings holding it moved as his mouth opened and closed. The way he did not carry a hatred or distain for these souls like most in Hell did. "You take such pride in your work," I commented.

"Keith, the Powers that rule Creation took the pitiful remnants of damaged souls then combined them to produce me. They did not have to use souls; they could have let them slip from eternity in the furnaces that bring all those who live in this place heat. But instead, they shaped and formed a body and a soul, producing what now sits before you. I am grateful for their consideration. I am grateful for their gift of consciousness. Then to allow me the honor of picking the bits and pieces I find pleasant, so I can build for myself a body which we are told is not unlike that of The Father's. It is not often I am allowed to walk the Plane in this form, but when I do, I do not take for granted the honor contained in that act. I am proud to, in some small way, reflect The Father's work." He paused and looked down for a second and finally when he was ready again he met my eyes, "My Lord.." he raised a finger to stop my objection, "...My existence is to bring pain. My sin is pride. These souls failed The Father and have, through me, been given the opportunity to make amends. It does not matter where or how I am asked to serve. I shall do so with every fiber of my being."

I don't know why but I gently reached out and touched his face; he leaned into it as a child does at a parent's touch. "I have met Fallen, Archangels, Judges and more souls than I can count. If only The Father could have created something as humble and pure as you I dare say Hell would not be as crowded and you would have more time to explore who you are. Thank you for this interview."

He looked at me in surprise. "Those are probably the kindest words I have ever heard, I thank you as well, Lord Keith. You might not like that title, but in these borrowed eyes, it is deserved."

He stood and walked to the door leading outside. I followed him. He walked a distance from the Keep and with great care removed his tunic, tights and other clothing, folding them and setting them on the ground next to him. Then reaching up with one hand he pulled the ties holding the lacing together and like biscuits leaving a tube he expanded out and grew. His tentacles reached down and folded the skin and placed it carefully on top of the clothing. Then finally he lifted the face, its laces hanging loose and set it on top. As he took the bundle in a single tentacle, he began to rise into the air as he continued to grow larger. Finally, when he reached the roof of the vast cavern, he attached himself. I didn't see where the parcel of possessions went. With sudden speed his arms traveled across the expanse, grasping three different souls, moving them to the forest and slamming them down, impaling them on their posts of pain as the cries began again. He had gone back to work, punishing those who, on this plane at least, deserved the suffering awaiting them.

As I turned and walked back into the Keep, I found Cemal standing there. I looked up toward the ceiling one last time. "You know, he is probably the noblest creature here."

# Entry 216

Realizing Cemal was outside our room I asked. "Did you come looking for me?"

"No, Master, I did not, I wanted to stretch my legs. I have been in our room for a while, and both the other Masters are out right now as well. This one thought it was a good time to look around. I hope Master does not mind."

Shaking my head, I replied, "Of course not, you're as free to move about the Plane as anyone else. Just be careful." The boy nodded his understanding. "Come, we can walk together. I just interviewed Detaltuchiaca..." I explained as I pointed up.

"Yes, he is very kind," answered the boy as we headed down the path through the forest. The screams of pain just background noise we barely noticed. We did watch a thorn bush snake up a newly planted soul. His cries grew louder as the thorns themselves started to bud and pierced his tough, scaly skin.

As the light started to dim toward evening (yes I can tell the difference now, it is subtle and really more visible in the forest due to the shadows) we noticed a small campfire off in the distance. "That is strange," I said as we turned off the path and started to work our way through the posts and thorns. I noticed they parted, the thorns that is, as we approached and moved back after we'd past. I guess if you weren't the soul they were assigned to they didn't bother you.

I looked down to find Cemal was holding my arm; I wasn't sure if he was scared or trying to slow me down. Either way, we froze when we heard a growl behind us and turned just in time to see a warthog looking creature, about four feet tall, bound out from behind a thick set of bushes. I screamed as he grabbed me, knocking me to the ground. Had I not thrown my arms up to stop him, his sharp teeth would have torn out my throat.

In the confusion, I lost sight of Cemal until I saw the creature on top of me fly across the clearing slamming into one of the posts and sliding to the ground. The next thing I realized I saw Cemal descend, his wings flapping furiously as he landed on the creature's chest. His arm came back and that was when I noticed he wasn't as I remembered him. With a vicious swipe, the boy's now six inch taloned claws cut through our attacker's flesh, amputating his hand. As quickly as the battle started, it was over. I heard a sharp, loud squeak, and then the creature didn't move again.

Cemal climbed off and turned to me. What I saw wasn't the little innocent slave boy I'd grown to know. Instead of the cute little mouth, the slit now traveled from his left ear to his right. His mouth was open, revealing several rows of razor-sharp teeth. As he moved to stand, I looked at his hand to verify they were now talons with six-inch scalpel sharp nails. His feet were the same way. His body was covered with a glistening sheen of what appeared to be sweat. I gasped and stepped back as he began to change, already tears were flowing down his face. Forgetting, the sight of his mouth reducing down in size, I ran up to try to comfort him, but he jumped back yelling "No Master, you cannot touch me."

I've been in Hell long enough to know what a warning sounds like, so I froze in place. He continued to transform. His body, which I'd not noticed had grown more muscular, shrank back down as his claws returned to the little demon hands I'd become used too. When he'd finished changing and was standing nude before me, he again looked like the little servant boy I'd cared so much for. "What in the Hell did I just see?"

Looking up at me with sheepish eyes still wet with tears he said, "Master, this one might not have had a chance to tell you everything about himself. Boy hopes you will forgive him and..." he paused as his hand coming up over his mouth in a gasp, "Ohh.. please Master do not send me away...please..." he began to cry harder.

"Can I touch you now?" I asked getting the answer as he ran up and fell into my arms weeping. "OK, calm down. First, what was that? And second, why in the world would I send you away?"

He clung to me for several seconds before looking up and in short gasps started to explain. "Master, boy has a defense in case he is attacked, or his master is threatened."

I let him go so I could sit down. "So you turn into a fierce beast when threatened?"

He gave me a shy smile. "Well...sort of, maybe a little."

I laughed, "A little? Cemal that had to be one of the most terrifying things I've seen in a while. I'm impressed."

"You are not angry?"

"Of course not, if anything I'm relieved. I'd always been worried about you going out to get supplies and stuff. That is why I always left you in the room and retrieved them myself. Now that I know you can defend yourself I feel a lot better."

A new wave of tears and sobbing flooded his face. "Oh thank you, Master. My defense is instinct, and this one has little control over it."

"Did Usis know about your special skills?" I asked, already suspecting I knew the answer.

"In a way he did Master, he asked this one if he had any protections. This one explained to him, but was never asked to demonstrate." I nodded. I had a feeling Usis knew. I shook my head, now missing my companion now even more.

"Your reaction speed was amazing. You reacted faster than I could've, not that I have any defenses in the first place."

"That is why Master needs to carry through with his plan. It will give Master defenses, and as Mater Elick has pointed out, Hell is a dangerous place. You will need to cast a strong image or you will always be at the mercy of those who think they are stronger."

I smiled and hugged him again. "Thank you, I've had many good councils from Kitar, Gabriel, and Elick but hearing that from you is all I needed to help me decide. You, my boy, I trust more than anyone else with me right now."

As we stood up and walked back to the body of the attacker my hand again found my mouth. The right side of his body, the amputated arm, his shoulder and most of his chest had melted away. Turning back to

Cemal to find him with a sheepishly look as he peaked around me, I asked, "What did you do to him? This doesn't look like just your claws."

"That is why boy stopped Master from touching him. When boy is attacked his body becomes coated with a slimy gel, it is really disgusting if truth be told. If any creature touches it, the toxin enters their bloodstream paralyzing them and then slowly starts to dissolve them until there is nothing left but a puddle of goop."

"That sounds disgusting."

"Oh, it is, boy feels like he has been rolled in slime but it is worse for the attacker," he said, pointing to the quickly disappearing warthog. "Not only are they paralyzed, but they stay conscious through it all until their head dissolves in excruciating pain. The only reason you cannot hear his screams of agony is due to the paralysis."

My gaze traveled between the boy and the creature several times. "Well, he is one ugly looking son of a bitch."

"Not for much longer Master. He will soon be a handsome puddle of sticky green goop." I smirked at the boy's description until I heard him hiss and assume an attack stance. I spun around to find a group of creatures standing several feet away staring at us.

Jumping in front of me Cemal hissed, "Do you want some of this? Just try to attack my Master."

The center one raised his hand. "We mean you no harm," pointing to the creature that was now just arms, legs and head, his torso nothing more than a puddle, "he was not with us."

# Entry 217

"Who are you?" I asked.

Looking back over his shoulder at me already partially changed, Cemal hissed, "Does Master want me to ensure they are not dangerous?"

"Down there, bruiser. They don't seem a threat." I looked back at the new visitors and added, "Though it might not be a bad idea if you explain who you are. The quicker, the better, I think my boy here is still in a fighting mood."

Again, the center one spoke, "We are just gypsies that live amongst the damned."

"You are not damned souls?"

"Some of us are My Lord. We have been freed by the Fallen that lives in the cave across the Plane."

"You mean Raguel?"

"Yes, My Lord…"

I interrupted him, "Keith, just call me Keith."

"Yes Keith, if you would like to join us we were about to sit down to a meal."

We followed the group back. It consisted of about five other creatures besides the one who was clearly their leader. Toward the mountain but still surrounded by the forest of suffering was a small clearing with another ten or so souls and Demons sitting around a fire. Most jumped up when they saw us but were quickly told to relax. It seems the warthog creature Cemal had killed had been terrorizing them for weeks. They were quite pleased to be rid of him.

I looked them over, almost instantly recognizing Tinolic, the Piaston from when I first arrived on this plane. Walking over to him, I said, "Raguel said he was going to talk to you."

"He did, My Lord, and we told him our story. He did not see it as a reason for reincarnation. He did offer us the option to be freed to live in exile here amongst the others who have escaped the tortures we so richly deserve."

Cocking my head to the side, I asked, "You're satisfied with that? If you feel you deserve punishment why did you leave?"

"We are content, My Lord. The Most High explained that here we would minister to the souls of those wandering as exiles amongst the planes. It is a calling we think we can fulfill better than we did before."

"Between the Planes? I know the route, and the doors are always locked."

"It seems there are other, secret ways that few know of. Tunneled over time for various nefarious reasons. This is Hell after all, who knows what plans lurk in the minds of men."

"I can't argue with you there. Well if you are...content...then I will be as well. This has to be better than the tortures planned for you."

"Yes indeed."

I'm not going to go into all the details of that night; it was just a bunch of creatures living hidden away, running when chased and hoping to make eternity a little less awful. Their stories were stories of desperation in most cases. They survived by carving pieces off the blasphemous sinners impaled all around them. When I made it back to the Keep, I asked Gabriel what he thought about souls running free on the planes, or even if he knew. You can imagine the answer to the latter part. Of course, he knew, what he did not do, was care. There were too many souls in Hell, and some had escaped. I'd been assured there were a lot, and I would probably meet more on the remaining planes. Therefore I chose not to record these. Like everything else, I know there is more to this part of this story than meets the eye but right now I had other things on my mind. Something about seeing them reminded me of my future, which reminded me of the hearts, which reminded me of Usis, which reminded me of what my only goal was. Therefore, after having dinner with them, I returned to the Keep.

# Entry 218

When we made it back to my room, I found Kitar and Elick in a state. "Where the Hell have you been?" barked Kitar.

"I thought you could always locate me." Waving him off, I told him, "Anyway, Cemal and I want for a walk."

"A walk," growled Kitar, "Do you not know how dangerous that is?"

I raised an eyebrow. "You seem to be slipping old boy. Did you not know our young companion here has got game?"

"Got WHAT..." yelled Kitar in almost a bark. "What is game.."

I waved. "It's an old Earth saying meaning, he has secret skills."

"Well, of course, he does, he is a Demon."

I walked up with a smile on my face until I was almost nose to muzzle with my irate guide. "Well it seems someone left that little bit of information out. Is there anything else you would like to tell me about while we are opening surprises?"

This time it was Elick who spoke. "We have left out a great many things. Do you wish to know all that Creation holds or save Usis? Choose your priorities."

I gave him a dangerous look. "I better not be being played by you as well. You might be immortal but now so am I and if you think I can be a bitch in the short term just imagine what I must be like for eternity. I want to go get my lover." Trying to not sound like a total bitch, I added, "And thank you all for your help."

I heard Kitar say something under his breath. "What did you just say?" I asked.

"We were talking about what the future holds, and it reminded me of a quote from one of your world's philosophers. 'He that hath wife and children hath given hostages to fortune; for they are impediments to great enterprises, either of virtue or mischief'."

"Wow, that's deep." Turning to Cemal, I said, "Would you mind preparing my dinner." The boy looked at me oddly and then glanced at the table. "I'm thinking thinly sliced."

Picking up the box like what I was asking was no big deal Elick added, "Yes, three of the primary and one of the secondary."

Cemal thought for a second. "Please allow this boy to make sure he understands. The primary is the one Master's companion has not eaten as much of, correct? And the secondary is Master Usis' primary. Oh, is this going to be confusing? May this one label them?"

"Good point, yes, you're in charge of them now. Label them as you see fit."

"We are talking about hearts from The Host, you realize that right?" added Kitar with a hint of indignation in his voice.

"Fine, then wrap them in silk, drape them in gold, but figure out how to mark which is which since they are both going to be disappearing more quickly now."

Cemal walked over and picked up the box, as he passed by Kitar he patted him on the chest twice, "Don't worry, Lord Judge, this boy has it covered. Just have a glass of wine and go sit down and act smug. We all have our skills."

Kitar's mouth dropped in shock as Elick and I burst out laughing. "You know, Kitar, I think the boy is starting to fit in nicely."

As the boy walked out with the plate, Kitar, in a rare show of desperation, grabbed me by the arm. "Do you really want to become one of the monsters?"

Gripping him by both sides of the head so our eyes met, I looked at him intensely. "Look at me, use that special sight of yours...." I was yelling, "Go ahead do it. You'll find that sometimes you must become the monster to save what you hold dear. It doesn't matter what your outsides look like or your actions, as long as they are for the right reasons and deep down you, at least, remember the person you wish to hang on to. I'll take on the shell of a monster to save Usis because not to try means I've already become one, and that's not something I'm prepared to spend eternity knowing."

We started at each other for a long time. Finally, he said, "And I will be there standing behind you to remind you of that scared soul I met oh so long ago."

"It's all I ever wanted from you Kitar, that and your friendship."

"Well then you have both."

# Entry 219

Cemal walked back in and set the plate on the table. Walking over I sat down with a smile. He'd done it up nice, complete with garnishes just like a high-end sushi restaurant back when I was living. I looked up and found him. "Thank you." He simply bowed. I found Kitar, then Usis, then as the door opened Gabriel walked in.

We watched the Angel walk across the room carrying an extremely ornate goblet and a dusty bottle of wine. He set both down, picked up the bottle, removed the cork and poured half a glass. "This goes better with heart."

I reached down and took the four slices, all exactly the same thickness. I lifted them to my lips and brought them onto my tongue. I chewed. They had no taste, or I was numb, I'm not sure which. I reached down, taking the goblet and took a drink of the wine.

I turned to them. "Keep the readers up to date. We have brought them this far. Until I awake."

# Entry 220 (Elick)

The Clitovic crawled up on the table; it had recorded Keith's last entry. I had the creature read it back as Keith passed out, slumping down in his chair. The hearts' effect did not take as long as expected. Gabriel reached behind Keith's head and under his legs, picked him up and carried him to the bed, laying him down almost reverently. As he finished, he turned, inclined his head to both Kitar and I and left.

We will get back to you when there is something new to report.

# Journal of a Deadman

## Volume 6 – Violence

## Alexander Collas

To the many people who have supported me during this process. To my Mother, Kyler, and Patrick, thank you. To everyone who has suffered through my moody writing days I cannot tell you how much it means. I would also like to thank Jim, the kind of fan any author would kill for.

Burning this book will allow you to contact Lucifer if you follow the directions inside. Remember, if it doesn't work, you will need to purchase another copy and try again.

"Remember what you must do
when they undervalue you
when they think
your softness is your weakness
when they treat your kindness
like it is their advantage.

You awaken
every dragon,
every wolf,
every monster
that sleeps inside of you
and you remind them
what hell looks like
when it wears the skin
of a gentle human."

- Nikita Gill

# Entry 221 – Cemal's Entry

"This one does not understand. What am I to do?" grumbled Cemal with a sigh.

"Do as you were instructed. Write your impressions of what has occurred since Keith began to consume the hearts of The Lovers," instructed Kitar.

Stomping, Cemal said, "I understand that part, but who will care? Who would want to read something by a simple slave like this one?"

"You do have a point there, but that does not change your orders. As to whom might read what you have written, well that would be everyone in the Nine Creations, at least that is what The Dark Lord hopes."

"No… this one does not carry the stature to address that many of anything without their permission. Master does realize that, right? Everyone in the nine Creations is a lot of living, right? This one is not sure he can or should do this. This one is not a writer; this one is a slave."

"To be completely accurate you are a cheeky overzealous slave that is currently arguing about something his Master, Keith, has instructed him to do. So, write." Looking around, Kitar added, "Why are we having this argument. As you yourself have pointed out, you are a slave. So, follow the orders given, which entails more writing and less debate."

"Fine… first, you Master, and with all due respect, are overly grumpy and a somewhat growly puppy doggie, as Master likes to call you since being honest is what Master, you that is, not my real Master, has suggested we do." Looking back with a huff and lifting his hands, he points to the large bug-like creature sitting on the table. "Where do I start?"

"That is your decision. Dictate your comments and the anacrateloc will take them down, and Keith can edit them when he wakes up."

Pausing Kitar adds, yelling, "and Keith does not call me a puppy doggie!"

"But… OK fine… boy is allowed to say, you, Master, are an 'overbearing, loudmouth sanctimonious pain in the ass' but not a puppy doggie. Does this one have this correct?" Stopping and looking at the anacrateloc with a wrinkled nose, Cemal adds, "Wait. If my Master, you know my real Master is going to edit this ones writing, why can't we just wait until Master awakens so Master can write it?"

"Did you call me sanctimonious? Where did you learn such a word?"

"Master Keith has been teaching this one. He says this one must learn to curse better. If one is to stand on his own feet, then one should do so occasionally by having the right words to remove others…feet that is." Pausing and looking up with a puzzled expression while biting his lower lip, Cemal asks, "Did this one not use the word correctly?"

"No, you used it correctly."

"So, Master agrees he is sanctimonious?"

"CEMAL…"

(Now is a good place to step in. This is Keith, and I'm doing the aforementioned editing which is how I know this conversation happened. I instructed the bug, or Anacrateloc, to record most of the conversations when he was in the room so I could add context later when I was preparing these entries for you the reader. Anyway, I'm not in the story yet, so I'll shut up and go back to being unconscious, well at least at this point in the entries.)

"Fine…" Cemal turned, and leaning into the multi-legged creature, said, "Hi, this one is called Cemal." Looking back over his shoulder, he asked, "Is that good? Is that where this one should start?"

"CEMAL! What are you doing?" barked Kitar again as he watched the boy use the corner of a cloth to dust the top of the nasty looking recording creature.

"It is dirty. Does anyone clean this creature?" Looking at the anacrateloc, the slave adds, "Do you not bathe?"

"CEMAL, WRITE!"

"Fine..."

Several weeks have passed, and for Master Keith's safety, we have left the Overlord's Keep on Blasphemy. Boy will leave the telling of where to one of the other Masters as instructed. My Master has awoken six times, each time in a lot of pain. Master's body looks horrible, and he spends most of his consciousness, screaming. This one quickly feeds him more of The Lovers, their hearts, and that seems to settle him back to sleep. Master Elick says that Master is still not conscious, it is just his body responding to changes. This one always keeps pieces ready to feed Master. Rarely does this one abandon his vigil. He is my Master. And a good one.

As boy is sure, all Master's readers remember Master Keith died in life and ended up in Hell where he has been traveling with a Judge from the Judgement Plane where souls are...well...judged, named Master Kitar. You have met him; he was the one yelling earlier, you know the puppy doggie. Master also travels with a companion named Usis. He has led to Master's current problem. See Master Usis has been abducted by a Fallen, Lord Leviathan, who is the Overlord of the Seventh Plane of Violence and Great Grandfather to Master's other traveling companion, Master Elick. The only other member of Master party is this one. This boy is a construct and was gifted to Master Keith to serve him as Master sees fit.

At some point during their travels, Master Keith and Master Usis were abducted by The Lovers, two Fallen who were imprisoned here in Hell. As boy understands, both Masters were tortured but eventually freed by Lord Lucifer. The Dark Lord it seems allowed Master Usis to vent his anger and revenge upon The Lovers. Master Keith did not know. At some point Master Usis during his tortures ripped the hearts from the two Fallen. My Master discovered on the last Plane, Blasphemy, that Master Usis had begun eating slices of one of the hearts. Boy is not clear of the reasons, but it seems it was to keep Master Usis's love safe, that love would be my Master. Upon finding out, my Master decided to rescue his companion when he reached the Seventh Plane and to ensure or at least help aid his success Master decided to start consuming pieces of the hearts as well. Master's hope is that by consuming both hearts, he will gain the powers of two Fallen, thus giving him an advantage in whatever is to come. That is why my Master is unconscious. His body has begun to change, and this boy is very worried about him. He is a good Master, understanding, considerate and does not yell, well at this one anyway. This one can think of nothing else to tell you, so thank you for listening, it was an honor.

Turning back to the room Cemal yells, "Master this one has completed the entry. Please tell us we will never be required to do this again, it is hard."

# Entry 222

Greetings sinners, this is the Lord Judge Kitar. Until Keith awakens to resume his duties, Lord Elick and myself are tasked with keeping you updated. It is my goal never to allow that little slave familiar to come near the Anacrateloc again. As you have no doubt observed it was a complete waste of time.

"This one did not do that badly," growled Cemal.

Enough of the chitchat. Keith is currently still incapacitated. He is waking more often, but only to scream about his suffering, therefore, for our sanity more than his, we are keeping him unconscious. A few days ago his skin started to sluff off in large greasy chunks. We expected this. The muscles underneath are continuously weeping a cloudy red liquid which would appear, if from the living, to be blood but which is in fact suffering. In addition to the skin loss, his body has also sluffed off his toes, fingers, ears, nose, as well as his hair. He is, at best a bloody skinless torso with only nubs for limbs. He is, as we expected, in the beginning stages of an extreme transformation.

As the boy pointed out, we have left the Plane of Blasphemy. Elick also petitioned The Dark Lord for permission not to distribute any of the entries from the time Keith entered the Sixth Plane until his current issues are resolved. If you are curious why, well it is simple, just like you, those wishing Keith harm can receive updates if they intercept his scribblings. Therefore, what you are reading has already occurred and is in our past. Lord Lucifer ordered us to continue writing the entries as we went, so his wishes are being followed. This ensures future events do not bleed into or alter what The Dark Lord wishes told and how, that being Keith's tour of his Planes. As you can imagine, even though you are reading this in our past, we too have no idea of the outcome at this point.

Currently, Keith has consumed ten slices of both The Lovers hearts. We will not know what his new form will be until the transformation is complete. The only complication we have seen thus far is he has not been recovering as quickly as Usis did, we are not sure the reason for this. Never in the memory of The Host or Hell has a mortal soul, or anyone for that matter, consumed one of The Host's hearts. True The Lovers were Fallen, or more accurately cast out, but still, never has a member, past or present, of The Host been destroyed in such a way. Why Lord Lucifer allowed Usis to take his revenge, like so many other things, is a mystery. We are not even sure if The Dark Lord knew. We can only assume he did. Between this entry and the previous one you should now be up to date. I will end the entry here and in closing say we look forward to your arrival in Hell.

# Entry 223

Greetings, again it is Kitar. Elick suggested it was time to update Keith's readers on the current status of their journalist. Full disclosure, Keith's Anacrateloc was also getting jittery. In case he has never used the "bug" creature's name before it is called an Anacrateloc. Just like Cemal and the Detaltuchiaca this creature as well is a construct. Keith will eventually tour the facilities on the Eighth Plane used to create such accessories.

Not being a writer, these entries may not be as interesting and most certainly far less emotional and overly dramatic as when Keith writes them, but then this is a status report nothing more.

According to Elick, Keith's body has taken a far more extreme transformation than that of his companion. Let's see, as stated earlier Keith's skin was cracking and falling off, unlike the rest of his body his legs below the knees not only lost its skin but the muscles as well, leaving only bone. We both agree that this is the initial preparations for his body to grow hooves of some kind. His fingers, which had also fallen completely away are now starting to regrow as well. From the new bone structure, it appears they will be longer than his original digits. This too is not uncommon since his fingers will probably be more like talons than human digits. From all of this, we can tell, Keith's final appearance should be closer to a classic Demon or one of The Fallen, unlike Usis.

Since the last entry, it was decided that we would no longer allow Keith to awaken, even temporarily, his mood and suffering are too extreme. Yes, mood, we never let him awaken fully but when he was even partially conscious, he became a real handful. This decision proved to be even more inspired once the muscles on his face started to atrophy and fall off leaving his head looking like little more than a skull. Since that time the muscles, just like the legs and hands, have again begun to regrow and his body is starting to undergo a bulking up. Everywhere that the new form feels it needs to expand the old construct, it will tear or sluff off the surrounding tissue in favor of regrowing its newer form. As you can imagine this entire process has become more an exercise in waste disposal than in tending for an injured patient. Cemal has been forced to haul away great heaping pans full of suffering soaked human tissue as well as change his Master's bed materials several times a day. In many ways, Keith's resting area has begun to resemble the torture pits he has often written about.

At first, both Elick and I worried more about the outcome than the process. That has since changed. We have both begun to spend large amounts of time by Keith's bed studying the transformation in minute detail. We are getting to watch The Father's creation energy at work. The very substance all of Creation uses to remain energetic. Now before our eyes, it is slowly sculpting Keith's old body into something new. Though he is becoming closer to the creatures of Hell, in many ways, I find the entire process very spiritual and dare I say, holy. It is interesting to see how the speed of the process changes between feedings of the hearts. Once Keith is first fed, I can watch as the veins, tissue, muscles, and nerves snake along his raw, red flesh, building the new pathways his new body will need to function. I have taken to recording the progress in much finer detail then I am sharing here with you. Maybe one day you will be able to visit the great library in Pandemonium and read my account of the work. As I was saying, the speed of his recovery is visible and quick right after he consumes the heart and continues for the next few days. It begins to slow until it is clear the creation energy contained within the slices has been depleted and his pain, like that of hunger, begins anew.

Since Keith's face has sluffed off Cemal is now required to pulverize the slices of heart into a sticky paste which is then forced down his throat using a wide flat stick. Keith's body has not ceased to function; his digestive system is still working. Do not misunderstand, when I say digestion it might lead you to believe it is like that of the living, which it is not. It is simply a transfer of energy. The body converts the physical tissue, which contains creation energy and then absorbs it leaving no waste behind. In this case, with Keith, it is the hearts. It could be anything, the flesh of a damned, processed suffering, it all is simply small amounts of The Father's energy used to continue and repair the creature who consumes it. The amount of energy a soul has is also directly dependent upon their comfort level. Therefore if a soul refuses to consume any food here in Hell, they will not cease to exist but only suffer due to the starvation the soul will feel from its depleted energy reserves. It is a common torture, that of depriving a soul of sustenance, therefore, making them suffer greatly.

One last thing, Keith's cock has fallen off. I only mention this since it seems to hold a special importance to him. He was, and probably will be again, very proud of it, leaving it in full display with his nudity far more than I deemed necessary or appropriate. Call me a prude if you will, and yes most of Hell is nude, but I expect more from a representative of one of The Powers, Fallen or otherwise.

# Entry 224

Again, it is I, Kitar with an update. This most certainly will be my last; our writer has quite literally begun to pull himself together. The entirety of his body, including his head, is now covered in thick scabs. His care has grown far less gruesome, something Cemal seems happy about, the only mess coming from when he shifts in his sleep breaking open one of the scabs causing it to weep.

It is clear Keith has begun taking on the aspects of what most certainly will be his final appearance. His precious cock has returned. His legs are still raw but fully formed, and he will have the classic cloven hoof which is common here in Hell, even Lord Lucifer has them. His fingers are now half again as long and the nails, which are black, have begun to form. His head has undergone the most dramatic change, so much so we are not sure if he will even be recognizable once his transformation has concluded. His ears have finished growing and are sized well for his body and pointed, as are his teeth. His horns have started to grow and are currently about eight, of his world's, inches long, curved upwards and three fingers around.

What else? Oh, Elick believes that since Keith has, from the start, consumed both hearts, the strength of The Father's creation energy is going to ensure he is by far more suited to his surroundings than his companion will be. Which is to say, he will carry more of the appearance of a Demon than Usis does. As far as Usis is concerned, which I have purposely left out of my updates, he is still unconscious, and Elick will probably keep him so for a considerable time to come. It will just be easier. This being the case, Elick has been visiting the Seventh Plane more often, since his choice to keep the young companion in a coma has caused Lord Leviathan to turn over care to Elick. As you should no doubt guess, he is not happy that Elick is not allowing Usis to awaken. I think that is it. Things are moving forward with very few interruptions; therefore, I will no longer update you and leave the next entry to Keith when his recovery allows.

# Entry 225

Well hello, this is my first entry since waking up in Hell. I don't mean the location of Hell but in my own personal Hell. Yes, this is Keith. I survived, what that means I'm still not sure. I'm awake. I awoke in amazing pain, but that was sated by me eating a couple of pieces of the hearts. Now I'm comfortably numb, have lots of energy so I'm sneaking in an entry while I can because I'll probably pass out again soon, so try not to be surprised if this entry ends curtly.

Here is what I know. I'm no longer in Gabriel's Keep, and no one will tell me where exactly we are. Being flat on my back and barely able to move I can't even tell you about my appearance. I've felt around. My arms are almost immobile, and my entire body's encased in a giant scab. When I first awoke and tried to move, I split open a scab on my arm causing a disgusting puss and a smell like a dead cat to escape. Kitar assured me this wasn't unexpected; he didn't say it wasn't bad, he just said it wasn't unexpected. I've been in Hell long enough to know he isn't telling me something, but then it seems they're all not telling me something. I tried to corner, well verbally corner, Cemal but that didn't work either. With the amount of pain it causes to move my normal tact of throwing a fit doesn't work. All I can do is lie here and give surly looks. To no great surprise that doesn't seem to work with Hellspawn.

This will have to be all for now; I can feel I'm starting to slip again into sleep. I wanted to get an entry written while I could, it's the only thing I have any control over, and right now I need that. And yes, I've learned these won't be published until this mess has concluded. I understand why, and fully agree with Lord Lucifer that I should keep writing regardless. Talking to you, even through these pages, is all I've got left, my life is gone, my companion is gone, and now even my body is no longer the one I remember. If it weren't for the journal, I probably would've already slipped away from eternity. Plus, as has been proven all too often, there's no telling when the shit's going to hit the fan in this accursed place and events of the past, if not taken down, would just be forgotten. So, in closing its good to talk to you again, even from a distance.

# Entry 226

Awake again, this time I'm feeling amazingly better. I'm still weak and scabbed over, but even those are starting to flake off in some places. When I awoke, already in a bad mood, I discovered Elick was nearby and decided to take my foul mood, discomfort and general bitchiness out on him. Isn't that his job?

I watched quietly as he took a seat on the floor beside my bed, well pallet; I'm on the ground. He said before I could even get started, "I know you have lots of questions..." He looked around, indicating our surroundings. "First we need to see if one of your new abilities has taken effect. Hellborn and Powers should not be able to be traced or ease-dropped upon by anyone but Lucifer. He can find us anywhere."

Now that was useful information.

I watched as his wings extended and he rose a foot or so off the ground and hovered in midair. As he raised his arms as his entire body began to glow, lighting the area where we were staying. As his energy (magic, who knows what to call it) traveled outwards I saw the hairs on Cemal's arm, who was kneeling beside the bed, begin to stand like they do when around static. For a long time nothing happened until finally Elick relaxed and settled back beside me on the ground pulling his wings in behind him.

"You no longer can be traced, which is good. What I am about to tell you everyone in our group already knows. We are no longer in Hell, to be more accurate we are no longer anywhere. We are in the void. This is the space where The Father worked, creating what we now call Creation and The Eternal city. If you remember this is also where The Father cast Lucifer and his followers after the Great War as well as where The Dark Lord created the initial firmament which became Hell."

"Wait we're nowhere? This looks like somewhere to me. To be honest, this looks like an old burned out storefront," I added, already my head was starting to hurt.

"That is very astute because a ruined storefront is precisely where you are. It is in one of the discarded creations scattered throughout the void," Elick explained as my eyes grew wider.

"A discarded creation? Ok, take this slow so I can understand and eventually write about it," I directed.

Before Elick could continue Cemal coughed getting our attention. "Does Master think he will need more heart before Master Elick begins?"

I looked at Elick. "Only if we're certain it won't knock me out. I don't want to lose this train of thought."

"I think you will be fine; you have been sleeping more now out of exhaustion than because the hearts are acting as a sedative. You might get sleepy, but you need to start pushing through that. It is time for you to get up and around."

So much for that, they did knock me out but only for a couple hours. Since we are continuing where we left off I'm not starting a new entry.

"Picking up from earlier, let's start with what the Hell a discarded creation is?" I asked groggily.

"I will try to keep this simple but it is important to remember the void is never taught or talked about by the Powers. Everything I know we have learned through Xia. Before The Father started anything he existed in The Void (yes, now that I know it's a title, I'm capitalizing it). Where he came from, where The Void as a construct came from, I do not think anyone knows. In the center of The Void, he created a platform, again I do not know why. Next, he created someone to share eternity with, that was Lucifer, The Dark Lord, The Firstborn, The Morningstar. From that point forward there were two. The Father and the Son. Are you good so far?" asked Elick. I simply nodded.

"As I said before, do not waste your breath asking 'why' or 'what' because I do not know. What you need to pay attention to, and I am not embellishing, is how important Lord Lucifer is to Creation."

I smirked. "Yes, you are embellishing but it's justified. Continue."

Elick shrugged. "Keep in mind, I will be using words like "time," and "millennia," but neither had been created yet. There was no 'time.' Their inclusion is only as a place marker." Again, I nodded.

"The Father and Lucifer spent many millennia talking about what to create, what to do with The Father's limitless power within the vastness of The Void. The full scope of their discussions only Lord Lucifer or The Father knows. Historians can only address what came into being."

"Creation?" I asked.

"Yes, or more accurately the Creation(s) we have now. Many more were created and destroyed during this process but let us not jump ahead."

"Wait, this could get confusing. When I have referenced Creations in the past, it has been the physical constructs where the living live. Are you using it in the same manner?"

"No, but I see the problem. We tend to call the entirety of The Father's creation, Creations."

"That's what I thought. If I write The Father's creation, Creations, it's going to confuse the hell out of everyone. Is there another word we can substitute?"

"How does the word Construct work for you? As I recall its definition is "to build or form, by putting together parts? I know that also refers to creatures like Cemal, hence why they are named as such, but that usage will not be relevant for in this discussion."

"That works. As you pointed out it's only for the purposes of this explanation. Go on."

"A lot of what I am going to tell you, that I am certain of, is due to the proximity I have had to Lord Lucifer by being a family member of one of the Fallen. The Father wanted to create more beings to populate his construct. Lucifer agreed. As The Father went off, metaphorically speaking, to decide what these being would look and act like, what powers they would have, Lucifer began the construct of a place for them to call home, what would later be named The Eternal City."

"Wait, Lucifer built The Eternal City?" I asked surprised.

"The first version of it, yes. As I understand, it was not as large or as grand, that came later. It is important to keep in mind that both The Father and Lord Lucifer had no frame of reference to what things should look like, how they should work. We take something like a building, a chair, a tree, well everything really, for granted but at that time these 'things' had not even been conceived of yet. This is why the first buildings and creations were so slow in being developed. The Father, at least, had some idea what he wanted his physical creations to look like. Most creatures, Lucifer, me, you and to some extent most of the living were made in his image, but not exclusively, as you have seen on Gluttony, he tried many variations. Most of which did not work out."

"This is the reason almost all the damned I've encountered, not all, but most have legs, arms, a head and torso of some variation."

"Correct. The Father created the Creation (right term this time) and then left enough of his spark behind to allow galaxies, planets, and stars to coalesce and if successful eventually evolve to contain life."

"Still, are all trees and the like the same?"

"There are many extremely different manifestations in a few Creations but due to the laws The Father created for the overall workings of each Creations many similarities exist than not. In some he did introduce differences, a greater gravity, a different dominant element, variations in the governing laws. By doing this, those Creations evolutions followed different paths, some successful, some not. Which brings us back to this Creation," He motioned around him. As I started to ask a question he held up a finger. "I will get there, I know what you are going to ask. Where was I? Right, this is one of the discarded Creations. Somewhere during its evolution The Father determined something ultimately was not going to work, and therefore he terminated it."

"So why the buildings and such?"

"What his reasoning for terminating this Creation when he did is anyone guess. But let's not get distracted. The Father created ultimately twelve successful Creations; I think that is right, to be honest, I do not recall. Of those twelve only nine remain. There were ten until recently when Hell and The Host attempted, and successfully raptured their first Creation since The Father left."

"They can do that?"

"To be more accurate, it was not Hell and The Host as much as Lord Lucifer and Michael, only together do they have the power for such a large undertaking. Before, The Father could do it on his own, but they are not he, at least that is what they want us to believe."

"Interesting. Go on," I said now agreeing with Elick's earlier point that we didn't want to get distracted. I know this is interesting and you're probably as curious as I am, but it really isn't within the context of what and why I'm writing the journals.

"At some point, the initial Creations were stabilized, yours being one of them. This did not stop The Father from continuing to experiment. He now had several successful Creations with hundreds of sentient species scattered amongst the millions of worlds, with many more still in flux. But by now the news had gotten out that the living, in the Creations which were successful, had been given souls and the ability to procreate. This is when the first stirrings of derision began amongst The Host. The Father, as I understand it, tried to solve the problem by ignoring it. He had his mind on other things, new Creations. As the number of working creations increased so did the trash left over from the failed ones. Instead of destroying them and reabsorbing the creation energy like he had originally done, The Father just raptured and discarding them. Literally tossing them in a corner to deal with later. Well, later never came. The Great War happened, and Lucifer left The Eternal City. We are told that after The War and his first born abandoning him that he lost all interest in this Construct and simply left, to where no one knows. In the end, there were ten working Creations, and several dozen destroyed discarded ones. This is one of them."

I won't lie I laid there with my mouth open. This wasn't the simple maturation of Hell, and the souls consigned there, this was the working of The Father. "Are you telling me that we're in a destroyed Creation. Is it not just a city? A world? A solar system or galaxy but an entire Creation and there are dozens like this?"

"Yes, that is percisely what I am telling you. We are in one of the less damaged but still equally as dead ones."

"Wait, when you say destroyed, if I'm lying in a bed in a storefront, how is it destroyed?"

"Ok, maybe discarded is a better word. What ultimately terminates a Creation is The Father, or now Lucifer and Michael setting in motion the process to end the Creation's ability to recycle The Father's spark contained within that Creation. Therefore, things wind down and grind to a halt. The souls are judged, and the physical construct is either reabsorbed by The Father or discarded like this one was. It is now nothing more than a dead shell open to The Void."

I took a deep breath. Don't worry I'm not giving up yet. "First, define 'Open to the Void'."

"When you can get up and around you can visit the destroyed city and see the jagged hole in the distant sky. It is an opening to The Void. If The Void were completely dark, which it is not, it would be impossible to see the rupture since the hole would blend into the background. But The Void has a faint glow due to the fires of Hell, and therefore the rupture is discernable against the slightly lighter Void. This Creation only has the single rupture; in most the entire top of their globe has been ripped off. As you can imagine, all these partial Creations used to be solid and self-contained, if you traveled to the bottom of the globe which housed the creation you would find the remains of the billions of worlds piled like so much discarded trash."

My mouth moved several times, but I don't think my mind was capable of building the words needed to form a sentence. Finally, all I could come up with was, "You said most of the souls. Are there still creatures living in these things?"

"Not living, obviously. There are souls still scattered throughout these Creations. We are not sure why and since they can't cause any harm or in any way affect the rest of the Construct, they have been mostly ignored to live out eternity trapped on these ruined worlds. You will see some if we stay here long enough."

"Ok one last thing, you said the mechanisms that allows the Creation to recycle The Father's spark ceases to run. What mechanism?"

"You have met the mechanism which starts the process to end a Creation. We have just left his Keep." He paused waiting to see if I'd figure it out, which I did.

"Gabriel."

"Correct, Gabriel's horn has the necessary ruins inscribed into it, and only he contains the ability to activate those ruins by playing the horn. That specific horn, blown by that Power starts the shutdown process for any given Creation. Now you can see why The Great War was more than just a family squabble. All the members of The Host have given tasks to perform to keep Creation running. If Gabriel had fallen with Lucifer instead of staying loyal to The Father, Lucifer would have had the mechanism by which to end Creation completely and thus The Host as well."

"Do you think he would have?"

"No, it would mean his end as well, but regardless of that, I do not think he is or was that angry about the way things played out. Many still believe the reasons for the war are not accurate or accidental."

Shaking my head, I said, "Screw that, I'm not getting into the politics of The Host. As my world and you once said, that is way above my pay grade."

"Indeed."

# Entry 227

I broke this conversation into two entries, mainly because the history lesson was over and the part about my little conundrum began.

"Why did you bring me here? We had Gabriel's protection, didn't we?" I asked.

"Yes and No..." answered Elick. I hate that answer and by reflex sat up and started to yell. My anger faded quickly as a wave of pain washed over me and several scabs burst open in a tsunami of puss so pungent it cased even Cemal and Elick to cringe. Oh yeah, it's that gross.

"Don't even start that shit with me," I growled slowly lowering my weeping carcass back onto my mat as Cemal scurried off to find towels.

"If you would shut up, stop stinking and listen you would understand. Gabriel was more than willing to continue hosting you at the Keep, but Great Grandfather sent two soldiers to abduct you. When Gabriel sent them back as ashes, he then turned up himself demanding he turn you over. It did not deteriorate into violence, but the mild skirmish of swords being drawn and crossed as several servants of The Host arrived to render assistance. They stood no chance against Grandfather, but it was a matter of principle. He would have to strike down a representative of The Host again, and even Grandfather did not want to cross that bridge for you. Then with the added insult of Gabriel turning his back and closing the door in his face, Grandfather left without you and a bit less of his pride."

"Shit," was all I could think to say.

"Exactly. I did not find out this had happened until Grandfather returned to the Keep. I was with Usis. He started ordering his troops to suit up because he was going to take Blasphemy by force."

"Can he do that?"

"No, he can't do that," answered Elick in a 'are you kidding' type of tone. "He can try but all Hell, pardon the pun, would have broken loose. In some ways it did. Lucifer did not show up in person, but he got his message across when over a third of Grandfather's soldiers burst into flame and were consumed from the inside out. Shortly after a small messenger demon arrived with a note, which simply read, "No!" Grandfather got that message. While the Keep was in an uproar over Lucifer toasting over four thousand soldier demons, I snuck out with a plan. I flew back to Blasphemy, told Gabriel I had an idea and needed your body and that my idea would keep you safe and get us out of his hair. I knew he would like that part, he agreed. I did not tell him what my idea was because no one knows about this place. I mean they know about the broken Creations but not that we have a base here. To make a long story longer, I brought you here."

I thought for a moment. "Yeah, but won't Leviathan just question you?"

Shaking his head, Elick answered, "No, he knows I will not tell him. He knows he cannot torture me unless he wants to capture me himself. Plus, and here is the good part, there is a good probability he will not even know your missing for some time."

"Why?" I asked intrigued.

"Easy, we are not in any construct. We are in none of the Creations, not the nine of the living, Hell or The Host; we are in The Void."

"I understand that, but I guess I'm missing the point."

"You see, we are outside of time."

"WHAT...Ouch..," I barked as I busted a scab on my side causing Cemal to run for towels again. "We're not in time? What does that mean?"

"Right now, little to no time has passed in Creation which includes Hell and The Host."

"Little to no? So not none?" I was starting to get brain fried.

"No, not none. Time passes in The Void just incredibly slowly. Therefore, it will be a while before Great Grandfather, with all his problems, discovers you are missing. We could keep you here for years, even decades of their time and very little would pass for us. This offers us several advantages."

My mind was racing with possibilities, but I was starting to wear down so instead of interrupting I just let him ramble on.

"First, you are lost to everyone. No one would imagine we would bring you here or for that matter very few even know The Void exists and other than The Powers even fewer know of the destroyed Creations."

"So how did you learn?"

"As you can guess, it was not me…"

I had to interrupt, "Xia?" He nodded, and I knew it already.

"Yes, he brought us here a while back."

"So how do you get into The Void?" I had to know.

"Through the window," answered Elick matter-of-factly.

I felt smart in that second. "The one on the Fourth Plane?" I asked.

Surprised Elick answered, "Yes. That's right you have been in the Overlord's private room." I nodded. "See very few people are ever granted an audience with him and to be honest many have probably forgotten about the window's existence. Xia entered a pact with the Overlord which allows us to travel freely through and back at will."

"So, no one can get here?"

"The Most High can, but they do not need to travel via the window. They can just will themselves where they wish to be, including here."

"OK, well that's your first reason for bringing me here which leads me to believe you have more." I won't lie, I was impressed.

"Yes, as a matter of fact, I do. Secondly, you will be able to heal more quickly and fully without having to worry about attacks. Thirdly, we will be able to train you to fight, both hand to hand and magical. And lastly, the best reason, when my Grandfather finds out he will be insane with anger, which will help throw him off his game for the battle. It is a small advantage, but every little bit helps. Add to that, your new appearance, which if we play our cards right, he will not know about, allowing you, once we reenter Hell to move more freely than would be possible if you remained in your old human form. He will have assassins looking for you."

Elick sat back completely satisfied with himself. I know you're wondering why I haven't asked the obvious question. To be honest, I haven't been able to shut Elick up long enough to ask.

"Cemal, do we have wine..." (No, that wasn't the question. Shut up, gawd.)

"Yes, Master," he answered and ran off.

Once he was back and I'd downed half the goblet, I turned a serious eye to Elick. "How is Usis and won't he be worried if I don't show up for decades? I don't want him to feel like we've abandoned him to the anger of your Great Grandfather."

"He will not. He is still and should remain unconscious. Not only does this have the added charm of pissing off Grandfather, but it will also ensure he is not harmed and can heal at his own speed. If I can manage it, he will not be waking up any time soon. Therefore your absence will go unnoticed," answered Elick.

"That seems risky on your part. Won't Leviathan punish you?"

"I did not do it; I brought in an elixir from the eighth plane labs to knock him out. Do not worry I have the antidote. This is for the best."

"Can't you smuggle him out as you did me?" I already knew the answer. I didn't know why and that was what I was after.

"No..." (see, told you), "Grandfather has guards all around the room who check on him constantly as well as servants replacing his bedclothes. Plus, he immediately tripled the sentries after Lord Lucifer sent his little message."

I had to laugh, "Little Message? He destroys, what did you say, four thousand demons, and it's a little message?"

"That is how things work around here. If you will recall, The Dark Lord wiped out almost all the souls on the Fifth Plane at one point during your visit." I'd forgotten, or maybe I never knew they were serious. I remember the Overlord mentioning it, but I thought she was being dramatic.

"So Usis is unconscious? Why do I get the feeling there is something you're not telling me?"

"There are lots of things I am not telling you. I think the one you are hinting at is as to the other reason. Usis' body had already begun the transformation from consumption of Enepsigo's hearts; it seems that when we introduced Zephar's heart as well, the process reset itself and started anew."

"What exactly are you saying?" I asked, frozen in terror.

"Which part did you not understand? His body began rebuilding itself a second time. The changes which had already occurred dropped away and his transformation began anew. I can see that look on your face, and it is too late and too dangerous to change anything at this point. He is unconscious therefore not in pain, as such."

"AS SUCH..." I bellowed then closing my eyes I took a deep breath trying to calm my nerves. This getting upset thing was starting to set back my healing. In a calm, almost too calm voice I added, "I need you to do me a favor. Since we cannot seem to get that slave Sigos gave me to go where I need him, I want you to find me something to write on. Yes, I know it'll be flesh, that's fine. I'm going to write Usis a letter, which you can deliver. I want him to hear from me and know he's in my thoughts. If he's in pain, don't force him to return one, even discourage it. Since we can't talk, there's no reason why we can't at least communicate."

"I think that is a great idea," answered Elick. "I will get you the supplies later tonight while you rest." As if on cue Cemal appeared beside me with my latest helping of heart.

"How much remains of the two hearts?" I asked as I looked down at the three slices. Remember, I'm eating two slices of my primary heart, which was Zephar's, and one of Usis' primary heart, Enepsigo's. This we are hoping will merge the effects.

"Master, there is roughly half of Zephar's heart and a little less than a quarter of Enepsigo's," explained Cemal.

"Should I increase the amount of the Zephar's heart I'm consuming?"

"We might want to swap them out. Increase the amount of Enepsigo's heart for you and Zephar's for Usis. This will speed Usis' second transformation as it will yours, which is almost complete. The sooner you are up and around we can start your training. If my estimates are correct, based upon your emerging strength, I would imagine it will be you who will fight Grandfather, which is his preference anyway. Therefore, we might want to give you more of both to up your powers."

I thought on that for a few minutes. "There's no way that could negatively impact Usis, is there?"

Shaking his head, Elick replied, "No, it should not. His body has entered the scabbing phase, so he is only just behind you. This means the hearts have done their transformational work. Any additional contribution will be toward your powers, which you will need if you expect to stand against my Grandfather. You are the center of this whole drama, Keith, whether you like it or not. You will always be his target. Since we have already started down this road, we would be remiss if we did not make you as powerful as possible. You are a piece on the chess board now, and our strength lies in the fact no one knows your moves or what powers you possess."

"A piece on the chess board..." I repeated to myself. How far I've come. "So you're suggesting two slices of Enepsigo and one slice of Zephars?"

"No, I am suggesting two slices of each. We continue Usis on one slice of each until the hearts run out."

"And you are sure this won't hurt him in any way? If so, I have no problem with it," I agreed.

As Cemal ran off to cut one more, I finished my wine. "You know I still find this eating hearts thing disgusting?"

"Yes, but necessary, if you had not chosen this path there was a serious chance Usis and your days together would have been over. Keep reminding yourself of that. Now rest and I will take Usis' next dose to him and arrange to get you some writing materials."

As Cemal handed me the plate, I said, "Elick, I want to get Usis back and make Leviathan pay for all the pain he has subjected us to. He is your Great Grandfather, so I need you to understand he *will* suffer for this and hope you have my back."

Neither said anything for several seconds until finally, Cemal added, "That is all fine but for now eat your hearts, my Master."

Elick nodded and walked off in silence. As I closed my eyes feeling the energy of the hearts travel through my body, I thought about how I'd just said I'd find my revenge against Leviathan. How many times have they told me about their adversarial relationship? Now, because of the hearts, I too had become a piece on Hell's chess board. I couldn't help wondering who was ultimately planning the next few moves, and how the game could be won, me or Elick. We both wanted to take down this particular king. The question was who wanted it more and what were they willing to sacrifice?

# Entry 228

When I awoke my first thought was, "Where was Kitar yesterday?"

As I awoke and opened my eyes above me was the same gray destroyed ceiling I'd seen throughout my convalescence here on the floor of this rotting world, my only light that of the small fires scattered throughout our campsite. Cemal was across the room working on something; I couldn't tell what, so I lay there studying what I should've already been familiar with, this ruined space. The floor was filthy, only disturbed by the imprints of the hooves of those who cared for me. I found Cemal's, and Elick's but there were others. This led me back to Kitar. I started looking for his paw prints and there were some, so he was here in The Void with us. What I'd find out later was he'd taken the opportunity of my unconsciousness to explore this desiccated world. I thought I should be pissed, him running off while I couldn't, but it wasn't in me. He was doing something that made him happy and not just fussing over me. I decided to be happy for him instead.

The right and back walls were littered with a myriad of different sized shelves, all discarded in a mass and piled to the ceiling like the room, or maybe the world had quickly been tilted to one side. The front wall of the shop looked like it might have been glass at one time, or whatever passed as glass on this world. The shelves weren't like the shelves we had; these were more detailed, something like you'd expect to find in a fantasy convenience store, all scroll work and curves. Before I could realize what had happened my thoughts had jumped me and my mind found itself back home, on Earth. All of our little shops and mega stores now standing empty — just starting to build up their layers of dust. The packages of food, now rotten and ready to blow away in the first breeze. Were they piled in a corner or still neatly stacked as was their way. Was there even a breeze. I wonder if Xia killed everything, the animals, the plants. Was all that food going to waste?

I was pulled from my musings by the feeling of a goblet being gently introduced to my hand (yes Cemal is amazing) and Kitar was there as if summoned, at the front of the shop. I looked over and found him staring at me. I shrugged. "I never even knew I cared that much for the place."

"It was your home," answered Kitar. He was doing one of the judge things he so enjoyed. I was surprised it worked on the new me. The 2.0 me.

"I never even knew I missed it. I wouldn't want anyone to end up here. I guess I liked knowing I would or could get news of how Earth was doing, of what they'd become," I frowned, "but then I guess that's been answered. Their...our...depravity in the end was enough to even upset Hell. It's quite a distinction. I guess I should feel proud. I don't though." I shrugged again as he pulled over a crate and took a seat.

Come to find out, it hadn't been yesterday when I was last awake but two weeks ago. Thank Gawd for this "out of time" thing, or I'd be frantic.

As I slowly awoke and asked groggy questions Kitar regaled me with stories of his exploration. I could tell he was trying to get my mind off Earth. As I said before, I was happy to see him enjoying himself, but I could feel that mood waning. I wanted to get up. This whole mess, if you overlooked the abduction and our bodies turning into demons, might've been good for everyone.

As we talked, I pulled back the covers doing a cursory check of my body. I could feel I was moving better, even if it was just my arms. Also, and I know this will sound strange, but already I missed not having toes to wiggle, something I didn't even know I took for granted until they were gone. It was and is still quite unsettling. But I kept trying and all that did was remind me they weren't there anymore and I wasn't me anymore.

Kitar stopped talking and watched me taking inventory of my new body. The scabs were starting to flake off, naturally this time. "Did Elick force me to sleep for two weeks?" I asked.

"Yes, the last time you were allowed to awaken you kept setting your progress back. He now feels you are about ready to try standing and getting used to moving in your new body...WITH assistance. You need to get your old muscles back in shape and begin training the new ones."

"It seems I'm still mostly scabs. Isn't moving going to hurt them?" Reaching over, he plucked one off revealing red puffy skin underneath.

"They are just hanging on due to inactivity. Getting up will help them sluff off."

I took a deep breath, returning my attention to the ceiling while Cemal and Kitar sat quietly beside me. Every once in a while, I'd lift a clawed hand and look at my fingers or flex my knee or lift my leg high to see the hooves. I shook my head, hooves, I had hooves. I'll save the full description for later, when I'm sure the changes are complete. I will say, I'm bulkier, have hooves, real fucking hooves and to be honest, other than the toe thing, they're pretty amazing. "I have a question. Is it the constant laying down that's caused my entire spine and back to hurt? It's killing me." I asked as Cemal tried to hide a laugh, even Kitar smirked.

"No, we noticed you shifting a lot in your sleep. It was then we realized..." Kitar paused when he heard a cough and corrected, "...actually Cemal realized what the problem was." Motioning to the boy he added, "Go ahead, your discovery, you tell him.

With a huge smile, Cemal announced like he was revealing the winner of a prize, "Master, you have a tail, and..."

"I have a tail. Oh help me up, I have to see it," I blurted, almost jumping out of bed.

"and...," again said Cemal but I wasn't listening.

"...being on your back had caused it to bunch. It will be one of the bigger challenges of your new body, learning to sit with a tail," finished Kitar but I wasn't listening to him either.

Kitar motioned for the boy to take the other side and together they helped me stand for the first time in I don't know how long. I swayed on my feet...I mean hooves... as Cemal let out a bark of surprise. "Master, watch the tail. You just spanked this boy." I spun around trying to see the new appendage causing them both to release me. I had made it halfway around before I began to fall forward. All of the sudden I was no longer touching the floor.

Wide eyes I looked at Cemal to see him smiling even wider. "Like this boy was trying to say, Master, um and...Master now has wings as well."

As they flapped, and my tail swished from side to side, I felt a pair of strong hands grab me around the waist and set me back on the ground. "Slow down."

"Take a breath and relax," instructed Kitar as Cemal brought over a create and they lowered me down onto it. I barked in pain and stood quickly back up, "As I said, you will have to take it slow until you learn how to move your tail out of the way."

"Master, calm yourself, take a couple of deep breaths and then when you are ready concentrate on your tail. Imagine lifting it as high as it will go. In time Master it will be just like your arms and legs, it will do what you want it to without you having to focus on it."

Following Cemal's suggestion, I took a few steadying breaths and then concentrated on my tail and to my surprise I felt it lift just like I'd imagined. "Now take a seat slowly, the mechanism that connects your tail to your spine will displace allowing you to sit normally. After you have done that Master, then try to relax it. It should find its own way to lay."

I felt my tail wiggle several times and then the pressure against my back vanished. "Perfect Master, like this boy said. "In time it will become natural."

"Tell me, if we have control of our tails like that why is it some demons I've met are always moving theirs while others almost never move. Is that a choice?"

"No. You have felines on your world, right? It is dependent upon the creature. Some can use their tail as another appendage; they can use it to lift, as a weapon, many different ways. Some tails are nothing more than a tail which hangs or moves based on mood. You being able to control yours so quickly tells me you will probably have control of it to a greater degree. That does not mean it won't flick involuntarily at times. Take your favorite obsession, Xia Morningstar. His tail is always going. He can use it with great dexterity, but when he is not consciously trying to use it for something it still tends to move and flick at varying speeds based upon his mood. Most in Hell know if you see his tail making short quick snaps behind him someone is about to be in a lot of pain," explained Kitar.

I'd like to say I did more on my first outing out of bed, but I'd be lying. Comal brought over the hearts, and I was asleep before I knew what happened. But I'd made it out of bed, and for the record, I'd also made my first flight…hehe, if you call not falling on your face a flight. I'm glad my wings, at least know what they're doing. I cannot believe I have wings and a tail, that is so fucking cool.

# Entry 229

I'm starting this entry by asking if you know the old earth saying, "as obvious as the nose on your face?" In case you're wondering why, it's because yesterday when I discovered my tail and wings, I missed what should've been so obvious as to be the first thing I discovered. To give you a hint before we start this next entry, let's revise the saying. Now it should read, "as obvious as the massive fucking horns on your head." Yup, that's right.

I sat nude and winced at Cemal's fastidious removal of scabs as he slowly coaxed them off my torso. My nudity isnt based in my incessant need to annoy my guide but more as a confirmation of the suspicion that my body had grown bigger. None of my clothes fit any longer. I was thicker and much more muscular. Though my skin appeared red, Kitar believe this to be a temporary anomaly which would change as I completed healing. As I sat there, my neck hurting, I reached up to rub my face and found what I couldn't believe I'd not already discovered. Horns. Yes, I have horns, huge horns. "How'd I miss these?" I blurted out in surprise.

"Your body has probably already compensated for them Master. As big as yours are you should be able to shift your eyes up and see the bottoms of them."

I did as Cemal suggested and sure enough, I could see them extending out in front of my head by a good foot. "They look huge. Tell me what they look like," I begged, both horrified and excited simultaneously as I began to run my hands along their contour.

From behind me I heard the familiar voice of Kitar. "As you can feel they extend from your temples just below your hairline and travel forward and slightly down for about a foot in front of your head before they curl upward and eventually back and down in a smooth arch. The tip of the horns are facing down and stop about a foot and a half above your head. As you have noticed, they are thick where they meet your forehead, maybe about as round as the middle of your lower arm but come to a razor-sharp point at their tip. It is quite an impressive rack."

"For the record, I wouldn't say my body had adjusted since my neck is killing me."

"That makes sense, you don't feel them, as such, but since you have been laying down for the last few months, your body has not had the chance to build up the strength to carry around your new head weight. I would have thought this minor adjustment to the size of your head would not have caused much discomfort. That neck has had been carrying around a pretty big head for quite a while now."

I looked down at Cemal. "Did he just make a joke?"

"Sound like he did Master," answered Cemal as he plucked another scab, causing me to wince. "Woops, boy does not think that one was ripe yet," he added with a grin.

Let's take inventory; I told you I'd wait until I was sure, well I think I am now. The only thing we're not sure about is skin color but at this point everyone seems to think it's going to be red. So here is what I've got: Massive horns, Big ass hooves with furry canon bones, a barbed tail (I don't think I mentioned that in the last entry since my wings caught my attention), wings that look a lot like bat wings with black bones and dark gray membrane. I'm larger, more muscular and have really long fingers with stupidly sharp nails.

Oh and something else I noticed that I only comment out loud about as a means to annoy Kitar, "Did you notice the cock? It's huge, and those nuts are like tennis balls. Boy this is going to come in handy... get it hand...y."

As hoped Kitar sat shaking his head as Cemal volunteered from behind me as he pulled off another scab, "Master has a nice ass as well. If Master does not mind this one pointing that out."

That got the growl I was hoping for from Kitar as I added, "I can't see my backside so thank you for pointing that out, my boy."

"How are you feeling?" asked Kitar, trying to ignore the both of us.

"Not bad, I seem to have more energy than I had before. Is there a chance we can sit outside? I'd love a change of scenery, and I would like to see the city I keep hearing about."

"We can arrange that," answered Kitar as Cemal stopped and ran ahead.

As they led me out front, I got my first look beyond the shattered corpse of my current home. Directly in front was a small clearing. Based upon the assorted chairs, tables and goblets, I assumed this is where the others were relaxing as I suffered into my new body. My interest in that was short lived as I began rubbernecking in an attempt to see my surroundings. Kitar and Cemal led me to a chair. I was only brought back when I heard Cemal bark in a louder than normal voice, "Master, TAIL..." causing me to pull it up as they lowered me down.

With a spark from Kitar's finger, several smaller campfires sprang to life lighting the area around us. I was sitting in an old wooden chair, which from the sound of it, wasn't too happy with my new-found bulk. In addition to the other chairs I've already mentioned I saw a small cushion made out of what looked like a folded blankets on the ground beside a crate of wineskins. I knew instantly what it was and still didn't approve. My suspicions were confirmed when Cemal walked over and bowed down on it.

What caught my attention had been fleeting and completely vanished the moment Kitar lit the fires. I was struck dumb for a couple of seconds until finally, I said in a chocked voice, "Can you kill the fires for a second?" Kitar started to say something. "Please?" I interjected, cutting him off.

With another snap, we were plunged back into darkness. First Kitar then Cemal began to speak but I shushed them, and together we sat in awkward silence in the pitch blackness of this dead world. Now if you have been reading my entries, you already know what I noticed. I'm not sure noticed is the right word. It was dark, real dark, not the greyness that was Hell, that always dusk where colors are muted and things seem a bit unreal. This was total and complete blackness. I found a tear running down my face; in the complete absence of light, when I could see nothing, I was again back home just for a second. A place where darkness was common and something to be ignored. Don't ignore it, enjoy it, it's one of the things you will lose at death.

Finally breaking the silence, I said, "Sorry, it's the darkness. It's been so long."

As I heard Kitar sit down in a chair beside me, Cemal said, "It scares me." Though tears were running down my cheeks, I smiled at that simple revelation. This little one who could be so fierce was scared. He had stood with Lucifer, before a member of The Host and here in the total blackness he was afraid of something he had never seen or experienced.

"Look up," instructed Kitar and I did. "Do you see it, focus your eyes, just stare."

It took a while but then a massive ragged shape resolved in the skies above us. It was barely discernable, just a hint of it lit ever so slightly from behind. "What is that?" I asked unable to put context to what I was seeing.

"That is the rupture in this Creation opening it to The Void."

"It looks like broken glass in a globe just like Elick said."

"Yes, because that is precisely what it is. Except instead of being a glass globe it is a Creation."

"What's the dim light behind it?" I asked.

"That is the light from Hell's fires shinning into The Void."

"But not The Eternal City's light?"

"No, they do not allow that to travel downwards onto Creation and Hell in fear those unworthy might see it."

"How big is it?" I asked.

"To use one of your favorite words, massive. In your world's terms it would be billions, maybe trillions of light years across."

I stopped trying to comprehend it and just stared. This was a vastness the minds of the living, present or past, were not capable of understanding.

"I have never asked, but how does someone the size of man work on things so large?"

"Explain your question. Who are you referring too? The Father?"

"Yes."

"He is not our size when he chooses not to be. None of the Powers are, they maintain the size you have seen because it makes it easier to work with the damned and to move in nine Creations. Their familiar size, I have been told, is out of habit now more than choice. Lucifer could fill The Void with his presence if he chose to, making a Creation little more than a marble in his palm."

As silence retook us, I could hear Cemal's teeth chattering; he was truly terrified. As if to punctuate my thought I felt him move closer and tightly wrap himself around my leg. "Please can you make it end?" he said timidly.

"Yes, Kitar please," I said as the fires sprung to life.

# Entry 230

I awoke from another bout of sleep. My body seems to be reaching the end of its rebuilding if that's what you want to call it. Now the hard part, learning to use all these new accessories. I'm not sure about referring to myself like a car or a computer, but there you are. Cemal sets out more heart, commenting that I seem to be consuming energy faster now that I'm at the end of the process. To me they're becoming like my morning coffee, an old earth drink, giving me energy at the start of each day. They don't put me to sleep anymore. I down them with the ever-present goblet of wine as Cemal helps me stand. I stumble and fall back, then try again. Walking in hooves is a real challenge, you wouldn't believe how important your toes are in the process of walking, hang on to them is all I can say. (It's twice now I've brought up toes, I miss those little guys.)

"Where's Kitar?" I asked.

"Out exploring, Master. As has become his custom."

"I hope to join him soon," I said as I took another tentative step. It appears the way hooves grow are partially to help the walker maintain their balance. Unlike others who hooves are straight down from the knee, mine has two knees, so to speak, one where it should be, then the bone goes backwards about a foot ending in another knee which then redirects another bone forward which ends in the hoof. To me it looks like what the more vicious Demons have instead of the standard satyr type like Lucifer, Cemal and Elick have.

"Do you have any idea why my hooves aren't the straight kind like yours?" I asked Cemal as he helped me take another step.

He shook his head. "No idea Master. This one can tell you that most Demons who have hooves like yours are usually bigger, as you have become." He was right; I think my new height topped out at about ten feet, which isn't big for The Powers when they're in show-off mode, but overall it's taller than the standard residents of Hell. "Does Master remember what kind of hooves The Lovers had?"

"No when I was with them, I didn't spend much time thinking about physiology," I answered.

"Of course, Master, this one apologizes for the comment."

"No need to, it's a good question," I answered as I rubbed his head.

As I took a few more steps, I started to get the rhythm. To explain what it's like and why it's so different, because of the strange bend where I'm not used to one, the entire process seems mechanical. What I mean is I must deliberately pick up, move forward and then set down the hoof as I lean forward for the next step. I'm sure I'll get used to it, but right now if I don't do it right, I tumble forward or back based upon the way I was leaning at the time.

"You are getting much better Master," encouraged Cemal as he helps me to a chair. Fortunately, my wings have my back. (HAHA I made a funny.) They won't let me fall on my face or onto my ass. They step in, without prompting, and keep me aloft. I still can't fly, but everyone says that'll come in time. Elick told me stories of him standing on a cliff and leaving craters below as he jumped and fell. He said learning to fly causes more injury to one's pride than one's body. Though all Hell born go through this learning curve. Mine is more difficult because I've had other kinds of feet and a preconceived notion of who should and shouldn't be able to fly.

After I'm seated Cemal ran off to get wine. Drinking and eating are as much of an adventure as everything else now. I have new teeth, well I used to have teeth, now I have fangs, razor-sharp fangs. I have on more than one occasion sliced open my lip or tongue after biting myself. My new tongue is long and pointed, can't wait to try that out. I haven't grown used to the changes, but I'm taking it day by day. I spend more time now awake sitting in the darkness with the fire out than asleep or recovering. Cemal still hangs onto my leg, but the conversation seems to help his nerves. My other past time is just staring at myself in one of the many reflective surfaces scattered throughout the destroyed wreckage. They thought I'd look different, but once my face had grown back and settled in, I can still see me in the new me. The other surprise, at least to Kitar, was I turned out to be dark blue with patches of black, no specific pattern, not red like he'd thought.

I'm still me. I don't know why I feel the need to keep saying that. I guess because I spend so much time contemplating my new appearance, I feel I need to remind everyone I'm still Keith. Maybe it's me who needs to hear that more than you. Kitar thinks that will change in time. As my confidence grows, we will see. I hope I get more confidence, but I don't want to lose the me that I am. The last thing about my body, since I have no plans of giving another update are my fingers. They're seriously a challenge, being so long and like the teeth, the nails are sharp, and it's easy to cut myself and others. Cemal has little scratches all over him where I've attempted to give him a reassuring pat only to cut him by accident. I've also speared the bug several times when my fingers have slipped. Of that I'm not sorry, little fucker.

Now for the city or the remains of it. It wasn't human, but in many ways, it reminds me of home. There are shops, streets, sidewalks, toppled trees, they don't decay, and lots of rubble and emaciated remains scattered around the area. There's a pile of corpses stacked up behind the rubble just off the clearing where we're staying. Cemal told me they hid it so not to upset me. The bodies lay where they fell and needed to moved when we arrived. I agree, that's rough. I spent some time yesterday looking at one of the bodies. Like I said they don't decay, but they do dry out, they looked elven to me, pointed ears, tall, and thin. With what I can tell from the city and its residents, it was probably a beautiful place before The Father grew bored with it. Some of the buildings, like the one we are staying in, are only single story, but many, especially off in the distance look like they could've been fifty or sixty stories at one time, many are now broken off, their jagged teeth pointing to the hole in the universe which was once this creation.

I'm sure it's as hard for you as it is for me to wrap my head around the fact that the hole isn't in this planet's atmosphere but the universes. It's like looking into deep space and finding part of it missing. I never really paid attention to space stuff when living but as Kitar said the rupture has to be hundreds of millions of light years across to be visible from this planet. As I understand it, this is one of the Creations which advanced far enough in their evolution to become technological. The Father destroyed and discarded it not because the bodies didn't take the souls, they did, but because he couldn't breed out of them their inherent violence. Kitar said this Creation was probably one of the first ones when The Father still believed he could create a more passive, loving creature. As we all know, he eventually gave up on that dream, since most of the species I've encountered, from the many creations and worlds, all tend to have a violent streak. I guess the apple doesn't fall far from the tree.

So instead of spending pages and pages describing this place, since we will be leaving, and the detail really doesn't matter. Just picture one of the big cities on your world, violently rip the tops off the tall buildings and drop them beside their bases, darken everything and cover it with a thick layer of bodies, debris, and dust, lots of dust. So an apocalypse, and you'll have this place.

# Entry 231

Everyone is away, even Cemal. It's one of those rare times when I'm completely alone. We've been having small attacks from the creatures that inhabit this place but that isn't what I want to talk about. I'll cover them later. Right now, I've moved away from the main area and am sitting on the floor in what might've been a restaurant. There are lots of tables and chairs spilled all over the room. I needed to be alone to write this. Completely alone.

I'm changing. Not so much myself, the self I've always been. But in a deeper fashion. I've started having dreams. First it was of my life while living, with brief flashes of how my mother, my father, people I knew felt, or thought, or was motivated. If I focus, normally by accident, on an aspect of their life I see all the factors leading up to them being the person they were at that point in their existence. All the things that made them or led them to their actions.

I saw my sister, we never really got along. I saw one of the days we were fighting, yelling and screaming at each other. She barked something, I can't remember now what it was, in the dream it struck me and I fixated on it. In a blink of the preverbal eye, I saw what led her to scream that, not the fight, or anything that day but back further, years before. It was one night late, everyone was in bed and she had watched something on TV which had scared her. She quietly crept out of her room and headed down the hall. I could see all of this like I was hovering behind her, which I wasn't. I saw me, asleep as she passed my room. She made it to my parents' room and she, we now, heard them talking. They were discussing the two of us, my sister and myself. She listened at how they said things came easier for Keith, he had a penitent for creative things. How he, me, would probably be gay, they had seen me watching the males in sporting events not the girls. My father in an offhanded remark said that my sister would probably be lucky to find a man early in life, she wasn't the prettiest girl around. My mother was horrified, and my father quickly clarified that to him she was a jewel, but facts were facts, and she was sort of homely. They both hoped she'd grow out of it. Not only for her own happiness, like looks equaled happiness, but because she'd need something. She was smart, average smart but not like Keith who was really intelligent. He easily picked up on things and didn't need to be instructed twice. If this wasn't the worst thing a girl a year shy of her teens to hear it was made worse when they both laughed as my mother said, "they can't all be brilliant."

My sister ran back to her room, threw herself on her bed and cried herself to sleep, what had scared her now forgotten. She learned that night that she had something worse to fear in a family of achievers, normality. Time jumped forward again, as altercation after altercation poured past the back of my eyes. That was the day we stopped being siblings and became competitors and adversaries. I'd never known what had caused my sister to hate me so, now I knew, and I think in that knowing, I realized I missed my sister. She'd died a few years later in a car accident erasing any chance of us ever finding each other, but then I guess it never would've happened anyway. I followed a few years after that.

# Entry 232

Today Elick came back but not by himself. Three other Hellspawn accompanied him. I'm not guessing here, it was clear they were like him. As they landed, I stood and carefully walked to meet them as Kitar and Cemal emerged from our current home.

Elick came over with a big smile on his face. "Cartos, Alcraw, Balthazar I would like to introduce you to The Dark Lord's writer, Keith."

I watched as the Hellspawn named Cartos walked closer and then around me. I had to look up to even see his face; he was a good thirty feet tall with flaming hair and huge wings with vicious looking talons on the end. His body was covered with dark red scales like a snake. "You are this writer I have heard so much about. Elick told me what you did. You know that's pretty stupid right?"

Stifling a growl, I simply answered, "You're not the first to suggest that."

"Cartos is Beelzebub's son," explained Elick.

I raised my eyebrows. "Son? Not Great-Grandson? And it is an honor to meet you."

Cartos rolled his eyes. Before I could say anything else, the next Hellspawn, Alcraw, came forward. "Xia would love you. I think you have caused more trouble in your short time here than he has in his whole storied existence."

"I cannot say, My Lord, based upon all I've been told so far, I fear I'd have to be far more ambitious to even rival Lord Morningstar on one of his lazy days," I said with a smile, causing Alcraw to burst out laughing. He was a more manageable size, just a bit taller than me at probably just over eleven feet. His horns were a true crown of horns, there must have been a dozen starting with two small sharp numbs just above his nose and then moving back in a v pattern until halfway up his scalp in the middle of the long white ponytail two huge horns curled back like an Addax or something. His skin had spotty scales in patches on his chest, back, down the tops of his arms and legs. His skin itself was a forest green and the scales a ruddy reddish color. His tail was long and barbed about every three inches with, what had to be, six-inch spikes.

Finally, Elick placed his hand behind the final Hellspawn almost forcing him to come forward. "This is Balthazar."

He stepped forward and reached out a hand as if to shake. It was one of the first times in a while were anyone offered to shake my hand. I noticed the other three stiffen. Balthazar's long black fingers wrapped around mine and held tight as I felt something like electricity coursing through my veins. I tried to pull away, but he was far stronger than I was, his arm didn't even move as I struggled. When he released I all but fell back, being caught by my wings. As he stepped away, he said, "The transformation was successful."

I started to lunge when I saw Elick shake his head. "Explain Balth."

Before I tell you what he said let me get the description out of the way, it's one of the easiest. He was equal in height, ten feet. His hair, what I could see of it, was pitch black, anime black as was everything about him, his body, face, wings, hooves, horns, everything. Pitch black like coal dust, no light reflected off his body, the only reflective part was the dead black eyes. He has to be one of the most disturbing creatures I've seen in a while. Knowing what I know now, what you're about to learn, I can also include in his description that I could feel the power pouring off him, like standing too close to a transformer.

"Did you not say this one has been consuming both Zephar's and Enepsigo's hearts?"

"Yes, when Keith decided to consume the hearts, we thought it best to give him both. He will have to go up against Leviathan after all."

"It has been successful. He carries both of their powers," explained Balthazar.

It was Kitar who asked the next question. "Equally?"

"Ah Lord Judge, we will see how Xia feels about his Great-Grandfather freeing you. It was Xia, as I recall, who installed you."

"Yes, My Lord, it was," answered Kitar.

"Does he have the power to do what we need done?" asked Elick.

Inclining his head, as little blue streaks of static danced between his loose hair. "Yes, if trained and somewhat lucky. He very well might be able to send The Lord of Violence to the Hatchery. To be so crude as to break down his power, I would say he is exactly balanced between physical strength and magical power." As the corners of his lips turned up slightly, he met my eyes. "You are going to become very dangerous. If there were not already a target on your back, there would be now. Creatures wanted your proximity now you have only increased how much they will covet your other powers and want to possess you. On a high note, at least, you should have the power to protect yourself." Turning to Elick, he concluded, "I would also suggest no one other than those inside this circle and the few you have been forced to tell find out how this happened."

"Meaning?" asked Elick.

"Think about it," was all Balthazar said as he waited. Finally, eyebrows went up.

"Good point, Balth. It would become an open season for The Powers' hearts. Good catch," boomed Cartos causing any intact windows to explode outwards. Kitar, Cemal and I all recoiled from the pain in our ears.

"Cartos, please use your indoor voice. You will kill the rabble," commented Alcraw.

As much as it hurt when Cartos spoke, I was still focused on Balthazar as he walked around me. Poking his head from behind he said, "I will teach him how to speed up the final bit of his transformation." Then almost to himself, he added, "Yes, this one will be interesting."

I turned back to Elick and raised an eyebrow. "Balth will be training you in Magic. He is...forgive me for being so crass, Balth... one of the most magically powerful beings you will ever meet. He could probably go toe to toe with Lord Lucifer if it were purely a battle of magical abilities."

Looking back at the Black Hellspawn, I asked, "How is that possible?"

"No one is sure, and I am not telling," answered Balthazar causing Cartos to add in a much more tolerable voice, "nor are they willing to ask. Our dear friend here looks meek but do not let that fool you, his temper rivals that of The Fallen."

"Yes, you are fortunate Balth is on our side. He is probably one of the few, if not the only one who could teach you strong enough magic to be effective against Leviathan in such a short amount of time," added Alcraw.

Elick smirked, "And it does not help that they hate each other."

All four, including Balthazar, said, "true."

"Can you fly yet?" asked Cartos causing the others to chuckle. It must be a private joke.

"Not really, my wings seem to have a mind of their own. They will keep me from falling off the damn hooves, but I cannot stay aloft," I answered.

"Not a problem. I will teach you," said Cartos.

# Entry 233

Well, a lot has happened since the last entry, just three days ago. That night after Elick's group arrived, I consumed the hearts under the scrutiny of Balthazar. I'm pretty sure to everyone else this entire idea of rescuing Usis is a fool's mission, but to him, it's more of an experiment. Don't get me wrong, I heard them talking and none of them are sure if this is going to work. The upside is even when they think I'm not listening, which is becoming easier due to the strength of my new hearing, they still don't discount the possibility that I, or more importantly, we could pull this off. What they'd left out was how they planned to help. The very thought of them being willing to stand with me made me feel both honored but probably a little more curious. I wonder what they know that I don't.

Anyway, I went to bed after having my heart slices only to be awoken a short time later with my body wracked in convulsions and unimaginable pain. Since what happened, happened to me, I can only give you a second-hand report. Here is my discussion after the fact and contained therein should be most of the information you need to know.

-------------------------------------------

As I awoke the second time, I found myself not only tied to the bed but gagged as well. My panic shot through the roof. Struggling to free myself I felt hands, hands I knew, reach up and undo the gag.

"What the fuck!" I screamed.

"Master, Masters Elick and Balthazar felt it would be safer if you were restrained until you awoke to see if there would be another episode," explained Cemal.

After untying me he rushed out to let the others know I was awake. As I rubbed the rope marks on my wrists, I decided to let them come to me. Yes, I was pissed.

"You have decided to rejoin us," commented Elick as he walked in.

"Not only that but without the wanton destruction. Which is good. The city is a mess already," added Balthazar.

I shook my head. I had no idea what the fuck they were talking about. They invited me to look for myself. I got up and went outside and fell back against the building in shock at the devastation which lay around us. I mean the city wasn't exactly in peak condition to start with, but now there wasn't anything left. Even the destruction was destroyed. Where the dusty remains of buildings had once been there were now piles of rubble. All around us the buildings which had still been standing were little more than smoldering husks of the original structures.

"What happened? It looks like a bomb went off." I asked.

"To be more precise, a Keith went off," explained Elick.

"To be even more precise, your powers awoke," corrected Balthazar.

"It looks like they awoke pissed off," I said.

"This is the very reason Belth suggested we bring you out here in the first place."

I pointed to our magical shadow. (Yes, that is exactly what he looks like a shadow.) "You were the one who suggested this place?"

"After Elick told me what you were doing I had a feeling when your powers manifested there might be fallout. You were after all going from nothing to the powers of, not one, but two Powers. To be honest, I am surprised it was not more destructive. The planet still remains."

I made a small circle. "No one was hurt, were they?" I could tell two things right off the bat. From Balthazar and Elick's eye roll, they saw that as a ridiculous question but more importantly from Cemal's little hoof kick in the dirt I knew something had happened. "What are you not telling me?"

Shaking his head, Elick said, "Nothing, we had to shield your little minion here because the blast almost blew him apart."

I ran over and dropped down to my knees in front of Cemal, grabbing him and looking him over. "Are you alright?"

I felt an arm reach down and help me up. "Yes, yes, yes, we shielded him before the blast reached him. He is fine. Correct, boy?"

I looked down as he nodded his head. "Do I need to feed him a couple of pieces of that heart to strengthen him up? I don't want any of our family hurt, not only Usis or Me but Cemal as well."

I thought nothing of my comment until I saw the two stunned faces of Balthazar and Elick and then looked over to find Cemal on his knees weeping. "What?" was all I could muster.

"You are offering the boy a piece of the Hearts?" said Balthazar. It was like I had told him he had just won the lottery.

"If both Usis and myself are powerful enough as far as I'm concerned all of you can finish it off. If it will make you more powerful, I'll even go as far as insisting since we're all going into this together. As for Cemal, if it will make him safer like I said I insist." As I finished speaking Cemal ran over and hugged me tightly.

I discovered not only were Elick and Balthazar in conference, but Cartos and Alcraw were with them. To round out the impromptu meeting in walked Kitar. "Oh gawd, what's happened? Everyone but Keith looks like they just...well...What did he do now?"

Now it was my turn to roll my eyes. "Your confidence is overwhelming. I just offered them all, you included, a slice or two of the heart(s) if we are sure my 'evolution' is complete."

Great, now Kitar had the same look as the rest of them. The only difference is he was still in the early phases of shock where the other four eyes were shifting between me and the backpack Cemal kept the hearts in.

"Are you serious?" asked Elick.

"What's the big deal? We're all about to go up against one of the strongest, most...evil...creatures in Hell. Do you think he'll limit his anger to Usis or me? To be honest, like I said, I think I'm insisting. Otherwise, you guys could prove to be, pardon the oversimplification, weak links. I'm pretty sure I'm going to need all the help I can get."

"He gets cocky quick," commented Alcraw.

"You have no idea," answered Kitar, rolling his eyes this time. I just smiled a smugly. There is already too much eye rolling in this entry.

Looking back to Balthazar, Elick asked, "Is he done?"

"Most certainly. He could use more just to pump up his regeneration and strength but from this point on its mostly cosmetic."

I shrugged. "Sounds like it's heart all around. Cemal, will you prepare the plate?" I said as a realization hit me, and I won't lie, I couldn't suppress my grin. "Oh wait, Kitar are you going to have a slice? I know how uptight you've been about this whole idea." I turned to our all-mighty judge sitting flat on his ass on the ground looking like he'd been hit by a brick. We all watched him until he looked up, his mouth moved several times, but no words came out. When his eyes met mine, I raised an eyebrow and shrugged a shoulder. "You said you would do whatever was necessary to ensure my protection. Well, my friend, now I'm offering you a chance to for you to perform your duties to your satisfaction. It will also help me keep a promise I made to you, to do what I could to protect our family, something you're a part of, in return."

He nodded with a smile. I'm still not used to doggy smiles. It's like I just rubbed his belly or behind his ear.

"No more than one slice each," said Belth loudly. "Both Alcraw and I will take a piece of Zephar's and give Elick and Cartos a slice from Enepisgo." Tapping his chin, he looked at the judge, "I think you need Zephar's as well. As for the boy…."

I cut him off. "Cemal gets one of both." I heard objections starting but held up a single finger, and they went quiet.

"After you have the portions prepared let us look to see how much is left. I want Keith and Usis to have at least a couple of more helpings," added Elick.

Once Cemal had the servings ready both Belth and Elick examined what remained of The Lovers' hearts. "This is good; both should be able to get at least three more portions in the same combination as before. Being at the bottom of the hearts, the portions will be smaller overall but still enough."

"Wait, how is this going to affect all of us to consume the same hearts? We have conjectured that Usis and Keith will be able to communicate and who knows what else since they share the same Powers creation energy. Is this going to tie us into them as well?" asked Alcraw.

"I would not think so since it is so little. I expect all this will do is augment and strengthen our already existing powers not introduce new ones," answered Balthazar. "We might be able to sense each other, but that too would probably be a bonus." Looking down to Cemal as he brought the platter back, he supplied, "How this will affect a construct though is anyone guess."

That got my attention. "It won't hurt him, will it?"

"I would not think so. He is, after all, nothing more than flesh, bone and Creation energy to start with, just not Creation energy from something like one of The Fallen."

"As long as you're sure," I added as we all reached for our slices. That is all of us but Cemal and Kitar. I took the plate from the boy's hands with the three remaining pieces and walked over to Kitar, who was still sitting on the ground. I picked up his piece and offered it to him, he took it, eyed it laying limply between his fingers. As he closed his eyes and consumed the piece, I smiled at how he looked like he was taking holy communion.

Once Kitar finished I turned and went and kneeled before Cemal. His eyes went wide in shock. Taking the first slice, I held it up to his mouth much like a wafer in communion and said, "I told you that you were part of this family. Now I have the opportunity to prove it. Now eat."

He took the first piece with tears rolling down his face. As I reached down to retrieve the last one I felt him lean forward and kiss me on the forehead. I offered him the second slice which he again hesitantly took, chewed and swallowed. As I started to stand, he said, "Thank you, Master. This boy will always serve you with love and gratitude."

"We will see about the 'serve' thing once this is over," I commented. I was surprised when he placed a very firm hand on my shoulder stopping me from standing.

"No Master, this boy was made to serve. This boy, regardless of what gifts or love Masters bestows upon him, will always wish to remain in your service just as I am. It allows this one to show his gratitude in the only way he knows how."

I nodded. "But should that desire ever change, let me know, and we will discuss it then."

"Yes, My Master."

I could hear the finality in his tone. I knew that request to be freed would never come.

# Entry 234

Later that night as I was starting to wind down, I found Kitar by himself in our repaired sitting area. "You've been quiet," I commented as I sat down beside him.

For a long time, he didn't speak. "Keith, you are becoming quite a leader. Your sharing of the hearts today came as a complete surprise. Though the others, well besides Elick, might not have shown their astonishment as much as I did, they were equally if not more taken aback."

"I don't understand why. It's not just about me; it's about all of us. Losing you, Elick, Cemal, or any of them though maybe not a devastating as if I lost Usis..." I paused, "...no as much as Usis, just in a different way. I would be equally as upset. You, Cemal and Usis are my family now, Elick to a lesser degree but that is only due to time, not loyalty or trust."

"Keith, to you it is logical to protect those around you. You do not think about it; it is just who you are. Other than myself and Usis, the rest of our group has spent their entire lives in Hell. Generosity is not part of their comprehension. To them, it is more of a weakness. Here you use those who can help you for as long as they can and then you move on. If they are hurt or destroyed in the process no one thinks twice about it. It is the price of doing business. You are not that way."

"I hope I'm never that way. Maybe that's why this place is like it is. Maybe that's why both The Host and Hell can't find it in their hearts, pardon the pun, to forgive the sins of the past and move on. Holding a grudge is called Wrath, I've seen the Plane. I wouldn't sacrifice one of you to save myself. What good is such a victory? It would be hollow and serve to do nothing but give me my own private Hell in which to spend eternity. No, we're family and friends. We rise or fall together."

"I guess I needn't fear for your humanity. You seem to be all you ever were and instead of letting this place or your circumstances making you harder, it has made you pliable and strong."

"If you don't sway in the wind, you break. If I've learned anything in Hell, it's that it plays upon our rigidness, for in that steadfastness it finds and exploits our sins and our weaknesses."

"How you have evolved. The very things that brought you here, your desire to be separate and apart, are the very things you have shed. You have grown instead into a very caring and giving heart. I know it has been said to tedium, and I must repeat it again, The Dark Lord chose well in choosing you. There is no doubt as to his wisdom because you have fulfilled his faith in you at every turn. What I wonder is if they are asking themselves, why? Why did Lord Lucifer choose someone who would soften and become more like The Host's picture of humanity instead of hardening and becoming what is expected of a servant of Hell."

As I turned to go back in, I saw Cemal asleep on his little pallet beside my cot. The hearts had almost instantly affected him, "Do you think he will be OK?"

Kitar turned and nodded. "So many new things are being explored here today. The living consuming the hearts of The Powers. Now Hellspawns doing the same. But as for Cemal, not only are we in uncharted waters with how the hearts will affect him but also how being treated as a person will. Constructs are manufactured to be tools, yet you elevated him, made clay into a person and shown him the same respect you have shown us. I might dare say a little more."

"He serves. It's what he wants to do. He sees his entire existence as a duty. It only seems fair that I see one of my duties as the responsibility to ensure he never questions the logic of his own choices." As I finished, I walked back inside and crawled in bed. I could feel the hearts or maybe just the events of the day starting to draw my eyes closed as well.

# Entry 235

I'm going to compress the next few days into a couple of entries. A lot happened, none of it boring, the problem is, in what order. I feel I should put the attack in first. I know the last few entries have been touchy-feely, which having been in Hell for as long as I have makes it feel a bit tripe. Still, let's do the new body stuff first and then we can get to the fresh horrors, both real and imagined, that existed in this dead Creation.

I'm proud to report I've got the hooves issue pretty much solved. I don't fall over anymore. My body has healed, and my new enormous cock is starting to show signs of life. I only bring that up because Kitar is reading over my shoulder. See it worked, he left.

As for my wings, well that's another story completely. You know, flying isn't as easy as all these demons and Powers make it look. I did learn why Cartos volunteered to teach me and why everyone chuckled when he did. It seems that he has spent his entire life being too big, too clumsy and uncoordinated. To hear him tell it, the only reason he learned to fly as well as he does is because Lord Morningstar, yes Xia, helped by taking him to the top of one of the mountains on the Great Plain and repeatedly chucking him off. He says you can still see the twenty feet tall Hellspawn craters at the base of the rock face. I know I said twenty, he was younger, but thank you for paying attention.

Now that I've told you that little tidbit of information, I'll explain how it pertains to me. Yes, you're bright if you're smiling, that is the way the mother fucker taught me to fly. Hauling me to the top higher and higher buildings and chucking me off. And yes, there are pissed off writer craters scattered around this wreck of a city now as well. Like that wasn't bad enough, all this was being done with an audience down below, cheering and betting how hard I'd hit this time. You know Hell is full of assholes.

The upside to these lessons is it does instill a certain bit of urgency to focus during them. It's amazing how a hard, rocky ground rushing toward your face can encourage one's mind to figure out how to get your damn bat wings to save your ass.

Surprisingly it didn't take long to learn the mechanics of flying. The way the wings are attached all spans from the shoulder blades. I'm not going to write a technical manual, but I'll say that an entire group of muscles and additional bones are overlaid above and below the shoulder blades. I sent some time looking at Kitar's back. He wasn't pleased but allowed it. Yes, I pulled rank. If you look on yourself, you will see that you can move your arms more or less independently of the bones on your back. Starting out I had a hard time flying and manipulating my arms and hands at the same time. This is mainly because my mind didn't understand the changes and thus how to manage sending commands to my wings which were not also interpreted by my arms and hands. I spent a lot of time with my arms either paralyzed or flailing about. The way wings work is I send subtle changes in direction and speed using the bones, nerves, muscles, and membrane of the wings to adjust pitch and stuff, sort of like opening and closing your fingers. The only time I need to multitask my shoulders is when I make extreme adjustments, course corrections or I am flapping them to gain speed or become airborne. I've been assured that in time my brain would learn to separate the differences in the commands to my wings and those to my arms and I can confirm this because I'm starting to get the hang of how to control them. I still tumble to the ground way more than I'd like, but with my new body, it tends to do little real damage. Don't think it negates the pain. It still fucking hurts to hit the ground after being tossed off a thirty-story building.

As for the rest of the body, my tail is still a challenge and fucking sore at this point, mainly because I keep forgetting to move it when I sit. It has become so predictable the entire group sounds like they just did one of those Greek plate things and yells "Opa!" each time I bark and stand up quickly. This both annoys me and amuses the hell out of Cemal, who tends to skip the celebratory yell in favor of just falling down laughing. I'm still not sure which bugs me more, though I'm leaning toward Cemal's giggling since he supposed to be a servant. Would you listen to that, how uppity I'm getting? I guess he better keep laughing if for no other reason than to keep me in my place.

A little more about new compatriots. Cartos, who it seems is Lord Morningstar (Xia's) best friend, is by far the most laid back. Think of that clumsy good-natured guy you knew in your youth. He's huge, quick to laugh and bring others to laugh. If I were to define his role within the group it'd be muscle, because he's all muscle. He's the force behind the others' intelligence and cunning. It's also important to note that his father is Lord Lucifer's second-in-command. Balthazar is, of course, the silent, intense and dangerous type. Its amazes me how little is known about him. I've probed several times but gotten nowhere. That just leaves Alcraw, which is the most charismatic. What I've managed so sus out is that he's their spy, which I can understand. He tends to blend into about any surrounding and has a nasty tendency of appearing just as he begins to speak, freaking the hell out of me.

News from Elick about Usis has been good and bad. See now they have me doing it. The good part is Usis' healing is complete. The first part of the bad news is Elick refuses to tell me what he looks like, he says it's a surprise he won't spoil. I'm guessing he must look good since every time Elick says that he follows up with the fact he will be holding me to that three-way. Like I'd say no. I've been alone, sick, and now have a huge new dick I want to try out.

Many other things have happened, and I'll cover in them in the upcoming entries.

# Entry 236

After a long day of training, both flight and combat, I retired to my cot, exhausted and sore. It didn't feel like I'd been asleep long when I realized I was in another dream.

Though many aspects have already started to fade, the ones which remain are too powerful to ignore. Unlike the last dream about my life this one wasn't; it was from the perspective of The Lovers. I can't say which. It might have been bits from both since the images were at times disjointed.

If you don't remember, by the time we were abducted The Lovers had been melded together, back to back, nothing more than emaciated husks, imprisoned in a cave between the Planes of Hell. These Cast Out, as they are known, were neither Fallen or Host any longer for you see they had chosen not to choose when the Great War started. When it eventually ended those who didn't fight for either side were cast out only to face an eternity lost in The Void.

As I understand it, Lucifer eventually relented, allowing those refugees to carve out a place for themselves in the mountains surrounding the Planes of Hell. Their own little reality. I've met several during my travels. Unfortunately for many, that wasn't enough, and they tried to overthrow him and seize Hell for themselves. They failed. The Lovers, after a couple of attempts, were eventually confined to a cave and joined back to back, so they could never look upon each other again. It was a way to ensure they felt the pain of separation. See, they loved each other deeply.

To keep this short and not turn it into a history lesson about events already recounted in these Journals, I'll cut to the end. After being tortured by the two Cast Out angels, Lucifer showed up, freed us and allowed Usis to exercise his darker desires of revenge upon them. His souvenir were their hearts.

This dream appears to be from before the Fall so for simplicity I'll stick with their future genders when I refer to them. Otherwise this could get very confusing. Something else I think you should remember; the dream is disjointed and not always understandable, but then we're dealing with The Powers and The Host, something I'll never see firsthand.

Zephar is with a group of other angels. They all seem tall, or maybe it's just that I feel so small in this dream. They're arguing. They've listened as Lucifer and The Father fought, all of Creation shuddering from the waves of anger emanating from the two beings. Before you ask, yes, The Father is there, but to my memory, he is nothing but a blur. I can hear his voice and can tell you that when he speaks and is calm, it's like the very fibers of my being are being drawn to him. The longer I hear him, the more I understand just how hard it must've been to decide to reject him and walk away.

In the dream I have no sense of time, but it seems like they have been locked in conflict forever. Lucifer wants The Father to stop his madness, his obsession with these Creations, not because he fears them or what they could mean. He sees how it's affecting the rest of the Powers as well as the stable Creations. The Father, no longer the careful architect, has become manic. He creates realities, watches them grow and fail, and then tosses them away like a child disappointed with a toy. The Void, previously a clean space for The Father to build is now nothing more than a jumble of Creations, many of which have already failed or on the verge of failing.

My dream shifts and this time I see through Enepsigo's eyes. She (again her future designation) is standing while others scream at her. I'm not sure scream is the right word, but I can see the anger rolling off them like waves. The bodies of the lesser creatures in The Host, who come within range, are ripped apart from the intensity of The Power's emotions. I recognize someone out of the corner of Enepsigo's eye; it's Gabriel.

She turns her head and there is Lucifer. He is as I've never seen him before, but then so was Gabriel. Their eminence, their power and presence is all engrossing. The light of their existences are beacons so bright that eternity should glow just from them being.

Now she is sitting and beside her sits Zephar. She looks down to see them holding hands. She looks up to him, and he to her.

The vision jumps again, and now we're in another crowded room. I only hear bits and pieces of what Lucifer is saying. (I almost typed The Dark Lord, but he's isn't yet. He is the Prince of Light.) He's explaining that all of Creation, their very existence he fears is at risk. The Father no longer speaks to him. He stays out in The Void on that platform lost in his distractions. His body is there, but his spirit moves through the expanse as Creations blink in or out existence. The speed so boggling that his strength and power dumbfound even The Host...

# Entry 237

That's when I'm shaken awake, first by Cemal screaming that we were under attack and then by a blast hitting the building.

I jumped up, fell, jumped up again, fucking hooves I swear. "What's happening?" I barked as Elick hurried into the room.

"It appears the creatures inhabiting this planet have massed for an attack," he explained.

"You look like you don't believe that," I said. Finally getting my feet below me, I catch the sword Elick tosses to me. "What the fuck am I supposed to do with this?"

"Not cut off your nuts would be a good start. If attacked, fight, remember your training," answered Elick as a firebolt flew across the clearing just outside the store. "Just stay back and if anything that is not one of us comes near you swing the pointy side at it." Turning to run back outside he points to Cemal. "Boy, it is time for you to shift. Help protect your Master."

In the guttural tone of the demon beast locked inside him, he barks, "Where else would I be? I care nothing about the rest of you if My Master is in danger." I watch as he shifted, his mouth splitting back to his ears as it filled with rows of razor-sharp teeth. His body became slick with a paralytic acid, and his fingers and toes turned into talons. He let out a vicious roar and sprang from the room.

Both Elick and I did a doubletake. "If he were not so cute, I would be worried about him," added Elick, the two of us following my blood hungry slave into the fray.

What I saw when I made it outside was staggering. Kitar, Cartos, and Alcraw were all in hand to hand combat with dozens if not hundreds of these creatures. To say it was combat might be over-glorifying it a bit. The Powers and Judge were tearing through them like they were tissue paper. The one I hadn't located was Balthazar until I saw a blast of black energy shoot across the clearing, destroying at least twenty percent of the attacking mob. I traced it back to where I thought it came from to find him holding off thousands of attackers further from town. I watched in awe as he floated some ten feet off the ground with huge concrete blocks the size of cars, torn from the structures around him, rotating in a circle around his body. When he raised his hand, I could see the glowing runes dancing across his palm. With a barely perceptible flip he'd send one of the massive boulders flying into the crowd where it would roll end over end bowling them down as plumes of dust filled the air.

I know I haven't described these things, and to be honest, considering what I know now I'm not even going to bother. If you need an image think of any zombie or post-apocalyptic creature you want. Their bodies were emaciated and dusty with limbs, heads, entire sections missing, yeah that should do it.

I ceased to be an observer and became a participant when I heard Cemal hiss from behind me. Spinning around what I saw wasn't one of this creation's discarded souls but a fully armored Demon some twelve feet high. "Elick, we have a problem," is all I could think to yell.

Cemal, on the other hand, had no problem figuring out what to do. As Elick yelled, pulling the Demon's attention away, Cemal lunged, found a bit of skin and buried his teeth. Already his goo was eating through the armor. The Demon screamed in both surprise and pain, then with his free hand knocked Cemal off, sending him flying into the center of the clearing and a horde of this world's inhabitants. I watched as the vicious claws of our little slave boy tore into the group, pulling them apart. He wasn't my boy anymore; he was a creature of hell and a pissed one at that.

Connecting steel brought me back to my problem. Turning Elick was there and engaged with the partially paralyzed Demon, who was bringing his sword up in a halfhearted block as Elick danced around him picking him apart. As the two battled I heard Elick say to the Demon has was fighting, "You need to go back to the Keep," growled Elick as he swung his sword, clipping the Demon on the arm opening a fresh wound.

"You know we cannot do that," answered the Demon. "Our Lord has sent us to bring the damned to him."

In a hiss, Elick barked, "If you wish to visit the Hatchery on this day it is your choice. I would suggest you return to my Great Grandfather and tell him he will not be getting Keith today or ever. Now decide, a message or your head, which would you prefer me to send back?"

Elick didn't give the Demon a chance to respond, with a great twirl his sword came around separating the body from the now silent but still talking head.

"This is Leviathan's work it seems?" I said rather obviously as I turned to find another of the large Demons right on top of me. I didn't think. I blocked a blow from his sword, pushing the tip into the dirt. My blade hand circled so quickly I didn't even realize I'd moved it and pushed forward, through the armor, the Demon and out his back as my other hand's long talons cut across his throat ripping his head off. As the creature dropped to the dusty ground, I turned wide eyes to Elick as I placed a hoof on the Demon's chest and pulled out my sword.

"It would seem," he said.

I realized after the battle was over, it wasn't me who did that. It was Enepsigo's training working through me.

The fight went on for a while. No one seemed to be worried about me anymore. I was dancing between the residents of this plane like I knew what the fuck I was doing. Occasionally when too many would engulf me, I'd see Cemal leap in to help, all teeth and claws.

As the number residents declined I saw off in the distance about twenty more armored Demons. "This looks bad," I heard from beside me. It was Alcraw. "Your Great-Grandfather seems to have forced our hand."

As they raced off to stop the attack, I turned to find Cemal lopping across the plain. With a mighty jump he landed on the back of one of the Demons as chunks started flying from its torso. I needed to learn to pay attention. I felt a clawed hand grip me by the shoulder, opening up wounds as he spun me around. I lifted my sword to attack but it was quickly knocked away. "Tell me where the writer is, and I will spare you," it growled as saliva dripped from its fangs. I realized he didn't know who I was.

As we both responded to a scream, I took the distraction as an opportunity to jump back out of reach. Before I could bring my sword to bear Cemal landed on Demon's chest and began tearing him apart. With amazing speed, he spun around, slapping Cemal off as a bark of pain come from my boy as he flew across the clearing. My anger flared. I dropped my sword as I shoved one of my clawed talons through the opening Cemal had created on Demon's armor. I was blind with rage. I felt my hand hit something solid as my head came forward and my fangs buried themselves in his face. As he wrestled to free himself my hand grasp the long boney column. I pulled with all my might as I released his face from my mouth. With a massive and disgusting rip, the creature's entire spinal cord came out through the front of his chest as what was left collapsed to the ground.

Alcraw ran up. I heard him say "Well, damn," as he parried an attack, "I cannot believe he sent so many just to retrieve you and how did he even find us?

I didn't realize how loud the battle was until everything stopped as someone barked, "Enough." In unison, we all turned to see Balthazar float into the center of the clearing as dozens of orbs circled his body in wide arks. Above his head was now a halo of blue-black runes sending out flashes of energy destroying whatever they hit. "How dare Leviathan send these pathetic creatures against me." As the last word left his mouth, we were all blown off our feet by the wave of energy that burst from his body.

I looked up to see him lower himself to the ground as Elick helped me back to my feet. Looking around there was no one left, the Demons, the souls, all dead. "He seems angry," I remarked still trying to catch my breath.

"It is not anger. He is insulted. It appears Great-Grandfather did not take us as much of a threat and sent low-level Demons."

"Low Level?" I added in disbelief. "This is what you call low level?"

Searching the battlefield, I found Cemal with his face buried in the chest cavity of one of the Demons he'd dispatched. "Cemal, what are you doing?" I shouted.

Looking up he sheepishly, he smiled. "It contains energy."

I just shrugged. "Not an issue, just gross, carry on."

Taking in the devastation, it was clear this battle was over.

I walked back and started to help the others set up our common area. Most of the chairs were still in one piece. As I righted a crate we used as a table, I saw Alcraw pull a wineskin out and fill several dusty goblets. Cartos plopped down a distance away -- remember he is like thirty feet tall and always ablaze. "It appears our hiding place is no longer a hiding place."

"It seems. The awakening of Keith's powers is probably responsible for notifying Great-Grandfather of our location."

"Where will we go? I'm not ready to face him so we can't go to his Plane, which should be next," I remarked.

"We were not going there next anyway. We decided it best to take you to the Eighth Plane while you train and gain strength. You can tour it while there, and we will worry about the Seventh after...," Elick was interrupted.

"...after we rip that fucker's heart out and consume it for dinner," growled Balthazar. Energy was still rippling off him like heat on concrete in the middle of a summer's day. This was Hell level mad.

"Won't Leviathan, otherwise known as 'that fucker,' come after us there?" I asked, trying to ignore the pissed off Hellspawn.

"No, the Overlords of Fraud and my Great-Grandfather are bitter enemies. He would not dare set foot on their Plane and any soldiers he sends the Overlords will deal with for us. We should be safe there," explained Elick. (In case your curious, Elick didn't refer to the Overlords of Fraud as "the Overlords" I added that, he used their names. You'll get them when we get there.)

"What about Usis? If your Great-Grandfather is sending people to capture us, I can't imagine he is treating Usis very well. And how will you check on him?" My voice was rising as the pit in my stomach grew.

"Don't worry; I am going to deliver your challenge while the others get you to the Eighth Plane. He will scoff at me, but that is no different than any other time."

"How will that help?"

"Once the terms of the challenge are agreed to he will be honored bound to protect Usis, since he is technically the prize."

"PRIZE!!" I barked.

"Calm yourself. The capture of an important person, be it The Dark Lord's writer's companion or one of the children of Hell's royals have protocols that no one would dare overstep. In so doing brings The Dark Lord into play and no one wants that. He is very rigid when it comes to his rules."

In a sarcastic tone, Balthazar snapped, "Just like The Hosts, Powers never change."

"If we have nothing else to do here, you four get everything together and get Keith to the Eighth Plane. They are expecting us. I will go visit my Great-Grandfather and let him know of his soldiers' defeat."

"Tell him I am coming for him," growled Balthazar.

"Fine, I will make sure not to do that," answered Elick as his wings extended and he shot into the sky.

# Entry 238

As Elick left we heard a noise just outside the clearing. Everyone except Balthazar tensed as he yelled, "There he is. I knew I left one laying around here somewhere!"

As they started across the square, I was instructed to stay behind. You can imagine how well that went, or for that matter how well I paid attention, I didn't. But as we ran, I did get distracted; it was the damage we'd caused since our arrival. I was brought here unconscious but just from the time I awoke until now a lot had happened. The most severe being when my powers awakening, then add to that the attack and there was nothing left standing. The building which had survived a disgruntled Creator couldn't weather four Hellspawns, a writer and his slave. I'm starting to think, if this were my home, I'd have attacked us too. Anyway, when I reached the other side of the clearing, I found my guardians gathered around one of the Demons. It had survived but only barely. All that remained was the top quarter of its torso and his head. Pieces of organs, bone, flesh, and blood were splayed out like a Pollack painting around what little was left.

"How is he still alive?" I asked.

Raising his hand, Balthazar answered, "That would be me. I'm not allowing this one to escape."

Alcraw smiled at Balthazar. "Yes, he will make an acceptable gift for Kritanta. I will enjoy seeing what he does to this one."

"Indeed," added Balthazar with an evil grin.

"What am I missing?" I asked.

"Remember the Overlords of Fraud have a standing hatred for Lord Leviathan. Handing over one of his soldiers will be the perfect gift upon our arrival," explained Alcraw.

"Very good idea, Alcraw."

"Then it is settled. Let's pack and get ready to move out. You need to be under their protection before Elick's Great-Grandfather finds out what happened.

As I was packing the few things I possessed, mainly Usis' and my backpack, I remembered something Elick had said earlier. "Kitar, why am I healing so much faster than Usis? I mean, for a long time he wasn't doing well at all."

"If I were to guess it could be any of several possibilities. You are wearing Lucifer's amulet, which protects and more importantly heals you quickly. You received better care than I am sure Usis did and finally you did not go through a long period of, for lack of a better word, power starvation. You have been regularly fed since you started, unlike Usis. If you had not discovered the hearts, there is no telling what shape your little companion would be in now."

"But Usis has an amulet as well. Why didn't that help?"

"His amulet is tied to you, as an extension of yours. Yours, on the other hand, was blessed directly by Lord Lucifer. That makes it much stronger. Usis' amulet is little more than an announcement to those who see it that its wearer is one of your protectorates and thus by extension one of The Dark Lord's."

"If he isn't with me, he isn't protected?"

"He is, it still carries The Dark Lord's seal but does not directly report to him."

My eyes went wide as I picked up the necklace. "This thing reports to Lucifer?"

"In a way. It will let him know if something adverse happens to you. How much more it does, I cannot say. If I were to guess, it probably does send occasional reports."

"It's just a necklace."

"Nothing is 'just' if it carries Lord Lucifer's seal..." Pausing, he walked over, lifting the amulet off my chest and closing his eyes. "Just as I suspected. There is a soul contained within. I am sure it can communicate with The Dark Lord if you are in danger, need assistance and probably if you start being...well...too you."

"Being too me? What the fuck does that mean?"

"A spoiled brat," offered Cartos as he strolled past us. Trust me it wasn't a surprise, as big as he is it's like having an earthquake roll past.

"Nice, all of you, nice," I growled as I heard a snicker behind me. "Oh do you agree with them, MY boy?"

"Master, I would never say such a thing about you," answered Cemal.

I smiled pleased until I noticed everyone else was smirking, then I got it. Looking back at him and raising an eyebrow, I asked, "You'd never say it? The question is, would you think it?"

Looking up at the great rupture in the sky Cemal spread his wings, lifting himself into the sky, "Master Elick should be at Lord Leviathan's Keep by now. Should we not be going?"

This got a laugh from me as well. I know me.

Together we followed his lead and lifted into the air. This was going to be the first big test of my flying abilities. To travel out of this Creation and then through The Void, whatever that is. In all honesty, my concern wasn't the ability to fly but more the endurance. I've found it very exhausting to fly thus far.

"I will hang back and ensure our charge does not falter," commented Cartos as he moved in beside me.

As we flew up over the ruined world, I got my first good look at the landscape. It was heartbreaking. Though destroyed you could see the central city where our little derelict shop had lived. Leading out were the veins of the many roads, now ruined, lined by the remnants of houses, hamlets, and villages with expanses of what had probably once been farmland — all lying dead like a corpse lost in a war long forgotten. I started to say abandoned but see that would've been the wrong word and in a lot of ways disrespectful. For you see the residents of this world were still here, the dried-up husks of their bodies lay where they fell. They like their world were the bones of a civilization trampled in the blink of a god's eye. Only through these journals would these nameless people in this nameless world be remembered. It harkened the old saying, "but there by the grace of god go I."

"Hang on; you have never done this before. Take my hand," Cartos instructed, so I did, and Cemal took mine, and with a blinding speed we shot across the open expanse of this ruined creation. The world which had once been our home now nothing but an ever-shrinking marble in the blackness of nothing.

"How are we going so fast?" I yelled to Cartos.

"I have not had the opportunity to teach you how to accelerate. With the vast distances of these Creations or The Void it would take millions of years to travel the distances involved at our original speed," he yelled back.

The acceleration was mind numbing as together we shot across the vastness of this once living universe. We passed dozens of dead worlds as the rupture grew larger before us. Finally, we broke through and for the first time I looked back to see the collection of discarded Creations, now nothing more than a pile of shattered balls discarded by a bored and angry child.

Turning my head away from what was, I saw what is, The Void. Though I didn't count them, it was easy to find the current Creations, the bright black marbles still filled with life floating in a sea of nothingness. It struck me how that description was mine not those who ruled this place, The Host and Hell. To them, these living universes were little more than a sustainable fuel source used to power their existence. They meant nothing to them. I looked up into a blinding light; it was like looking at the sun, when in fact it was looking toward The Father, for that brief glimpse was all I'd probably ever see of The Eternal City.

I found the nebula I'd seen, oh so long ago, from the window on the Fourth Plane, I knew it was feeding new resources into an active Creation somewhere beyond my sight. As we continued to race downward, I turned my attention to our destination, Hell. Just like the living and dead creations, it was a massive globe, easily ten times the size. Where it differed, was its complete blackness, no light escaped. That is not to say that it wasn't lit, for it was, from below. Flames, billions of miles high, licked at its sides. These were the furnaces fed by the suffering of the souls The Powers grew in the nine tiny greenhouses called Creation.

As we grew closer, the heat began to increase eventually becoming stifling. I heard a sound to my left and looked to see Cartos take a deep breath. "Home," was all he said with a smile. We were now traveling across the sooty surface of the great globe. I couldn't help but feel like we were fighter jets traveling over the black landscape of some forgiven land. Cemal pulled up beside me, tears running down his face, "There…" he pointed to a small opening in the side of the smooth surface. As we grew closer, I began to see the wisps of the minerals snaking from the small opening. I turned to trace its path only to find it now lost on the other side of Hell's massive surface.

With great speed, we approached the opening — such a small window looking out onto The Void. We zipped through and again set or feet upon the Planes of Hell. We paused just long enough to greet the Overlord of Greed. With respect I bowed to the little childlike creature as the Hellspawns all marched past paying no attention to its resident. Once we were outside, on the plane itself, Balthazar cast a spell around the group, rendering us invisible as we rose only to descent down into the pit and the Eighth Plane.

I moved over beside Cemal and let a little lightning bolt fly, hitting him in the ass. As his head shot around, preparing for an attack, I smiled innocently at him, revenge for the comment back on the broken Creation.

# Entry 239

Well, here we go again, a new Plane and new horrors. My job resumes, again I'm Hell Journalist. It's been made clear that regardless of my own personal dramas, my primary duty is to The Dark Lord. So, I'll be touring and writing about this plane, the Eighth Plane, the Plane of Fraud and Deceit.

I know, I know, I say this every time, but boy was this Plane not what I'd expected. Normally I first describe the Keep, usually the most predominant feature, but oh no, no, not here. It's big if it's the building I think it is for you see it is easily lost in the city in which it sits. Yes, a real city ...not town ...not village but full fucking city. A full fucking futuristic city to boot. But still, neither the Keep or the city are the main features of this Plane.

The main feature are the lakes, two at the top, on a plateau which takes up clearly two thirds of the Plane, and a third at its base hundreds of feet below. I'll start with the lowest one. If I were to guess, by itself, it's as big as the entirety of the Sixth Plane. The two at the top together are twice the size. As you can see, this Plane is enormous, at least four times that of the last Plane I visited.

The city proper rests on a flat artifical (origianlly it was going to be manmade, but that just didn't seem right) island extending out from the cliffs between the two upper lakes overlooking the bigger one hundreds of feet below. Now if that isn't enough, both of the top lakes were damned. I mean real damns, holding back the millions of gallons of what I can only guess is suffering. To give any of you from Earth, which at this point shouldn't be many, reading this a perspective, the Hoover dam in Nevada was only 726 feet tall, and these must be twice that height. When we arrived, flying over the Plane, the gates of the two upper lakes were open letting the liquid suffering cascade down in violent waterfalls into the lower lake below. Take a moment, I know it's a lot to take in.

Now if you've been following these journals, you know that all the souls on the seven planes, though I haven't visited the Seventh yet, are tortured for no other reason than to produce suffering. It's serves as the main accelerant used to fuel the intense fire of the furnaces. Though your world might revolve around your local star, all that background radiation your scientists keep talking about and can't explain, is, in fact, the heat produced using the suffering inflicted on the former residents of the nine Creations. In short, you.

Flying across the Plane we swooped down to sail a few feet above one of the lakes when I noticed that the churning water isn't caused by tides but by millions, maybe billions of souls all struggling to stay afloat. As we get closer to the city more and more detail started to emerge. I remember playing a game back on Earth called SWTOR. There was a city there named Nar Shaddah, this resembles that. Very Blade Runner-ish. Lots of neon, tall glass buildings with broken or boarded up windows, trashy streets, and strange looking creatures scurrying about. When we entered the city, I also learned that with my new wings, the speed and complexity of navigating through the narrow corridors becomes more difficult as I begin to grow exhausted.

As we swooped around a tight corner, there before us stands a building which doesn't initially look like it should fit in. As we grew closer and more detail revealed itself, it became evident that it really does. As you've probably guessed this is the Keep for the Plane. Where the other buildings are glass and metal this one is stone with dark black windows. The primary feature isn't the building as much as what hangs from the exterior walls of its fifty plus stories, row after overlapping row of robots, cyborgs, whatever you want to call them. The entire structure covered from top to bottom in bodies like a mechanical puppet maker storing his overcrowded stock along the shop walls. The taller ones, if they have feet, hang down onto the creatures below them. Their thrashing damaging the faces and torsos of those they've spent eternity kicking while they all flap and make all manner of noise.

Now before you get started, I'm thinking the same thing. Where in Hell, pardon the pun, did they get skyscrapers, steel, glass, and technology? How many times have they said that Hell didn't have advanced tech simply because they dealt with too many races, from too many worlds, from too many times? Clearly, again, that was just what they said in their unending mission not to give me insight into the Lower Planes.

I was still in shock as we landed in front of the Overlord's Keep. Before I could even get a word out Kitar jumped in with what I just wrote. "You know we were told not to tell you about future Planes. On the upside, there are no more Planes after this one, so ask away." Smart ass.

Adding to what Kitar had just said, Alcraw chimed in with, "And it is probably tactically relevant at this point that you know more than less about what you are walking into." Where's he been all my death?

So, being me, I maintain that professional demeanor I'm know for and start screaming as I jump up and down like a twelve-year-old, "That's what I've been saying from the start."

They all stand there, arms crossed, waiting patiently for my fit to pass. Which is does. After which I just push past all of them and remind myself that this journey's almost done. Wow, this journey is reaching an end. Well, that's amazing...

Before anyone could knock or just walk in the front door, it opened and we're greeted by a little, almost identical clone of Cemal.

"Brother," yelled the little creature, "you are home."

With a broad smile, Cemal squealed as he ran over and threw his arms around the other one. Turning back to me, he said, "Master this is another of this one's generation. Its name is Jacob." (Pay attention to that last part, it's going to be important on this Plane.)

"It is nice to meet you, Jacob. I can't believe how similar you two look," I commented.

"We are of the same batch, my Lord," answered Jacob.

Now before you get confused, he is in many ways like Cemal, but his hair was longer and orange, so easy enough to tell apart. The other major difference I noticed, once he opened the door fully, was it had no genitalia of any kind. All you gender-rights people can get upset if you want but he is staying a he for me. If by chance you don't like that you can take it up with my new 10-foot-tall demon frame when you fucking get here. I was a big supporter of gender rights when I was alive, but to be honest with you, it makes writing about a person incredibly difficult. I will say knowing what I know now, having settled into the Plane, this issue will come up again.

This is where I'm going to end this entry. I'll get to the Overlords, the interior of the Keep, which is fucking amazing, and what I discovered as the rudimentary definition of Fraud and Deceit later. Trust me it's far more encompassing than you imagine. I can now understand why its technically the last Plane if you don't count the Great Plane that is.

# Entry 240

I tried, for a change, to enter the Keep with a more cavalier attitude, mainly for your benefit. I didn't want to write again about how I was stopped in my tracks to stand stunned at the outrageousness of this specifics Plane's idea of horror. Well the problem is I sorta was, and I sorta did, so fuck. Well not stunned but impressed for a change. See this Keep was not horrific, it was like a video arcade on crack. Confusing, busy, loud and alive.

The long dark lobby traveled the length of the building, its floors and walls constructed from black veined marble. Down the center was a walkway which bisected the two sides of the massive chamber. As we entered, led by Jacob, I noticed a lot of creatures coming and going. The entire room was abuzz with activity, both from the workers and the many video screens of various sizes positioned in large clumps throughout the space. The majority of workers seemed mostly to be from the same species, if that's the right word. "Who are those...things?" I asked pointing to one of the creatures.

"They are seekers," answered Kitar.

These Seekers were each about seven feet tall with thin, pale bodies, long arms and no distinguishing marks of any kind. Their skin was stark white and appeared to have been pulled too tightly around the underlying frame. So much so that at each curve and pressure point I could see the puckered folds where the flesh had been forced to compensate for the change in direction. As one walked away, I looked to find an expected scar running down their back where clearly the skin had been pulled tight, bunched, stitched together and the extra snipped away. The other odd thing about these creatures was their head and hands. Their heads were smooth and egg-shaped with no eyes, ears, mouth or nose. Each of the creature's bodies were long and lanky, their arms hanging down to almost their knees with fingers at least three times the normal length. They were all nude with no genitalia but considering there were little more than an animated featureless humanoid shape; I didn't expect any. I realized after studying them for a moment; they weren't of the same species, they were all the same. These had to be constructs of some kind.

"Should that mean something?" I asked, a little annoyed that Kitar had interrupted instead of allowing Jacob to answer.

"No. It will later," was his answer which annoyed me even more.

"Whatever," I said as we stopped about a third of the way into the lobby.

"Our Lordship is on the way. This one has been instructed to keep you here," the boy said as he smiled at Cemal.

After all the Planes and all the introductions, I'm used to this awkward first meeting. Usually, it's a lot of posturing where we either learn we're welcome or we're not. I occupied myself by getting a better lay of the land. On both sides of the massive chamber were passages leading into smaller hallways. These are where the Seekers kept vanishing into after entering through a series of doors at the far end of the chamber. I continued to study the sleekness of the lobby; it wasn't opulent, it wasn't even lavish, just utilitarian. As I watched, one of the Seekers came in the back, stood looking around before going over where it began to slowly move its hands across the little jeweled glowing pimples running in long vertical lines along all the wall. For several seconds it just stood there, perfectly still. I watched as its right hand stopped over a red stone, it then inclined its head and plucked it from its resting place on the wall and hurried off toward the back door. I started to ask but was interrupted by Jacob.

"Our Lord has arrived," he said as we all turned to find a creature from a Giger painting floating toward us. My eyes went wide, see I knew it would happen. She/He/It was mechanical. From the waist up it had an exquisitely detailed mat black torso with golden scrollwork around the nipples, down the sides and along the shoulders. Its head had all the normal trappings of a face, but like the rest of its body, it was black with golden eyebrows, nose ring, and pouty lips, which curved into a smile. It had four arms, two in the normal location and two just below. Each mat black hand was capped off by golden fingernails. As I said, it was floating toward us, for it had no lower body, as such. Instead of a pelvis, legs, and feet, there were dozens of snaking tentacles dancing below its torso. They appeared to all move randomly, floating just high enough so to only occasionally brush the floor. The final touch were its wings, only the cartilage, no membrane, also made from gold like the rest of the accents on this exquisite creature. Yes, I'm already in love with the look of Fraud's Overlord, so I braced myself expecting the typical 'you are not welcome here' speech as it spent the next few minutes explaining what it'd heard about me and why that would not be allowed in its Domain.

As it grew closer, we all stepped back as long arching sinews of electricity shot from the ends of each of its tentacles, traveling the twenty or so feet to the walls where it danced from one little-gemmed dimple to the next. Occasional the lighting would strike one of the Seekers dissolving it into nothing but dust as it dropped to the floor in a pile. Never once did the Overlord remove its eyes from me.

Yes, I've mentioned them twice now, the walls are covered in these little gems. In many ways they reminded me of cabochons from a rock shop. Initially I thought they were just decoration, and they might be, but I think not. The faceless figures kept going to them, studying them with their hands, then snatching one and rushing away. Now the Overlord's tendrils of lightning are dancing across them as it approaches. I made a mental note to find out more later.

I watched in rapt fascination until it stopped just a couple of feet in front of us. "Might this one have the honor of introducing you to our beloved Overlord Kritanta," said Jacob as he went to his knee. We followed suit, well Cemal, Kitar and I did, the Hellspawns remained standing.

"You may call me Death. Please rise so I may get a look at you," ordered the Overlord as I listened hoping to get a read on what gender it assumed and wasn't surprised to find it was neither masculine nor feminine. What it did have was a soothing, gentle voice with just a touch of process behind it, like a computer which had been taught to speak properly.

Rising I looked up and smiled. It towered over me. "Greetings, My Lord, I'm Keith, and it is an honor to be in your domain. If you will allow me to introduce my travel companions, Lord Judge Kitar, and my dear friend Cemal."

Kitar rose. "It is an honor, I have heard so much about you My Lord."

I watched as what I thought were immovable lips shifted slightly into a straight line. "You Lord Judge carry much baggage and reputation with you. One must wonder upon your transgressions to be punished in this way?"

"Punished?" asked Kitar.

"Yes, to be forced to act as an escort to a soul...," it turned to look at me as its lips again shifted, "...regardless how exalted that soul might be, through The Dark Lord's domain."

Not missing a beat, Kitar replied, "Once you get to know him, I am sure your opinion will change. It is important to note as well, My Lord Death, I was not forced. I choose this assignment."

"Do not mistake me as being blind to this one's abilities. He was after all chosen by our Lord; there is much about him I hope to learn." Death paused and leaned in close, so close in fact our noses almost touched. "I see remnants of my brothers as well. Yes, indeed, you might just survive your coming tests and bring Violence's lord low. That is, of course, if these boys can ever get you trained."

"I've been told you're rooting for my success. Might I ask why?" I don't know why I asked that.

"I am indifferent in all honesty. But if a side must be chosen, then yes, I would enjoy watching you force that pathetic worm take a knee."

"Worm?"

Alcraw spoke from behind me. "Leviathan."

Nodding, my gaze hardened. "He took someone I care for very much. I have every intention of fulfilling that wish for you."

"I appears you believe you do..." it said as it rose again to its full height. Clapping two of its hands it turned its head towards Jacob. "Take Lord Lucifer's representatives companions to their rooms on the 45th and see to their needs." Looking back to me it added, "I require you to come with me." Without waiting the Overlord turned and began to float away. Looking to my companions for guidance I saw the three Hellspawns shooing me, so I rushed to catch up.

# Entry 241

The room Death led me into appeared to be its quarters. It was simple in a futuristic sort of way. The walls were the same black marble, all littered with several dozen monitors showing everything from the lobby to what looked like torture stations. In addition to the thrones, there were tables in the back of the room filled to overflowing with electronic and mechanical parts, another couple of normal chairs, several tables, and two bowing genderless slaves. What I found strange were all the candles. I mean lots, several dozens of all shapes and sizes and all lit. It was very romantic; I mean...well...yeah?

The Overlord floated to the pair of thrones and began the interesting process required for it to sit. The throne it used, the right one, had a hole in the center of the seat and I watched as it rose high into the air, pulled its tentacles together and lowered itself down until its torso rested against the seat's hard marble base. "Please join me," it said as it snapped causing the slaves to rush off only to eventually return with a single goblet. "Please. As you can imagine, I do not partake."

As I took a seat, I studied the second throne which remained empty. Unlike the other, this one appeared normal. Strangely with the candles, the clutter on the table and just the overall feel of the room, this was one of the first Overlord quarters I'd seen where it felt lived in, like someone had made a home here and were not just occupying an official residence. I liked it.

"I would think not, what with shorting out and all," I hadn't meant to say that out loud and was surprised when the Overlord laughed an electronic laugh.

"Yes, yes indeed. You are quite brave coming with me without any companions after having just arrived. I am sure you realized that was foolhardy?"

I shrugged. "Everyone motioned for me to follow. If I've learned anything, it's to trust those around me..." I lifted my amulet from under my tunic. "...plus, I do have Lord Lucifer's protection, and my journey so far has been littered with foolhardy decisions."

"If our Lord were in Hell at this time, I might agree, but he is not. Therefore I would suggest more caution."

"Should I be worried?"

"Not at all, if I wanted to harm you there are far better ways than letting you into my chambers. Out on the Plane would seem more suited for such an attack, with the added benefit of not messing up my floors."

"That's kind of what I thought as well. Plus, we've been led to believe you've expressed an interest in assisting us in this particularly difficult time and for that I extend a lot of trust and gratitude."

"You are very well spoken. It is clear you have embraced the lessons learned from your travels. You are correct; I am willing to help you. It is, even as we speak, escalating the tensions between myself and that miserable worm holding your companion."

"How so?" I asked.

"Lord Leviathan has already sent soldiers to my Plane insisting when and if you arrive that I turn you over immediately... Insisting is a bit of an understatement, it was more of a command." Again, it laughed.

"And?"

"And what? I sent his representatives back with a message. That being that I had no intentions of acquiescing to his demands and as long as you are here you are under my protection." Pausing it added, "not that the representatives could verbally convey my message since only small parts, vital I am sure to the gendered, were returned to their Lord and Master. Still, I have no doubt he will sus out the message's intent." Again a laugh. I liked this creature.

"I'd imagine that would muddy the message a bit, but being so succinct, I'm sure he'll decipher the symbolism."

"Indeed. Now to why I brought you here so quickly. First, to extend to you my welcome and cooperation. I am assuming you are not abandoning your duties to our Lord Lucifer. If you have entertained such ideas, I would strongly suggest you rethink that decision."

"I'm fully aware I have a job to do and regardless of my current issues I'll continue doing it. It wouldn't be wise to also have The Dark Lord angry at me as well."

"An accurate assessment. Your companions have suggested, and I concur, that my domain would be a more suitable place to train for your somewhat ill-advised encounter with the worm in hopes of reacquiring your companion. Lastly, I believe you intend to interview we Overlords during your stay, thus, I am giving you an opportunity to do so now."

I looked around, a bit stunned and on the spot. "Normally I save that for when I know more about the Plane you rule over."

"That makes sense where the Plane is concerned. I thought first, we could deal with your curiosity as to why I am, well, like this," it said, motioning to its mechanical body. "Questions about my realm can be addressed as you learn more about it. This cuts down on the time you require of me and to be honest, understanding me will help you understand my Plane better as you encounter it."

"Reasonable points. I guess the first and most obvious question, at least from my perspective is, and forgive my bluntness, what are you?"

Again, a laugh. It liked to laugh. "I am Fallen."

"You're a robot, mechanical, cybernetic? I'm not sure which word to use and not be insulting."

Death shook its head. "They are all insulting but only from my perspective, not yours. After all your world had only just scratched the surface of mobile sentient beings as of the time of Lord Morningstar's visit, in that regard, if it helps, keep in mind, that most interactions with our Dark Lord's wayward grandchild often end with something or someone being inconvenienced in some way."

"Inconvenienced? He destroyed it."

"Yes, well, when it comes to moderation, he has been known to be found wanting."

"So, it seems. As to the level of technology, I'll have to take your word on that since I left many years before Xia passed judgment and sentenced it to extinction."

"I find it interesting you are not more passionate about your world and its passing?"

"I've long since made my peace with that news. And to be honest, I might not be happy that it happened, but if Earth continued upon the path it was traveling when I died I can, unfortunately, fully understand their fate."

Death paused for a long second; I could tell it was studying me. "That is a very enlightened observation. I am impressed. As for what I am. To understand that you must know a little about my past, if you will indulge me."

"It would be a great honor to learn your history. Thank you."

We sat in silence for several minutes, I've grown used to this. When it came time to learn about the Powers, they either jumped in like a child at the beach, with enthusiasm or, as was the case here, a languid transition into memories they most probably choose not to revisit often.

"In the beginning my job in the greater scheme of what The Father was building was unclear. Many, like Gabriel, Lucifer, and Michael, all had purposes, predetermined roles. Us, lesser..." it inclined its head in a strikingly human way, "...Powers had not yet found our place. When The Father approached me I was told he needed an avatar to help set up, manage and create for the souls of the living a transition to the afterlife. When I accepted he anointed me the Angel of Death."

"Yes?" it added as I took a long drink of my wine, finishing it. I felt the slight touch and turned to find one of the genderless servants kneeling beside me with a pitcher. I took more as Death continued.

"Then the troubles began. At first just hints of the conflicts to come, Lucifer leaving council meetings before they had concluded. The whispering of groups about decisions The Father had made. As time passed and Lucifer more steadfastly refused to see Father's ambition for his Creations both sides started to shore up their followers, so they approached me. First Raphael who wanted to ensure, that even if "actions had to be taken" against Lucifer that the smooth transition of souls would continue. I, at first, assured them I would continue to do my job. It might sound like a significant role, which it eventually became, but at this point in our past, few living, if any, were manifesting souls and thus little traffic was transitioning from Creation into Eternity. When more began to arrive, a real problem developed into what to do with them. They left it to me, but as of yet, there was no place to house them. At first, we just sent them back. It would have been a long-term solution if The Father had not wanted to continue creating unique souls, and not just recycle the old ones."

It paused again, its black shiny orbs cast up and off, lost in thought. "The conflicts continued to escalate. Lucifer and Father were growing less and less patient with each other, both, were beginning to refuse even to hear the other one out." Again there was a long silence. "We could see the effects this was having on our Dark Lord. He had never been shut out before. He had always had Father's ear, his shoulder when in doubt, and a value to his words. Not anymore, they were no longer talking.

As you can imagine the day finally came when it was clear sides needed to be chosen, and we were all going to be forced into a decision. Souls were arriving more rapidly now, either from the stable creations or the abandoned ones Father discarded as failures. I continued to do my job. I made my voice heard when asked; I did not care, I had procedures, processes that needed to be handled, cleaned up, and refined. Then Beelzebub visited me in hopes of swaying me toward Lucifer's side. While he was there, Raphael also came, and both started to aggressively lobby me for a decision, now, not later. In anger I expelled them both and in protest shut down all the processes of death, trapping the souls of the dying in their pathetic rotting shells of meat. It did not take long for the cries of agony from those in pain as their bodies decayed to be heard in the Halls of the Most High." It cast its head down and buried its face in its metal hands.

When it looked back up, he continued, "Then Father visited. He never visited. I was not important enough to merit consideration. I was a functionary — a program, nothing more. We argued. He ordered me to restart the ascension for the souls, I refused. I felt that until those in 'power' chose to deal with the growing gluttony of souls with no place to go, and stop their ridiculous squabbling, I would not, in the mercy Father had taught us, allow any more souls to enter eternity."

It met my eyes. "Here is the start of the War. I do not know how many creatures know the first action, the spark. It was not Lucifer's. It was mine. See our argument had spilled out onto the streets of The Eternal City. Father and I yelling, well me yelling, Father ordering. When my back was literally against a wall, he reached out to grasp my cloak. I am still not sure why, but I slapped his hand away and in a vicious growl, I can still hear, said, 'you will not touch me' to which he struck me hard across the face answering my insolence with 'I am your Father, you are my servant, my child, I will do with you as I see fit." That was the end, or more accurately, the beginning. I rose slowly, carefully to my feet. Off in the distance, I saw over Father's shoulder Lucifer and his new generals standing, watching. It happened so fast. I drew my sword and swung at Father. He, of course, was no longer where my sword passed, he had moved. In a panic I turned to find him standing behind me. The anger in his eyes was palatable. The very foundations of Creation shook and before I could react he drew his mighty sword. I knew it was my end. As is clear, I was wrong. Father bellowed, "how dare you?" as the instrument of his wrath moved forward, ready to cut me down."

It paused. I was on the edge of my seat. I swear I almost yelled, "Get on with it." I didn't though.

"Just as Father's sword finished its upward arch and started down it encountered something which changed eternity forever..." It smirked. "That is an odd line. Father's blade met another's as I fell to the ground. As all of The Host looked on there stood in the plaza of The Eternal City, amongst such splendor, two immovable forces locked in a stare. For you see, Lucifer had blocked The Father's blow with his own sword. The only thing in Creation strong enough to withstand Father's wrath. It was then, I'm told, the war began."

"You were told? Were you not there?"

"No, for with a simple look Father destroyed me, well he would have if not again for Lucifer's actions. What I tell you now is as it was told to me later. I did not exist as such at this point. Lucifer used his power and captured my essence, there is no word for what we are, thus saving me from oblivion. In anger, The Dark Lord turned back to face Father and said, 'you have drawn first blood. You have betrayed your promises. You have proven yourself to be false. You have lied and deceived. I, your Morningstar, will not stand while you betray all that you instilled in us, your children. I now judge you unworthy.' The fighting began. The war raged for years..." It paused and leaned into me. "Have you ever wondered why Our Dark Lord had been saddled with the mark 666? It is not only in your culture but in all. It is known as The Mark of the Beast when it is in all actuality, the mark of the dead. For you see, 666 followers of The Father, our brothers, are how many were wiped from Eternity by Lucifer during The Great War. It is not his shame; it is his battle count, it is his pride. That is my history."

I sat panting, so many questions had just been answered.

It continued, "When the time came, and the war was over, Lucifer using his power came to meet me in whatever place he had placed me to spare my existence. He offered me my old body, as he also explained how those who had left, the Fallen, had chosen a new form. He showed me his, the opposite of the divine, the antithesis of what their old forms had been. We talked about many things, the outcome of the war, the starting of Hell, the gendering of the Fallen, call it a status report if you will.

"It was during this conversation when Lucifer in passing told of how some of The Father's discarded creatures had advanced to a point where they were manufacturing sentient beings. This was a joke between The Dark Lord and myself. See The Father had struggled for quite a long time with that very problem. How to make his creations intelligent. Now his little monkeys were replicating and surpassing his struggles like they were nothing. In that conversation, I found my decision. You must understand, my hatred, yes hatred, for Father was so blinding as to be focusing. I asked Lucifer if he could wait. If I could reside in this place until a mechanical body could be created to house my essence. This surprised even our Dark Lord. I explained that The Father, he was no longer my Father, had betrayed me and therefore if I was to survive, I would serve only Lord Lucifer and at no point would my countenance ever resemble something The Father had made or constructed. I rejected him not only as my sovereign but also as my creator.

"During our discussions, Lucifer explained how The Host, as they now called themselves, hated how the talking monkeys were reproducing, advancing and in many ways rejecting all that The Father gave them for their own creations, as you would call it, their virtual worlds. I knew then; I would become a fraud. I wanted to reside in the technology the living were creating to replace the one who had failed us, The Father. As you can imagine, this pleased Lucifer greatly. But being the fair being he is, he explained how my decision would cause many in The Host to reject me as one of their brothers. That was fine, in fact, it was what I wanted. Lucifer left me, and for many years I resided in nonexistence until the day he came for me and gave me the power to build my shape using only technology created by the living. I have built several forms, one of which you see before you and to this day I stand, as I did so long ago, as a monument of opposition against our Father, the true betrayer of all he created."

Death was now standing at one of the windows in the room looking out. I'd not even realized it had moved. For a long time, it stood in silence. It motioned for me to join it. As I looked out over the lakes in the distance it added, "Is it not sad? I spent so many years working to develop a way to give you living a life after your time in Creation was completed, and it has come to this. Billions of your kind fighting just to stay afloat in a lake of their own making with no hope for a reprieve. They will tire and sink to the bottom to eventually be crushed. Their bare essence, like wine, only to flow down and through the rest of Hell until their time ends as the fuel for the furnaces which keep their Creations alive. It is not a very happy reality but reality it is none the less."

We stared out across the Plane of Fraud. Finally, I finished my wine, turned and bowed. "Thank you; it was truly an honor to hear your story. But I'll not lie, I need time to process what you've told me before there is even a hope of me finding a question to ask."

"This is the reason I felt we should talk first. Feel free to return when you have more questions. I will arrange to have my brother here as well. Good day, young one."

I took that as a dismissal, bowed, and turned to leave. The Overlord instructed the young genderless slave to show me to my quarters. Just as we were about to walk out, I looked back. "Why no genders on your constructs?"

"Gender is a weakness. It was created to fulfill a task. I see no good in it past that. In truth, they are nothing more than constructs of the mind, a manufacturing tool used to create more of a species. We, the Powers, and you, the living, were not created to define yourselves by something so narrow as a gender. The devices placed between your legs and in your body were not intended to tell those in Creation who you are. They were placed there to ensure you could continue to recreate yourselves. It is sad how many in Creation have now embraced their gender as a definition of their very existence. They do not understand that by doing so, they are doing little more than limiting the existence they hope to define, and very narrowly at that. A gender is a tool, if used properly it can expand your horizons, if not, it only limits your scope."

I left, and by the time I was back in the main hall, I already felt a little less full. Death was clearly now a presence in my very being and already I longed to return.

# Entry 242

As I followed the servant through the Keep my curiosity about the gems only grew stronger. They were everywhere. I asked the slave several times but to no avail. Either he didn't know or wasn't willing to volunteer the information. In lots of ways, the entire first floor was pretty much living up to my first estimations of the place, a post-apocalyptic hotel lobby, even down to the elevator. When we reached our floor, I was surprised to find two guards, one standing on each side of the lift. In our new room, Kitar was by the windows and Cemal setting up our customary bar and buffet.

"We were beginning to worry about you," commented Kitar as I walked in.

"The Overlord just wanted a chat. I can tell its very efficient. I hate calling it an it, but I feel he or she is even more inappropriate. Kritanta, is that its name, thought if I understood its personal story before seeing the Plane it would help put things in context. Did you know she...he...fuck...it was the spark that started the war?"

"Seriously? For some reason I always assumed he was not that important in the greater scheme of things," commented Kitar.

"If managing the machinery which oversees the transitions of souls into eternity is a 'little thing' then yes, I would agree. Which clearly, I do not. Where's everyone else?" I asked.

"They are settling into their rooms; we have the whole floor."

"I suppose up this high there's no balcony. As strange as it sounds, I need some air."

"Master, there is a very spacious one, would Masters like to have their dinner there?" asked Cemal.

I nodded. "Yes, and how are you feeling?"

"This one is feeling great Master, this boy thanks --"

I cut him off. "I know, and you're welcome."

As if he was a cold splash of water Kitar added, "That does not change the fact that the table will not set itself or dinner serve itself."

"As Master Growl wishes, so shall this one fulfills," answered Cemal.

"Kitar be nice," I barked.

"Do not worry, Master. This boy understands the pressure Lord Judge was under in his earlier position and how such an important job would require one to have a stick firmly lodged up their ass." He smiled, bowed and turned to head off to who knows where, but just before he left earshot, we heard, "and if that stick is any indication, Master was paid very well."

I burst out laughing as Kitar growled, "You need to do something about that boy's discipline."

"He has tons of discipline. He also doesn't take shit from anyone, and I like that considering the shit we find ourselves in. Now, where's this balcony?" I asked.

As he led me across the room, I couldn't shake the feeling I was in some futuristic sci-fi film. "This place is overloading my brain. It's just so different."

"Keep in mind this and the Great Plane are not like the Planes of punishment you have seen before. From this point on you leave Hell's business of Torture. These last two planes are about the running of Hell and to a certain degree Creation as a whole."

If I was going to say something I didn't. The view from our balcony stopped me dead. We were on the forty-fifth floor after all. High enough to be able to look down the canyons of tall buildings to the mountains beyond. Above us, vulture-like creatures circled in the neon-lit glow in the top of the cavern. Just outside the city, I could barely see the churning turbulence of lakes of suffering. "Where is the passthrough?"

"They only come in to this plane; there is no out. If a soul made it this far, it is the end of the line," answered Kitar.

"What about the Great Plane?"

"One must have distinguished themselves either while living or in death to become a resident of the Great Plane. You could say its invitation only. Be that invitation an actual invite or simply the soul has been pressed into servitude to one of the residents of Hell's Capital and surrounding plane."

"That's Pandemonium, right?"

"Yes, it was the first city built and in many ways is a darker version of The Eternal City," explained Kitar.

"That makes sense, I guess. Are there any torture stations?"

"Not really. There is some torture in the traditional sense. Most souls at this point, either being singularly guilty of Fraud or Deceit or their base sin is so extreme as to fall into Fraud or Deceit are sent here because they don't fit in anywhere else. Plus, you must keep in mind they have already spent time on all the other Planes before getting to this one. Most of the Plane's punishments happens in the chambers beneath the upper lakes."

"Wait, they can be here if their base sin isn't one of this Plane's sins?"

"Yes, think of it like this. Many sins, when taken to their natural conclusion, will eventually reach a point where it is less about intent and more about how to achieve the goals of their sin through deception. Lust taken to its extreme may still be the sin of Lust but when deceit or fraud is introduced into the mix and becomes the catalyst by which the soul practices their Lust they pass from the relatively lesser sin of Lust into the greater sin of Fraud. Understand?" asked Kitar.

"I guess, I'd always assumed this plane was a blow off Plane. You're making it sound like all roads..." I paused and laughed. "I was about to say, all roads lead here, but in point of fact, I guess they do. So why are some of the fucks on Blasphemy not here instead of on the Plane we just left? Everything about religion is about fraud and deceit."

"First, I would have thought by now that opinion would have changed. Secondly, Blasphemy is the exception since their sins are against The Father himself and punished not by Hell's system but instead by The Host's."

"Ok, that makes sense. Also, for the record, though I might've been wrong about the fact Heaven and Hell exist, it doesn't change the fact that most of what is taught by the living is a lie. In the case of the Catholic Church back on Earth, a means to an end, which in their case were pedophilia and world control. Speaking of that, where are the Popes? I didn't see any on Blasphemy."

"There were a few on the last Plane in the audience at the Great Hall but to be honest, they, like many of the high clergy of other worlds, are considered a commodity and most of them end up in servitude or entertaining on the Great Plane."

"They've become the Demon butt-boys of Hell?"

"That is one way of putting it, yes."

"I like that idea. Maybe if I live through this, I'll get me a Pope Benedict dancing go-go boy for the house."

"Sorry that will not be happening, someone as evil as he gets promoted to full Demon status."

I hadn't even noticed Cemal setting a small table behind us; I was too wrapped up in the view. I described the plane as we flew over, but from here, and without moving I could get a good look at it. If I walked over and looked from either side of the balcony, I'd be transported out of Hell and into a futuristic city. If it wasn't for the trouble Usis was in I'd probably could've enjoyed this place.

"Your dinners are ready Masters," said Cemal, bowing deeply.

"Very formal, what's the occasion?" I asked.

"Boy feels he should adhere more closely to his training while on his creation Plane. One never knows when eyes are watching, Master."

"Wise idea, boy, anything to get you to show more respect," groused Kitar.

Still kneeling, Cemal bowed deeper, adding, "Master, this one is always respectful, though sometimes playful."

I shook my head. "Don't mind him, Cemal. I've known Kitar for decades now, and his mood is like the Planes of Hell, varied and often disturbing."

As we ate, we worked out a plan of attack for the Plane. I'll admit though worried about what's to come on the Seventh Plane; it's a relief to be working again. Remember I've been doing this for a very long time now, so it's become a welled oiled machine. Well right up to the point where all Hell breaks loose, and people start running around screaming. I know the one screaming is normally me.

During dinner as we laid out the plans, I realized I didn't have as much stress about this Plane as all the others. Why wasn't I as stressed? All I could come up with was because of the transformation. Before I'd always been apprehensive about traveling to a new Plane, but now with my new appearance it gave me a sense that I'm not as...I don't know...vulnerable as before.

# Entry 243

I guess to start this entry I'd like to talk first about Kitar. I know I spend a lot of time bitching about his temperament. It helps to remember he spent thousands of years as a judge. He welcomed souls to Hell, determined their sins and assigned them to their punishment. That has to take a toll over time. Kitar and I spend a lot of time in each other's company, and we do get along, very well in fact. I dare say we enjoy each other's companionship.

I asked him, "What confuses me is if this Plane is less about sin why does it have such an extensive city? There has to be something more."

"There is, and you will discover it in time. You just got here. Acclimate yourself."

"I know, I'm just in sensory overload right now. I don't want the details yet. I prefer to let that happen naturally." Yes, I rolled my eyes. I hate when it happens naturally. It usually means things are about to go to shit. "So other than whatever this city is about, is there anything else you think we shouldn't miss?"

"You will probably want to visit the wineries and the labs. They are on this Plane," explained Kitar.

"Finally, I get to see how they make wine," I said as I took a sip.

"We will see if your excitement holds up after the tour," grinned Kitar. "What I think will help you understand this Plane, without saying too much, is to understand how souls are utilized. Souls coming onto this Plane whose sins were rooted in earlier sins are no longer of concern. They are thrown into the lakes to suffer the trials contained therein. The city and Keep deal with a very specific type of sin. In this case, sin might not be the right word. It is more about the denial of The Father's gift because the soul chooses to either move their consciousness into a manmade construct or they were manufactured by man but eventually met the requirements to have a soul."

"You've completely lost me."

"Let's first take the denial of The Father's gift. What that means is the soul was born in a vessel created by the Father's spark, such as you and I were when you were born..."

"Flesh and blood?"

"Correct, or some derivative thereof. Due to the technological advances of their species the soul now have the opportunity to extend their lives by migrating from the living 'host' to a mechanical one. The Host sees this as a betrayal of The Father's gift, and thus their sin becomes Fraud since their existence is just that. They have turned down The Father's gift, choosing instead to pretend they are alive and not to enter eternity at their designated time. Are you keeping up so far?"

"I think so. That is why the Overlord calls itself as well, a Fraud. It's like AI or VR I guess."

"Or more to the point, as demonstrated with Death, a synthetic, but yes. When the soul, for whatever reason, is released or leaves the mechanical construct they then enter eternity and are judged and sent here." He could see a question and answered it before I had to ask. "The release could be any reason, war, malfunction, any number of things. More often than not it's a voluntary choice because the soul just tires of 'living'. Once they arrive on Fraud and no longer having a vessel to reside in, their soul is now housed in one of the soul gems you saw down in the lobby."

"So that's what those are," I barked.

"Yes. It is best you reserve your questions on that until you are touring. That will help give you context."

"I agree, but why not put the soul back in their original body? You know, the one they were born with."

"Simple, as far as The Host and Hell are concerned, they turned their backs on The Father's gift, so Death assisted in creating a torture specific to these creatures. They become power sources, for lack of a better word. The energy contained in their souls is what imbues the constructs Hell has grown so dependent on."

"There is a soul inside creatures like the Hellhounds and Cemal?"

"Actually, in the case of Cemal or other such advanced constructs, there are pieces of many different souls. Different aspects are picked and chosen based upon the construct's eventual function. Take Cemal, for example. The souls used to create him, or his class, are normally more submissive creatures who understand and can embrace servitude and enjoy it. With Cemal having demon traits I am sure aspects of other souls were used to instill the necessary aggressive nature he needs to transform and attack with no remorse."

"Wait, so are you saying that Cemal's personality is not his but a dead living?"

"At first probably but based upon the skills of the construct's creator the souls should eventually merge and allow the construct to assert its unified personality. As in Cemal's case, I can assure you that smart ass nature was not part of his original design."

Looking over to Cemal who'd been strangely quiet, I asked, "Is that true?"

"Yes, Master. This boy can remember when the seven souls used to construct this one were implanted. They did not merge initially and often asserted themselves, either separately or collectively. As time went on, the I that I am began to take control and the souls became all parts of a single, which is this Cemal."

"Is it just you now or can you still interact with the individual souls used in your creation?" I asked.

"Most certainly, Master. Each of the souls used have specific characteristics the creator wanted in this construct. Therefore they all had skills and now that we work together provide suggestions on how best to deal with specific situations. We are one but also seven individuals with a single overseer now, which is the construct you know as Cemal."

"You can just say 'me'. I don't like it when you don't refer to yourself as a person. Many people think there are different voices inside them which help them make decisions or choose courses of action. I often said, while living, that I had thirteen voices in my head. We worked together, but just like you, those voices all had dominant traits. Thus, in different situations, I'd take advice from the collective group or sometimes one individually."

Leaning in, Kitar commented, "That is very interesting. It explains a lot about you. Did your world not see that as a psychological disorder?"

"If it wasn't controllable it probably would have become one. But to use Cemal's words, 'the me that I am' was able to manage and control it. Often it was like a board meeting in my head, and still is, where all the different voices were screaming suggestions on how to deal with a specific situation. It can be overwhelming. That is why you will see me sitting alone, quiet, so often, I'm dealing with or confer with of one or more of my internal voices."

"If Master will forgive, being a construct and having 'voices' as Master calls them. This might explain why The Dark Lord chose you Master as his writer. Is it incorrect for this boy to guess that due to those voices, each being almost its own entity, that they tend to catch things you as the host missed and later will assert them back into your memories as you write?"

"That is exactly what they do. It's hard to explain but each looks through my eyes, and each almost has its own memory and processing power within my head. They will remember or contribute their own observations, ones I as the host did not even register at the time."

We all jumped as Alcraw spoke behind us. No one even heard him walk in. "I can assure you the little slave is correct. It is why Lucifer chose you. It again will add an interesting twist to your new situation. As time goes on, and you learn the subtleties of your new powers you very possibly will be able to manifest a separate form, a specter as such, to send out independently. This will allow you to be in, as the living like to put it, more than one place at a time."

"Oh wow, that'd be cool."

"It can be, but it also can be very taxing. Many users of such abilities tend to keep their host secluded using only their avatars as their connection to the outside realms and world. It is one of the ways The Powers enter Creation. Lord Lucifer can step into Creation, but due to the enormity of his presence, he will often choose instead to send part of himself into Creation to address a specific task. In the case of mages and magical based creatures here in Hell the process is reversed, they often leave behind one of the avatars to do research while they go out and deal with their lives."

"OK, let me think on that. We're getting bit trippy," I added, rubbing my head. "Can you do this, Alcraw?"

"No, it is specific to The Powers and a few other gifted creatures. As hard as it is to admit you are probably morphing into something greater than we are as Hellspawn. That is one of the reasons everyone is interested in seeing how this plays out."

"That would also explain why you guys said we needed to keep it amongst ourselves," I added.

"Yes, imagine if you could elevate yourself to being almost as strong as The Powers but consuming their essence. It would bring all sorts of chaos to Hell and The Host."

"Oh good, another thing I need to worry about. On the surface, the ability sounds great, but with this being Hell and all, I'm sure they'll find a way to turn this into something to kick my ass."

"You are starting to learn," said Alcraw with a smile. "We Hellspawn grow up knowing that our strengths and how they can be used against us. That somewhere around the corner someone is just waiting to exploit a weakness. Therefore, Hellspawns like Xia tends to destroy first and then ask questions."

I just nodded. I was hoping for a little more of a positive note than, Yup, it sucks. "Anyway, moving on. Back to our original discussion. You said first let's deal with the souls which denied The Father's gift. Now explain how the purely synthetic, which were created by man, meet the requirements to obtain a soul."

"Keep in mind they must reach a certain level of consciousness first. They can't just be reasoning machines or fast computational entities. These creatures, and yes, we can use that word at this point, must be independent, self-taught and internally self-governing beings. If they reach that certain point where they no longer meet the definition of a machine, both in design, understanding, and consciousness, then by the very nature set forth by The Father in his initial parameters of what constituted 'the living', the spark of Creation energy in them becomes sufficient to bring into manifestation a soul. In many ways, they're no different from a child when they reach the point of accountability. At that moment the being becomes divine."

"Divine?"

"In the sense that the Creation's spark, which resides in everything, is sufficient to awaken in The Father's eyes."

"You're telling me, the living can create a creature from mechanical parts which can have a soul and go to The Host or Hell?"

"Your concept is right but not quite. First, mechanical parts imply metals and such; there are creatures on this Plane which were manufactured with materials similar to those of a living creature birthed from a parent. Now there are mechanical beings as well, but almost always, if they have met the requirements to house a soul, the only reason they are still metallic is purely an aesthetic one. Secondly, there are no non-Father created entities in The Host, as far as The Powers, both Fallen or Holy are concerned they are Frauds. Not only the artificial entities but their creators are both considered abominations in the eyes of The Father and thus The Host."

"An artificial being that is created by man bears little difference from the 'constructs' created here in Hell."

"Exactly," answered Alcraw.

"But now here is where it gets interesting," said Kitar.

"Like it's not already?" I added.

"As you have already seen, the Overlord for this Plane is mechanical. Kritanta lobbied and eventually received permission to house these beings here on Fraud but not to punish them. In his eyes, their creation was a sin performed by their creator and not by them. I am not saying that some have not committed sins of an earlier Plane but again, since Fraud is the highest ranking of the sins, they would be consigned here. Interestingly enough, the sin for which they will spend eternity in Hell is probably the first sin they performed which is also the gift they received causing them to sin in the first place. Simply becoming aware."

"All artificial beings are sent to this Plane and are not subjected to punishment?"

"Correct, in so much that they are not tortured. If you wish to be technical, since they have The Father's spark, their natural inclination is to be in his presence. Instead, they are denied that and will spend eternity in the city below."

After our discussion, I dismissed everyone including Cemal for the night. Usis weighed heavy on my mind, so I decided to escape to a place I used to enjoy, New York. Dragging a chair around I found a spot on the balcony where I could look out over the busy city street instead of something which would remind me of Hell. Here I'd lose myself in a fantasy for just a few hours. As I sat down, I growled having again forgotten that damn tail. With a drink in hand, I closed my eyes and became lost in thought. Sometimes my mind was back home, others it was with Usis as we relived some of our grand adventures. Even the bad ones still had him in them, and right now that made them far less traumatic. How long had he been gone? I didn't know. I wanted him back. I guess if I made a decision that night, it was to either rescue my companion or die trying, well as close to dying as I could get. To be honest, deciding to save Usis at any cost was the easy part. What wasn't as easy was which of the two options I preferred, rescuing him and continuing to live a life in Hell or just passing into eternity and then it would all be over.

# Entry 244

I awoke some hours later still in the chair. The last thought I remember from the night before was Usis, and the first thought this morning was him as well. I chuckled to myself. Here I'd just recently eaten an angel's heart but felt I no longer had one of my own; it was with him, wherever he was.

Hearing the jostling of metal behind me my first reaction was alarm. Turning quickly, I saw Elick standing in the middle of the room with his arms outstretched as Cemal worked around him carefully removing his armor. I sat and watched until the handsome, pale Hellspawn stood nude. He smiled and knelt before the boy who quickly pulled the tunic over his head and fastened it around the wings. As Elick rose Cemal took a worn belt and pulled it around the Hellspawn's thin waist. Handing him his boots the boy bowed to both of us and rushed away to get us drinks.

Walking over Elick took a seat beside me and as he pulled his boots on I noticed his sword learning against the building. "Good Morning," he said.

"You are looking as handsome as always, My Lord," I said with a smile.

He just nodded as Cemal reemerged with a tray and goblets. Elick took one and handed it to me then took the other. With his first sip he relaxed back letting out a deep breath.

I asked, more to break the ice, "Does it have a name?"

"Does what have a name?"

"The City?"

"You know, I am not sure."

"Do I need to ask?" He knew what was on my mind.

"No, you do not. It is why I am sitting here," he answered.

"So?"

"Grandfather (he says Grandfather but in actuality it's Great Grandfather) is somewhat upset. I am not sure if that is a result of the failed attack, where we are, why we are here, or simply because he has no idea what we are up to. It was wise to leave none of the soldiers living. It probably was not so wise to send one of the bodies back in the shape it returned in."

"What do you mean? We did not send a body back."

"I am not sure. The note was from Kritanta. With their mutual hatred I would not put it past him to have done this as a goad."

"Oh well, maybe it'll throw him off his game a bit. I can use all the help I can get. Now... why are you stalling? Is the news about Usis that bad?" I asked.

"Usis is fine. I might even say better than fine. His body is healed, and he seems to have no negative ramifications from the transition. I let him awaken and told him to keep up appearances of being feeble minded and weak. That is mainly so they do not try to force him into answers he should not give or does not know and then conjecture, the latter they would take as a lie."

I laugh at this. "He should be able to pull that off. I guess you still won't tell me what he looks like, will you?"

"Not going to happen."

"I can't remember, does he even know what I did? I mean this." I said running my hands up and down my body like Vanna White.

"No, I think that discussion should be between the two of you upon your reunion. I have told him we are putting together a plan to free him once we arrive on the Plane."

"Please tell me you didn't tell him I was going to be fighting. All he would do is worry."

"No, he has no idea. Like you he pressed but I told him he would see in time. In case you have not gleaned it from our conversation so far, he is now considered a prisoner."

"He's what?"

"I could not keep him asleep any longer. Grandfather was about to step in, and we could not have that. After the attack and the subsequent partial return of his guard I decided there was no viable way to keep Grandfather from forcing the issue. So, I let him awaken, it appears to have been a good decision."

"How so?"

"He is using his charm and cooperating with Grandfather's scientists to try to figure out his transformation. He has not told them the truth and I have suggested that he not. Oh, you will like this part. He is using his skills to wipe the scientist's minds at the end of each session. Therefore, when they return to give their report, they cannot remember anything damaging. I was there for a couple of the meetings. His scientists not wanting to admit they have no memory of the examinations are making shit up. It is quite funny."

I laughed. It was good to see Usis was getting back to his old self. "How long do you think it will be before we can rescue him?"

"You, my friend, need to continue to hone your skills. Both Balthazar and I are going to start working with you more intensely. You are already showing good progress, but you are a long way from being a challenge to Grandfather."

"I like that plan. There doesn't appear to be a whole lot to see on this Plane, so I should have time."

"You are wrong there. There is plenty for you to explore and write about. It is subtler than the earlier Planes. I personally would also suggest you get some time in with the Overlord. He also can give you insights into Grandfather that even I don't have."

"Fine. I want to get down into the city today. In a lot of ways this reminds me of home. I'd like to take advantage of its familiarity. As for training, you two set the schedule and I'll comply."

# Entry 245

That afternoon a slave I'd not seen before dropped by with a message from Balthazar saying he wanted to see me. I pulled on a tunic, no tights and followed the boy out into the hall. Getting a good look at it this time I notice paintings covered every wall. There are stark white marble topped tables laden with statues along the length of the hallway. Some I recognized as gods from my old world, most though I didn't. DeSade would hate this place, it's too sterile. The slave led me to a door where he knocked then opened it and we entered.

Unlike my room, this one wasn't as scantily furnished. Don't get me wrong; it's nice and functional just not up to the standard I normally get. (Listen to me, I'm not getting the five-star treatment, and already I'm ready to bash the place on Yelp.) Realizing how pretentious my thought was I reached around, and Gibb slapped myself. All of this internal dialog and external acting out took about fifteen seconds. When my attention returned to the boy, I found him staring at me with a look like he thought I'd lost my mind. We won't tell him, I arrived in Hell with like thirteen voices and had recently added two more. So yeah maybe.

"Master, I've brought the other Master as you requested."

I give the boy a strange look. "If there's more than a couple of people in the room that could get very confusing."

"You have no idea," he replied with a smirk as he bowed and left. I'm impressed.

"They are all made to be sociable," I heard Balthazar say.

"Gee thanks. I was starting to think he/she/it was warming up to me."

"I guess we can cut a hole in it wherever you get an itch and you can do with it as you will."

"Oh please. Gawd. Did you need something other than throwing me off my lunch?"

"Of filleted souls' flesh, no I think you will be fine."

"You suck," I growled.

"On occasion but not now. Let's spend some time with your magical training."

"I can use all the help I can get. So far it's been like teaching a cow to whistle."

"Not sure what a cow is but if they have lips, it probably can be done. As for teaching you magic, you are underselling yourself. You have already shown a degree of competence with electrical magics. I just think you need more practice and training on the different types. It will help focus your abilities as well as liberate the memories you carry from The Lovers."

"What soul will I be searching?"

"Zephyr's."

Suddenly a light goes on. He gives me that smile a teacher gives their dim student when they finally get it. "The dreams."

"Exactly, clearly you have the ability to access The Lovers' memories and I am confident that if you delve a little deeper, you will find answers to questions and maybe even help while you spar or cast."

"Wait, that is sounding eerily like they reside inside me. Please, please tell me that's not what you're telling me?"

"Not exactly, their consciousness no longer exists, your little boyfriend saw to that. Well, Lucifer probably...but he worked through your boyfriend allowing him to take the necessary steps. Their knowledge and memories should be available to you both."

I want to say I remember the last part of that sentence, but I don't. I heard it later when buggy played it back. Yes, buggy follows me around now most of the time. Being a big bad Demon with wings seems to have crimped in his style. He can't hang from my back anymore. Something I'm sure he's more upset about than I am. If his reaction the last time he tried is any indication, I think I taste bad.

Anyway, all I got was the first part. "Wait, what do you mean Lucifer probably did?"

"I said that because you are going to have to learn to focus. Tell me how what Lucifer did or did not do has any impact upon what you are here to learn. Leviathan is going to use mind games. If you have not noticed, it is one of our primary characteristics. You need to focus and not get distracted by every little thing. Understand?"

"I see your point. Now, what did you mean by Lucifer probably did?"

Balthazar let out a long slow breath and then shot a bolt of fire about the size of a tennis ball across the room hitting me in the chest, setting my tunic on fire as I cried out in pain. "Maybe you are correct; cows cannot be taught to whistle."

As I danced around trying to put out the fire or remove the tunic, I heard over my cries, "Use your mind, extinguish it, you idiot."

Still consumed in flames, I turned. "Did you just call me an idiot?"

"Father's nuts, this is going to be challenging," cursed (I think) Balthazar as the last bits of tunic fell from my now nude body. I looked down and started to turn. "Where are you going?"

"To get clothes?"

"No, stay nude, I do not think it will help you focus, but at least it gives me something to look at while I struggle not to send you to the Hatchery."

I sauntered up to the black Hellspawn. "You see something you like?"

Faster than I can react, he spun me around and bended me over, grabbing my tail and lifting my ass. "I am not sure, let us find out."

I barked in surprise and escaped as he burst out laughing. "Can we get down to business now?"

"See we are both learning. I have learned you are, in fact, trainable and you have learned to take these sessions a little more seriously, right?" he says with a most disturbing grin. His pointed teeth are red, which doesn't help in the least.

"Yes, yes... I think I get it. What would you like to teach me today, ol wizened and wise teacher?"

"Don't push it or I will."

# Entry 246 – Magic Training

(I'm separating this entry since it's the first time I talk about Balthazar's training. As you've probably already gleaned from earlier entries, I've been training since I woke up and could move. I love it; it makes me feel less of a victim in this place. Plus, I want to send Leviathan to the Hatchery and then be waiting when he emerges, so I can send him back. With each passing day, with each new lesson, with each conversation, I grow angrier. I want Usis back, but now as much, I want revenge as well. It's not only about Leviathan taking my companion it's about every fucking moment since I awoke in Hell. All the suffering and the pain I've been through. I want to make manifest so someone else can feel what I've felt, and I've chosen my victim, Leviathan.

I'm telling you some of my training so you can understand what I'm taking in with me. I hate writers who just pull a new skill out of their ass because they wrote their characters, or in my case myself, into a difficult situation. Now it's my ass and I want you to see what's in there.)

Reaching down he picked up two metal balls, handing one to me. It was gold and heavy and about a foot in diameter. It felt solid. "As I have said many times, the first thing you need to learn is to settle your mind and FOCUS. Here in a room, among friends, that is easy. We have to get you to the point where you can do it when you are in the heat of battle."

Having taken yoga some while living and well just having not run away screaming after some of the things I'd seen in Hell I thought I had this. Closing my eyes, I took a deep breath.

In a softer tone, Balthazar said, "Good, now open your eyes and focus on the ball in your hand. Reach out with your consciousness and will it to rise an inch or so above your palm."

I made a face as the ball rose. "Okay, seriously didn't we do this shit like a while back?"

Smiling, he then added, "The ball contains a gift Usis gave Elick for you. It is in a small chamber in the center of the otherwise solid ball. If you want the gift, you will have to get it out without destroying it."

"But how?" I didn't wait for an answer I just started to focus. Nothing happened.

"Did I mention, each second you fail the chamber grows smaller. You have about 10 minutes before its contents are destroyed and absorbed, becoming unrecoverable."

I started to reach for the ball when he added, "Nope, you cannot touch the globe, it must remain floating."

"But…"

"I think about five seconds have passed."

I focused on the ball; already I was sweating. "We haven't done anything like this before. What the fuck? You have something from Usis and are willing to destroy it to teach me a lesson? You want to be the next person I fight?" Yes, I was angry and getting more so by the second.

"If you wish to challenge me once you have defeated Leviathan, I will gladly introduce you to the Hatchery. The Dark Lord did want you to tour all of Hell, after all." He smiled.

I swear I saw a glint in his eyes. I was getting frustrated, and that's what he wanted. What else could upset me in Hell at this point? "You suck," I added.

"Revisiting old dialogs will not solve the puzzle."

This went on for several minutes, probably five. I turned the ball, heated the ball, nothing worked. In frustration, I tried to explode it, and that is when I heard a sound from Balthazar. I looked up, "Is that a sound of fear or am I on the right track?"

"The latter. Here is a hint, all magic is just the manipulation of Creation energy, often down at the molecular level."

That was a hint, and I caught it. I stopped the ball from moving and closed my eyes, taking another second to calm my thoughts. I pictured the ball in my mind's eye. I heard a voice say "right." It wasn't Balthazar.

I ignored it and started to zoom in, closer and closer until all I could see was gold. Again, I heard the voice, "See all that matter? Tell it to move."

I did as instructed. I could feel the surface of the ball warping.

"Look closer. See all that space between those molecules." I tried what was suggested. There it was, between the very building blocks use to construct the ball.

"Now you want what is inside. Look at all that empty space; it would be so simple just to expand it." I tried. At first nothing, then I noticed one of the molecules move just a tiny bit...

"Careful, don't break them apart, it would cause a chain reaction, push the whole molecule out of the way...Yes, that is the way."

My head was starting to hurt from concentration as my mind yelled about how much time this was taking. "Open your eyes," said Balthazar.

I almost lost focus when I saw the remains of the ball. It was in millions of tiny pieces, all suspended in the air in front of me. There was nothing inside. I turned in anger to Balthazar as the pieces fell to the floor. "There is nothing, you lied," I was raging both with anger and disappointment.

He shrugged. "Did I ever say it was that ball?" He answered as he looked down at the other one.

He didn't finish his comment before I had the other ball lifted into the air and ripped apart. I reached inside the mass of metal and snatched the small piece of parchment as the shards dropped forgotten to the floor.

*"I was instructed to write something and promised it would get to you. I am not sure what to say, but then it does not matter, just knowing you are going to read this is enough. That you will soon hold something that I have held. Keith, you are my soul, my heart and my eternity. I love you and miss you so very, very much. I hope we can be together soon."*

I was in tears. I have no idea how long I was lost in my own euphoria. I read the note several times, and each time again I was lost. These were Usis' words. He'd written this. He'd sent me a lifeline.

I looked up to find Balthazar standing patiently. I jumped to my feet, raced over and threw my arms around him.

"Um...that is not necessary and to be honest, not my style," he complained.

"Then you are going to hate this," I said as I grabbed the back of his head and locked him in a deep kiss. He didn't pull away. It had to be due to shock, not because he couldn't. Finally, when I let go and stepped back, he looked like he was about to faint. I'd achieved my goal and smiled.

"Thank you," I said softly.

We walked to his sitting area and ordered wine. "I think you have made your pleasure quite clear. Take a minute and pull yourself together. There is more to your training today." My eyebrows shot up, but he quickly added, "No more notes, sorry. What I want you to do is remember the feelings you needed to open that second ball, the sheer uninterrupted focus you used. You always need to be that focused. Distractions are just that, and they waste your potential. To us Powers, intent is our strongest weapon. All of Creation is malleable, we must believe in ourselves and our goals. I have one question; how did you figure out how to solve the puzzle?"

As I took the glass, I looked around. I'd forgotten about the other voice. "Who else was here during the exercise. Someone walked me through the process of looking at the molecular level."

"I was hoping that would happen. We picked a lesson with a lot of emotional importance. We were hoping your desire to break into the sphere would also help break down the walls between you and the parts of The Lovers inside you. I am glad to see it worked."

"It was one of the Lovers?"

"It had to be, no one else was here," he answered.

The idea of them so conscious inside me was worrying. I decided to let it go, I had other questions. I ate the hearts, so I need to accept the side effects. I focused on my new-found powers. "How extensive is this ability?"

"Explain?"

"I ripped apart that ball, but can I rebuild it into something else?"

"Of course. You have control over Creation energy. Once you can drill down far enough, anything you imagine is available to you. Look around, Lord Lucifer made the very firmaments of Hell in the blink of an eye and later the Planes. The Father understood the process so well he manifested Creation as easily. What we have to discover is how much of that energy do you have and can control. That will ultimately define your power."

I sat stunned, sipping my wine. "Can I change myself?"

"Some can, some can't. Cartos has never been able to master shape manipulation. He has made a fine mess out of trying. Xia, on the other hand, can do it without much trouble. He used to change his body constantly. The trick he liked the most was forming his wings out of his back. Even The Most High normally have to concentrate to manipulate their form, to Xia it was little more than an afterthought. One he used to good effect as well, I might say. We think it has to do with a sense of self. As I recall your world did not have magic, right?"

"There was a lot of talk about it in our literature but no. I mean some people like Wiccans claimed to use magic, but I'm not sure I ever believed that shit."

"As I recall you did not believe in this shit either, meaning The Host and Hell. Being wrong seems to be within your comfort zone. Your world's magic, at least in the second manifestation, was a passive magic. Worlds, where it is employed in daily life, are considered to have active magic. Meaning that the difference in forces is more like a push compared to a nudge, if you will. The living work with the powers present in their worlds, their planet and their creation where we do not. The Powers, which in this case are anyone not born of the living..."

I started to say something, but he held up a finger.

"...you and Usis are an exception because you have been allowed to consume the essence of one of the Most High, it does not matter if they were Fallen. Therefore, for all practical purposes, you are no longer born of the living. You can consider your transition from your living form to your new form a rebirth. The Father's Creation energy rebuilt you into the creature the energy you consumed expected you to be. How powerful or successful that transformation was is yet to be seen."

"I'm growing uncomfortable with this implication I'm a Power. I'm just simple Keith, like I've always been."

"See that is one of the first misconceptions you will need to release yourself from, or you will never attain your full potential. The Living are very limited, by design. The only part of your new personification which thinks you are still an ex-living is your mind and you must abandon that belief if you hold any hope of expanding your potential. Remember what I said about Xia's sense of self. He is probably the third strongest creature in Hell."

"You being the second?" I asked with a smirk.

"I was given an intellect therefore it has and probably never will be tested to find out. I am comfortable not knowing."

"Or more to the point, anyone else knowing. I'd imagine."

"There is that," he said with a mock toast from his glass.

When I didn't say anything he continued, changing back to the earlier topic, "Where the living almost exclusively manipulate the energies around them, we (The Powers) can draw from the energies within Creation. It can be something as simple as the power contained within a living creature to the almost endless supply held within the suffering which flows here in Hell. We can also use that energy to create something from nothing, using only our inner strength but that should be limited to dire circumstances or when no other source is available, for you will tire."

"Wait when you say, 'powers contained within a living creature' you're not saying drain the life force from a living person or a soul, are you?"

"Yes, I am. But it is not limited to a creature; it can be plants, animals or just the atmosphere within a Creation. Even the void of space within your creations carry immense amounts of energy. Some civilizations eventually can detect it. I think even your world gave it the name of dark matter, a name we here in Hell liked. It is everywhere. When a Creation was created The Father put enough Creation energy into that manifestation to ensure it could not only produce the necessary structures for things like universes but also the living. Everything in a given creation is connected. That Creation energy continues to recycle until the creation is raptured. Which, to put it simply, is the disabling of the mechanisms needed to recycle The Father's Creation energy. As you have seen in the discarded creations, The Father left quite a bit of Creation energy behind when he did not absorb it back into himself. For as long as I can remember The Powers have been trying to figure out how to reclaim that energy. There is enough in those old constructs to probably power the rest of Creation for billions of millennia."

As he finished, he motioned for me to look at my hand. My mouth fell open when I looked down to find a small gold ball floating about three inches above my palm. "What the fuck?"

"The biggest mistake people make when learning to use magic is, they try too hard. It is not normally that easy, but then you have a couple of skilled beings helping out."

"They were in pieces?"

"Yes, they were, and yet while we talked, you coalesced bits of the old balls into a new one. I think that is enough for today. Try to gain more control, and once you are confident, find heavier things to lift, take apart, and rebuild into something new. I would suggest you try some destruction powers as well. But be careful, I do not think it will go over well if you blow up the Keep. You might want to practice that specific skill out on the Plane.

"Lastly, and do not roll your eyes, spend some time each night meditating. See I said not to do that. You not only need to find that source of power within you but also see if you can have a little chat with the memories of your two new voices. Think of them as a book, you know the information you need is in there, you just have to find it and have access to it in a pinch. Also, when doing your meditation do not leave out fighting skills. You have two authorities in there, learn to utilize them."

# Entry 247

I spent most of that afternoon working on Balthazar's lessons. By the evening I was able to pull things apart and put them back together. The statues in the hall proved very useful for this. Not sure how the Overlord will feel about me rearranging her art, literally. Like that wasn't hard enough, the entire time I had Cemal sit with his hands about a foot apart while I wove a small gold ball between his outstretched hands. I'd become obsessed with getting better and as fast as I could.

I won't lie. Not only was this fun but it also stroked that sense of control I was so needing at the time. As the evening light started to dim, I had dinner and then went out on the balcony to try my hand at this meditation thing.

Like I said I'm not going to a spend ton of time discussing the intricacies of my training. It has little to do with the reasons for these journals. There isn't much to say about the physical stuff, I mean how much can you say about how to swing a sword. It's a skill learned by doing, not by reading about it. As for magic, if your world facilitates the use of magic then there are probably far better sources on the subject than me. If your world doesn't, no amount of description will help you understand how it feels. In case you're wondering, normally when I say I'm glossing over something it's more at the advice of Kitar. He has become, not so much my editor as my content advisor.

I will speak to meditation though. When I was living, my world had many different words for meditation: praying, meditation, quiet contemplation, walking, basically anything that left you alone in silence with your mind. I always thought it was bullshit, but I've always done it. While alive, when I wrote, I called it 'thinking.' For proof, if you read my entries, it's always there, me sitting on the balcony of this Plane or that, by myself, lost in thought, wondering how to write the next entry.

I sat after that last session with Balthazar and the afternoon and evening with Cemal and my new-found powers. I wouldn't let anyone in. When Cemal was exhausted I dismissed him as well and went out to give this meditation thing a shot. I wanted it to fail, really, I did, oh but it didn't. It was like The Lovers were sitting, waiting to ambush me.

It took me a while to settle my mind and then, as Balthazar suggested, I focused on Zephar's mind, asking for guidance with my magic. I don't know what I was expecting, but it most certainly wasn't a barrage of images with someone talking like the tape was on fast forward. At first, I couldn't control the amount of information going into my head. It's like it had all been lying sleeping like a land mine waiting on an unsuspecting leg. I screamed and kept screaming. In the back of my mind, my real mind I guess, I could hear people rushing in, the activity around me. I saw Creation, the void, the Eternal City, the way he placed his fingers when casting the harder spells. The simpler ones didn't need any physical movements or words. All that was necessary was the intent, the pulling in of the power, or if none was available, the creation of it from the stray Creation energy. Once the intent merged with the power to fund it, it was the simplest thing to push it out into reality where it would follow its instructions and execute my intent.

I felt a hand on my shoulder, then like being slapped another voice, a face, in my head, it was Balthazar, "What did I tell you about blowing up the place. Wake up now, those you are not scaring you are pissing off."

And like that, I was back in the meditation pose. What had changed other than Cemal hiding under the bed, Kitar smoking and Alcraw laughing his ass off in what remained of my room.

"Did I do that?" I asked weakly.

"Did he do that?" barked Alcraw as his laughter caused him to double over in pain. "It's probably not wise to pump a soul full of two Powers and then leave him unsupervised to practice his magic. What did you think would happen, Bel?"

"OK, point taken," answered Balthazar as he helped me stand up. As I walked in a slow circle, he put his arm around me. We were both looking at the remains of one of the chairs. "Let us start simple, put the chair back together."

"What? How?"

"Do you remember what it looked like before you blasted it with lightning?"

"I blasted it with lightning?" I said in shock as they nodded.

"That was not the question. Do you remember what it looked like?" repeated Balthazar in an eerily calm voice.

"I think so," I answered as Cemal crawled out from under the bed, ran to the other room and returned dragging another chair just like the destroyed one.

"It looked like this, Master," he said smiling, panting and as I looked over at the chair he was holding he squeaked, dropped the chair and dived under the bed again. Were we all heard from beneath, "This one has complete confidence in master's abilities."

"Now look at that chair. Good idea, boy, by the way," commented Balthazar as he bent down to see under the bed. As he returned standing, he added, "Once you have the image firmly affixed in your mind, use your power to draw energy into you and then simply will the chair back together. Set your will, put it out and impose it upon reality."

As the shock of my surroundings wore off, I began to enjoy the whole process. I did as he suggested. I walked around the intact chair a couple of times and then back over to the broken one. In my mind, good thing I'm creative by nature, I imagined the chair intact. Once I was satisfied, I reached out, Creation energy was all around me, and grabbed onto some and started to let it flow into my body. As the energy continued to flow, so did the clarity of the image of the chair. Finally when it was clean and crisp in my mind's eye, I concentrated and pushed that image out.

At first, nothing happened, then slowly I started to notice the pieces of the destroyed chair beginning to move closer together. I could hear

Balthazar urging me on, "Yes, that's it, keep the image focused in your mind. Do not push out too fast." I did as he instructed, slowly spooning energy into the broken parts. To my surprise, they began to piece back together, like a jigsaw puzzle. After a couple of minutes, the chair was again together but still a mess, the parts I'd destroyed completely were still missing.

"Very well done. Using the extra energy inside you move the image of the chair in your head out and onto the real chair. Carefully, do not try to force it, just picture the image floating over and then setting down on top of the one in reality. Good, good."

I did as he instructed and to my surprise the two chairs eventually matched up, the real one and the image of one.

"Now, if you like the way it looks, just mentally say 'Amen'."

I spoke the words, and to my and everyone else's surprise, the two images came together and where there had been an exploded chair, there was now a completely repaired, as good as new, one.

I smiled as Cemal crawled from under the bed, letting out a loud whoop. He then ran over and threw himself into it. "Master, it is solid, you did it."

I looked over to Balthazar as he removed his hand from around my shoulder. "It will get easier with practice. In time you will not need to focus on all the steps necessarily. Your mind will understand what you want, and your intent will just make it happen. In the blink of an eye."

"I just imagine something and then will it to be so?" I asked.

"Basically yes. You are using Creation energy, therefore anything you can imagine you can create, alter or impose your will upon, be it a creature or reality itself. Just keep in mind, the bigger the goal, the more energy it takes to achieve said results. Something like fixing a chair takes very little, where if you wanted to create a Creation from scratch you would need a force of will, the energy and the determination of The Father to impose such a complicated construct upon the whole of Creation. That is why mages like myself have strongholds off in the middle of nowhere. That way we can work on slowly increasing our power without too many things being destroyed. This is your first step into a Creation you have never seen before."

"So, it's not only fixing a chair, or combat, it can create that chair from scratch with nothing to work from?"

"Absolutely. You had parts of the old chair. They just helped reduce the cost of the casting. Had there been nothing to start with, it would have taken more energy to impose the image in your head upon reality. But it can be done easily with enough practice. You can be as strong of a mage as you wish to be, it is all up to you and your devotion to the craft. By that I mean, practice, practice, practice."

"Wow."

"That's enough for today. I heard you wanted to see the city. We can plan to go out later this evening. Elick will be back, and you need to continue your combat training. Like the magic, it will probably help to sit for a while and see if you can get in touch with Enepisgo and her store of training information. She was a formidable warrior. If you can tap into that, you just might stand a chance against Leviathan when the time comes."

"From a magical perspective, where would you say I am?"

"To be honest, your power and understanding are at a master's level. What you need to do, just like if you were injured and destroyed your legs, you need to relearn how to walk. Zephar's knowledge has given you the understanding. It is your job to help your mind wrap itself around the workings."

I nodded and took the goblet Cemal was proudly bowing and offering up. "One last question if you don't mind?"

"Go ahead."

"Would you consider training and working with me when all of this is over?"

Raising an eyebrow, he gave me a curious look. "You mean if you survive? It is an interesting proposal. I will think about it."

# Entry 248

Just as I finished dressing, Elick landed on the balcony. As normal everything stopped...he'd gone to check on Usis.

He was smiling. He was smiling big. I started smiling, for no reason. It just seems the thing to do.

Walking over to me, he tossed a scroll on the table.

"What's that?" I ask.

"It appears you are not the only writer," he answered with a shrug as he went to pour two goblets. For a second, I wondered where Cemal was, but my attention kept returning to the roll of skin.

"What do you mean?" I ask as together we took a seat. I'm still staring at the scroll. I can feel the apprehension. "Do you mean? Another one!"

"You realize there is a solution or more accurately an answer to all of your questions?"

I snatch it off the table, pull off the tie and open it. It is...

"You got the ball open, good for you. Do not be surprised if Usis does not mention that letter. I told him to write you like you had not seen it."

"Didn't that make him suspicious?"

"Of course."

"But you didn't explain?"

"Of course."

"I hope I don't become as much of an ass as all the rest of you guys are."

"I am sure there is no fear of you becoming any more of an ass than you already are. Creation energy can do a lot but let's not ask for miracles. Now read."

A letter from Usis.

*Greetings my love,*

*I hope this letter finds you well and your anger at my actions has not turned your affections away from me. Elick told me how you learned about my deceit, and for that, I am truly sorry. It was never my wish to hide anything from you or to let you down in any way.*

*I know you are concerned and to be honest so am I. I do not worry about my future or what this horrible Leviathan might do to me. My only fear, one that tears at my very soul, is that I will never get to look upon your face again.*

*My heart sank when I learned you had skipped this Plane in favor of the next. Elick said it was for specific reasons but would not tell me what they were. All he assured me was that it was in preparations for freeing me and returning us to each other. I so want that to be true, but my heart and my deceit eat at me like a hungry hellhound and I fear your anger is what has led you to abandon this Plane.*

*I guess the only remaining thing I can say, and I say it with all my heart, is you are my life, my world and my eternity. If my deceit has hardened your heart to me, then I will take any punishment or pain gladly, for there is nothing Hell can imagine that could hurt as badly as knowing I lost your love.*

*With that, I will continue to believe what Elick has told me and hope one day soon to see your face and if that day ever comes, I pray my appearance will not turn you away.*

*With eternal devotion and love,*

*Usis*

(Since I'm writing this after the fact, I don't feel like I'm a complete ass by pointing out at this time how well written that letter is. I'm stunned. Not because I didn't think Usis was smart enough or even capable, I just didn't know he was that capable yet.)

I was crying as I finished the letter and gripped it to my chest. The room was silent, but I didn't notice at first. I'd been lost in the words and the fear of my most beloved. He had no idea what we were doing, what I'd done. He didn't know my only goal was to return him to me.

"You have to explain to him what is happening," I said to Elick as reality came back to me.

"We cannot, and you know that. It would not only jeopardize the mission, but it would also put Usis in danger. Great Grandfather might destroy him just to be rid of the possible implications attached to you staging a rescue attempt."

"What implications?" I barked, instantly angry.

"Like having to send The Dark Lord's writer to the hatchery?" answered Alcraw.

"Yes, they cannot know. Not yet," added Balthazar.

"Can I at least send him a letter in return?" I asked, now begging.

Elick moaned. "Please don't tell me you want to write it now. I thought we were going out on the town. This place is quite something."

Shaking my head, I said, "No I need time to think about what to write which will put his mind at rest without saying too much or more to the point, being too obvious about it. As for going out on the town, now we must. Otherwise I'll just sit and sulk all night."

"There you go. Let us find some entertainment so we may enjoy ourselves while we bask in the glory of your incessant sulking. For I am confident that no matter where we are you will be doing just that for the majority of the evening," said Kitar. I turned and scowled at him even more so because he was probably right.

"Great," said Alcraw as he clapped his hands and everyone rose. I looked over to see Cemal kneeling in the corner.

"You best get dressed in something other than that little loincloth. You're coming too." Turning to Elick, I asked, "Can you get him a tunic, some tights ...and shoes please."

To my surprise, Cemal barked in a serious tone, "No, not shoes, Master please."

I laughed. "Ok fine, no shoes."

It was then I noticed all three of the Hellspawns were staring at me, "What?"

"Taking a slave on a night out?" asked Alcraw.

"Ok, let's get one thing straight, Cemal is a servant, not a slave. He only remains a servant because it makes him happy. What he is, above all other things, is part of this family. Therefore when the family goes out for an evening, he will not be left behind."

Everyone nodded and even chuckled when Cemal said as he walked by, "Don't worry Masters, this one will still fill your wine goblets. This one can't have the big bad Lords of Hell spilling something all over those fancy clothes."

After we'd all dressed and reassembled in the common room only one member was still missing, Cemal. I knocked on the door leading to his room, he yelled he was coming, but he never came. Finally, Alcraw went in after the boy. A few seconds later he came back out, "I think you will need to rethink your plan," Alcraw said.

"What?" I remarked as I marched to the door and entered. Cemal was there, dressed in his tights and tunic. He was handsome, and he was crying. "What's wrong? You look wonderful."

He sniffled and started several times but never really got out what was upsetting him. I took a seat on his sleeping mat (Yes, I don't approve either but he insists. I wanted him to have a normal bed.) and pulled him close. Holding him to my chest I stroked his hair until he calmed.

"Now tell me what's wrong?"

Looking up with his puffy red eyes, well puffy red, red iris', and red tears, lots of red, he said, "Master, this boy was excited at first. The thought of wearing clothes like the Masters wear. Going into town as the Masters do."

"But?"

"But that is not this boy. This boy is your servant and in that this one carries a certain pride. As I (he rarely said 'I') got dressed it just did not feel right Master." Again, he started to cry. "This one is sorry, Master."

"For what?" I was trying not to smile; he was after all so cute.

"For disappointing you, Master. Boy wanted to go. Boy wanted to dress as Master wished. But...but..."

Enough was enough. Lifting his head until his eyes met mine I said in a gentle but firm tone, "Cemal, being part of a family means you're accepted just the way you are. I don't want to change you; you're perfect in my eyes. If you don't want to wear different clothes, then don't, it's just that simple. You're you, and you're part of this group. I made the mistake of thinking you wanted a night off from being a servant, but I guess that was a mistake. You were made, I still can't get over that part, to be who you are, and you're wonderful. If you're proud to be my servant and be seen with me, then I'm more than proud to be your Master and would be honored to have you by my side in any way you feel comfortable."

He smiled, and I hugged him close. "Get changed, we will meet you in the common room."

I stood and walked out as he hopped up and started stripping. I returned to a room full of smirks, "What?"

"It is his nature," said Balthazar.

"Why didn't someone tell me. He's a wreck."

"If you are going to own servants and live in Hell you need to learn these things for yourself. Find your own path as to how you treat and discipline those in your charge. Consider this another lesson. It is not all magic and fancy swords," explained Elick.

Shaking my head, I heard the door behind us close and Cemal was standing there in a very nice loincloth, with a silk looking wrap around his shoulders. As he grew closer, I saw arm, wrist and ankle bands of gold and gems. It was Alcraw who gave himself away. "I knew you were going to fail in your little endeavor..."

"As it seems everyone did," I snarked.

"Well yes, so I brought him some clothes fitting an honored servant in a master's household."

I could see the reluctant happiness in Cemal's still red and puffy eyes. "And I wouldn't have him any other way."

# Entry 249

As we stepped off the elevator, I noticed a handsome man leaning against a column. It appeared he was waiting for us. "Mind if I join you?"

"I'm guessing you know who this is?" I asked mainly based on the reactions from my little group. Kitar and Cemal dropped to a knee while the Hellspawns nodded like they were greeting a peer.

Kitar answered which surprised me because for some reason he's been keeping a low profile. Sure, he made the one remark before we came down but still, he isn't his normal snarky, chatty self. This, of course, sends up warning flags since him being quiet is sort of like walking through a minefield on a moonlit night, it might look peaceful, but that much silence just means someone's about to explode. "It's Kritanta, The Overlord," he answered which replaced my concern about him with disbelief.

I took another look. Where earlier Death had been an imposing creature with tentacles instead of legs and a golden torso, this new version was a thin, handsome androgynous male about my height with long black hair. I could tell it was synthetic but considering what I knew about the Plane, I understood what I was seeing. The only thing I recognized from earlier were the eyes. They still carried their weight. "You look different."

"I cannot very well join you for a night out on the town looking like myself. Everyone would behave differently. It would cause too much of a stir for you to get a real sampling of the Plane. I thought this more appropriate for our outing."

"You do this a lot?" I asked.

"I would think it would be foolish to answer that question, now wouldn't it?"

"I see your point," I said as I motioned for him to lead. "It's your town. Will you do us the honor of giving us a tour?" As we walked, I added, "You realize by coming with us you're on the clock." The wrinkled eyebrows told me he had no idea what I was saying, "Meaning, you're invited to add commentary about the city you rule and its workings which I'm sure will lead to questions on my part."

Stopping the in middle of the street, oblivious to the crowds who had to quickly change course so as not to run into us, he again gave me a confused look. "I thought that is why I said I was accompanying you?" Looking back to Hellspawns he added, "Are you sure this is THE writer who has caused previous Overlords to breathe a sigh of relief as he left? He seems a bit slow."

"I'm just a soul, not all of us can be a machine with an Angel trapped inside. So maybe cut me a break," I smirked hoping it didn't come off the snarky.

"That is what you were; you are not that soul any longer. You are a Power, an Angel as you call it. As for the body, if you want one, I can have one arranged, but point taken. This way."

As we worked our way through the busy crowds, I was all smiles. It was like being in a Blade Runner movie. The buildings were tall, the streets crowded with all manner and shapes of beings. Each pushed their way through the litter-strewn din of neon signs and ratty open storefronts. To top it off, it was raining, not hard just a drizzle. Again, I must be slow tonight; it took a second to register, it was raining. "Rain?"

"As such, it is not water but suffering. We run it up from the lakes, vaporize and release it, where it condenses on the cavern ceiling and then returns to the city and lakes in the form of rain. We capture some but the rest serves to wash away any accumulated bits of souls which helps keep the city clean."

"I've had suffering strike me before. It's like three weeks of bad nightmares in the blink of an eye."

"It is for anyone who can suffer from such emotions. As for why you are not, that is simple. The suffering of the living can no longer affect you, you are Divine. You really should think before you speak."

Normally that last bit would piss me off, but the one thing which has gotten through my thick head is that I'm talking to both a computer and a Fallen. One is bad enough but combined, and I bet the operating system would be called Condescending 2.0. "Really, well that's a perk," I added rolling my eyes. To be safe, I looked back to find Cemal hoping that he wasn't susceptible. He was rubbernecking and smiling from ear to ear, so clearly not.

We walked for a while. The city was massive. I mean I knew it was big because I almost didn't make it to the Keep when we flew in, but still, on foot brought it to a whole new scale. Like Cemal, before long I was doing the loose neck tango. The neon was in every language, offering free upgrades, sex, booze, books, and of course food, lots of food. That surprised me. The variety of synthetics was absolutely astounding. What I quickly noticed was how they didn't seem to want to look too human or living if you know what I mean. There was lots of shiny skins, openly articulated limbs, and blinking piercings. Overall most were humanoid shaped, but that is where the parallels ended.

As my stomach grumbled, the Overlord turned. "Yes, I am taking us to a restaurant I find particularly enjoyable. You like noodles; I think your world called it Udon or Soba."

"I love Japanese. I guess you just answered my question about how often you go out incognito."

Looking back over his shoulder the Overlord said to no one in particular, "Look he worked that out all on his own." He turned back to me with a mischievous grin. "Yes, Overlords can have a sense of humor. If you would like I could have one installed in your judge. I am not sure he would be compatible, but a hammer and a few tacks and I bet we could get it to stick."

Most of our group barked with laughter as Kitar humphed behind me.

"It seems the punishments for the living sentenced to Fraud are kept less obvious?"

"Unlike many of the other Planes, this one's rewards (there's that word again) are more integrated and less structured, less noticeable.

Since most of the residents are synthetic, they are not here for punishment but to find a home. They are here because no one else will have them, but I will."

"Do you come out as yourself often, and if not, is this your standard form when spying?"

"I am offended dear boy; I am not spying, just...overseeing" There was that smile again. "To answer your question, yes, I visit the city in my earlier appearance, normally for more formal visits where I want those I encounter to know their Overlord walks amongst them. Otherwise, I use a variety of forms. It is one of the benefits of being synthetic, there is no limit to what we can look like."

"I didn't mean to offend, forgive me. But... what about your essence or soul, I mean how is that transferable? Is it transferable?"

"Ahhh here we are," he said as we stopped at a lunch counter; the only seating were stools along the stainless-steel counter. Behind it was a synthetic who had the classic tragically dirty white apron and crappy ass chef's hat. I slapped my hands together as we headed over. I did notice the slightest nod from the Overlord causing all the current customers to pick up their things and scurry off.

"How did you do that?"

"I had them come earlier and keep the place busy, ensuring..."

"You didn't have to pull rank?" I said.

"Yes, after all, I went to all the trouble of changing forms."

"Clever," I said as we saddled up to the bar. The Overlord ordered and before I knew it there were Vietnamese style spring rolls while we watched the cook go through the intricate process of preparing our soup. "In case you haven't heard I do not get distracted easily. Where is the soul or in your...maybe in our... case, essence?"

"You start with the big questions. In the living, the soul permeates the entire physical being. That is why these schemes they create to extend their lives never work. I think your world tied freezing, both the full body and sometimes just the head. They can market it any way they want, it is nothing more than a frozen dead head. The soul leaves its physical form at the moment of death. Now, in the case of data dumps, transfers where the mind, and everything that makes that person who they are, are moved into a synthetic housing, be it robotic or virtual, then the soul is moved as well. When I created the process, I conveniently choose the act of death as the trigger for the ascension. This proved fortuitous later when the living learned to transfer their souls to synthetic entities."

"So, it wasn't planned from the start?"

"No."

"Maybe you can answer a question no one seems to want or be able to. What is a soul?"

"The living's soul is an amalgamation of all that you become. That is why children don't have souls; they are not enough of themselves yet to have come into enlightenment. As for The Powers, which you can now call yourself, or those related to The Powers, our essence is who we are, regardless of the substrate in which it is housed. That is why when our current body becomes damaged beyond repair our essence transfers down to The Hatchery where it takes a Lucifer imposed time-out. Since the process of losing our body and being transferred is so traumatic, it can take a while for an essence to re-find itself. Once it does, then it can start working on constructing a new original appearance. Many take a trip to The Hatchery, whether voluntary or not, to rebuild themselves. Think of it as a fresh start."

"It sounds like the ability to shift this form..." I motion to my body, "is not that common. As it was explained earlier it has something to do with a sense of self. Someone like Xia who can do it so easily probably understands who they are more fully than say others?"

"I would dispute that conjecture. There is nothing in Creation with a higher or better sense of self than The Powers, and most cannot shift easily, at least not as Lord Morningstar does. Often, they only can accomplish it with great effort or when they are entering Creation. Then they are required to construct a form, though many decide instead to be hosted by a living being. I would even go as far as suggesting it is the opposite. Xia has always had questions about his birth, so much so it has been an underlying issue most of his life. I think his ability is due to his more fragile sense of how he sees himself. Arguably since The Father began creating other Creations and creatures The Powers have had their sense of self shaken, but instead of becoming more flexible many instead became far more rigid in their views of their place in The Father's overall construct."

"Do we, The Powers that is, have hearts?"

"I was curious if you had made that logical leap as of yet. No, we do not."

"Then how?" I asked.

"Think about it. I am confident you already know the answer. Whether you like that answer is a different matter entirely."

I was distracted by a bowl of soup which had just been placed in front of me, and oh gawd, did it smell good. I dug in, as did we all, all conversations stopping. That was until what the Overlord had just said sank in. "Lucifer."

"I would suggest you not say that name quite as loud; half the street just jumped under something or started looking for escape routes. But yes, The Dark Lord. Therefore, what do you extract from that realization?"

I sighed. "That he forced, I'm guessing, their essence into those hearts so Usis could find them and eat them. Fine, but how did he know? Was that the time thing?"

He shrugged as he took a big bite of noodles. "No idea, probably not. Our Lord is a very good judge of character; he probably rolled the dice in hopes that your little boy toy would see his good fortune as an opportunity. Which, in fact, he did."

"I get the feeling, to use your words, that Lord Lucifer rolls the dice a lot?"

"You have no idea. Our dear missing Father insisted things have order. Why his first creation was tantamount to walking chaos is anyone's guess."

"The Father is OCD?"

"I am not sure I would say that to him, but it does not change the truth of the statement. He created checklists before Creation even knew what it was going to look like. I am sure they are still floating around in The Host someplace."

We ate the rest of our meal in silence; I finished first. Spinning around on my stool - I cannot tell you how happy that simple act makes me, so much so I had to take a couple of more laps – When I stopped, while the others finished, I relaxed and watched the crowded street parade past. It was still raining, and as normal, there was a mix of those who tried to cover their heads not to get wet and those who didn't give a shit. I observed for a while, trying to pick out the species I'd seen before, that was until a giant red blob of flesh and weeping wounds came slithering toward us. It looked like a pile of red hash browns in the shape of a half ball with three random arms and a giant eye hanging from a stalk a couple of feet in front of it. As it slithered by it left a red trail that was quickly washed away by the rain. "What the fuck is that?" I blurted out.

Alcraw turned, noodles hanging from his mouth, all the way to the bowl. "Looks like a failed experiment."

When The Overlord turned he confirmed, "Yes, Ezera has more heart than he needs for his creations. Since he made it, regardless how much a failure or how hideous it is, he cannot bring himself to destroy it."

"He just lets them go to roam the streets?" I ask.

"I would think the answer to that question is self-evident. Normally they don't last long," explained the Overlord.

"I can imagine, something that squishy only needs a hole and I bet it would feel great," threw in Cantos.

Remember he doesn't talk much, and now we see why. I looked up, thirty feet tall, remember, "Really, that's just fucking gross."

"Don't knock it till you have just emerged from the Hatchery; your cock has just grown back, and you have a Demon sized case of blue balls. Then even a three-legged hooker with syphilis scars leaking green puss as body parts fall off looks good." Yup, you guessed it, that was enough to finish pretty much everyone's dinner.

I smirked. "Really, all you guys live in Hell, and I'm sure you've seen what they do to the souls, and that puts you off your dinner?"

Cartos laughed loudly. "I think it is more due to memories of past dates than revulsion. Alcraw here..." He never finishes, just smirks.

"Hey, don't mock it until you try it and then squeegee it off the next morning," added Alcraw. "She was sexy...if not just a bit weepy."

With that, I changed the subject, if for no other reason than to keep my noodles down. "So the labs. I'm assuming that was from a lab and this Ezera is one of the, what do I call them, creators?"

"You are correct on both accounts," says the Overlord.

"Can they just make anything, Creation's Lego set, so to speak?"

"Pretty much, they have their orders to fill. The young ones, new to the craft are encouraged to experiment. It is how they learn to use souls and manipulate flesh."

As Death finishes another couple walks by, these two clearly synthetic. "So let me get this straight. If the living created them and they are completely synthetic and the 'spark' as you call it is strong enough to manifest a soul, they end up down here to live out eternity. No torture? No punishment? No fear of the furnaces? Wait, it just hit me, this place isn't as hot either."

"You are correct on all accounts excluding one. There are several options other than the living creating the synthetics. Many races that reside here in Hell have thousands of years between their creation and the original breakthrough by their living creators. Creatures like themselves created these beings."

"That leads to an interesting question. Are there any 'species' which would be considered synthetic but have a, I'm not even sure the word, a biological design like that of the living?"

"Yes, there are several 'species' which are considered the ultimate blasphemy. These races can trace their lineage back to mechanical, composite beings whom eventually recreated The Father's design using flesh, bone, and blood. The difference is most, but not all, are not born of parents but are still manufactured or gestated in labs or manufacturing facilities. As for your other question, the temperature, the furnaces do not vent on this Plane."

"The heat fucks with the electronics?"

"Exactly."

This was all very interesting. The question crossed my mind if humans from Earth would ever reach this point but then I remembered, that would never happen, we're extinct.

After dinner, we continued to stroll the streets. I not only delighted in the city but also in Cemal as he wandered around, peaking in windows and shops, pointing things out, no matter how distracted he got he was never more than a few feet away from me for very long. I can see in his eyes the familiarity with this place. To me this was a Plane of Hell, to him, it was home.

At one point I stopped to look in a store with wide-eyed amazement. The shop itself was narrow and deep, along the walls were hundreds of bins, shelves and hanging racks with a staggering variety of parts, I don't know any other word for it. The place was filled with synthetics, mostly mechanical here, "The downside of having a mechanical body is over time it wears down, it is thus necessary to give some of the more inventive species room to set up fabrication facilities to ensure our population stayed repaired," explained the Overlord. "Mind you these shops only deal with cosmetic alterations. The real workshops are located elsewhere on the Plane."

Walking in I saw what looked like a barber's chairs. In one was a shiny robot looking humanoid laid out as a technician tried different orbs in the creature's eye socket, explaining its specifications. It was interesting the way they were picking out parts like a human would choose hair color, contact lenses, shoes, or piercings. Walking back, I rejoined the group who were leaning against a wall across the street. "You guys didn't want to come in?"

"We assumed you wanted to see what was happening in the shop. If a band of Hellspawns walks in there is little chance you would have achieved your goal," explained Balthazar.

As I caught up with the Overlord, I asked, "I have another question. What is with all the destroyed but still active synthetics hanging from the exterior of the Keep?"

"Those are souls who choose a synthetic body over a Father created form. When they arrived due to the parameters I set for such beings, their bodies came with them. Had it not they would have been placed in a soul stone. The living who arrive with synthetic bodies are shunned by both The Host, Hell and most of the residents of this Plane. They are truly outcasts. We hang their bodies from walls of the Keep until one of their personality traits is needed in the labs or one of our residents wishes to refurbish them to participate in matches or mutilation sports offered by many of the clubs and entertainment venues across the city."

See I knew if I waited long enough this plane would take the Hellish turn. And there it was. "When their mechanical form is destroyed, what becomes of them?"

"They end up in the Hatchery, often becoming the primordial gel which those still trying to find themselves use for nourishment."

(I think I wrote earlier that those who transferred from a flesh body were allowed to live untortured, but I can't remember. If so, then sorry, since I got this new information directly from the Overlord's mouth, I trust her over anyone else.)

# Entry 250 (Part 2)

I separated the walk through the city from the club. For your gore fans, this is the chapter for you...enjoy)

Alcraw led us on a winding trip through the city, eventually stopping at a loud neon-lit bar.

"You are not serious?" said The Overlord.

"Why? Listen, it's Earth music," commented Alcraw almost defensively. The other three Hellspawns were trying to hide laughs.

I looked around Alcraw to get a peek into the club. The door was open, guys and girls were dancing naked both on the street and in the bar, and some of them were cute. More importantly, and I mean way more importantly Marylin Manson's voice was blasting from the inside. "You can't take this from me, Forbidden in Heaven and useless in Hell." With that I made an executive decision. "We need to go in here," I said as I started for the door.

I heard Alcraw add, "See?" I didn't see or hear The Overlord's response.

As we stepped into the bar many questions about this Plane were answered. See I was starting to think it was just a Haunted Mansion on steroids, but then I got a whiff of the suffering. You can judge me if you want. I'm not saying I like the smell. But after this many years and this Plane being such a drastic change it was a little comforting to be surrounded by something I recognized, suffering and screams covered with a liberal dose of heavy metal music. See when I say it that way it doesn't sound so bad, does it? OK, I know it still does.

The place was darkish, and the music so loud it hurt our ears. I could tell everyone but the Overlord was loving it. We pushed our way through the seriously crowded dance area. The pushing part is a bit of an overstatement, with four Hellspawns, one being over thirty-feet tall and covered in flames, the crowd parted like a drunk Moses at a beach party. Remember Hellspawns are the royalty of Hell, they're both respected and feared in equal measures.

We found a booth in the back, a huge curved one with a table in the middle; Hell must like these things, De Sade had them too. The waitress came over and was promptly sent away with our drink orders and instructions to have a server with a bit more...cock deliver them. While we waited, I took in the details of the bar.

This entire Plane is throwing me off. To be honest, it makes me feel old. I'm used to, maybe even comfortable with, the non-technological Hell. This plane feels like one of those traveling Raves designed to milk drug-addled, testosterone-driven gays of their money and souls. Are their straight raves? I wonder. I know I used a similar description about the Club inside the Keep on Lust. There though it was part of a classic building whose overseer was the Marquis De Sade, so a lot could be forgiven, plus it was a punishment. Here though, it just seems...I don't know like Hell was purchased by a big budget movie producer from the 20th century on Earth.

The club itself looked to take up the entire first floor. On every side, the walls were black tinted glass with bright chrome moldings looking out over the streets of the city. On two walls were long bars with various places for dancers to slither and move. (Remember when I say slither, I'm not talking about a dance style as much as the fact some of the dancers had tentacles.) In the center of the room was a massive raised round mirrored stage/dancefloor filled to overflowing with all forms of creatures grinding and moving. The forty-foot-high ceiling was clearly designed for the comfort for all sizes of Demons; even Cartos didn't have any problems. A couple of times he had to duck to avoid the flashing lights, but otherwise, everyone who should've been having fun seemed to be. The ones who weren't were the souls chained up around the club also for the guest's enjoyment.

As we entered, I said it smelled of suffering. First along the back wall, were booths, ours being one of them, and to each side in the empty spaces were both synthetic and biological soul suspended spread eagle in front of curtains of torture implements hanging from chains, I guess they didn't want anyone stealing them. Several of the souls were currently occupied, so to speak. A fleshy creature was very methodically having his body flayed into super thin strips which were then piled on a plate by a patron and taken back to the booth to be slow roasted over a small flame pit. I guess a sort of Korean BBQ. In another area a synthetic, from the damage it looked like one from the Keep walls, it was hanging from the ceiling by a single chain as several other synthetics used rotary grinders to strip away the soul's outer casing slowly. "Does that hurt the creature?" I asked the Overlord.

"Pain is different for a synthetic. It is not like a soul's pain. What that one would experience is the growing drone of warning lights and systems failures as parts of its body are destroyed. It's not physical pain, as such, but he knows where it is headed and he is incapable of doing anything about it. It has probably already run a dozen scenarios letting it know how long the current progress will take to finally destroy is carapace enough to short him out and thus end his existence. Since he experiences time in the billionth of seconds, to him this torture and the inevitable end are lasting an eternity. So, he does not feel pain, but the prolonged knowledge of the inevitable is equal in almost all ways." When the Overlord finished, he leaned over taking a closer look. "That model might have pain sensors. If so then he would be experiencing a simulated version of what his coding sees as pain."

"Couldn't he turn that off if needed?" I asked.

"Possibly, though if his tormentors are worth their carbon, they would have disabled its ability to do so." Then as if on cue the creature let out an artificial screech as several areas across its body started to spark. "It will not be long now; he just entered a cascading failure. Oh, look at that, the short one has stepped in to halt the process, bad luck for the one in the chains."

I watched as the 'short one,' one of the torturers pulled out tools and began working on their victim. It looked like he was repairing him. "So, he is stopping it from dying."

"So, to speak, yes."

Turning my attention back to the club, I watched the crowd dance as I looked for other details to share. There were in the floor, scattered around the club, several wide pits with mesh over them. Looking at

Alcraw, since he seemed to know the place, I asked, "What are those? Is there someone down there?"

Pointing up he directed my attention to more dancer/acrobats suspended from the ceiling swinging and twisting from chains and platforms. "It is for them...just watch. I would hate to spoil the surprise."

Well spoil it he didn't, and the wait wasn't long. As the song came to an end, I noticed the chains which bound each of the suspended dancers' wrists and ankles. The wrists secured to the ceiling and the one around their ankles went down and through the grates in the floor. As another piece of music started, one I would later discover was sort of the anthem for this activity, the crowd scurried away, making room around the pits as the chains retracted, pulling the dancers taught. At first, I thought they were going to rip the dancers in half but again I was wrong. As the grates retracted, strange looking machines emerged. The sides of the device were attached to the chain allowing it to climb while in the center was three long blades, each moving back and forth as well as up and down. Across the room where the other dancer was the device instead had two massive dildos filled with holes.

Unable to take my eyes off the first one, the closest, I watched as the device started to climb as the speed of the blades increased. Everyone at my table was wrapped in anticipation including the Overlord. I shook my head already knowing where this was going. The first screams came as the two outside blades started shaving off pieces of the creature's inner legs and thighs, throwing the slices into the crowd. I was able to look away until I heard a cheer punctuated by a blood curtailing scream. Looking back my hands went to my mouth as the center blade penetrated the creature between his legs as the outside ones became lodged temporarily in the joints connecting the creature's legs to his hips. It was then I realized why the blades also oscillated, for as the device rose pushing the center one deeper, the two side blades began to saw through the bones eventually snapping off the legs letting them fall into the pit below. I don't know how much detail you want but suffice it to say the two outside blades eventually removed the sides of the torso, the arms, and legs where the center blade wreaked havoc inside the creature until finally, he fell silent as the blade pierced the skull, destroying the head as the pieces of mutilated dancer fell into the pit. What I guess is important to remember was that the creature remained conscious, awake and suffering until the blade finally destroyed the skull.

Across the room, at the dildo device, something similar happened. The two large holey dildos entered the female in the two lower openings, using vagina and ass, and pushed up into her. It was at this point that dozens of long sharp needles about as long as your hand shot out and the entire thing started to spin completely pulverizing the center and lower torso to the screams of the victim and the cheers of the crowd as the bits of flesh, organs, and blood flew across the room in a confetti spray of carnage. In all honesty, this one was much worse than the first. See the first one destroyed the entire body including the head. The second one pretty much only ripped out the torso from the tits to her vagina causing the lower half with the legs to fall away while the upper torso, arms, and head were still intact with the creature still conscious as its organs twirled on the rotating devices. As they lowered her, still awake and screaming much to the delight of the audience, I started to ask what would happen to the body until I saw a Demon place her remains on a tray where it went over and presented it to one of the tables. "Dinner?" I said sarcastically.

"Yes, and they paid a premium for it."

The upside to my new form is I can't turn pale or green anymore when I get sick. When I was finally able to shake the horrors of what I'd just seen I turned back to my companions to find them all watching me.

"Two things..." I said very matter of factly. "First...Oh My Gawd, and Secondly...." I addressed the Overlord. "You allow this?"

"Of course, my dear. This might not be the Hell you have grown accustomed to but this is still Hell, and our job is still the production and processing of suffering. If it keeps the citizens happy well all the better."

"Where did you get the souls? I didn't see that many biological creatures on this plane...oh, wait, the lakes."

"Exactly, the proprietors of these clubs are free to go down and fish out whatever they need." Pausing for a second, it turned to Elick. "Is this not one of your establishments?"

My head snapped around as my eyebrows rose into my hairline. "Alcraw and I are partners. Xia owns the place."

I was about to say something when a spray of blood covered the table and I heard a scream. I turned in time to watch a Demon rip the spine out of one of the creatures chained against the wall and then bury his head in the soul's torso, spraying blood and gore across our table. Reaching over Alcraw tapped the guy on the back causing him to pull his head out. In a bored tone, he said, "Take your dinner someplace else. You are getting suffering all over our table." The creature started to say something until his intelligence kicked in as he studied our booth. I followed suit. There are four Hellspawns and me all with raised eyebrows just hanging on his next words. You guessed it, he pulled the soul off the wall and hurried off. What was amazing is how quickly the bar staff appeared, dragging in another soul to replace it.

Leaning over I whispered to Elick, "Is it possible since you have clout here to have maybe the two spots nearest us left vacant?"

Smirking, he snapped his fingers, summoning our waiter, yes, a male now, and explained who he was and before I knew it the bodies to each side of our booth were removed. As that was occurring, I realized, everything that had happened, the two dancers' torture and death, all occurred with disco lights still ablaze and most of the patrons watching as they danced. For a second the realization stunned me. It's happened several times during my travels, but that makes it no less overwhelming. To all these 'residents' this was nothing special, maybe even boring. It's just another night out at the club.

We drank, talked, and drank some more. Lots of drinking. Other than the occasional show the only significant point of interest was when someone attacked us. Imagine that; a few friends can't go out in Hell without some over muscled Demons thinking they can make a name for themselves. The cool part, if you want to call it that, was that while they were yelling Balthazar leaned over to me. "We are about to send this lot to the Hatchery; would you like to practice on one before we start?"

I was about to object until the biggest one turned and pointed to me. I thought he'd recognized me until he said, "Save that one, I want to fillet him and fuck all the holes."

I'm not sure why, maybe because I was drunk, but that pissed me off bad. Then something strange happened, time stopped. Everyone except those at my table were affected. The attackers, the people in the bar, the activity outside, all slowed down. Turning my attention back to the asshole, I focused, did the draw in energy thing, and then manifested a ball of lightning in the middle of his body. As you can guess he exploded. I mean like pasta sauce all over the walls exploded. As time resumed, I looked over at Balthazar and said, "Ooopps, I guess that was a little stronger than I thought."

"You think?" barked Alcraw as he broke out laughing. "We might need to work on your control…" He paused. "On second thought, seeing as you are going up against the Worm Lord maybe overkill is the best plan of attack."

My attention was drawn back when Elick said to the other three attackers, "Oh we forgot about you." He waved a hand, and they fell apart, literally, arms, legs, head, torso in pieces. Looking around at the stunned bar he announced in a loud voice, "Sorry for the mess, but well, help yourselves. Dinner is served."

It didn't take long for the crowd to pounce. I closed my eyes and waited for the ravenous mob to clean up the bits of ex-Demon. As the noise died down, I looked up to find two little hands holding a drink just a foot or so in front of me. "Master looks like he could use a drink, or two," said Cemal as he sat another one in front of me. "Surprisingly the bartender over there said these were on the house and he was really really sorry about the problem. There were a few more reallys, but this one thinks Master gets the point." What I liked was how he took his drink and giggled like he had been given a prize and scooted into the booth beside me. He took a sip, his back straight, his head held high as he looked around to see if anyone was noticing how he was acting like his Masters. The more I know Cemal the more I enjoy just watching him discover the wonders of being equal to those around him.

"I'm guessing your demonstration was why people fear Hellspawns so much?" I asked.

"What you did was great for a beginner, and you did it well. But growing up in Hell we learn quickly that the short, fast acts like what I did not only helps spread one's reputation but also cuts down on the number of future encounters. If you have a discussion with each person who tries to make their mark upon your defeat you will find yourself doing little else. We like using Xia as an example, so let us do so again. He was born with a target on his back. He is a member of The Morningstar family. He constantly had creatures picking fights with him. Sometimes it was to build up their reputation, others it was to strike at Lord Lucifer through him. I remember when he reached what we call his early adulthood, something snapped one day. With nothing more than a blink of an eye, he destroyed an entire arena full of creatures. And that was only the first, he learned quickly after that that to stop a fight before it starts with extreme violence cuts down on the conversation, the number of variables in the encounter, and more importantly the number of conflicts you will be subjected to in the future. Now he has the reputation you have heard about since you arrived. He is rarely challenged. That is not because they know he can destroy them, they do, but more importantly, they know he isn't going to waste his time on them. Someone would need to hit him fast and hard before he would even notice what they were doing, then he would just send them to the Hatchery and go on with his day. Now that you are in the position you are in, I would suggest you learn that lesson now; you are a soul who has been raised to become a Power and Lord Lucifer's writer which puts you in his circle. You have that target on your back now. As, dare I say, is currently being demonstrated by my Great Grandfather. All of Hell will be watching how this plays out and both you and he will have to live with the results for a very long time," said Elick as everybody just nodded.

"Listen to what he says. We all have had to learn it. Look where I am now compared to where I started. Your future is in your hands, and he is correct, the outcome of this single encounter will shape the rest of your eternity," added the Overlord.

Oh wow, just what I needed to hear. I know they're right, but we came out to relax. I guess that was the message of this story. If I want to 'just relax' first I must prove it's not wise for them to make me work on them. "Point taken but let's talk about what I did for a second since it was my first real use of my powers. Balthazar, why was it so strong? I didn't expect that. And why did time stop?"

"I think we just learned something. I agree with Elick, but I think what they do not understand is that for you that was a show of force. What I take away from this is when you are threatened you seem to react decisively. You need more training, and you do need to keep in mind what Elick said because he is correct. As for the strength, I am not sure if that was you or your benefactors but hang on to it. I also noticed the way you used the other two to draw your energy. That is a perfect way to clean up multiple targets. This was a good test of your reaction speed; it told us a lot about where we need to focus in your remaining training."

"As for the time issue, that is common for The Powers when they feel threatened or need to micro-control their interactions with their surroundings. As you grow more comfortable with your new form and your powers, you will discover many new traits that even Hellspawns do not have. You can choose to slow time in almost any event, but I would suggest you hold off until you have better control of your abilities. As Balthazar said, we learned a substantial amount about your talents tonight." answered the Overlord.

"Trust me I didn't think about using the others that way. I just didn't know where to get the energy, and I knew they had some," I said.

"See, that is reaction vs. overthinking. The Lovers probably helped you, but it's becoming clear with your reaction speed that you are in control of your powers and that is a major step toward surviving the upcoming battle," added Alcraw.

The rest of the night I drank alot, and it wasn't wine this time but booze. I know I should probably write more, at least about the creatures I saw but to be honest the night was mostly a blur after that. I woke the next morning in my bed with the first real hangover I've had in a while.

# Entry 251

As I stumbled out of my room, I had to grip the door to hold myself upright. What the fuck was in those drinks?

As I stumbled to the chair and carefully eased myself down I heard Cemal emerging from the service room. (Is that what you call it?) He was looking a little rough as well. "What the fuck was in those drinks last night?" I asked as he set a tray of food down in front of me.

"Master, this boy feels like his head is about to explode. Boy has never been allowed to consume Hellfire before."

"What the fuck is Hellfire?" I asked as I started to try food slowly. As I expected my stomach made threats.

"It is evil, Master, that is what it is..." The way he announced his feelings with such disgust written across his face I couldn't help but to laugh. "It is not a wine but an alcohol. As you might have noticed it is a bit stronger," said Cemal as Kitar came in, taking a seat at the table. He started to snap, his way of telling Cemal to get him breakfast, but stopped when I looked up through bloodshot eyes and raised an eyebrow. "Dear boy, would you be so kind as to fetch me some breakfast?"

Both Cemal and I smirked as he headed off to get food. "Why have I never heard of this stuff before? I would have thought De Sade would have tried to kill me with it."

Shaking his head, Kitar answered, "Hellfire rarely makes it up to the higher Planes. You will discover many things about this and the Great Plane which are different from the rest of Hell. When you visit the breweries, you will see how both wine and Hellfire are produced."

"Ok, that's answers that. What else do I need to know or see while we're here? I want this fast so I can get to the Seventh Plane, kill Leviathan and get my lover back."

"Ah business meeting time." Kitar smiled. "As I have already stated, the winery, the labs, the lakes and damned at the very least."

"I thought they were thrown in the lake?" I rubbed my head. This was going to be a very long day.

"Most are and those who do not immediately do make it there in time. As you have seen many are used as servants, entertainment and in the public shaming stations."

As Kitar talked, my stomach was still protesting the food I was determined to get down. He was on a roll, so I closed my eyes, calmed my breath, inhaled slowly and concentrated on my discomfort. In a shock of realization, I felt the spots where the pain was most intense. It was like having someone push my bare skin with a single finger, only it was in my stomach, a spot in my head, my arms, and back. I concentrated on each, one at a time, sending energy to their locations in hopes of helping the pain. I was making this up as I went along, but it worked. First my stomach, I found the location and in my mind's eye saw a ripple move across the spot, when it dissipated so did the discomfort. I did the same with the others with similar results. This was a good skill to know.

As I relaxed and opened my eyes, I saw Kitar studying me. "You just healed yourself, did you not?"

"I guess that's what I did. I remember Balthazar saying I could use the energy internally to calm and heal myself, but it would take time and practice. It was either try now or give back my breakfast."

"Might I say thank you for your choice and congratulations."

"Thanks, I guess," I replied as I started to finish my food. Yup, I felt better. "I think I want to get the brewery out of the way, but before that have you seen Elick?"

"Yes, last I heard he was with the Overlord."

"While I get some writing done, can you give him this..." I said handing him a scroll. "Ask him to deliver it to Usis and say please."

"Is that all?"

"No, find out when he wants to do the combat training. As you've probably ascertained, I'm finding the magical aspect of my new abilities far less taxing...well at least at this point, I'm sure that will change. The combat, on the other hand, I haven't gotten a grip on yet. I plan on meditating beforehand to see if I can make the same kind of connection with Enepsigo."

Taking the scroll, he said as he left, "I have no doubt your need for extra tutelage with a blade has nothing to do with the fact that when Elick trains you he does so almost nude."

I laughed. "He does, really? I've never noticed or for that matter haven't even an inkling what you're talking about."

Kitar pulled the door shut behind him as Cemal scurried from the other room. He was clearly still suffering. Again, I reached out and found the areas which were not right due to the poison we love to call liquor. I could tell it would only take a tiny bit of energy. Placing my hand on the left-over food, I dissolved and absorbed it. I reached out and healed those spots that were dragging my dear boy down. He stopped, and in shock turned and found me. I nodded. He set the dishes down and bowed deeply. "Oh thank you, thank you, thank you My Lord."

At first, I started to correct him then... I realized... If I'm- a Power, then I'd be called Lord. For a split second I thought about that, and then said, "It's just Master, if you must use a title, I would think only Lord Lucifer can give me the title of Lord."

"Yes, Master," he corrected.

# Entry 252

After I finished the entries and dressing, Kitar returned and we headed down to the lobby. As he talked to one of the little genderless slaves, I watched the Seekers running in and out with the gems. I wanted to know more about them but as Kitar concluded whatever he was doing, I decided to leave it for later. Today was about the Lakes. "You ready, let's get the Lakes out of the way?"

As we stepped outside, the first thing I noticed was it wasn't raining. Even Hell's standard grey was being kept at bay by the stark multicolored lights of the city. I guess there always on, which is good. They make the entire atmosphere seem less imposing. I'd always been comfortable in NYC at night when the streets were painted in shadows of blacks and greys. This reminded me of home, and in that memory, I found comfort.

We were halfway to the first lake when the attack came or would've come had they known my little secret. Just like the night before they still thought I lived in the body of that old scared human I used to be, which was good news. Leviathan hadn't found out yet about my transformation; we needed to keep it that way.

The two Demons appeared out of nowhere and had us both backed into an alley before we could gather our wits and react.

"Where is the writer?" the short red Demon barked at both of us. When I say short, he was still ten feet tall and built like the side of a building. Knowing the little I know now about constructs, which I assumed he was, told me this guy was made to be muscle. The body size, like a pumped-up caricature of one of the lizard creatures but complimented with massive fangs, clawed feet like that of a bird and a long tail ending in a metal spike. He was built to abduct or destroy. I felt my blood run cold, not from fear but anger. I wanted these guys dead, no...that's not right...I wanted them to suffer.

"Writer, you want Keith. You know he is under the protection of The Dark Lord. What do you think is going to happen to you when our Lord learns of this?" said Kitar.

Enough talk. As the Demon started to answer I stepped forward and rose to my full height as I motioned for Kitar to stay quiet. "He is safe, and you are dead. You do realize that, do you not?" I used Hell's speech. In case you've never noticed, no one in Hell uses conjunctions, it's more formal.

I could tell from the look on their faces they were confused. They had no idea who this Demon was. They poised to attack, but I cut them off. This was the second fucking attack in as many days. Glancing over their shoulders, I saw a bar full of damned and Demons. Good, I was going to need the energy. I'd use the souls. I didn't allow myself time to debate whether it was right or wrong. At the moment I didn't care. Reaching out I grabbed the threads of a dozen damned and pulled their energy into myself as their bodies dissolved. When I felt I had enough, I built an image of the Demons frozen and sent it out, instantly they went rigid. Out of the corner of my eye, I saw Kitar turn to me in surprise. I ignored it. I built the next image in my mind and again sent it out causing their flesh to begin peeling away. An ungodly cry erupted from their lips as the scales which covered their body dropped off, piling up at their feet. The underlying skin began to roll up, first their legs, up over their torso, chest, face until coming together at the tops of their scalps. I plucked off the bloody rolls of spaghetti and let them drop to the ground. Let this send a message. I moved one of my hooves forward stepping on the flesh dissolving the mass and absorbing its energy. I pictured the parts of the body, the skin was gone, but there was still muscle, internal organs, and the skeleton. I also found their essence. It was strange like it was more than one, I ignored that. I locked their souls into their muscles. Then I reversed everything. I had no idea if this would work, but it did, well sorta. The skeleton was still inside, but now the outer surface of their muscles faced inwards, pushed together as their organs blossomed from their torso, spilling out onto the ground at my feet. I could hear the now muffled screams, so they were alive just turned inside out. Good.

With a blink I removed the paralysis and the two Demons dropped to their knees, ripping muscle and connective tissue where it wouldn't bend properly. Their entire bodies were a weeping river of inky black blood as it poured from their damaged frames. I turned and looked at

Kitar. "You did that?" he said. I could see more than shock in his eyes. He wasn't surprised but concerned at the disturbing viciousness of my reaction.

I noticed the crowd, all the business in the area had emptied, all eyes focused on me, "It might be time to exit stage left, don't you think?"

He nodded and followed me out of the alley. As I started for the Lakes, Kitar barked, "Where are you going?"

"To the Lakes. Wasn't that the plan?"

"Well, yes, but that was before the attack."

"No, I attacked, or can you not tell?" I barked as my anger flared again. "We're not doing this. I have a job to do. All of you have made that abundantly clear. It's also obvious that neither Leviathan, or anyone for that matter knows what I look like, so I'm safe, and I'm getting this job done, and then I'm saving my companion. If anyone gets in my way..." pointing down at the two writhing Demons on the ground, "...that is what will happen to them. Am I clear?"

He pointed to the two guards still on the ground. I dismissed it. "Don't worry about them, leave them to suffer. If for no other reason, then if they survive, they can go home and report to that fucktard Fallen what is protecting Lord Lucifer's little writer since it's clear he can't do it." I turned and started marching through the recoiling crowd.

I won't lie, this whole power thing is pretty cool. What these attacks have done more than anything else is drive Usis' message home. He's right; we need to be able to protect ourselves. Well, we can, and anyone who stands against us will suffer for it. I'm not sure I feel good about destroying those damned, but I have no problem killing these Demon fuckers who were born in this place. To quote Super Chicken, 'they knew the job was dangerous when they took it'."

I didn't have much time to concentrate before I was in the air. Someone had plucked me off the street and from my angle I couldn't tell who or what it was. All I could see is that I was being carried back to the Keep. We flew over the city and then just before running into a plate glass wall we shot up at a stomach-churning speed. Next thing I knew I was dropped onto our balcony. I turned, ready to attack, to find not only Kitar but Elick, Balthazar, and Alcraw there. "Where's Cartos, he wasn't hurt, was he?"

"Oh no, he is doing what he does best. When the attack..." said Elick.

Balthazar cut him off as he spat, "That was no attack, it was a fucking insult. Is he not taking us seriously? Does he not know what I can do to his pitiful little Plane?" He was pissed.

"As I was saying, when the attack started, we went to find you and Cartos went to stir up some trouble on Violence," said Elick calmly.

"Is that a good idea?"

"Keith, Leviathan is between a rock and a hard place, and I think he is about to realize it. You have Lucifer's protection, he has your companion, and now Lucifer's second in command's son is about to start ripping my dear great-grandfather's Plane apart while his two henchmen stagger home inside out. Nice job by the way."

Alcraw added as he pushed past us into the apartment, "You were just planning a rescue. If you cannot, we are now planning a war."

I walked over beside Elick and in a whisper asked, "Are you ok with that?"

"I chose my side when I took on this assignment."

"Why isn't Lucifer here? He could stop all of this in the blink of an eye," I barked.

"Literally. But if I had to guess, not only does he have his hands full, but to be honest, I am not sure he would intervene. This might be one of his little tests."

"Tests? I keep getting attacked."

"You are now a resident of Hell, Keith. You are a Power. You have been moved from the cheap seats and introduced into the game. Based on what just happened down in the city, it is good to see you are ready to play."

"PLAY!!"

"Like it or not, to someone somewhere this is little more than a game. Its time you realize that and start working on counter moves."

"I understand that, but where do I start. Thank gawd I have you guys. I have no idea how to fight this fight," I was screaming now.

"First by signing this," we heard from behind us. Turning we saw the Overlord standing in our room holding a scroll.

"What is that?" I asked, walking in the room.

"A formal challenge," Death answered. "Sign this, and Leviathan either has to relent or accept your request for a duel."

"A duel, how very old school."

"The oldest. Now sign it and let me get it in transit."

"Will that stop him? If I've learned one thing in my travels, you guys don't exactly play by the rules."

"We don't need rules. The challenge also states that you are under my protection until the match."

I lifted the necklace I wore. "I've been under protections. That doesn't seem to mean SHIT..." I yelled the last word at no one in particular, hoping he would hear.

"Exactly, that is why I'm putting you under mine. That is a slap in the face to not only Leviathan, who will see it as an act of war, but also our Dark Lord for not holding up his end of your agreement," explained the Overlord.

"That is a very dangerous game to play Kritanta," said Elick.

"And you know it will piss him off," offered Alcraw.

"It damn well better," added the Overlord as I walked over and signed the scroll. Just before he rolled it up, I saw Usis' name. Grabbing the scroll back I barked, "What is this?"

"It is a clause that if anything happens to your companion before the challenge is brought to fruition, then Lord Leviathan can consider himself at war with the 2nd, 6th, and 8th Planes."

"Wait, they agreed to this?"

"It was De Sade's idea," it explained as it walked, well floated, across the balcony handing the scroll to a little Demon just on the other side of the railing.

As the messenger flew off, I said, "Well thank you. I know there are underlying reasons for your actions but they are still greatly appreciated." The Overlord nodded. "I need a drink..." I said, but before I finished, I felt a goblet touch my hand. I looked down with a smile as Cemal waggled the bottle in his other hand.

"Boy will refill."

"That won't be necessary. Who's going with me to the Brewery?" I said finished my drink in one gulp.

"NOW?" barked Kitar.

"We have already had this discussion, so YES, NOW... I need to get this shit done. In case you don't remember, we have a war to fight."

# Entry 253

Ultimately only Kitar went with me, which was fine. The others, though powerful, would try to impose their narrative upon what I was seeing. I didn't want that. That all sounds high and mighty I know, but the truth was they didn't have any interest in taking me on a tour. It was one thing to train me to fight one of the meanest creatures in Creation, but another to 'hold my hand' as I visited the Breweries.

In the short time I was back in the room the weather changed. Now it was raining, I mean it was pouring. Maybe two hours had passed, and, in that time, it went from nothing to a downpour. As we stepped onto the street, I also noticed the reactions this time. Today I could see how it was affecting the unprotected souls. All along the street were dozens of damned curled in fetal positions crying while synthetics walked past oblivious to the suffering they were stepping over. We turned a corner to find a little human in a ball on the sidewalk screaming and clawing at her face. What little hair she had left was in loose patches all over her head, and the skin of her face hung in ribbons of red and pink noodles below deep tear streaked wounds. Mixed with the sounds of the rain striking the pavement were the now the familiar sounds of souls reliving all the pain of the suffering's former victims.

I slowed but wasn't allowed to stop. I felt Kitar's paw press into my back as he guided me down the street. As we approached one of the damns at the edge of the city, the gutters were no longer running with just the yellow puss colored suffering for it had now been tinged with streaks of red, the city's resident's contribution to Hell's ever-growing power reserve.

"So, they suck the suffer from the lakes and vaporize it causing it to rise into the top of the cave. It then condenses and rains untold sorrows down upon the city. The souls caught in the downpour experience the pains and horrors of the suffering's original owner, now all mixed together. This causes them to brutalize themselves as their own blood/suffering is added to the runoff which goes back into the sewers to be returned to the lake for the cycle to start again. Do I have that right?"

"Elegant is it not?" answered Kitar. "This way."

We turned down a side street which ended at a door. There was nowhere else to go but back. Kitar pulled out his key. Gawd, I forgot about those things. "That thing works here as well?"

"Of course, it is the Master's Key."

"Oh wait, I just got that, it's the MASTER'S key. Very clever. Is there anything it won't get into?"

"I do not know, I have never tried, nor would I recommend it. Remember where you are. Who knows what is behind doors you do not know anything about."

I interrupted, "And then we wake up in the Hatchery."

"Maybe the Lovers imparted some brains as well."

When he unlocked the door, we entered what looked like Anton Levey's living room back in San Francisco. Dark, bleak, nothing but a bored Demon leaning back in a chair reading a scroll.

Kitar coughed.

"Subtle," I said.

"Sorry we never get visitors and the ones we do I have instructions to send along, you know…"

"Yes, the Hatchery…I've heard this song before," I said.

"I am Lord Judge Kitar and this…."

I got to cough this time…to remind Kitar not to use my name. Remember I'm incognito in my new form.

"We have been sent by the Overlord to tour the Brewery," explained Kitar after realizing why I was coughing.

"Sure, you are. How am I to know that?" the Demon said as three more joined him from the door in the back of the room.

I wasn't in the mood for this, so I did what I do best, overreacted. I focused on one of the Demons, sucked the energy out of him, built a razor-sharp disk in my mind and materialized it in the center of the Demon's neck, then expanded it. As you can guess, it separated him from his head. As both halves dropped to the floor, I grabbed the head by the horns, handed it to one of the other Demons and said, "Could you run this back to the Keep so he can get the Overlord's authorization?"

"But…" was all the other Demons could manage. "He's dead, how is he going to get authorization?"

"Who replaces him if something like this happens and don't tell me it's the first time?"

"Well…er…that would be me, I guess."

"And who is running the head to the Keep?"

"Well…er…OH…you want me to get the permission," he said as he dropped his friend's head. "I see. I get it. I…yes…ok…well…then…I will be off."

Leaning down and picking up the previous demon's head I handed it back to him. "Don't forget your friend."

He looked at it, then me, then Kitar who smiled showing all his teeth. As he ran, and I mean ran out the door we had just entered I turned back to find the other two Demons had vanished. Looking up to Kitar, I asked politely, "Do you want the chair, or should I take it?"

He stood staring at me. "You are getting very rash. You just killed a Demon. Is this going to become a problem?"

"I've no idea. I don't know how often the opportunity might present itself. If I were to guess, it wouldn't become a problem but a solution. What I AM sure of is that I've put up with their bullshit for who knows how many years and sometimes I might just want to repay the favor. The question should be, is this going to be a problem for you?"

Shaking his head, Kitar answered, "No, not at all, it is just surprising. Out of curiosity, did you enjoy it?"

"What, cutting off his head? In all honesty, I was as surprised as you were. I didn't register what I was doing until I did it."

"See now that makes sense. It is probably Enepsigo's reaction more than yours."

"Wait...what are you saying? They might be able to control my actions?"

"Does that bother you?"

"Of course, it does. I don't want two psyco Powers taking control of my body."

"Well then you should have thought of that before you started munching on their hearts."

"You're fucking with me, aren't you?"

"It probably was Enepsigo's training which caused you to react like that, but yes, they will not be able to control you. You did as you were taught, trusted your instincts."

"So no taking over my body?"

"No."

"Then why did you say it?"

"You were getting a bit uppity. Now you are off balance and paranoid again, just like I like you. Plus, it might serve as a reminder not to run around attacking things. Oh, look our friend is back," said Kitar turning as the second demon returned. I had to laugh; he was still carrying the head.

"This way My Lords, if you please."

As he unlocked the door and Kitar and I turned to follow, I said under my breath, "you're a dick."

"I have one, yes. It is good to see it still works," replied my dear Judge as we followed the very friendly Demon holding a severed head.

Just inside the door were stairs leading down, lots of them. Fortunately, there was also a shaft, it was about twenty feet across and went straight down. "Stairs or fly?" asked Kitar.

Looking over the edge, "How far down it is?"

"All the way," he said as he and I both extended our wings. Walking to the edge, we stepped off and began to descend. Just as I was about to vanish into the pit, I heard a voice from above say, "I will just wait here, if you don't mind."

"No problem," I yelled.

Then from down below, I heard Kitar add, "And do not set that head down."

I had to laugh. He was a dick.

After descending several hundred feet, Kitar alighted on a balcony. I'd noticed several similar on our way down. "We passed a lot of doors. What are they?" I asked.

"Different workshops, torture chambers, the labs and the like."

"One at a time, right now booze," I added. I was surprised at how upset all these doors made me. I guess it wasn't the doors as much as the time they possibly symbolized — the time which was keeping me from Usis.

Kitar opened the doors and we stepped through. My first impression was the size; it had to be miles in every direction. The height of the ceiling, easily one hundred feet. The smells were that of burning flesh, so strong that even with the vastness of the space it still stung my eyes. It coupled with the heat, the smell of suffering and alcohol made the room stifling.

Two guards met us as we entered, both synthetic standing about fifteen feet tall. To all extents, Terminator look alikes.

"And who do we have here?" I heard before I saw a figure halfway across the room moving down the center aisle.

"Greetings, Klitog. It is Lord Judge Kitar and a friend."

As the creature grew closer, I began to make out a form. All through these journals, I've always had trouble trying to figure out how to describe some of the strange creatures. First, she was floating; I could see that. When she was finally close enough for me to get a better look, my reflexes caused me to take a step back, both in surprise and maybe disgust. Floating about three feet off the floor was a morbidly obese nude humanoid female. Now that's the easy part.

From the top down. I couldn't make out her face because it was covered in one of those straw hats as worn in rice fields back on Earth, from which hung a veil of filthy gauze covering her face. Her body was nothing but huge rolls of skin and breasts, big breast, hanging to her waist. Big fat arms rippled down until the fat formed cuffs over her tiny hands. All that existed of her lower half was her hairy female parts and upper legs ending at the knees. Below that, from each leg, hung dozens of cables of different diameters, all dragging the floor. In the left hand, she held a Khopesh sword about three feet long with a red pearl handle. In the right a beautifully detailed fan.

"Greetings, Kitar. Is this the writer I was told to expect?" asked Klitog.

Kitar looked around. We were alone other than the two guards. "Before I answer I need your promise to secrecy."

"Which means it is. I was informed he would eventually visit. But I was also told he was...is...humanoid. I assume this new form is the reason for your reluctance and your hope for my secrecy," she said as she waved the fan gently in front of her face.

As she snapped her fan closed and tucked it into a belt, she floated closer. When just inches from us, she turned to Kitar. "Dear, I never leave my post. This creature does not match the description of the writer given to me, which clearly now renders said description void. The issues on the Seventh Plane, the group of Hellspawn and Demons he has chosen to call companions, yourself included, are all reasons why I Klitog have no interest in involving myself with The Dark Lord's writer. He is trouble, plain and simple. And the last time I involved myself in the workings of the foolishness outside this room, I lost my legs. Not that I was attached to them, but still they were mine and did not taste particularly nice when I was forced to eat them."

"All good answers. May I present Keith, the Dark Lord's writer."

"Did you not understand what I just said? You most certainly may not present Keith, The Dark Lord's Writer. I will show you and this total stranger of whom I have no interest in meeting my purpose for existing. Said purpose is to produce the only beverage in all of Hell and The Host worth drinking." Before turning away her eyes brushed across mine as she added, "it is a pleasure not to meet you, whomever you are...this way."

As we walked, I leaned into Kitar. "Interesting."

"She does not get out much, so forgive her verboseness," he said in a whisper.

"And her exemplary hearing," she added from a few feet in front of us. "The brewery is broken into three sections. The largest being the common wine drunk by most of the residents of Hell. The other two sections are used for the creation of Hellfire and The Private reserve. Is there one you would prefer to start with?" asked Klitog.

"Since the common wine is well...the most common, let's start with it."

"Well said. Yes, friend of Kitar and total stranger to myself, we will start there."

I smirked as did Kitar as I nodded that I liked her.

We were not the only ones in this massive production and distribution facility. There were hundreds of synthetics moving about, all taller than me, at least thirty feet tall.

The center isle was a good hundred feet across and clearly the main artery for the entire facility. To the left, the view of the largest section of the brewery was blocked by metal casks stocked almost to the ceiling and running the entire length of the several-mile-long room. Each container measured about fifteen feet wide by twelve feet high and deep. I know that sounds large, but they were easily manageable by the large creatures responsible for working with them. More importantly is to keep those sizes in mind as the tour continues.

It seemed like we walked forever, which is fine for her, she didn't have feet or hooves. Eventually, we reached a long path leading through the casks and into the production area. Not only was the stock the full length of the chamber but also stacked several rows deep making this new hallway some two hundred plus feet in length. As we drew nearer, and the cries of pain grew louder, it was clear souls were used during the distalation process.

"Am I correct that the liquid suffering collected from all the above Planes is the basis for the beverages?" I asked.

"Yes, it is the main ingredient along with some flavoring and tempering agents."

"What does that mean?"

In the main production area, we stopped at a cask turned on its side with its top off. "I will walk you through the process as we prepare this cask," she said.

"Start from the beginning please."

"The preliminary step of purification really cannot be shown since it occurs in a closed system. The suffering is pipped down from the lakes above and run through a series of filters."

"Filters? What kind?"

"As I said it is a closed system, so an explanation will need to suffice. We use an aquatic creature from I think the fourth creation for the purification. Each creature measures about seven times the length of a cask (so about 105 ft) and are bottom dwellers on their world specifically suited for purification of whatever liquid they are submerged in. In each chamber, there are three of these creatures. They are secured in such a way that the front half of their body is in the raw intake area and the back half in the purified reserve chamber. When the first chamber is filled the creature inhales the suffering, digests and removes all the particulate matter and a portion of the actual experiences contained within the liquid. Once it has worked its way through their system, it is expelled through their anus and stored in a purified state ready for the next step."

"So wait, they consume the suffering, which I know causes whomever it touches to experience all the pain and agony of the creature who created it. They remove part of that pain, absorb the nasty bits that might have traveled down with the raw liquid and then piss out a clean and pure product?" I was already getting sick, and we were only at the first step.

"Yes, though the word 'pure' is purely subjective. They are only the first filter for the pain and not a very good one at that. They, at best, remove ten percent of the suffering. As for the rest of your oversimplification, yes you are correct. The result is a beautiful translucent pale green liquid. You will see it as we move to the next step."

As we walked over, I watched as one of the large synthetics began to fill a cask with green liquid. For our convenience they turned one on its side for us to stand on, allowing us to see into the tank they were filling. They continued filling this cask until it was about eighty percent full. At which point the Brewer motioned for another synthetic to bring over three very tall thin damned. These creatures were extremely pale, beefy but super skinny and had a strange sickly-looking skin. Once in the work area, they were arranged facing out, in a little triangle, and bound tightly together like a bunch of sticks.

"These souls are one of the most prolific in all of Creation. Their race has spread across and populated millions of planets in their home Creation. The reason for their abundance is their skin." She explained as the three creatures were lifted and held just above the tank, I could already see where this was going. "Their skin is porous allowing them to inhale just about any atmosphere and through a natural process they convert it into something their bodies can use, allowing them to survive. It is quite remarkable."

As she finished, the three were lowered into the cask. Their cries silenced as they sunk beneath the murky surface. "It took us a while to discover that three Uedkestesa were all we needed to cause the cascading chain of events in a single vat. What happens now is the cask is sealed…" As she explained the lid was lowered, closing the large container. "…and then moved to storage where it will remain for about ten years. During this time the Uedkestesa's natural systems will experience and absorb all the remaining suffering. When the process has completed, their systems will go into shock due to what they have endured causing them to release the final flavoring component as well as the deep red color expected in the wine."

It was a good thing I was blue otherwise I'd have been green. To make matters worse Kitar leaned over and said, "You do love that wine. I cannot begin to guess how much you have consumed in your time in Hell." I jabbed him in the ribs.

"Once the process has completed what happens to the creatures?" I asked.

"This is where the real art comes into play. See the casks must be monitored regularly by our tasters to determine the perfect time to remove the Uedkestesa and bottle the final product."

Closing my eyes slowly I re-asked a question I knew I wasn't going to want the answer too. "Again, what happens to the used creatures once they are removed from the tanks."

"They are taken and stored in a large soundproof chamber in the back of the facility, so we do not have to listen to the insufferable wailing of the millions of Uedkestesa we have stored. It becomes quite unbearable. Ultimately though, the suffering saturated creatures are used in the Hellfire manufacturing process. Since it is the next logical stop. If you follow me, I can show you that procedure."

"Before we leave, since this is the standard drink of Hell, on all the Planes, how much of this stuff do you use in a year?" I asked.

(Remember I do the conversions for you. A time system was set up in both Hell and The Host back at the beginning of Creation. It is somewhat equivalent to many of the living planets standard year throughout Creation. This is due to what scientists call the "Goldilocks" zone, that area around a star where planets are most likely to have life. And it isn't that way by accident. The Father set up the system to ensure that once the seed for creation has been planted, evolution can occur and over time create life. So for most sentient species in all nine Creations a year is pretty close to the same.)

She stopped and thought for a moment. "I am not sure of the exact amount but somewhere around seventy to eighty million casts."

"And how much do you have on hand at any given time?"

"Considering each cast takes ten years to reach fermentation, we have around twelve years' worth at any given time," she explained as we walked across the massive production area, through some more stacks of casks.

Now just stop and think about that. Seventy million casts a year, with twelve years' supply on hand. That is 840 million casks of wine. Use that number to help wrap your head around the size of this place.

# Entry 254 (Hellfire)

As we entered the next area, I was introduced to a fresh Hell. It's important to remember just last night I'd drunk a lot of this stuff; now I got to see how they make it. From what I was seeing my stomach was most certainly not going to approve of the production process.

Standing with my cute fanged mouth hanging open, the Brewer smirked and said, "So picking up where we left off, the first part of the process is much the same, the initial purification that is. Though with Hellfire we do purify a second time. This is quality shit. Once the liquid is almost completely clear we add it to the casks. As you can see, these are golden casks instead of silver like the other ones."

"What is that?" I ask pointing to the few dozen fire pits with screaming creatures turning on spits.

"That is what makes Hellfire so damn tasty. See where this process differs is we do not need to remove the suffering from the liquid. The only creatures who can consume Hellfire and survive are those who were either made in Hell or rule it or The Host."

"Meaning?"

"Meaning The Fallen, The Host, Hellspawn, Demons, and constructs. Well, constructs that are not synthetic..." she added as she tapped her arm, making a muffled metallic clanking sound.

Oh, that's right. I missed that earlier. When she turned around to lead us to the production area, I noticed that her skin was pulled over a metal frame and laced up the back. It doesn't fit, its pulled together like a corset, her armature and mechanical parts all visible from the back. If not on this creature it would be cool.

"OK, I think I understand. Go on..."

"Good. Remember the Uedkestesa from earlier. Here is why we kept them. We retrieve two of the Uedkestesa from storage and add a Hodels and a Melsock (not going to describe them. You'll understand why soon). They are then bound together, put on the spit and roasted until nice and toasty. As you can hear, this does not dampen their enthusiasm for their suffering; they just keep screaming like it's going to do some good. Oh look, there is a set being pulled off the fire right now, instead of telling you, we can watch," she said as she led us to where two of the large synthetics were removing the four severely burnt screaming souls from the fire.

"Next they are unbound and taken to the grinder," she explained as I froze.

"The what?"

"Grinder, of course."

As you can imagine this is where Kitar poked me in the ribs to let me know he is smiling. He stayed silent but for some reason that didn't reduce my urge to punch him.

As the screams reached a new order of magnitude, I covered my mouth with a hand trying to keep an emotionless face. I watched one of the synthetics unceremoniously shove each of the four souls into a grinder while the other turned the crank. If you think I'm talking like sausage or ground beef you'd be wrong. These guys were coming out pulverized, chips and pieces, all dripping into a bucket. My human side was sickened by this display while the writer and 'been in Hell too long' side watched and noticed how each of the souls stare down to watch themselves being slowly consumed and spit out by the circular blades. I find it surprising they'd watch themselves. I saw several groups ground up that day, and almost all of them did it. Don't you find that interesting? Well, maybe not. Anyway, as you can guess each continued to watch and scream until eventually, the noise ended when their upper torso and head were devoured by the mill. Oh and since I'm in the mood, when they get to the head it's often necessary to use a big baseball bat like stick to get the head down into the grinder. There's an upside and downside to that. The upside is their unconscious before their head, or what's left of it, enters the grinder. The downside is well their last view of eternity is their skull being pulverized by a big robot with a baseball bat.

"Once the seasoning (I just let that comment go by) is prepared and added to the liquid, we then take any one of several different species - you are a human, right?" I nodded. "Not your species, you are very bland – and add them in for a little extra kick. (Yes, they're conscious.) Then the cask is sealed."

I just nodded. I was quickly reaching overload at this point. I was spending lots of time exploring the back of my teeth with my tongue.

"Next the cask is carried over to a warming station and heated for several minutes."

I had to laugh; it's like this process just can't not get worse. What she was saying is that one of the big guys picks the cask up and deposits it on a fire.

"I thought gold had a low melting point?"

"Not here. The metal is specially created for this purpose."

"So it's an alloy, not pure?" I asked.

"That is correct. Once the cask is properly heated, it is then stacked and stored for no less than fifty years. After which time it is opened, strained to remove any stray bits and the soul, which are discarded, and then bottled."

# Entry 255 (Divine Wines)

Again, I'm separating the last liquor into a separate entry. If you didn't catch it earlier, the Royalty of Hell and The Host have a private reserve.

As we walk to the final area, I asked the painfully obvious question. "Why can't The Host or for that matter The Fallen just turn water into wine or manifest something out of thin air?"

"Those are all good questions and ones I unfortunately in my lowly state do not have the answer for."

"I understand, at this point, that's my go-to answer as well."

"Right, so the same process is followed until we get to the roasting of the souls. Now here is a note you might find interesting. Due to this specific characteristic of the vintage, both The Fallen and The Host can consume the liquor. I have on more than one occasion been sent a message from Lord Lucifer letting me know how he and some of his more Hostly visitors have enjoyed my creations. I once received a note from Michael himself. I have it in my quarters." You could see the pride radiating from her.

"That is a glowing endorsement indeed. What makes their wine different from the others?"

"Instead of using the four souls like in Hellfire, we use high ranking religious leaders who have betrayed The Father's trust."

Though this surprised me, I couldn't and didn't try to hide my smile. I turned to Kitar, raising an eyebrow, grinning ear to ear. "Remember on Blasphemy, after the souls were forced to face their sins, they rose to the top of the Plane to be tormented by flies? Every few years when our Brewer here runs out of stock the oldest are harvested from Blasphemy and brought down here to be processed into divine wine," he explained.

"And The Host can drink this?" I ask.

"Remember The Host rules Blasphemy. Therefore, the stock is cleansed before it is sent here for processing. Due to the type of sin, coupled with the initial processing being done by a representative of The Host, neither side finds it objectionable. If we have a truly exalted damned pass through, then they are used for a fourth and much rarer vintage which only goes to The Dark Lord's Keep."

"Exalted Damned?" I asked.

"From your world, that honor would be reserved for someone like your Popes."

"Ahh, the guys who rule over the child molesters. The big wig fucktards, I see," I added.

"Exactly," said Kitar.

"Can I get a couple of bottles of this stuff? I want some Pope wine."

"You will need to take that up with The Dark Lord."

"I'll do that," I said still grinning. I want Pope wine, that would be a great karmic thing I think.

"If you wish to see the process, I can show you, but it differs little from the Hellfire procedure," she added. "Are there any questions?"

"Not really, it seems straight forward. Gross but straight forward."

"There is one additional fact you might find interesting," said Kitar. "Since the suffering is not diluted in both the Hellfire and the Divine reserve to remove the pain it is mostly pure, even augmented due to the additives. Therefore, it is useful to creatures like ourselves... (he motions to him and me) ...in replenishing our energy reserves. As you have already learned your body stores a certain amount of Creation energy allowing you to manifest magic without needing to draw from an outside source. These wines, just like rest, helps you replenish that."

"That's really helpful information. I'll keep that in mind. I can drink this stuff now, right?"

"Yes," he answered.

As Kitar was explaining the added benefits, I kept noticing the Brewer studying me, like she was looking for something. When I couldn't ignore it anymore, I blurted far more bluntly than I had intended, "What?"

"I did not expect you to be like... well...that? I was under the impression you were human."

"I was. It's a long story..."

"One which you will not be learning and as I emphasized earlier one you will not be repeating. Is that clear?" said Kitar in that stern judge tone.

"Yes, Lord Judge," she said as she bowed. "Both of you are doing the service of our Lord and to have you here and allowing me to show you my purpose is a very great honor. I would never dream of spoiling it by betraying your trust."

I bowed back to show my respect. We worked our way back to the front of the Brewery, said our farewells, flew up and returned to the Keep. In case you're interested, I drank very little that night. It took a few days before I could get past the process and back to drinking with sincerity. Oh, and we finally let the guard Demon set down his friend's head, which like a good Demon, he was still holding when we made it back to the top.

# Entry 256

Today the Overlord returned asking to speak with me on the balcony. Needless to say, it worried me especially after he didn't get right to the point, so I made conversation while my stomach tried to burrow its way into my hooves. I decided to punt and get some work out of the way. "Tell me about these lakes. Do I need to visit them? Close up I mean?"

"There is not much to see. There are three lakes in the system. The top two are reservoirs for the suffering produced on the earlier Planes. In your units of measurements, they are roughly fifteen miles long and about ten wide, each about five hundred foot deep."

"And the souls?"

"As souls enter the Plane we dispose of them in the lakes. This serves two purposes. First, being submerged in all that suffering causes each soul to experience all the pain of all the souls before them, from all the earlier Planes. Secondly, and more importantly, there are still impurities in the water. By tracking down and consuming these impurities it gives the souls a temporary respite from their anguish. This helps clean and purify the suffering before it flows down into the lower reservoir.

"The damns you see blocking the two lakes serve several purposes. They hold back the liquid to form the upper lakes. Secondly, as the suffering flows through the locks most of the liquid goes through another purification removing the final bits of particulate matter. Then any overflow due to inefficiency in the speed of collection is vaporized and projected into the cavern ceiling where it rains down across the city and the back half of the Plane not covered by the upper lakes. That is why our city is extended out over the lake below. The rain not only keeps the city clean, it also ensures any souls deserving of punishment within the city or on the lower plane suffers as well."

"I'm impressed. It's a very efficient system."

"You toured the Brewery, correct?"

"Yes, after seeing the distillation process, I took a few days off drinking. I'm not sure I'll ever want Hellfire again."

"Because of how it is manufactured?"

"That and the fact it knocked me on my ass."

"It can do that. You would not have been given the opportunity while you were a damned. If a soul consumes Hellfire the suffering is unendurable. Even Hell's punishments pale in comparison. At one point they thought of streamlining the system by feeding it to everyone who appeared at our gates. The amount of time it took to produce proved to be a problem. Now it is reserved for the Powers, Demons and any other creatures not once living. I have heard it acts as a quite effective intoxicant."

"Very effective. If don't mind I do have one question, the reserve vintage? Kitar said it helps restore our energy reserves. Can I get some before I travel to the Seventh Plane? Considering all that is coming up it might come in handy, and I can't count on any resources or cooperation from Leviathan."

"Good thinking. I will arrange to have a case or two delivered to take with you."

"Are we going to continue having problems with Leviathan's goons? I want to ensure I can keep writing, I've discovered it helps take my mind off of other issues. I know at this point it's a sore spot."

"As far as I am concerned, we are at war with Lord Leviathan. He has sent soldiers into my domain more than once and sent them here to assassinate guests under my protection. His emissaries will be found and expelled, and we will be sending soldiers to secure the areas you are about to tour. Nothing is going to get through to you again."

"Thank you, My Lord."

"It is my job, nothing more."

"I'm sure it has nothing to do with the fact you...um, hate...well hate might be too strong a word...Lord Leviathan."

"I can assure you, dear boy; hate is not too strong of a word. It is, in fact, the precise word to use. Now if you will excuse me, I need to attend to the torture of our two visitors."

"More?" I said with concern.

"Far from it. These are the ones you tortured by turning inside out and locking them in their bodies, for which I am grateful. Now my people get to see what they can learn employing more traditional forms of coercion."

"Why?"

"They are guests are they not? They entered my Plane with intent to do a guest harm, did they not? Have we not covered this? I plan on rewarding them for a very long while. As you said yourself, working helps take our minds off our other problems. I bid you well, Keith."

I bowed as The Overlord left. Back in the apartment, I said, "It seems I don't need to see the lakes. The Overlord filled me in on their purpose. What's next? Let's get this Plane out of the way. It's time to get moving."

"I agree the lakes are relatively straight forward in their function and purpose," commented Elick. "I have your message; I am going to fly up and see the fireworks when Great Grandfather finds out there is a new player no one knows about who dispatched his soldiers in a single blow, then delivered them into the hands of Kritanta. It should be worth the trip. I will deliver your message as well. Remember, I will only allow Usis to read it. I will not allow him to keep it; we cannot take that risk."

"I was going to suggest the same thing. Be careful my friend, I will see you upon your return. Wait before you leave, I have a question I'm hoping one of you knows the answer to. The Overlord said the lakes were five hundred feet deep. What happens to the souls that get pushed under the water?"

Balthazar took the question. "I can answer that. They not only are subjected to the pain of all the suffering, but they do it with the misguided belief they are drowning. Of course, they cannot, breathing is not necessary any longer, but their bodies refuse to believe that. What I guess the Overlord left out is there are dozens of Scylla which patrol the upper waters and Hydras which patrol the depths. Most stray bodies eventually get eaten."

"Well shit, I was on the verge of blowing off the lakes, but now I want to see a Scylla and a Hydra," I replied in an extremely overly spoiled bratty tone.

"Do not worry; we can fly over later and see if we can spot any. It is probably safest to fly anyway. Then we will get you a treat afterwards, if you are good," joked Balthazar. It's good to see he picked up on my joke.

"With you delivering a challenge to Grandfather, by rights that should cease any further actions against you. He is honor bound to wait until you meet face to face," added Elick.

"Honor bound? Seriously?" I commented with a smirk.

"We don't have a lot of rules, and any created by the individual Overlords are often overlooked when needed. This falls into the dictates of Lord Lucifer. It would be very unwise even for my Great Grandfather to ignore those," commented Elick, "I am off now, you guys take care of him. I will be back in the morning for your weapons training."

"Will do and be safe."

# Entry 257

My Dearest Usis,

I received your letter and to say it lifted my spirits and brightened even this dark place would be such a disservice to its actual effect.

I miss you. I think of you every moment my mind will release me from the horrors of not having you by my side. As for your concern. I know about your changes, not specifically, Elick won't give me details but assures me I'll be very pleased. To be honest, though, your looks, though wonderful isn't why I love you, it's your heart and your soul, my dear. Please never doubt your importance to me. The living say, 'I will love you forever', then death comes, with us that is no longer a concern and therefore I can say with confidence that I will, indeed, love you forever.

At first, I wasn't happy about the decision you made, the hearts that is. Over time it has become not a source of stress or concern because I understand its intent. You did what you thought needed to be done in hopes of ensuring our safe existence after my obligations to The Dark Lord are complete. There will never be a way to be angry at you for such a caring act. It not only told me that you cared for our wellbeing but also that you were planning for our long-term future, something we've never really discussed. In your act I hope I've received my answer.

I'm well and will be making my way to you soon. Take care of yourself and do not let them harm you. I look forward each time Elick visits you, for his return brings you just a little closer to me.

Remember, my dear, my feeling for you and the love my heart carries for you has never waned, and with each day I grow more determined to have us again side by side.

Take care and know you are on my mind.

Keith

# Entry 258

*I stood in a bright room. The white marbled walls veined in gold flowed up to a painted ceiling and down to a delicate mosaic floor. To my left, the only opening was a balcony leading out to a view my mind couldn't comprehend. But I knew this place; I'd lived here for millions, no billions of years. It was The Eternal City.*

*I reached out a hand, and a servant was there with a goblet of wine. It was heavy, the wine sweet and aromatic. I looked to the girl, dressed in a Grecian tunic. She bowed as I dismissed her. As I took a sip, I heard feet on the balcony behind me. "Where have you been and for so long?"*

*"Father sent me to Alteia to deal with their awakening," answered Enepsigo.*

*I turned as my lips curve into a smile. "How did it go?"*

*"Not well, sadly they will be forsaken."*

*"No surprise, more and more of Father's little monkeys are turning our representatives away. Remember his first, Earth. What did they do? I cannot recall."*

*"Hung him from a tree."*

*"Oh, that is right." I laughed even though I knew I shouldn't. "It amazes me how when Father finally sends someone to confirm for the living their deepest desire, if we exist, how they often call them liars and torture them. Oh well maybe at some point Father will realize his mistake and end this folly."*

*"You sound more like Lucifer every day. What do you think about their latest tiff?"*

*"It is what it is. Father's firstborn has always been strong willed."*

*"Many think he should rule, and Father should rest. Create his dream and retire there."*

*"That will never happen. He is too stubborn and obsessed with those silly creations."*

I awoke with a cry, my body covered in sweat. This time it wasn't sadness or despair, but wonder. I'd seen The Eternal City. Cemal bounded into the room already in his Demon form. I held up a hand. "It's alright, Cemal, just a dream."

He shifted back, the glow leaving his body. "Another dream, Master? They are happening more often."

"No need to remind me. This one, other than its content, reminded me of something from Gabriel's Plane. Did you ever get a chance to talk to his servant? What was his name?"

"Zacul, Master, and yes this one did as Master wished."

"And?"

"This one would like to report the conversation went well, and there is much to tell. My brother (He calls all slaves his brother or sisters.) lived in the third Creation." Cemal started talking, and before I realized what was happening, I held up a finger, and he went silent. It stopped. No wait there it was. I latched onto it. I could see their conversation. Time had shifted, and I was watching them talk.

Shifting back, I explained this new development to Cemal. Just for a second, I mean a millisecond, I saw fear which he covered instantly with an outward expression of joy. "That is wonderful, Master."

I gave him a hard look; he was lying. "Why are you lying to me?"

His face all but melted. "Master?"

"I saw the fear, the apprehension that crossed your face. Why?"

"It is nothing, Master."

"Cemal?" I said in a warning tone. Not too harsh but it got the point across.

"This one is just afraid if Master..." he paused, "...evolves too far there will not be a need for this one any longer." I won't lie I read his thoughts; he was telling the truth. Yes, this was a new skill I discovered just now.

I pulled him in close. "That will never happen. Cemal, I'm not sure how many times I have to tell you this. You're not a slave; you're a friend, more to the point, you're family. I never had a child but if I did I imagine I would feel for them the same way I feel for you and that will not...cannot...change. Now come here and let me read your experience. This is new to me, it just manifested." He moved over and curled into my lap; I put my arms around him as he leaned back against my chest. Get your mind out of the gutter, I just said 'like a child' remember. I see nothing sexual in him. O.K. he does have a nice ass, but its pride not lust.

Before I got a chance to start, he asked, "Does it scare you?"

"What?"

"All these new powers."

"Sometimes, yes. Other times it's not that they scare me it's more like they shake my sense of myself. Just when I'm starting to feel I'm me again, well as me as I can be and look like a Demon, something happens, and I'm back to square one. Right now, I judge each new ability in the context of how I can use it to get Usis back."

I could see the events in my mind's eye, but they were direct representations of the interview. I wanted Cemal to fill in gaps, explain things and give his take. That was after all why I had him do it.

"Let's start with the obvious, did you get his history? You know, before his death?"

"This one asked, but he refused to tell me. He said it was another time, another life and he did not wish to relive it."

"Interesting considering he is in The Eternal City. He had to have lived a pretty decent life. As we all know, that is one hard ticket to get."

"They give tickets for The Host?" asked Cemal with a wrinkled brow.

"No, it's just an expression. OK, so no back story. Where was he willing to start?"

(Note: I'm going to intermingle my visions of Cemal's story with his telling. There are parts he doesn't see as important that I think are. He is good at telling the story as he remembers it, but he leaves out some of the images Zacul gives him. An example is his arrival at The Host.)

The first thing Zacul related to Cemal was the moment he awoke after death. I found it interesting considering, as I've recounted in this Journal my arrival in Hell, the differences between the two.

I awoke on the shores of a river, my body in the same condition it was at my death, my head having been crushed by a cab. He, on the other hand, awoke in a small park. He said he stood for several seconds confused until a person came walking up the path, stopping a foot or two away. He said the representative was the most strange but beautiful creature he'd ever seen.

They turned and walked up the path, the "angel" explaining that he, Zacul, had lived a very rare and special life. A life of meaning. A life deserving to stand in The Father's company.

They approached the gates to The Eternal City. He said the wall first struck him, it enclosed everything. (As I watched the replay of his thoughts the wall caught my attention as well. I'd heard so much about it. My question upon seeing it was, what were they protecting themselves from?) There were buildings of many heights both inside and out. He would later learn that most of those outside the walls were houses. Some of the protected buildings inside were like glorious cathedrals rising high into the clear sky with massive towers filled with balconies.

As they approached the gates, three other Angels walked down to meet them. There were no lines like in Hell, no great masses of souls. Today, as with most days, it was just one, him. The center Angel stopped before them and smiled. "Welcome, Zacul, we have reviewed your life and find it divine. You young one are deserving of an eternity without suffering. We invite you to set down the burdens of your old life and join us here, in the city of our Father."

Zacul started to cry at this point during his telling. At first, I like Cemal, thought it was the joy of reliving such an intense memory but come to find out it wasn't.

The welcomed him in, the city was a fairytale, his words not mine. I thought back to my dream from the night before. Had I not had it I'm not sure what my image of a "fairytale" would've been, but now I knew. I'd seen the city. Its tall white spires gilded in golds and silvers. The road which under the right light could have appeared gold as well. I know it wasn't, don't ask me how. I'd have to have been pulling from one of The Lover's memories. I remember when I thought it was gold how my mind corrected me saying, "We would never place such beauty beneath the feet of talking monkeys."

He talked about how rarely The Powers came down to street level. It was then I remembered, again from my dream, the balcony that Enepsigo landed on. They had wings; they didn't mix with the souls. I think I had an "of course" moment.

He went on and told how life in The Eternal City was in many ways no different than life when he was living. They had rooms, small, single bed, some personal effects they would acquire over time. Normally something the artisans made, little trinkets, statues of The Father, what we would call religious paraphilia. They were provided for, their food, drink, he made friends. Their days filled with jobs and mandatory rallies where they sang the praises of The Father. Everything revolved around serving The Powers.

Zacul, having worked in metals during his life, was assigned to the foundries. One day, when an order of laculic (a metal like gold or iron) was completed, he was instructed by one of the Lesser Powers to deliver the precious alloy to the Power who'd ordered it. It'd been one of the hardest requests he'd seen since starting there. The Power who ordered it demanded the mixture and purity be to an exacting standards. The Power was Gabriel.

He explained how difficult and in many ways demeaning it was to seek an audience with one of the Children of The Father, the Most High.

I remember him pausing. Cemal said he seemed stuck. In my view he was gauging what he should or shouldn't say, or how he should say it. Cemal was good at getting him to open up.

He went through the process to deliver the metal sheeting. Every time he talked about his delivery something kept causing an itch in my brain like I was missing something and then I got it. It was Gabriel, and he needed metal. He recalled being given a small alabaster disk by the lesser power and told it would allow him into the building. He found the entrance; it was in an alley and almost invisible. Inside was a simple room with a pedestal. He placed the disk in the slot and was instantly standing in a different white room with an ornate door on one wall.

Again, Zacul started to tear up, the difference from the first time was instead of tears of sadness there was a hint of happiness. I remember thinking, as cynical as I might be, that I'd hoped there would be happiness in this story. I'd spent years submerged like a drowning man in sorrow; I needed to believe the it wasn't this way for everyone. I'd learned during my time in Hell how much "we," the living, were despised by The Powers. I wanted, no needed, to hear there was still happiness somewhere in someone's eternity. That all stories didn't end in pain.

He continued after a few minutes. Cemal, bless his heart, had gone over and poured his fellow slave a drink. With the same respect he shows me when he serves, he extended the same to his brother. It was a touching moment, for both Zacul and me, you could see it in his eyes. Again, my cynicism kicked in. Cemal, a creature of Hell, created here, never having seen any other reality, always without fail treated everyone with respect. I was so proud of him at that moment.

He knocked, and another servant answered the door. At first, he didn't think he would get to enter. He could just barely see Gabriel sitting with his head down at a desk. He was deep in thought. Zacul handed the metal over, and just before the door closed, they both heard, "Come in, little one."

I will record this in Zacul's words. "I remember stepping into the room. I caught a glimpse of his Lordship as I dropped to a kneeling position on the pink marble floor, my head bowed. I heard him push his chair back and come around the table. The clack, clack, clack of his shoes against the floor. He stopped just in front of me. He was wearing boots, I know now they are his favorite, they are white and lace up to his knee. He knelt before me and with a finger under my chin he lifted my face. I met his eyes. Time stopped. I don't know how else to say it. I became lost in the depths contained inside those orbs. He was dressed in a simple tunic and tights but none of that mattered. It was the slight smile he wore that filled the room. "What is your name?"

"Zacul, My Lord."

He looked up. "What did he bring?"

"The metal Master was expecting."

"Oh yes, I recall it being ready. Go place it on my desk," he instructed. He goes to stand, but stopped, his finger is still under my chin. After removing it he stood. Turning to his servant, he said, "You may leave."

"In life I had never bowed, now here in my eternal reward I find myself on my knees."

"The boy bowed and slipped quietly from the room. I had not noticed until just that second as the boy walked away that he was nude."

Cemal asked. "Really? Do Powers you know....?"

I would have asked the same question, good for Cemal.

Zacul explained, "No, Master, not as such. See unlike The Fallen; The Powers do not have gender assigned to them. They often choose a gender, normally masculine, but as you have seen with my Master, there is still the refinement of the feminine gender as we the living would define it. They do, or at least my Master does, show affection when he is so inclined."

After the boy was gone, Gabriel had Zacul fetch him a drink from a bar at the far end of the room. He served Gabriel who was now sitting on one of the several couches and for a long time they talked. After several hours he was dismissed. He was surprised how Gabriel asked about his life. How closely the Angel paid attention to his every word. It made him feel, for that little bit of time, like Gabriel had nothing more important in all of Creation to do other than listen to him tell his story. I know it doesn't matter but I was proud of Gabriel for giving Zacul that small gift. The boy needed it.

Zacul explained that any sadness or more accurately disappointment he might have felt about how they were treated in The Eternal City evaporated with that encounter. "See the living are welcome only by an old edict of The Father's. But he is gone now, so it is only out of respect that they still observe his wishes. The Powers, due to their feelings about the living and how it led to the Great War and eventually The Father's disappearance, do not necessarily like the souls living in The Eternal city. That is why, citing an obscure comment made by The Father about allowing the souls of those who are worthy to serve for eternity in The Host, they see the living as nothing more than servants. Some even assigning us the title of slave. My Master is not one of them, though he most certainly holds the souls of the living in distain.

"Where in Hell your eternity is torture and pain. In The Host, those few of us who are allowed to enter will spend our eternity as servants. We are responsible for ensuring the city is kept running and up to the standards the Powers would expect. We are told time and time again always to be prepared for The Father's return. There are several classes of entities in The Eternal City. The souls of the living being the bottom caste where The Most High, as their name implies, are at the top. There are lesser powers who live amongst the souls. These are often souls as well, but they have in some way distinguished themselves as being almost divine."

I could have kicked Cemal for not exploring that more, but he didn't.

Finally, and yes, I know this is a long entry. Zacul explained how one day he was again summoned to Gabriel's quarters. He was told by the power (little p) that he needed to take his personal effects with him. He received the disk, and with a fear, so great his hands were shaking he transferred up to Gabriel's apartment. When he entered, Gabriel told him he would serve him now. Which is what he has been ever since. When pressed Cemal did manage to get him to admit that it's not all harp music and halos. Gabriel, like all the other Powers, has a temper and was very free when demonstrating his displeasure.

Cemal pushed a little more, I think as much for himself as for Zacul. It took a while, but he did get the boy to explain that accompanying Gabriel to Hell for his time on Blasphemy had been a gift. Because each person tends to see their situation within the scope of their own experiences. After his first stint in Hell, he saw The Eternal City in a different light. He said it hadn't changed but in contrast to what the alternative was, it truly was a reward to be allowed to live there. He was honored to serve under Gabriel. Yes, he had a temper, but he was overall a wonderful person. His life was filled with happiness once he got past his own hang-ups about being a servant. He said he understood that Hell wasn't as much the place but more the lack of the other place. His afterlife wasn't as he'd been told it would be while living but in contrast to what it could've been, the struggle it had been while living to be the type of person who was allowed to walk through those gates had been worth the sacrifice.

There is what the interview added up to. I'm sure you like myself would've liked more. But after they reached the part where Zacul became Gabriel's personal servant the boy would no longer give details. Clearly, Cemal understood, he said it was a code between their masters and themselves. Since Cemal is mine, I can't say I dislike knowing they are judicious with their master's personal information.

I want to add something Zacul said toward the end, after the official interview was over and he could see the disappointment in Cemal's face. Part of this is a repeat of some of the things he said earlier but I'm including it in its entirety, as he said it.

"Brother, understand any sadness I carried about my service in The Eternal City is only because of my preconceptions of what I thought it would be. Having served my Master as long as I have and having been in the room during many private conversations, I can safely report that those preconceptions are the folly of the living. We, not the Host, want to believe we will be welcomed in and be placed on pedestals and extolled for our wonderful deeds while living. It is us wanting to believe we are special and that is just not true. The Powers do honor those few of us who live lives of distinction, but we are still only there due to a technicality. If more time had passed between the time The Father created us and the Great War, The Father might have made his wishes clearer. He might, as many believe, have made a different place for the souls of the living outside The Eternal City. But all they have to go on are his wishes as stated before he left. Most of those comments, as I understand, were made in the heat of an argument with Lucifer and the council when he would grow angry. He would end the conversation by saying if a soul did ascend, they were to be welcomed home. It is not something The Most High wanted, quite the opposite. They saw The Host as their home, and The Father as their Father, we were just side effects of his misguided experiments."

Cemal thanked him, and that was the end of that.

# Entry 259

I wandered down to the main lobby wanting to spend some time in the Keep like I did the others. If I'd been welcomed on the Plane, I'd almost always enjoyed the Keeps. Often, due to my protected status, the Keeps seemed to be reasonably immune to the drama that saturated the halls of Hell like the screams of its residents.

As I emerged from the elevator, I realized I was alone. How did that happen? No escorts? I wandered through the lobby, taking this turn or that, just exploring. The eyeless creatures scurried about doing whatever it was they did. As one entered from the back, I decided it was the one I was going to tail. As it passed, I waited half a breath then followed it down one of the side halls.

It entered a large room made from the same stone as the rest of the Keep. The floor, walls, and ceiling were all mirror smooth marble pulsating with tens of thousands of soul stones attached to every surface. I stopped just inside the door and watched my mark as it found the wall it needed. Opening its hand flat, it skimmed its palms slowly down the rows of glowing crystals. Every few seconds it would stop, occasionally inclining its head, until finally finding what it was looking for, then it plucked the soul from the wall and scurried from the room.

As I turned to leave, I saw another little flying humanoid creature with hummingbird wings zip past me into the room. On his belt hung a bag, he reached in and pulled out a hand full of crystals. Sorting through them for a second, he took one and placed it in the empty spot created by the creature I had been following.

Racing to catch up I realized as I stepped into the lobby that all the fucking guys looked the same. I had no idea which one mine was. I guess it didn't matter, they're all doing the same job and probably going to the same place. So I just picked another one. As I was about to take off I noticed a ripple go through all the creatures in the lobby. I shook my head and turned to find Alcraw walking toward me as everyone else dropped to a knee and bowed as he passed. "Does that get old?"

"What?"

"The bowing and stuff?"

"It's according to how you look at it. I am a Hellspawn, the son of Molock. To not bow to me is to slight my family, my Father in by extension The Dark Lord himself."

"So, it doesn't bother you if it's not out of respect."

"I could care less their motives; they bow because I am one of The Powers. Why they bow, or their motives for doing so are insignificant to me, just as the creatures are. Are you currently occupied?"

"I was hoping I'd escaped and could take my time and look around."

"That is perfectly fine if that is what you wish. Elick suggested I take a turn with you to test how your fighting skills are coming along. He thinks you need more variation in your training."

"Great, just what I need someone else to kick my ass."

"He said the same thing, which was one of the incentives for me. I have not gotten to humiliate a soul in a while."

"You make it sound so appealing."

"It is inconsequential how it feels. Your time on this Plane will soon end, and your destiny awaits. You have a date with one of Hell's Generals, and his sword of office, forged and given to him by The Father. You can rest assured that will be his weapon of choice."

I faced Alcraw. "Sorry if I sounded short. Actually, I think I would welcome your company. We haven't had any time to get to know each other."

"Fine, let's go to the training grounds," he said as he turned and started back toward the main entrance. As I ran to catch up one of my wings flapped out hitting two passing creatures and knocking them against the wall. "I thought you could retract those things. You are becoming a menace." Alcraw said with a chuckle.

"They are retracted."

"No, I mean completely. Remember all that talk about Xia. I swear that is the problem with all you...talk, talk, talk, never getting anything done. Have you even tried to shift?"

"No, I think it was on the list of things to teach me, but we've never gotten around to it since it has little to do with the battle or the Plane. So, this isn't retracted?" I said looking up seeing the points arching just at the edges of my vision.

"No, let's see if you can fully retract them."

"Here? Right this second?"

"Sure, why not or would you prefer we have another long discussion about it, then maybe get around to trying it in a thousand years or so. It seems to be the way things are working right now."

"Fine...damn, you're grumpy. What do you want me to do?"

"Close your eyes and picture your wings shrinking. Picture them becoming like liquid metal."

I did as he asked. I tried to picture them shifting, to be more fluid, to become smaller. I understood the basic idea. Cartos and I had talked one night, he told me about his inability to change his body in any way. But having tried for so many years he had a great grasp of the mechanics. They'd always assumed it was because the flames were permanent, making his body hard to convert. That led me to ask what fuel powered his flame, if any. He said it was just part of his nature. They would, however, increase and decrease based upon his mood and intentions. In many ways it was like magic, he pulled from the things around him to feed his energy needs. He recounted how it was instrumental in bringing him and Xia closer together. Xia doesn't flame all the time but when he grows angry his body often becomes covered in blue flames so hot many have seen him melt his jewelry as rivers of metal flowed down his chest and arms.

I also found out why he was so reclusive, rarely going with us to tour the Plane or on nights out on the town. He has to power up, for lack of a better description, before he goes out or his body will automatically start pulling energy from the damned around him. He can wipe out an entire room in a single evening.

As I concentrated, I felt a ripple travel up my spine. "That is good, but segregate it to your wings, you are changing the whole back of your torso." I did as he said and within a few minutes just the wings were shimmering. "Good, now tell your body you want to absorb that matter back into yourself."

It took several tries, but I managed to do it, my wings were gone. Sadly, my back looked like a failed science experiment. "That is good, you will need to work on smoothing out the look, but now at least we know you can transform. And you learned about a new ability without a lot of talk."

"Do I just visualize it like I do when I'm forming something using energy?"

"It is exactly the same. Just visualize what you want and then manifest it. It does not matter if it is an attack, a wingless back or a full set of wings. Now bring them back. You will need your wings during training."

I found out quickly that bringing them back was far easier than hiding them. My body knew what it considered my base state, so returning to it was no problem at all.

We headed across the city. The streets were still as crowded, but the rain had stopped. I think I was driving Alcraw crazy, which seems easy, because I kept stopping as I saw different creatures. One to catch my attention was outside this take-out joint. Not sure what they were selling. It was a ten-foot long purple warty lizard creature, with an oversized torso, a long muzzle like a crocodile, complete with teeth, three human-looking legs, two in the back and one on its chest just below its head. It walked on all three legs; there wasn't a way for it to stand up. What caused me to notice it wasn't only the creature itself but when a small possum thing tried to run under it, a tongue shot out from its underside grabbing the rodent and pulling it into a huge mouth filled with even more teeth. It slurped, chewed as little bits of the small creature fell to the ground. Those were quickly snatched up by a seven-foot-tall bird creature with a tongue as long as it was tall.

"You coming?"

"Sorry, there seem to be more varieties of mutated creatures here than I've seen anywhere else in Hell."

"You clearly have not been paying attention. It is the same everywhere. But here the less common varieties are due to the labs; they are always coming up with new variations."

"See what confuses me is these things remind me of paintings back on earth from the Middle Ages. They're more what my world pictures Hell to look like."

"That makes sense, most of the living that astral project or are pulled down here often land on the Great Plane where they take back their memories of the things they see. Some go to the other Planes but very few. Only Higher Demons or above really have the skill necessary to bring a soul, even temporarily to Hell. There are some Damned who have the skills, but they have often apprenticed under a more trained magical master to learn the craft."

"The living can come to Hell?"

"At times, normally they are extremely powerful or skilled and have either dedicated themselves to The Dark Lord or one of his Generals, Hellspawns or the Greater Demons."

"I've never met any."

"Like I said most go to the Great Plane."

"As for the art. You're saying that after seeing the Great Plane, they assume that's what all of Hell looks like?"

"Correct," laughing he added, "It is also not uncommon for a summoner here in Hell to hold their rituals in a place which will ensure the living they are working with are sufficiently impressed with what they see."

"Stage dressing? They make it look like the commonly accepted version of Hell, so the living don't get the idea that there are noodle shops and bars visited by the run of the mill working Demons?"

"That is an oversimplification, but none the less accurate. Ah, here we are."

# Entry 260

I'm breaking this entry into two. Elick showed up just as we were about to get started. I want to cover what he said was as well as my combat training. Oh, and a spoiler alert, swords are heavy.

"I've always wondered. If The Father is this nice old guy who believes in peace and love, why did he equip all The Powers with swords as their symbol of office?"

"We both know from the start that premise of your analogy is not correct. The Father has never been about peace. Look at the books he gave each of the worlds. Even in their basest form there is more aggression than love."

"Well I know the Bible and Quran are that way. Just curious which one are you referring to?"

"The Bible, that other one has nothing to do with The Father. The Quran was an experiment early on by one of Lucifer's Generals. He wanted to see if they could send propaganda to the living in hopes of speeding along The Father's failure with his talking monkeys. It was a rousing success. As for the Bible, where did The Father ever show love and peace? As I recall from class, when we studied your world, most of his actions were vicious, often killing the person or persons which upset him."

"But he preached peace and love?" I wasn't defending The Father as much poking at Alcraw.

"And what is the first rule of Creation? What do we keep telling souls over and over? Even The Father said it. Let me give you a hint, what will they be judged by?"

"By their acts, not their words. So, it's do as I say not as I do?"

"Exactly. The Father can destroy at will because to him you are nothing more than playthings. For you to kill yourselves is in many ways the living trying to subsume The Father's authority. Look at this Plane. Look at how many synthetic beings are by their nature violent as well. They were created by the living who were created by The Father, who at his core used destruction as his means of Creation. Look at all the wasted civilizations still floating destroyed in The Void," Alcraw said.

I already knew the answer. "So you're saying that violence isn't learned but instead a trait accidently installed by a creator who knew no other way to deal with conflict. He by his very nature was violent, so it was only logical that such tendencies would be passed on to his creations, who would eventually pass them on to theirs."

"Exactly. Now here is a strange quirk to add to this discussion. Synthetic races whom eventually make even more advanced replacements of themselves often program out violence completely. Does this not lead you to believe, like many here in Hell do, that The Father when he started trying to create life was maybe too immature himself to have ever be successful in his endeavors?"

"Greetings everyone," said Elick, cutting off what was turning into a deep discussion. I needed to corner Alcraw more often.

"You're back. How did it go?" I asked. I could hear the nervousness in my voice.

He led me to a bench against the wall, only making me more nervous. "He is good." (He knew I was only interested in Usis.) "He was very touched by your scroll. It is interesting how both of you are dancing around the changes in your bodies. I assured him the two of you would soon be back together."

"But?"

"After the meeting with Great Grandfather, I can see it happening sooner than expected."

"Why? What happened?"

"He signed the challenge, agreeing to the battle. He was more amused than serious. He saw signing it as a way to humor all of us, unwilling to believe we could actually think there was any doubt about the outcome. He does not see how a soul can defeat an entity like himself. What worked in our favor was Beelzebub was there with a message from The Dark Lord which I was instructed to give to you, as well. He wants all parties involved to be know he sanctions this challenge. He also wanted it made clear that all hostilities were to stop until both combatant's step into the arena. As a direct warning to my Grandfather, Lucifer ordered that you, Keith, were to be allowed onto the Plane, reunited with your companion and not hindered in the execution of your duties for him. In exchange for Grandfather's cooperation, it was also agreed that if he wins the both of you will be turned over to him to do with as he chooses."

"WHAT?"

"Keith, remember, at that point your duties to The Dark Lord will have been completed, and he will have no further use for you. You are the one issuing the challenge. You cannot expect him to force one of his generals to comply and not preemptively attack and then also tell him that there will be no reward if he wins the challenge. You rolled the dice; now you have to deal with the risks involved."

"Believe it or not, I do..." No one spoke for several seconds until I added, "So I just need to finish this Plane, and then Usis and I can be reunited?"

"It would appear so. I encourage you to take your time. I know you are eager to return to Usis but rushing to Great Grandfather's Plane would set in motion everything else involved in the visit, not to mention being extremely unwise."

"Why?" I asked.

"You need to start thinking more than one step ahead," said Alcraw with a laugh. Turning to Elick, he added, "May I?" to which Elick nodded for him to continue.

"You issue a challenge. I can assure you that pissed Lord Leviathan off. Then to add insult to injury, our Lord sends his second in command to deliver a message and a warning, which can easily be seen as a slight. So, what does he do? He now agrees to a challenge he is sure he will win. Knowing Lord Lucifer as he does and knowing he has opted to step into the middle of this mess, he can assume The Dark Lord understands more of the variables than probably either of the involved parties do. One of those variables we know Lucifer knows, that we also know Leviathan does not know, is that you are now a Power as well. Which should lead you to wonder what variables favor Leviathan that we do not know. Thus, Leviathan agreed for you two to be reunited hoping you will rush to his Plane where he holds sway. There he can monitor, without getting involved, your training and planning from a distance. Not knowing about the hearts, he also does not know you have become relatively proficient at magic. More importantly you have also, in equal but opposite measures, proven you are not overly proficient in hand to hand combat. These are all cards in the deck, the ones he does not presently know about needs to stay that way."

It doesn't take an Einstein to realize that if I were not careful, I could easily be played. "I see your point."

"Keith, this is as much a combat lesson as is spending time with a sword. You have challenged a creature who has for trillions of years helped plan the course of entire Creations. Great Grandfather is not thinking a couple of moves ahead; he is thinking entire games ahead. We were all hoping he would see this challenge as so insignificant as to not think about it at all. Now that has changed, by Lord Lucifer getting involved everyone is starting to look for what they have missed, knowing something is not as it seems. You must do the same. Each move you make publicly at this point must be thought out in detail. You have to find a variable which everyone is still overlooking that you can exploit," added Elick.

"How am I supposed to compete with Leviathan in that aspect?"

"You are new to this; we are not. We have been trained in the games of Hell since birth. That is why we are here, that is why the others are here. They all have something to offer you. Use it."

"Point taken. We need to watch out for his minions, his servants," I say remembering a movie I saw once.

"I am not following you."

"In a movie back on Earth called 'Becket,' King Henry II after promoting his dearest friend to the position of Archbishop of Canterbury finds that his friend, Tomas Becket, instead of deciding to do Henry's bidding was going to do God's or the Church. As time went on and this became more of a problem their friendship fell apart. Henry knew he couldn't attack Becket since he was a bishop of the Church. One night after drinking he poured his sorrows out to his generals. Telling them how Becket was becoming such an insurmountable problem for him and his ability to rule his country. Them being loyal to their Lord and Master, the King, took it as a hint that since Henry couldn't move against Becket, they needed to. One night when they knew Becket was in Westminster Abbey, they entered, locked the doors and executed the bishop seeing it as a duty to their King. My point is, Leviathan may not be able to watch, or attack me directly, but if he makes his displeasure known what is the chances one of his loyal Generals or soldiers won't see it as their duty to do what their Lord and Master cannot?"

I could see such pride in their faces as they looked at each other. "He learns quickly," commented Alcraw.

"You are correct, Keith. That document only ensures Grandfather will not order someone to move against you; it does not guarantee that someone loyal to him will not take it upon themselves, seeing it as a way to curry favor." To Alcraw, Elick added, "has he has gotten no better?"

"You are here, find out."

In the flash, Elick's sword appeared at his side and was drawn and headed toward my head. That wasn't the surprising part, what was is the sword I had picked to spar with met Elick's midstride.

You think I was surprised you should've seen their faces; they were both stunned. Don't be fooled Elick quickly recovered, bringing his sword around and in from the left. I dropped mine, and as our blades came together in sparks, I forced the tip of his to the ground.

Again, he recovered, stepping forward into an attack. In a split second, I tried something I'd never tried before. I blocked, used the information from earlier and reformed my wings, then flapped once pulling myself back 20 feet outside his range. I heard Alcraw clap as Elick dropped his sword to his side as his eyes moved between us.

"I just realized your wings were gone," he announced.

"I taught him. Imagine what he could learn if you don't jabber endlessly," snarked Alcraw. "On a whim I had him try to retract them, he was able to with his first try. It was a bit messy, but he got it done."

"But to reform them so quickly, that is amazing."

"I agree," added Alcraw. "Tell me how you work out such a complicated strategy so quickly?"

"I'm not sure what you mean."

"You countered, decided to form your wings, brought them forth which took thought, then pulled yourself backward out of range. Explain how you made those decisions."

I could already see Elick nodding. "I didn't, I just reacted."

"That is what I thought. Your mind did not give you a chance to second guess Enepsigo's skills."

"Ohhhh...," I said.

"The underlying lesson here is what?" asked Elick.

"Trust my instincts. I keep hearing that." I answered.

"You have the skills to fight. Like the other day in the city, you used magic without really forming a plan. You just reacted. Work with that," said Elick.

"You are a writer; some might say a thinker..." Alcraw smiled evilly, "we have always assumed your biggest problem was going to be acting on instinct and not over-thinking your attack."

"That does not mean don't plan. As you become more comfortable and start seeing how your opponent fights, their technique, you should be able to chart their next attack and exploit their weaknesses.

What I am not sure of is if you will have the time to become comfortable enough with yourself to trust those reactions so that you can study theirs during a battle," explained Elick.

With a smile, I raised my sword and pointed it toward him. "There's only one way to find out. Let's dance."

For the next several hours we sparred and slowly by forcing myself to relax and not second guess I was able to press the attack instead of just defending myself. There was no chance I'd beat him, but at least this time I didn't look like a complete idiot. I got better but more importantly, today's practice gave me a determination and understanding about what I needed to start doing and what to look for. Up until now, I wasn't even sure I wouldn't die with my own blade by my own hand, let alone win a battle. Now I was feeling the blade as an extension of myself and less a clumsy tool. I still had to figure out how to combine this with magic, because I had far more confidence in those skills.

In case you wonder why I haven't talked more about the combat training reread the paragraph above. I sucked and I really didn't see the need to chronicle my failures. Plus, as I said before, sword fighting in a word is boring unless you're one of those gifted authors who can bring it to life. I'm not one of them.

# Entry 261

When I got back to the room it was empty. This is becoming a thing. A good thing, but still a thing. At first, I ignored the noise across the darkened apartment. Then froze when I heard it again, this time I listened and turned just in time to see this strange little creature flying toward me with a dagger in its hand.

I squeaked, I know not very butch, as those reflexes people keep telling me to use kicked in, I let loose a fire ball toward the creature and missed. As it darted to the left, I followed up with another and missed again. As it raced around the room, I continued sending blast after blast at the damn thing. Yes, I kept missing. Finally, as the little creature zigged, my fire ball zagged it hit him square in the chest. As he dropped to the floor screaming the fireball quickly consumed him. In a few seconds the cries of pain stopped followed by all movement.

That's when I heard a second one. It had seen me set its cohort on fire so it took off running toward the balcony. In the split second I took to decide what to do, it froze in place, mid-air, mid-run.

"Did you intend to blow up the room? I sure hope that was the plan otherwise your aim sucks." I heard from behind me. Before I knew what I was doing I materialized my sword (how the fuck did that happen?) and spun around toward the sound. As the rotation of my head caught up with my swing, I realized it was Balthazar.

"Oh Shit," I barked trying to stop but by now it was being carried by its own momentum. That is until it stopped. Not slowed but stopped. Hard. My arms and chest felt like I'd just hit the side of a brick wall with a baseball bat. When my watering eyes cleared the sword's edge was several inches from Balthazar's neck, "Nice swing," he said as he walked by. Letting the sword drop to my side I turned and followed him across the room. I know I should've been focused on everything and anything but the fact he was shirtless. I had never even seen him without that hooded cloak he wore. I stared.

"You had your chance," he said with a smile as he stopped in front of the little creature, adding, "Well, well, well, what do we have here?

Seems we have a guest." Turning back to me, he asked, "Did you invite an imp up? Not really your style, is it?"

"What, ohhhh, No!" I barked. "Him and the other one were in the room when I got here."

"Oh that's right. Can you do anything without making a mess?" he asked as he looked around the burning room. "We should probably do something about that. Boy, there is Imp all over the floor. Be so kind as to clean it up."

I don't know where Cemal came from but there he was, with a rag and a disapproving look in his face. "Master, was it your intention to burn down the room?"

"No..." I growled as Balthazar pointed to the remains of the toasted imp. You'd think it would be drier, I set it on fire after all.

Cemal looked at it, then at the spots of fire, then Balthazar, then me, then back at the imp. "This is gross. Master's room is already on fire, would he like to take another shot to finish it?"

"You just don't want to clean up the mess," I said as Balthazar and I walked over to the creature.

"Master's assessment of the situation would be accurate," said the boy as he knelt down. "Owwww...owwwww... who knew imps were so...well...squishy."

Turning my attention to the imp we'd captured I could now apprise it without having it attack me. It couldn't have been more than maybe three feet tall. He was humanoid with a bloated grey body wearing nothing but a loincloth. The wings on his back looked in worse shape than he did. In a lot of ways, he reminded of a bald pug with long pointy teeth (I love saying that) which were more brown than white.

About then, and right on que, Kitar, Elick and Alcraw burst in the room. "Are we being attacked?" barked Alcraw as he looked around the room.

"No, our little writer here said he felt cold," commented Balthazar in the driest of tones.

"What the Hell? Why are you burning down the room?" barked Kitar as he started putting out the fires.

"I think he was practicing his aim. If this is the case, in that respect your weapons training is failing miserably."

"Hey, I almost took your head off with my sword," I retorted.

"Yes, keep believing that if it helps. As for being attacked, there is this," commented Balthazar as he picked the still frozen little imp out of the air by his hair. "I think we have a spy." Turning to the creature he asks very nicely in baby talk, "Are you a spy?" (Yeah, try to picture a Hellspawn doing baby talk. It's not cute like he hoped, its creepy.)

It didn't answer.

"You probably need to unfreeze it first," added Elick as he joined Kitar putting out our room.

"Oh right," said Balthazar as he snapped his fingers with his other hand. "Good thing my friend here came to your rescue. I was about to see how many pieces I could make out of you for being rude. Now answer the question."

Which the little thing did not.

"Now he's being rude," smirked Alcraw who was still leaning in the doorway watching.

"Bel, why don't you set him down and let's find out what he knows," said Elick in that normal low seductive tone. Don't ask me why interrogating a little imppie thing makes me horny. It's probably not the imp interrogation as much as the extremely well-muscled thin physique of Balthazar which I swear I'm still not staring at.

"What do we do with him?" I asked.

Surprisingly all eyes went to Balthazar who was still studying the creature quiet closely. "I think I have an idea. This could serve as a bit of training for our pyro here. If no one else minds?" explained Balthazar looking around to Elick and Alcraw, who both shrugged.

"I would also like to point out his aim was with fire balls not a blade. It think this one is on you, Bel, not us," added Elick.

"Really, that is what you are focusing on?" laughed Balthazar.

"Training how? You want me to blow him to bits? If Leviathan sent him, I won't have any problems with that," I asked.

"Please, Master, no, the room cannot take much more," cried Cemal in a mock pitiful tone.

My head snapped around as the others start laughing. He just smiled and did that bowing thing. I think that's his way of getting out of trouble.

"No. What I have in mind turns the table back on your beloved Great Grandfather. First, we will teach the young one here how to enslave it. Secondly we will also instruct him how to install motivations discouraging our new spy from revealing his enslavement as well as some mild incentives to obey any commands he might be given." Turning to me he added, "do you have any problems with that?"

"He is a spy for Leviathan, right?" I asked.

"Correct."

"The person holding my companion?"

"Correct."

"The Fallen whom I'm going to fight and probably be killed by?"

"Also Correct...." I gave him a sharp look, "...absent a miracle. Better?"

"No, not really." Now it was my turn to lean down. "Will this process be painful?"

"On you or him?"

"Him...wait, will it be painful on me?"

Shaking his head, he replied, "No, not on you... on him probably."

"When do we start?" I say with my own evil grin which really didn't seem to be working.

The Demon looked up. "Fine, do you worst. The one I was sent to find clearly is not here. Once I return with no information I will be tortured anyway, it might as well be you. Wait..." he looked at Elick, "are you not the Master's great-grandson. Oh, it's going to be torture for both of us."

"Wait..." I said, "we just entered an agreement with Leviathan to cease all hostilities. Is this going to violate that?"

"No, as you can see, he is still sending..." explained Elick then he stopped turning to the creature. "When were you sent?'

"Will answering your questions keep me from being tortured?" he asked.

Leaning down and almost hissing in the creature's ear Balthazar said, "It will not stop your punishment, but it will assist in assessing the degree. How badly do you want to suffer?"

"Just yesterday, My Lord," he answered as a look of terror grew in his eyes.

I don't know, everyone's worrying about me losing my humanity, especially Kitar. As Balthazar stood, I stepped in to talk to the little Demon. "This is what's going to happen. I'll promise you won't be tortured just punished if you let us down. The amount of pain you suffer, if any, is completely in your hands." I found myself doing the same thing which had been done to me since arriving in Hell. Reaching down, with one finger, I placed it under his chin and lifted his head till our eyes met. "Do you understand?"

"Yes, My Lord."

"Good. Let us begin," I said.

Over the next few hours Balthazar taught me how to enslave the little creature. Believe it or not, it's a lot like reprogramming. In two areas of his mind we installed different feelings. First in the time prior to me walking into the room, we created a deep loneliness, a longing, an unending sadness for something missing he couldn't describe. Next, from the second he saw me that ache ended. He felt fulfilled. He had found his purpose for existing, me. Each time he fulfilled one of my wishes the ecstasy he would experience was like an addictive drug. Therefore, if he didn't reveal he was a spy, if he did something to aid me, anything which served my interests rewarded him a massive wave of pleasure.

After we were confident he was enslaved we added the second part, punishment. Here Balthazar did most of the work. He again programmed the creature with levels of disappointment. If he overlooked something small which could aid us it would be nothing more than a feeling of disappointment. If he even thought about giving away his mission, he'd physically become ill, this would grow in severity based upon how strong the urge was. If he resolved to reveal his enslavement and took steps to do so, like going to see Leviathan or someone in power, just as the words formed on his lips, he'd drop dead.

The final step was the most important to me, we installed an ability to see and hear through the little guy's body. We set it up so Alcraw, Elick, Balthazar and myself could access his vision and hearing as well as give him new commands. Unlike the last spy, this time I wouldn't be a passive visitor but able to direct his actions and watch their outcome through his eyes.

After the three Hellspawns were sure all the magic was in place and working they released the creature. I went and sat down beside Kitar. He'd been too quiet. "Do you think this is a mistake?" I asked.

At first, he didn't answer. "I understand your intentions and cannot say I disagree. I am just unsure about how I fell about enslaving a creature to your will."

"So, you do not approve?"

"I did not say that. To be honest, the creature is nothing more than a construct. He was created as a tool and you are using him as such."

"He breathes, thinks and has self-realization. Should him being a construct matter?" I asked.

"To be honest, Keith, that is a question you will need to answer within yourself. You are now not only a resident of Hell but stand the potential to be a powerful one. Even if you are defeated no one but Lucifer can destroy you. How you see and treat the damned, Demons and created creatures is entirely up to you."

"You need to test the connection," I heard Alcraw say from across the room.

That is when it struck me that I'd never really thought about life after getting Usis back. Who I was? Who had I become? Who would I be? I know I've been writing about all that's happening, all my dreams of the future. But only the immediate future, not down the road. It hadn't really sunk in. I looked around, everyone was staring at me. Taking a deep breath, I realized if I've learned anything its not to let anyone know the weaknesses. I just closed my eyes and tried to settle my mind. Then reached out for the connection with the imp.

At first nothing happened and then there in the blackness I saw a small light. I turned my attention to it and willed my mind that way. In a flash the light grew bigger and took shape, it was the creature. I continued to zoom in until I entered the back its head.

I swayed as my vision shifted from my own to that of the creature's as he stumbled catching himself on a cart parked on the side of a path. "Master, careful you almost knocked me on my ass," the creature barked to no one at all. Passersby didn't pay any attention.

"Can you hear me?" I thought.

"Yes, Master."

"Good, I was just testing the connection. Next time don't give me away when I visit. Keep our conversations in your head. Is that clear?"

"Yes, Master."

"Get back to Leviathan's Keep and see if you can find a way to check on my companion. I know he's there but I've no idea where. I'll check back with you soon."

"It will be an honor Master and thank you for trusting me with a chance to please you," the creature said. Being in his mind, seeing and feeling what he was, I could read his excitement at being given a task and a chance to fulfill it. He started to run, racing toward the Keep. His only desire to find Usis so he could feel more pleasure by pleasing me.

# Entry 262

I was surprised at how when I broke the connection, I was disoriented. They said it was normal and would become easier with more practice, even an hour later at dinner; I was still a bit off. I didn't eat much and couldn't tell you what the conversation was about. While Cemal was clearing the dishes I announced, "I need something to distract me from this afternoon. What's left on this Plane to visit?"

"Just the labs or Cathedral."

"The Cathedral, what is that?"

"It is the beginning of the trials for the clergy of false religions or those who chose to usurp The Father's duties, placing themselves between him and his children."

"Wait, I thought Blasphemy dealt with those punishments."

"That is their ultimate destination. You met the lesser clergy, like that Bakker fellow. They go directly to Blasphemy but..." Kitar paused and thought. "Your world's Priest and Popes, for example, begin their trials here."

"What differentiates them from the others?"

"As you can imagine, few sins are worse than trying to presume yourself equal with The Father. The clergy does it when they place themselves between The Father and his children. Where the living slip up is when they presume to pass judgment on others. Both are considered unforgivable. The clergy are first sent to Fraud to atone for the ways they misguided their flock then they travel to Blasphemy to face their punishments there."

"Ultimately being raised into the cavern to await their turn in the brewery?"

"Correct."

"Let's pay them a visit so that I can scratch them off the to-do list."

In the lobby, we bumped into the Overlord. "Greetings, young one. What is your destination today?"

"We're going to see the Cathedral," I said. To my ears, it sounded more like a question than an answer. I looked to Kitar to make sure I had the right name. He nodded.

"That region is an important part of my realm's responsibilities. I think you will find it interesting," it said. As we turned to walk off, I heard the Overlord add, "Please don't burn it down."

# Entry 263

We made our way back to the passage leading to the Brewery and descended deeper. Several hundred feet this time. I noticed the temperature rising the deeper we went; it was getting hotter, much hotter. When we touched down, we were standing in a small room with a door. I know, another door. This one so hot it was practically glowing red.

As Kitar opened the door the heat almost knocked me off my feet. It wasn't the temperature as much as the texture of the air. It was dense almost like walking through red hot cotton candy. I was glad to see the physical heat doesn't appear to have much effect on my body any longer.

"Why's it so hot? I thought this Plane was cooler," I asked.

"Do you want me to tell you or do you want to do your job?"

I found us standing in a dimly lit cavern which appeared to be as big as the brewery. The walls and ceiling were half barrel shaped curving up from the floor and becoming lost in the gloom overhead. The room was tiled with rough bricks, each about a yard square. The only light came from the stones which were currently glowing a dull red, probably the source of the heat. This room appeared to be little more than a giant kiln. In many ways, it looked like Hell's version of the old catacombs below some of the French and English cathedrals. Which I guess makes sense, they called it The Cathedral, after all.

Before me was a ragged line of battered and beaten souls waiting patiently for whatever was next. As we entered, I could see in their eyes that lost defeated look of creatures whose privileged lives had ended only to now be facing an eternity of pain and torment. I motioned for Kitar to lead; he had a way with crowds. As ordered, he barked, I love saying that, and two guards appeared from each side. They talked quietly for a few seconds, then Kitar motioned for me to follow him to the right side of the room where a separate path led to the front of the queue of endless souls.

"All these souls are clergy from different creations. They are waiting to see the Seekers at the front of the line," explained Kitar

I didn't see the need to ask any questions at this point; I knew when we reached the Seekers I'd get most of the answers I needed. Plus, I was, as usual, busy taking in the assortment of different species. Normal I look for any humans, and there were plenty in line. I found the last three popes, John Paul 2, Benedict, and Francis. I nudged Kitar and pointed. "Those three guys over there were the Popes of The Catholic Church while I was living. I don't see John Paul I, but then I don't think he lasted but a week or so."

"Do you wish to use them as case studies?"

"Not yet, let's see what happens and then I'll decide. They have a lot to be held accountable for." Before I could expound my attention was drawn away as we arrived at the front.

We stopped and stood near the wall as we watched the dozen or so Seekers at tables doing their thing. In a lot of ways, this was all very reminiscent of the DMV.

In a respectful tone, Kitar approached one of the Seekers and introduced us. Though every Plane had them, this was probably the first time I'd ever talked to one of Hell's sorters of sin. As always, they were represented as naked wrinkled old crones with saggy tits and long tangled white hair down to their waist through which crawled hundreds of tiny maggots.

"Greetings, my Lady, if you would be so kind as to take a moment, we come as a representative of The Dark Lord. My friend here is tasked with telling Hell's story."

Turning but not rising, she studied me. When her dark red pupil-less eyes locked on mine I stumbled and grasped Kitar. I was no longer in the Cathedral, I was back in my life, living, at first as a child and then quickly, so quickly as to become lost in vertigo, my mind flashed forward through the events of my life, its sins and the acts which led me to this place. I screamed as the images stopped and I collapsed to the floor.

As my vision cleared and I was again in The Cathedral, I found Kitar standing over the Seeker whose hand was on her cheek as she was picking herself up off the floor. It didn't take long to realize Kitar had slapped her.

"You will never turn your gaze upon the servants of Our Lord Lucifer again, is that clear?" barked Kitar, angrier than I'd seen him in a while.

I rushed over and extended a hand helping the frail old crone back into her chair. Once she was seated, she looked up again, causing me to flinch. "Do not worry the Lord Judge has made his warning clear. I will not turn my gaze upon your sins again," she said in a raspy voice. To Kitar she added, "Forgive us, Lord Judge, it has been a very long time since we have been allowed to look upon a soul and not upon their transgressions. How may I be of service?"

"Do you have a room with more privacy?" he asked.

"This way, please," she says as she leads us to a door off to the side of the chamber. Now for clarity, I feel it's important to remind you I've only explained the front third of the chamber. Where the souls await judgment. Behind the Seekers, in the remaining two-thirds, are thousands of souls hanging upside down from the ceiling over coals.

She led us to a room no bigger than fifty feet square with only benches against each wall. As she invited us to sit, she asked, "How may I be of service, Lord Judge?"

"Before I start, I need you to understand that what I am about to tell you must not be repeated under any circumstances. Even to one of the Fallen or their Generals," explained Kitar.

Smiling a crooked toothless smile, the Seeker responded, "I have seen his existence. I understand your concern. I have not spoken to anyone but the damned in a million years. What would ever give you the impression that will change anytime soon?"

"I understand, it just needs to be made clear."

"Is there to be another uprising? You know, Lord Judge, those such as myself do not involve themselves in the petty politics of the Master's realm."

"No, there is not to be an uprising. What you cannot repeat by orders of Lord Lucifer is the appearance of the soul here with us now. This is Keith, Lord Lucifer's writer," explained Kitar in the form of an introduction.

"Lord Judge, my overstep...." She rubbed her jaw, "...showed me more than a simple soul from Earth in Creation 1. Inside him is now housed two of The Powers, or The Fallen, or The Cast out, whichever name you might wish to assign them."

"And that is what you must never reveal."

"As Lord Judge wishes. How might I be of service?"

"Keith here is writing of his journeys through Hell. Now we are here, and I would like you to explain what happens in The Cathedral. Start with the lines leading to you, Seekers."

Nodding, the partial smile never faded. Turning to me she began, "My sisters and myself are nothing but taskmasters. It is our job to welcome a damned soul consigned to our charge and to task them with their next punishment."

"Next? They're punished and then return? Why?" I asked.

"See, young one, each of the souls in this place was at one point, while living, patriarchs and matriarchs of their bastardization of The Father's teachings."

"Like the Popes from my world. They ran the Holy Roman Church."

"Exactly, my boy."

"What is their sin?" I remembered what they told me earlier, but I wanted to her describe it.

"Each of these souls took upon themselves the sins of their flock. They lead their sheep to believe they were the intermediaries between the living and The Father. That unto itself would have only destined them for Blasphemy. Where their more serious sin began is when they also attempted to usurp the powers of The Father. They led their followers to believe they, a living soul, had the power to condemn, judge and more importantly forgive these souls of their sins."

"And they were wrong?"

"Acutely."

"So that explains why they're here, what's their punishment?"

"As I have just said, they took upon themselves the sins of their flock. Now they are here, and it is time to pay for those sins. The Father in his eternal wisdom has accepted these souls' offer to absorb their flocks' sins. Therefore it is now time for them to visit the applicable Planes and serve out their punishment in unison with the sinner to whom they falsely absolved."

"Wait, so they suffer every sin of every person that confessed to them at the same time as the actual sinner does?"

"Forgive me. When I say in unison, I only mean, as well. The soul itself is only consigned to the Plane befitting the sin they most celebrated during life. The blasphemous usurper will suffer every sin confessed to them and then falsely forgiven."

"So, you're saying; the actual soul goes to say Gluttony because that was the ruling sin in their life. Where the priest who claimed to have forgiven them will suffer for every sin they forgave regardless if it's the sinner's main sin or not."

"Yes, the soul who sinned was not forgiven, for no living has that power. Their souls are still weighed down with the burden of their transgressions. Since these intermediaries choose to step between The Father and his lambs and to accept the sins of the souls in their flock. The Father feels they should be willing, even eager to suffer in their steed."

I started laughing. I started laughing hard. Finally, after all this time in Hell, I found a sinner who got exactly, down to the letter, what they deserved. Oh, but wait it gets better.

After I had stopped laughing, I asked, "On a serious note, what about the sins they allowed?"

"That is too broad a question. Please explain your meaning," asked the Seeker.

"Out there I saw three popes from during my life. All three of them resided over and ignored one of the churches biggest scandals and in no subtle way, condoned it. The Catholic church had a problem with priests raping children and nuns. I'd hope that sin doesn't only fall upon the pedophile priests who betrayed so many but also upon the leaders who turned a blind eye?"

"I will answer this," interrupted Kitar. "Your world's Catholic Church is a perfect example of a sadly common bigger problem. That being when The Father's houses become houses of sin instead of houses of divinity. To put it bluntly, no one in that religion during the time of the atrocities will ever see The Eternal City."

"Not even the members of the religion?"

"No one. The flock supports all houses of worship. They not only attend but fund those houses. Like in the case of your Catholic Church, when the congregation becomes aware of the atrocities and continues to allow those who are committing or allowing the sins to stay in power, then they are condemning their own souls to eternal damnation. Simply put, they become participants of the said sin. It falls upon those congregations, at the cost of their souls, to ensure those who have committed and sanctioned these atrocities are pulled down and cast out of The Father's house. By not doing so, they become damned as well."

"Perfect, I couldn't think of a better thing to happen to all those self-righteous pricks who allowed their children to be molested and continued to follow the fuckers who did it, good for Hell."

"I will forward your approval to The Dark Lord. I am sure he will be relieved," snarked Kitar.

"My next logical question is what is the additional punishment for all these pricks who allowed it happen?" I asked.

"Though it may not meet with your approval, that specific sin is not singularly accounted for since it is not present across all the Creations. It is clumped in with the many other overriding atrocities these souls collectively have done. What ultimately becomes of them falls under the purview of another component of this Plane," answered Kitar.

"Fine, what else happens here?"

"You say that like this is not enough."

"Well it's enough, but it's sort of like a temp service for perverted priests, there isn't much to see."

"True, but you have written about the distillery already, and that should provide the visual component for what these souls are destined for...cooked, ground, decanted, and served to The Dark Lord himself," smiled Kitar.

"Great now I have that image in my head as well. You suck," I added. Then turning to the Seeker, I said, "Thank you for your time."

"It was a pleasure, young one. May The Dark Lord be with you for what you have to come," she said as we walked back into the main hall.

I was about to ask what she meant when it sounded like a bomb went off. There was this massive whoosh sound, and then the entire room shook. "What the fuck?"

"That is another component of this chamber. The reason for its shape and size," explained Kitar. "As you have no doubt noted, this room has been steadily growing warmer. That is because it is a giant kiln. (See, I told you.) The flames of the furnaces come up from just below this room and curve around it continuing their journey to the seventh and ultimately venting on the sixth, if you recall. They heat this chamber to an unbearable temperature if you are a soul." He pointed toward the lines. All the priests' feet looked like little more than burned steaks weeping their own juices. As they moved, they had to pry them loose from the hot stones, often leaving bits behind.

"They heat the chamber just to torture the priests' feet? I like it but isn't that a bit of overkill," I said.

"That is not the purpose of the fire, just a side effect. The purpose is what lies above us. Come, I will show you."

We went back to the shaft and started up, I thought we were leaving, but Kitar stopped at an archway just a couple of hundred feet up. We entered. As we landed, Kitar pushed me to the floor as a massive club slammed into the wall above us. I came up ready for a fight when I heard Kitar announce in a loud voice, "We are here on The Dark Lord's business."

"Normally it is a good idea to lead with that before landing," answered a booming voice.

"You did not give us a chance. Now could you kindly remove the club from the wall so that we may stand."

"Oh yes, that, sorry, reflexes and all," said what I could now say was a giant. No other word for him, he was every bit of a hundred feet tall with a ram's head, just like Khnum from Egyptian mythology. Oh, and because it's a trend with me, their (yes, there are two of these guys) cocks were twice as tall as I am, the new me not the little human me. "That cock would leave a mark," I said as Kitar elbowed me.

"Forgive our interruption but Lord Lucifer..." The two giants dropped to a knee and bowed causing the entire chamber to shake. "...has instructed me to show his servant around." Before I got a chance to object, I got another elbow. That's right they can't know who I am, I keep forgetting.

Standing the first giant, the one with the club said, "I am Mactar, and this is Puctar. How may we be of service?"

"We are interested in an explanation of this chamber and its workings as well as the duties you perform," instructed Kitar.

"It will be an honor; we so rarely receive guests."

Walking over, Mactar, clearly the talkative one, placed his hand on a massive lever. Easily three times as long as I am tall. "Puc do not pull your lever just show our guests where it is," instructed Mactar as the other giant placed a hand on an identical lever. Then pointing to the long-charred stones running along the walls on both sides of the chamber he explained, "When these two levers are pulled it opens the flues from the furnaces down below the Cathedral. The flames then engulf that chamber and flood this one in Hell's fires."

I had to interrupt. "If you pull the levers aren't you also set ablaze as the chamber fills?"

"Yes, My Lord, but to no consequence. Both Puc and I are fire Demons; the flames do not affect us."

"Oh, there are types of Demons?" I said turning to Kitar, "If they are fire Demons, what am I?"

"I am pretty sure you are a new class, maybe the obstinate class. Your skill is to ease the suffering of those in the torture pits with your endless complaining about the conditions around you. Thus making the suffering soul feel less reluctant to be hit across the head with a massive club or to have their heads cut off thus ending the limitless droning on of the vicious Lord of bitching."

"Seriously? Did you make that up on the spot or have you been rehearsing it in your room at night?"

"Guess you will never know," said Kitar with a shrug. I was shocked, not only had he balled me out, but he'd done it with a sense of humor. That more than anything else worried me.

"Shall I continue?" Mactar asked a little confused.

Both Kitar and I nodded.

"The Cathedral then begins to heat up. After a cycle, when the stones encasing the chamber glow bright red, we release the levers closing the flues. Puc then goes to the large lever on the back wall while I go to this one here…" It was opposite the one he'd holding before. "…Puc pulls his lever which opens the doors above us…" We looked and could barely see the outlines of the doors which took up a good portion of the curved ceiling. "…flooding this chamber with suffering from the lakes above instantly turning it to steam. Here is where it gets tricky. I must wait just a half a moment for the suffering to engulf the entire chamber then I pull this lever opening the vents allowing the steam to be released into the Plane above."

"Does all the suffering convert to steam?" I asked

"Most of it, what does not is consumed the next time we open the furnaces."

Turning in amazement to Kitar, I said, "That is where the rain we keep seeing comes from."

"Correct. It is one of several techniques employed in the final cleansing of the suffering before it flows to the Great Plane. The condensation is either gathered in the reservoirs circling the massive domed ceiling or rains down upon the city. Some returns to the two top lakes, but that is of no concern, it will eventually be processed. There is currently such a glutton of suffering we could power the furnaces for millennia before needing to refill the lakes."

We thanked the giants and excused ourselves as they hurried to get back on schedule and open the furnace flues. I didn't want to be there for that. When we finally made it back up and out the door, I wasn't surprised to see that it was raining. "That is a very ingenious system. I feel like we missed something though. Remember the souls in the back part of the cathedral, what are they for?"

"The ones over the coals?" asked Kitar.

"Yes."

"They are souls who still need to suffer the sins of their flock, but due to the overflow on the given Plane, it is determined these souls can be held back to suffer time over the coals instead of the designated sin. This does not excuse them from their other punishments only from the one for a specific soul on a specific plane," answered Kitar.

I nodded, now you see why I skipped it. They are just overstock. As we stepped onto the street, I added, "One question, a bit off topic. "Should I be worried about what the Seeker said?"

"No, she cannot see the future, but most in Hell probably know by now that Keith, the human Keith, is going to do battle with a Fallen. She wished you luck because she knows."

"Something we want very few others to do, right?"

"Within reason, we might need to let others know in the course of you touring."

"But no one knows I'm in this form and I still have the protection of this, right?" I asked picking up the amulet Lucifer gave me.

"Yes, why?"

"Good, get lost. I want a night out on the town."

"By yourself?"

"Yes..."

"Keith..."

"I'm a big mean looking Demon with two Fallen in my head and an amulet of protection from the guy who owns the place. I think I'll be fine."

"As you wish, if you are not back by morning, I am sending out the Hellspawns."

"There's no need to get mean."

"Just saying," commented Kitar as he turned and headed off.

I was grinning from ear to ear, finally a night to myself. I can't even remember when the last one was.

# Entry 264

I watched Kitar vanish into the crowd and eventually around a corner. Leaning back against the door I felt my wings push into my back. Standing up straight I concentrated and again was impressed at the way they simply liquified and absorbed into my body. I took a few extra moments and pictured my back, or at least what I thought a back should look like and felt the fluid skin slip into place. This is going to make dressing so much simpler; you have no idea how hard it is to get a tunic over wings. If you are like me, your mind has already started trying to work on it. Demonic tunics, I guess angelic ones as well, fasten in the back. It's like putting a coat only in reverse. That is why I need Cemal to help me dress now.

As I started onto the street, which wasn't very crowded I looked up into the rain to see if I could find the reservoirs Kitar had mentioned but had no luck. They were just too high.

I strolled down the street; it appeared I looked high enough on the food chain to have creatures moving out of the way as I walked by. Don't get me wrong it wasn't like they were making a path, they'd bow their head slightly and walk around me. I strolled around for a while, letting the rain wash over me. Occasionally I'd spot some souls huddled together under an overhang or piece of worn leather trying to hide from the suffering. I could tell when a drop made it through; you would see one of the creature's wince, start crying or clawing at their body.

I was happy to see most of the shop signs I could read even though they were in different languages. Synthetic beings were also not affected by the rain went about their business stopping at shops, chatting, living what would otherwise be considered a normal life. I know you want to know what they looked like, the majority were humanoid in one form or another, what I mean by this is they had a torso, at least one head, a set of arms, sometimes more, and several legs, often just the standard two. They had languages; some spoke in soft lulling almost sing-song tones while others were like that little robot in *Star Wars* and just beeped and clicked.

As I crossed one of the main streets, I noticed a lot of flashing lights coming from a few storefronts down the road. That was my queue, so I headed that way. I found what I was looking for, the entertainment section. As I was reading the club signs, a barker stepped out and with a very extravagant bow introduced himself as Avacar.

"Greetings, My Lord. It appears you have not consecrated your fine physique with any adornments. His lordship must be young. Could I interest you in some markings or ornamentations?"

"Markings or adornments? What do you mean?" I used my commanding/booming voice...hehe, he flinched.

"Please, my Lord, this way," he said as he straightened and headed into his little shop. Immediately I realized he did tattoos and piercings. I was sold.

He went to the back of the shop and brought out a small case with dozens of sets of jewelry in them. "Forgive me for being so blunt but is your Lordship prone to bursting into flames?"

"Flames? You mean I can on my body?" Hell, I didn't know if I could bring up flames. Concentrating I extended my arm and sure enough, my entire arm burst out in red flames, "Well, I guess yes."

"Very nicely done My Lord, beautiful color. So normal metals are out." He fished around in the display and pulled out a set of rings with a ball and a chain with Lord Lucifer's pentagram hanging from the end. "Might I suggest these, they would match My Lord's handsome necklace."

I'd forgotten to tuck it under my tunic and as he reminded me my hand went to it without thinking. "Yes, I think that would be great," I said.

He smiled as I sat on the table he had motioned too. Before I could explain he would need to help me with my tunic, he was already behind me undoing the latches. At first, I was surprised, but I guess working in Hell you figure out how to get to people's body if you're in the piercing business. He unhooked it and pulled it over my arms leaving it to rest on my lap. Some customers must be sensitive about nudity, but I can't imagine how with almost the entire population on all the Planes running around naked.

Coming back around, without warning, he reached up and pinched my nipples hard. I barked, and he jumped. "You do that again without telling me first I might need to bend you over for a few moments," I joked trying to cover my embarrassment.

He started sweating. "Just kidding," I added. "Carry on."

"Yes, My Lord," he answered as he pulled out a vicious looking needle which looked way longer than it needed to be. I took a deep breath; I guess I shouldn't have expected any of those cool guns, you know the hepatitis spreaders used in malls. Grabbing a nipple, again without warning, he jabbed the needle through lengthwise and out the other side. Before I even registered the poke, he had it out, and the ring in and was on to the next. Again, a sharp pain and now I wore two shinny Kitar raggers. I figured these should be worth a good hour or two worth of hysterics. Smirking that gave me an idea. I always did like piercings.

"How is that, My Lord? They look very handsome. So nice in fact, My Lord might wish to start going topless. A nice harness would show them off wonderfully," he said while I was sorting through the box of jewelry.

"I like that idea," I said as I handed him a simple barbell piercing. If you don't know what that is, it's exactly like it sounds, a straight piece of metal with a ball on each end. One or both of the balls can be unscrewed allowing the piercing to be changed or removed. Pulling my tunic away so he could get a good look of my endowment, I said in a firm tone, "I want that...here," as I lifted the shaft and indicated the underside of the cock right below the head. I think it's called the frenum.

"Yes, My Lord and a very nice choice of jewelry, the metal should hold up if his Lordship decides to flare up," he chuckled at his joke as he took my cock, massaged it a couple of times, I don't know if that was to help the process or just to make me happy, I didn't ask. This time I won't lie, I closed my eyes. A sharp needle that close to little Keith was more than I could watch. He didn't wait, I felt him pinch the skin, and then he pushed, and I sucked in a breath. When I opened my eyes, I saw the store owner, a strange looking synthetic, smiling at me like he'd just won a prize. Looking down I had to admit it looked great.

"Very nice, what's the charge?" I asked.

He stepped back as his hand went to his chest, he was actually clutching his pearls, "For such an exalted Demon as yourself My Lord, no charge. Please just tell your friends where you got them."

"That I can do. I'm sure one of my guides will be down to see you tomorrow," I said, not mentioning it would probably be to strangle him. Details. Details.

As I got redressed, I realized something; I'm still cut. I can grow hooves, wings and a fucking tail but I can't get my foreskin back? I thought about trying that morphing thing like with my wings, but I wasn't sure if that would interfere with the new piercing. Plus, screwing up my wings and never flying again is one thing, messing up my cock, well some things are just not worth the risk. I decided I'd have to spend some time contemplating my cock when I got back to my room. Yes, I know, as you can imagine with Usis gone, I've spent a lot of time with the ol boy of late, too much time. But then Hell is stressful and any port in the storm to help relax.

# Entry 265

I found a club just down the avenue from the piercing shop. I could stay on this Plane for years and probably never learn as much about how the synthetics feel about the living as what I learned that night.

It is called "The Open Wide Club."

As usual, the music attracted me to the neon-emblazoned club with two golden humanoid synthetic Demons standing guard to each side of the door. As I started to enter, they both stepped in front, blocking the entrance. It was almost like they sensed something. I need to remember to ask what that's about; it's happened a couple of times now.

When it was clear I was visiting their establishment and equally clear that I wasn't rabble they stepped aside, bowing their heads slightly as I entered. The first thing I noticed, and that is saying a lot, was the odor. It smelled like rotting flesh. At first, this wouldn't seem odd, if Hell had a smell it would be just that, except remember this is a synthetic Plane. But not the inside of the club, per se, we'll revisit this shortly. The second note of interest was how packed the bar was.

I'm going to give you an overview description instead of first impressions; they were misleading.

The walls were covered, with few visible gaps, in flayed torsos. You read that right, living torsos. The right wall was two species; I noticed it first because one of the species was human, the other an alligator-like creature with a torso much like ours. The rows of humans and alligator bodies alternated. The humans were upside down, and the alligator's right side up, arranged so their heads were beside each other. The torsos were split across the shoulder blades to the center, and then down, just before the cut reached the groin, the slice veered off and continued along the front of the legs. The skin and meat on the chest and legs had been peeled away from the bones and lay open like a set of shuttered windows and tacked back against the wall. The souls were close enough not to overlap, but very little wall space was visible. The ribs were still intact but empty, the internal organs all removed. Along the floor was a long grate of flames running the length of the wall. For lack of a better way of putting it, they were being cooked low and slow.

The back wall was far less interesting from an artistic standpoint; it was just cages, the biggest on the bottom working up to smaller ones on top, all filled with a variety of creatures. The last wall, the left one was mercifully empty with a stage and four dance poles. I shook my head. This was probably going to be an upsetting night but then what could they do that I hadn't seen already?

Scattered around the main floor and on a balcony at the top of a set of stairs were booths and tables with an assortment of stools. The bar, as seemed to be the custom, was round and in the center. There was a dancer at each end; neither took my fancy since I had no idea what species they were or even really what I was seeing. Arms, legs, and heads all over the place and that was just one of the two dancers.

As I struggled to get my bearings, I was approached by a little gremlin looking thing. "Would My Lord like a something to drink? A table or booth possibly?"

"A booth, in the back out of the way if possible. If there's a show then one with a view of the stage," I instructed, trying to sound authoritative.

"As his Lordship wishes," said the creature, motioning me to follow.

I was led upstairs to one of the small private booths. It'd probably held about three people with room for a slave to kneel at the foot of the table. Looking over the railing, I could see the crowd below with a perfect view of the stage. "Great spot, thank you. Bring me whatever food and wine you might have," I said internally cringing at what I knew was the next question.

"Would My Lord like reptile or primate?" See I knew that's what he was going to ask.

"I think reptile tonight," I answered with a bit of trepidation. I'm sure I've eaten human at some point during my stay in Hell, since all meat is from souls, but I didn't want to look into the eyes of the creature I was about to think tasted like chicken.

"Very good, My Lord. Will his Lordship be requiring a servant tonight?" the goblin asked.

I didn't get a chance to answer. "We will take two. Send up two humanoid males, young, attractive and well hung," said Balthazar as he entered taking a seat. "Also, send someone back to the Keep and have them bring back some real wine."

The goblin froze in fear. At first, I didn't know why and then it struck me. With a smirk I looked over. "I didn't know I was going to have company tonight. What brings you out, Balthazar?"

As the imp started to breathe again he rushed away with a wave and a, "as My Lord wishes." Balthazar hit me across the chest with the back of his hand.

"Why did you spoil my fun?"

"You knew he didn't know who you were?"

"Of course, I rarely visit the Planes. I pride myself in being unknown, and you take away all my fun."

"Oh well, that doesn't negate my question. Why are you here?"

"I am Hell's Royalty, I do not need a reason, but if I were to give one, I would say I wanted to get away from everyone, and you are not totally unpleasant company."

"Always the charmer. I'll take that as a compliment, and while we're telling truths, I realized quick I was in over my head when I discovered humanoid was on the menu. So, it's good to see you."

"You did not order it, did you? The reptile is better."

"That's what I got."

"Enjoy it while you can, very few remain. Between the ones sent to the furnaces before the destruction of their world at their own hands, we will not be getting any more. I dare say these might be the last in all of Hell and we are lucky enough to get to dine on them before they vanish from eternity."

"Charming. Seriously charming."

"You are about to spend eternity, E.T.E.R.N.I.T.Y in Hell. Like it or not, the living who are here for their 'sins' have something to do. The rest of us have to deal with a life which rarely changes. After you have spent a few millions of years here, you will discover that when something unique or limited comes along, you will be racing to get in line like the rest of us."

We heard a small cough and turned to find two extremely hot guys kneeling before us. The first taller thinner one was flesh tone, four arms, and the rest standard issue. The other one had interesting opalescent scales like a snake, with everything – arms, legs, torso, and cock – in normal quantities. He had pointed ears, and there was something about his voice which caught the attention of the freshly pierced little Keith. When I saw his pointed teeth and spiked tongue, I yelled a bit too eagerly, "I call dibs on snake boy."

Balthazar raised an eyebrow, I think, then said, "Well it sounds like you are mine," he added patting his lap.

They bowed set the platters of food on the table and excused themselves returning a few minutes later with several bottles of wine and two goblets. After opening and pouring, each took their positions on our respected laps.

Yes, Yes, I know…Usis. If I've said it once, I've said it a hundred times. He wouldn't want me passing this up. So never forget I am now and always will be thinking of him, thank you.

We ate and drank for a while, talking about nothing in particular. Balthazar, determined to continue my training, kept pointing at creatures and suggesting things I might do to them. It ranged from every time a guy sat his drink down, I'd move it one way or another to setting that same guys hair, well tentacles, on fire when he started screaming at us from the first floor. Oh and yes Balthazar was right, the alligator guy has a great flavor. I mean once you've drunk enough to get past the fact that if so inclined you could walk down and thank him personally.

The little snake boy had a name there's no way I could pronounce, so I resorted to calling him, Adam. They were quite good at their job, both serving and satisfying. As much as I enjoyed Adam's attentions, I have to say I was more interested in watching how Balthazar played with his little slave. I'd almost always, I think always actually, had sex with former living. It was interesting how a Hellspawn not only treated the boy, which was, as you would imagine, brutal at times but also very tender at others. He also used his magic to enhance the passions of both himself and the slave. Little pops of electricity, heightened senses, magically not letting the boy release until he was so consumed with lust and desire that his screams when he finally came caught the attention and applause of the entire room.

By the time the show started the two boys were worn out and curled together asleep in the corner. Balthazar and I settled down to some serious drinking as the entertainment began. I already knew this was going to be a test since every time I'd seen one of Hell's shows I usually ended up throwing up and needing to be carried out.

Tonight's was horrific, but I guess I've reached a point where it just doesn't affect me as adversely. I'm not sure if that is good or bad, it just is. The show started with the Master of Ceremonies coming to the stage and welcoming everyone to the bar. As he gave his welcomes and mindless babble, I asked Balthazar, "If this Plane is mostly synthetic why are they so fascinated with the living?"

"It is not the living; it is the bodies of the living. To be a resident of this Plane and not consigned to it means you were never organic. Synthetic beings seem to have an endless fascination with the bodies of those who were alive."

"Sort of like the living have an unquenchable desire to know what the afterlife is and often fixate on what The Host, Hell, Angels and Demons are like?"

"I could see a correlation. Remember in many ways, if you follow the logical programming of the beings who are synthetic their creators are the living. So yes, I would say their fascination with them is in many ways equal to the livings fascination with The Powers."

"But why the….," I tried to think of the right word, "anger. No that's not it. Obsession with mutilation, torture, and humiliation. It can't be the same reasons as those here in Hell tasked with punishing the living for their sins."

"Oh no, take a second and look at this club. Most of the patrons are synthetic. Still, they are pulling pieces off the roasting souls and eating them. This is not an inherent need to punish for the lives they led, its simpler than that, it's a hatred of the life itself. As has been evident many times in your journals, there is an anger at learning that those who were supposed to be divine are as flawed as you are, and you did not even believe in The Powers or an afterlife. Imagine what those who did must feel when they arrive and eventually learn that those who run Creation are as imperfect as those they created. If you extrapolate that out, unlike with The Father and the Creations, where he was flawed and created something more flawed, those who are synthetic are often far more perfect than their creators. Imagine how disappointing that must be. Their arrival in Hell is often first met with cold curiousness. When they learn they are not going to be tortured but were instead sent here to live out eternity, they then turn those all-powerful minds to learning about the rest of Hell and what has become of the living who created them. This often leads to not only anger but more to the point, disappointment on so many levels. First, they find out their makers were a pale comparison to them intellectually. Then when discovering there was an afterlife, they become angry at all of Creation. They feel they are more than what The Father made, but in that self-envisioned perfection they still will never see The Eternal City being instead forced to live out eternity with creatures flawed from their very inception."

He looked at me and smiled. "Remind you of anyone?"

I nodded, "Oh yes, it sounds a lot like the single Power I've met, Gabriel. If he's an example, they've many of the same characteristics as the synthetics. Bars like this, the devouring of flesh, the humiliation of the souls, the petty toying and tortures are simply their way of acting out their disappointment?"

"Exactly, and with their micro-detailed minds, the tortures they inflict are more subtle, vicious and cruel than those which happen on all the other Planes. Their attention to detail does not allow them to see a single soul as just another in an endless line of creatures. The synthetic sees each soul as a singular exploration into the investigation of pain and humiliation."

"Why do I get the feeling that one of the reasons Lucifer, and whoever else, allowed this Plane to exist in its current state is so they could have an eager group of scientists working to refine new and horrible ways of bringing a soul to task."

"Very astute. That is precisely why the Overlord was allowed to carry out her plan on this Plane. While we are young and still learning, we are often brought here to watch, write reports and study new and creative ways to expand and intensify the amount of suffering a specific species can endure before turning into little more than kindling. That is why Xia almost exclusively refers to souls as kindling or cordwood; he has had a lifelong obsession with pain and how to better inflict it. If we could not find him in his normal haunts, he was either in the void practicing on souls or here in the clubs or down in the labs."

"This entire conversation makes me think of a couple of lines from a song by a group called Concrete Blonde back on Earth – I told the priest don't count on any second coming, god got his ass kicked the first time he came down here slumming, he had the balls to come, the gall to die and then forgive us, no I don't wonder why I wonder what he thought it would get us," I swear I've quoted this song before in the journals, but I can't remember. Either way, it got a big laugh out of Balthazar.

"That is one of the running jokes. When a species reaches its collective age of accountability, meaning its time they learn of the higher powers who run creation, the Powers send a representative to that creation in hopes of finding that 'perfect' civilization The Father was sure would develop. All that ever happens is the emissary is tortured and sent back with their tail between their legs. Did not your world hang yours?"

"Not rope hang, but we hung him from a cross. Good thing too, it would be disturbing to see two billion Catholics making the hung from a noose sign." We both laughed at that. "What happens if they fail this test, as we did?"

"The Host cuts off all connections with that civilization thus leaving them to fend for themselves. That is why after your little hanging you never heard from any of The Father's representatives again. You were for all intents and purposes, abandoned."

By the time my attention turned back to the stage it was covered in blood, the crowd was cheering for more and pieces of whoever had performed were being drug off. The reason I skipped the stage show is that it's gratuitous carnage and serves no real purpose at this point. It was souls consigned to this or one of the other planes; they are shipped around based upon need. There is just too much other stuff to cover.

Balthazar and I had a pretty good time. He's strange and try as I might I really couldn't get much personal information from him. Which after a while became frustrating for both of us. For him because I kept trying, and for me because I kept failing.

# Entry 266

When I left, Balthazar had awoken the two boys and was starting his next round. I slipped out and headed back to the Keep. I'd thought about going again with snake boy, but my conscious would only let me get away with one, anything after that and a pouty-faced Usis popped into my mind. As I walked back I felt something strange on my chest and reached up to scratch only to wince as I pulled the ring in my left nipple.

By the time I made it back I was thankful for the respect the crowd kept showing me by moving out of the way, the city was crazy busy. When I opened the door, I found something which had been becoming more and more regular, silence and solitude. This was completely abnormal for Kitar who I found in his room asleep. He sleeps curled up like a puppy on a pallet on the floor; it's so cute. Anyway, I have to believe this new less overly protective trend has to do with my new body and skills. Whatever the reason I'm not going to complain about it.

I crept to the other door though I don't know why. Before I opened it I could already hear Cemal's snoring. Boy, can that boy make a racket. I crept in and waited until a snore ended then positioned my hands over two bottles of wine, as his next snore shook the room, I grabbed them and raced quickly out.

Out on the balcony, I popped one open as I took a seat and stared across the city. After downing about half the bottle, I closed my eyes focusing on the enslaved Demon from the day before. To my surprise, I was looking through his eyes.

I sent a thought into its mind. "Hi, it's me, you know your Master?"

It let out a squawk and then threw its hands over its mouth. The other servants in the vicinity didn't seem to notice. Guess that's the luck of being in Hell, silence is suspect, screaming is not. "Please do not do that again. I could have dropped dead right here," it said.

"You can die?"

"I have no idea, but if you do that too often, we will find out. How might I serve you, Master?"

"You're not speaking out loud, are you?"

"Do I look like an idiot?"

"Wow, cocky for someone I can turn inside out with a thought. Look around. I want to see what the place looks like," I said. This was sort of cool.

I watched as he walked around the Keep, looking up toward other floors and down corridors. I won't describe it here, at some point I'll see it firsthand, so I'll tell ya then. How do I know I'll see it, you ask? Well, I know my job, and I know Lord Lucifer will not let anything interfere with that job. It is one of the perks of working for a god, in many respects. What I'll tell you now and what I did find interesting and a bit disturbing are the number of soldiers in Leviathans Keep, they're everywhere.

At every hallway, beside many of the doors, in long rows in the main galleries, stood big ass Demons, red and imposing with huge pikes, all frozen at attention. Creatures scurried about, like at any keep, but here they were not informal or manic, their movements were determined, precise and intended. These were soldiers, not slaves.

The creature worked his way up, finding an archway he gave me a view of the landscape. I will say this; it was Violence. Not the simple innocent violence the living can muster, but a determined lust filled ferocity of creatures who only goal was to produce suffering and regret.

Once while the creature was wandering about talking to himself, well actually me, he dropped to a knee, and his eyes fell to the floor as he froze. I heard the clanging of metal, the distinct sound of nails upon marble and the deep booming voice of my adversary. As the creature lifted his head, he turned to watch Leviathan receding down the hall with two of his lieutenants. My blood ran cold with both hate and fear.

As he wandered through the structure, through his ear, I heard conflict. This wasn't the tortured pain of souls reaping their rewards; this was controlled, intended conflict. He followed it and eventually emerged in a courtyard full of soldiers, Lucifer's soldiers, or so one would assume. Leviathan was after all one of his Master's Generals, but I noticed something strange. They didn't wear The Dark Lord's signet on their armor. It was the marking of the house Lancestrider, Leviathan's house, and name.

I had to wonder if this was normal or was there something bigger brewing? A rogue general planning a coup while his master was away. I don't know, and for that matter, I didn't care, I...we...whomever would deal with him soon enough, plus having Lucifer discover a plot could only be good for me at this point.

Finally, when I'd seen all I wanted to see, and the long night was starting to bear down upon my shoulders, I instructed the creature to find a specific room, a special room, which he did. Standing on each side, in all their imposing ferocity, were two soldiers. The creature snuck back around and gathered a bottle of wine, fresh goblets, a tray and returned explaining he'd been sent to refresh the prisoner's cupboard. He had told me it wouldn't be his first time, since his return he'd become one of the housekeepers, as instructed.

The soldiers nodded, and the imp opened the door and looked in. There sleeping in the bed was a Demon. Not just any Demon. My Demon. My Usis.

This was my first glimpse of him in his new form. I was relieved, shocked and pleased but most of all I was crying. It's been a while since tears have come uninvited to these eyes, the wonderstruck writer long ago replaced by this Demon encased in his invisible protective walls of his own making.

See, he wasn't a scaly Demon from the fantasy novels, much like myself, much like most of those here. He was a smooth, sleek creature taken more from the pages of Egyptian mythology.

He was still short, well for a Demon, maybe seven feet tall. His body was long and muscular, much like it had been when he was a soul. His skin was dark, almost black covered in what appeared to be a downed fur. Where my feet ended in hooves, his were like those of a dogs, like Kitar's. The fingers, on the one hand, I could see were long and delicate with two-inch-long bright red nails ending in points. His face like that of Anubis, the jackal, he had a long dolichocephalic snout like a greyhound. His eyes appeared to slant up, but since they were closed it was hard to tell. To be honest, they seemed to disappear when shut. His ears are what lead me to think Egyptian, they were short and stood up straight with deep red interiors. It was then I noticed the striations in his fur, the black red stripes which ambled lazily across his body. He lay curled against his furs so that I couldn't see the front of his body, but he was wearing a loincloth. I had the creature just stand there for what felt like hours as I watched his chest rise and fall, his shifts, the way a finger would come up to scratch an ear. He was no longer the Usis taken from me, but he was still beautiful. He was still perfect. And my heart still held its love for him.

When the sleepy stirrings became more frequent, I knew he'd awaken soon, so I instructed the creature to leave. It had been wonderful to see my love again. The ache in my heart was almost more than I could bare. I wanted him not in a bed as I watched from afar though other creatures' eyes. I wanted him with me, in our bed where the vision of him could be absorbed into my soul through my own eyes.

As the creature left, I was still in tears. The gut-wrenching pain was almost more than I could bear. I needed to be with him. We needed to be together.

I instructed the creature to leave the Keep and wander off into the throngs of suffering waring souls. There, once I was sure he was away, and no one would notice, I sent forth a command, and his body exploded. I couldn't risk becoming obsessed, so I had to remove the avatar, my mind couldn't keep dragging me back, causing me to forsake the work I needed to do to bring him back to me.

Almost the instant the little creatures head exploded it struck me like a physical assault that I'd just destroyed a being. It didn't matter; it was a construct. Cemal was 'just' a construct. I had to tell myself the truth I did it for my own selfish reasons. The meter by which I measured my humanity. Kitar was always worried about stepping down another notch like a battery slowly losing its power.

I opened my eyes to a crowd; they were all standing there quietly. It was Elick who broke the silence, "You destroyed the spy?" Yes, it was a question.

I answered in a whisper, "It's just too tempting. I would spend all my time there." He nodded as he and Alcraw turned to go back in. I heard him say, "Aw love, whether above or below someone dies so others may love." I looked away; I didn't want to see the look in Kitar's eyes. I started crying anew, for so many different reasons.

# Entry 267

I rested, ate, chatted for a bit and decided, yet again, it was time to do something to occupy my mind which was with each passing day becoming more a jumble of confused activity. So we headed to the Labs. Kitar never said anything about what I'd done, and neither did I. I knew his opinion and he knew my reasons, but more to the point he knew I knew it had been a mistake.

We trekked back into the city but always toward the lakes. Everything on this Plane was under the lakes. Not only because of the space it provided but also, in the case of the Labs, the ready access to the flow of suffering, which was the energy that powers the creation process.

As we stepped through the door, I could feel the magic and technology sizzling in the air like the static from a thunderstorm. The atmosphere was positively alive. Again, this place appeared enormous, not measured in yards but miles.

The chamber was the flat black stone which made up the Planes. The walls and floor were all polished to a sheen. The only interruptions in the massive expanses of black were the two doors, the entrance and another, and a sharped edged reservoir which bisected the entire space flowing with puss green suffering fed from a waterfall on the back wall. Workstations litter the room, each with their own lighting. They poxed the room with glowing islands of suffering lost in a void of inky blackness. A void so complete as to consume the edges and height of the chamber.

The other almost overwhelming feature was its silence. When I say silence, don't get me wrong, there were sounds just not the sounds I'd grown used to in both abundance and volume throughout my travels. Hell has a constant gale of cries which pirouette through the planes like a hurricane ripping through a coastal town. Here, the relaxing sound of cascading suffering from the back of the room mixed with the hushed conversations of Labs technicians created an uncomfortable normality. I'd often said I wished there was an escape from the cries. Now that I had it, I found it disturbing. Occasionally a minor interruption would bring back the Hell I knew. The sound of a soul being drug to a table as fresh raw materials for one of the craftsmen. So harsh and savage was the single cry just before being snuffed out that the lone voice shook me more than the choruses I was now lamenting.

Before I get to the technicians and their work, I want to address the most significant presence in the room, the cascading waterfall of suffering. A large section of the back wall was nothing but a never-ending flow of the putrid green liquid cascading from the lakes above to the lake below. We were looking through a mile-long section of one of the damns. Just inside were the mechanisms used to divert part of the flow into the chamber and through the reservoir running down its center.

Hell's population consists of several distinct groups; The Royalty which govern. The torturers who put into practice what the inventors create. Both always looking for new and horrible was to extract just one more drop of that precious liquid from a damned soul. Then there are the residents and constructs, which you have seen throughout my travels and finally the souls who grease the wheels with their pain so all those who hate them can continue their misguided existences.

I think the most substantial change in the way I see Hell has happened during my travels. When I arrived, I believed the tortures were forced upon souls as a form of punishment. I saw it as revenge by The Powers upon the powerless abandoned by a misguided Father. But now more than ever I see it as a choice the souls make throughout the course of their lives. They pick and choose their sins, sculpting for themselves the pains they will spend eternity enduring. In our/their defense, I also believe that The Father through his lack of understanding instilled in the living a latent urge to sin in the misguided hope it would never be explored. It's there where Lucifer stepped in. He taught the living the differences between good and evil, if such a concept exists, and gave them the ability to choose, with their own minds, their eternity, their pain, their own personal transgressions. The Father promised them free will; Lucifer gave it to them.

Lastly, toward the back where the storage areas, two types. On the left side of the chamber were the fledgling constructs and to the right, those physical damned who would be used for parts to create the abominations of Hell.

Turning to my entourage, they all came, even Cemal, I asked, "So how are we doing this?"

It was Cemal who bounced up and ran off returning a few seconds later dragging a creature by his sleeve. "Master, this is this one's creator. Master Skedwe, this is this one's owner and most wonderful Master."

I smiled both at the Demon (I'm not sure what he is yet) because of the introduction, the confused look on his face and the joy in Cemal's eyes at getting to introduce me. "It is a pleasure, Skedwe. I hope I pronounced that right?"

"Close enough..." he answered as he swatted Cemal's hand off his robe. "Have you brought this one back to have some of his exuberance removed. I feared we might have installed too much..." He paused trying to think of the word.

"Bounce?" I added.

"Yes, yes indeed, bounce. Entirely too much bounce," he agreed as we both looked down to see Cemal with his lip stuck out, "Oh stop pretending to pout. We did not build you with any of that." Looking up and finally seeing who was with me he unconsciously straightened his robes, "Oh my, such distinguished guests. How might I be of service?"

"I am sure you have heard about the writer The Dark Lord has tasked with documenting his domain, this is he. We are here so he can see how The Lab plies its craft," answered Alcraw.

"Keith has recently undergone a personal transformation, and I must warn you against sharing that information. You will tell no one how he now appears. Those of us with him, the Overlord and of course, The Dark Lord know along with a limited few. Yourself now included.

There will be no reprieve if you violate our trust, am I clear," said Elick gravely.

"Oh yes, My Lord. We here are known for our discretion."

"I knew we could trust you."

This was all getting too grave. "So you're the administrator of these facilities?" I asked.

"Yes, My Lord."

"And you made my boy here?"

"Yes, Cemal was an experiment. A Demon from Pandemonium named Hactar commissioned him. He requested a happy, carefree servant."

"You did very well then. Cemal is most certainly carefree." Looking between them both I added, "If Cemal was a commission why was he serving in Wrath's Keep?" I asked. I cannot tell you how strange it was to be talking about a thinking creature as if they were a car or a sports coat.

Looking at Cemal, Skedwe asked, "Would you like to answer your Master?"

"My original Master made several bad decisions and was sent to the furnaces to finish out eternity," answered Cemal. His head was down, and eyes were cast down toward the floor.

"You miss him?" I asked.

"No Master, he was very mean. This one just feels bad for not feeling bad about his plight."

"When his commissioner found himself no longer in need of a servant Cemal was returned here to the labs to be reassigned. For a time, he assisted me here in the labs. Eventually, he was sent to Wrath for reasons which are unclear," he explained, but I knew there was more.

"But if you had to venture a guess?" I asked as I gave Elick a hard stare. I had a feeling I knew the answer. When I looked back, Skedwe was also looking at Elick questioningly.

"Tell him; he already suspects," answered Elick.

"Lord Elick came and took Cemal to Wrath's Keep some time ago. As I have already explained, the reasons were not disclosed."

"You little shit, did you just pawn this explanation off on me?" laughed Elick.

"Yes, My Lord, it does appear I have," answered the Demon.

I turned to Elick and raised an eyebrow. "Lord Lucifer felt you needed a servant, so he had me find one that suited your temperament and…"

"…had him placed in the service of one of the Overlord's I'd be visiting so to appear I discovered him on my own. Aww but see, I think you might have just pulled the same stunt Skedwe here just pulled."

"Why?" asked Elick.

"Because Usis found Cemal, interviewed him and recruited him to our service. The Overlord just formalized it. So, my question to you my dear handsome caretaker is, did my companion have a hand in this little ruse as well?"

I must be getting better. I had the head of Hell's Labs, several Hellspawns, a slave and a Judge all fidgeting. "Not at first, Cemal was stationed on Wrath in hopes he would prove to be a good fit for you and your companion," explained Elick.

Cemal's face went from worried to scared. I could see it in his eyes. His fear I would reject him. "Well, then I'll have to give my thanks to Lord Lucifer for his foresight and concern for my happiness. I couldn't have thought of a better person to add to our little family than Cemal."

Everyone breathed a sigh of relief.

# Entry 268

As with many places I have written about in Hell, due to the expanse, I'm focusing on specific parts individually. As with the Labs, I depend on you my readers can extrapolate what I'm about to explain into thousands of similar workstations.

It's important to remember this Plane is one of the first we've where we see the utilization of the suffering collected. First with the Brewery and now here with the creation of entirely new sentient beings. To be honest, it's the first time we'll get to see the divinity of Hell in action as well.

The mechanism at the back of the room, which brought the suffering into the space would be pushed out into the falls. It would capture a large ladle of the liquid to store until needed to refill the trough running down the center of the chamber. I'd see servants, much like Cemal, run to the channel and scoop up a dipper full of the liquid and then rush back offering it up to the creator working at the bench.

"I'm in your hands, lead the way," I asked.

"Yes, please this way," answered Skedwe walking into the expanse. "The labs are spread out across three levels, this and the two below. Each specializing in a specific area of study." As he led us to the back, he stopped at a set of cages. "Here we store a variety of different souls, with an assortment of temperaments. The ones on the left have were pampered to some extent, where the ones to the right, far less so, many undergoing strategic abuse to bring forth the personality the client has requested. After we are satisfied with their development, they are given over to their future owner who can fine-tune the behavior traits they wish the construct to retain once transferred to their new body." Seeing the confused look on my face he added, "such constructs include Hellhounds, Guards, Consorts and the like."

"Oh, like I saw with, oh what was his name, Dozer, The Dark Lord's Hellhound?"

"Yes, that is an excellent example. The Dark Lord himself chose that soul from a race of now-extinct creatures; there could be no higher honor. Once the species was determined, we then educate and install a sense of rigid adherence to Lord Lucifer's wishes. The hellhound then has an unwavering ferocity in its execution of The Dark Lord's instructions. Due to its training, its intelligence was increased dramatically as well as its sense of justice as Lord Lucifer understands it. Thus, it could comprehend the nuances of the instructions given as well as the ramifications if someone, Power or otherwise, chose to violate said instructions in its presence. It is a masterwork of craftsmanship if I do say so myself. Do you understand?"

"I think so, your explanation combined with what I remember from earlier. I guess my question is what keeps it from modifying its behavior over time?"

"The construct?"

"Yes."

"If the owner does not wish their construct to evolve, say they need them for a specific task, then the reasoning and learning capabilities of the creature are removed at the time of insertion. This ensures the constructs temperament will remain static from that point on, for the most part."

"Meaning?"

"No one can be sure what will happen in the future. Just like any other creature with The Father's spark, time will only tell how or if it will develop."

"If the construct does change, what happens then?"

"If the owner is no longer satisfied the construct will be destroyed and a new one produced to take its place. Most constructs have a limited life span, for lack of a better phrase, to start with anyway. The souls of the living used are very unstable. Thus the construct will start to breakdown at some point."

I turned and looked at Cemal who was again staring at the floor. "Yes, Balthazar said that's what was happening with Cemal here," I explained.

Lifting Cemal like he was weightless Skedwe set him on a table. "What are you doing?" I asked as I bounded to Cemal's side.

"I am checking to see how this construct is holding together," explained Skedwe.

I started to object when I felt Elick touch my elbow and motion for me to remain quiet. At first, I wasn't sure why, then Skedwe's brow started to furrow, and over the next few moments a look of complete bewilderment slowly washed across his face. I realized what Elick wanted to see. "What has happened to you child?" Turning to us he added, "This is most peculiar, this construct..."

"His name is Cemal," I corrected.

"Yes, Yes, of course, Camal here is not losing cohesion if anything he...well...no long is drawing energy from the souls used in his construction. It's as if he has..."

"Become a real boy?" I inserted thinking of Pinocchio.

"Yes, yes indeed, it is exactly as if he has become a real being. This is extraordinary," exclaimed the mage.

At this point Elick stepped in. "Some things have occurred which has facilitated some changes in the young slave..." as he put his arm around the mage's shoulder, he added, "changes which it would be best not discussed or researched. Doing so could lead to problems with not only us but our Lord as well, if you take my meaning."

Stepping away as if he had discovered Cemal was radioactive he said in a worried voice, "Yes, of course, My Lord. It is not my place to question the actions of ones such as yourself let alone our Lord and Master."

"Based upon your assessment though, you would say Cemal will no longer be having the issues other constructs would have?" I asked.

"My Lord, your young 'boy' here is, for all intents and purposes, no longer a construct, therefore no."

Clapping my hands together, I said excitedly, "Did you hear that, my boy? You are a being now, not a construct." I hadn't needed to tell Cemal since he had collapsed into tears.

Jumping down off the table he ran up and gave me a big hug. "Thank you, Master, thank you."

Pulling him away with a smile still plastered across my face, I said, "So as you were saying?"

It took Skedwe a while to get his head back in the game. He led us around showing us the different workstations. But finally, when he'd shaken off the surprise of Cemal's ascension, as he kept calling it, he brought us to a particularly ugly creature's work area. The mage himself had four standard humanoid arms and a highly modified head. What was disgusting about him is he was a giant fly. His head, instead of having a lower jaw had a large set pinchers, no nose and two bulbous eyes with dozens of lenses. The skin which covered his body was an off grey-green with rigid course hairs sprouting from dozens of places in little clumps. Instead of a butt he had a long tail which ended in a cactus-like bulb full of short, sharp barbs. Oh, and he had a set of ram horns, but crusty, flaking and also covered with short prickly little hairs. What I couldn't figure out is why he was so hard to see clearly, it was like he was slightly out of focus.

"If you have the time Lords, (there was a name said here of the fly guy, but I have no idea what it was, it sounded like it had at least 30 letters), is ready to perform a transfer," he explained as he pointed to the inanimate hellhound body lying on the table.

"Absolutely," I answered.

The fly guy (that's his name now) summoned a huge Demon over who scooped up the hellhound carcass, and together we followed him to a clearing near the back. Etched on the floor was a massive pentagram. To give you some reference on size, the center of the pentagram was a good twenty feet across holding a large altar about ten feet long, six feet deep and tall. The lines of the pentagram itself were small canals carved into the hard stone floor. At each corner of the star stood a tall gold candle holder with a blood red candle sitting upon it. (I know how very gothic this sounds, but they had to have gotten it somewhere I guess.)

The Demon lay the hellhound on the altar as flyboy summoned over five emaciated creatures. Their translucent dried skin hugged their skeletal bodies like an unwrapped mummy. The creature's eyes were nothing more than sunken black pits. Their nose and lips rotted away exposing a mouth full of sharp teeth. Below the waist, the creatures had no body just long ragged strips of tattered skin. What made them even more disturbing was how they glowed from an orange flame blazing in their chest illuminating the ribs cage. Around their head floated a golden glowing crown of angelic symbols.

The five figures positioned themselves at each of the points of the Pentagram. The Demon left the circle as the flyboy entered to stand behind the altar. From the back of the room, we heard a commotion and turned to see the Demon hauling one of the aggressive souls behind him by the foot. The Demon drug the soul into the center of the pentagram on the other side of the altar as flyboy muttered a spell causing it to go rigid, its arms and legs locking as it rose to float even with the hellhound.

"As you can probably imagine, the reason we immobilize them is to ensure they do not attack the necromancer," explained Skedwe.

I looked to find the rest of my group only to see Elick and Alcraw talking between themselves as they leaned bored against the wall.

As I turned back, fly boy started to chant as the five avatars reached out a boney finger touching the wicks of the candles causing them to burst into flame. As the candles grew brighter the room around us faded until it was just the pentagram and nothing more. We stood at the edge of the darkness a couple of feet back from the working circle.

When the shroud of darkness was complete, the five joined in, their chanting adding to the strength of the flyboy's. Louder and louder their voices grew, each swaying slightly from left to right. Then out of the corner of my eye, I saw movement by the suspended soul, he was bucking against his invisible bonds. At first, there were just moans but as the chanting grew so did the cries from the suspended form.

As the sounds of chanting and anguish grew steadily, I saw blue flames appear at the feet of the sacrifice. At first, they were small delicate flames, then like the chants, they began to grow consuming first the feet, then legs of the creature. I hadn't thought the cries could grow louder, but they did. As the flames continued up the body, blisters appeared and then popped dripping more suffering, accelerating the intensity of the flames. The creature's balls ruptured as the fire continued up the chest, the cries turning to wails of agony as the five avatars abandoned their posts and started toward the body. They floated over, forming a circle around the creature now fully engulfed.

Then with one loud grunt, the chanting stopped, the cries stopped, all sound stopped as the body dropped to the ground no longer suspended. As it hit the floor with a sickening thud the flames went out, and the five avatars descended on it, ripping and tearing at the flesh and innards consuming it hungrily. As they ate the glow in their chest began to strengthen. When finally, the corpse was nothing but bones, the avatars glowed with blinding intensity.

I heard Skedwe mutter something, as shading descended over my eyes like I'd just put on sunglasses. Now I could see the avatars as they turned and began to move toward the inanimate hellhound. As they encircled the altar, flyboy stepped forward and grasped the face of the hound pulling its mouth open as the avatars brought their razor-sharp nails up to their chest, plunging them in, ripping their chest open. The light again increased by magnitudes, then grasping their ribs they broke the front off with a sickening snap as the flames burst forth. With amazing speed, flyboy, with his free hands, grasped each of the balls forcing them into the hellspawn's mouth, shoving the last one in up to its elbow.

The five avatars dropped to the ground now nothing but empty sacks of bones and torn skin, their stretched faces with hollow eyes staring out into nothingness.

Flyboy slid his arm out and slammed the creature's mouth shut. In a language I could understand it started saying "Take the gift. Ingest it. Use it." It was almost like he was begging, encouraging the Hellspawn to respond.

And that is precisely what it did. Not much at first, just a twitch of his foot. I would have missed it had not Skedwe prodded me pointing. "It is taking the soul."

Skedwe waved his hand slightly causing the shading over my eyes to fade. I noticed then that the blackness that had surrounded the pentagram had dissolved as well, replaced by three Demons, one holding a collar and chain. As the Hellspawn started to spasm, then kick, the Demon rushed forward securing the collar around its neck. Just in time, for not a second later the creature bounded up onto its feet on the altar. Its body glistening blue-black, its eyes glowing bright yellow with flames licking from the sockets. As it grew stronger, it raised its head and in a triumphant howl let the room know it had been born. Turning fast a paw shot out and ripped open the chest of the Demon standing closest. I heard a "tsk tsk tsk" come from Skedwe. Luckily that wasn't the Demon holding its leash. Like a fool flyboy leaned in and whispered something into the beast's ear. To my surprise, it calmed and with a tug followed the Demon across the room.

"What did he say?" I asked in a hushed voice.

"(Flyboy's name) will always be his creator. Therefore, he will always hold sway over the beast, loyal second only to its new masters once they have performed a bonding ritual."

Skedwe turned and walked off leaving me standing staring in stunned surprise. As flyboy walked off, I turned to my companions. "That is how they make constructs?" I asked.

"Yes and No..." I growled. I hate that answer, "Yes, it is how they make constructs of a lower caste. No, it is not the process for the complicated ones like your slave here or those who serve as attendants to the Powers of Hell. You will see that when we reach the lowest level," answered Elick.

"I thought the tracks in the pentagram would be used? And there were none of those gemstones."

"They are for more advanced insertions, not something as simple as a hellhound," explained Elick.

"Are the avatars dead? Well...you know what I mean."

"No, they have just used up their energy. They will be taken to their temple to recuperate."

# Entry 269 (2<sup>nd</sup> floor)

On the second floor the first thing that struck me was the smell. I mean the cries were there but how many times can I comment on them.

"What am I looking at? I mean I know what I think I'm looking at but please enlighten me?"

"It is what it appears to be," answered Kitar.

"A butcher shop?"

"Yes and no…" He smiled. "One of its function is exactly that. This is one of the meat preparation facilities."

"Gawd. I didn't realize there was such organization. I mean I knew Hell had to have infrastructure, but this is staggering. Among the many other questions why Fraud? I'm assuming all these souls are from this Plane?"

"And that assumption would be incorrect. If a body is beyond a quick regeneration in one of the recovery areas it is sent here to be processed for food. This is not the only such processing plant, just the largest."

"Oh, right the heads. I remember, I can't remember which Plane now, had the mountains of heads. So, the bodies are sent here but the head is kept?"

"Correct. If the head becomes damaged during the punishment process, then the soul will blink out and end up as goo in the Hatchery or sent directly to the furnaces.

"Let's not get into that," I said as I turned slightly green, well wait what color does a blue person turn when they turn green? I don't know, anyway, "What's the second purpose?"

"That would be the main reason for the services provided on this floor," explained Skedwe. "Here the various types of raw material are prepared to build the construct's bodies. If you would follow me."

He headed down the rows of long tables. I guess for you horror nuts I should probably tell you what I'm seeing. It was several miles in every direction of long tables with thousands of Demons filleting and dismembering bodies on a mind-boggling scale. I stopped and looked up one of the rows. The Demons stood on the left facing the table. The walkway behind them was twice to three times as wide as it needed to be. Behind and between every two Demons was a wheeled wagon where the butchered parts were being deposited. On the backside of the table, in front of the Demons, were other creatures rolling even more carts with bodies stacked ten or more feet high. As one of the Butchers would finish, another soul would be tossed on the table in front of them. Now as you might have ascertained already, these souls were conscious and fully aware of what was about to happen. There seemed to be two types, those who were still pleading and begging and then the silent ones, whom I can only imagine had resigned themselves to their fate. Afterall they made it to the last real Plane, so they'd eaten untold others who'd been processed in this room or one very much like it. The guys pushing the carts had the tough job, the souls wouldn't sit still, I imagined it like trying to stack live fish, they just kept flopping all over the place. Wow that was crude.

As we stood there the Demon Butcher (not of fleet street) finished the soul he was processing and barked for another one. The creature with the cart rushed over and deposited a yellowish looking humanoid with gills onto the table. This soul was one of the ones still begging for mercy. I could see the tears streaming down its face. I was already preparing myself for what was to come. I'd learned long ago to assume the worst, at least then I'd be halfway to what was actually going to happen.

The screaming didn't last long as Skedwe pointed out as the Demon slit the creature's throat. "The first step is always to shut it up. They are dreadfully noisy."

Next the Demon – I started to say 'with no compassion' but then I realized to them this was no different than what humans did to cattle on earth - slit the soul open from neck to vagina. He reached in and ripped out the organs, throwing them into a deep trough in the floor. I heard a lot of growling and tearing so I'm guessing there's something down there. Then, with quick exaggerated strikes he removed the hands and feet. Dropping them into the big cart. To my surprise, he ran his blade along the center of the creature's legs and started to peel the flesh from the bone with great care.

"They fillet the souls?" I asked before my mind got a handle on the insensitivity of the question.

"Not always, this particular species is considered a better cut and is processed with more care than the majority of the other souls," he explained. As if to punctuate his comment he pointed to the table just behind the one I'd been watching where a new soul had just been delivered. Unlike the gilled soul, this one was common, I'd seen many of them during my travels. The butcher wasn't as careful. He cut the throat, slit the chest open, removed the innards and here is where things changed. He didn't start a meticulous filleting process. From the legs working up he began segmenting the body into roughly one-foot pieces. Though the throat was cut the soul was flailing, its eyes wide with both pain and horror as it watched its body being dismembered. When the Demon reached the top of the legs, he next moved to the arms where he repeated the process until only the torso and head remained. Mercifully he removed the head at this point, tossing it on the floor where its face still moved and distorted feeling each strike of the Butcher's cleaver. He separated the torso down the middle, the sound of the massive blade cutting through the spinal cord was sickening. After the torso was halved, he sectioned it like he'd done the appendages, tossing all the pieces on the cart behind him

"Why isn't the soul destroyed during this process?" Before he could answer, I answered myself. "Oh that's right, the head. So that means they never dissect the head?"

"Correct, that would cause the soul, well the head at least, to be destroyed thus sending them to the hatchery. We do, at times, get instructions to destroy the heads for a certain period when the Hatchery is running short of primordial food used in regenerating its residents."

As he finished, I turned my attention back to the gilled creature only to find nothing left. The body was just a stack of very well proportioned and boned fillets. The Demon barked and a different Demon came running over and took the soul meat away.

"These aren't added to the carts?" I asked as I put a hand on Kitar's shoulder to steady myself. After this long it stuck me odd that it was still making me queasy, so much so that I had to steady myself several times, reaching out to grip a table or one of my companion's shoulders.

"No, being as high quality as they are, they will be distributed separately," answered Skedwe.

"Something for you to keep in mind, Keith. Those like ourselves..." Elick motioned to the Hellspawns, "...we will place orders for specific species, and they will be delivered to the Keeps. Most of the food you have been served has been the better cuts since you have dined so often in the Overlord's home. They would not risk serving someone of your "status" (yes, he did air quotes, the fucker) the slop the damned and lesser workers of Hell are given. You may have never noticed, since your pallet is not as refined, but the food you consume when visiting the towns is often the lesser cuts."

There was something about this whole process, first with the wine and now this that was making me consider being Vegan. A Vegan in Hell. Sort of sounds like an oxymoron.

"With that let's move on to the construct processing part of this floor. I'm starting to reach overload."

"I was wondering if that was going to happen. It will only make the next part more enjoyable," added Kitar. The fucker.

# Entry 270 (Construct processing)

I reviewed my notes several times trying to figure out how to break this next section into a couple of entries, but sadly there isn't a way, so bear with me. I know a lot of journal time has been spent here in the Labs, but there are several events which happened that need recording. I'll say before starting, in retrospect, the creation of a hellhound was nothing compared to what was required to create a construct like Cemal.

As Skedwe led us to the back of the room, past all the food prep stations, he began to explain what we were approaching. What he said I've no idea, my head was pounding, and I was still queasy from all the gore surrounding me. Or so I thought.

Kitar stopped and looked me over. "Do you need to rest? Is this one of your panic attacks?"

I rolled my eyes. "No, I'm just feeling a bit woozy. I think it's the heat, the smells, and the visuals. It's not quite panic attack level yet. Don't worry, its nothing."

Along the back wall of the chamber were probably five hundred (I'm guessing) large square vats, each holding several thousand gallons, each with a queue of souls trailing back into the blackness. This was one of the few places where I saw Demon guards by the dozens patrolling the lines. What I also noticed was that all the souls in each line were the same species.

Seeing what happens to the damned, I'll keep this short. I think you'll get the point. The souls are marched up the steps to a platform beside each vat. They were then unceremoniously shoved into a pulper, ground up and deposited in the tank below as nothing more than a chunky soup. I looked at Kitar. "They're so quiet." Unlike everywhere else these souls were stoic. There was no crying, begging, nothing.

"The guards help. If there is any emotional outbursts, it normally occurs in the line. When it is their time, most have reconciled themselves with what is to come. Keep in mind, by now they have been to every Plane, spent years being punished and suffered untold agonies. I would venture a guess they see what is before them as the end, their suffering will soon be over," explained Kitar.

"Which isn't right, is it?"

"No, their bodies, as you will soon see, will become the clay employed in the construct creation. Passing through this process, the grinders that is, also traps their souls in their bodies, ensuring it is available to the sculptors below."

"Wait. If they're in pain the whole time, does a construct feel their agony?"

"Not precisely. In some cases, they do, as when we create torture Demons, Hellhounds or other creatures of aggression. In those cases, all the souls involved in the process will eternally be present offering their pain to the final build. The Hellhound you witnessed being given life first had to be sculpted. Since you will see the process of sculpting a new construct I thought it best not to skip around. Keep in mind; all constructs start with the biomass contained in the vats. As for pain, the parts of the souls used in a construct as detailed as Cemal allowed a respite. They no longer feel the pain caused to their original bodies," explained Skedwe.

"But only the amount of the goo used?" I asked pointing to the vats.

"Correct. Think of it as putting salve on a burn. The rest of your body might be in pain, but the area affected by the lotion feels relief. The souls as a whole, might still be suffering if some of their mass remains in the vats, but the parts removed and used cease to suffer, thus reducing the overall agony the creatures are in," added Kitar.

"Ok, I think I understand. Now how is this used? You keep talking about sculptors?"

"Please this way," said Skedwe as he led us away from the vats toward another set of stairs.

(Note: Most of these souls eventually gave in to the pain as the metal teeth consumed their bodies. Often the shrieks started around the upper legs and continued until the grinder consumed the head. Some, more than I would've thought possible, never made a sound. They took their fate in silence as their old form slipped finally forever from eternity. It was a force of will, and dare I say courage; I know I'd never have had.)

# Entry 271 (Construct Creation)

As we were on our way down to the third level a sudden wash of vertigo hit me, and I fell against the wall. Kitar was there first to catch me. I knew he'd been watching me but I'd ignored it.

"Are you alright?" he asked.

I held a hand up and took a couple of stabilizing breaths. "I'm fine, like I said I think it's all the stimuli. Let's keep going."

I didn't lie, I felt fine physically it was my head and eyes which were acting up, my senses. For just a few seconds the surroundings changed. What had all morning been hollowed out rock became something else for second, it was like the whole place was made of flesh. It was gone as quickly as it appeared.

Balthazar was to me in the blink of an eye. Like a doctor he came over grabbing my face and looked into my eyes. "Exactly what is occurring? Explain what you are feeling to me in detail."

Still leaning against the wall, I said, "It's not a feeling, it was vertigo. My eyes keep acting up, one second I see one thing the next something else."

"Meaning?" asked Elick as he and Balthazar exchanged looks.

"It's been happening for a couple of days. I just thought it was the night out or something."

"Focus, Keith. What just happened?" There was a force in Balthazar's voice.

"The room shifted, one second it was rock, then the floors changed...." Skedwe started to say something but was quickly silenced with a look from the whole group.

"Then?" Balthazar prompted.

"I don't know, it's like the entire place was made of flesh."

Through my blurry eyes I could see everyone nodding. Whatever this was they understood it. Believe it or not, that made me feel better, at least someone knew what the fuck was going on.

"The next phase of your transformation has begun. I was curious if you would progress further, fully transforming or remaining a hybrid."

"What?" I sat on the steps. Which for the moment were again stone.

Turning to our Skedwe, he asked, "Do you have a room that can be damaged?"

"I can take you to one of the large insertion rooms. They are well fortified. Might I enquire what is happening?" Though I could see fear in his eyes, it was interspersed with curiosity. This was the scientist at work.

"Our young friend here has been incrementally transforming into what you see before you. It appears the next phase has begun," explained Elick as he and Balthazar grabbed me under the arms dragging behind Skedwe as he led us across the chamber. "We need to get him someplace safe. Every other time this has happened it has been extremely destructive."

I felt like one of those patients who show up at the hospital with their guts hanging out or a president when the secret service whisked them off the stage fearing a rational person has finally decided to end their idiocy. In other words, I was not moving, I was being moved.

I was ushered into a large room with a pentagram carved into the floor. That is all I saw before everything vanished with a wave of Elick's hand. "Get him some wine."

I'd like to say they were overreacting, but the shifts had started to happen more frequently. It was making me nauseous. It wasn't just the walls anymore, the whole room and my companions themselves were morphing.

"My wings are trying to come out. I didn't summon them," I said with worry. They'd never tried to force themselves out after I'd retracted them.

"Let them, your body is trying to revert to its natural state, don't fight it," said Balthazar as he helped me sit up. I felt a goblet touch my hand. Looking over I saw Cemal with a worried look on his face.

"Should he be in here? If this is going to be violent, will it harm him?" I asked between gulps. I was sweating heavily now.

"Good point. Everyone except Hellspawns out...Now," barked Alcraw.

Reaching over I put a hand on Cemal's arm. "Don't worry it's just for your safety."

"I know, Master," he said as he and Skedwe were pushed from the room.

"Just relax, whatever is happening is going to happen whether you like it or not. Just let it play itself out," said Elick as he wiped my forehead.

I was scared. The other times it has just happened, or I'd blacked out, this time I was conscious, present and aware.

"Keep telling us what you are seeing," instructed Balthazar.

"It's hard to describe, so many things are happening, it's overwhelming."

"Pick one and say it, then the next. Do not be so damn anal."

"The walls keep changing to what looks like muscle tissue. All of you are almost glowing. When it shifts the sound is overwhelming. It's like millions of people are screaming in my head." As I explained it happened again, causing me to grip my ears trying to cover them. "It keeps getting louder and more intense."

I heard myself screaming now as well.

That was the last thing I remembered before passing out.

# Entry 272 (Creature construction, take 2)

I woke to a thunderous roar in my ears. Again, I gripped my head, then as quickly as it started it stopped. Opening my eyes, I saw we were in the same room but there were no sounds, nothing at all.

"I can't hear."

"Yes, you can, I deafened you to all external stimuli until we get a grasp on this," explained Balthazar. "Everyone say something so he can see he is fine." They did and I could hear them all.

"Let me explain what we know. This is probably the last phase of your transition. We have been anticipating it, not sure when or if it would even happen."

"But why all the noise?" I asked, tears running down my face.

"Your mind has opened to Creation. What you are hearing are all the voices of the living?"

"Why me?"

"It is not just you, all Powers have this ability. That specific metamorphosis is one even we do not have. Only The Fallen and The Powers can hear the voices of Creation."

"How do I stop it? Please, please tell me there is way to make it stop?" I was begging.

"Keith, first you must calm yourself. This is new to all of us. We never thought we would ever see, let alone assist, in the birth of a Power. If I understand what is occurring, it should have no problem helping you come to grips with this new development. First calm yourself, then focus your mind, just like with any other magic."

Focus my mind? Calm myself? The world...the universe was spinning, visions of things I didn't even understand were flipping past my eyes at a nauseating speed. Then I heard a voice, but it didn't sound like my companions. It wasn't coming from my ears. I tried to focus, I knew that…no wait…those voices. I started to scream as the visions grew faster. "Listen to our voice."

I felt Balthazar's hand, I gripped it.

"Take one of your breaths," their synchronized voices said in perfect harmony. I did as they requested. "Another." I felt my body relax.

"Good. You are now part of us, as we are part of you. We are working from the inside, you will need guidance from the outside. For there we are powerless. You must trust Abaddon." The voices faded away.

My mind raced. Had I ever heard that name? Again, I squeezed Balthazar's hand.

"Keith, you must tell me what is happening," said Balthazar softly but with a sharp edge.

"They told me to find someone," I said, my voice sounded unfamiliar, like I'd swallowed a pound of nails. I felt Balthazar's hand tighten for just a second then relax.

"Go on, who did they say could help you?"

"Abaddon," I whispered, my throat so sore from my screams.

I heard Balthazar chuckle. "Well, damn."

"Abaddon, how can he help you? He has not been seen or heard from since The Fall. To be honest no one knows if he even still exists. To most born in Hell see him as little more than a myth," said Elick.

"I heard my father mention him once. He called him The Demon of The Pit because they say he resides in The Void and viciously protects his privacy. When he left The Host he refused to come to Hell with Lucifer. No one knows why."

"Your father always was a dick…" Balthazar went silent and none spook for what seemed like an eternity, "…I needed time. I was angry at everyone after the war. Both sides had been so stubborn and so, so wrong. When Lucifer manifested Hell's firmament I continued to fall, refusing to join him. I did not want to see anyone, talk to anyone, not

Lucifer, not Father, no one. I fell for eons. So far into The Void that even the lights of The Host and Hell began to dim in the distance. It was there I made my home and set out to explore the sides of our powers we had always been discouraged from visiting."

"Balthazar your...but how...why?" said Alcraw. I could hear the disbelief in his voice.

"I had my reasons," answered Balthazar.

"But I have known you all my life," said Elick.

"I rejoined Lucifer's army when Xia was born."

"Why..."

"Lucifer sought me out and asked me to return. He said he...well Xia would need me," explained Balthazar. "Forgive me, my friends."

"Why did you never tell us?" I heard Alcraw say.

"I made them promise to hide my identity as long as possible. Then..." I heard sadness in his voice, "...I met all of you. Hell's new generation and in you I saw hope. I strove to stay apart, alone but you...Elick...you needed a friend, Xia, all of you were like me...outcasts. Leviathan was so...the way he treated you...unnecessary. As time passed, I remembered what it was like to have friends again. To be part of a group. To not be alone. For the first time in millennia I felt included. You have no concept how lonely The Void can be."

"Do the other Fallen know? Does...Xia know?"

"I cannot hide myself from my brothers. Their silence was only maintained through fear...fear of not only me but Lucifer as well. As for Xia, no he does not know. I am the one who introduced him to The Void. A place for all of us to escape the pain of Hell. For all of you it was a place to hide from the demands heaped upon your shoulders. For me, it was home, a place to lament with my memories. In Lucifer I still saw the Morningstar, that bright light. But deeper...I could see his lingering pain. What he did he did not do out of choice but...then Xia came along, so many questions. As he grew...so much like his Great Grandfather."

I cut Elick off. "Um...guys...Hellspawns and apparently really mean ass Fallen, remember me, Keith, still a bit fucked up here."

There was a long pause then Elick said, "Yes, finish this. I can only speak for myself, but you have always been a true friend. That is something rare. I cannot say I forgive you, but I will listen and...and...you will talk this time. You will explain yourself. Ultimately it changes little."

This is one of those times when it felt like millions of years passed in seconds. I could feel the waves of energy, hurt, anger, betrayal and then maybe, acceptance and forgiveness wash over me from first Elick, then Alcraw and Cartos.

"No one must know."

"Trust me, that much we understand," added Alcraw and the others agreed.

"That includes you Judge."

"It does not matter what I have become, I am still little more than a soul. As you wish, My Lord." I could hear reverence and awe in his voice.

"Keith?"

"Fine, I hang out with Lucifer, what the fuck do I care who you are? Now fix me."

I heard him chuckle. "Maybe all of us should tour Hell as the soul of a living. Your tenacity is impressive."

"Get on with it...um..." I said, pausing no longer sure what to call him.

"I am still Balthazar, use no other name. Now let us get this done. Picture creation..." I started to ask how, "...just think of what you saw in the Void. Nod when you have the image in your mind."

It took me some time but eventually I remembered what I'd seen when we were flying back toward Hell. I firmly locked that image in my mind's eye. I nodded.

"Good, now imagine all the sounds in creation, do it any way you want, as sound waves, colors, it does not matter. Then encompass the entirety of the firmament."

I did as he suggested and nodded again. All of creation was now encapsulated inside a red ball.

"Good, now start slowly shrinking the size down until it is small enough to only rest in your head or a small distance around you. I would suggest, to start, make it fit your body like a glove."

This was pushing my imagination but eventually I was wearing a red body suit in my mind. I nodded.

"Now, before you start, let me remind you that if this works you will not hear us like this anymore. So be careful. Now manifest into creation a desire to not hear anything outside that shell. Be specific or you will deafen yourself. I am going to keep talking to give you a gauge. Once my voice cuts off, give me a nod." It took me quite a while to get it right but eventually, with Balthazar's coaching all sound stopped and his voice went silent. For a couple of seconds there was nothing, total calm and then I heard someplace off to my right a small sound. I turned to find Kitar tapping a nail against one of the large golden candle holders.

"I can hear that," I said. I heard my voice.

"Can you hear me?" asked Elick.

"Yes." Everyone breathed a sigh of relief.

"Ok, that took care of that emergency."

"So, it is gone for good?" I asked.

"No, I will work with you and help you learn control. Eventually you will be able to listen to any specific creature, world or Creation. As large a scope as you wish. The only ones you will not be able to hear are The Powers both here in Hell and The Host, The Overlords and Hell's Royalty like the Hellspawns. It's the same as when you manifested, it stopped anyone from being able to ease drop on you."

I swallowed hard. "Now can you explain you guys' appearance. They look like they are wearing glitter where you seem to be shifting between multiple forms. More importantly why is this room now made from meat?"

"You want to take this one?" Balthazar said to Elick with that familiar smile which until just that second had vanished from between the friends. It was tentative laced with hope.

"Coward..." he said with a broad grin as he turned to me. Now I was nervous, "...honestly we were expecting this to happen at some point. All of Hell will appear differently now. The living mind, as amazing as The Father might have made it, cannot comprehend creatures like ourselves, the Powers and the true nature of much of Creation. The walls are an example, it substitutes, making flesh into stone, creatures into something less disturbing and so forth. Some minds, actually most minds, at some point will shift, as time passes, and the securities of their living world fall away thus leaving them less equipped to substitute. When this happens, they do like you just did and start to see Hell as it really is. It is almost like a reset on the horrors they are experiencing. Without their illusions, Hell is reborn anew, and the old horrors become fresh and the suffering so much more acute. It causes even the most jaded and apathetic souls, used to their punishments, to cower in terror as the true nature of The Dark Lord's realm is revealed."

"It's like a saying on my world — 'everyone has their own version of Hell' — I just didn't realize it was literal."

"Yes, the Hell you have seen and written about is accurate, to you. It will convey The Dark Lord's intent but it most assuredly will not look for another soul as it did for you."

"Here is an interesting fact you asked about a few weeks ago in a roundabout way. Do you remember asking me why images of Hell created by the artists from the living worlds are so much more gruesome than what you have seen?" asked Beelzebub as I nodded. "When a Power or one of Hells Mages contacts the living world for whatever reason, not only do they often stage what the soul sees prior to the vision but since they are projecting their images upon that living soul, it sees what is projected. This vision is not clouded by the soul's defense mechanisms; thus, they often see a far more realistic version of Hell than those who are newly arrived."

"OK, way too deep. Tell me this, there is nothing to panic about, right?" I was now officially at my freak out level again.

"Nothing in the least. If it helps, you might very well have just completed the transformation process. We really will not know until you are put in extreme danger. That tends to bring out any latent powers."

"Then we should know soon enough. Help me up," I asked. I paused. I heard something strange. I smiled as I realized what it was. I didn't need divine senses to hear the sniffles outside the door. "And would someone please let Cemal back in, he's having a nervous breakdown."

While the others were distracted, I leaned into Balthazar. "You will tell me more."

In a whisper he added, "Deal but much will soon be revealed."

Great another cryptic fucking answer. Just want I needed. I shook my head. "I refuse another plot twist, nothing more until I get Usis back."

"You are absolutely correct, nothing more until I say otherwise. Understand, little Demon."

"That's Power, not Demon, as I recall," I said raising an eyebrow and straightening my back.

"Barely," he scoffed with a grin.

# Entry 273 (Creature construction, take 3)

I'd like to note before we finally get to the construct floor that I was here for a long time. I wanted to see the entire process. I'm going to describe the steps but not in full detail.

After Cemal was allowed in and spent his customary time looking me over while not looking like he was looking me over, I managed to get my feet, well hooves, back under me. "Is there some conspiracy going on I should know about?" I asked.

"Conspiracy? Whatever do you mean?" asked Kitar. He was the first to answer, but it got everyone's attention.

"It seems every time we start this stage of the journey, meaning the building of constructs, something happens to interrupt my tour."

"It would seem that way, I agree but rest assured it is not the case." This time it was Elick. I think they thought I was about to have one of my fits.

"In that case, let's get the show on the road," I said turning to Skedwe.

"Now?" blurted Kitar as expected.

"Yes now. We're not leaving only to come back. As everyone keeps pointing out, I'm a fucking Power now, and I'll be fine. By the Powers invested in me, let's do this," I said sounding all strong and powerful. If Cemal hadn't giggled, I might have pulled it off.

"If you are feeling up to it, as you wish. Skedwe after you," said Elick.

As Skedwe led us through the new chamber to my unending concern I noticed how things had changed; everything was different. Where the labs had initially been carved from the stone of the Plane, now the floors, walls, and ceiling were made of muscle tissue complete with veins, and paper-thin sheets of pale fat tissue. The entire surface not only looking like a human abdomen or back stripped of skin but moved as such, every so often it'd ripple like it was taking a breath in or letting one out. The third floor was longer than wide, both distances still enormous. The length as long as the second and first floors. The most significant difference was the height, where the earlier chambers ceilings vanished in the depths of darkness this floor was only forty feet or so tall.

Down both sides were what I could only call cubicles, three-sided rooms with open fronts. Between each was a door leading into one of the private chambers like the one I'd just emerged from. All the walls went entirely to the ceiling and were made from the same fleshy looking substance as the rest of the chamber and lit by fire sconces belching black smoke. In all the cubicles were piles of boxes and supplies stacked on shelves with one wall covered in hanging tools. Today most of the cubicles were filled with activity which were focused on the massive table which took up most of the space. Each table had to be at least twenty feet wide by forty long, upon which lay differently shaped bodies in various stages of completion.

"So how are we doing this. Will it be too much of an inconvenience to see the process from beginning to end?" I asked.

"You are a Lord of Hell now Keith, nothing is an inconvenience if you want it," whispered Alcraw from behind me.

"No, my Lord, if you will honor us with the time required, we can demonstrate the entire creation process from beginning to end. If it pleases you, we will use one of the more completed bodies since the shaping phase is more time consuming than informative," answered Skedwe.

"I still want you to at least verbally walk me through that process. Lead the way."

As he walked, he explained what was happening as I studied the bodies stretched out on the tables in various stages of completion. In each of the ten or so cubicles we visited some were nothing more than piles of sludge while others, almost complete. The constructs varied from creatures as small as Cemal to others so big they hung off the sides and ends of the table. At each stop, he would inspect the work and instruct the sculptor to explain what part of the creative process he was currently performing.

Over the course of these few tables, Skedwe managed to show us the entire construction process. Remember the vats of ground up souls on the floor above that is the clay used to build these new creatures.

"We cannot create creatures from scratch; only The Father has that ability, the Powers might be able to in a limited way, I do not know. We use the deconstructed souls you saw above as the biomass in the building process. As you have seen in each step the ingredients used are key to the final product. Each vat above holds a different species, and each species contributes a wide variety of different characteristics to the final product. Take Cemal here...." explained Skedew until I stepped in.

"Let's not, I'm still not comfortable with the fact he came from this process so let's talk in more abstract terms and not use examples which have served me dinner," I said.

"As his Lordship wishes. When a client comes to us wanting a construct built, we first discuss the features needed in the new creation. It can be anything from timid serving class or worker to something as brutal as an assassin, guard or full fledge Demon. Once we understand the personality, which has little impact on this stage of the process, we talk about the physical characteristics desired in the new build. As you have no doubt noted many constructs fall into, but are not limited to, a few similar physical types. Demons, for example, most often are required to look menacing. Most clients request the construct emulate what The Fallen have chosen as their base form, meaning hooves, horns, tail, etc. Basically, as you appear now. Once we understand the desired appearance, we then drill down and start defining the responsibilities the construct will be asked to perform or endure..."

"Endure?" I interjected.

"Yes, take for example the constructs assigned to manage the humidity vents here on this Plane. They not only needed to endure the flames from the furnaces but also long submersion as they fill the vats with suffering. Where Cemal...," I started to say something, but he held up a hand, "...no specifics, was required to be attractive and timid as well as have an ability to shift into his Demon form instantly.

That form includes a head transformation to facilitate the elongated mouth full of teeth, as well as the ability to excrete from his pores a paralytic gel, his hands and feet become talons with razor-sharp nails and lastly a profound alteration in his base personality. So, as you can see, we can fulfill just about any need."

He stopped when he saw Elick motioning for him to get on with it. I chuckled. "It seems Hellspawn should have had more patience added during construction."

"Indeed, my Lord, but I can assure you that impatience is a base characteristic of most of Hell's Royalty," chuckled Skedew, garnering a glare from almost everyone but me. "As is no doubt obvious the prep work is critical. We are after all bringing a creature into existence, and it's such a waste of time and resources when the client is not satisfied, and we are required to scrap them." I ignored how he mentioned creating a living creature and then how they would scrap it in the same sentence.

"Once the needs of the construct are determined we match as many of the physical properties to the raw material you saw above. With great care a formula, or mixture if you will, is determined and then the biomass is ordered and mixed into a substrate."

"Wait, so to oversimplify, you are saying that you build a recipe, I need two cups of this creature, three of this, one of this other one, and so on?"

"That is not oversimplifying My Lord, the quantities are greater than cups, but otherwise your characterization is accurate. To ensure consistency, the architect who worked with the client will also be performing the construction, seeing it through to completion." He stopped at a cubicle, motioning for the Demon inside to carry on. "Here we go. Ixide is just about to begin. What you see on the table is the substrate, and from the grit and specks of green, I can see this creature is destined to be a guard class. The green is from the Ogheia, a very vicious creature. Continue, Ixide, do not mind us."

We watched as the foul-smelling meat concoction was spread out on the table with a trowel. Sorry, that's what it looked like. After several minutes Ixide had a humanoid shaped meatloaf about fifteen feet tall and half as wide built on the table. As I watched, I couldn't help noticing the little bits of bone and hair. "That isn't very clean; it still has hair and bone in it."

"Of course, most creatures evolve with the correct ratio of tissue to solids necessary to support their frame. Therefore, when we produce the raw materials upstairs, we leave all the particulate matter mixed in. Under most circumstances regardless of the size of the construct, the necessary skeletal structure will be fashioned to support the body created."

Ok, even I'll admit that was interesting and more than a little impressive.

When the crude form was completed, Ixide stepped back inviting me to review his work. "Having never seen the process I'll probably ask some dumb questions. The first being, it looks very crude?"

"This is just the roughing of the form my Lord; the detail will be added once Ixide starts to bring the form together."

"Makes sense. Is that when you add the wings, horns, and hair?" I asked.

"Yes, all the detail work is done after we have an acceptable form. This process does not fail often, but there are times when we do not maintain cohesion."

"Understood, please continue," I said as I stepped back.

For the first time, I saw the energy extend from Ixide's hands as the figure began to rise from the table. Ixide walked to its feet and placed both hands on the creature. Slowly the light began to creep up the figure's body, first enveloping his feet, then legs, groin, torso, arms and finally the head. When fully encased the form began to ripple and bubble, never losing its base form.

"What's happening?" I asked Elick.

"He is separating the soft from the skeletal material. Watch."

In wonder, I watched as the meaty mass separated from the solid matter floating higher and out of the way. As he turned his attention to the skeleton, a servant started to place bowls of different compounds on the table. I watched as the little bits of chipped white shards began to arrange themselves, pulling together until a rough skeletal structure floated before us. "In his mind's eye, he is manifesting what he wants the skeleton to look like. You will notice how things begin moving around the body," added Elick.

"What's he doing?"

"After he has the skeleton has been pulled together, he will begin to augment it. This is done to strengthen parts of the body based upon the build and duties of the specific construct. It is not uncommon for a battle construct to have most of its skeleton encased in a metal plating. That is what is about to happen here; I recognize the substance in the large container. Also, they will strengthen his shoulders and back for a large set of wings and his arms to ensure they can survive the impact of using some types of weapons."

As we watched a thick cord of the substance began to snake its way up from the container. Starting at the lower legs, the little tornado of dust began moving between the individual bones coating them with a thin layer of the powdered metal, turning the skeleton from white to almost black.

When the bones were coated, Ixide's hands began to glow a deep red. I knew what was going to happen. He was heating the dust. I watched as slowly the powdered metal began to liquify, slipping into all the tiny crevasses missed by the dust. The way Ixide swayed and moved I could see the skill required to heat the different parts just enough to ensure the desired layer of metal adhered to the bones. Not a wasted drop hit the table.

By the time he finished the bright red glowing bits of bone had not only came together to form a complete armature but were coated in a layer of metal. Again, the color of the magic changed as the heavy stone top of the table slide away revealing a tank of pale green liquid. It was suffering. The glowing skeleton began to slowly lower into the liquid until with a great hiss and a flourish of steam he was covered. "He's tempering it?" I asked. Elick nodded.

The process of building the skeleton probably took about two hours. There were other small adjustments made. As they had said, Ixide strengthened the shoulder blades, adding more layers of metal to support the wings. He also added strength to the bottoms of its femurs and cannon bones; this was to support the demands of creature's weight on his hooves. The metal coating process occurred a total of three times. Once Ixide and Skedew were satisfied with the frame, which now also included the armature for the wings, as Elick said they were enormous, the horns and claws, they were ready to build the body.

The skeleton was kept in place as the meaty pulp was lowered covering the bones, leaving just the earlier loosely shaped humanoid form.

Slowly over the next several hours, Ixide worked his way up from the hooves bringing detail to the Demon's form. In a lot of ways, it reminded me of the rendering process used to create the realistic movie special effects. The first pass was rough, forming the muscles, tendons and internal structures. On the second pass, he added more detail, refining what was already there and creating new sections. When satisfied he ran the skinless creature through a series of gesticulations to test all the joints and range of motion. Finally, in a series of three passes, he added the skin, wing membranes, hair, and other details until what floated before us was a truly exquisite study in terror.

Its hooves were large and black. Its body was covered from head to knee in deep red scales which Ixide added one at a time. Its tail was a good six feet long, equipped with hundreds of razor shape barbs. His massive hands and fingers ended in the metal nails created at the beginning of the process. Its face though covered in smooth small scales still held an almost serene look. I asked and was told that the fierceness came more from the personality than the build. Don't get me wrong; he had massive fangs, large pointed ears and a rack of horns coming from the sides of his head which curled up and back over his skull only to then curve forwards sharply where they ended in razor-sharp points a good two feet in front of its head. As you noticed I called him a 'he' you can imagine how I knew that. As was the case with most of the Demons in Hell he had a thick three-foot-long horse cock. Overall this was a powerful Demon.

With a smile, Skedwe turned to me. "What does his Lordship think?" I stood there for a few seconds with a blank look on my face until Elick nudged me and I realized he was talking to me. I'll never get used to this title.

"Normally I would say it looks terrifying but having seen the process it's amazing." Both Skedwe and Ixide bowed their heads as their smiles widened.

Rubbing his hands together he added, "Now let's get down to work and see if we can animate this boy."

We followed the two and the floating Demon body toward one of the private rooms. After my last experience, my skin prickled a bit as I entered. As everyone was getting things situated, I leaned over to Cemal. "Does it bother you to see this process? I mean, knowing you were like this once?"

Shaking his head, he replied, "No, Master, it was a bit unsettling at first, but after I returned, I assisted in thousands of creations."

Only when I returned my attention to the room did I notice there were again five avatars standing in the corner. The servants who had followed us in were arranging the candlesticks at each of the points of the pentagram, remember its carved into the floor. It will be important this time. As I watched, I heard whimpering in the dark recesses only to find several cages of ragged souls awaiting whatever atrocity required their participation.

After the newly constructed creature was positioned in the center of the pentagram I was motioned over to a small table against the wall where I saw several small gems. "Finally, I've seen these things since I arrived. Please tell me you're about to explain their purpose?" I said.

"Yes, in each of these five stones is a different soul, each with an aspect to be installed into the construct."

"Only a single aspect? If you pull a part of the soul out what happens to the rest of it?" I asked pretty sure of the answer.

"It is destroyed. We use what we need and discard the rest. Once the procedure is complete the gems will be sent to the furnaces for disposal," answered Skedwe.

Yup, I had a feeling that was the answer.

Skedwe clapped his hands and chairs, well thrones really, were brought in and placed in a line a few feet in front of the door. Between each, a table was set with a goblet and a bottle of wine. "I have seen to your Lordships' comfort while you observe the installation. They can take a while and seeing how his Lordship wishes to observe the entire process I just thought..."

"Thank you, Skedwe," said Alcraw as he walked over and took a seat. I noticed as I found my chair that I was the only one not with a servant bowing just to the left in front of my assigned table. I looked over to Cemal and smiled. He slipped over with a grin and knelt as he reached up and poured me a glass. "My Lord," he added as I took my seat. Elick sat beside me and moved the table. "Good plan, I'm sure I'll have questions," I said.

# Entry 274 (the Ritual)

To make sure you have the full cast of characters and the layout, there is my group and me. We are seated in front of the doors. Skedwe is by the soul stones. Ixide is inside the pentagram holding a long staff with a black glowing crystal on its cap. As I studied the room more closely, I saw the pentagram was far more complicated than I initially noticed. Outside the circle of the central pentagram was another circle about a foot away. Inside this outer space were five smaller pentagrams, each at a point of the big center star. Above the smaller pentagrams outside the large outer ring were five additional circles, not pentagrams, each attached to the outer ring as well as the inner smaller pentagram. Does this make sense? Finally, there are five avatars as well and a bunch of caged souls. That is everyone. Oh, of course, the construct, who is in the center.

Leaning over to Elick, I asked, "This is a complicated setup. Two sizes of pentagrams, circles carved into channels in the floor, then the avatars, souls and soul gems?"

"Yes, keep in mind what they are doing. The Dark Lord created this ritual in the first days of Hell. As I understand, when Hell began to grow, they realized they needed more workers, so Lucifer created the Demon stock. As you can imagine this got cumbersome. Over the course of several decades, he worked with our most talented sorcerers and developed a method for each of the steps in the creation process. What you see before you is nothing more than a very elaborate workaround of what Lord Lucifer did. The steps must be exact, or the entire procedure fails and must begin again."

"Wow."

With three strikes of his staff, Ixide brought all conversation to a halt. "We are here to install a personality into this new servant of The Dark Lord. Seeing how we have guests, I will caution everyone from any interference. The personality we are creating today is a bodyguard, and therefore those involved must ensure their concentration never wains."

Turning to face the construct, Ixide raised his staff and began an incantation. (Don't even think of asking for what this spell was. They made it clear in no uncertain terms that I'm would not be revealing such a powerful bit of magic to the living world. So, you're out of luck.)

His voice started low, almost reverently. Several times I heard Lucifer's name intoned. As he chanted the avatars moved to each point of the pentagram and began lighting the five black candles. Servants brought the soul stones from the table, and once the avatars finished, they took each stone from the servants, who then quickly retreated into the shadows.

Holding the gems in both hands, the avatars knelt, bowed their heads and brought the gem up, touching it to their foreheads. After a few seconds, they bent forward and placed the crystal into a small gold lined indention in the center of the smaller pentagrams where it began to glow. Rising slowly, they took their positions beside the candles joining Ixide in his chant. I could feel the power being summoned into the room as the atmosphere began to grow heavier.

As the chanting grew in strength over the next few verses so did the intensity of the stones. When it didn't appear they could grow any brighter, with a rap of his staff the room fell silent.

"He is about to start installing the aspects of the construct's personality. Not only are the traits of each installation important but also the order there installed. Think of it as working from the bottom up. The last trait will be the most dominant. It is not just personality traits installed but species-specific characteristics as well. These can be installed using the qualities of the personalities in the stones as well as the very cells of the creatures which made up the substrate. They both hold racial memories which the builder can bring forwards if they wish certain attributes to exist in the constructs personality," explained Elick quietly.

"Can they tell me which aspects you are installing beforehand?" I asked.

In a loud voice, Elick said, "Explain each aspect your using, please." This announcement garnered Elick a sharp look from Skedwe.

Skedwe looked to Ixide, nodding for him to explain. "There are five stones in this installation, your Lordships."

"Can there be more?"

"Yes, as many as needed."

"Cool... carry on," I said as I tapped Elick on the arm and silenced him. That got me a look.

"The first personality, the least predominant will be language, which comes from a Hidged. Secondly is Cunning from an Ugesge. Third will be intelligence from a Qizesgesde. The fourth trait will be viciousness from the humans, and finally, the ruling trait will be loyalty, from the Icccesegs."

"He doesn't know does he?" I whispered to Elick.

"What that you were once human, I would assume not," he answered, not even trying to hide his grin.

"Forgive me for reminding My Lords but once we start, we cannot pause, so if there are no more questions..." He looked around the room. When his eyes met mine, I indicated I didn't have any, "...then let us begin."

I leaned forward in anticipation of seeing how this process would occur. From the center of the circle, Ixide stamped his staff and with a mighty voice and a wave of his hand ordered the souls to present themselves. The five crystals flared brightly as figures appeared above their respective stone. They looked like holograms, but I learned later they were more like spirits, or ghosts. What caused me to think of holograms was how they flickered as they floated above their crystal.

In a whisper to Elick, I said, "Remind me why these souls are in stones instead of their bodies like everyone else?"

"Remember the Plane you are on. These creatures were born in a body given them by The Father but abandoned it in favor of an artificial shell. When they pass into eternity and arrived in Hell, they were encased in the stones to be used as building materials for constructs."

"Oh, so why does that body look like a bird?" I asked pointing to one of the spirits.

"That is its Father-given body. We do not recognize its synthetic form after death."

I shrugged. I guess that made sense.

I studied the souls, mainly the human. As the flickering subsided and the manifestations stabilized, I could see the bodies writhing in agony, their mouths open in silent cries. The five avatars now moved into the outer circle of the pentagram, each placing themselves in front of one of the souls. Unlike the avatars I'd seen during the Hellspawn creation process, these were not glowing. They were just emaciated dried husks.

As Ixide stamped his staff yet again and started chanting the avatars let out a vicious roar as their long talons lunged forward digging into the spirits. There was no blood, suffering or viscera; it was purely a visual dismembering as the avatars devoured the spirits piece by piece. There might not have been any physical carnage, but in the eyes of the spirits, you could see the realization and pain as their souls were ripped apart. The silent looks of terror I found more horrific than all the cries in Hell. Their heads thrashed back and forth, sometimes stopping and looking directly at us as if pleading for us to intervene.

It was shortly after the avatars had begun feeding when I noticed the first stirring of the light in their chests. As they continued to devour the souls the intensity grew steadily as the gems started to dim. I could feel the weight and suffering of their diminishing souls as it pressed down upon my shoulders.

As the last bits of the souls vanished in a blurred slur of filaments the stones shattered, leaving nothing behind but dust.

With another stamp of Ixide's staff, the construct went rigid in the center of the pentagram, as all chanting stopped. As he moved in front of the first avatar, the one for language, servants brought five of the souls from the back and placed one in each of the small pentagrams. Unlike the souls in the stones, these were physical beings.

"From you, I call forth language, find those abilities in your sacrifice and offer them forth," Ixide ordered.

They stood motionless for the longest time then the avatar started to spasm. The convulsions grew stronger until final it vomited up a muddy deep green glowing orb of puss into its cupped hands. As the creature presented it to Ixade, they both began to chant as the glowing globe rose. The ball traveled the distance to the construct where it circled around and forced itself into its mouth as the body started to shudder. When the last of the orb was consumed the Demon screamed as a bright light was expelled from its mouth, arched around its body and hit the avatar in the chest.

Ixide turned as the energy struck, still chanting. He motioned to the soul restrained behind them. In a single movement, the avatar lunged at the soul-gripping both sides of its head with its hands bringing their lips together as a gagging scream arose from the throat of the damned.

"The avatar is ejecting the remains of the soul used for the construct into the sacrifice. It is an excruciating process. Its host already occupies the body of the damned and now it is being forced to assimilate another. The first never accepts the second soul willingly."

When the avatar released the head of the sacrifice its body dropped to the floor as Ixide made a motion and ordered, "Silence," causing the suffering soul to go quiet as it writhed in agony.

For the sake of expediency, this same process happened four more times with each of the creatures summoned from the stones. By the time the body of the construct had settled for the fifth time, the avatars lights had gone out, the candles were almost burned down, and a body lay suffering at each of the five points of the pentagram.

Ixide moved back to the front of the construct in the center of the pentagram as it lowered to its feet and then down onto its knees. Now at eye level, Ixide lifted its eyelids checking its pupils, like a doctor, as the avatars moved back into place and again began to chant. Five more souls were brought forward; the avatars took the damned by their hair lifted them off the ground. When Ixide was sure everyone was ready he brought the tip of his staff down once more. In unison, with a single long fingernail, the five avatars cut the throats of the struggling souls as blood began to flow down their bodies and into the small indentations carved into the floor. When the pentagrams were filled with the essence of the sacrificed souls, the chanting of the avatars rose in volume. Ixide lifted a dagger and carved an upside-down pentagram into the forehead of the construct and said, "Amen," as the entire room went black. I felt a hand on my arm letting me know nothing was wrong. Slowly, as the chanting died away and the light returned, I saw Ixide standing in front of a now animated construct. I heard a sniffle and looked down to find Cemal lost in the joy of the new birth.

The Demon which hours before had been little more than a muddy slush of ground up flesh was now awake and conscious.

In a commanding voice, Ixide said, "When you are transferred to your master and named your powers will become available to you. Until that time you will mind those who work for me. If anything ever happens to that Master, and they can no longer command you, I want you to return here for reassignment. You will serve your Master with no regard for yourself or others. Only The Dark Lord, Lucifer Morningstar and his family will hold more sway over you than your Master. Do you understand? Speak?"

In a surprisingly smooth voice, the construct bowed his head and said, "Yes, My Lord."

Placing a hand upon the creature's head, Ixide said, "Good. I know you are famished from your exertions today. We have provided five souls with the remains of those used to create you. You may consume them for both their energy as well as the thrill of feeding upon the damned. If your hunger is not sated, we will bring more souls until you are satisfied. Remember young one, serve your Master well. Bring only glory to Hell and The Dark Lord. You are now free to feed."

The construct didn't even wait for the echoes of Ixide's words to fade before he raced across the room and tore into one of the writhing bodies. I just sat watching the newly born Demon shove pieces of the damned into its mouth. Eventually, I had to look away, he was making a mess. His eagerness or maybe it was hunger so intense he was destroying the bodies more than devouring them. At one point he stopped eating, his face covered in blood, intestines, and meat dangling from his hands, and threw back his head, laughing in pure delight. This was not a beast who'd ever known the pains of existence. This was the delight of a small child at Christmas, and in suffering, he found his joy. I know I knew this already, but there was something in this single demonstration that helped me understand Hell all the better. Those Demons in the torture pits didn't understand the pain they were inflicting. To them it was little more than their divine Dark Lord letting them bask in the joy of their existence. To a soul, Hell was a punishment, a place to suffer for eternity, but to those who were born here, this was a playground filled with joys and delights.

Skedwe came over as we finished our wine and stood. "Are your Lordships satisfied with the demonstration?"

All eyes turned to me. I handed Cemal the glass and in a shock of revelation froze as he took it, this is how they made him. "Is this how you made my boy? My sweet, gentle boy?"

Nodding, Skedwe replied, "Yes, My Lord, but he was not so gentle initially. His hunger was as intense as this one here..." he said as he motioned to the newly created Demon. "...it was not until his Master named him that his programming engaged, and he became the creature you hold dear. In all honesty, Cemal has exceeded his design and has become a work I am personally very proud of."

"So, do they grow and learn as they age?"

"Of course, unless their future Master does not wish them too. Otherwise, they are sentient beings, capable of their own decisions, mistakes, and achievements. Their programming ensures they are at their root, the creature requested, but that does not limit their abilities to develop over time."

"As for our visit, it was very enlightening. I thank both you and Ixide for your patience at our interference, and if there is nothing else, I need to get back to the Keep and make a few notes."

Everyone in the room bowed as Elick led us out into the main chamber and through a door at the far end of the room which led to the tunnels back to the Keep.

# Entry 275

We were met in the lobby of the Keep by one of Death's genderless slaves. "Our Lords invites you to their chambers this evening."

"I'd be honored. We're just returning from the labs. Do I have the time change my clothes and relax for a few minutes?" I answered.

"Yes Master, someone will be sent to collect you in a few hours," the slave said.

"We will be ready," commented Elick as he turned, heading toward the elevators.

"Forgive me, Lord Lancestrider, my masters have extended only a single invitation to Master Keith. There were no others included," explained the slave before he turned and hurried away.

I put a hand on Elick's shoulder. "That's fine. I don't think I've anything to worry about, wouldn't you agree?" I asked.

He simply nodded.

It didn't take me long to get paranoid. "Do you think there's anything to worry about?" I asked.

"If you are not safe in the Overlords' quarters you most certainly are not safe on their Plane. And you seem to be safe there, so...."

The knock came a couple of hours, a bottle of wine, and a change of clothes later. By then I was as ready as my traveling companions were for me to leave.

I've described the Overlords' quarters before, so I won't rehash old entries, the only difference tonight was there were two figures. I was almost certain the creature sitting on the right throne was Death, though like the first night he was wearing a different body. It was the one on the left which caught my attention. This one was different, stunning even; I had to force myself to look away. Bowing to both, I directed my distracted comments to Death, "You look different again tonight. Forgive me for saying, more feminine."

That is when the new creature spoke. I thought my legs were going to give out. Where Death had a mechanical, distant voice, this one didn't. It was humanoid with pale greyish blue skin. I know that sounds odd, but it wasn't, it was like a pastel color from a royal pallet. The way he sat, even before speaking, told me volumes about his personality. He was relaxed across his throne with one leg draped over the arm of the chair like a figure almost bored or maybe wanting to allure an enemy into its graces. His face was lovely, smooth and flat with delicate features. His slanted eyes were thickly lined in black and then complimented in shades of blue, green and magenta. He wore long flowing silk robes of pale blue and mauve, so delicate as to barely conceal the long lines and curves of his youthful body. The sleeves of the robes ended in chains at the top of his hands which continued down to wrap around his fingers. Attached to the back of his robe and draping over his head hung a cowl of the same liquid silk flowing back from the edge of his hairline. Over its shoulders and arms hung a red gossamer shawl. Its neck, fingers, and wrists were covered in jewelry and on its forehead was a golden pentagram which slowly rotated, "He is very diplomatic, this one. I was going to mention the form you chose tonight myself wondering if it was a ploy for the boy's attention. If memory serves, his attention does not lean towards the feminine." Its voice was like a soft blanket on a cold day. I shivered just a bit.

"Please do not start in on the poor child before being introduced," scolded Death.

"Is it wise to lecture me on your slight?" added the creature as he shifted slightly on his throne giving me a vailed glimpse of his manhood.

"Let us take a moment to correct that now. Keith, it is an honor to present to you my companion, Life. Together we are responsible, with our counterpart Eternity, of managing populations in the many Creation worlds," she said.

As I bowed Life noticed my slight smile. "It is an honor," I said.

"And appears in some way to be amusing as well. Please share," asked Life.

"Forgive me your…Lordships but you commented on Death's appearance tonight and…again forgive me if I am blunt… but you as well are extremely…. eloquent."

Looking to Death with a broad grin Life nodded his approval. "You were accurate my dear, he has developed well past the rough weeping creature we received reports on so long ago." Shifting his eyes back to me, he continued, "I like to think of Life as being eloquent in all its forms — something to be prized. No matter how long one has lived, as has been proven by our beloved brothers, Zapars and Enepsigo, it can end quite simply. It is often said that what Life loans to the living, Death collects from the dead. It is a well-balanced partnership."

"So, you rule together?"

"In some respect yes. Life has no interest in the maturations of Hell, as his name implies, he tends to be more watchful of those who have not yet earned their eternal reward," explained Death.

"As you can imagine we work closely together which is good since we have always been very close," added Life.

"Due to our duties within Creation, it is often necessary for one of us to travel into the worlds of the living, leaving the other behind."

"You travel into Creation; I'm not sure I've ever heard of an Overlord leaving their realm," I commented.

"Small one you have left behind the tawdry business of our Lord's Domain and have begun your journey into its oversight," Life paused and looked at Death with a tender smile. "My brother and I are facets of the same gem. Eternity completes us; sadly he does not reside on Fraud choosing instead to make his home on The Great Plane. Together we oversee the functions of the living."

"What exactly does that mean, oversee the functions of the living? I asked.

"It is our responsibility to monitor the populations of specific Creations, galactic structures, down to the planetary level. We study how a species' existence is affecting their world and that of others. Then through global acts, we cull or accelerate populations and growth. This ensures an overly negative species does not damage their ecosystems, be it that of the single planet or in the cases of space-faring races, their galactic communities," answered Death.

"So, any kind of massive event on a planet or solar system can be seen as an 'act of god'? I asked.

"It could but not accurately, since often it is Hell who institutes such events. We consult with The Host to ensure all treaties and agreements are adhered to. But rarely do they really care about what becomes of a Creation since to them, and to be fair to us as well, the living are superfluous. It has fallen upon Hell, and more specifically Death and I, to manage because it was our jobs before The Great War. Since then we have simply continued because, as you have no doubt observed, most of the living will eventually reach our doorsteps and not The Host's."

"Where does Eternity fit into this partnership?"

"It is often Eternity's decision to remove a species from that Creation's landscape completely. He sees things on a much longer scale than either Death or I choose too. Since the three of us have differing views on the motivations and outcomes of The Great War, The Father's Creations and so forth, together we offer a balanced approach to Creation management."

"How so?" I asked.

"Take something as simple as how we choose to present ourselves. As you can see, I choose to free myself of The Father's form where Life here embraced it, dare I even say perfected it, in many ways. This is why my dear Life is often sent to The Host to negotiate or cajole the Powers there; I refuse to recognize them as anything more than puppets to a misguided, delusional and absentee Father."

"Let us not travel that path this evening," Life quickly said trying to hide an obvious aggravation resting just below the surface.

"I would agree. You have presented me with many new concepts. I couldn't even guess what line of questions I'd need to ask you at this point. We've moved into a completely different realm of Hell's functions. As you've both said, this is Hell's management more than its suffering production, for lack of a better way to put it. What I do understand so far, and correct me if I'm wrong, you two are unlike any the other Overlords encountered on my travels and few have intrigued me as much as the two of you have. How you still interact with Creation and The Host. Life's unquestioning allure and struggle to find a middle ground where you Death seem to be more cut and dry in your estimations of Creation and The Powers." I smiled. "Which I guess is how both, life and death, are often played out for the living. Realizing now the subtleties you both employ it brings me back to your appearances and my initial question, Death why did you choose to be more feminine this evening?"

"I did some research, and I am led to believe that males from your planet see females as less threatening," he explained.

With a smirk, I asked Life, "If that is the case, and Death choose this form to put me at ease. What might I might I interpret from your appearance?"

"Anything you wish. I chose for my appearance to be far less fluid. This is as I always am," answered Life.

"Not precisely true my dear, as I choose not to be threatening, I believe you chose those robes with more acute reactions in mind," I couldn't see the humor but could easily hear it in Deaths remarks.

"I have nothing to hide; I find the newly born Power intriguing," answered Life with a subtle raise of his eyebrow. I think he was hitting on me.

"As for females not being threatening, I'm not sure I agree. Clearly you've never met my mother, she was far from 'less threatening'."

In an almost imperceptible movement, I saw Death glance to Life who subtly nodded, Death returned his attention to me. "Actually, we have, and yes I could see that."

The casualness of the admission caught me off guard. I know I've written very little about my life while I lived. That wasn't by accident. I didn't dislike my life, but then I didn't like it either. It was what it was, and now as I look back, its duration was just about as long as it needed to be. Any more and it would have become tedious, I think.

It's strange this came up. I've several times thought about giving some insight as to the history of your tour guide but had always turned away from the idea. I know, if I had an editor here in Hell, one I worked with that is, they would've probably suggested I give some back story. But I don't, and since I don't feel the need to rehash the past, I won't.

"You knew my mother?"

"Not directly, she was on this Plane for a while. Her life for one reason or another centered around Fraud."

"Really? I'm not sure how. Would you care to elaborate?"

"I neither care or not, she was guilty of fraud because she worked with The Dark Lord to help prepare you for your life after death," answered Life.

"So, she knew? She knew Lucifer?" I barked growing angry.

"Calm yourself. She knew his guise. Not who he was or what the future held for you. She was just a willing participant in the process of ensuring you had the training you needed to prepare yourself if by chance you made it to Hell."

"If by chance. So it wasn't planned?"

"Lord Lucifer did not destine you to our company. What he did, as I understand it, was to see in you certain aspects which would be conducive for his chronicler. He then went about ensuring you had the proper perspective, nothing more. If you require more than what I have offered, you will need to take that up with Our Lord himself." She paused, clapped her hands twice (a very human trait) and said, "A drink?" as two slaves scurried into the room with a tray, goblets, and wine. The one was genderless and went directly to Death. The second was probably one of the most handsome males I've ever seen. He too was nude but flush and pink with a health I only recalled in memories. His body was toned, his muscles rippled but not intrusive to his overall appearance, his manhood hug full and proud.

It was then I noticed both overlords watching me, "What? Your servant is very handsome. So full of..." I paused and smiled.

"Life. Yes, he is," answered Life.

I took the goblet, didn't say thank you and drank it down. I was in a foul mood. I want Usis back. I want this issue with Usis over. I want to stop being a pawn in games I don't know about. I want to be happy again. Well as happy as Hell will allow. I want someone else's problems to bother me, not my own.

"I sense your anger; it is a lost ship in this storm. You are looking for something to focus your intense gaze on, and here there is little that cares. Plus, as you no doubt know, it is also misplaced. Your anger is at Leviathan if I were to be so bold as to venture a guess. With that being the case, we have secured something upon which you can focus that newly born demonic rage."

Again, with a clap two slaves hustled in and pulled open one of the great slabs of black marble, revealing a compartment. It wasn't the space or the fact I hadn't seen it before which became the focus of my attention. It was the huge Demon chained inside.

"Who is that? And why is he chained up?" I asked.

"He is one of Leviathan's top generals. He was captured just this morning trying to infiltrate our Keep...OUR KEEP," the Overlords barked in unison.

"And why?" I asked then walked around to stand in front of the Demon. "Wait, let's let him answer that." Leaning in, so our faces were just inches apart I asked, "Why are you here?"

At first, he didn't answer. I turned to the Overlords and shrugged. Death gave me what I guess was her version of a smile. "This is Hell. He is chained awaiting...have you learned nothing during your travels?

You are now a Power, what is the customary reward for those who disappoint us?"

Placing my hand on its arm, I let a charge of electricity flow through my fingers into the prisoner. To his credit, he didn't make a sound. "Was that not enough? I can do more," I said in a low hiss. "All we want is to know why you're here?"

"To clean up what My Lord cannot," he answered.

"And that would be?" I said in a deadly tone I didn't even know I had.

"That damned The Dark Lord has been protecting. Give him to me, and we can all be free of his meddling."

"Meddling? Now that is interesting. Who's meddling? The Dark Lord? Surely that opinion cannot be good for your health?" I said.

From behind me, I heard, "That is what you got from that? That he might upset Lord Lucifer? That is all you read in his statement?"

I looked back and wrinkled my eyebrows. Well, where they had been?

"Not so bright I see. He is here to relieve his Lord, that would be Leviathan, of his little problem. That would be Keith. You know the damned HUMAN soul who has been touring the Planes. He came to destroy him...Keith...the Human," I wasn't as dim as it appears Life thought I was, I got it, well I finally got it after his first 'human' comment. As my eyebrows went up in understanding Death added, "There it is."

"What exactly are we going to do with him? Wait...I want him to suffer. I want him to suffer fully and without mercy," I growled.

"Do you think we invited you to this little meeting to talk about how we dress? You need to learn to be proactive, to fight back. All that pent-up hostility needs an outlet, and Lord Lucifer has seen it in his non-existent heart to send you a stress reliever."

"Lucifer sent him?" My fists were now clutched as electricity danced between my fingers and horns.

"Young one, surely you have realized nothing happens on these Planes that The Dark Lord does not have knowledge of. If something happens, he may not be its originator, but if it continues past conception, you can be sure he has a hand in its outcome. Do not make that face; you have known that for a while. Now are you going to drink wine and talk all night, or do you wish to send Leviathan a message?" Replied Life almost impatiently, as if he was growing tired having to explain to a small child.

I'm not sure what they wanted me to do, but the options started to rush through my head like a torrent of waves after a flood. I needed to control my anger. I needed advice. I knew what I wanted to do, rip him to pieces. Instead, I said like an idiot, "I want to talk to Elick and Kitar, there is too much at stake.

"See therein lies the challenge. It is time for you to step forward and stop peaking from behind the armor of those who stand before you. This offer has a limited life expectancy....," Life said before being interrupted.

We all turned to find a massive vicious looking Demon, well Fallen actually, standing in the doorway. Death dropped to a knee while Life rose more slowly and in a motion as fluid as his robes lowered himself as well. "My Lord," they said in unison.

This Fallen was huge. He strolled into the room like he owned the place. With each step, sparks flew from his hooves as the building shook beneath him. He left behind hoof prints in the hard stone as he walked forward.

In all aspects, this was the image Creation had of a Demon. His body was covered in dark red scales and rising from his head were curved horns all of seven feet long but small compared to the rest of him. His eyes turned toward me, and for several seconds, while I stood trying not to shake, he apprised me. Still having said nothing with a flick of his hand, he caused all the furniture between him and the prisoner to slide violently against the walls. He walked over and stopped before Leviathan's general. Leaning down so their eyes could meet, he said, "Did your master send you?"

Any defiance the general had dissolved, "Yes, Lord Beelzebub."

Nodding the Demon, who I now knew to be Lucifer's second in command, turned to me. "Gather your companions. We leave for the Seventh Plane," he ordered as he turned toward the door.

"Excuse me. Sorry for interrupting and all, but can we take him with us?" I asked pointing to Leviathan's general. "I have an idea."

Giving me a sideways glance, he reached out and gripped the general by the front of his armor ripping him from his prison. The chains which suspended him held causing his arms and legs below the knees to be ripped off and left behind. Looking back at me he said in a commanding voice, "Did you not hear my orders?"

# Entry 276

I returned to our room to find everyone gathered in the sitting area, "So you know?" I asked as I walked in.

Kitar turned, "Know what? We were just talking about what else needed to be done on this Plane before we inevitably have to travel to the Seventh."

"There is nothing left, trust me," I said flatly as I ordered Cemal to start collecting our things.

"That is not exactly true; there are several more areas you need to visit to complete your tour," explained Balthazar.

"Well according to Beelzebub who is waiting downstairs in the Overlords' quarters there is nothing else since he has ordered us to get ready to leave."

"What? Is Beelzebub here? But...," exclaimed Elick.

"If you have a but, you're welcome to go downstairs and voice it."

"What caused Lord Lucifer's, head of Command, to visit and order such a drastic change of plans," asked Kitar suspiciously.

"It could be the General chained up in the Overlords' quarters that was sent by Great Granddaddy," I explained as I noticed Cemal packing our bags.

"Great Grandfather sent someone here after signing the agreement. I am guessing to assassinate you?"

"If his story is credible. Death and Life had just presented the general to me as a gift to do with as I pleased when Beelzebub showed up and announced in no uncertain terms that we were leaving with him. Who is waiting... yes WAITING downstairs?"

"Well there it is, time to go face the music," added Balthazar as he headed out to pack.

"Everyone downstairs in five minutes," I said.

"Master, your clothes are packed," added Cemal.

Now it was just Elick and myself alone in the room. "I have a few ideas about how this first meeting should go," he said.

"Don't worry about it, I've already decided how I plan to introduce myself."

"And that would be?"

"The faster you get packed, the faster you will find out."

Walking over he gave me a hard stare. "Keith this is no game."

My anger exploded before I had a chance to check it as my body burst into flames. "I'm tired of hearing that. Do you think there's been a single minute since that son of a bitch imprisoned my companion that I've thought this was a game? This is far from it, and nothing short of The Dark Lord himself is going to stop me from ripping Leviathan's heart out, consuming it and returning Usis to me. Am I clear?"

He nodded a couple of times as he headed for his room he added over his shoulder, "Hang onto that anger, you will need it."

Right before Elick left I added as the flames went out, "I'm sorry for being short. This whole Plane has been like pulling a bandage off too slowly. The wait to get Usis back has been eroding my mood something dreadful. I'm ready for it to be over, win or lose. I'm not sure I care anymore."

With a devious smile, Elick said, "You? In a bad mood. No. Who would have ever noticed?" He winked as he walked out. I changed clothes, come to find out, they don't make tunics fireproof even in Hell. I think I see a business opportunity. Well if we survive.

We met in the lobby to find Death and Beelzebub waiting, the later very impatiently. "Are you sure you want this brought along?" asked Lucifer's second in command pointing to the appendage free general.

"Yes, but not by you. I have an idea," I answered. It was interesting, almost amusing to see the different reactions. Elick, Balthazar, Alcraw, and Kitar all rolled their eyes where Beelzebub smiled.

"And that idea would be?" he asked.

"I'm guessing they don't know you're here or are, excuse me for saying, pissed..." I waved with my hands around a couple of times, "I'm guessing this is your pissed look?"

My companions cringed as the general's smile peaked through. "Lord Lucifer said you were a handful. Yes, this is my...pissed...look."

"Good, and am I correct in assuming you are coming with us?"

"Yes, I need to have a word with Leviathan."

"About sending this?" I motioned to the general now hanging from Elick hand.

"Yes..."

"Good. Elick give him to Cartos to take with us and if you don't mind Lord Beelzebub could you hang back until the appropriate moment to join us."

"How will I know when this 'appropriate moment' is?" asked Beelzebub now clearly curious.

"Oh, you'll know, trust me."

"As you wish."

I turned to Death, "Please extend my thanks to Life, and I'd like to thank you for your help and advice. You've allowed me to gain the strength for what is to come, and for that, I'm...eternally...grateful. Your Plane has been a respite in a storm I'm not sure I'll weather."

"It was my pleasure as well, be careful, young one," answered Death.

Outside we found Cartos waiting with his father. Though Beelzebub towered over the rest of us, he was dwarfed by his son. "I'm surprised the size difference has not caused any issues," I said to Elick as we emerged from the front door of the Keep.

"Normally Lord Beelzebub is as tall; he is showing amazing respect to you by not changing his size."

I didn't even ask; we're on our way to the Plane of my lover's captor. I explained to Cartos what I needed and asked him to trust me because I planned to ask a very odd favor when we reached Leviathan's Keep. Everyone but Beelzebub was now fidgeting with nervousness. After all these years, I have to say it was terrific to, for at least a second, have the upper hand.

We took wing and together ascended the great pit and onto the Plane of Violence. As we emerged, I looked around, though my mind wanted to focus on what was to come my training forced me to take in the new area. It, like my soul at that moment, was bleak and barren. It was a large flat expanse filled with waring souls, the only landmark was the massive Keep rising out of the center of the plane, it, like its owner, making sure nothing stood above it.

We were met by several of Leviathan's soldiers who flew up to flank us, but only briefly, for no sooner had they arrived then they burst into flames and fell in great spiraling arches to the ground below. We continue toward the Keep. Its stark and unwelcoming façade showed to be impervious, only a few windows and balconies breaking up the vast black expanse. It appeared to be little more than a massive black crypt. In the center of the Keep's arched roof, high above the Plane, was a great cauldron in which burned a flame. It had to have been over three hundred feet tall. I'd learn later it was fueled by those who served Leviathan but, in some way, didn't live up to his expectations. It wasn't like the furnaces, so the creatures cast in weren't consumed, they just burned endlessly. The Plane was insufferably hot. We swooped down, following Elick, and landed on the bridge leading to the Keep's entrance. Beelzebub had hung back and wasn't in sight. The Hellspawns and Kitar moved in front of me, but I pushed past as the massive doors cracked open. And there before me finally stood my adversary... Leviathan, his pale black body of stars encased in his massive dragon armor.

I swallowed and turned to Cartos. "May I have the head?" I announced in a booming voice. Without missing a beat, the massive thirty-foot-tall Hellspawn lifted high the torso of the general and with a look of pride ripped its head from the body and handed it to me. Everyone's mouth was agape even Leviathan's.

Turning back as my body burst into flames and my wings flared out behind me, I walked forward with the head of the general hanging by his hair from my hand. "You have something of mine, and as an act of goodwill I'm returning something of yours," I announced in a loud voice as I tossed the head at The Fallen's feet.

Nothing and no one moved for several seconds, and then Leviathan roared, "How dare you?" as he drew his sword. Balthazar stepped forward as his sword of office appeared in his hands, "Think twice, little brother."

With our eyes locked on each other, I could feel the anger rolling off Leviathan's body. He was so focused he didn't notice what was happening until the entire Keep convulsed. I knew who had just landed and turned to watch as my companions parted as Beelzebub walked casually up the drawbridge.

As he stepped even with me, he said in a warning tone, "I would suggest you sheath that sword, Leviathan, unless of course, you plan on using it on me. You have a pact not to harm, attack or threaten Keith until the two of you face each other on the field of battle. A pact which I understand you have already broken many times thus turning our Lord Morningstar's eye toward your Plane."

"I have no plans to harm that pitiful thing, but this Demon has overstepped himself."

That is when I stepped in again. Being braver than I ever thought I would be, I wasn't thinking, just acting, trusting those instincts everyone had suggested I give more council. "See therein lies the confusion. Please, I beg your forgiveness, Lord Leviathan, in my eagerness to return your general to your loving embrace I neglected to introduce myself, I am Keith, The Dark Lord's writer."

Looking first at me and then turning his attention to Beelzebub he barked, "What kind of game are you playing here? That is not the insignificant bug I encountered back on the Fifth Plane. He most certainly was not a Demon."

"This might be the time for you to stop reacting and look more deeply, old friend," encouraged Beelzebub.

Leviathan walked closer, so close in fact we now stood nose-to-nose and locked my gaze. For several seconds there was silence and then he stepped...no almost fell back in shock. "How can this be?"

"Is there any reason I need to continue this subterfuge?" I asked Beelzebub.

"Even if you tried it would not stay a secret for long. So please continue, I am curious to see the reaction," answered Lucifer's General as Leviathan's eyes shifted back and forth between us.

It was now my turn to step forward, and to my surprise, with each step I took he fell back one, "See Lord Leviathan, the last Fallen to challenge myself and my companion were The Lovers..."

"The Dark Lord destroyed them..." he said as he turned his attention to Beelzebub, "the Dark Lord destroyed them for this and then raised it up?" He pointed at me dismissingly as his anger flared.

"Not exactly, you might want to let him finish," answered Beelzebub who was not even trying to hide his enjoyment.

Leviathan turned his steely gaze back to me, and I'm not sure, but I think I saw just a hint of understanding. "See Lord Lucifer didn't destroy them. He left their punishment to Usis and myself..." leaning in again so our faces were only inches apart, "...and we ripped their souls out and consumed them."

Wide-eyed, no longer hiding his shock, Leviathan all but fell back as his eyes again went to Lucifer's General. "That is how it happened. I have it from Lord Lucifer himself. You see, old friend, your anger over your son being bested now puts you in direct conflict with the first creature ever to consume not just one but two of our brother's essences. What you see before you is the first Power born to Creation since Father gave us life. This is that pathetic creature you met on the Fifth Plane." Looking past Leviathan Beelzebub added, "No offense."

"None taken. Now since we've cleared all that up can you have someone show us to our rooms? I need to record my arrival on your Plane in my Journal for all Creation to read. Plus, I'm assuming the conversation you're about to have with Lord Beelzebub you would prefer to happen in private," I said as I walked into the Keep like I owned the place.

Elick pushed past everyone, his eyes locked on me and his mouth hanging open, "I will show our guests to their quarters Great Grandfather."

Never looking back, I heard each of my companions greet Leviathan and then follow closely behind. The reason I never looked back is simple, at this point I'd consumed all my existing courage. I'm pretty sure I was about to faint.

When we finally made it up the stairs and into the room, I collapsed in a heap on the floor. I lay panting and in shock for several minutes until I regained control of my nerves. Looking up I found the entire group still standing by the now closed doors staring at me. "What?"

"Where in all that is holy did you muster that from?" bellowed Kitar.

"What?"

"That..." was all Kitar could get out as he stammered and pointed at the door.

"Oh that. Well to put it simply, I winged it."

Everyone in the room jumped, including myself, in shock when a roar of laughter burst from Balthazar's lips. "That will go down in the annals of Hell as one of the best-played introductions in history. You, a lowly soul managed to throw the mighty Lord Leviathan completely off his game. Ohhhh, it is truly an honor to watch The Dark Lord's wisdom at work."

"I have to agree. Well played, boy," added Alcraw. "Is there wine?"

"Yes please, lots," I added still collapsed on the floor. Before the sound of my request faded Cemal appeared beside me with a golden goblet and in a very formal move knelt and offered it up with such grace, "Your wine, Lord Keith."

Everyone in the room dropped to a knee as well and together bowed their heads. When Elick looked up, he said, "Yes all questions or doubts have been quelled, you are most certainly Lord Keith after this..." he paused and stood adding under his breath, "I mean if you survive the battle," and started laughing.

# Entry 277

We all turned when we heard a whistle from Alcraw who was standing on the balcony. "It appears Lord Lucifer is serious."

We all rushed over to see a large contingent of The Dark Lord's elite soldiers landing on the bridge leading to the Keep. There had to be a couple of hundred of them. We were high enough that we couldn't hear the conversation between Leviathan and Beelzebub, but there wasn't any doubt it was heated.

Like that wasn't enough I heard the door slam shut behind us to find Kitar leaning against it. "New development."

"What, hasn't this day had enough surprises? I just had to play like I had balls. I could use a break," I said as we started to hear beating on the door.

Kitar still wasn't explaining why he'd decided to act like a demon barricade. "I am not saying it is a bad thing as such. The timing might be considered less than fortuitous. I think it is safe to say this encounter. Keith will prefer to take privately."

"What Kitar, spit it out," I barked.

"Is that yu, Kitar? Are you blocking this fucking door? Let me in or so help me I will rip your balls off, you mutt. Open this fucking door," came a voice I knew all too well. It had a little more ferocity than I remembered, but it was him.

"Step out of the way, Kitar," I asked calmly.

Bowing his head slightly Kitar stepped to the side as the door flew open. A nine-foot-tall (he was taller than I thought) angry cross between a house cat and Anubis fell into the room and crashed to the floor, still cursing. "I heard Keith's voice," Usis said as he stood. First, he found Kitar and growled, then Elick and moved on to the other Hellspawns he hadn't met yet. His eyes moved right past me. For a second, I was hurt, then I remembered I didn't exactly look the same either. When Usis found Cemal he smiled sweetly. "Hello, young one. I know you will not lie to me. Where is my companion?" The tone of his voice sent chills down more backs than just my own.

Cemal, bless him and his evil streak. He bowed, walked over and with a single finger pointed at me, "Master, your companion wishes to see you."

Our eyes locked. Usis looked around but didn't need to say anything; everyone was rushing for the door, more than one with a smirk on his face. The room was empty by the time Cemal knelt before my companion and presented a goblet of wine. "Master, the wine you will probably be needing, if not already, shortly this one would imagine."

Usis took the goblet, rubbed Cemal's head, mussing his hair. "Yes, thank you, you are dismissed."

Cemal slowly walked toward the door only stealing a glance back over his shoulder to smile at me and with his eyes suggested I move. As the door closed, I heard Usis say, "Keith?"

"Hello, my love," I answered with a sheepish smile. "Something's different. Have you changed your hair?"

"A little. By chance have they provided you with a mirror recently?" he said as he looked me over, downed his wine, and walked over to refill it. Turning he raised the bottle and shook it. I finished mine and joined him. No words were spoken as he poured the wine. Strolling over, swinging the bottle between two long black fingers he pulled a chair over and then took a seat across the table and motioned from me to the chair.

"You don't want me to sit beside you?" I asked innocently.

"Not yet, I want to study you a bit more, and I have not decided if I am mad at you yet or not."

"What is there to be mad about?" again I asked innocently, trying not to smile.

"You do realize I am going to kill Elick. You know this, right?"

I took the chair. "But why? He was instrumental in keeping us informed about each other's wellbeing." I was baiting him. I was in shock. I had no idea what to do or say. I fell back on things I knew, sarcasm. This wasn't how I'd planned our reunion.

"Wellbeing!!!" he screeched. "Wellbeing! You're a Demon. How --" He stopped when I raised a finger.

"Well, technically I think WE are Powers, not Demons..." I corrected causing his ears to stand straighter as he stamped a paw and growled. Oh, gawd was it cute. Taking a long breath, he set the goblet on the floor and rested his elbows on his knees and buried his face in his hands. "You ate the heart as well."

We sat in silence for a long while. Finally picking up his glass, he said, "That whole eating parts of both hearts was your idea, right?"

"Yes, it was all I could do considering."

"Considering what. I wanted to protect you."

"And who was going to protect you? And now that I sort of ended up having to fight Leviathan to get you back. Eating part of the hearts was the only way we could think of to give me a fighting chance," I said and instantly realized he knew nothing about that either.

He slowly rose from his chair as I heard him muttering, "He kept us informed.... he kept us informed...," all the time while walking to the door. When he reached it, he flung it open and screamed at the top of his lungs, "You left out the fucking part about my companion becoming a Demon! He kept us informed, my ass..." And slammed the door so hard the room shook.

I sat back in the chair. Usis wasn't upset...Usis was mad.

He marched over still in full fury and threw himself onto the couch as he refilled his glass. He sat the bottle down never taking his eyes off me. I didn't dare speak. For a long time, we sat in silence. Finally, he said, "You look good."

I got up and went over to couch, pulled my wings in and sat down beside him. "Wooo... what did you just do?" he asked.

"The wings get in the way, haven't you noticed that? I learned how to absorb them."

"Look at you, even good at being a Demon," he said as he smiled and offered me his goblet. I took a sip and handed it back. I could see the winds of his furry starting to fade though he was fighting to hang on them. With a gentle hand I took his chin and turned his head till our eyes met. I leaned in and kissed him, he has a muzzle, it's strange, but we figured it out. As we separated, I whispered, "I love you. I missed you more than my heart can ever tell you. You know that, right?"

"Well it would make that whole fighting a Fallen for me thing a little awkward otherwise," he said in a quiet voice as the damn broke. He threw his arms around me and started to cry. Not just cry, it was an ocean of grief, pent up pain from all that had happened to us. As you can imagine before long, I had joined him. For what seemed like eternity we cried, hugged, curled into each other, talked, then cried some more.

I brought him up to speed on the impending battle. The pack, both of us, were required to sign. How it ensured I could do my job. How Leviathan had broken it. Usis asked a lot of questions, and I did my best to answer them. I'll say, based upon what he told me, when he was awake Leviathan hadn't mistreated him, which was a relief. So much so I had to fight to hang on to my furry. Usis had been through a tough time, being alone and transforming. As much as I hated Leviathan, I couldn't help but feel grateful that he hadn't made it any harder. I also needed to thank Elick. All the time he was gone I'd seen it as him being away from me, when in fact, I should've seen it as him being with Usis. There was little more I would've asked.

All night we heard noises outside the door and ignored them. The entire group was probably there, or at the very minimum Cemal with orders to run reports back. Finally, when we'd said all we needed or wanted to say, at least for the moment, I said, "We should probably let everyone in. Are you up to the questions?"

"It will be nice to be with friends again. It's been very lonely. Elick has helped, the little fucker," he said as he sat up. Before he let me go, he said with a look that froze my blood, "We are going to kill Leviathan, slowly, brutally and with so much pain his cries will pale all the other suffering in Hell."

"It was my intention," I said. I think he thought he was revealing a great secret, but I'd already known for a while.

# Entry 278

As everyone made it back in Cemal went to work getting everyone drinks while they introduced themselves to Usis. It took several minutes for me to realize someone was missing.

"Where is Elick?" I asked casually.

"Keith," I heard Kitar say with a note of warning in his voice.

"Where is Elick?" I asked again.

"He was summoned to his Great Grandfather's study. I tried to go with him, but the guards refused to let anyone tag along," answered Balthazar.

"Guards? He sent guards to get Elick?" I said trying not to sound like I was getting upset. I realized I failed when all conversation stopped; everyone turned their attention to me.

"Keith...," cautioned Kitar.

I spun on my heels so quickly it caught everyone off guard, "You want to take that tone with me one more time?" I marched over till Kitar and I were nose not nose, "Do you? DO YOU?" I barked as I sat my wine on the table and headed for the door, materializing my wings on the way.

"What are you going to do?" barked Kitar in his judge tone as he ran past me throwing himself across the door.

Without even thinking, with a swipe of my hand, he flew across the room and slammed into the wall. I stopped at the door and turned, "No one comes with me. That means you as well, my love. I need to set some parameters, and anyone more will diminish the show of strength," I said as I turned and marched down the hall. Thankfully no one followed.

It took me longer than I expected to make it downstairs. When I arrived in the lobby, I asked where Leviathan's office was and how to get there. I guess it made sense that no one questioned me, I was after all just a Demon looking for the Lord of the Keep.

Soon I didn't need direction; I could hear the raised voices. I took a deep breath; there were two guards outside the door. As I walked closer, they stepped in front and crossed their pikes, blocking my path. I shook my head and said quietly, "Move." They didn't comply. Then I heard Leviathan bark, "You will fall into line, or I will send you and that upstart to the Hatchery."

That was my cue. With a wave the doors to the study were thrown open as both guards flew back into the room consumed by flames. "We'll be making one thing clear. You have your marching orders, Overlord, and while I'm here they damn well better be in service to me. I don't give a shit who you think Elick is or what his relationship to you might be, right now he has been drafted by Lord Lucifer to serve as my guide and that circumvents any plans The Dark Lord's servants, such as yourself, might have for him. Therefore, everyone traveling with me is under mine and The Dark Lord's protection so if you have anything to say you will direct it through me."

By the time I finished Leviathan had grabbed his sword in hand. As he came into range I materialized both my swords. Yes, two, that's something new. I knew I had one. The shock of me holding both The Lovers swords, one in each hand, brought Leviathan up short. "Now have I made myself clear. You'll get your day, until then I have a job to do and by the Gods, I'm going to do it. Elick with me," I barked as I turned and marched from the room.

When Elick caught up, I stopped and looked back to find Leviathan standing where I had left him. I added, "You can forgo the arrival banquet the more civilized Planes have thrown upon my arrival. I think we can agree that neither of us wishes to spend any more time than necessary in the others company."

Elick and I walked back to the room in silence. That was as long as it lasted. The moment we were in and had the door closed, all Hell broke loose.

First Kitar started in, still rubbing his back, "What did you do and what do you think you are doing? Are you trying to get yourself sent to the Hatchery?" I ignored him, but Elick didn't.

"Both encounters with my Great Grandfather so far have accomplished something which very well might prove invaluable. He is not living up to the expectations Grandfather had of him. Some might even say Keith's strategy was the only way to deal with an entity like him. It is a good strategy if he does not push it too far." Turning to Balthazar Elick then added, "What concerns me more is this sudden aggressiveness? Do you think it's part of his manifestation?"

"Without a doubt. He has two Powers in him. They do not by their very nature put up with an excessive amount of posturing. If eternity and The Great War has taught us anything, it is that there will always be a level of competition between those of equal or close to equal status. Keith has been elevated to that level and as you just pointed out, if he does not overextend himself, he can play upon that," answered Balthazar.

"Knocking your friends around might be overextending," barked Kitar.

"What did I miss?" asked Elick.

"Nothing, when Keith went to find you Kitar tried to stop him, and with a wave Keith sent him sailing across the room," explained Alcraw with a bigger smile than it seemed Kitar cared for.

"Yes, I would limit those types of activities," added Elick.

"That takes care of what happened up here, now fill us in on what happened with Leviathan," asked Balthazar.

Elick explained the argument and how when Leviathan drew his sword; I materialized two swords.

"Wait, you materialized both Zapar's and Enepsigo's swords? At the same time?" said Balthazar with a look of surprise.

"Yup," was all I said.

"Do it again."

I concentrated and with little trouble was able to manifest both swords again. Balthazar came over and studied them. "Those are their swords. That is very interesting. I knew you could draw one, but I never thought you would have access to both of them. Dematerialize them; I want to try something."

I did as he asked.

Walking over he stood in front of Usis. "Have you been training with your powers?"

Usis shook his head. "Some things come naturally, but I have not had any training."

"You have seen the two swords now. Close your eyes and focus on them. Use your will and summon them to your hands."

It took a while, but with Balthazar's patience and some basic instructions on using his force of will, eventually Usis was able to summon first one and then two swords.

"Now for the next experiment. Keith summon the swords again," instructed Balthazar.

I did as he instructed, and we all watched as they dematerialized from Usis hands and appeared in mine.

"Interesting. I suspected you both could not summon them simultaneously. If I were to guess, Usis probably cannot summon them from you unless you allow it, you have more training and to be honest are just more powerful. He should be able to if you allow it."

We tried and yes, he could if I released my hold on them. To me it felt like a gentle tugging along with some innate understanding Usis was requesting the two blades.

We talked until we heard what sounded like guards marching up the hall toward our rooms. Instantly everyone was on high alert. For a long time, no one moved, we just stood there, weapons drawn, spells crackling and Cemal in demon form. Finally, someone knocked. We all jumped as several spells bounced off the stones surrounding the door.

"Maybe someone should open it," I said as they all turned and looked at me like they wanted me to do it.

"You are the one with the protective amulet," volunteered Kitar.

"Bitch, as I recall you're the one protecting me remember. I don't open doors; I hide behind couches, that's the way this works."

"For the love of Lucifer," barked Alcraw as he walked across the room and threw the door open.

The captain of Beelzebub's guards looked into the room. Upon seeing all of us in battle stance he turned back to one of his commanders, "You were right, I will pay you tomorrow." Looking back, he said with a smile, "Stand down; we are under orders to guard this wing while you rest. Our soldiers will be just outside the door. Just letting you know," he said as he turned with a snicker and barked for his men to assume their posts.

As Cemal closed the door, I heard Alcraw say, "This should end sooner than later, or we may very well could end up blowing each other back to the beginning of Creation. Night..." He left out the door headed to his room.

In short order, everyone left leaving Usis and I alone. We looked over when we heard a cough. There stood Cemal pointing to a set of goblets, several bottles of wine and some snacks he'd dug up (probably literally). He walked over and with two dramatic gestures measured mine and Usis' width with his hands, then went to the bed and compared our sizes to the bed. "Should fit." He then crawled up, cut the size in half, found the center of the bed, and jumped up and down several times adding, "should hold." As he climbed back down, nodding his approval, he walked past us toward the door finally adding, "As Master has said several times tonight...carry on," then bowed and left.

I looked over at Usis who was shaking his head and laughing. "You picked him, just remember that," I added.

"I know, and he is doing a fine job from what I can see."

# Entry 279

I remember when I didn't have any problems writing about sex in the journals, now though it seems different. I guess then it was an experience and not as personal, it might still be with someone other than Usis. I did several drafts of our first night back together but discarded all of them. It just didn't seem right. We'd been apart for years, all the struggles of Hell paling when held against the scale of the pain our absence meant to one another.

I think the other reason there's so little to write about is because there's not much to tell about the actual sex. After we got past the changes in our bodies and back down to the souls who inhabited them it changed from what you'd call sex and became more about passion and intimacy. Like it or not when a person's appearance changes dramatically while two people are together it does affect their relationship, as it did with ours. Don't worry this isn't going to be some lament about a love that was no longer. There was love, and the sex was good, it was passionate.

I guess every time this happens its different for those involved. Looking back, I can see how it'd be hard. I remember several times during our intimacy I'd look at the creature in bed with me and miss my Usis only to chide myself; he was here. Still, my mind would say, 'yeah...but.' Then at one point he spoke, said something inconsequential but in it I heard the familiar voice, and it reminded me that he was going through the same feelings, I wasn't me anymore either.

Read that last part again, what I just wrote, 'I wasn't me anymore either,' that was the moment everything changed. I stopped and sat up; he lay there with a tear leaking from his eyes.

"You don't want me anymore do you?" he said.

"It's not that. Tell me honestly, in all the time you imagined what it would be like when we got back together was it like this?" I asked.

"No.... but...," he started crying hard, "I don't want to lose you. I still love you."

I took him into my arms and hugged him close. Standing I took his paw and led him to the couch, poured us wine and we cuddled up together. We sat in silence for a long time. Finally I said, "I don't think these two bodies need each other yet. These souls need to be reunited with their lovers." Pulling him close so he laid against my chest, I could see over his head but not really him, and he could see my arms but not me, we started talking. We went all the back to the beginning, to when we met, then worked our way forwards, all the tears, hard moments, laughs, the fun, what little there is in Hell. We talked, and at a certain point, the bodies were forgotten because we were strolling together through our memories, all the times we'd been together. For hours we revisited the horrors, failures, and victories, we'd had as a couple, fought our way through them again. Eventually, when we came back to the room we were sitting in, the bodies looked different. In the simple act of reconnecting we found a new familiar. This new normal found its home and no longer were they strange bodies, strangers to each other. We weren't a Classic Demon and an Egyptian Demon anymore; we were Keith and Usis. And together the two lovers went to bed and made love, for finally we were reunited.

# Entry 280

We awoke with a start the next morning. The sounds from the hall told me immediately we were under attack. Usis and I were both out of bed in a flash; he hung back while I materialized my two swords (I like this two-sword thing) and threw the door open. As expected, several of Lucifer's guards had engaged what I can only guess were Leviathan's Demons, and they were pushing the attack. Leviathan's men had positioned themselves in the hallway leading to our rooms. At first, I thought they'd made a huge mistake by underestimating me until I heard Usis bark and turned to find two soldiers rushing in from the balcony. I slammed the door shut again. I'd like to say my training didn't let me hesitate, but I knew then as now, it wasn't me, it was my new guests, the lovers, and their training. With a quick thought, the forming of an idea, and then forcing of it into reality, several sharp blades formed and within seconds the Demons fell to the floor in several pieces. The next thing I knew the dismembered ex-soldiers exploded covering the surrounding area in viscera, including Usis.

"Well shit, that did not work," he barked with a look of disgust.

"Did you do that?" I barked as I was trying to get my head around what to do next.

"Yes, not very well it seems."

"Yeah, you probably need to stay back."

"Throw the door open, and I'll attack," he barked indicating he wanted a sword. It didn't take him long to realize I wasn't relinquishing them.

"Nope, you remember the plan," I said as I sent a blast of energy at the door blowing it off the hinges. The flying shrapnel tore through the hall almost hitting Balthazar, but at the last second, he pushed it away.

As my mind came to grips with the attack, I realized I was sick of this shit, which also meant I was pissed, beyond pissed I was furious. We weren't going to get a moment of peace until this little problem between Leviathan and myself was over. In that split second, I decide to fuck the plan; we're dealing with this here and now. Looking down the hall, I discovered Leviathan had come to the same conclusion. He was standing there with his sights set on me.

I looked back at Usis and nodded. "This isn't how we planned it but hang back, and I'll see what I can do."

Just as I started to send out a spell to deal with the soldiers, they were all consumed in flames. Leviathan turned to find me as confused as he was. His attention snapped around when he heard something behind him. Balthazar was standing there with his arms crossed amidst the remains of his soldiers. "I do not believe this is how The Dark Lord intended this encounter to play out, but it is time for it to end. I have taken care of the riff-raff so you two boys can play," he said as several more Demons on the balcony behind me went up in flames. As Balthazar walked by, he stopped beside Leviathan and added, "You are lucky your fight is not with me. You will fight fair, or it will be, and we both know you do not want that, little brother."

"Send him to the Hatchery," he said. "I am going down to deal with his soldiers."

By now I wasn't only holding both swords of office, but my entire body was ablaze in blue flames.

I started down the hall, the heat radiating off me consuming everything in its wake, the marble on the walls was shattering as I passed from the heat.

In response, Leviathan shifted as well, and I thought he was intense before. His entire star filled upper body began to blaze a purple-black flame as his lower torso and legs shifted becoming a long serpent. This was the creature of the abyss that had often filled the tales of the living. This was The Leviathan. He rose to his full height, he towered over me by a good ten feet, but I didn't care, it was time to dance.

"You put on a good show, little soul, but even you should see you stand no chance against me. You might have bested two weak rejected outcasts, but they are not one of the Mighty Fallen," taunted Leviathan.

"Or are you? While we're posturing and making our big fight scene speeches, does Lucifer know about all the troops you're training in secret? I've traveled the Planes and have learned to spot the powerful Overlords; you're little more than a mockery. How Lord Lucifer gave such responsibility to something so pathetic is beyond me. Come at me, let's dance so I can start my day right by feasting on your heart."

His anger flared, and before I could react, he was on me. Shit, I forgot my wings. I quickly materialized them, pulling myself out of range. The tip of his sword grazed my chest as the end came back smoking. The heat of my body affected his sword; we were both surprised. The cut hurt... bad. I shook it off.

I did a couple of cross attacks forcing Leviathan to block the first and dodge the second. Over the next few attacks and parries, while we tested each other, we worked our way down the hall back toward the common area.

Where his attacks were precise and hitting the mark more times than not, I was flailing, getting lucky a couple of times, but never connecting. By the time we were in the larger chamber able to maneuver I was already dripping blood or whatever it is I leak, from half a dozen shallow wounds. He had one across and down his arm, that was my only hit, but it was deep.

All I was doing was keeping up, blocking his attacks but in the long term this wasn't going to work, he kept getting in hits. He was slowly picking me apart. Several times I tried spells but learned quickly, the weak things I knew were worthless against a Power as strong as my opponent, he just brushed them off. I could understand now what Balthazar had said about needing to learn stronger attacks. Nothing I could do could even touch him, but I was kicking his Keep's ass if that counts for anything.

Over time as he scored more hits, I began to fall back working my way around the parameters of the room. Elick yelled something, but I couldn't hear what he said, but I guess my mind did. I felt it relax as the Lovers reflexes immediately took control. As we dodged and parried, I began to see patterns in Leviathan's moves. As the fight progressed and my confidence grew slightly, I noticed fewer of his lunges were hitting their mark as more of mine were finding their target. I was beginning to push him back. It was then I realized I had a better chance in the hallway since there was less room for his massive frame to maneuver. To be honest, it had as many drawbacks as advantages, but at least I could score a strike. The Keep was enormous, but it wasn't made for a creature as big as Leviathan when he was fully resolved. I swear he kept growing and he was using that fucking tail like another weapon. I'd ignored it until after making a successful strike causing him to spin, he knocked me back, sending me flying a good twenty feet across the room.

"You are good, little monkey, but it's time for you to set your weapons down and submit to your superiors," he taunted.

"You think you're going to win. Lucifer will eat you alive," I taunted. It was all I had.

"You know as well as I do if Lord Lucifer wanted this over it would have already ended. He does not care about you, boy; you have done your job; your usefulness has expired."

My anger flared and I pinwheeled my swords pushing him back. He was underestimating me. He didn't understand the anger and hatred of the living mixed with an eternity of disappointment from the two Powers which now inhabited my soul. With several targeted strikes I pushed him back against the wall leading into our rooms. He was starting to have trouble moving; he was too big to get through the remains of our doorway. I had him boxed in.

As his back hit the wall behind him to my surprise it exploded inwards, opening his way into our chamber. I smiled internally; this fight was now over; he just didn't know it yet.

"You broke the terms of this contract," I barked.

"You think that matters? Did you ever think a pathetic talking monkey could defeat a Fallen? That was your creatures' problems all along;

you never respected your betters. Alone, you never stood a chance. If you thought those who rallied to your side were going to help you then you have learned nothing about Hell." He motioned to Elick and the other Hellspawns. "They know better than to pick a side because of what will happen to them once I am done with you. You are alone, boy, and this is over." His next strike was so powerful it drove me to a knee. I barely blocked the following blow as it pushed me onto my back.

"No, you're wrong. I've never been alone, and your arrogance, as always, will serve as your downfall. See there are two of us," I screamed as the swords vanished from my hands, leaving me unarmed. It was enough of a surprise to stop Leviathan's attack for the split second I needed. Before he could recover and what I said registered, I saw Usis appear behind him, flying through the air as the two blades materialized in his hands. Leviathan heard the sound, but it was too late. He turned just in time to see the two crossed swords find his scaled neck and connect. A cheer went up from behind me as the Fallen's head lifted just inches and began a slow spin away from his body. Usis came down hard in a mass of swords and limbs, coming to rest in the middle of the still writhing body of our advisory.

I relaxed as the head rolled toward me, the frozen look of shock letting me see that life was still there. Balthazar barked for me to destroy it.

I reached down grabbing the head and brought it up to look my adversary in the eyes, "I was never alone, you fucker," I bellowed as every ounce of magic in my body was forced outward to devour the Fallen's head in a mass of blue flames. Right before it blinked out of existence, it exploded destroying the entire side of the Keep. The flash was so bright it blinded me. For several seconds there was nothing, total silence, my body felt weightless as it hurled through the air. As I found the ground, blackness took me.

# Entry 281

A conversation awoke me. I opened my eyes to find myself in a bed that wasn't my old room, but I guess that made sense, the last thing I recall was it being blown to bits.

What caught my attention was two voices. One was Beelzebub's, and the other was The Dark Lord himself. Now he shows up.

"Our little warrior appears to have awoken," said Lucifer.

I sat up slowly. Gawd, did I hurt. "Forgive the tone, My Lord..."

"But..." he prompted with raised eyebrows.

"Where the fuck have you been?" I asked. Though my voice was calm, it none the less has the desired effect on the rest of the room. Beelzebub smirked as Kitar cringed. What mattered was Lucifer, and he just chuckled.

"I know you living, present or past, might believe you are the center of the universe, but you are wrong. Far more important things needed my attention. And as is often said about me, I like being proven correct. I finally realized what you needed. It is in your nature. We needed to stop handling you and let you sink or swim on your own. And for what it is worth, you did very well."

"Is Leviathan dead?"

"Of course not, it will be a few weeks before he wakes up in the Hatchery. Then it should take him some time to pull himself back together and get out."

I shook my head. "Then all this bullshit starts again? He will come after me."

"You need not worry yourself about that. Leviathan might be rash, but he is rational, and once he and I have a sit-down, you will have little to fear. Which brings me to the other reason for my visit." Turning he found Elick. "You are now Overlord of Violence. Your Great Grandfather will be spending some time relearning what it means to even think about challenging me. The Plane is yours, short of the excessive army he was foolishly building. I sent them and the souls that made them to the furnaces."

"What now?" I asked stopping Lucifer who was already on his way out of the room with his second-in-command.

Without looking back, he shouted, "I would suggest you get some rest and recover, things are about to get busy both here in Hell and in The Host. It is time you get started on the real reason I brought you here."

I've spent enough time with Lucifer to know that last part needed to concern me, but sadly that realization came a few seconds too late. He was already gone.

Getting out of bed I discovered I was nude by Kitar handing me a tunic. I smirked and waved it away. "Did you guys enjoy my battle, which is an excellent way of saying 'Where the fuck were you?'"

"You seem to be asking that question a lot this morning," commented Elick.

"Well, Overlord, in case you haven't noticed I've been forced to wing it a lot lately," I said Overlord with emphasis just to rub it in. It worked as Elick shook his head. I could tell his friends were enjoying the new stress The Dark Lord had heaped upon the handsome Hellspawn's shoulders because they kept slapping him on the back and toasting him.

Balthazar added, "The biggest pacifist in Hell is now in charge of Violence. It might work, you know. In a few years you can have Creation's worst killers all making doilies for the Royal houses. It might be a decent torture for them," he said as they burst out laughing.

"That is all fine and good but on to more important issues," interrupted Elick clearly trying to change the subject. "How in the Hell did you dispatch Grandfather?"

"You didn't see it?" barked Usis. They all shook their heads. "What good is performing a miracle if no one is paying attention."

"I know right," I added as I looked around for Cemal. "Is the boy alright? Where is he?" The answer came in the form of a muffled voice from the other room. "The keep is not running well right now Master; the new Overlord is not very organized. There are not many processes in place. This one just found wine...It is wine Master is wishing, is it not?"

"Exactly. Be patient my boy, I hear the new Overlord of V.I.O.L.E.N.C.E is cute but a little slow on the uptake," I said with a smile.

"Really you too?" barked Elick.

Over the next hour I filled them in on how the battle had happened and more to the point how Usis and I had developed a plan the night before while we were talking. Oh yeah, that might be one of the reasons I left so much out of that entry.

"You two planned that attack strategy?" asked Alcraw.

"Do you think that could happen by accident. For a while there I wasn't sure I was going to be able to get Leviathan turned around with his back to the room. Usis can move pretty fast but the first rule of this whole plan was not to underestimate Leviathan's abilities," I explained.

"Wise. It is amazing he did not notice," added Elick.

"You see that was Usis' idea actually and with a little..."

"Very little," injected Usis with a smile. Great another smiling dog. It doesn't matter how long I'm in Hell dogs smiling is just creepy.

"...help from you. See Usis said it was your idea that he feigns weakness. Since you had him keep up that ruse for so long, it was only natural that Leviathan would overlook him. Then when we discovered we could transfer the swords by simply summoning them, everything came together in my mind. I hadn't planned it to happen this soon, but we both agreed we'd stay on our toes and take the first opportunity presented."

"Wait you did not spend the whole night having sex?" asked Balthazar with a sound of disappointment.

"Not all, but after we had a plan and got over the shock of each other's new bodies well....," smirked Usis, "...I will tell you... if you ever get a chance, have Keith do that changing body size, length, and thickness thing on you. Oh boy..."

I had to laugh as we watched everyone in the room, except Kitar, zone out trying to think of the possibilities. Elick was the first to return to the present. "I have to hand it to you; it was a great plan. Swords of Office were probably the only weapons you could have used to take him down."

I didn't miss the implications of what he'd just said, "Wait, if they were the only ones, what exactly was the plan before us discovering I could summon them?"

"Well you see, we did not have one. We were hoping Lucifer would show up and put an end to this. Or more to the point, arrange for you to have something that would work. Sometimes we just have to have a little faith."

"Faith? FAITH? You were leveraging my future on faith?" I barked.

"If it makes you feel any better, we had started working on a plan to rescue the two of you from the hatchery," added Kitar dryly. I just shook my head.

"Yeah, I'm glad you kept that bit of confidence to yourself."

"What it proves Keith, whether you like it or not, is that you are ready to assume your role here in Hell. No one is sure what it is yet, you are an anomaly, but you are now one of The Powers and in being such will have certain responsibilities."

"That's all good and fine, let's cross that bridge when we get to it. Right now, I'm sure the new Overlord needs to inspect his Plane and in doing so can show me around," I said as I started the process of getting dressed. Pausing I asked, "Is there a town on this Plane? I'd love to get out for a while without the overriding fear of being hunted down and killed."

"You should keep that fear. This is still Hell," answered Elick. "As far as a city, Grandfather would not allow such frivolity on his Plane; this is…was, I guess, a military installation but in the back corner by the barracks is a tavern. Since it is mostly soldier Demons, it tends to be rougher in both appearance and temperament than those you have seen. I will need to make an appearance at some point. Since Balthazar, Alcraw, and Cartos have been reassigned why don't we gather there tonight for one last evening before you move on to the Great Plane and they off to their new duties."

# Entry 282

As we stepped out of the Keep, I realized this was my chance to explain the differences in Hell since the illusions had dropped. This was the real Hell. Thinking back, I realized the changes had begun for me on Fraud, but with that Plane being glass and steel the differences were more subtle and harder to see. Here, on Violence, the new vs. the old Hell was night and day.

The first significant change was the color, I mean of the whole Plane. No longer was it that dusky grey of a day right before sunset. It was still as dark, but now the entire atmosphere was tinged with oranges/reds almost like the night sky engulfed in forest fires. Which I guess for Hell made sense.

Like the other Planes, this one was little more than a massive cavern, several miles in each direction and hundreds, if not thousands of feet tall. The earlier Planes were surrounded by vast mountains as is this one but not as expansive. Elick told me that what I was now seeing existed on most of the Planes. The outside walls which formed the physical cavern were still stone, but the mountains weren't there any longer. They were now great jagged ranges of bodies swamped with flies rising hundreds of feet from the hard-stone floor, here and their pockets of flames would escape consuming the flesh causing the souls to cry out. He told me, and I believed, that the living mind was incapable of this level of understanding. It could not comprehend the sheer quantity of bodies needed to build the glistening flesh and jagged bone mountains which enclosed the horrors contained on the Planes.

As strange as it sounds, what I found interesting about this revelation was how it explained the numbers of souls contained in Hell which to my reckoning never added up. All the Planes are full to overflowing but if you take into consideration the enormity of eternity, the nine Creations with millions of sentient worlds and the quintillions of souls soon to be exiled to this place the numbers become staggering. I'm still not sure if the numbers make sense, but then I have no way of knowing how many are in the furnaces or waiting to be thrown in. On Violence alone the mountains encircling the Plane had to span almost a hundred miles around. Add the height of several hundred feet and a depth rivaling that, and it doesn't take long for the mind to become boggled by the number of bodies needed to construct such an expanse. Yes, if you're just not getting it, these aren't mountain ranges of hard stone but of discarded souls, broken and battered, still conscious and suffering. Their cries of pain have become the background music for all of Hell.

Now if that isn't enough, we have the Keep. If you remember when we arrived, I offered a cursory overview, but my mind was on the impending confrontation with Leviathan, so several details went overlooked. The Keep is still little more than a massive box of black stone with a huge fire beacon on top. What I hadn't noticed was how all the exterior walls were covered in short spikes, probably a foot long, each with a head impaled upon it. Millions of these heads. It gave the whole structure an eerie movement as the mouths articulated up and down in silent cries of pain while vast committees (yes, that is the right word) of carrion birds swoop in, plucking bits of flesh and muscle from the silent souls.

As we walked out onto the Plane, Elick took me around to the mounting stations. Here the souls who'd fallen in the wars which raged across Violence were dumped to await their punishment. See the heads on the Keep were not just damned souls; these are the creatures who'd fallen in combat. In everything about this Plane, I could see Leviathan. His hatred for what The Father had created. His need to find the best. His total lack of forgiveness for those who didn't achieve his vision of perfection. Forget the damned, what struck me, was this was the environment Elick was raised in. This was the legacy his Great Grandfather had tried to force upon him.

The Demons in charge of these stations were massive creatures, each more than fifty feet tall. Their only purpose was to shuck the bodies of the discarded souls keeping only the heads which they impale upon vacant spikes. Where only a skull remained, the vultures having devoured the flesh and muscle, it was plucked off and tossed onto a pile of skulls which rose as high as the Keep itself.

I know I'm harping, but I even see Leviathan in this stack of souls. I see his need to impose, his desire to be something bigger or maybe just again what he was. Think about it; we are talking about a Fallen, a former member of The Host who's only desire is to puff up his chest. This is the arrogance of pride, plain and simple. Lucifer, say what you will about him, he stood up against his creator, a creature who created everything with a vision he himself eventually forgot. In Lucifer, there's still a level of nobility. Many who rule here in Hell still carry that same dignity, but not on this Plane, not this Fallen. He was, and I guess will continue to be nothing but a pathetic creature with memories of what he was and a misguided belief of what he hopes to be again.

At the mountain of skulls, I was introduced to the next abomination living here on this Plane. These were multiarmed behemoths, their fat bodies covered in scars and wounds as their six long arms used pitchforks to spear the discarded skull, piling them into huge wheeled carts.

I heard the whoosh before I saw the flames of Hells furnace's burst up from great fissures just this side of the mountains. As the intense heat washed across the Plane it incinerated large swaths of the waring souls. When it reached us, I felt the wave of pain causing my skin to sting, then the cooling relief of the protective shell Elick cast around us. It raged for several minutes, the flames splashing against the cavern roof high above us. As quickly as they appeared, they died away leaving nothing but a glowing red orifice in the rocky ground. It was in this lull when the skull tenders rushed their huge trollies over and dumped its contents, the skulls of the damned, into the glowing fissures.

"What are they doing?" I asked.

"Disposing of the remains. The fissures lead directly to the furnaces, there the souls will begin their final stretch in eternity."

"I don't understand. Let's say one of these souls as it moved down through the Planes headed here to Violence, is first cut, that bit of flesh devoured by some creature. Then on another Plane, they lose an arm, which lays discarded on the ground or devoured by the rat things. They finally make it here where they eventually fall in battle. Once that happens, their heads are removed, the bodies going who knows where, and placed on spikes to be picked clean by the vultures. This leaves bits and pieces of that one soul strewn all over Hell. Now you say that the skull is loaded into a cart and dumped in a fissure which leads down to the furnace's where they are ultimately destroyed. I guess my question is, with bits and pieces everywhere, when or how does the soul blink out of existence?"

"The furnaces, though they are great fires are in actuality, soul devourers, the flames are just the physical manifestation of the souls as they are consumed. Once any part of the creature is introduced into the fires of Hells furnaces and consumed, any remaining parts scattered across the Planes will rot and melt away. The sheer number of souls contained in the mountains you see surrounding just this Plane would overwhelm Hell's workers if they had to haul them all down to the furnaces. Therefore, the tenders, the large Demons around the Keep, also work the mountains of souls removing the heads to be sent down and incinerated. Once the head no longer exists the rest of the body which is still here on the Plane will begin to rot."

I just shook my head, "It seems like I've gotten bits and pieces but never the full story."

"Keith you have to understand, Hell is bigger than any of us. You probably come closer to a fuller understanding now than anyone you have met on your travels, other than Lucifer and few of the Powers who work or visit here."

"The power it must've taken to create all of this. It never stops amazing me," I said looking around.

"You have no idea how strong the children of The Father are. The strength of even the weakest of the Powers eclipses my abilities as thoroughly as mine do the living. The Lovers were an example of the weaker Powers. As hard as all that is to grasp, if you try to factor in Lucifer and Michael's strength, we are all nothing more than insects beneath their feet. No one has any idea how strong Lord Lucifer truly is. Even after The Father gifted Michael with his powers many in

Creation still believe it in no way approaches The Dark Lord's strength. Remember he created all of Hell in a single thought. He overrode The Father's creations and gifted his followers with the ability to procreate. Something The Father was so against he allowed a war to tear his Creation apart. After all of this, instead of standing to face Lucifer, he walked away leaving his first son to do as he wished. Was that out of devotion or simply the realization he could not stop it? Of this, we may never know. So you see Keith, no one knows the full story. You have received bits and pieces of facts and conjecture though out your travels not because things were kept from you but simply because no one understands it all. But that is what Lord Lucifer wanted, for a human to walk the Planes of Hell. A living soul with its limited understanding to struggle to piece together the wonders of Creation in a way that other living could comprehend. In that, I think you have done your job and it is for that reason that I believe you are being allowed to become one of The Powers yourself. For from this point on, a living soul will not be telling his story, a Power will and in that telling is a different story."

I sat down. For some reason after all the build-up to the battle and it ending as it did and now my mind being plunged back into the enormity of Hell and what I'd seen during my time here, I was overwhelmed anew. I'd like to say we toured the rest of the Plane. I saw it like I said before it was just one great war. A war waged by souls saturated with a need to hurt and destroy. The concept that they were dead and could lay down their weapons, rest from their struggles, was incomprehensible to them. For into eternity, they brought their vendettas with the hope of exercising them on any and all their weapons of vengeance could strike down.

We walked back in silence. At one point I stopped and found in the distance one of the massive tenders, so much bigger than me, but there on the mountain of souls nothing more than a speck. We made it back to our room where Usis waited. He spent the rest of the afternoon catching up with Cemal as I struggled to put down what you just read. Once I was satisfied, I took a nap, the revelations of all that had gone unexplained due to my limited eyes picked at me like one of those carrion birds consuming a skull. Had my job been for naught? Had I failed you, the living? Had I not gotten across how horrific this place is and why you should struggle never to be sent here? I don't know; I did the best I could. It's strange how my mind went back to one of the first bits of advice given to me by Kitar all those eons ago, "Don't become like them, hang onto yourself." How many times have I referenced that conversation during these journals and now here I am, one of them? Was I still Keith? Who had I become, what would be my role? I didn't know. Like life, I now stood naked against eternity with no understanding of myself or my purpose — a simple Demon in the land of horrors with no sense of who or what lay before me.

As my mind raced over these realizations, I felt someone shake me. I awoke to find Usis smiling. "Are you alright, my love? You were thrashing in your sleep."

I nodded. "What time is it?"

"We need to leave for the Tavern soon, or we will be late."

# Entry 283

I thought about describing the inside of the Keep since I only did it through the eyes of that imp we'd enslaved, but why, what it was isn't any longer and what it will become it hasn't become yet. I decided to skip it in favor of just saying: Tonight, the Keep it was abandoned. When we made our way to the main hall where we found Elick talking to a couple of Demons as the others stood around waiting.

"This place looks like a tomb," I commented as we walked up.

"While you have been sleeping, we have been cleaning house. Most of the soldiers were extremely loyal to Great Grandfather, so much, so they thought about starting a revolt," explained Elick.

"They what? Do we need to be armed?" I barked, looking around like I was about to be attacked.

"No, they are all gone now. Elick here will be needing to order a whole new batch of Demons in the next few weeks."

"You killed them all?" I was shocked.

"You say it like it was hard. Just a wave of Balthazar's hand and they were all consumed by flames. Sort of fitting. Anyway, you ready to go?" explained Elick.

"Sure…" I said, stunned that I'd slept through a coup.

Seeing my look, Alcraw said was we took wing, "You will get used to it. They happen a lot when power shifts on the Planes."

The flight over Violence told me what I already suspected about the Plane and why I have pretty much ignored it. It was just wholesale war. In some areas, it looked as if groups of superior souls had organized and were brutalizing the weaker creatures for their own sport but otherwise hacking and slaying. When we landed, I asked Elick about it.

"There are souls which employ violence to get their way in life even though they are physically or mentally inferior to those they try to inflict their will upon. To Hell it does not matter if you are a competent fighter or not. If you recall, it is one's actions which matter not the reason behind them, at least in the case of Violence. Therefore, if an otherwise inferior soul chooses to use aggression and brutality as a means of achieving their goals while living, they will discover upon their arrival in Hell that they will be assigned to Violence since that is the vehicle they choose in life. As you have seen as we flew over, once they arrive here they discover they are not equipped for the rigors of this Plane and are often turned into slaves or simply tortured by the other souls. We do not discourage such behavior since it only serves to punish the weak for using violence as a means to live. This also, over time, allows our overseers to find the truly vicious souls. These damned then are often sent to the labs to be installed in hellhounds or Demons like the one you witnessed earlier. What the living do not seem to grasp is the way they live their life will ultimately determine where they spend eternity and if you are a weak version of whatever sin category you choose to specialize in you probably will be at the bottom of the rung when you reach Hell and thus your punishment will be far more severe.

"We call them Bullies back on Earth." I followed Elick as we made our way through the array of buildings scattered on each side of a rocky path. "Are these barracks?" I asked.

"Yes, most of which will be demolished. With what this Planes does there is little need for a standing army, we have a strong enough group of guards to ensure the souls cannot gain the upper hand."

"Is that a problem?"

"More so on this Plane than the others. With these soul's root sin being violence, which often translates to leaders of wars when they were living, they tend over time to try to band together and overthrow their guards and overseers. One of my ongoing conflicts with my Great Grandfather was what I called his laziness in administrating his Plane. Things will be changing here soon. Anyway, tonight is not about business. Let's relax and celebrate your victory."

I'm not sure what I expected from a military tavern, but I was impressed. It was dark, non-descript and crowded with a variety of

Demons. I could tell these were the working-class Demons; they were just hanging out after a long day on the job. Another surprise was the live music. The band consisted of what had to be three constructs with a lead singer looking to be a mix between a lizard and a hamster. She was strange but had a great voice. We found a large table in the back with comfortable chairs designed for a Demon's body. As we settled in a couple of handsome servants came running up to take our orders. I was surprised at how well cared for they were.

"Are those new?" asked Balthazar, "They don't look like your Great Grandfather's type."

"Yes, I had them brought up from one of our clubs in Pandemonium. I arranged to have males here tonight, but there will be girls as well."

"Are you going to allow the clientele to enjoy them?" asked Alcraw and I knew exactly what he meant. Abuse them, in other words.

"Not the staff, if they want to bring in something from out on the Plane, that's fine. I will probably even encourage it. But like I just told Keith, no business tonight. This might be our last night together for a while with all that is happening." I saw a look travel around the table and when all the eyes settled on me, I raised an eyebrow.

"Do not worry this time it is not bad. As you know, I have been tasked with getting this Plane back in order, and it has to be done quickly; otherwise those who might want to challenge my authority will try."

"As for us, we were just doing a favor for Elick. Your issue with Leviathan is over, so we need to get back to our duties to The Dark Lord," explained Alcraw. There was something in their looks which told me I wasn't getting the whole story. I let it go. If I'd grown used to anything it was not knowing what the Hell is going on.

"Makes sense. The only issue I've got is I'm not sure what to do now. Do I head to the Great Plane? We can work that out later; I still have Kitar I'm guessing?" I asked looking over to get a nod from our judge. "Good, well tonight like Elick said, no business lets have some fun. I think I've earned it, after all, I've just kicked a Fallen's ass."

With that everyone yelled, "Here, here," as we clanked the newly delivered drinks and toasted my victory.

We spent the night relaxing and hitting on the cute little servants. Overall not much happened. At one point, Usis asked if I minded if he went back to the Keep since he was still feeling the effects of his change. It hadn't gone as smoothly for him, but then I guess that makes sense since he didn't have a band of Hellspawn to help him through the process. He insisted I say, but if I'm honest, I hadn't planned on leaving, I needed some downtime. Don't write anything into that, we're fine maybe even better than fine but with all the buildup to the battle, for it to end so anticlimactically has just stripped me of all the nervous energy I'd been surviving on. When Usis left Kitar and Cartos went with him. This has never been Kitar's kind of thing, and Cartos was more of a loner.

"If you don't mind one question, what is going to happen when your Grandfather gets out of the Hatchery? I mean I know Lord Lucifer said he planned on dealing with him, but I can't believe he's just going to take this change laying down, so to speak," I asked.

"No, he will not. This is more of a slight than you can imagine. He has never liked me, my ways or my associations," Elick said as he was interrupted.

"He means Xia and me," interjected Balthazar.

"Why you? I mean I can sort of understand Xia but..."

"Many of the Fallen tend to shun me since they know who I am. Due to my reclusiveness and the stories which have built up over time, I am a mystery. Powers don't like things they don't understand."

"In case you have not figured it out Keith, when Grandfather found out Balthazar was involved, he probably rethought his entire plan. Our little black buddy here has more than once turned the tides of war between Fallen and even The Powers a couple of times. Not knowing what I know now I understand why they tend to retreat when he stands against them," explained Elick.

I shrugged. "I'm hoping we will all remain in touch. Since what is going to happen to me after all this is anyone guess."

"Don't worry, our Dark Lord pays his debts, and you have done him many favors with your tour and your recent victory. You and Usis will be set up in Pandemonium. At first, I would have said an apartment, but now with you being a Power and all, you might get a Keep, who knows. A lot of it will be up to you."

We fell quiet again, none of us talking. This journey is over for me, like it or not, even if I'm asked to write about the Great Plane it won't be like these journals. Eventually, Balthazar and Alcraw headed out leaving just me and Elick.

"I need to head back to the Keep," he said.

"If you don't think it will cause any problems, I think I'll stay."

"No one will dare bother you. Trust me every eye in this place is on you. The stories have already started to circulate. I will see you back at the Keep in the morning, and we can figure out what is next," he said as he stood and left.

I sat as the night drifted on, several times the crowd thinned out and then grew again like waves washing up on a beach. I don't know I guess I felt empty. So much energy had gone into getting Usis back, and now that he is I feel like I don't have a direction. So much lay before us, we needed to rekindle a love that hadn't faded, but we were different people now simply because of the amount of time we'd been apart. Don't get me wrong; we're secure in our relationship, it's just that usual uncomfortableness when you were away for a long time and then come back together with no idea of what the future holds.

When the room went quiet, I was lost in thought and didn't notice for a second, but it only took a second. With all the dangers in Hell, it doesn't take you long to realize when the atmosphere changes. I looked up and immediately knew what had changed. Standing in the door was a massive Demon with a duel set of horns which curled from the front and sides of his head encasing a long ponytail pulled back behind him. His lean muscular body was black tinted in a mottled green. His hands ended in black talons and his hooves were some of the biggest I'd ever seen and covered in a thick hair. His face was handsome, striking actually, and accented by a small pentagram between his eyebrows. He wore a harness and loincloth with a massive sword of office hanging from a thick belt at his side. He stood in the doorway with an intense look which chilled the room, his tail swishing behind him like it had a mind of its own. As his eyes moved over the crowd, several of the lesser Demons popped out of existence on the spot, the goblets they were holding dropping to the floor with a chatter. This was a Demon of massive power.

My heart froze when his eyes met mine, and he started across the room, the crowd not only parting but dropping to their knees and bowed to him.

"You are the writer?" he said in a smooth deep voice with such authority I almost passed out.

"Yes, My lord," was all I could say.

"The one who just defeated this Plane's Overlord, is that correct?"

"Again, yes, My Lord."

He let out a great laugh. As he looked down, I could see his fangs pressing against his bottom lip. He pulled out the chair opposite me and motioned for a drink. We sat across from each other in silence until a goblet was placed in front of him. He kicked back his chair onto two legs as he propped his hooves up on the table. Raising an eyebrow, he again focused his gaze upon me. "I hear you have requested an interview. Well here I am," he said as I realized this was Xia Morningstar.

Thank you for reading the

Journal of a Deadman series.

Made in the USA
Columbia, SC
04 May 2021

36767978R30417